THE OXFORD LIBRARY OF
SHORT NOVELS

THE
OXFORD LIBRARY OF
Short Novels

Chosen and Introduced by

JOHN WAIN

Volume II
Conan Doyle to Conrad

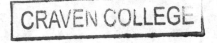
GUILD PUBLISHING
LONDON · NEW YORK · SYDNEY · TORONTO

This edition published 1990 by
Guild Publishing
by arrangement with Oxford University Press

Introduction and selection © *John Wain 1990*

C.N 2127

Printed in England by
Clays Ltd, St Ives plc

Contents

Sir Arthur Conan Doyle
THE SIGN OF FOUR
1889

SIR ARTHUR CONAN DOYLE was born in Edinburgh of
Scottish Roman Catholic parents. He came of a literary and artistic
family, his grandfather being 'Dicky' Doyle, who was one of the group
of radical journalists who founded *Punch* and the designer of the jaunty
cover it kept for over a century. Arthur Conan Doyle studied medicine
at Edinburgh University, where he was particularly impressed by a
celebrated surgeon, Dr Joseph Bell, under whom he did part of his
training. Bell set a high value on accurate diagnosis, and drilled
his students into assembling every scrap of information that could
contribute to this and considering it from every angle.

Sherlock Holmes, who applies the same method to the solving of
criminal cases, appeared in the first book Conan Doyle published,
A Study in Scarlet (1887), and then in *The Sign Of Four*, but he did
not begin to exert his magnetic sway over the public until a series
of short stories featuring him, and later collected as *The Adventures
of Sherlock Holmes,* began to appear in *The Strand Magazine* in 1891.
A long series of Holmes stories followed, plus other books of a light
and engaging nature, notably *The Exploits of Brigadier Gerard* (1896)
and *The Lost World* (1912).

Conan Doyle, a man built on a large scale both mentally and
physically, participated in many areas of life. He worked in a field
hospital during the South African war, and later defended the British
Government's action in going to war with the Boers, in a pamphlet
that was translated into twelve languages and widely distributed
in Europe in an attempt to counter anti-British propaganda which
depicted the war as crude colonialism. In May 1909 he took up
the cause of a man named Oscar Slater, who had been convicted
of murder and robbery in Glasgow; Slater had been condemned to
death but the sentence had been commuted to life imprisonment, and
Doyle, convinced on the evidence that the man was innocent and that
it was a case of mistaken identity, worked for nineteen years and finally
had his sentence quashed and compensation paid.

Conan Doyle is one of the authors, like Dickens or Gogol, who 'cre-
ate a world'. Holmes and his friend Watson, from their lodgings at
221B Baker Street, sally out into a Victorian London that is as familiar
to us as the place we live in, and the clutter of Holmes's life—his

Stradivarius, his old Turkish slipper stuffed with shag tobacco, his row of scientific monographs—is like the clutter of our own. Small wonder that an enormous pseudo-scholarship has grown up around the exploits of the lean, hawk-eyed detective and the courageous and well-meaning, but slightly slow-witted Indian Army doctor, retired from the Service, whose old wound still troubles him in rainy weather. Discrepancies of date and place are anxiously discussed and reconciled where possible (what was Holmes doing between these dates?) quite as if the characters had lived and breathed. Conan Doyle was an excellent spinner of tales, but his other recurrent characters, Brigadier Gerard or Professor Challenger, were never paid this compliment. Holmes and Watson are familiar figures wherever books are read.

I. THE SCIENCE OF DEDUCTION

SHERLOCK HOLMES took his bottle from the corner of the mantelpiece, and his hypodermic syringe from its neat morocco case. With his long, white, nervous fingers he adjusted the delicate needle, and rolled back his left shirt-cuff. For some little time his eyes rested thoughtfully upon the sinewy forearm and wrist, all dotted and scarred with innumerable puncture-marks. Finally, he thrust the sharp point home, pressed down the tiny piston, and sank back into the velvet-lined armchair with a long sigh of satisfaction.

Three times a day for many months I had witnessed this performance, but custom had not reconciled my mind to it. On the contrary, from day to day I had become more irritable at the sight, and my conscience swelled nightly within me at the thought that I had lacked the courage to protest. Again and again I had registered a vow that I should deliver my soul upon the subject; but there was that in the cool, nonchalant air of my companion which made him the last man with whom one would care to take anything approaching to a liberty. His great powers, his masterly manner, and the experience which I had had of his many extraordinary qualities, all made me diffident and backward in crossing him.

Yet upon that afternoon, whether it was the Beaune which I had taken with my lunch, or the additional exasperation produced by the extreme deliberation of his manner, I suddenly felt that I could hold out no longer.

'Which is it today,' I asked, 'morphine or cocaine?'

He raised his eyes languidly from the old black-letter volume which he had opened.

'It is cocaine,' he said, 'a seven-per-cent solution. Would you care to try it?'

'No, indeed,' I answered, brusquely. 'My constitution has not got over the Afghan campaign yet. I cannot afford to throw any extra strain upon it.'

He smiled at my vehemence. 'Perhaps you are right, Watson,' he said. 'I suppose that its influence is physically a bad one. I find it, however, so transcendingly stimulating and clarifying to the mind that its secondary action is a matter of small moment.'

'But consider!' I said, earnestly. 'Count the cost! Your brain may, as you say, be roused and excited, but it is a pathological and morbid process, which involves increased tissue-change, and may at last leave a permanent weakness. You know, too, what a black reaction comes upon you. Surely the game is hardly worth the candle. Why should you, for a mere passing pleasure, risk the loss of those great powers with which you have been endowed? Remember that I speak not only as one comrade to another, but as a medical man to one for whose constitution he is to some extent answerable.'

He did not seem offended. On the contrary, he put his fingertips together, and leaned his elbows on the arms of his chair, like one who has a relish for conversation.

'My mind', he said, 'rebels at stagnation. Give me problems, give me work, give me the most abstruse cryptogram, or the most intricate analysis, and I am in my own proper atmosphere. I can dispense then with artificial stimulants. But I abhor the dull routine of existence. I crave for mental exaltation. That is why I have chosen my own particular profession, or rather created it, for I am the only one in the world.'

'The only unofficial detective?' I said, raising my eyebrows.

'The only unofficial consulting detective,' he answered. 'I am the last and the highest court of appeal in detection. When Gregson, or Lestrade, or Athelney Jones are out of their depths—which, by the way, is their normal state—the matter is laid before me. I examine the data, as an expert, and pronounce a specialist's opinion. I claim no credit in such cases. My name figures in no newspaper. The work itself, the pleasure of finding a field for my peculiar powers, is my highest reward. But you have yourself had some experience of my methods of work in the Jefferson Hope case.'

'Yes, indeed,' said I, cordially. 'I was never so struck by anything in my life. I even embodied it in a small brochure, with the somewhat fantastic title of "A Study in Scarlet."'

He shook his head sadly.

'I glanced over it,' said he. 'Honestly, I cannot congratulate you upon it. Detection is, or ought to be, an exact science, and should be treated in the same cold and unemotional manner. You have attempted to tinge it with romanticism, which produces much the same effect as if you worked a love-story or an elopement into the fifth proposition of Euclid.'

'But the romance was there,' I remonstrated. 'I could not tamper with the facts.'

'Some facts should be suppressed, or, at least, a just sense of proportion should be observed in treating them. The only point in the case which deserved mention was the curious analytical reasoning from effects to causes, by which I succeeded in unravelling it.'

I was annoyed at this criticism of a work which had been specially designed to please him. I confess, too, that I was irritated by the egotism which seemed to demand that every line of my pamphlet should be devoted to his own special doings. More than once during the years that I had lived with him in Baker Street I had observed that a small vanity underlay my companion's quiet and didactic manner. I made no remark, however, but sat nursing my wounded leg. I had had a Jezail bullet through it sometime before, and, though it did not prevent me from walking, it ached wearily at every change of the weather.

'My practice has extended recently to the Continent,' said Holmes, after a while, filling up his old briar-root pipe. 'I was consulted last week by François le Villard, who, as you probably know, has come rather to the front lately in the French detective service. He has all the Celtic power of quick intuition, but he is deficient in the wide range of exact knowledge which is essential to the higher developments of his art. The case was concerned with a will, and possessed some features of interest. I was able to refer him to two parallel cases, the one at Riga in 1857, and the other at St Louis in 1871, which have suggested to him the true solution. Here is the letter which I had this morning acknowledging my assistance.'

He tossed over, as he spoke, a crumpled sheet of foreign note-paper. I glanced my eyes down it, catching a profusion of notes of admiration, with stray '*magnifiques*', '*coup-de-maîtres*', and '*tours de force*', all testifying to the ardent admiration of the Frenchman.

'He speaks as a pupil to his master,' said I.

'Oh, he rates my assistance too highly,' said Sherlock Holmes lightly. 'He has considerable gifts himself. He possesses two out of the three qualities necessary for the ideal detective. He has the power of observation and that of deduction. He is only wanting in knowledge, and that may come in time. He is now translating my small works into French.'

'Your works?'

'Oh, didn't you know?' he cried, laughing. 'Yes, I have been guilty of several monographs. They are all upon technical subjects. Here, for example, is one "Upon the Distinction Between the Ashes of the Various Tobaccos." In it I enumerate a hundred and forty forms of cigar, cigarette, and pipe tobacco, with coloured plates illustrating the difference in the ash. It is a point which is continually turning up in criminal trials, and which is sometimes of supreme importance as a clue. If you can say definitely, for example, that some murder had been done by a man who was smoking an Indian lunkah, it obviously narrows your field of search. To the trained eye there is as much difference between the black ash of a Trichinopoly and the white fluff of bird's-eye as there is between a cabbage and a potato.'

'You have an extraordinary genius for minutiae,' I remarked.

'I appreciate their importance. Here is my monograph upon the tracing of footsteps, with some remarks upon the uses of plaster of Paris as a preserver of impresses. Here, too, is a curious little work upon the influence of a trade upon the form of the hand, with lithotypes of the hands of slaters, sailors, cork-cutters, compositors, weavers, and diamond-polishers. That is a matter of great practical interest to the scientific detective—especially in cases of unclaimed bodies, or in discovering the antecedents of criminals. But I weary you with my hobby.'

'Not at all,' I answered, earnestly. 'It is of the greatest interest to me, especially since I have had the opportunity of observing your practical application of it. But you spoke just now of observation and deduction. Surely the one to some extent implies the other.'

'Why, hardly,' he answered, leaning back luxuriously in his armchair, and sending up thick blue wreaths from his pipe. 'For example, observation shows me that you have been to the Wigmore Street Post Office this morning, but deduction lets me know that when there you dispatched a telegram.'

'Right!' said I. 'Right on both points! But I confess that I don't see how you arrived at it. It was a sudden impulse upon my part, and I have mentioned it to no one.'

'It is simplicity itself,' he remarked, chuckling at my surprise—'so absurdly simple that an explanation is superfluous;

and yet it may serve to define the limits of observation and of deduction. Observation tells me that you have a little reddish mould adhering to your instep. Just opposite the Wigmore Street Office they have taken up the pavement and thrown up some earth, which lies in such a way that it is difficult to avoid treading in it in entering. The earth is of this peculiar reddish tint which is found, as far as I know, nowhere else in the neighbourhood. So much is observation. The rest is deduction.'

'How, then, did you deduce the telegram?'

'Why, of course I knew that you had not written a letter, since I sat opposite to you all morning. I see also in your open desk there that you have a sheet of stamps and a thick bundle of postcards. What could you go into the post-office for, then, but to send a wire? Eliminate all other factors, and the one which remains must be the truth.'

'In this case it certainly is so,' I replied, after a little thought. 'The thing, however, is, as you say, of the simplest. Would you think me impertinent if I were to put your theories to a more severe test?'

'On the contrary,' he answered; 'it would prevent me from taking a second dose of cocaine. I should be delighted to look into any problem which you might submit to me.'

'I have heard you say that it is difficult for a man to have any object in daily use without leaving the impress of his individuality upon it in such a way that a trained observer might read it. Now, I have here a watch which has recently come into my possession. Would you have the kindness to let me have an opinion upon the character or habits of the late owner?'

I handed him over the watch with some slight feeling of amusement in my heart, for the test was, as I thought, an impossible one, and I intended it as a lesson against the somewhat dogmatic tone which he occasionally assumed. He balanced the watch in his hand, gazed hard at the dial, opened the back, and examined the works, first with his naked eyes and then with a powerful convex lens. I could hardly keep from smiling at his crestfallen face when he finally snapped the case to and handed it back.

'There are hardly any data,' he remarked. 'The watch has been recently cleaned, which robs me of my most suggestive facts.'

'You are right,' I answered. 'It was cleaned before being sent to me.'

In my heart I accused my companion of putting forward a most lame and impotent excuse to cover his failure. What data could he expect from an uncleaned watch?

'Though unsatisfactory, my research has not been entirely barren,' he observed, staring up at the ceiling with dreamy, lack-lustre eyes. 'Subject to your correction, I should judge that the watch belonged to your elder brother, who inherited it from your father.'

'That you gather, no doubt, from the H.W. upon the back?'

'Quite so. The W. suggests your own name. The date of the watch is nearly fifty years back, and the initials are as old as the watch; so it was made for the last generation. Jewellery usually descends to the eldest son, and he is most likely to have the same name as the father. Your father has, if I remember right, been dead many years. It has, therefore, been in the hands of your eldest brother.'

'Right, so far,' said I. 'Anything else?'

'He was a man of untidy habits—very untidy and careless. He was left with good prospects, but he threw away his chances, lived for some time in poverty with occasional short intervals of prosperity, and, finally, taking to drink, he died. That is all I can gather.'

I sprang from my chair and limped impatiently about the room with considerable bitterness in my heart.

'This is unworthy of you, Holmes,' I said. 'I could not have believed that you would have descended to this. You have made inquiries into the history of my unhappy brother, and you now pretend to deduce this knowledge in some fanciful way. You cannot expect me to believe that you have read all this from his old watch! It is unkind, and, to speak plainly, has a touch of charlatanism in it.'

'My dear Doctor,' said he, kindly, 'pray accept my apologies. Viewing the matter as an abstract problem, I had forgotten how personal and painful a thing it might be to you. I assure you, however, that I never even knew that you had a brother until you handed me the watch.'

'Then how in the name of all that is wonderful did you get these facts? They are absolutely correct in every particular.'

'Ah, that is good luck. I could only say what was the balance of probability. I did not at all expect to be so accurate.'

'But it was not mere guess-work?'

'No, no; I never guess. It is a shocking habit—destructive to the logical faculty. What seems strange to you is only so because you do not follow my train of thought or observe the small facts upon which large inferences may depend. For example, I began by stating that your brother was careless. When you observe the lower part of that watch-case you notice that it is not only dinted in two places, but it is cut and marked all over from the habit of keeping other hard objects, such as coins or keys, in the same pocket. Surely it is no great feat to assume that a man who treats a fifty-guinea watch so cavalierly must be a careless man. Neither is it a very far-fetched inference that a man who inherits one article of such value is pretty well provided for in other respects.'

I nodded, to show that I followed his reasoning.

'It is very customary for pawnbrokers in England, when they take a watch, to scratch the number of the ticket with a pin-point upon the inside of the case. It is more handy than a label, as there is no risk of the number being lost or transposed. There are no less than four such numbers visible to my lens on the inside of this case. Inference—that your brother was often at low water. Second inference—that he had occasional bursts of prosperity, or he could not have redeemed the pledge. Finally, I ask you to look at the inner plate, which contains the keyhole. What sober man's key could have scored those grooves? But you will never see a drunkard's watch without them. He winds it at night, and he leaves these traces of his unsteady hand. Where is the mystery in all this?'

'It is as clear as daylight,' I answered. 'I regret the injustice which I did you. I should have had more faith in your marvellous faculty. May I ask whether you have any professional inquiry on foot at present?'

'None. Hence the cocaine. I cannot live without brain-work. What else is there to live for? Stand at the window here. Was there ever such a dreary, dismal, unprofitable world? See how the yellow fog swirls down the street and drifts across the dun-coloured houses. What could be more hopelessly prosaic and material? What is the use of having powers, doctor, when one has no field upon which to exert them? Crime is commonplace, existence is commonplace, and no qualities save those which are commonplace have any function upon earth.'

I had opened my mouth to reply to this tirade, when, with a crisp knock, our landlady entered, bearing a card upon the brass salver.

'A young lady for you, sir,' she said, addressing my companion.

'Miss Mary Morstan,' he read. 'Hum! I have no recollection of the name. Ask the young lady to step up, Mrs Hudson. Don't go, Doctor. I should prefer that you remain.'

II. THE STATEMENT OF THE CASE

MISS MORSTAN entered the room with a firm step and an outward composure of manner. She was a blonde young lady, small, dainty, well gloved, and dressed in the most perfect taste. There was, however, a plainness and simplicity about her costume which bore with it a suggestion of limited means. The dress was a sombre greyish beige, untrimmed and unbraided, and she wore a small turban of the same dull hue, relieved only by a suspicion of white feather in the side. Her face had neither regularity of feature nor beauty of complexion, but her expression was sweet and amiable, and her large blue eyes were singularly spiritual and sympathetic. In an experience of women which extends over many nations and three separate continents, I have never looked upon a face which gave a clearer promise of a refined and sensitive nature. I could not but observe that, as she took the seat which Sherlock Holmes placed for her, her lip trembled, her hand quivered, and she showed every sign of intense inward agitation.

'I have come to you, Mr Holmes,' she said, 'because you once enabled my employer, Mrs Cecil Forrester, to unravel a little domestic complication. She was much impressed by your kindness and skill.'

'Mrs Cecil Forrester,' he repeated, thoughtfully. 'I believe that I was of some slight service to her. The case, however, as I remember it, was a very simple one.'

'She did not think so. But at least you cannot say the same of mine. I can hardly imagine anything more strange, more utterly inexplicable, than the situation in which I find myself.'

Holmes rubbed his hands, and his eyes glistened. He leaned forward in his chair with an expression of extraordinary concentration upon his clear-cut, hawk-like features.

'State your case,' said he, in brisk, business tones.

I felt that my position was an embarrassing one.

'You will, I am sure, excuse me,' I said, rising from my chair.

To my surprise, the young lady held up her gloved hand to detain me.

'If your friend,' she said, 'would be good enough to stop, he might be of inestimable service to me.'

I relapsed into my chair.

'Briefly,' she continued, 'the facts are these. My father was an officer in an Indian regiment, who sent me home when I was quite a child. My mother was dead, and I had no relative in England. I was placed, however, in a comfortable boarding establishment at Edinburgh, and there I remained until I was seventeen years of age. In the year 1878 my father, who was senior captain of his regiment, obtained twelve months' leave and came home. He telegraphed to me from London that he had arrived all safe, and directed me to come down at once, giving the Langham Hotel as his address. His message, as I remember, was full of kindness and love. On reaching London I drove to the Langham, and was informed that Captain Morstan was staying there, but that he had gone out the night before and had not returned. I waited all day without news of him. That night, on the advice of the manager of the hotel, I communicated with the police, and next morning we advertised in all the papers. Our inquiries led to no result; and from that day to this no word has ever been heard of my unfortunate father. He came home with his heart full of hope, to find some peace, some comfort, and instead——'

She put her hand to her throat, and a choking sob cut short the sentence.

'The date?' asked Holmes, opening his note-book.

'He disappeared upon the 3rd of December, 1878—nearly ten years ago.'

'His luggage?'

'Remained at the hotel. There was nothing in it to suggest a clue—some clothes, some books, and a considerable number of curiosities from the Andaman Islands. He had been one of the officers in charge of the convict guard there.'

'Had he any friends in town?'

'Only one that we know of—Major Sholto, of his own regiment, the 34th Bombay Infantry. The Major had retired some little time before, and lived at Upper Norwood. We communicated with him, of course, but he did not know that his brother officer was in England.'

'A singular case,' remarked Holmes.

'I have not yet described to you the most singular part. About six years ago—to be exact, upon the 4th of May, 1882—an advertisement appeared in *The Times* asking for the address of Miss Mary Morstan, and stating that it would be to her advantage to come forward. There was no name or address appended. I had at that time just entered the family of Mrs Cecil Forrester in the capacity of governess. By her advice I published my address in the advertisement column. The same day there arrived through the post a small cardboard box addressed to me, which I found to contain a very large and lustrous pearl. No word of writing was enclosed. Since then every year upon the same date there has always appeared a similar box, containing a similar pearl, without any clue as to the sender. They have been pronounced by an expert to be of a rare variety and of considerable value. You can see for yourselves that they are very handsome.'

She opened a flat box as she spoke, and showed me six of the finest pearls that I had ever seen.

'Your statement is most interesting,' said Sherlock Holmes. 'Has anything else occurred to you?'

'Yes, and no later than today. That is why I have come to you. This morning I received this letter, which you will perhaps read for yourself.'

'Thank you,' said Holmes. 'The envelope, too, please. Postmark, London, S.W. Date, July 7. Hum! Man's thumb-mark on corner—probably postman. Best quality paper. Envelopes at sixpence a packet. Particular man in his stationery. No address. "Be at the third pillar from the left outside the Lyceum Theatre tonight at seven o'clock. If you are distrustful bring two friends. You are a wronged woman, and shall have justice. Do not bring police. If you do, all will be in vain. Your unknown friend." Well, really, this is a very pretty little mystery! What do you intend to do, Miss Morstan?'

'That is exactly what I want to ask you.'

'Then we shall most certainly go—you and I and—yes, why, Dr Watson is the very man. Your correspondent says two friends. He and I have worked together before.'

'But would he come?' she asked, with something appealing in her voice and expression.

'I shall be proud and happy,' said I, fervently, 'if I can be of any service.'

'You are both very kind,' she answered. 'I have led a retired life, and have no friends whom I could appeal to. If I am here at six it will do, I suppose?'

'You must not be later,' said Holmes. 'There is one other point, however. Is this handwriting the same as that upon the pearl-box addresses?'

'I have them here,' she answered, producing half-a-dozen pieces of paper.

'You are certainly a model client. You have the correct intuition. Let us see, now.' He spread out the papers upon the table, and gave little, darting glances from one to the other. 'They are disguised hands, except the letter,' he said, presently; 'but there can be no question as to the authorship. See how the irrepressible Greek ε will break out, and see the twirl of the final ς. They are undoubtedly by the same person. I should not like to suggest false hopes, Miss Morstan, but is there any resemblance between this hand and that of your father?'

'Nothing could be more unlike.'

'I expected to hear you say so. We shall look out for you, then, at six. Pray allow me to keep the papers. I may look into the matter before then. It is only half-past three. *Au revoir,* then.'

'*Au revoir,*' said our visitor; and with a bright, kindly glance from one to the other of us, she replaced her pearl-box in her bosom and hurried away.

Standing at the window, I watched her walking briskly down the street, until the grey turban and white feather were but a speck in the sombre crowd.

'What a very attractive woman!' I exclaimed, turning to my companion.

He had lit his pipe again, and was leaning back with drooping eyelids. 'Is she?' he said, languidly; 'I did not observe.'

'You really are an automaton—a calculating machine,' I cried. 'There is something positively inhuman in you at times.'

He smiled gently.

'It is of the first importance,' he said, 'not to allow your judgment to be biased by personal qualities. A client is to me a mere unit, a factor in a problem. The emotional qualities are antagonistic to clear reasoning. I assure you that the most winning woman I ever knew was hanged for poisoning three little children for their insurance-money, and the most repellent man of my acquaintance is a philanthropist who has spent nearly a quarter of a million upon the London poor.'

'In this case, however——'

'I never make exceptions. An exception disproves the rule. Have you ever had occasion to study character in handwriting? What do you make of this fellow's scribble?'

'It is legible and regular,' I answered. 'A man of business habits and some force of character.'

Holmes shook his head.

'Look at his long letters,' he said. 'They hardly rise above the common herd. That *d* might be an *a*, and that *l* an *e*. Men of character always differentiate their long letters, however illegibly they may write. There is vacillation in his *k*'s and self-esteem in his capitals. I am going out now. I have some few references to make. Let me recommend this book—one of the most remarkable ever penned. It is Winwood Reade's "*Martyrdom of Man*". I shall be back in an hour.'

I sat in the window with the volume in my hand, but my thoughts were far from the daring speculations of the writer. My mind ran upon our late visitor—her smiles, the deep, rich tones of her voice, the strange mystery which overhung her life. If she were seventeen at the time of her father's disappearance she must be seven-and-twenty now—a sweet age, when youth has lost its self-consciousness and become a little sobered by experience. So I sat and mused, until such dangerous thoughts came into my head that I hurried away to my desk and plunged furiously into the latest treatise upon pathology. What was I, an Army surgeon with a weak leg and a weaker banking account, that I should dare to think of such things? She was a unit, a factor—nothing more. If my future were black, it was better surely to face it like a man than to attempt to brighten it by mere will-o'-the-wisps of the imagination.

III. IN QUEST OF A SOLUTION

IT was half-past five before Holmes returned. He was bright, eager, and in excellent spirits, a mood which in his case alternated with fits of the blackest depression.

'There is no great mystery in this matter,' he said, taking the cup of tea which I had poured out for him; 'the facts appear to admit of only one explanation.'

'What! you have solved it already?'

'Well, that would be too much to say. I have discovered a suggestive fact, that is all. It is, however, *very* suggestive. The details are still to be added. I have just found, on consulting the back files of *The Times*, that Major Sholto, of Upper Norwood, late of the 34th Bombay Infantry, died upon the 28th of April, 1882.'

'I may be very obtuse, Holmes, but I fail to see what this suggests.'

'No? You surprise me. Look at it in this way, then. Captain Morstan disappears. The only person in London whom he could have visited is Major Sholto. Major Sholto denies having heard that he was in London. Four years later Sholto dies. *Within a week of his death* Captain Morstan's daughter receives a valuable present, which is repeated from year to year, and now culminates in a letter which describes her as a wronged woman. What wrong can it refer to except this deprivation of her father? And why should the presents begin immediately after Sholto's death, unless it is that Sholto's heir knows something of the mystery and desires to make compensation? Have you any alternative theory which will meet the facts?'

'But what a strange compensation! And how strangely made! Why, too, should he write a letter now, rather than six years ago? Again, the letter speaks of giving her justice. What justice can she have? It is too much to suppose that her father is still alive. There is no other injustice in her case that you know of.'

'There are difficulties; there are certainly difficulties,' said Sherlock Holmes, pensively; 'but our expedition of tonight will solve them all. Ah, here is a four-wheeler, and Miss Morstan inside. Are you all ready? Then we had better go down, for it is a little past the hour.'

I picked up my hat and my heaviest stick, but I observed that Holmes took his revolver from his drawer and slipped it into his pocket. It was clear that he thought that our night's work might be a serious one.

Miss Morstan was muffled in a dark cloak, and her sensitive face was composed, but pale. She must have been more than woman if she did not feel some uneasiness at the strange enterprise upon which we were embarking, yet her self-control was perfect, and she readily answered the few additional questions which Sherlock Holmes put to her.

'Major Sholto was a very particular friend of Papa's,' she said. 'His letters were full of allusions to the Major. He and Papa were in command of the troops at the Andaman Islands, so they were thrown a great deal together. By the way, a curious paper was found in Papa's desk which no one could understand. I don't suppose that it is of the slightest importance, but I thought you might care to see it, so I brought it with me. It is here.'

Holmes unfolded the paper carefully and smoothed it out upon his knee. He then very methodically examined it all over with his double lens.

'It is a paper of native Indian manufacture,' he remarked. 'It has at some time been pinned to a board. The diagram upon it appears to be a plan of part of a large building with numerous halls, corridors and passages. At one point is a small cross done in red ink, and above it is "3.37 from left" in faded pencil-writing. In the left-hand corner is a curious hieroglyphic like four crosses in a line with their arms touching. Beside it is written, in very rough and coarse characters, "The sign of the four—Jonathan Small, Mahomet Singh, Abdullah Khan, Dost Akbar." No, I confess that I do not see how this bears upon the matter. Yet it is evidently a document of importance. It has been kept carefully in a pocket-book; for the one side is as clean as the other.'

'It was in his pocket-book that we found it.'

'Preserve it carefully, then, Miss Morstan, for it may prove to be of use to us. I begin to suspect that this matter may turn out to be much deeper and more subtle than I at first supposed. I must reconsider my ideas.'

He leaned back in the cab, and I could see by his drawn brow and his vacant eye that he was thinking intently. Miss Morstan and I chatted in an undertone about our present expedition and its possible outcome, but our companion maintained his impenetrable reserve until the end of our journey.

It was September evening, and not yet seven o'clock, but the day had been a dreary one, and a dense drizzly fog lay low upon the great city. Mud-coloured clouds drooped sadly over the muddy streets. Down the Strand the lamps were but misty splotches of diffused light, which threw a feeble circular glimmer upon the slimy pavement. The yellow glare from the shop-windows streamed out into the steamy, vaporous air, and threw a murky, shifting radiance across the crowded thoroughfare. There was, to my mind, something eerie and ghost-like in the endless procession of faces which flitted across these narrow bars of light—sad faces and glad, haggard and merry. Like all human kind, they flitted from the gloom into the light, and so back into the gloom once more. I am not subject to impressions, but the dull, heavy evening, with the strange business upon which we were engaged, combined to make me nervous and depressed. I could see from Miss Morstan's manner that she was suffering from the same feeling. Holmes alone could rise superior to petty influences. He held his open note-book upon his knee, and from time to time he jotted down figures and memoranda in the light of his pocket-lantern.

At the Lyceum Theatre the crowds were already thick at the side-entrances. In front a continuous stream of hansoms and four-wheelers were rattling up, discharging their cargoes of shirt-fronted men and beshawled and bediamonded women. We had hardly reached the third pillar, which was our rendezvous, before a small, dark, brisk man in the dress of a coachman accosted us.

'Are you the parties who come with Miss Morstan?' he asked.

'I am Miss Morstan, and these two gentlemen are my friends,' said she.

He bent a pair of wonderfully penetrating and questioning eyes upon us.

'You will excuse me; miss,' he said, with a certain dogged manner, 'but I was to ask you to give me your word that neither of your companions is a police-officer.'

'I give you my word on that,' she answered.

He gave a shrill whistle, on which a street arab led across a four-wheeler and opened the door. The man who had addressed us mounted to the box, while we took our places inside. We had hardly done so before the driver whipped up his horse, and we plunged away at a furious pace through the foggy streets.

The situation was a curious one. We were driving to an unknown place, on an unknown errand. Yet our invitation was either a complete hoax—which was an inconceivable hypothesis—or else we had good reason to think that important issues might hang upon our journey. Miss Morstan's demeanour was as resolute and collected as ever. I endeavoured to cheer and amuse her by reminiscences of my adventures in Afghanistan; but, to tell the truth, I was myself so excited at our situation, and so curious as to our destination, that my stories were slightly involved. To this day she declares that I told her one moving anecdote as to how a musket looked into my tent at the dead of night, and how I fired a double-barrelled tiger cub at it. At first I had some idea as to the direction in which we were driving; but soon, what with our pace, the fog, and my own limited knowledge of London, I lost my bearings, and knew nothing, save that we seemed to be going a very long way. Sherlock Holmes was never at fault, however, and he muttered the names as the cab rattled through squares and in and out by tortuous by-streets.

'Rochester Row,' said he. 'Now Vincent Square. Now we come out on the Vauxhall Bridge Road. We are making for the Surrey side, apparently. Yes, I thought so. Now we are on the bridge. You can catch glimpses of the river.'

We did indeed get a fleeting view of a stretch of the Thames, with the lamps shining upon the broad, silent water; but our cab dashed on, and was soon involved in a labyrinth of streets upon the other side.

'Wandsworth Road,' said my companion. 'Priory Road. Larkhall Lane. Stockwell Place. Robert Street. Coldharbour Lane. Our quest does not appear to take us to very fashionable regions.'

We had indeed reached a questionable and forbidding neighbourhood. Long lines of dull brick houses were only relieved by the coarse glare and tawdry brilliancy of public-houses at the corners. Then came rows of two-storied villas, each with a frontage of miniature garden, and then again interminable lines of new, staring brick buildings—the monster tentacles which the giant city was throwing out into the country. At last the cab drew up at the third house in a new terrace. None of the other houses were inhabited, and that at which we stopped was as dark as its neighbours, save for a single glimmer in the kitchen-window. On our knocking, however, the door was instantly thrown open by a Hindu servant, clad in a yellow turban, white, loose-fitting clothes, and a yellow sash. There was something strangely incongruous in this Oriental figure framed in the commonplace doorway of a third-rate suburban dwelling-house.

'The sahib awaits you,' said he, and even as he spoke there came a high, piping voice from some inner room.

'Show them in to me, khidmutgar,' it cried. 'Show them straight in to me.'

IV. THE STORY OF THE BALD-HEADED MAN

WE followed the Indian down a sordid and common passage, ill-lit and worse-furnished, until he came to a door upon the right, which he threw open. A blaze of yellow light streamed out upon us, and in the centre of the glare there stood a small man with a very high head, a bristle of red hair all round the fringe of it, and a bald, shining scalp which shot out from among it like a mountain-peak from fir-trees. He writhed his hands together as he stood, and his features were in a perpetual jerk—now smiling, now scowling, but never for an instant in repose. Nature had given him a pendulous lip, and a too visible line of yellow and irregular teeth, which he strove feebly to conceal by constantly passing his hand over the lower part of his face. In spite of his obtrusive baldness, he gave the impression of youth. In point of fact, he had just turned his thirtieth year.

'Your servant, Miss Morstan,' he kept repeating, in a thin, high voice. 'Your servant, gentlemen. Pray step into my little sanctum. A small place, miss, but furnished to my own liking. An oasis of art in the howling desert of South London.'

We were all astonished by the appearance of the apartment into which he invited us. In that sorry house it looked as out-of-place as a diamond of the first water in a setting of brass. The richest and glossiest of curtains and tapestries draped the walls, looped back here and there to expose some richly-mounted painting or Oriental vase. The carpet was of amber and black, so soft and so thick that the foot sank pleasantly into it, as into a bed of moss. Two great tiger-skins thrown athwart it increased the suggestion of Eastern luxury, as did a huge hookah which stood upon a mat in the corner. A lamp in the fashion of a silver dove was hung from an almost invisible golden wire in the centre of the room. As it burned it filled the air with a subtle and aromatic odour.

'Mr Thaddeus Sholto,' said the little man, still jerking and smiling. 'That is my name. You are Miss Morstan, of course. And these gentlemen——'

'This is Mr Sherlock Holmes, and this Dr Watson.'

'A doctor, eh?' cried he, much excited. 'Have you your stethoscope? Might I ask you—would you have the kindness? I have grave doubts as to my mitral valve, if you would be so very good. The aortic I may rely on, but I should value your opinion upon the mitral.'

I listened to his heart, as requested, but was unable to find anything amiss, save, indeed, that he was in an ecstasy of fear, for he shivered from head to foot.

'It appears to be normal,' I said. 'You have no cause for uneasiness.'

'You will excuse my anxiety, Miss Morstan,' he remarked airily. 'I am a great sufferer, and I have long had suspicions as to that valve. I am delighted to hear that they are unwarranted. Had your father, Miss Morstan, refrained from throwing a strain upon his heart, he might have been alive now.'

I could have struck the man across the face, so hot was I at this callous and off-hand reference to so delicate a matter. Miss Morstan sat down, and her face grew white to the lips.

'I knew in my heart that he was dead,' said she.

'I can give you every information,' said he, 'and what is more, I can do you justice; and I will, too, whatever Brother Bartholomew may say. I am so glad to have your friends here, not only as an escort to you, but also as witnesses to what I am about to do and say. The three of us can show a bold front to Brother Bartholomew. But let us have no outsiders—no police or officials. We can settle everything satisfactorily among ourselves, without any interference. Nothing would annoy Brother Bartholomew more than any publicity.'

He sat down upon a low settee, and blinked at us inquiringly with his weak, watery blue eyes.

'For my part,' said Holmes, 'whatever you may choose to say will go no farther.'

I noded to show my agreement.

'That is well! That is well!' said he. 'May I offer you a glass of Chianti, Miss Morstan? Or of Tokay? I keep no other wines. Shall I open a flask? No? Well, then, I trust that you have no objection to tobacco smoke, to the balsamic odour of the Eastern tobacco. I am a little nervous, and I find my hookah an invaluable sedative.'

He applied a taper to the great bowl, and the smoke bubbled merrily through the rosewater. We sat all three in a semi-circle, with our heads advanced and our chins upon our hands, while the strange, jerky little fellow, with his high, shining head, puffed uneasily in the centre.

'When I first determined to make this communication to you,' said he, 'I might have given you my address; but I feared that you might disregard my request and bring unpleasant people with you. I took the liberty, therefore, of making an appointment in such a way that my man Williams might be able to see you first. I have complete confidence in his discretion, and he had orders, if he were dissatisfied, to proceed no further in the matter. You will excuse these precautions, but I am a man of somewhat retiring, and I might even say refined, tastes, and there is nothing more unaesthetic than a policeman. I have a natural shrinking from all forms of rough materialism. I seldom come in contact with the rough crowd. I live, as you see, with some little atmosphere of elegance around me. I may call myself a patron of the arts. It is my weakness. The landscape is a genuine Corot, and, though a connoisseur might perhaps throw a doubt upon that Salvator Rosa, there cannot be the least question about the Bouguereau. I am partial to the modern French school.'

'You will excuse me, Mr Sholto,' said Miss Morstan, 'but I am here at your request to learn something which you desire to tell me. It is very late, and I should desire the interview to be as short as possible.'

'At the best, it must take some time,' he answered; 'for we shall certainly have to go to Norwood and see Brother Bartholomew. We shall all go and try if we can get the better of Brother Bartholomew. He is very angry with me for taking the course which has seemed right to me. I had quite high words with him last night. You cannot imagine what a terrible fellow he is when he is angry.'

'If we are to go to Norwood, it would perhaps be as well to start at once,' I ventured to remark.

He laughed until his ears were quite red.

'That would hardly do,' he cried. 'I don't know what he would say if I brought you in that sudden way. No, I must prepare you by showing you how we all stand to each other. In the first place, I must tell you that there are several points in the story of which I am myself ignorant. I can only lay the facts before you as far as I know them myself.

'My father was, as you may have guessed, Major John Sholto, once of the Indian Army. He retired some eleven years ago, and came to live at Pondicherry Lodge, in Upper Norwood. He had prospered in India, and brought back with him a considerable sum of money, a large collection of valuable curiosities, and a staff of native servants. With these advantages he bought himself a house, and lived in great luxury. My twin brother Bartholomew and I were the only children.

'I very well remember the sensation which was caused by the disappearance of Captain Morstan. We read the details in the papers, and knowing that he had been a friend of our father's, we discussed the case freely in his presence. He used to join in our speculations as to what could have happened. Never for an instant did we suspect that he had the whole secret hidden in his own breast, that of all men he alone knew the fate of Arthur Morstan.

'We did know, however, that some mystery, some positive danger, overhung our father. He was very fearful of going out alone, and he always employed two prize-fighters to act as porters at Pondicherry Lodge. Williams, who drove you tonight, was one of them. He was once light-weight champion of England. Our father would never tell us what it was he feared, but he had a most marked aversion to men with wooden legs. On one occasion he actually fired his revolver at a wooden-legged man who proved to be a harmless tradesman canvassing for orders. We had to pay a large sum to hush the matter up. My brother and I used to think this a mere whim of my father's; but events have since led us to change our opinion.

'Early in 1882 my father received a letter from India which was a great shock to him. He nearly fainted at the breakfast-table when he opened it, and from that day he sickened to his death. What was in the letter we could never discover, but I could see as he held it that it was short and written in a scrawling hand. He had suffered for years from an enlarged spleen, but he now became rapidly worse, and towards the end of April we were informed that he was beyond all hope, and that he wished to make a last communication to us.

'When we entered his room he was propped up with pillows and breathing heavily. He besought us to lock the door and to come upon either side of the bed. Then, grasping our hands, he made a remarkable statement to us, in a voice which was broken as much by emotion as by pain. I shall try and give it you in his very own words.

' "I have only one thing," he said, "which weighs upon my mind at this supreme moment. It is my treatment of poor Morstan's orphan. The cursed greed which has been my besetting sin through life has withheld from her the treasure, half at least of which should have been hers. And yet I have made no use of it myself, so blind and foolish a thing is avarice. The mere feeling of possession has been so dear to me that I could not bear to share it with another. See that chaplet tipped with pearls beside the quinine-bottle? Even that I could not bear to part with, although I had got it out with the design of sending it to her. You, my sons, will give her a fair share of the Agra treasure. But send her nothing—not even the chaplet —until I am gone. After all, men have been as bad as this and have recovered.

' "I will tell you how Morstan died," he continued. "He had suffered for years from a weak heart, but he concealed it from everyone. I alone knew it. When in India, he and I, through a remarkable chain of circumstances, came into possession of a considerable treasure. I bought it over to England, and on the night of Morstan's arrival he came straight over here to claim his share. He walked over from the station, and was admitted by my faithful old Lal Chowdar, who is now dead. Morstan and I had a difference of opinion as to the division of the treasure, and we came to heated words. Morstan had sprung out of his chair in a paroxysm of anger, when he suddenly pressed his hand to his side, his face turned a sickly hue, and he fell backwards, cutting his head against the corner of the treasure-chest. When I stooped over him I found, to my horror, that he was dead.

' "For a long time I sat half distracted, wondering what I should do. My first impulse was, of course, to call for assistance; but I could not but recognize that there was every chance that I would be accused of his murder. His death at the moment of a quarrel, and the gash in his head, would be black against me. Again, an official inquiry could not be made without bringing out some facts about the treasure, which I was particularly anxious to keep secret. He had told me that no soul upon earth knew where he had gone. There seemed to be no necessity why any soul ever should know.

' "I was still pondering over the matter, when, looking up, I saw my servant, Lal Chowdar, in the doorway. He stole in and bolted the door behind him. 'Do not fear, sahib,' he said; 'no one need know that you have killed him. Let us hide him away, and who is the wiser?' 'I did not kill him,' said I. Lal Chowdar shook his head and smiled. 'I heard it all, sahib,' said he; 'I heard you quarrel, and I heard the blow. But my lips are sealed. All are asleep in the house. Let us put him away together.' That was enough to decide me. If my own servant could not believe my innocence, how could I hope to make it good before twelve foolish tradesmen in a jury-box? Lal Chowdar and I disposed of the body that night, and within a few days the London papers were full of the mysterious disappearance of Captain Morstan. You will see from what I say that I can hardly be blamed in the matter. My fault lies in the fact that we concealed not only the body, but also the treasure, and that I have clung to Morstan's share as well as to my own. I wish you, therefore, to make restitution. Put your ears to my mouth. The treasure is hidden in——"

'At this instant a horrible change came over his expression; his eyes stared wildly, his jaw dropped, and he yelled, in a voice which I can never forget, "Keep him out! For Christ's sake, keep him out!" We both stared round at the window behind us upon which his gaze was fixed. A face was looking in at us out of the darkness. We could see the whitening of the nose where it was pressed against the glass. It was a bearded, hairy face, with wild, cruel eyes and an expression of concentrated malevolence. My brother and I rushed towards the window, but the man was gone. When we returned to my father, his head had dropped and his pulse had ceased to beat.

'We searched the garden that night, but found no sign of the intruder, save that just under the window a single footmark was visible in the flower-bed. But for that one trace, we might have thought that our imaginations had conjured up that wild, fierce face. We soon, however, had another and more striking proof that there were secret agencies at work all round us. The window of my father's room was found open in the morning, his cupboards and boxes had been rifled, and upon his chest was fixed a torn piece of paper, with the words, "The sign of the four," scrawled across it. What the phrase meant, or who our secret visitor may have been, we never knew. As far as we can judge, none of my father's property had been actually stolen, though everything had been turned out.

My brother and I naturally associated this peculiar incident with the fear which haunted my father during his life; but it is still a complete mystery to us.'

The little man stopped to relight his hookah, and puffed thoughtfully for a few moments. We had all sat absorbed, listening to his extraordinary narrative. At the short account of her father's death Miss Morstan had turned deadly white, and for a moment I feared that she was about to faint. She rallied, however, on drinking a glass of water which I quietly poured out for her from a Venetian carafe upon the side-table. Sherlock Holmes leaned back in his chair with an abstracted expression and the lids drawn low over his glittering eyes. As I glanced at him I could not but think how, on that very day, he had complained bitterly of the commonplaceness of life. Here at least was a problem which would tax his sagacity to the utmost. Mr Thaddeus Sholto looked from one to the other of us with an obvious pride at the effect which his story had produced, and then continued, between the puffs of his overgrown pipe.

'My brother and I,' said he, 'were, as you may imagine, much excited as to the treasure which my father had spoken of. For weeks and for months we dug and delved in every part of the garden without discovering its whereabouts. It was maddening to think that the hiding-place was on his very lips at the moment that he died. We could judge the splendour of the missing riches by the chaplet which he had taken out. Over this chaplet my brother Bartholomew and I had some little discussion. The pearls were evidently of great value, and he was averse to part with them, for, between friends, my brother was himself a little inclined to my father's fault. He thought, too, that if we parted with the chaplet it might give rise to gossip, and finally bring us into trouble. It was all that I could do to persuade him to let me find out Miss Morstan's address and send her a detached pearl at fixed intervals, so that at least she might never feel destitute.'

'It was a kindly thought,' said our companion, earnestly; 'it was extremely good of you.'

The little man waved his hand deprecatingly.

'We were your trustees,' he said. 'That was the view which I took of it, though Brother Bartholomew could not altogether see it in that light. We had plenty of money ourselves. I desired no more. Besides, it would have been such bad taste to have treated a young lady in so scurvy a fashion. "*Le mauvais goût mène au crime.*" The

French have a very neat way of putting these things. Our difference of opinion on this subject went so far that I thought it best to set up rooms for myself; so I left Pondicherry Lodge, taking the old khidmutgar and Williams with me. Yesterday, however, I learnt that an event of extreme importance has occurred. The treasure has been discovered. I instantly communicated with Miss Morstan, and it only remains for us to drive out to Norwood and demand our share. I explained my views last night to Brother Bartholomew, so we shall be expected, if not welcome, visitors.'

Mr Thaddeus Sholto ceased, and sat twitching on his luxurious settee. We all remained silent, with our thoughts upon the new development which the mysterious business had taken. Holmes was the first to spring to his feet.

'You have done well, sir, from first to last,' said he. 'It is possible that we may be able to make you some small return by throwing some light upon that which is still dark to you. But, as Miss Morstan remarked just now, it is late, and we had best put the matter through without delay.'

Our new acquaintance very deliberately coiled up the tube of his hookah, and produced from behind a curtain a very long, befrogged top-coat with Astrakhan collar and cuffs. This he buttoned tightly up, in spite of the extreme closeness of the night, and finished his attire by putting on a rabbit-skin cap with hanging lappets which covered the ears, so that no part of him was visible save his mobile and peaky face.

'My health is somewhat fragile,' he remarked, as he led the way down the passage. 'I am compelled to be a valetudinarian.'

Our cab was awaiting us outside, and our programme was evidently prearranged, for the driver started off at once at a rapid pace. Thaddeus Sholto talked incessantly, in a voice which rose high above the rattle of the wheels.

'Bartholomew is a clever fellow,' said he. 'How do you think he found out where the treasure was? He had come to the conclusion that it was somewhere indoors: so he worked out all the cubic space of the house, and made measurements everywhere, so that not one inch should be unaccounted for. Among other things, he found that the height of the building was seventy-four feet, but on adding together the heights of all the separate rooms, and making every allowance for the space between, which he ascertained by borings, he could not bring the total to more than seventy feet.

There were four feet unaccounted for. These could only be at the top of the building. He knocked a hole, therefore, in the lath and plaster ceiling of the highest room, and there, sure enough, he came upon another little garret above it, which had been sealed up and was known to no one. In the centre stood the treasure-chest, resting upon two rafters. He lowered it through the hole, and there it lies. He computes the value of the jewels at not less than half a million sterling.'

At the mention of this gigantic sum we all stared at one another open-eyed. Miss Morstan, could we secure her rights, would change from a needy governess to the richest heiress in England. Surely it was the place of a loyal friend to rejoice at such news; yet I am ashamed to say that selfishness took me by the soul, and that my heart turned as heavy as lead within me. I stammered out some few halting words of congratulation, and then sat downcast, with my head drooped, deaf to the babble of our new acquaintance. He was clearly a confirmed hypochondriac, and I was dreamily conscious that he was pouring forth interminable trains of symptoms, and imploring information as to the composition and action of innumerable quack nostrums, some of which he bore about in a leather case in his pocket. I trust that he may not remember any of the answers which I gave him that night. Holmes declares that he overheard me caution him against the great danger of taking more than two drops of caster-oil, while I recommended strychnine in large doses as a sedative. However that may be, I was certainly relieved when our cab pulled up with a jerk and the coachman sprang down to open the door.

'This, Miss Morstan, is Pondicherry Lodge,' said Mr Thaddeus Sholto, as he handed her out.

V. THE TRAGEDY OF PONDICHERRY LODGE

IT was nearly eleven o'clock when we reached this final stage of our night's adventures. We had left the damp fog of the great city behind us, and the night was fairly fine. A warm wind blew from the westward, and heavy clouds moved slowly across the sky, with half a moon peeping occasionally through the rifts. It was clear enough to see for some distance, but Thaddeus Sholto took down one of the sidelamps from the carriage to give us a better light upon our way.

Pondicherry Lodge stood in its own grounds, and was girt round with a very high stone wall topped with broken glass. A single narrow iron-clamped door formed the only means of entrance. On this our guide knocked with a peculiar postman-like rat-tat.

'Who is there?' cried a gruff voice from within.

'It is I, McMurdo. You surely know my knock by this time.'

There was a grumbling sound and a clanking and jarring of keys. The door swung heavily back, and a short, deep-chested man stood in the opening, with the yellow light of the lantern shining upon his protruded face and twinkling, distrustful eyes.

'That you, Mr Thaddeus? But who are the others? I had no orders about them from the master.'

'No, McMurdo? You surprise me! I told my brother last night that I should bring some friends.'

'He hain't been out o' his room today, Mr Thaddeus, and I have no orders. You know very well that I must stick to regulations. I can let you in, but your friends they must just stop where they are.'

This was an unexpected obstacle. Thaddeus Sholto looked about him in a perplexed and helpless manner.

'This is too bad of you, McMurdo!' he said. 'If I guarantee them, that is enough for you. There is the young lady, too. She cannot wait on the public road at this hour.'

'Very sorry, Mr Thaddeus,' said the porter, inexorably. 'Folk may be friends o' yours, and yet no friends o' the master's. He pays me well to do my duty, and my duty I'll do. I don't know none o' your friends.'

'Oh, yes, you do, McMurdo,' cried Sherlock Holmes, genially. 'I don't think you can have forgotten me. Don't you remember the amateur who fought three rounds with you at Alison's rooms on the night of your benefit four years back?'

'Not Mr Sherlock Holmes!' roared the prizefighter. 'God's truth! how could I have mistook you? If instead o' standin' there so quiet you had just stepped up and given me that cross-hit of yours under the jaw, I'd ha' known you without a question. Ah, you're one that has wasted your gifts, you have! You might have aimed high, if you had joined the fancy.'

'You see, Watson, if all else fails me, I have still one of the scientific professions open to me,' said Holmes, laughing. 'Our friend won't keep us out in the cold now, I am sure.

'In you come, sir, in you come—you and your friends,' he answered. 'Very sorry, Mr Thaddeus, but orders are very strict. Had to be certain of your friends before I let them in.'

Inside, a gravel path wound through desolate grounds to a huge clump of a house, square and prosaic, all plunged in shadow save where a moon beam struck one corner and glimmered in a garret window. The vast size of the building, with its gloom and its deathly silence, struck a chill to the heart. Even Thaddeus Sholto seemed ill at ease, and the lantern quivered and rattled in his hand.

'I cannot understand it,' he said. 'There must be some mistake. I distinctly told Bartholomew that we should be here, and yet there is no light in his window. I do not know what to make of it.'

'Does he always guard the premises in this way?' asked Holmes.

'Yes, he has followed my father's custom. He was the favourite son, you know, and I sometimes think that my father may have told him more than he ever told me. That is Bartholomew's window up there where the moonshine strikes. It is quite bright, but there is no light from within, I think.'

'None,' said Holmes. 'But I see the glint of a light in that little window beside the door.'

'Ah, that is the housekeeper's room. That is where old Mrs Bernstone sits. She can tell us all about it. But perhaps you would not mind waiting here for a minute or two, for if we all go in together, and she has had no word of our coming, she may be alarmed. But, hush, what is that?'

He held up the lantern, and his hand shook until the circles of light flickered and wavered all round us. Miss Morstan seized my wrist, and we all stood, with thumping hearts, straining our ears. From the great black house there sounded through the silent night the saddest and most pitiful of sounds, the shrill, broken whimpering of a frightened woman.

'It is Mrs Bernstone,' said Sholto. 'She is the only woman in the house. Wait here. I shall be back in a moment.'

He hurried for the door, and knocked in his peculiar way. We could see a tall old woman admit him, and sway with pleasure at the very sight of him.

'Oh Mr Thaddeus, sir, I am so glad you have come! I am so glad you have come, Mr Thaddeus, sir!'

We heard her reiterated rejoicings until the door was closed and her voice died away into a muffled monotone.

Our guide had left us the lantern. Holmes swung it slowly round, and peered keenly at the house, and at the great rubbish-heaps which cumbered the grounds. Miss Morstan and I stood together, and her hand was in mine. A wondrous subtle thing is love, for here were we two, who had never seen each other before that day, between whom no word or even look of affection had ever passed, and yet now in an hour of trouble our hands instinctively sought for each other. I have marvelled at it since, but at the time it seemed the most natural thing that I should go out to her so, and, as she has often told me, there was in her also the instinct to turn to me for comfort and protection. So we stood hand in hand, like two children, and there was peace in our hearts for all the dark things that surrounded us.

'What a strange place!' she said, looking round.

'It looks as though all the moles in England had been let loose in it. I have seen something of the sort on the side of a hill near Ballarat, where the prospectors had been at work.'

'And from the same cause,' said Holmes. 'These are the traces of the treasure-seekers. You must remember that they were six years looking for it. No wonder that the grounds look like a gravel-pit.'

At that moment the door of the house burst open, and Thaddeus Sholto came running out, with his hands thrown forward and terror in his eyes.

'There is something amiss with Bartholomew!' he cried. 'I am frightened! My nerves cannot stand it.'

He was, indeed, half blubbering with fear, and his twitching, feeble face peeping out from the great astrakhan collar had the helpless, appealing expression of a terrified child.

'Come into the house,' said Holmes, in his crisp, firm way.

'Yes, do!' pleaded Thaddeus Sholto. 'I really do not feel equal to giving directions.'

We all followed him into the housekeeper's room, which stood upon the left-hand side of the passage. The old woman was pacing up and down with a scared look and restless, picking fingers, but the sight of Miss Morstan appeared to have a soothing effect upon her.

'God bless your sweet, calm face!' she cried, with an hysterical sob. 'It does me good to see you. Oh, but I have been sorely tried this day!'

Our companion patted her thin, work-worn hand, and murmured some few words of kindly, womanly comfort, which brought the colour back into the other's bloodless cheeks.

'Master has locked himself in, and will not answer me,' she explained. 'All day I have waited to hear from him, for he often likes to be alone; but an hour ago I feared that something was amiss, so I went up and peeped through the keyhole. You must go up, Mr Thaddeus—you must go up and look for yourself. I have seen Mr Bartholomew Sholto in joy and in sorrow for ten long years, but I never saw him with such a face on him as that.'

Sherlock Holmes took the lamp and led the way, for Thaddeus Sholto's teeth were chattering in his head. So shaken was he that I had to pass my hand under his arm as we went up the stairs, for his knees were trembling under him. Twice as we ascended Holmes whipped his lens out of his pocket and carefully examined marks which appeared to me to be mere shapeless smudges of dust upon the coconut-matting which served as a stair-carpet. He walked slowly from step to step, holding the lamp low, and shooting keen glances to right and left. Miss Morstan had remained behind with the frightened housekeeper.

The third flight of stairs ended in a straight passage of some length, with a great picture in Indian tapestry upon the right of it and three doors on the left. Holmes advanced along it in the same slow and methodical way, while we kept close at his heels, with our long, black shadows streaming backwards down the corridor. The third door was that which we were seeking. Holmes knocked without receiving any answer, and then tried to turn the handle and force it open. It was locked on the inside, however, and by a broad and powerful bolt, as we could see when we set our lamp up against it. The key being turned, however, the hole was not entirely closed. Sherlock Holmes bent down to it, and instantly rose again with a sharp intaking of the breath.

'There is something devilish in this, Watson,' said he, more moved than I had ever before seen him. 'What do you make of it?'

I stooped to the hole, and recoiled in horror. Moonlight was streaming into the room, and it was bright with a vague and shifty radiance. Looking straight at me, and suspended, as it were, in the air, for all beneath was in shadow, there hung a face—the very face of our companion Thaddeus. There was the same high, shining head, the same circular bristle of red hair, the same bloodless countenance. The features were set, however, in a horrible smile, a fixed and unnatural grin, which in that still and moonlit room was more jarring to the nerves than any scowl or contortion. So like was the face to that of our little friend that I looked round at him to make sure that he was indeed with us. Then I recalled to mind that he had mentioned to us that his brother and he were twins.

'This is terrible!' I said to Holmes. 'What is to be done?'

'The door must come down,' he answered, and, springing against it, he put all his weight upon the lock.

It creaked and groaned, but did not yield. Together we flung ourselves upon it once more, and this time it gave way with a sudden snap, and we found ourselves within Bartholomew Sholto's chamber.

It appeared to have been fitted up as a chemical laboratory. A double line of glass-stoppered bottles was drawn up upon the wall opposite the door, and the table was littered over with Bunsen burners, test-tubes, and retorts. In the corners stood carboys of acid in wicker baskets. One of these appeared to leak or to have been broken, for a stream of dark-coloured liquid had trickled out from it, and the air was heavy with a peculiarly pungent, tar-like odour. A set of steps stood at one side of the room, in the midst of a litter of lath and plaster, and above them there was an opening in the ceiling large enough for a man to pass through. At the foot of the steps a long coil of rope was thrown carelessly together.

By the table, in a wooden arm-chair, the master of the house was seated all in a heap, with his head sunk upon his left shoulder, and that ghastly, inscrutable smile upon his face. He was stiff and cold, and had clearly been dead many hours. It seemed to me that not only his features, but all his limbs, were twisted and turned in the most fantastic fashion. By his hand upon the table there lay a peculiar instrument—a brown, close-grained stick, with a stone head like a hammer, rudely lashed on with coarse twine. Beside it was a torn sheet of note–paper with some words scrawled upon it. Holmes glanced at it, then handed it to me.

'You see,' he said, with a significant raising of the eyebrows.

In the light of the lantern I read, with a thrill of horror, 'The sign of the four'.

'In God's name, what does it all mean?' I asked.

'It means murder,' said he, stooping over the dead man. 'Ah! I expected it. Look here!'

He pointed to what looked like a long, dark thorn stuck in the skin just above the ear.

'It looks like a thorn,' said I.

'It is a thorn. You may pick it out. But be careful, for it is poisoned.'

I took it up between my finger and thumb. It came away from the skin so readily that hardly any mark was left behind. One tiny speck of blood showed where the puncture had been.

'This is an insoluble mystery to me,' said I. 'It grows darker instead of clearer.'

'On the contrary,' he answered, 'it clears every instant. I only require a few missing links to have an entirely connected case.'

We had almost forgotten our companion's presence since we entered the chamber. He was still standing in the doorway, the very picture of terror, wringing his hands and moaning to himself. Suddenly, however, he broke out into a sharp, querulous cry.

'The treasure is gone!' he said. 'They have robbed him of the treasure! There is the hole through which we lowered it. I helped him to do it! I was the last person who saw him! I left him here last night, and I heard him lock the door as I came downstairs.'

'What time was that?'

'It was ten o'clock. And now he is dead, and the police will be called in, and I shall be suspected of having had a hand in it. Oh, yes, I am sure I shall. But you don't think so, gentlemen? Surely you don't think that it was I? Is it likely that I would have brought you here if it were I? Oh, dear! oh, dear! I know that I shall go mad!'

He jerked his arms and stamped his feet in a kind of convulsive frenzy.

'You have no reason to fear, Mr Sholto,' said Holmes, kindly, putting his hand upon his shoulder; 'take my advice, and drive down to the station to report the matter to the police. Offer to assist them in every way. We shall wait here until your return.'

The little man obeyed in a half-stupefied fashion, and we heard him stumbling down the stairs in the dark.

VI. SHERLOCK HOLMES GIVES A DEMONSTRATION

'NOW, Watson,' said Holmes, rubbing his hands, 'we have half an hour to ourselves. Let us make good use of it. My case is, as I have told you, almost complete; but we must not err on the side of over-confidence. Simple as the case seems now, there may be something deeper underlying it.'

'Simple!' I ejaculated.

'Surely,' said he, with something of the air of a clinical professor expounding to his class. 'Just sit in the corner there, that your foot-prints may not complicate matters. Now to work! In the first place, how did these folk come, and how did they go? The door has not been opened since last night. How of the window?' He carried the lamp across to it, muttering his observations aloud the while, but addressing them to himself rather than to me. 'Window is snibbed on the inner side. Framework is solid. No hinges at the side. Let us open it. No water-pipe near. Roof quite out of reach. Yet a man has mounted by the window. It rained a little last night. Here is the print of a foot in mould upon the sill. And here is a circular muddy mark, and here again upon the floor, and here again by the table. See here, Watson! This is really a very pretty demonstration.'

I looked at the round, well-defined muddy discs.

'That is not a footmark,' said I.

'It is something much more valuable to us. It is the impression of a wooden stump. You see here on the sill is the boot-mark, a heavy boot with a broad metal heel, and beside it is the mark of the timber-toe.'

'It is the wooden-legged man.'

'Quite so. But there has been someone else—a very able and efficient ally. Could you scale that wall, Doctor?'

I looked out of the open window. The moon still shone brightly on that angle of the house. We were a good sixty feet from the ground, and, look where I would, I could see no foothold, nor as much as a crevice in the brickwork.

'It is absolutely impossible,' I answered.

'Without aid it is so. But suppose you had a friend up here who lowered you this good stout rope which I see in the corner, securing one end of it to this great hook in the wall. Then, I think, if you were an active man, you might swarm up, wooden leg and all. You would depart, of course, in the same fashion, and your ally would draw up the rope, untie it from the hook, shut the window, snib it on the inside, and get away in the way that he originally came. As a minor point, it may be noted', he continued, fingering the rope, 'that our wooden-legged friend, though a fair climber, was not a professional sailor. His hands were far from horny. My lens discloses more than one blood-mark, especially towards the end of the rope, from which I gather that he slipped down with such velocity that he took the skin off his hand.'

'This is all very well,' said I; 'but the thing becomes more unintelligible than ever. How about this mysterious ally? How came he into the room?'

'Yes, the ally!' repeated Holmes, pensively. 'There are features of interest about this ally. He lifts the case from the regions of the commonplace. I fancy that this ally breaks fresh ground in the annals of crime in this country—though parallel cases suggest themselves from India, and, if my memory serves me, from Senegambia.'

'How came he, then?' I reiterated. 'The door is locked; the window is inaccessible. Was it through the chimney?'

'The grate is too small,' he answered. 'I had already considered that possibility.'

'How, then?' I persisted.

'You will not apply my precept,' he said, shaking his head. 'How often have I said to you that when you have eliminated the impossible, whatever remains, *however improbable*, must be the truth? We know that he did not come through the door, the window, or the chimney. We also know that he could not have been concealed in the room, as there is no concealment possible. Whence, then, did he come?'

'He came through the hole in the roof?' I cried.

'Of course he did. He must have done so. If you will have the kindness to hold the lamp for me, we shall now extend our researches to the room above—the secret room in which the treasure was found.'

He mounted the steps, and, seizing a rafter with either hand, he swung himself up into the garret. Then, lying on his face, he reached down for the lamp, and held it while I followed him.

The chamber in which we found ourselves was about ten feet one way and six the other. The floor was formed by the rafters, with thin lath-and-plaster between, so that in walking one had to step from beam to beam. The roof ran up to an apex, and was evidently the inner shell of the true roof of the house. There was no furniture of any sort, and the accumulated dust of years lay thick upon the floor.

'Here you are, you see,' said Sherlock Holmes, putting his hand against the sloping wall. 'This is a trap-door which leads out on to the roof. I can press it back, and here is the roof itself, sloping at a gentle angle. This, then, is the way by which Number One entered. Let us see if we can find some other traces of his individuality.'

He held down the lamp to the floor, and as he did so I saw for the second time that night a startled, surprised look come over his face. For myself, as I followed his gaze, my skin was cold under my clothes. The floor was covered thickly with the prints of a naked foot—clear, well-defined, perfectly formed, but scarce half the size of those of an ordinary man.

'Holmes,' I said, in a whisper, 'a child has done this horrid thing.'

He had recovered his self-possession in an instant.

'I was staggered for the moment,' he said, 'but the thing is quite natural. My memory failed me, or I should have been able to foretell it. There is nothing more to be learned here. Let us go down.'

'What is your theory, then, as to those footmarks?' I asked, eagerly, when we had regained the lower room once more.

'My dear Watson, try a little analysis yourself,' said he, with a touch of impatience. 'You know my methods. Apply them, and it will be instructive to compare results.'

'I cannot conceive anything which will cover the facts,' I answered.

'It will be clear enough to you soon,' he said, in an off-hand way. 'I think that there is nothing else of importance here, but I will look.'

He whipped out his lens and a tape measure, and hurried about the room on his knees, measuring, comparing, examining, with his long, thin nose only a few inches from the planks, and his beady eyes gleaming and deep-set like those of a bird. So swift, silent, and furtive were his movements, like those of a trained bloodhound picking out a scent, that I could not but think what a terrible criminal he would have made had he turned his energy and sagacity against the law instead of exerting them in its defence. As he hunted about he kept muttering to himself, and finally he broke out into a loud crow of delight.

'We are certainly in luck,' said he. 'We ought to have very little trouble now. Number One has had the misfortune to tread in the creosote. You can see the outline of the edge of his small foot here at the side of this evil-smelling mess. The carboy has been cracked, you see, and the stuff has leaked out.'

'What then?' I asked.

'Why, we have got him, that's all,' said he. 'I know a dog that would follow that scent to the world's end. If a pack can track a trailed herring across a shire, how far can a specially-trained hound follow so pungent a smell as this? It sounds like a sum in the rule of three. The answer should give us the——But, halloa! here are the accredited representatives of the law.'

Heavy steps and the clamour of loud voices were audible from below, and the hall door shut with a loud crash.

'Before they come,' said Holmes, 'just put your hand here on this poor fellow's arm, and here on his leg. What do you feel?'

'The muscles are as hard as a board,' I answered.

'Quite so. They are in a state of extreme contraction, far exceeding the usual *rigor mortis*. Coupled with this distortion of the face, this Hippocratic smile, or "*risus sardonicus*", as the old writers called it, what conclusion would it suggest to your mind?'

'Death from some powerful vegetable alkaloid,' I answered, 'some strychnine-like substance which would produce tetanus.'

'That was the idea which occurred to me the instant I saw the drawn muscles of the face. On getting into the room I at once looked for the means by which the poison had entered the system. As you saw, I discovered a thorn which had been driven or shot with no great force into the scalp. You observe that the part struck was that which would be turned towards the hole in the ceiling if the man were erect in his chair. Now examine this thorn.'

I took it up gingerly and held it in the light of the lantern. It was long, sharp, and black, with a glazed look near the point as though some gummy substance had dried upon it. The blunt end had been trimmed and rounded off with a knife.

'Is that an English thorn?' he asked.

'No, it certainly is not.'

'With all these data you should be able to draw some just inference. But here are the regulars; so the auxiliary forces may beat a retreat.'

As he spoke, the steps which had been coming nearer sounded loudly on the passage, and a very stout, portly man in a grey suit strode heavily into the room. He was red-faced, burly, and plethoric, with a pair of very small, twinkling eyes, which looked keenly out from between swollen and puffy pouches. He was closely followed by an inspector in uniform, and by the still palpitating Thaddeus Sholto.

'Here's a business!' he cried, in a muffled, husky voice. 'Here's a pretty business! But who are all these? Why, the house seems to be as full as a rabbit-warren!'

'I think you must recollect me, Mr Athelney Jones,' said Holmes, quietly.

'Why, of course I do!' he wheezed. 'It's Mr Sherlock Holmes, the theorist. Remember you! I'll never forget how you lectured us all on causes and inferences and effects in the Bishopgate jewel case. It's true you set us on the right track; but you'll own now that it was more by good luck than good guidance.'

'It was a piece of very simple reasoning.'

'Oh, come, now, come! Never be ashamed to own up. But what is all this? Bad business! Bad business! Stern facts here—no room for theories. How lucky that I happened to be out at Norwood over another case! I was at the station when the message arrived. What d'you think the man died of?'

'Oh, this is hardly a case for me to theorize over,' said Holmes, drily.

'No, no. Still, we can't deny that you hit the nail on the head sometimes. Dear me! Door locked, I understand. Jewels worth half a million missing. How was the window?'

'Fastened; but there are steps on the sill.'

'Well, well, if it was fastened the steps could have nothing to do with the matter. That's common sense. Man might have died in a fit; but then the jewels are missing. Ha! I have a theory. These flashes come upon me at times. Just step outside, sergeant, and you, Mr Sholto. Your friend can remain. What do you think of this, Holmes? Sholto was, on his own confession, with his brother last night. The brother died in a fit, on which Sholto walked off with the treasure! How's that?'

'On which the dead man very considerately got up and locked the door on the inside.'

'Hum! There's a flaw there. Let us apply common sense to the matter. This Thaddeus Sholto *was* with his brother; there *was* a quarrel: so much we know. The brother is dead and the jewels are gone. So much also we know. No one saw the brother from the time Thaddeus left him. His bed had not been slept in. Thaddeus is evidently in a most disturbed state of mind. His appearance is—well, not attractive. You see that I am weaving my web round Thaddeus. The net begins to close upon him.'

'You are not quite in possession of the facts yet,' said Holmes. 'This splinter of wood, which I have every reason to believe to be poisoned, was in the man's scalp where you still see the mark; this card, inscribed as you see it, was on the table, and beside it lay this rather curious stone-headed instrument. How does all that fit into your theory?'

'Confirms it in every respect,' said the fat detective, pompously. 'House full of Indian curiosities. Thaddeus brought this up, and if this splinter be poisonous, Thaddeus may as well have made murderous use of it as any other man. The card is some hocus-pocus—a blind, as like as not. The only question is, how did he depart? Ah, of course, here is a hole in the roof.'

With great activity, considering his bulk, he sprang up the steps and squeezed through into the garret, and immediately afterwards we heard his exulting voice proclaiming that he had found the trap-door.

'He can find something,' remarked Holmes, shrugging his shoulders; 'he has occasional glimmerings of reason. *Il n'y a pas des sots si incommodes que ceux qui ont de l'esprit!*'

'You see!' said Athelney Jones, reappearing down the steps again; 'facts are better than theories, after all. My view of the case is confirmed. There is a trap-door communicating with the roof, and it is partly open.'

'It was I who opened it.'

'Oh, indeed! You did notice it, then?' He seemed a little crest-fallen at the discovery. 'Well, whoever noticed it, it shows how our gentleman got away. Inspector!'

'Yes, sir,' from the passage.

'Ask Mr Sholto to step this way.—Mr Sholto, it is my duty to inform you that anything which you may say will be used against you. I arrest you in the Queen's name as being concerned in the death of your brother.'

'There, now! Didn't I tell you?' cried the poor little man, throwing out his hands, and looking from one to the other of us.

'Don't trouble yourself about it, Mr Sholto,' said Holmes; 'I think that I can engage to clear you of the charge.'

'Don't promise too much, Mr Theorist, don't promise too much!' snapped the detective. 'You may find it a harder matter than you think.'

'Not only will I clear him, Mr Jones, but I will make you a free present of the name and description of one of the two people who were in this room last night. His name, I have every reason to believe, is Jonathan Small. He is a poorly educated man, small, active, with his right leg off, and wearing a wooden stump which is worn away upon the inner side. His left boot had a coarse, square-toed sole, with a band round the heel. He is a middle-aged man, much sunburned, and has been a convict. These few indications may be of some assistance to you, coupled with the fact that there is a good deal of skin missing from the palm of his hand. The other man——'

'Ah, the other man?' asked Athelney Jones, in a sneering voice, but impressed none the less, as I could easily see, by the precision of the other's manner.

'Is a rather curious person,' said Sherlock Holmes, turning upon his heel. 'I hope before very long to be able to introduce you to the pair of them. A word with you, Watson.'

He led me out to the head of the stair.

'This unexpected occurrence,' he said, 'has caused us rather to lose sight of the original purpose of our journey.'

'I have just been thinking so,' I answered; 'It is not right that Miss Morstan should remain in this stricken house.'

'No. You must escort her home. She lives with Mrs Cecil Forrester, in Lower Camberwell, so it is not very far. I will wait for you here if you will drive out again. Or perhaps you are too tired?'

'By no means. I don't think I could rest until I know more of this fantastic business. I have seen something of the rough side of life, but I give you my word that this quick succession of strange surprises tonight has shaken my nerve completely. I should like, however, to see the matter through with you, now that I have got so far.'

'Your presence will be of great service to me,' he answered. 'We shall work the case out independently, and leave this fellow Jones to exult over any mare's-nest which he may choose to construct. When you have dropped Miss Morstan, I wish you to go to No. 3, Pinchin Lane, down near the water's edge at Lambeth. The third house on the right-hand side is a bird-stuffer's; Sherman is the name. You will see a weasel holding a young rabbit in the window. Knock old Sherman up, and tell him, with my compliments, that I want Toby at once. You will bring Toby back in the cab with you.'

'A dog, I suppose?'

'Yes, a queer mongrel, with a most amazing power of scent. I would rather have Toby's help than that of the whole detective force of London.'

'I shall bring him then,' said I. 'It is one now. I ought to get back before three, if I can get a fresh horse.'

'And I', said Holmes, 'shall see what I can learn from Mrs Bernstone, and from the Indian servant, who, Mr Thaddeus tells me, sleeps in the next garret. Then I shall study the great Jone's methods and listen to his not too delicate sarcasms. "*Wir sind gewohnt dass die Menschen verhöhnen was sie nicht verstehen.*" Goethe is always pithy.'

VII. THE EPISODE OF THE BARREL

THE police had brought a cab with them, and in this I escorted Miss Morstan back to her home. After the angelic fashion of women, she had borne trouble with a calm face as long as there was someone weaker than herself to support, and I had found her bright and placid by the side of the frightened housekeeper. In the cab, however, she first turned fair, and then burst into a passion of weeping—so sorely had she been tried by the adventures of the night. She has told me since that she thought me cold and distant upon that journey. She little guessed the struggle within my breast, or the effort of self-restraint which held me back. My sympathies and my love went out to her, even as my hand had in the garden. I felt that years of the conventionalities of life could not teach me to know her sweet, brave nature as had this one day of strange experiences. Yet there were two thoughts which sealed the words of affection upon my lips. She was weak and helpless, shaken in mind and nerve. It was to take her at a disadvantage to obtrude love upon her at such a time. Worse still, she was rich. If Holmes's researches were successful, she would be an heiress. Was it fair, was it honourable, that a half-pay surgeon should take such advantage of an intimacy which chance had brought about? Might she not look upon me as a mere vulgar fortune-seeker? I could not bear to risk that such a thought should cross her mind. This Agra treasure intervened like an impassable barrier between us.

It was nearly two o'clock when we reached Mrs Cecil Forrester's. The servants had retired hours ago, but Mrs Forrester had been so interested by the strange message which Miss Morstan had received that she had sat up in the hope of her return. She opened the door herself, a middle-aged, graceful woman, and it gave me joy to see how tenderly her arm stole round the other's waist, and how motherly was the voice in which she greeted her. She was clearly no mere paid dependent, but an honoured friend. I was introduced, and Mrs Forrester earnestly begged me to step in and to tell her our adventures. I explained, however, the importance of my errand, and promised faithfully to call and report any progress which we might make with the case. As we drove away I stole a glance back, and I still seem to see that little group on the step—the two graceful, clinging figures, the half-opened door, the hall-light shinning through stained glass, the barometer, and the bright stair-rods. It was soothing to catch even that passing glimpse of a tranquil English home in the midst of the wild, dark business which had absorbed us.

And the more I thought of what had happened, the wilder and darker it grew. I reviewed the whole extraordinary sequence of events as I rattled on through the silent, gaslit streets. There was the original problem: that, at least, was pretty clear now. The death of Captain Morstan, the sending of the pearls, the advertisement, the letter—we had had light upon all those events. They had only led us, however, to a deeper and far more tragic mystery. The Indian treasure, the curious plan found among Morstan's baggage, the strange scene at Major Sholto's death, the rediscovery of the treasure immediately followed by the murder of the discoverer, the very singular accompaniments to the crime, the footsteps, the remarkable weapons, the words upon the card, corresponding with those upon Captain Morstan's chart—here was, indeed, a labyrinth in which a man less singularly endowed than my fellow-lodger might well despair of ever finding the clue.

Pinchin Lane was a row of shabby, two-storied brick houses in the lower quarter of Lambeth. I had to knock for some time at No.3 before I could make any impression. At last, however, there was the glint of a candle behind the blind, and a face looked out at the upper window.

'Go on, you drunken vagabond,' said the face. 'If you kick up any more row, I'll open the kennels and let out forty-three dogs upon you.'

'If you'll let one out, it's just what I have come for,' said I.

'Go on!' yelled the voice. 'So help me gracious, I have a wiper in this bag, an' I'll drop it on your 'ead if you don't hook it!'

'But I want a dog,' I cried.

'I won't be argued with!' shouted Mr Sherman. 'Now, stand clear; for when I say "Three", down goes the wiper.'

'Mr Sherlock Holmes——' I began; but the words had a most magical effect, for the window instantly slammed down, and within a minute the door was unbarred and open. Mr Sherman was a lanky, lean old man, with stooping shoulders, a stringy neck, and blue-tinted glasses.

'A friend of Mr Sherlock is always welcome,' said he. 'Step in, sir. Keep clear of the badger, for he bites. Ah, naughty, naughty! would you take a nip at the gentleman!' This to a stoat, which thrust its wicked head and red eyes between the bars of its cage. 'Don't mind that, sir; it's only a slow-worm. It hain't got no fangs, so I gives it the run o' the room, for it keeps the beetles down. You must not mind my bein' just a little short wi' you at first, for I'm guyed at by the children, and there's many a one just comes down this lane to knock me up. What was it that Mr Sherlock Holmes wanted, sir?'

'He wanted a dog of yours.'

'Ah! that would be Toby.'

'Yes, "Toby" was the name.'

'Toby lives at No. 7 on the left here.'

He moved slowly forward with his candle among the queer animal family which he had gathered round him. In the uncertain, shadowy light I could see dimly that there were glancing, glimmering eyes peeping down at us from every cranny and corner. Even the rafters above our heads were lined by solemn fowls, who lazily shifted their weight from one leg to the other as our voices disturbed their slumbers.

Toby proved to be an ugly, long-haired, lop-eared creature, half spaniel and half lurcher, brown and white in colour, with a very clumsy, waddling gait. It accepted, after some hesitation, a lump of sugar which the old naturalist handed to me, and, having thus sealed an alliance, it followed me to the cab, and made no difficulties about accompanying me. It had just struck three on the Palace clock when I found myself back once more at Pondicherry Lodge. The ex-prizefighter McMurdo had, I found, been arrested as an accessory, and both he and Mr Sholto had been marched off to the station. Two constables guarded the narrow gate, but they allowed me to pass with the dog on my mentioning the detective's name.

Holmes was standing on the doorstep, with his hands in his pockets, smoking his pipe.

'Ah, you have him there!' said he. 'Good dog, then! Athelney Jones had gone. We have had an immense display of energy since you left. He has arrested not only friend Thaddeus, but the gate-keeper, the housekeeper, and the Indian servant. We have the place to ourselves, but for a sergeant upstairs. Leave the dog here and come up.

We tied Toby to the hall table, and reascended the stairs. The room was as we had left it, save that a sheet had been draped over the central figure. A weary-looking sergeant reclined in the corner.

'Lend me your bull's-eye, sergeant,' said my companion. 'Now tie this bit of card round my neck, so as to hang in front of me. Thank you. Now I must kick off my boots and stockings. Just you carry them down with you, Watson. I am going to do a little climbing. And dip my handkerchief into the creosote. That will do. Now come up into the garret with me for a moment.'

We clambered up through the hole. Holmes turned his light once more upon the footsteps in the dust.

'I wish you particularly to notice these footmarks,' he said. 'Do you observe anything noteworthy about them?'

'They belong,' I said, 'to a child or a small woman.'

'Apart from their size, though. Is there nothing else?'

'They appeared to be much as other footmarks.'

'Not at all! Look here! This is the print of a right foot in the dust. Now I make one with my naked foot beside it. What is the chief difference?'

'Your toes are all a cramped together. The other print has each toe distinctly divided.'

'Quite so. That is the point. Bear that in mind. Now, would you kindly step over to that flap-window and smell the edge of the wood-work? I shall stay over here, as I have this handkerchief in my hand.'

I did as he directed, and was instantly conscious of a strong tarry smell.

'That is where he put his foot in getting out. If *you* can trace him, I should think that Toby will have no difficulty. Now run downstairs, loose the dog, and look out for Blondin.'

By the time that I got out into the grounds Sherlock Holmes was on the roof, and I could see him like an enormous glow-worm crawling very slowly along the ridge. I lost sight of him behind a stack of chimneys, but he presently reappeared, and then vanished once more upon the opposite side. When I made my way round there I found him seated at one of the corner eaves.

'That you, Watson?' he cried.

'Yes.'

'This is the place. What is that black thing down there?'

'A water-barrel.'

'Top on it?'

'Yes.'

'No sign of a ladder?'

'No.'

'Confound the fellow! It's a most break-neck place. I ought to be able to come down where he could climb up. The water-pipe feels pretty firm. Here goes, anyhow.'

There was a scuffling of feet, and the lantern began to come steadily down the side of the wall. Then with a light spring he came on to the barrel, and from there to the earth.

'It was easy to follow him,' he said, drawing on his stockings and boots. 'Tiles were loosened the whole way along, and in his hurry he had dropped this. It confirms my diagnosis, as you doctors express it.'

The object which he held up to me was a small pocket or pouch woven out of coloured grasses, and with a few tawdry beads strung round it. In shape and size it was not unlike a cigarette-case. Inside were half-a-dozen spines of dark wood, sharp at one end and rounded at the other, like that which had struck Bartholomew Sholto.

'They are hellish things,' said he. 'Look out that you don't prick yourself. I'm delighted to have them, for the chances are that they are all he has. There is the less fear of you or me finding one in our skin before long. I would sooner face a Martini bullet myself. Are you game for a six-mile trudge, Watson?'

'Certainly,' I answered.

'Your leg will stand it?'

'Oh, yes.'

'Here you are, doggy! Good old Toby! Smell it, Toby, smell it!' he pushed the creosote handkerchief under the dog's nose, while the creature stood with its fluffy legs separated, and with a most comical cock to its head, like a connoisseur sniffing the *bouquet* of a famous vintage. Holmes then threw the handkerchief to a distance, fastened a stout cord to the mongrel's collar, and led him to the foot of the water-barrel. The creature instantly broke into a succession of high, tremulous yelps, and, with his nose on the ground, and his tail in the air, pattered off upon the trail at a pace which strained his leash and kept us at the top of our speed.

The east had been gradually whitening, and we could now see some distance in the cold, grey light. The square, massive house, with its black, empty windows and high, bear walls, towered up, sad and forlorn, behind us. Our course led right across the grounds, in and out among the trenches and pits with which they were scarred and intersected. The whole place, with its scattered dirt-heaps and ill-grown shrubs, had a blighted, ill-omened look which harmonized with the black tragedy which hung over it.

On reaching the boundary wall Toby ran along, whining eagerly, underneath its shadow, and stopped finally in a corner screened by a young beech. Where the two walls joined, several bricks had been loosened, and the crevices left were worn down and rounded upon the lower side, as though they had frequently been used as a ladder. Holmes clambered up, and taking the dog from me, he dropped it over upon the other side.

'There's the print of wooden leg's hand,' he remarked, as I mounted up beside him. 'You see the slight smudge of blood upon the white plaster. What a lucky thing it is that we have had no very heavy rain since yesterday! The scent will lie upon the road in spite of their eight-and-twenty hours' start.'

I confess that I had my doubts myself when I reflected upon the great traffic which had passed along the London road in the interval. My fears were soon appeased, however. Toby never hesitated or swerved, but waddled on in his peculiar rolling fashion. Clearly, the pungent smell of the creosote rose high above all other contending scents.

'Do not imagine,' said Holmes, 'that I depend for my success in this case upon the mere chance of one of these fellows having put his foot in the chemical. I have knowledge now which would enable me to trace them in many different ways. This, however, is the readiest, and, since fortune has put it into our hands, I should be culpable if I neglected it. It has, however, prevented the case from becoming the pretty little intellectual problem which it at one time promised to be. There might have been some credit to be gained out of it, but for this too palpable clue.'

'There is credit, and to spare,' said I. 'I assure you, Holmes, that I marvel at the means by which you obtain your results in this case, even more than I did in the Jefferson Hope murder. The thing seems to me to be deeper and more inexplicable. How, for example, could you describe with such confidence the wooden-legged man?'

'Pshaw, my dear boy! it was simplicity itself. I don't wish to be theatrical. It is all patent and above-board. Two officers who are in command of a convict guard learn an important secret as to buried treasure. A map is drawn for them by an Englishman named Jonathan Small. You remember that we saw the name upon the chart in Captain Morstan's possession. He had signed it on behalf of himself and his associates—the sign of the four, as he somewhat dramatically called it. Aided by his chart, the officers—or one of them—gets the treasure and brings it to England, leaving, we will suppose, some condition under which he received it unfulfilled. Now, then, why did not Jonathan Small get the treasure himself? The answer is obvious. The chart is dated at a time when Morstan was brought into close association with convicts. Jonathan Small did not get the treasure because he and his associates were themselves convicts and could not get away.'

'But this is mere speculation,' said I.

'It is more than that. It is the only hypothesis which covers the facts. Let us see how it fits in with the sequel. Major Sholto remains at peace for some years, happy in the possession of his treasure. Then he receives a letter from India which gives him a great fright. What was that?'

'A letter to say that the men whom he had wronged had been set free.'

'Or had escaped. That is much more likely, for he would have known what their term of imprisonment was. It would not have been a surprise to him. What does he do then? He guards himself against a wooden-legged man—a white man, mark you, for he mistakes a white tradesman for him, and actually fires a pistol at him. Now, only one white man's name is on the chart. The others are Hindus or Mohammedans. There is no other white man. Therefore we may say with confidence that the wooden-legged man is identical with Jonathan Small. Does the reasoning strike you as being faulty?'

'No: it is clear and concise.'

'Well, now, let us put ourselves in the place of Jonathan Small. Let us look at it from his point of view. He comes to England with the double idea of regaining what he would consider to be his rights, and of having his revenge upon the man who had wronged him. He found out where Sholto lived, and very possibly he established communications with someone inside the house. There is this butler, Lal Rao, whom we have not seen. Mrs Bernstone gives him far from a good character. Small could not find out, however, where the treasure was hid, for no one ever knew, save the major and one faithful servant who had died. Suddenly, Small learns that the major is on his deathbed. In a frenzy lest the secret of the treasure die with him, he runs the gauntlet of the guards, makes his way to the dying man's window, and is only deterred from entering by the presence of his two sons. Mad with hate, however, against the dead man, he enters the room that night, searches his private papers in the hope of discovering some memorandum relating to the treasure, and finally leaves a memento of his visit in the short inscription upon the card. He had doubtless planned beforehand that, should he slay the major, he would leave some such record upon the body as a sign that it was not a common murder, but, from the point of view of the four associates, something in the nature of an act of justice. Whimsical and bizarre conceits of this kind are common enough in the annals of crime, and usually afford valuable indications as to the criminal. Do you follow all this?'

'Very clearly.'

'Now, what could Jonathan Small do? He could only continue to keep a secret watch upon the efforts made to find the treasure. Possibly he leaves England and only comes back at intervals. Then comes the discovery of the garret, and he is instantly informed of it. We again trace the presence of some confederate in the household. Jonathan, with his wooden leg, is utterly unable to reach the lofty room of Bartholomew Sholto. He takes with him, however, a rather curious associate, who gets over this difficulty, but dips his naked foot into creosote, whence come Toby, and a six-mile limp for a half-pay officer with a damaged *tendo Achillis*.'

'But it was the associate, and not Jonathan, who committed the crime.'

'Quite so. And rather to Jonathan's disgust, to judge by the way he stamped about when he got into the room. He bore no grudge against Bartholomew Sholto, and would have preferred if he could have been simply bound and gagged. He did not wish to put his head into a halter. There was no help for it, however: the savage instincts of his companion had broken out, and the poison had done its work: so Jonathan Small left his record, lowered the treasure-box to the ground, and followed it himself. That was the train of events as far as I can decipher them. Of course, as to his personal appearance he must be middle-aged, and must be sunburned after serving his time in such an oven as the Andamans. His height is readily calculated from the length of his stride, and we know that he was bearded. His hairiness was the one point which impressed itself upon Thaddeus Sholto when he saw him at the window. I don't know that there is anything else.'

'The associate?'

'Ah, well, there is no great mystery in that. But you will know all about it soon enough. How sweet the morning air is! See how that one little cloud floats like a pink feather from some gigantic flamingo. Now the red rim of the sun pushes itself over the London cloud-bank. It shines on a good many folk, but on none, I dare bet, who are on a stranger errand than you and I. How small we feel, with our petty ambitions and strivings, in the presence of the great elemental forces of Nature! Are you well up in your Jean Paul?'

'Fairly so. I worked back to him through Carlyle.'

'That was like following the brook to the parent lake. He makes one curious but profound remark. It is that the chief proof of man's real greatness lies in his perception of his own smallness. It argues, you see, a power of comparison and of appreciation which is in itself a proof of nobility. There is much food for thought in Richter. You have not a pistol, have you?'

'I have my stick.'

'It is just possible that we may need something of the sort if we get to their lair. Jonathan I shall leave to you, but if the other turns nasty I shall shoot him dead.'

He took out his revolver as he spoke, and, having loaded two of the chambers, he put it back into the right-hand pocket of his jacket.

We had during this time been following the guidance of Toby down the half rural villa-lined roads which lead to the Metropolis. Now, however, we were beginning to come among continuous streets, where labourers and dockmen were already astir, and slatternly women were taking down shutters and brushing doorsteps. At the square-topped corner public-houses business was just beginning, and rough-looking men were emerging, rubbing their sleeves across their beards after their morning wet. Strange dogs sauntered up and stared wonderingly at us as we passed, but our inimitable Toby looked neither to the right nor to the left, but trotted onwards with his nose to the ground and an occasional eager whine which spoke of a hot scent.

We had traversed Streatham, Brixton, Camberwell, and now found ourselves in Kennington Lane, having borne away through the side streets to the east of the Oval. The men whom we pursued seemed to have taken a curiously zig-zag road, with the idea probably of escaping observation. They had never kept to the main road if a parallel side-street would serve their turn. At the foot of Kennington Lane they had edged away to the left through Bond Street and Miles Street. Where the latter street turns into Knight's Place, Toby ceased to advance, but began to run backwards and forwards with one ear cocked and the other drooping, the very picture of canine indecision. Then he waddled round in circles, looking up to us from time to time, as if to ask sympathy in his embarrassment.

'What the deuce is the matter with the dog?' growled Holmes. 'They surely would not take a cab, or go off in a balloon.'

'Perhaps they stood here for some time,' I suggested.

'Ah! it's all right. He's off again,' said my companion, in a tone of relief.

He was indeed off, for after sniffing round again he suddenly made up his mind, and darted away with an energy and determination such as he had not yet shown. The scent appeared to be much hotter than before, for he had not even to put his nose on the ground, but tugged at his leash and tried to break into a run. I could see by the gleam in Holmes's eyes that he thought we were nearing the end of our journey.

Our course now ran down Nine Elms until we came to Broderick and Nelson's large timber-yard, just past the White Eagle tavern. Here the dog, frantic with excitement, turned down through the side gate into the enclosure, where the sawyers were already at work. On the dog raced through sawdust and shavings, down an alley, round a passage, between two wood-piles, and finally, with a triumphant yelp, sprang upon a large barrel which still stood upon the hand-trolley on which it had been brought. With lolling tongue and blinking eyes, Toby stood upon the cask, looking from one to the other of us for some sign of appreciation. The staves of the barrel and the wheels of the trolley were smeared with a dark liquid, and the whole air was heavy with the smell of creosote.

Sherlock Holmes and I looked blankly at each other, and then burst simultaneously into an uncontrollable fit of laughter.

VIII. THE BAKER STREET IRREGULARS

'WHAT now?' I asked. 'Toby has lost his character for infallibility.'

'He acted according to his lights,' said Holmes, lifting him down from the barrel and walking him out of the timber-yard. 'If you consider how much creosote is carted about London in one day, it is no great wonder that our trail should have been crossed. It is much used now, especially for the seasoning of wood. Poor Toby is not to blame.'

'We must get on the main scent again, I suppose.'

'Yes. And, fortunately, we have no distance to go. Evidently what puzzled the dog at the corner of Knight's Place was that were two different trails running in opposite directions. We took the wrong one. It only remains to follow the other.'

There was no difficulty about this. On leading Toby to the place where he had committed his fault, he cast about in a wide circle and finally dashed off in a fresh direction.

'We must take care that he does not now bring us to the place where the creosote-barrel came from,' I observed.

'I had thought of that. But you notice that he keeps on the pavement, where as the barrel passed down the roadway. No, we are on the true scent now.'

It tended down towards the river-side, running through Belmont Place and Prince's Street. At the end of Broad Street it ran right down to the water's edge, where there was a small wooden wharf. Toby led us to the very edge of this, and there stood whining, looking out on the dark current beyond.

'We are out of luck,' said Holmes. 'They have taken to a boat here.'

Several small punts and skiffs were lying about in the water and on the edge of the wharf. We took Toby round to each in turn, but, though he sniffed earnestly, he made no sign.

Close to the rude landing-stage was a small brick house, with a wooden placard slung out through the second window. 'Mordecai Smith' was printed across it in large letters, and underneath, 'Boats to hire by the hour or day.' A second inscription above the door informed us that a steam-launch was kept—a statement which was confirmed by a great pile of coke upon the jetty. Sherlock Holmes looked slowly round, and his face assumed an ominous expression.

'This looks bad,' said he. 'These fellows are sharper than I expected. They seem to have covered their tracks. There has, I fear, been preconcerted management here.'

He was approaching the door of the house, when it opened, and a little curly-headed lad of six came running out, followed by a stoutish, red-faced woman with a large sponge in her hand.

'You come back and be washed, Jacked,' she shouted. 'Come back, you young imp; for if your father comes home and finds you like that, he'll let us hear of it.'

'Dear little chap! cried Holmes, strategically. 'What a rosy-cheeked young rascal! Now, Jack, is there anything you would like?'

The youth pondered for a moment.

'I'd like a shillin',' said he.

'Nothing you would like better?'

'I'd like two shillin' better,' the prodigy answered, after some thought.

'Here you are, then! Catch!—A fine child, Mrs Smith!'

'Lor' bless you, sir, he is that, and forward. He gets a'most too much for me to manage, 'specially when my man is away days at a time.'

'Away, is he?' said Holmes, in a disappointed voice. 'I am sorry for that, for I wanted to speak to Mr Smith.'

'He's been away since yesterday mornin', sir, and, truth to tell, I am beginning to feel frightened about him. But if it was about a boat, sir, maybe I could serve as well.'

'I wanted to hire his steam launch.'

'Why, bless you, sir, it is in the steam launch that he has gone. That's what puzzles me; for I know there ain't more coals in her than would take her to about Woolwich and back. If he'd been away in the barge I'd ha' thought nothin'; for many a time a job had taken him as far as Gravesend, and then if there was much doin' there he might ha' stayed over. But what good is a steam launch without coals?'

'He might have bought some at a wharf down the river.'

'He might, sir, but it weren't his way. Many a time I've heard him call out at the prices they charge for a few odd bags. Besides, I don't like that wooden-legged man, wi' his ugly face and outlandish talk. What did he want always knockin' about here for?'

'A wooden-legged man?' said Holmes, with bland surprise.

'Yes, sir, a brown, monkey-faced chap that's called more'n once for my old man. It was him that roused him up yesternight, and, what's more, my man knew he was comin', for he had steam up in the launch. I tell you straight, sir, I don't feel easy in my mind about it.'

'But, my dear Mrs Smith,' said Holmes, shrugging his shoulders, 'you are frightening yourself about nothing. How could you possibly tell that it was the wooden-legged man who came in the night? I don't quite understand how you can be so sure.'

'His voice, sir. I knew his voice, which is kind o' thick and foggy. He tapped at the winder—about three it would be. "Show a leg, matey," said he: "time to turn out guard." My old man woke up Jim—that's my eldest—and away they went, without so much as a word to me. I could hear the wooden leg clackin' on the stones.'

'And was this wooden-legged man alone?'

'Couldn't say, I am sure, sir. I didn't hear no one else.'

'I am sorry, Mrs Smith, for I wanted a steam launch, and I have heard good reports of the——Let me see, what is her name?'

'The *Aurora*, sir.'

'Ah! She's not that old green launch with a yellow line, very broad in the beam?'

'No, indeed. She's as trim a little thing as any on the river. She's been fresh painted, black with two red steaks.'

'Thanks. I hope that you will hear soon from Mr Smith. I am going down the river, and if I should see anything of the *Aurora* I shall let him know that you are uneasy. A black funnel, you say?'

'No, sir. Black with a white band.'

'Ah, of course. It was the sides which were black. Good morning, Mrs Smith. There is a boatman here with a wherry, Watson. We shall take it and cross the river.'

'The main thing with people of that sort,' said Holmes, as we sat in the sheets of the Wherry, 'is never to let them think that their information can be of the slightest importance to you. If you do, they will instantly shut up like an oyster. If you listen to them under protest, as it were, you are very likely to get what you want.'

'Our course now seems pretty clear,' said I.

'What would you do, then?'

'I would engage a launch and go down the river on the track of the *Aurora*.'

'My dear fellow, it would be a colossal task. She may have touched at any wharf on either side of the stream between here and Greenwich. Below the bridge there is a perfect labyrinth of landing-places for miles. It would take you days and days to exhaust them, if you set about it alone.'

'Employ the police, then.'

'No. I shall probably call Athelney Jones in at the last moment. He is not a bad fellow, and I should not like to do anything which would injure him professionally. But I have a fancy for working it out myself, now that we have gone so far.'

'Could we advertise, then, asking for information from wharfingers?'

'Worse and worse! Our men would know that the chase was hot at their heels, and they would be off out of the country. As it is, they are likely enough to leave, but as long as they think they are perfectly safe they will be in no hurry. Jones's energy will be of use to us there, for his view of the case is sure to push itself into the daily Press, and the runaways will think that everyone is off on the wrong scent.'

'What are we to do, then?' I asked, as we landed near Millbank Penitentiary.

'Take this hansom, drive home, have some breakfast, and get an hour's sleep. It is quite on the cards that we may be afoot tonight again. Stop at a telegraph office, Cabby! We will keep Toby, for he may be of use to us yet.'

We pulled up at the Great Peter Street Post Office, and Holmes dispatched his wire.

'Whom do you think that is to?' he asked, as we resumed our journey.

'I am sure I don't know.'

'You remember the Baker Street division of the detective police force whom I employed in the Jefferson Hope case?'

'Well?' said I, laughing.

'This is just the case where they might be invaluable. If they fail, I have other resources; but I shall try them first. That wire was to my dirty little lieutenant, Wiggins, and I expect that he and his gang will be with us before we have finished our breakfast.'

It was between eight and nine o'clock now, and I was conscious of a strong reaction after the successive excitements of the night. I was limp and weary, befogged in mind and fatigued in body. I had not the professional enthusiasm which carried my companion on, nor could I look at the matter as a mere abstract intellectual problem. As far as the death of Bartholomew Sholto went, I had heard little good of him, and could feel no intense antipathy to his murderers. The treasure, however, was a different matter. That, or part of it, belonged rightfully to Miss Morstan. While there was a chance of recovering it I was ready to devote my life to the one object. True, if I found it, it would probably put her for ever beyond my reach. Yet it would be a petty and selfish love which would be influenced by such a thought as that. If Holmes could work to find the criminals, I had a tenfold stronger reason to urge me on to find the treasure.

A bath at Baker Street and a complete change freshened me up wonderfully. When I came down to our room I found the breakfast laid and Holmes pouring out the coffee.

'Here it is,' said he, laughing, and pointing to an open newspaper. 'The energetic Jones and the ubiquitous reporter have fixed it up between them. But you have had enough of the case. Better have your ham and eggs first.'

I took the paper from him and read the short notice, which was headed, 'Mysterious Business at Upper Norwood'.

About twelve o'clock last night, [said the *Standard*] Mr Bartholomew Sholto, of Pondicherry Lodge, Upper Norwood, was found dead in his room under circumstances which point to foul play. As far as we can learn, no actual traces of violence were found upon Mr Sholto's person, but a valuable collection of Indian gems which the deceased gentleman had inherited from his father has been carried off. The discovery was first made by Mr Sherlock Holmes and Dr Watson, who had called at the house with Mr Thaddeus Sholto, brother of the deceased. By a singular piece of good fortune, Mr Athelney Jones, the well-known member of the detective police force, happened to be at the Norwood Police Station, and was on the ground within half an hour of the first alarm. His trained and experienced faculties were at once directed towards the detection of the criminals, with the gratifying result that the brother, Thaddeus Sholto, has already been arrested, together with the housekeeper, Mrs Bernstone, an Indian butler named Lal Rao, and a porter, or gatekeeper, named McMurdo. It is quite certain that the thief or thieves were well acquainted with the house, for Mr Jones's well-known technical knowledge and his powers of minute observation have enabled him to prove conclusively that the miscreants could not have entered by the door or by the window, but must have made their way across the roof of the building, and so through a trap-door into a room which communicated with that in which the body was found. This fact, which has been very clearly made out, proves conclusively that it was no mere haphazard burglary. The prompt and energetic action of the officers of the law shows the great advantage of the presence on such occasions of a single vigorous and masterful mind. We cannot but think that it supplies an argument to those who would wish to see our detectives more decentralized, and so brought into closer and more effective touch with the cases which it is their duty to investigate.

'Isn't it gorgeous?' said Holmes, grinning over his coffee cup. 'What do you think of it?'

'I think that we have had a close shave ourselves of being arrested for the crime.'

'So do I. I wouldn't answer for our safety now, if he should happen to have another of his attacks of energy.'

At this moment there was a loud ring at the bell, and I could hear Mrs Hudson, our landlady, rising her voice in a wail of expostulation and dismay.

'By heavens, Holmes,' said I, half rising, 'I believe that they are really after us.'

'No, it's not quite so bad as that. It is the unofficial force—the Baker Street irregulars.'

As he spoke, there came a swift pattering of naked feet upon the stairs, a clatter of high voices, and in rushed a dozen dirty and ragged little street arabs. There was some show of discipline among them, despite their tumultuous entry, for they instantly drew up in line and stood facing us with expectant faces. One of their number, taller and older than the others, stood forward with an air of lounging superiority which was very funny in such a disreputable little scarecrow.

'Got your message, sir,' said he, 'and brought 'em on sharp. Three bob and a tanner for tickets.'

'Here you are,' said Holmes, producing some silver. 'In future they can report to you, Wiggins, and you to me. I cannot have the house invaded in this way. However, it is just as well that you should all hear the instructions. I want to find the whereabouts of a steam launch called the *Aurora*, owner Mordecai Smith, black with two red streaks, funnel black with a white band. She is down the river somewhere. I want one boy to be at Mordecai Smith's landing-stage opposite Millbank to say if the boat comes back. You must divide it out among yourselves, and do both banks thoroughly. Let me know the moment you have news. Is that all clear?'

'Yes, guv'nor,' said Wiggins.

'The old scale of pay, and a guinea to the boy who finds the boat. Here's a day in advance. Now, off you go!'

He handed them a shilling each, and away they buzzed down the stairs, and I saw them a moment later streaming down the street.

'If the launch is above water they will find her,' said Holmes, as he rose from the table and lit his pipe. 'They can go everywhere,

see everything, overhear everyone. I expect to hear before evening
that they have spotted her. In the meanwhile, we can do nothing
but await results. We cannot pick up the broken trail until we find
either the *Aurora* or Mr Mordecai Smith.'

'Toby could eat these scraps, I dare say. Are you going to bed,
Holmes?'

'No; I am not tired. I have a curious constitution. I never
remember feeling tired by work, though idleness exhausts me
completely. I am going to smoke and to think over this queer
business to which my fair client has introduced us. If ever man
had an easy task, this of ours ought to be. Wooden-legged men
are not so common, but the other man must, I should think, be
absolutely unique.'

'That other man again!'

'I have no wish to make a mystery of him to you, anyway. But
you must have formed your own opinion. Now, do consider the
data. Diminutive footmarks, toes never fettered by boots, naked
feet, stone-headed wooden mace, great agility, small poisoned
darts. What do you make of all this?'

'A savage!' I exclaimed. 'Perhaps one of those Indians who were
the associates of Jonathan Small.'

'Hardly that,' said he. 'When first I saw signs of strange weapons, I was inclined to think so; but the remarkable character of
the footmarks caused me to reconsider my views. Some of the
inhabitants of the Indian Peninsula are small men, but none
could have left such marks as that. The Hindu proper has long
and thin feet. The sandal-wearing Mohammedan has the great
toe well separated from the others, because the thong is commonly
passed between. These little darts, too, could only be shot in one
way. They are from a blow-pipe. Now, then, where are we to find
our savage?'

'South American,' I hazarded.

He stretched his hand up, and took down a bulky volume from
the shelf.

'This is the first volume of a gazetteer which is now being
published. It may be looked upon as the very latest authority.
What have we here? "Andaman Islands, situated 340 miles
to the north of Sumatra, in the Bay of Bengal." Hum! Hum!
What's all this? Moist climate, coral reefs, sharks, Port Blair,
convict barracks, Rutland Island, cottonwoods—— Ah, here we

are! "The aborigines of the Andaman Islands may perhaps claim the distinction of being the smallest race upon this earth, though some anthropologists prefer the Bushman of Africa, the Diggers of American, and the Terra del Fuegians. The average height is rather below four feet, although many full-grown adults may be found who are very much smaller than this. They are a fierce, morose, and intractable people, though capable of forming most devoted friendships when their confidence has once been gained." Mark that, Watson. Now, then, listen to this. "They are naturally hideous, having large, misshapen heads, small, fierce eyes, and distorted features. Their feet and hands, however, are remarkably small. So intractable and fierce are they, that all the efforts of the British officials have failed to win them over in any degree. They have always been a terror to shipwrecked crews, braining the survivors with their stone-headed clubs, or shooting them with their poisoned arrows. These massacres are invariably concluded by a cannibal feast." Nice, amiable people, Watson! If this fellow had been left to his own unaided devices, this affair might have taken an even more ghastly turn. I fancy that, even as it is, Jonathan Small would give a good deal not to have employed him.'

'But how came he to have so singular a companion?'

'Ah, that is more than I can tell. Since, however, we had already determined that Small had come from the Andamans, it is not so very wonderful that this islander should be with him. No doubt we shall know all about it in time. Look here, Watson; you look regularly done. Lie down there on the sofa, and see if I can put you to sleep.'

He took up his violin from the corner, and as I stretched myself out he began to play some low, dreamy, melodious air—his own, no doubt, for he had a remarkable gift for improvisation. I have a vague remembrance of his gaunt limbs, his earnest face and the rise and fall of his bow. Then I seemed to be floated peacefully away upon a soft sea of sound, until I found myself in dreamland, with the sweet face of Mary Morstan looking down upon me.

IX. A BREAK IN THE CHAIN

IT was late in the afternoon before I woke, strengthened and refreshed. Sherlock Holmes still sat exactly as I had left him, save that he had laid aside his violin and was deep in a book. He looked across at me as I stirred, and I noticed that his face was dark and troubled.

'You have slept soundly,' he said. 'I feared that our talk would wake you.'

'I heard nothing,' I answered. 'Have you had fresh news, then?'

'Unfortunately, no. I confess that I am surprised and disappointed. I expected something definite by this time. Wiggins has just been up to report. He says that no trace can be found of the launch. It is a provoking check, for every hour is of importance.'

'Can I do anything? I am perfectly fresh now, and quite ready for another night's outing.'

'No; we can do nothing. We can only wait. If we go ourselves, the message might come in our absence, and delay be caused. You can do what you will, but I must remain on guard.'

'Then I shall run over to Camberwell and call upon Mrs Cecil Forrester. She asked me to, yesterday.'

'On Mrs Cecil Forrester?' asked Holmes, with the twinkle of a smile in his eyes.

'Well, of course, on Miss Morstan too. They were anxious to hear what happened.'

'I would not tell them too much,' said Holmes. 'Women are never to be entirely trusted—not the best of them.'

I did not pause to argue over this atrocious sentiment.

'I shall be back in an hour or two,' I remarked.

'All right! Good luck! But, I say, if you are crossing the water you may as well return Toby, for I don't think it is at all likely that we shall have any use for him now.'

I took our mongrel accordingly, and left him, together with a half-sovereign, at the old naturalist's in Pinchin Lane. At Camberwell I found Miss Morstan a little weary after her night's adventures, but very eager to hear the news. Mrs Forrester, too, was full of curiosity. I told them all that we had done, suppressing, however, the more dreadful parts of the tragedy. Thus, although I spoke of Mr Sholto's death, I said nothing of the exact manner and method of it. With all my omissions, however, there was enough to startle and amaze them.

'It is a romance!' cried Mrs Forrester. 'An injured lady, half a million in treasure, a black cannibal, and a wooden-legged ruffian. They take the place of the conventional dragon or wicked earl.'

'And two knights-errant to the rescue,' added Miss Morstan, with a bright glance at me.

'Why, Mary, your fortune depends upon the issue of this search. I don't think that you are nearly excited enough. Just imagine what it must be to be so rich, and to have the world at your feet!'

It sent a little thrill of joy to my heart to notice that she showed no sign of elation at the prospect. On the contrary, she gave a toss of her proud head, as though the matter were one in which she took small interest.

'It is for Mr Thaddeus Sholto that I am anxious,' she said. ' Nothing else is of any consequence; but I think that he has behaved most kindly and honourably throughout. It is our duty to clear him of this dreadful and unfounded charge.'

It was evening before I left Camberwell, and quite dark by the time I reached home. My companion's book and pipe lay by his chair, but he had disappeared. I looked about in the hope of seeing a note, but there was none.

'I suppose that Mr Sherlock Holmes has gone out?' I said to Mrs Hudson as she came up to lower the blinds.

'No, sir. He has gone to his room, sir. Do you know, sir,' sinking her voice into an impressive whisper, 'I am afraid for his health?'

'Why so, Mrs Hudson?'

'Well, he's that strange, sir. After you was gone he walked and he walked, up and down, up and down, until I was weary of the sound of his footstep. Then I heard him talking to himself and muttering, and every time the bell range out he came on the stairhead, with "What is that, Mrs Hudson?" And now he has slammed off to his room, but I can hear him walking away the same as ever. I hope he's not going to be ill, sir. I ventured to say something to him about cooling medicine, but he turned on me, sir, with such a look that I don't know how ever I got out of the room.'

'I don't think that you have any cause to be uneasy, Mrs Hudson,' I answered. 'I have seen him like this before. He has some small matter upon his mind which makes him restless.'

I tried to speak lightly to our worthy landlady, but I was myself somewhat uneasy when through the long night I still from time to time heard the dull sound of his tread, and knew how his keen spirit was chafing against this involuntary inaction.

At breakfast-time he looked worn and haggard, with a little fleck of feverish colour upon either cheek.

'You are knocking yourself up, old man,' I remarked. 'I heard you marching about in the night.'

'No, I could not sleep,' he answered. 'This infernal problem is consuming me. It is too much to be baulked by so petty an obstacle, when all else had been overcome. I know the men, the launch, everything; and yet I can get no news. I have set other agencies at work, and used every means at my disposal. The whole river has been searched on either side, but there is no news, nor has Mrs Smith heard of her husband. I shall come to the conclusion soon that they have scuttled the craft. But there are objections to that.'

'Or that Mrs Smith has put us on a wrong scent.'

'No, I think that may be dismissed. I had inquiries made, and there is a launch of that description.'

'Could it have gone up the river?'

'I have considered that possibility too, and there is a search party who will work up as far as Richmond. If no news comes today, I shall start off myself tomorrow, and go for the men rather than the boat. But surely, surely, we shall hear something.'

We did not, however. Not a word came to us either from Wiggins or from the other agencies. There were articles in most of the papers upon the Norwood tragedy. They all appeared to be rather hostile to the unfortunate Thaddeus Sholto. No fresh details were to be found, however, in any of them, save that an inquest was to be held upon the following day. I walked over to Camberwell in the evening to report our ill-success to the ladies, and on my return I found Holmes dejected and somewhat morose. He would hardly reply to my questions, and busied himself all the evening in an abstruse chemical analysis which involved much heating of retorts and distilling of vapours, ending at last in a smell which fairly drove me out of the apartment. Up to the small hours of the morning I could hear the clinking of his test-tubes, which told me that he was still engaged in his malodorous experiment.

In the early dawn I woke with a start, and was surprised to

find him standing by my bedside, clad in a rude sailor dress with a pea-jacket, and a coarse red scarf round his neck.

'I am off down the river, Watson,' said he. 'I have been turning it over in my mind, and I can see only one way out of it. It is worth trying, at all events.'

'Surely I can come with you, then?' said I.

'No; you can be much more useful if you will remain here as my representative. I am loth to go, for it is quite on the cards that some message may come during the day, though Wiggins was despondent about it last night. I want you to open all notes and telegrams, and to act on your own judgment if any news should come. Can I rely upon you?'

'Most certainly.'

'I am afraid that you will not be able to wire to me, for I can hardly tell yet where I may find myself. If I am in luck, however, I may not be gone so very long. I shall have news of some sort or other before I get back.'

I had heard nothing of him by breakfast-time. On opening the *Standard*, however, I found that there was a fresh allusion to the business.

With reference to the Upper Norwood tragedy, [it remarked] we have reason to believe that the matter promises to be even more complex and mysterious than was originally supposed. Fresh evidence has shown that it is quite impossible that Mr Thaddeus Sholto could have been in any way concerned in the matter. He and the housekeeper, Mrs Bernstone, were both released yesterday evening. It is believed, however, that the police have a clue as to the real culprits, and that it is being prosecuted by Mr Athelney Jones, of Scotland Yard, with all his well-known energy and sagacity. Further arrests may be expected at any moment.

'That is satisfactory so far as it goes,' thought I. 'Friend Sholto is safe, at any rate. I wonder what the fresh clue may be, though it seems a stereotyped form whenever the police have made a blunder.'

I tossed the paper down upon the table, but at that moment my eye caught an advertisement in the agony column. It ran this way:

LOST.—Whereas Mordecai Smith, boatman, and his son Jim, left Smith's Wharf at or about three o'clock last Tuesday morning in the steam launch *Aurora*, black with two red stripes, funnel black with a white band, the sum of five pounds will be paid to anyone who can give information to Mrs Smith, at Smith's Wharf, or at 221B Baker Street, as to the whereabouts of the said Mordecai Smith and the launch *Aurora*.

This was clearly Holmes's doing. The Baker Street address was enough to prove that. It struck me as rather ingenious, because it might be read by the fugitives without their seeing in it more than the natural anxiety of a wife for her missing husband.

It was a long day. Every time that a knock came to the door, or a sharp step passed in the street, I imagined that it was either Holmes returning or an answer to his advertisement. I tried to read, but my thoughts would wander off to our strange quest and to the ill-assorted and villainous pair whom we were pursuing. Could there be, I wondered, some radical flaw in my companion's reasoning? Might he not be suffering from some huge self-deception? Was it not possible that his nimble and speculative mind had built up this wild theory upon faulty premises? I had never known him to be wrong, and yet the keenest reasoner may occasionally be deceived. He was likely, I thought, to fall into error through the over-refinement of his logic—his preference for a subtle and bizarre explanation when a plainer and more commonplace one lay ready to his hand. Yet on the other hand, I had myself seen the evidence, and I had heard the reasons for his deductions. When I looked back on the long chain of curious circumstances, many of them trivial in themselves, but all tending in the same direction, I could not disguise from myself that even if Holmes's explanation were incorrect the true theory must be equally *outré* and startling.

At three o'clock in the afternoon there was a loud peal at the bell, an authoritative voice in the hall, and, to my surprise, no less a person than Mr Athelney Jones was shown up to me. Very different was he, however, from the brusque and masterful professor of common-sense who had taken over the case so confidently at Upper Norwood. His expression was downcast, and his bearing meek and even apologetic.

'Good-day, sir; good-day,' said he. 'Mr Sherlock Holmes is out, I understand?'

'Yes, and I cannot be sure when he will be back. But perhaps you would care to wait. Take that chair and try one of these cigars.'

'Thank you; I don't mind if I do,' said he, mopping his face with a red bandanna handkerchief.

'And a whisky and soda?'

'Well, half a glass. It is very hot for the time of year; and I have had a good deal to worry and try me. You know my theory about this Norwood case?'

'I remember that you expressed one.'

'Well, I have been obliged to reconsider it. I had my net tightly round Mr Sholto, sir, when pop he went through a hole in the middle of it. He was able to prove an alibi which could not be shaken. From the time that he left his brother's room he was never out of sight of someone or other. So it could not be he who climbed over roofs and through trap-doors. It's a very dark case, and my professional credit is at stake. I should be very glad of a little assistance.'

'We all need help sometimes,' said I.

'Your friend Mr Sherlock Holmes is a wonderful man, sir,' said he, in a husky and confidential voice. 'He's a man who is not to be beat. I have known that young man go into a good many cases, but I never saw the case yet that he could not throw a light upon. He is irregular in his methods, and a little quick perhaps in jumping at theories; but, on the whole, I think he would have made a most promising officer, and I don't care who knows it. I have had a wire from him this morning, by which I understand that he has got some clue to this Sholto business. Here is his message.'

He took the telegram out of his pocket, and handed it to me. It was dated from Poplar at twelve o'clock. 'Go to Baker Street at once,' it said. 'If I have not returned, wait for me. I am close on the track of the Sholto gang. You can come with us tonight if you want to be in at the finish.'

'This sounds well. He has evidently picked up the scent again,' said I.

'Ah, then he has been at fault too,' exclaimed Jones, with evident satisfaction. 'Even the best of us are thrown off sometimes. Of course this may prove to be a false alarm; but it is my duty as an officer of the law to allow no chance to slip. But there is someone at the door. Perhaps this is he.'

A heavy step was heard ascending the stair, with a great wheezing and rattling as from a man who was sorely put to it for breath. Once or twice he stopped, as though the climb were too much for him, but at last he made his way to our door and entered. His appearance corresponded to the sounds which we had heard. He was an aged man, clad in seafaring garb, with an old pea-jacket buttoned up to his throat. His back was bowed, his knees were shaky, and his breathing was painfully asthmatic. As he leaned upon a thick oaken cudgel his shoulders heaved in the effort to draw the air into his lungs. He had a coloured scarf round his chin, and I could see little of his face save a pair of keen dark eyes, overhung by bushy white brows, and long grey side-whiskers. Altogether he gave me the impression of a respectable master mariner who had fallen into years and poverty.

'What is it, my man?' I asked.

He looked about him in the slow methodical fashion of old age.

'Is Mr Sherlock Holmes here?' said he.

'No; but I am acting for him. You can tell me any message you have for him.'

'It was to him himself I was to tell it,' said he.

'But I tell you I am acting for him. Was it about Mordecai Smith's boat?'

'Yes. I knows well where it is. An' I knows where the men he is after are. An' I knows where the treasure is. I knows all about it.'

'Then tell me, and I shall let him know.'

'It was to him I was to tell it,' he repeated, with the petulant obstinacy of a very old man.

'Well, you must wait for him.'

'No, no; I ain't goin' to lose a whole day to please no one. If Mr Holmes ain't here, then Mr Holmes must find it all out for himself. I don't care about the look of either of you, and I won't tell a word.'

He shuffled towards the door, but Athelney Jones got in front of him.

'Wait a bit, my friend,' said he. 'You have important information, and you must not walk off. We shall keep you, whether you like or not, until our friend returns.'

The old man made a little run towards the door, but, as Athelney Jones put his broad back up against it, he recognized the uselessness of resistance.

'Pretty sort o' treatment this!' he cried, stamping his stick. 'I come here to see a gentleman, and you two, who I never saw in my life, seize me and treat me in this fashion!'

'You will be none the worse,' I said. 'We shall recompense you for the loss of your time. Sit over here on the sofa, and you will not have long to wait.'

He came across sullenly enough, and seated himself with his face resting on his hands. Jones and I resumed our cigars and our talk. Suddenly, however, Holmes's voice broke in upon us.

'I think that you might offer me a cigar too,' he said.

We both started in our chairs. There was Holmes sitting close to us with an air of quiet amusement.

'Holmes!' I exclaimed. 'You here! But where is the old man?'

'Here is the old man,' said he, holding out a heap of white hair. 'Here he is—wig, whiskers, eyebrows, and all. I thought my disguise was pretty good, but I hardly expected that it would stand that test.'

'Ah, you rogue!' cried Jones, highly delighted. 'You would have made an actor, and a rare one. You had the proper workhouse cough, and those weak legs of yours are worth ten pound a week. I thought I knew the glint of your eye, though. You didn't get away from us so easily, you see.'

'I have been working in that get-up all day,' said he, lighting his cigar. 'You see, a good many of the criminal classes begin to know me—especially since our friend here took to publishing some of my cases: so I can only go on the war-path under some simple disguise like this. You got my wire?'

'Yes; that was what brought me here.'

'How has your case prospered?'

'It has all come to nothing. I have had to release two of my prisoners, and there is no evidence against the other two.'

'Never mind. We shall give you two others in the place of them. But you must put yourself under my orders. You are welcome to all the official credit, but you must act on the lines that I point out. Is that agreed?'

'Entirely, if you will help me to the men.'

'Well, then, in the first place I shall want a fast police-boat—a steam-launch—to be at the Westminster Stairs at seven o'clock.'

'That is easily managed. There is always one about there; but I can step across the road and telephone to make sure.'

'Then I shall want two staunch men, in case of resistance.'

'There will be two or three in the boat. What else?'

'When we secure the men we shall get the treasure. I think that it would be a pleasure to my friend here to take the box round to the young lady to whom half of it rightfully belongs. Let her be the first to open it. Eh, Watson?'

'It would be a great pleasure to me.'

'Rather an irregular proceeding,' said Jones, shaking his head. 'However, the whole thing is irregular, and I suppose we must wink at it. The treasure must afterwards be handed over to the authorities until after the official investigation.'

'Certainly. That is easily managed. One other point. I should much like to have a few details about this matter from the lips of Jonathan Small himself. You know I like to work the details of my cases out. There is no objection to my having an unofficial interview with him, either here in my rooms or elsewhere, as long as he is efficiently guarded?'

'Well, you are master of the situation. I have had no proof yet of the existence of this Jonathan Small. However, if you can catch him, I don't see how I can refuse you an interview with him.'

'That is understood, then?'

'Perfectly. Is there anything else?'

'Only that I insist upon your dining with us. It will be ready in half an hour. I have oysters and a brace of grouse, with something a little choice in white wines. Watson, you have never yet recognized my merits as a housekeeper.'

X. THE END OF THE ISLANDER

OUR meal was a merry one. Holmes could talk exceedingly well when he chose, and that night he did choose. He appeared to be in a state of nervous exaltation. I have never known him so brilliant. He spoke on a quick succession of subjects—on miracle plays, on medieval pottery, on Stradivarius violins, on the Buddhism of Ceylon, and on the warships of the future—handling each as though he had made a special study of it. His bright humour marked the reaction from his black depression of the preceding days. Athelney Jones proved to be a sociable soul in his hours of relaxation, and faced his dinner with the air of a *bon vivant*. For myself, I felt elated at the thought that we were nearing the end of our task, and I caught something of Holmes's gaiety. None of us alluded during dinner to the cause which had brought us together.

When the cloth was cleared, Holmes glanced at his watch, and filled up three glasses of port.

'One bumper,' said he, 'to the success of our little expedition. And now it is high time we were off. Have you a pistol, Watson?'

'I have my old service-revolver in my desk.'

'You had best take it, then. It is well to be prepared. I see that the cab is at the door. I ordered it for half-past six.'

It was a little past seven before we reached the Westminster Wharf, and found our launch awaiting us. Holmes eyed it critically.

'Is there anything to mark it as a police-boat?'

'Yes; that green lamp at the side.'

'Then take it off.'

The small change was made, we stepped on board, and the ropes were cast off. Jones, Holmes, and I sat in the stern. There was one man at the rudder, one to tend the engines, and two burly police-inspectors forward.

'Where to?' asked Jones.

'To the Tower. Tell them to stop opposite to Jacobson's Yard.'

Our craft was evidently a very fast one. We shot past the long lines of loaded barges as though they were stationary. Holmes smiled with satisfaction as we overhauled a river steamer and left her behind us.

'We ought to be able to catch anything on the river,' he said.

'Well, hardly that. But there are not many launches to beat us.'

'We shall have to catch the *Aurora*, and she has a name for being a clipper. I will tell you how the land lies, Watson. You recollect how annoyed I was at being baulked by so small a thing?'

'Yes.'

'Well, I gave my mind a thorough rest by plunging into a chemical analysis. One of our greatest statesmen has said that a change of work is the best rest. So it is. When I had succeeded in dissolving the hydrocarbon which I was at work at, I came back to the problem of the Sholtos, and thought the whole matter out again. My boys had been up the river and down the river without result. The launch was not at any landing-stage or wharf, nor had it returned. Yet it could hardly have been scuttled to hide their traces, though that always remained as a possible hypothesis if all else failed. I knew that this man Small had a certain degree of low cunning, but I did not think him capable of anything in the nature of delicate finesse. I then reflected that since he had certainly been in London some time—as we had evidence that he maintained a continual watch over Pondicherry Lodge—he could hardly leave at a moment's notice, but would need some little time, if it were only a day, to arrange his affairs. That was the balance of probability, at any rate.'

'It seems to me to be a little weak,' said I: 'it is more probable that he had arranged his affairs before ever he set out upon his expedition.'

'No, I hardly think so. This lair of his would be too valuable a retreat in case of need for him to give it up until he was sure that he could do without it. But a second consideration struck me. Jonathan Small must have felt that the peculiar appearance of his companion, however much he may have top-coated him, would give rise to gossip, and possibly be associated with this Norwood tragedy. He was quite sharp enough to see that. They had started from their headquarters under cover of darkness, and he would wish to get back before it was broad light. Now, it was past three o'clock, according to Mrs Smith, when they got the boat. It would be quite bright, and people would be about in an hour or so. Therefore, I argued, they did not go very far. They paid Smith well to hold his tongue, reserved his launch for the final escape, and hurried to their lodgings with the treasure-box. In a couple of nights, when they had time to see what view the papers took, and whether there was any suspicion, they would make their way under cover of darkness to some ship at Gravesend or in the Downs, where no doubt they had already arranged for passages to America or the Colonies.'

'But the launch? They could not have taken that to their lodgings.'

'Quite so. I argued that the launch must be no great way off, in spite of its invisibility. I then put myself in the place of Small, and looked at it as a man of his capacity would. He would probably consider that to send back the launch or to keep it at a wharf would make pursuit easy if the police did happen to get on his track. How, then, could he conceal the launch and yet have her at hand when wanted? I wondered what I should do myself if I were in his shoes. I could only think of one way of doing it. I might hand the launch over to some boat-builder or repairer, with directions to make a trifling change in her. She would then be removed to his shed or yard, and so be effectually concealed, while at the same time I could have her at a few hours' notice.'

'That seems simple enough.'

'It is just these very simple things which are extremely liable to be overlooked. However, I determined to act on the idea. I started at once in this harmless seaman's rig, and inquired at all the yards down the river. I drew blank at fifteen, but at the sixteenth—Jacobson's—I learned that the *Aurora* had been handed over to them two days ago by a wooden-legged man, with some trivial directions as to her rudder. "There ain't naught amiss with her rudder," said the foreman. "There she lies, with the red streaks." At that moment who should come down but Mordecai Smith, the missing owner? He was rather the worse for liquor. I should not, of course, have known him, but he bellowed out his name and the name of his launch. "I want her tonight at eight o'clock," said he—"eight o'clock sharp, mind, for I have two gentlemen who won't be kept waiting." They had evidently paid him well, for he was very flush of money, chucking shillings about to the men. I followed him some distance, but he subsided into an ale-house; so I went back to the yard, and, happening to pick up one of my boys on the way, I stationed him as a sentry over the launch. He is to stand at the water's edge and wave his handkerchief to us when they start. We shall be lying off in the stream, and it will be a strange thing if we do not take men, treasure and all.'

'You have planned it all very neatly, whether they are the right men or not,' said Jones; 'but if the affair were in my hands I should have had a body of police in Jacobson's Yard, and arrested them when they came down.'

'Which would have been never. This man Small is a pretty shrewd fellow. He would send a scout on ahead, and if anything made him suspicious he would lie snug for another week.'

'But you might have stuck to Mordecai Smith, and so been led to their hiding-place,' said I.

'In that case I should have wasted my day. I think that it is a hundred to one against Smith knowing where they live. As long as he has liquor and good pay, why should he ask questions? They send him messages what to do. No, I thought over every possible course, and this is the best.'

While this conversation had been proceeding, we had been shooting the long series of bridges which span the Thames. As we passed the City, the last rays of the sun were gilding the cross upon the summit of St Paul's. It was twilight before we reached the Tower.

'That is Jacobson's Yard,' said Holmes, pointing to a bristle of masts and rigging on the Surrey side. 'Cruise gently up and down here under cover of this string of lighters.' He took a pair of night-glasses from his pocket and gazed some time at the shore. 'I see my sentry at his post,' he remarked, 'but no sign of a handkerchief.'

'Suppose we go down stream a short way and lie in wait for them,' said Jones, eagerly.

We were all eager by this time, even the policemen and stokers, who had a very vague idea of what was going forward.

'We have no right to take anything for granted,' Holmes answered. 'It is certainly ten to one that they go down stream, but we cannot be certain. From this point we can see the entrance of the yard, and they can hardly see us. It will be a clear night and plenty of light. We must stay where we are. See how the folk swarm over yonder in the gaslight.'

'They are coming from work in the yard.'

'Dirty-looking rascals, but I suppose every one has some little immortal spark concealed about him. You would not think it, to look at them. There is no *a priori* probability about it. A strange enigma is man!'

'Someone calls him a soul concealed in an animal,' I suggested.

'Winwood Reade is good upon the subject,' said Holmes. 'He remarks that, while the individual man is an insoluble puzzle, in the aggregate he becomes a mathematical certainty. You can, for example, never foretell what any one man will do, but you can say with precision what an average number will be up to. Individuals vary, but percentages remain constant. So says the statistician. But do I see a handkerchief? Surely there is a white flutter over yonder.'

'Yes, it is your boy,' I cried. 'I can see him plainly.'

'And there is the *Aurora*,' exclaimed Holmes, 'and going like the devil! Full speed ahead, engineer. Make after that launch with the yellow light. By Heaven, I shall never forgive myself if she proves to have the heels of us!'

She had slipped unseen through the yard-entrance and passed behind two or three small craft, so that she had fairly got her speed up before we saw her. Now she was flying down the stream, near in to the shore, going at a tremendous rate. Jones looked gravely at her and shook his head.

'She is very fast,' he said. 'I doubt if we shall catch her.'

'We *must* catch her!' cried Holmes, between his teeth. 'Heap it on, stokers! Make her do all she can! If we burn the boat we must have them!'

We were fairly after her now. The furnaces roared, and the powerful engines whizzed and clanked, like a great metallic heart. Her sharp, steep prow cut through the still river-water and sent two rolling waves to right and to left of us. With every throb of the engines we sprang and quivered like a living thing. One great yellow lantern in our bows threw a long, flickering funnel of light in front of us. Right ahead a dark blur upon the water showed where the *Aurora* lay, and the swirl of white foam behind her spoke of the pace at which she was going. We flashed past barges, steamers, merchant-vessels, in and out, behind this one and round the other. Voices hailed us out of the darkness, but still the *Aurora* thundered on, and still we followed close upon her track.

'Pile it on, men, pile it on!' cried Holmes, looking down into the engine-room, while the fierce glow from below beat upon his eager, aquiline face. 'Get every pound of steam you can.'

'I think we gain a little,' said Jones, with his eyes on the *Aurora*.

'I am sure of it,' said I. 'We shall be up with her in a very few minutes.'

At that moment, however, as our evil fate would have it, a tug with three barges in tow blundered in between us. It was only by putting our helm hard down that we avoided a collision, and before we could round them and recover our way the *Aurora* had gained a good two hundred yards. She was still, however, well in view, and the murky, uncertain twilight was settling into a clear, starlit night. Our boilers were strained to their utmost, and the frail shell vibrated and creaked with the fierce energy which was driving us along. We had shot through the Pool, past the West India Docks, down the long Deptford Reach, and up again after rounding the Isle of Dogs. The dull blur in front of us resolved itself now clearly enough into the dainty *Aurora*. Jones turned our searchlight upon her, so that we could plainly see the figures upon her deck. One man sat by the stern, with something black between his knees, over which he stooped. Beside him lay a dark mass, which looked like a Newfoundland dog. The boy held the tiller, while against the red glare of the furnace I could see old Smith, stripped to the waist, and shovelling coals for dear life. They may have had some doubt at first as to whether we were really pursuing them, but now as we followed every winding and turning which they took there could no longer be any question about it. At Greenwich we were about three hundred paces behind them. At Blackwall we could not have been more than two hundred and fifty. I have coursed many creatures in many countries during my chequered career, but never did sport give me such a wild thrill as this mad, flying man-hunt down the Thames. Steadily we drew in upon them, yard by yard. In the silence of the night we could hear the panting and clanking of their machinery. The man in the stern still crouched upon the deck, and his arms were moving as though he were busy, while every now and then he would look up and measure with a glance the distance which still separated us. Nearer we came and nearer. Jones yelled to them to stop. We were not more than four boats' lengths behind them, both boats flying at a tremendous pace. It was a clear reach of the river, with Barking Level upon one side and the melancholy Plumstead Marshes upon the other. At our hail the man in the stern sprang up from the deck and shook his two clenched fists at us, cursing the while in a high, cracked voice. He was a good-sized, powerful man, and as he stood poising himself with legs astride, I could see that, from the thigh downwards, there was but a wooden stump upon the right side. At the sound of his strident, angry cries, there was a movement in the huddled bundle upon the deck. It straightened itself into a little black man—the smallest I have ever seen—with a great, misshapen head and a shock of tangled, dishevelled hair. Holmes had already drawn his revolver, and I whipped out mine at the sight of this savage, distorted creature. He was wrapped in some sort of a dark ulster or blanket, which left only his face exposed; but that face was enough to give a man a sleepless night. Never have I seen features so deeply marked with all bestiality and cruelty. His small eyes glowed and burned with a sombre light, and his thick lips were writhed back from his teeth, which grinned and chattered at us with half-animal fury.

'Fire if he raises his hand,' said Holmes, quietly.

We were within a boat's-length by this time, and almost within touch of our quarry. I can see the two of them now as they stood: the white man with his legs far apart, shrieking out curses, and the unhallowed dwarf with his hideous face and his strong, yellow teeth gnashing at us in the light of our lantern.

It was well that we had so clear a view of him. Even as we looked he plucked out from under his covering a short, round piece of wood, like a school-ruler, and clapped it to his lips. Our pistols rang out together. He whirled round, threw up his arms, and, with a kind of choking cough, fell sideways into the stream. I caught one glimpse of his venomous, menacing eyes amid the white swirl of the waters. At the same moment the wooden-legged man threw himself upon the rudder and put it hard down, so that his boat made straight in for the southern bank, while we shot past her stern, only clearing her by a few feet. We were round after her in an instant, but she was already nearly at the bank. It was a wild and desolate place, where the moon glimmered upon a wide expanse of marshland, with pools of stagnant water and beds of decaying vegetation. The launch, with a dull thud, ran upon the mud-bank, with her bow in the air and her stern flush with the water. The fugitive sprang out, but his stump instantly sank its whole length into the sodden soil. In vain he struggled and writhed. Not one step could he possibly take either forwards or backwards. He yelled in impotent rage, and kicked frantically into the mud with his other foot; but his struggles only bored his wooden pin the deeper into the sticky bank. When we brought our launch alongside he was so firmly anchored that it was only by throwing the end of a rope over his shoulders that we were able to haul him out, and to drag him, like some evil fish, over our side. The two Smiths, father and son, sat sullenly in their launch, but came aboard meekly enough when commanded. The *Aurora* herself we hauled off and made fast to our stern. A solid iron chest of Indian workmanship stood upon the deck. This, there could be no question, was the same that had contained the ill-omened treasure of the Sholtos. There was no key, but it was of considerable weight, so we transferred it carefully to our own little cabin. As we steamed slowly up-stream again, we flashed our searchlight in every direction, but there was no sign of the Islander. Somewhere in the dark ooze at the bottom of the Thames lie the bones of that strange visitor to our shores.

'See here,' said Holmes, pointing to the wooden hatchway. 'Wᴄ were hardly quick enough with our pistols.' There, sure enough, just behind where we had been standing, stuck one of those murderous darts which we knew so well. It must have whizzed between us at the instant we fired. Holmes smiled at it and shrugged his shoulders in his easy fashion, but I confess it turned me sick to think of the horrible death which had passed so close to us that night.

XI. THE GREAT AGRA TREASURE

OUR captive sat in the cabin opposite to the iron box which he had done so much and waited so long to gain. He was a sunburned, reckless-eyed fellow, with a network of lines and wrinkles all over his mahogany features, which told of a hard, open-air life. There was a singular prominence about his bearded chin which marked a man who was not to be easily turned from his purpose. His age may have been fifty or thereabouts, for his black, curly hair was thickly shot with grey. His face in repose was not an unpleasing one, though his heavy brows and aggressive chin gave him, as I had lately seen, a terrible expression when moved to anger. He sat now with his handcuffed hands upon his lap, and his head sunk upon his breast, while he looked with his keen, twinkling eyes at the box which had been the cause of his ill-doings. It seemed to me that there was more sorrow than anger in his rigid and contained countenance. Once he looked up at me with a gleam of something like humour in his eyes.

'Well, Jonathan Small.' said Holmes, lighting a cigar, 'I am sorry that it has come to this.'

'And so I am, sir,' he answered, frankly. 'I don't believe that I can swing over the job. I give you my word on the Book that I never raised hand against Mr Sholto. It was that little hell-hound Tonga who shot one of his cursed darts into him. I had no part in it, sir. I was as grieved as if it had been my blood-relation. I welted the little devil with the slack end of the rope for it, but it was done, and I could not undo it again.'

'Have a cigar,' said Holmes; 'and you had best take a pull out of my flask, for you are very wet. How could you expect so small and weak a man as this black fellow to overpower Mr Sholto and hold him while you were climbing the rope?'

'You seem to know as much about it as if you were there, sir. The truth is that I hoped to find the room clear. I knew the habits of the house pretty well, and it was the time when Mr Sholto usually went down to his supper. I shall make no secret of the business. The best defence that I can make is just the simple truth. Now, if it had been the old major I would have swung for him with a light heart. I would have thought no more of knifing him than of smoking this cigar But it's cursed hard that I should be lagged over this young Sholto, with whom I had no quarrel whatever.'

'You are under the charge of Mr Athelney Jones, of Scotland Yard. He is going to bring you up to my rooms, and I shall ask you for a true account of the matter. You must make a clean breast of it, for if you do I hope that I may be of use to you. I think I can prove that the poison acts so quickly that the man was dead before ever you reached the room.'

'That he was, sir. I never got such a turn in my life as when I saw him grinning at me with his head on his shoulder as I climbed through the window. It fairly shook me, sir. I'd have half killed Tonga for it if he had not scrambled off. That was how he came to leave his club, and some of his darts too, as he tells me, which I dare say helped to put you on our track; though how you kept on it is more than I can tell. I don't feel no malice against you for it. But it does seem a queer thing,' he added, with a bitter smile, 'that I, who have a fair claim to half a million of money, should spend the first half of my life building a breakwater in the Andamans, and am like to spend the other half digging drains at Dartmoor. It was an evil day for me when first I clapped eyes upon the merchant Achmet and had to do with the Agra treasure, which never brought anything but a curse yet upon the man who owned it. To him it brought murder, to Major Sholto it brought fear and guilt, to me it has meant slavery for life.'

At this moment Athelney Jones thrust his face and shoulders into the tiny cabin.

'Quite a family party,' he remarked. 'I think I shall have a pull at that flask, Holmes. Well, I think we may congratulate each other. Pity we didn't take the other alive; but there was no choice. I say, Holmes, you must confess that you cut it rather fine. It was all we could do to overhaul her.'

'All is well that ends well,' said Holmes. 'But I certainly did not know that the *Aurora* was a clipper.'

'Smith says she is one of the fastest launches on the river, and that if he had had another man to help him with the engines we should never have caught her. He swears he knew nothing of this Norwood business.'

'Neither he did,' cried our prisoner — 'not a word. I chose his launch because I heard that she was a flier. We told him nothing; but we paid him well, and he was to get something handsome if we reached our vessel, the *Esmeralda*, at Gravesend, outward bound for the Brazils.'

'Well, if he has done no wrong we shall see that no wrong comes to him. If we are pretty quick in catching our men, we are not so quick in condemning them.' It was amusing to notice how the consequential Jones was already beginning to give himself airs on the strength of the capture. From the slight smile which played over Sherlock Holmes's face, I could see that the speech had not been lost upon him.

'We will be at Vauxhall Bridge presently,' said Jones, 'and shall land you, Dr Watson, with the treasure-box. I need hardly tell you that I am taking a very grave responsibility upon myself in doing this. It is most irregular; but of course an agreement is an agreement. I must, however, as a matter of duty, send an inspector with you, since you have so valuable a charge. You will drive, no doubt?'

'Yes, I shall drive.'

'It is a pity there is no key, that we may make an inventory first. You will have to break it open. Where is the key, my man?'

'At the bottom of the river,' said Small, shortly.

'Hum! There was no use your giving this unnecessary trouble. We have had work enough already through you. However, doctor, I need not warn you to be careful. Bring the box back with you to the Baker Street rooms. You will find us there, on our way to the station.'

They landed me at Vauxhall, with my heavy iron box, and with a bluff, genial inspector as my companion. A quarter of an hour's drive brought us to Mrs Cecil Forrester's. The servant seemed surprised at so late a visitor. Mrs Cecil Forrester was out for the evening, she explained, and likely to be very late. Miss Morstan, however, was in the drawing-room; so to the drawing-room I went, box in hand, leaving the obliging inspector in the cab.

She was seated by the open window, dressed in some sort of white, diaphanous material, with a little touch of scarlet at the neck and waist. The soft light of a shaded lamp fell upon her as she leaned back in the basket chair, playing over her sweet grave face and tinting with a dull, metallic sparkle the rich coils of her luxuriant hair. One white arm and hand drooped over the side of the chair, and her whole pose and figure spoke of an absorbing melancholy. At the sound of my footfall she sprang to her feet, however, and a bright flush of surprise and of pleasure coloured her pale cheeks.

'I heard a cab drive up,' she said. 'I thought that Mrs Forrester had come back very early, but I never dreamed that it might be you. What news have you brought me?'

'I have brought something better than news,' said I, putting down the box upon the table and speaking jovially and boisterously, though my heart was heavy within me. 'I have brought you something which is worth all the news in the world. I have brought you a fortune.'

She glanced at the iron box.

'Is that the treasure, then?' she asked, coolly enough.

'Yes, this is the Great Agra treasure. Half of it is yours and half is Thaddeus Sholto's. You will have a couple of hundred thousand each. Think of that! There will be few richer young ladies in England. Is it not glorious?'

I think that I must have been rather over-acting my delight, and that she detected a hollow ring in my congratulations, for I saw her eyebrows rise a little, and she glanced at me curiously.

'If I have it,' said she, 'I owe it to you.'

'No, no,' I answered, 'not to me, but to my friend Sherlock Holmes. With all the will in the world, I could never have followed up a clue which has taxed even his analytical genius. As it was, we very nearly lost it at the last moment.'

'Pray sit down and tell me all abut it, Dr Watson,' said she.

I narrated briefly what had occurred since I had seen her last. Holmes's new method of search, the discovery of the *Aurora*, the appearance of Athelney Jones, our expedition in the evening, and the wild chase down the Thames. She listened with parted lips and shining eyes to my recital of our adventures. When I spoke of the dart which had so narrowly missed us, she turned so white that I feared that she was about to faint.

'It is nothing,' she said, as I hastened to pour her out some water. 'I am all right again. It was a shock to me to hear that I had placed my friends in such horrible peril.'

'That is all over,' I answered. 'It was nothing. I will tell you no more gloomy details. Let us turn to something brighter. There is the treasure. What could be brighter than that? I got leave to bring it with me, thinking that it would interest you to be the first to see it.'

'It would be of the greatest interest to me,' she said. There was no eagerness in her voice, however. It had struck her, doubtless, that it might seem ungracious upon her part to be indifferent to a prize which had cost so much to win.

'What a pretty box!' she said, stooping over it. 'This is Indian work, I suppose?'

'Yes; it is Benares metal-work.'

'And so heavy!' she exclaimed, trying to raise it. 'The box alone must be of some value. Where is the key?'

'Small threw it into the Thames,' I answered. 'I must borrow Mrs Forrester's poker.'

There was in the front a thick and broad hasp, wrought in the image of a sitting Buddha. Under this I thrust the end of the poker and twisted it outward as a lever. The hasp sprang open with a loud snap. With trembling fingers I flung back the lid. We both stood gazing in astonishment. The box was empty!

No wonder it was heavy. The ironwork was two-thirds of an inch thick all around. It was massive, well-made, and solid, like a chest constructed to carry things of great price, but not one shred or crumb of metal or jewellery lay within it. It was absolutely and completely empty.

'The treasure is lost,' said Miss Morstan, calmly.

As I listened to the words and realized what they meant, a great shadow seemed to pass from my soul. I did not know how this Agra treasure had weighed me down, until now that it was finally removed. It was selfish, no doubt, disloyal, wrong, but I could realize nothing save that the golden barrier was gone from between us.

'Thank God!' I ejaculated from my very heart.

She looked at me with a quick, questioning smile.

'Why do you say that?' she asked.

'Because you are within my reach again,' I said, taking her hand.

She did not withdraw it. 'Because I love you, Mary, as truly as ever a man loved a woman. Because this treasure, these riches, sealed my lips. Now that they are gone I can tell you how I love you. That is why I said, "Thank God".'

'Then I say "Thank God", too,' she whispered, as I drew her to my side.

Whoever had lost a treasure, I knew that night that I had gained one.

XII. THE STRANGE STORY OF
JONATHAN SMALL

A VERY patient man was that inspector in the cab, for it was a weary time before I rejoined him. His face clouded over when I showed him the empty box.

'There goes the reward!' said he, gloomily. 'Where there is no money there is no pay. This night's work would have been worth a tenner each to Sam Brown and me if the treasure had been there.'

'Mr Thaddeus Sholto is a rich man,' I said; 'he will see that you are rewarded, treasure or no.'

The inspector shook his head despondently, however.

'It's a bad job,' he repeated; 'and so Mr Athelney Jones will think.'

His forecast proved to be correct, for the detective looked blank enough when I got to Baker Street and showed him the empty box. They had only just arrived, Holmes, the prisoner, and he, for they had changed their plans so far as to report themselves at a station upon the way. My companion lounged in his arm-chair with his usual listless expression, while Small sat stolidly opposite to him with his wooden leg cocked over his sound one. As I exhibited the empty box he leaned back in his chair and laughed aloud.

'This is your doing, Small,' said Athelney Jones, angrily.

'Yes, I have put it away where you shall never lay hand on it,' he cried, exultantly. 'It is my treasure, and if I can't have the loot I'll take darned good care that no one else does. I tell you that no living man has any right to it, unless it is three men who are in the Andaman convict-barracks and myself. I know now that I cannot have the use of it, and I know that they cannot. I have acted all through for them as much as for myself. It's been the sign of four with us always. Well, I know that they would have had me do just what I've done, and throw the treasure into the Thames rather than let it go to kith or kin of Sholto or Morstan. It was not to make them rich that we did for Achmet. You'll find the treasure where the key is and where little Tonga is. When I saw that your launch must catch us, I put the loot away in a safe place. There are no rupees for you this journey.'

'You are deceiving us, Small,' said Athelney Jones, sternly. 'If you had wished to throw the treasure into the Thames, it would have been easier for you to have thrown box and all.'

'Easier for me to throw, and easier for you to recover,' he answered, with a shrewd, side-long look. 'The man that was clever enough to hunt me down is clever enough to pick an iron box from the bottom of the river. Now that they are scattered over five miles or so, it may be a harder job. It went to my heart to do it, though. I was half mad when you came up with us. However, there's no good grieving over it. I've had ups in my life, and I've had downs, but I've learned not to cry over spilt milk.'

'This is a very serious matter, Small,' said the detective. 'If you had helped justice, instead of thwarting it in this way, you would have had a better chance at your trial.'

'Justice!' snarled the ex-convict. 'A pretty justice! Whose loot is this, if it is not ours? Where is the justice that I should give it up to those who have never earned it? Look how I have earned it! Twenty long years in that fever-ridden swamp, all day at work under the mangrove-tree, all night chained up in the filthy convict-huts, bitten by mosquitoes, racked with ague, bullied by every cursed black-faced policeman who loved to take it out of a white man. That was how I earned the Agra treasure, and you talk to me of justice because I cannot bear to feel that I have paid this price only that another may enjoy it! I would rather swing a score of times, or have one of Tonga's darts in my hide, than live in a convict's cell and feel that another man is at his ease in a palace with the money that should be mine.'

Small had dropped his mask of stoicism, and all this came out in a wild whirl of words, while his eyes blazed and the handcuffs clanked together with the impassioned movement of his hands. I could understand, as I saw the fury and the passion of the man, that it was no groundless or unnatural terror which had possessed

Major Sholto when he first learned that the injured convict was upon his track.

'You forget that we know nothing of all this,' said Holmes, quietly. 'We have not heard your story, and we cannot tell how far justice may originally have been on your side.'

'Well, sir, you have been very fair-spoken to me, though I can see that I have you to thank that I have these bracelets upon my wrists. Still, I bear no grudge for that. It is all fair and above-board. If you want to hear my story, I have no wish to hold it back. What I say to you is God's truth, every word of it. Thank you, you can put the glass beside me here, and I'll put my lips to it if I am dry.

'I am a Worcestershire man myself, born near Pershore. I dare say you would find a heap of Smalls living there now if you were to look. I have often thought of taking a look round there, but the truth is that I was never much of a credit to the family, and I doubt if they would be so very glad to see me. They were all steady, chapel-going folk, small farmers, well-known and respected over the country-side, while I was always a bit of a rover. At last, however, when I was about eighteen, I gave them no more trouble, for I got into a mess over a girl, and could only get out of it by taking the Queen's shilling and joining the 3rd Buffs, which was just starting for India.

'I wasn't destined to do much soldiering, however. I had just got past the goose-step, and learned to handle my musket, when I was fool enough to go swimming in the Ganges. Luckily for me, my company sergeant, John Holder, was in the water at the same time, and he was one of the finest swimmers in the Service. A crocodile took me, just as I was half-way across, and nipped off my right leg as clean as a surgeon could have done it, just above the knee. What with the shock and the loss of blood, I fainted, and should have been drowned if Holder had not caught hold of me and paddled for the bank. I was five months in hospital over it, and when at last I was able to limp out of it with this timber toe strapped to my stump, I found myself invalided out of the army and unfitted for any active occupation.

'I was, as you can imagine, pretty down on my luck at this time, for I was a useless cripple, though not yet in my twentieth year. However, my misfortune soon proved to be a blessing in disguise. A man named Abel White, who had come out there as an indigo-planter, wanted an overseer to look after his coolies and keep them up to their work. He happened to be a friend of our colonel's, who had taken an interest in me since the accident. To make a long story short, the colonel recommended me strongly for the post, and, as the work was mostly to be done on horseback, my leg was no great obstacle, for I had enough knee left to keep a good grip on the saddle. What I had to do was to ride over the plantation, to keep an eye on the men as they worked, and to report the idlers. The pay was fair, I had comfortable quarters, and altogether I was content to spend the remainder of my life in indigo-planting. Mr Abel White was a kind man, and he would often drop into my little shanty and smoke a pipe with me, for white folk out there feel their hearts warm to each other as they never do here at home.

'Well, I was never in luck's way long. Suddenly, without a note of warning, the great mutiny broke upon us. One month India lay as still and peaceful, to all appearance, as Surrey or Kent; the next there were two hundred thousand black devils let loose, and the country was a perfect hell. Of course you know all about it, gentlemen — a deal more than I do, very like, since reading is not in my line. I only know what I saw with my own eyes. Our plantation was at a place called Muttra, near the border of the North-west Provinces. Night after night the whole sky was alight with the burning bungalows, and day after day we had small companies of Europeans passing through our estate with their wives and children, on their way to Agra, where were the nearest troops. Mr Abel White was an obstinate man. He had it in his head that the affair had been exaggerated, and that it would blow over as suddenly as it had sprung up. There he sat on his veranda, drinking whisky-pegs and smoking cheroots, while the country was in a blaze about him. Of course, we stuck by him, I and Dawson, who, with his wife, used to do the book-work and the managing. Well, one fine day the crash came. I had been away on a distant plantation, and was riding slowly home in the evening, when my eye fell upon something all huddled together at the bottom of a steep nullah. I rode down to see what it was, and the cold struck through my heart when I found it was Dawson's wife, all cut into ribbons and half-eaten by jackals and native dogs. A little farther up the road Dawson himself was lying on his face, quite dead, with an empty revolver in his hand, and four Sepoys lying across each other in front of him. I reined up my horse, wondering which way I should turn; but at that moment I saw thick smoke curling up from Abel White's bungalow, and the flames beginning to burst through the roof. I knew then that I could do my employer no good, but would only throw my own life away if I meddled in the matter. From where I stood I could see hundreds of the black fiends, with their red coats still on their backs, dancing and howling round the burning house. Some of them pointed at me, and a couple of bullets sang past my head; so I broke away across the paddy-fields, and found myself late at night safe within the walls at Agra.

'As it proved, however, there was no great safety here, either. The whole country was up like a swarm of bees. Wherever the English could collect in little bands, they held just the ground that their guns commanded. Everywhere else they were helpless fugitives. It was a fight of the millions against the hundreds; and the cruellest part of it was that these men that we fought against, foot, horse, and gunners, were our own picked troops, whom we had taught and trained, handling our own weapons and blowing our own bugle-calls. At Agra there were the 3rd Bengal Fusiliers, some Sikhs, two troops of horse, and a battery of artillery. A volunteer corps of clerks and merchants had been formed, and this I joined, wooden leg and all. We went out to meet the rebels at Shahgunge early in July, and we beat them back for a time, but our powder gave out, and we had to fall back upon the city.

'Nothing but the worst news came to us from every side — which is not to be wondered at, for if you look at the map you will see that we were right in the heart of it. Lucknow is rather better than a hundred miles to the east, and Cawnpore about as far to the south. From every point on the compass there was nothing but torture and murder and outrage.

'The city of Agra is a great place, swarming with fanatics and fierce devil worshippers of all sorts. Our handful of men were lost among the narrow, winding streets. Our leader moved across the river, therefore, and took up his position in the old fort of Agra. I don't know if any of you gentlemen have ever read or heard anything of that old fort. It is a very queer place — the queerest that ever I was in, and I have been in some rum corners too. First of all, it is enormous in size. I should think that the enclosure must be acres and acres. There is a modern part, which took all our garrison, women, children, stores, and everything else, with plenty of room over. But the modern part is nothing like the size of the old quarter, where nobody goes, and which is given over to the scorpions and the centipedes. It is all full of great, deserted halls, and winding passages, and long corridors twisting in and out, so that it is easy enough for folk to get lost in it. For this reason it was seldom that anyone went into it, though now and again a party with torches might go exploring.

'The river washes along the front of the old fort, and so protects it, but on the sides and behind there are many doors, and these had to be guarded, of course, in the old quarter as well as in that which was actually held by our troops. We were short-handed, with hardly men enough to man the angles of the building and to serve the guns. It was impossible for us, therefore, to station a strong guard at every one of the innumerable gates. What we did was to organize a central guard-house in the middle of the fort, and to leave each gate under the charge of one white man and two or three natives. I was selected to take charge during certain hours of the night of a small isolated door upon the south-west side of the building. Two Sikh troopers were placed under my command, and I was instructed if anything went wrong to fire my musket, when I might rely upon help coming at once from the central guard. As the guard was a good two hundred paces away, however, and as the space between was cut up into a labyrinth of passages and corridors, I had great doubts as to whether they could arrive in time to be of any use in case of an actual attack.

'Well, I was pretty proud at having this small command given me, since I was a raw recruit, and a game-legged one at that. For two nights I kept the watch with my Punjaubees. They were tall, fierce-looking chaps, Mahomet Singh and Abdullah Khan by name, both old fighting-men, who had borne arms against us at Chilian Wallah. They could talk English pretty well, but I could get little out of them. They preferred to stand together and jabber all night in their queer Sikh lingo. For myself, I used to stand outside the gateway, looking down on the broad, winding river and on the twinkling lights of the great city. The beating of drums, the rattle of tom-toms, and the yells and howls of the rebels, drunk with opium and with bang, were enough to remind us all night of our dangerous neighbours across the stream. Every two hours the officer of the night used to come round to all the posts, to make sure that all was well.

'The third night of my watch was dark and dirty, with a small, driving rain. It was dreary work standing in the gateway hour after hour in such weather. I tried again and again to make my Sikhs talk, but without much success. At two in the morning the rounds passed, and broke for a moment the weariness of the night. Finding that my companions would not be led into conversation, I took out my pipe, and laid down my musket to strike a match. In an instant the two Sikhs were upon me. One of them snatched my firelock up and levelled it at my head, while the other held a great knife to my throat and swore between his teeth that he would plunge it into me if I moved a step.

'My first thought was that these fellows were in league with the rebels, and that this was the beginning of an assault. If our door were in the hands of the Sepoys the place must fall, and the women and children be treated as they were in Cawnpore. Maybe you gentlemen think that I am just making out a case for myself, but I give you my word that when I thought of that, though I felt the point of the knife at my throat, I opened my mouth with the intention of giving a scream, if it was my last one, which might alarm the main guard. The man who held me seemed to know my thoughts; for, even as I braced myself to it, he whispered: "Don't make a noise. The fort is safe enough. There are no rebel dogs on this side of the river." There was the ring of truth in what he said, and I knew that if I raised my voice I was a dead man. I could read it in the fellow's brown eyes. I waited, therefore, in silence, to see what it was that they wanted from me.

' "Listen to me, sahib," said the taller and fiercer of the pair, the one whom they called Abdullah Khan. "You must either be with us now, or you must be silenced for ever. The thing is too great a one for us to hesitate. Either you are heart and soul with us on your oath on the cross of the Christians, or your body this night shall be thrown into the ditch, and we shall pass over to our brothers in the rebel army. There is no middle way. Which is it to be — death or life? We can only give you three minutes to decide, for the time is passing, and all must be done before the rounds come again."

' "How can I decide?" said I. "You have not told me what you want of me. But I tell you now that if it is anything against the safety of the fort I will have no truck with it, so you can drive home your knife, and welcome."

' "It is nothing against the fort," said he. "We only ask you to do that which your countrymen come to this land for. We ask you to be rich. If you will be one of us this night, we will swear to you upon the naked knife, and by the threefold oath, which no Sikh was ever known to break, that you shall have your fair share of the loot. A quarter of the treasure shall be yours. We can say no fairer."

' "But what is the treasure, then?" I asked. "I am as ready to be rich as you can be, if you will but show me how it can be done."

' "You will swear, then," said he, "by the bones of your father, by the honour of your mother, by the cross of your faith, to raise no hand and speak no word against us, either now or afterwards?"

' "I will swear it," I answered, "provided that the fort is not endangered."

' "Then, my comrade and I will swear that you shall have a quarter of the treasure, which shall be equally divided among the four of us."

' "There are but three," said I.

' "No; Dost Akbar must have his share. We can tell the tale to you while we await them. Do you stand at the gate, Mahomet Singh, and give notice of their coming. The thing stands thus, sahib, and I tell it to you because I know that an oath is binding upon a Feringhee, and that we may trust you. Had you been a lying Hindoo, though you had sworn by all the gods in their false temples, your blood would have been upon the knife and your body in the water. But the Sikh knows the Englishman, and the Englishman knows the Sikh. Hearken, then, to what I have to say.

' "There is a rajah in the northern provinces who has much wealth, though his lands are small. Much has come to him from his father, and more still he has set by himself, for he is of a low nature, and hoards his gold rather than spend it. When the troubles broke out he would be friends both with the lion and the tiger — with the Sepoy and with the Company's Raj. Soon, however, it seemed to him that the white men's day was come, for through all the land he could hear of nothing but of their death and their over-throw. Yet, being a careful man, he made such plans that, come what might, half at least of his treasure should be left to him. That which was in gold and silver he kept by him in the vaults of his pal-ace; but the most precious stones and the choicest pearls that he had he put in an iron box, and sent it by a trusty servant, who, under the guise of a merchant, should take it to the fort at Agra, there to lie until the land is at peace. Thus, if the rebels won he would have his money; but if the Company conquered, his jewels would be saved to him. Having thus divided his hoard, he threw himself into the cause of the Sepoys, since they were strong upon his borders. By his doing this, mark you, sahib, his property becomes the due of those who have been true to their salt.

' "This pretended merchant, who travels under the name of Achmet, is now in the city of Agra, and desires to gain his way into the fort. He has with him as travelling companion my foster-brother, Dost Akbar, who knows his secret. Dost Akbar has promised this night to lead him to a side-postern of the fort, and has chosen this one for his purpose. Here he will come presently, and here he will find Mahomet Singh and myself awaiting him. The place is lonely, and none shall know of his coming. The world shall know of the merchant, Achmet, no more, but the great treasure of the rajah shall be divided among us. What say you to it, sahib?"

'In Worcestershire the life of a man seems a great and sacred thing; but it is very different when there is fire and blood all round you, and you have been used to meeting death at every turn. Whether Achmet the merchant lived or died was a thing as light as air to me, but at the talk about the treasure my heart turned to it, and I thought of what I might do in the old country with it, and how my folk would stare when they saw their ne'er-do-weel coming back with his pockets full of gold moidores. I had, therefore, already made up my mind. Abdullah Khan, however, thinking that I hesitated, pressed the matter more closely.

' "Consider, sahib," said he, "that if this man is taken by the commandant he will be hung or shot, and his jewels taken by the Government, so that no man will be a rupee the better for them. Now, since we do the taking of him, why should we not do the rest as well? The jewels will be as well with us as in the Company's coffers. There will be enough to make every one of us rich men and great chiefs. No one can know about the matter, for here we are cut off from all men. What could be better for the purpose? Say again, sahib, whether you are with us, or we must look upon you as an enemy."

' "I am with you heart and soul," said I.

' "It is well," he answered, handing me back my firelock. "You see that we trust you, for your word, like ours, is not to be broken. We have now only to wait for my brother and the merchant."

' "Does your brother know, then, of what you will do?" I asked.

' "The plan is his. He has devised it. We will go to the gate and share the watch with Mahomet Singh."

'The rain was still falling steadily, for it was just the beginning of the wet season. Brown, heavy clouds were drifting across the sky, and it was hard to see more than a stone-cast. A deep moat lay in front of our door, but the water was in places nearly dried up, and it could easily be crossed. It was strange to me to be standing there with those two wild Punjaubees waiting for the man who was coming to his death.

'Suddenly my eye caught the glint of a shaded lantern at the other side of the moat. It vanished among the mound-heaps, and then appeared again coming slowly in our direction.

' "Here they are!" I exclaimed.

' "You will challenge him, sahib, as usual," whispered Abdullah. "Give him no cause for fear. Send us in with him, and we shall do the rest while you stay here on guard. Have the lantern ready to uncover, that we may be sure that it is indeed the man."

'The light had flickered onwards, now stopping and now advancing, until I could see two dark figures upon the other side of the moat. I let them scramble down the sloping bank, splash through the mire, and climb half-way up to the gate, before I challenged them.

' "Who goes there?" said I, in a subdued voice.

' "Friends," came the answer. I uncovered my lantern and threw a flood of light upon them. The first was an enormous Sikh, with a black beard which swept nearly down to his cummerbund. Outside of a show I have never seen so tall a man. The other was a little, fat, round fellow, with a great yellow turban, and a bundle in his hand, done up in a shawl. He seemed to be all in a quiver with fear, for his hands twitched as if he had the ague, and his head kept turning to left and right with two bright little twinkling eyes, like a mouse when he ventures out from his hole. It gave me chills to think of killing him, but I thought of the treasure, and my heart set as hard as a flint within me. When he saw my white face he gave a little chirrup of joy, and came running up towards me.

' "Your protection, sahib," he panted; "your protection for the unhappy merchant Achmet. I have travelled across Rajpootana that I might seek the shelter of the fort at Agra. I have been robbed and beaten and abused because I have been the friend of the Company. It is a blessed night this when I am once more in safety — I and my poor possessions."

' "What have you in the bundle?" I asked.

' "An iron box," he answered, "which contains one or two little family matters which are of no value to others, but which I should be sorry to lose. Yet I am not a beggar; and I shall reward you, young sahib, and your governor also, if he will give me the shelter I ask."

'I could not trust myself to speak longer with the man. The more I looked at his fat, frightened face, the harder did it seem that we should slay him in cold blood. It was best to get it over.

' "Take him to the main guard," said I. The two Sikhs closed in upon him on each side, and the giant walked behind, while they marched in through the dark gateway. Never was a man so compassed round with death. I remained at the gateway with the lantern.

'I could hear the measured tramp of their footsteps sounding through the lonely corridors. Suddenly it ceased, and I heard voices, and a scuffle, with the sound of blows. A moment later there came, to my horror, a rush of footsteps coming in my direction, with a loud breathing of a running man. I turned my lantern down the long, straight passage, and there was the fat man, running like the wind, with a smear of blood across his face, and close at his heels, bounding like a tiger, the great, black-bearded Sikh, with a knife flashing in his hand. I have never seen a man run so fast as that little merchant. He was gaining on the Sikh, and I could see that if he once passed me and got to the open air he would save himself yet. My heart softened to him, but again the thought of his treasure turned me hard and bitter. I cast my firelock between his legs as he raced past, and he rolled twice over like a shot rabbit. Ere he could stagger to his feet the Sikh was upon him, and buried his knife twice in his side. The man never uttered moan nor moved muscle, but lay where he had fallen. I think myself that he may have broken his neck with the fall. You see, gentlemen, that I am keeping my promise. I am telling you every word of the business just exactly as it happened, whether it is in my favour or not.'

He stopped, and held out his manacled hands for the whisky-and-water which Holmes had brewed for him. For myself, I confess that I had now conceived the utmost horror of the man, not only for this cold-blooded business in which he had been concerned, but even more for the somewhat flippant and careless way in which he narrated it. Whatever punishment was in store for him, I felt that he might expect no sympathy from me. Sherlock Holmes and

Jones sat with their hands upon their knees, deeply interested in the story, but with the same disgust written upon their faces. He may have observed it, for there was a touch of defiance in his voice and manner as he proceeded.

'It was all very bad, no doubt,' said he. 'I should like to know how many fellows in my shoes would have refused a share in this loot when they knew that they would have their throats cut for their pains. Besides, it was my life or his when once he was in the fort. If he had got out, the whole business would come to light, and I should have been court-martialled and shot as likely as not; for people were not very lenient at a time like that.'

'Go on with your story,' said Holmes, shortly.

'Well, we carried him in, Abdullah, Akbar, and I. A fine weight he was, too, for all that he was so short. Mahomet Singh was left to guard the door. We took him to a place which the Sikhs had already prepared. It was some distance off, where a winding passage leads to a great empty hall, the brick walls of which were all crumbling to pieces. The earth floor had sunk in at one place, making a natural grave, so we left Achmet the merchant there, having first covered him over with loose bricks. This done, we all went back to the treasure.

'It lay where he had dropped it when he was first attacked. The box was the same which now lies open upon your table. A key was hung by a silken cord to that carved handle upon the top. We opened it, and the light of the lantern gleamed upon a collection of gems such as I have read and thought about when I was a little lad at Pershore. It was blinding to look upon them. When we had feasted our eyes we took them all out and made a list of them. There were one hundred and forty-three diamonds of the first water, including one which has been called, I believe, "the Great Mogul", and is said to be the second largest stone in existence. Then there were ninety-seven very fine emeralds, and one hundred and seventy rubies, some of which, however, were small. There were forty carbuncles, two hundred and ten sapphires, sixty-one agates, and a great quantity of beryls, onyxes, cats'-eyes, turquoises, and other stones, the very names of which I did not know at the time, though I have become more familiar with them since. Besides this, there were nearly three hundred very fine pearls, twelve of which were set in a gold coronet. By the way, these last had been taken out of the chest, and were not there when I recovered it.

'After we had counted our treasures we put them back into the chest and carried them to the gateway to show them to Mahomet Singh. Then we solemnly renewed our oath to stand by each other and be true to our secret. We agreed to conceal our loot in a safe place until the country should be at peace again, and then to divide it equally among ourselves. There was no use dividing it at present, for if gems of such value were found upon us it would cause suspicion, and there was no privacy in the fort nor anyplace where we could keep them. We carried the box, therefore, into the same hall where we had buried the body, and there, under certain bricks in the best-preserved wall, we made a hollow and put our treasure. We made careful note of the place, and next day I drew four plans, one for each of us, and put the sign of the four of us at the bottom, for we had sworn that we should each always act for all, so that none might take advantage. That is an oath that I can put my hand to my heart and swear that I have never broken.

'Well, there's no use my telling you gentlemen what came of the Indian Mutiny. After Wilson took Delhi and Sir Colin relieved Lucknow the back of the business was broken. Fresh troops came pouring in, and Nana Sahib made himself scarce over the frontier. A flying column under Colonel Greathead came round to Agra and cleared the Pandies away from it. Peace seemed to be settling upon the country, and we four were beginning to hope that the time was at hand when we might safely go off with our share of the plunder. In a moment, however, our hopes were shattered by our being arrested as the murderers of Achmet.

'It came about in this way. When the rajah put his jewels into the hands of Achmet, he did it because he knew that he was a trusty man. They are suspicious folk in the East, however; so what does this rajah do but take a second even more trusty servant and set him to play the spy upon the first? The second man was ordered never to let Achmet out of his sight, and he followed him like his shadow. He went after him that night, and saw him pass through the doorway. Of course, he thought he had taken refuge in the fort, and applied for admission there himself next day, but could find no trace of Achmet. This seemed to him so strange that he spoke about it to a sergeant of guides, who brought it to the ears of the commandant. A thorough search was quickly made and the body was discovered. Thus at the very moment that we thought that all was safe we were all four seized and brought to trial on a charge of murder — three of us because we had held the gate that night, and the fourth because he was known to have been in the company of the murdered man. Not a word about the jewels came out at the trial, for the rajah had been deposed and driven out of India; so no one had any particular interest in them. The murder, however, was clearly made out, and it was certain that we must all have been concerned in it. The three Sikhs got penal servitude for life, and I was condemned to death, though my sentence was afterwards commuted into the same as the others.

'It was rather a queer position that we found ourselves in then. There we were all four tied by the leg and with precious little chance of ever getting out again, while we each held a secret which might have put each of us in a palace if we could only have made use of it. It was enough to make a man eat his heart out to have to stand the kick and the cuff of every petty jack-in-office, to have rice to eat and water to drink, when that gorgeous fortune was ready for him outside just waiting to be picked up. It might have driven me mad; but I was always a pretty stubborn one, so I just held on and bided my time.

'At last it seemed to me to have come. I was changed from Agra to Madras, and from there to Blair Island in the Andamans. There are very few white convicts at this settlement, and, as I had behaved well from the first, I soon found myself a sort of privileged person. I was given a hut in Hope Town, which is a small place on the slopes of Mount Harriet, and I was left pretty much to myself. It is a dreary, fever-stricken place, and all beyond our little clearings was infested with wild cannibal natives, who were ready enough to blow a poisoned dart at us if they saw a chance. There was digging and ditching and yam-planting, and a dozen other things to be done, so we were busy enough all day; though in the evening we had a little time to ourselves. Among other things, I learned to dispense drugs for the surgeon, and picked up a smattering of his knowledge. All the time I was on the look-out for a chance to escape; but it is hundreds of miles from any other land, and there is little or no wind in those seas; so it was a terribly difficult job to get away.

'The surgeon, Dr Somerton, was a fast, sporting young chap, and the other young officers would meet in his rooms of an evening and play cards. The surgery, where I used to make up my drugs, was next to his sitting-room, with a small window between us. Often, if I felt lonesome, I used to turn out the lamp in the surgery, and then, standing there, I could hear their talk and watch their play. I am fond of a hand at cards myself, and it was almost as good as having one to watch the others. There was Major Sholto, Captain Morstan, and Lieutenant Bromley Brown, who were in command of the native troops, and there was the surgeon himself, and two or three prison-officials, crafty old hands who played a nice, sly, safe game. A very snug little party they used to make.

'Well, there was one thing which very soon struck me, and that was that the soldiers used always to lose and the civilians to win. Mind, I don't say there was anything unfair, but so it was. These prison-chaps had done little else than play cards ever since they had been at the Andamans, and they knew each other's game to a point, while the others just played to pass the time and threw their cards down anyhow. Night after night the soldiers got up poorer men, and the poorer they got the more keen they were to play. Major Sholto was the hardest hit. He used to pay in notes and gold at first, but soon it came to notes of hand and for big sums. He sometimes would win for a few deals, just to give him heart, and then the luck would set in against him worse than ever. All day he would wander about as black as thunder, and he took to drinking a deal more than was good for him.

'One night he lost even more heavily than usual. I was sitting in my hut when he and Captain Morstan came stumbling along on the way to their quarters. They were bosom friends, those two, and never far apart. The Major was raving about his losses.

' "It's all up, Morstan," he was saying, as they passed my hut. "I shall have to send in my papers. I am a ruined man."

' "Nonsense, old chap!" said the other, slapping him upon the shoulder. "I've had a nasty facer myself, but—" That was all I could hear, but it was enough to set me thinking.

'A couple of days later Major Sholto was strolling on the beach: so I took the chance of speaking to him.

' "I wish to have your advice, Major," said I.

' "Well, Small, what is it?" he asked, taking his cheroot from his lips.

' "I wanted to ask you, sir," said I, "who is the proper person to whom hidden treasure should be handed over. I know where half a million worth lies, and, as I cannot use it myself, I thought perhaps the best thing that I could do would be to hand it over to the proper authorities, and then perhaps they would get my sentence shortened for me."

' "Half a million, Small?" he gasped, looking hard at me to see if I was in earnest.

' "Quite that, sir — in jewels and pearls. It lies there ready for anyone. And the queer thing about it is that the real owner is outlawed and cannot hold property, so that it belongs to the first comer."

' "To Government, Small," he stammered, "to Government." But he said it in a halting fashion and I knew in my heart that I had got him.

' "You think, then, sir, that I should give the information to the Governor-General?" said I, quietly.

' "Well, well, you must not do anything rash, or that you might repent. Let me hear all about it, Small. Give me the facts."

'I told him the whole story, with small changes, so that he could not identify the places. When I had finished he stood stock still and full of thought. I could see by the twitch of his lip that there was a struggle going on within him.

' "This is a very important matter, Small," he said at last. "You must not say a word to anyone about it, and I shall see you again soon."

'Two nights later he and his friend, Captain Morstan, came to my hut in the dead of night with a lantern.

' "I want you just to let Captain Morstan hear that story from your own lips, Small," said he.

'I repeated it as I had told it before.

' "It rings true, eh?" said he. "It's good enough to act upon?"

'Captain Morstan nodded.

' "Look here, Small," said the Major, "we have been talking it over, my friend here and I, and we have come to the conclusion that this secret of yours is hardly a Government matter, after all, but is a private concern of our own, which, of course, you have the power of disposing of as you think best. Now the question is, What price would you ask for it? We might be inclined to take it up, and at least look into it, if we could agree as to terms." He tried to speak in a cool, careless way, but his eyes were shining with excitement and greed.

' "Why, so to that, gentlemen," I answered, trying also to be cool, but feeling as excited as he did, "there is only one bargain

which a man in my position can make. I shall want you to help
me to my freedom, and to help my three companions to theirs. We
shall then take you into partnership, and give you a fifth share to
divide between you."

' "Hum!" said he. "A fifth share! That is not very tempting."

' "It would come to fifty thousand apiece," said I.

' "But how can we gain your freedom? You know very well that
you ask an impossibility."

' "Nothing of the sort," I answered. "I have thought it all out
to the last detail. The only bar to our escape is that we can get
no boat fit for the voyage, and no provisions to last us for so long
a time. There are plenty of little yachts and yawls at Calcutta or
Madras which would serve our turn well. Do you bring one over.
We shall engage to get aboard her by night, and if you will drop us
on any part of the Indian coast you will have done your part of the
bargain."

' "If there were only one," he said.

' "None or all," I answered. "We have sworn it. The four of us
must always act together."

' "You see, Morstan," said he, "Small is a man of his word. He
does not flinch from his friends. I think we may very well trust
him."

' "It's a dirty business," the other answered. "Yet, as you say,
the money will save our commissions handsomely."

' "Well, Small," said the Major, "we must, I suppose, try and
meet you. We must first, of course, test the truth of your story. Tell
me where the box is hid and I shall get leave of absence and go back
to India in the monthly relief-boat to inquire into the affair."

' "Not so fast," said I, growing bolder as he got hot. "I must have
the consent of my three comrades. I tell you that it is four or none
with us."

' "Nonsense!" he broke in. "What have three black fellows to do
with our agreement?"

' "Black or blue," said I, "they are in with me, and we all go
together."

'Well, the matter ended by a second meeting, at which Mahomet
Singh, Abdullah Khan, and Dost Akbar were all present. We talked
the matter over again, and at last we came to an arrangement. We
were to provide both the officers with charts of the part of the Agra
fort, and mark the place in the wall where the treasure was hid.

Major Sholto was to go to India to test our story. If he found the box he was to leave it there, to send out a small yacht provisioned for a voyage, which was to lie off Rutland Island, and to which we were to make our way, and finally to return to his duties. Captain Morstan was then to apply for leave of absence, to meet us at Agra, and there we were to have a final division of the treasure, he taking the Major's share as well as his own. All this we sealed by the most solemn oaths that the mind could think or the lips utter. I sat up all night with paper and ink, and by the morning I had the two charts all ready, signed with the sign of four — that is, of Abdullah, Akbar, Mahomet, and myself.

'Well, gentlemen, I weary you with my long story, and I know that my friend Mr Jones is impatient to get me safely stowed in chokey. I'll make it as short as I can. The villain Sholto went off to India, but he never came back again. Captain Morstan showed me his name among a list of passengers in one of the mail-boats very shortly afterwards. His uncle had died, leaving him a fortune, and he had left the army; yet he could stoop to treat five men as he had treated us. Morstan went over to Agra shortly afterwards, and found, as we expected, that the treasure was indeed gone. The scoundrel had stolen it all, without carrying out one of the conditions on which we had sold him the secret. From that day I lived only for vengeance. I thought of it by day and I nursed it by night. It became an overpowering, absorbing passion with me. I cared nothing for the law — nothing for the gallows. To escape, to track down Sholto, to have my hand upon his throat — that was my own thought. Even the Agra treasure had come to be a smaller thing in my mind than the slaying of Sholto.

'Well, I have set my mind on many things in this life, and never one which I did not carry out. But it was weary years before my time came. I have told you that I had picked up something of medicine. One day when Dr Somerton was down with a fever a little Andaman Islander was picked up by a convict-gang in the woods. He was sick to death, and had gone to a lonely place to die. I took him in hand, though he was as venomous as a young snake, and after a couple of months I got him all right and able to walk. He took a kind of fancy to me then, and would hardly go back to his woods, but was always hanging about my hut. I learned a little of his lingo from him, and this made him all the fonder of me.

'Tonga — for that was his name — was a fine boatman, and owned a big, roomy canoe of his own. When I found that he was devoted to me and would do anything to serve me, I saw my chance of escape. I talked it over with him. He was to bring his boat round on a certain night to an old wharf which was never guarded, and there he was to pick me up. I gave him directions to have several gourds of water and a lot of yams, coconuts, and sweet potatoes.

'He was staunch and true, was little Tonga. No man ever had a more faithful mate. On the night named he had his boat at the wharf. As it chanced, however, there was one of the convict-guard down there — a vile Pathan who had never missed a chance of insulting and injuring me. I had always vowed vengeance, and now I had my chance. It was as if fate had placed him in my way that I might pay my debt before I left the island. He stood on the bank with his back to me, and his carbine on his shoulder. I looked about for a stone to beat out his brains with, but none could I see.

'Then a queer thought came into my head, and showed me where I could lay my hand on a weapon. I sat down in the darkness and unstrapped my wooden leg. With three long hops I was on him. He put his carbine to his shoulder, but I struck him full, and knocked the whole front of his skull in. You can see the split in the wood now where I hit him. We both went down together, for I could not keep my balance; but when I got up I found him lying quiet enough. I made for the boat, and in an hour we were well out at sea. Tonga had brought all his earthly possessions with him, his arms and his gods. Among other things, he had a long bamboo spear, and some Andaman coconut-matting, with which I made a sort of a sail. For ten days we were beating about, trusting to luck, and on the eleventh we were picked up by a trader which was going from Singapore to Jiddah with a cargo of Malay pilgrims. They were a rum crowd, and Tonga and I soon managed to settle down among them. They had one very good quality: they let you alone and asked no questions.

'Well, if I were to tell you all the adventures that my little chum and I went through, you would not thank me, for I would have you here until the sun was shining. Here and there we drifted about the world, something always turning up to keep us from London. All the time, however, I never lost sight of my purpose. I would dream of Sholto at night. At last, however, some three or four years ago, we found ourselves in England. I had no great difficulty in finding where Sholto lived, and I set to work to discover whether he had realized the treasure, or if he still had it. I made friends with someone who could help me — I name no names, for I don't want to get anyone else in a hole — and I soon found that he still had the jewels. Then I tried to get at him in many ways; but he was pretty sly, and had always two prize-fighters, besides his sons and his khidmutgar, on guard over him.

'One day, however, I got word that he was dying. I hurried at once to the garden, mad that he should slip out of my clutches like that, and, looking through the window, I saw him lying in his bed, with his sons on each side of him. I'd have come through and taken my chance with the three of them, only even as I looked at him his jaw dropped, and I knew that he was gone. I got into his room the same night, though, and I searched his papers to see if there was any record of where he had hidden the jewels. There was not a line, however, so I came away, bitter and savage as a man might be. Before I left I bethought me that if I ever met my Sikh friends again it would be a satisfaction to know that I had left some mark of our hatred; so I scrawled down the sign of the four of us, as it had been on the chart, and I pinned it on his bosom. It was too much that he should be taken to the grave without some token from the men whom he had robbed and befooled.

'We earned a living at this time by my exhibiting poor Tonga at fairs and other such places as the black cannibal. He would eat raw meat and dance his war-dance; so we always had a hatful of pennies after a day's work. I still heard all the news from Pondicherry Lodge, and for some years there was no news to hear, except that they were hunting for the treasure. At last, however, came what we had waited for so long. The treasure had been found. It was up at the top of the house, in Mr Bartholomew Sholto's chemical laboratory. I came at once and had a look at the place, but I could not see how, with my wooden leg, I was to make my way up to it. I learned, however, about a trap-door in the roof, and also about Mr Sholto's supper-hour. It seemed to me that I could manage the thing easily through Tonga. I brought him out with me with a long rope wound round his waist. He could climb like a cat, and he soon made his way through the roof, but, as ill-luck would have it, Bartholomew Sholto was still in the room, to his cost. Tonga thought he had done something very clever in killing him, for when I came up by the rope I found him strutting about as proud as a peacock. Very much surprised was he when I made at him with the rope's end and cursed him for a little, bloodthirsty imp. I took the treasure box and let it down, and then slid down myself, having first left the sign of the four upon the table, to show that the jewels had come back at last to those who had most right to them. Tonga then pulled up the rope, closed the window, and made off the way that he had come.

'I don't know that I have anything else to tell you. I had heard a waterman speak of the speed of Smith's launch, the *Aurora*, so I thought she would be a handy craft for our escape. I engaged with old Smith, and was to give him a big sum if he got us safe to our ship. He knew, no doubt, that there was some screw loose, but he was not in our secrets. All this is the truth, and if I tell it to you, gentlemen, it is not to amuse you — for you have not done me a very good turn — but it is because I believe the best defence I can make is just to hold back nothing, but let all the world know how badly I have myself been served by Major Sholto, and how innocent I am of the death of his son.'

'A very remarkable account,' said Sherlock Holmes. 'A fitting wind-up to an extremely interesting case. There is nothing at all new to me in the latter part of your narrative, except that you brought your own rope. That I did not know. By the way, I had hoped that Tonga had lost all his darts; yet he managed to shoot one at us in the boat.'

'He had lost them all, sir, except the one which was in his blow-pipe at the time.'

'Ah, of course,' said Holmes. 'I had not thought of that.'

'Is there any other point which you would like to ask about?' asked the convict, affably.

'I think not, thank you,' my companion answered.

'Well, Holmes,' said Athelney Jones, 'you are a man to be humoured, and we all know that you are a connoisseur of crime; but duty is duty, and I have gone rather far in doing what you and your friend asked me. I shall feel more at ease when we have our story-teller here safe under lock and key. The cab still waits, and there are two inspectors downstairs. I am much obliged to you both for your assistance. Of course, you will be wanted at the trial. Good-night to you.'

'Good-night, gentlemen both,' said Jonathan Small.

'You first, Small,' remarked the wary Jones as they left the room.

'You first, Small,' remarked the wary Jones as they left the room. 'I'll take particular care that you don't club me with your wooden leg, whatever you may have done to the gentleman at the Andaman Isles.'

'Well, and there is the end of our little drama,' I remarked, after we had sat some time smoking in silence. 'I fear that it may be the last investigation in which I shall have the chance of studying your methods. Miss Morstan has done me the honour to accept me as a husband in prospective.'

He gave a most dismal groan.

'I feared as much,' said he. 'I really cannot congratulate you.'

I was a little hurt.

'Have you any reason to be dissatisfied with my choice?' I asked.

'Not at all. I think she is one of the most charming young ladies I ever met, and might have been most useful in such work as we have been doing. She had a decided genius that way; witness the way in which she preserved that Agra plan from all the other papers of her father. But love is an emotional thing, and whatever is emotional is opposed to that true cold reason which I place above all things. I should never marry myself, lest I bias my judgement.'

'I trust,' said I, laughing, 'that my judgement may survive the ordeal. But you look weary.'

'Yes, the reaction is already upon me. I shall be as limp as a rag for a week.'

'Strange,' said I, 'how terms of what in another man I should call laziness alternate with your fits of splendid energy and vigour.'

'Yes,' he answered, 'there are in me the makings of a very fine loafer, and also of a pretty spry sort of a fellow. I often think of those lines of old Goethe: *Schade dass die Natur nur* einen *Mensch aus dir schuf, Den zum würdigen Mann war und zum Schelmen der Stoff*. By the way, apropos of this Norwood business, you see that they had, as I surmised, a confederate in the house, who could be none other than Lal Rao, the butler: so Jones actually has the undivided honour of having caught one fish in his great haul.'

'The division seems rather unfair,' I remarked. 'You have done all the work in this business. I get a wife out of it, Jones gets the credit; pray what remains for you?'

'For me,' said Sherlock Holmes, 'there still remains the cocaine-bottle.' And he stretched his long, white hand up for it.

Herman Melville

BILLY BUDD, FORETOPMAN
What Befell Him In The Year of
The Great Mutiny, Etc.

*c.*1891

HERMAN MELVILLE (1818–91) was born in the same year as
Walt Whitman and fourteen years after Nathaniel Hawthorne. These
three together form the first major focus of American literature; they
are the writers who first broke away from the English mould and
created a literature that really belonged to the new continent. Edgar
Allen Poe, born in 1809, had an originality that matched theirs, but
Poe, whose education was partly in England, seems somehow to be a
renegade European writer; his theories of poetry, which aroused little
attention at home, were so influential on the generation of Charles
Baudelaire that he has been described as 'the most important figure
in nineteenth-century French literature'. Hawthorne, Melville, and
Whitman, particularly the latter two, could never have been anything
but Americans. Their art springs from the decade when American
society consisted of a long, narrow strip of urbanization down the
East Coast, flanked immediately by the western areas, enormous
areas, of grain-growing, cattle-grazing land, and, further west still,
the wilderness. So much was still new and unexplored that an air of
discovery and enquiry was drawn into everyone's lungs; it was as if
Western Man had not earned the right to settle in, and exploit, this
huge land-mass until he had thought freshly over, and perhaps come
up with new answers to, absolutely fundamental problems of right
and wrong, conduct and responsibility, which Europeans, guided by
tradition and rooted in societies which had rubbed along somehow
for hundreds if not thousands of years, could go their lifetime without
needing to re-examine.

Melville's masterpiece, *Moby Dick*, is on the surface a realistic
account of a whaling voyage out of New England (Melville himself
went on such a voyage in 1841), but from the beginning few readers
can have been unaware of the gigantic symbols thrown like shadows
by the action; the immense ocean is the Unknown, the desperate

Captain Ahab and his sinister elemental foe the White Whale, are . . .
exactly what? Mankind, perhaps, engaged in their compulsive quest
for the truth, a quest that in the end will destroy them just as Moby
Dick's death-throes sink the *Pequod* and all who sail in her, except for
the one called Ishmael, the narrator, whose name, significantly, means
the one set apart.

　Melville lived an adventurous life, and some of his novels are frankly
documentary, picturesque romances about places which in those days
the ordinary person had no chance to visit, such as the South Seas
in *Omoo* (1842) and *Typee* (1846), though his motive in writing *White
Jacket* (1850) seems to have been an attempt to improve the naval
rating's harsh lot. But his strength always lay in the philosophical
narrative, whether one reads it as a precise allegory or a larger and
more shifting symbolism. His finest short story, *Bartleby the Scrivener*
(1856), is an example of this; *Billy Budd*, written in the last five years
of his life and not published until 1924, is another. Billy is an innocent
young man. He is more; he is Innocence itself. The story shows him as
a victim. He is more; he is The Victim personified, he is the insulted
and injured as they exist everywhere and at all times. Though credible
on a realistic level, he is an embodiment of sinlessness, not tainted by
human guilt. When the well-meaning ship's chaplain tries to impress
the young barbarian with ideas of death akin to those conveyed by the
skull, dial, and cross-bones on old tombstones and to bring home to
him the thought of salvation and a Saviour, Billy listens attentively,
not because it means anything to him 'but out of a certain natural
politeness'. In his case, just as punishment is meaningless, forgiveness
is irrelevant.

PREFACE

THE year 1797, the year of this narrative, belongs to a period which, as every thinker now feels, involved a crisis for Christendom, not exceeded in its undetermined momentousness at the time by any other era whereof there is record. The opening proposition made by the Spirit of that Age, involved a rectification of the Old World's hereditary wrongs. In France, to some extent, this was bloodily effected. But what then? Straightway the Revolution itself became a wrongdoer, one more oppressive than the kings. Under Napoleon it enthroned upstart kings, and initiated that prolonged agony of continual war whose final throe was Waterloo. During those years not the wisest could have foreseen that the outcome of all would be what to some thinkers apparently it has since turned out to be, a political advance along nearly the whole line for Europeans.

Now, as elsewhere hinted, it was something caught from the Revolutionary Spirit that at Spithead emboldened the man-of-war's men to rise against real abuses, long-standing ones, and afterwards at the Nore to make inordinate and aggressive demands, successful resistance to which was confirmed only when the ringleaders were hung for an admonitory spectacle to the anchored fleet. Yet in a way analogous to the operation of the Revolution at large, the Great Mutiny, though by Englishmen naturally deemed monstrous at the time, doubtless gave the first latent prompting to most important reforms in the British Navy.

I

(An inside Narrative)

IN the time before steamships, or then more frequently than now, a stroller along the docks of any considerable seaport would occasionally have his attention arrested by a group of bronzed marines, man-of-war's men or merchant sailors in holiday attire ashore on liberty. In certain instances they would flank, or, like a bodyguard, quite surround some superior figure of their own class, moving along with them like Aldebaran among the lesser lights of his constellation. That signal object was the 'Handsome Sailor' of the less prosaic time alike of the military and merchant navies. With no perceptible trace of the vainglorious about him, rather with the offhand unaffectedness of natural regality, he seemed to accept the spontaneous homage of his shipmates. A somewhat remarkable instance recurs to me. In Liverpool, now half a century ago, I saw under the shadow of the great dingy street-wall of Prince's Dock (an obstruction long since removed) a common sailor, so intensely black that he must needs have been a native African of the unadulterate blood of Ham. A symmetric figure much above the average height. The two ends of a gay silk handkerchief thrown loose about the neck danced upon the displayed ebony of his chest; in his ears were big hoops of gold, and a Scotch Highland bonnet with a tartan band set off his shapely head.

It was a hot noon in July; and his face, lustrous with perspiration, beamed with barbaric good-humour. In jovial sallies right and left, his white teeth flashing into view, he rollicked along, the centre of a company of his shipmates. These were made up of such an assortment of tribes and complexions as would have well fitted them to be marched up by Anacharsis Cloots before the bar of the first French Assembly as Representatives of the Human Race. At each spontaneous tribute rendered by the wayfarers to this black pagod of a fellow—the tribute of a pause and stare, and less frequent an exclamation— the motley retinue showed that they took that sort of pride in the evoker of it which the Assyrian priests doubtless showed for their grand sculptured Bull when the faithful prostrated themselves. To return——

If in some cases a bit of a nautical Murat in setting forth his person ashore, the Handsome Sailor of the period in question evinced nothing of the dandified Billy-be-Dam, an amusing character all but extinct now, but occasionally to be encountered, and in a form yet more amusing than the original, at the tiller of the boats of the tempestuous Erie Canal or, more likely, vapouring in the groggeries along the tow-path. Invariably a proficient in his perilous calling, he was also more or less of a mighty boxer or wrestler. It was strength and beauty. Tales of his prowess were recited. Ashore he was the champion, afloat the spokesman; on every suitable occasion always foremost. Close-reefing topsails in a gale, there he was, astride the weather yard-arm-end, foot in 'stirrup,' both hands tugging at the 'ear-ring' as at a bridle, in very much the attitude of young Alexander curbing the fiery Bucephalus. A superb figure, tossed up as by the horns of Taurus against the thunderous sky, cheerily ballooning to the strenuous file along the spar.

The moral nature was seldom out of keeping with the physical make. Indeed, except as toned by the former, the comeliness and power, always attractive in masculine conjunction, hardly could have drawn the sort of homage the Handsome Sailor in some examples received from his less gifted associates.

Such a cynosure, at least in aspect, and something such too in nature, though with important variations made apparent as the story proceeds, was welkin-eyed Billy Budd, or Baby Budd, as more familiarly, under circumstances hereafter to be given, he at last came to be called, aged twenty-one, a foretopman of the fleet toward the close of the last decade of the eighteenth century. It was not only very long prior to the time of the narration that follows that he had entered the King's Service, having been impressed on the Narrow Seas from a homeward-bound English merchantman into a seventy-four outward-bound, H.M.S. *Indomitable*; which ship, as was not unusual in those hurried days, had been obliged to put to sea short of her proper complement of men. Plump upon Billy at first sight in the gangway the boarding-officer, Lieutenant Ratcliffe, pounced, even before the merchantman's crew formally was mustered on the quarter-deck for his deliberate inspection. And him only he selected. For whether it was because the other men when ranged before him showed to ill advantage after Billy, or whether he had some scruples in view of the merchantman being rather short-handed; however it might be, the officer contented himself with his first spontaneous choice. To the surprise of the ship's company, though much to the Lieutenant's satisfaction, Billy made no demur. But indeed any demur would have been as idle as the protest of a goldfinch popped into a cage.

Noting this uncomplaining acquiescence, all but cheerful one might say, the shipmates turned a surprised glance of silent reproach at the sailor. The shipmaster was one of those worthy mortals found in every vocation even the humbler ones—the sort of person whom everybody agrees in calling 'a respectable man.' And—nor so strange to report as it may appear to be—though a ploughman of the troubled waters, life-long contending with the intractable elements, there was nothing this honest soul at heart loved better than simple peace and quiet. For the rest, he was fifty or thereabouts, a little inclined to corpulence, a prepossessing face, unwhiskered, and of an agreeable colour, a rather full face, humanely intelligent in expression. On a fair day with a fair wind and all going well, a certain musical chime in his voice seemed to be the veritable unobstructed outcome of the innermost man. He had much prudence, much conscientiousness, and there were occasions when these virtues were the cause of overmuch disquietude in him. On a passage, so long as his craft was in any proximity to land, no sleep for Captain Graveling. He took to heart those serious responsibilities not so heavily borne by some shipmasters.

Now while Billy Budd was down in the forecastle getting his kit together, the *Indomitable's* lieutenant, burly and bluff, nowise disconcerted by Captain Graveling's omitting to proffer the customary hospitalities of an occasion so unwelcome to him, an omission simply caused by preoccupation of thought, unceremoniously invited himself into the cabin, and also to a flask from the spirit locker, a receptacle which his experienced eye instantly discovered. In fact, he was one of those sea-dogs in whom all the hardship and peril of naval life in the great prolonged wars of his time never impaired the natural instinct for sensuous enjoyment. His duty he always faithfully did; but duty is sometimes a dry obligation, and he was for irrigating its aridity whensoever possible with a fertilising decoction of strong waters. For the cabin's proprietor there was nothing left but to

play the part of the enforced host with whatever grace and alacrity
were practicable. As necessary adjuncts to the flask, he silently
placed tumbler and water-jug before the irrepressible guest. But
excusing himself from partaking just then, dismally watched the
unembarrassed officer deliberately diluting his grog a little, then
tossing it off in three swallows, pushing the empty tumbler away,
yet not so far as to be beyond easy reach, at the same time settling
himself in his seat, and smacking his lips with high satisfaction,
looking straight at the host.

These proceedings over, the Master broke the silence; and there
lurked a rueful reproach in the tone of his voice: 'Lieutenant, you
are going to take my best man from me, the jewel of 'em.'

'Yes, I know,' rejoined the other, immediately drawing back the
tumbler, preliminary to a replenishing; 'yes, I know. Sorry.'

'Beg pardon, but you don't understand, Lieutenant. See here
now. Before I shipped that young fellow, my forecastle was a rat-pit
of quarrels. It was black times, I tell you, aboard the *rights* here. I
was worried to that degree my pipe had no comfort for me. But
Billy came; and it was like a Catholic priest striking peace in
an Irish shindy. Not that he preached to them or said or did
anything in particular; but a virtue went out of him, sugaring
the sour ones. They took to him like hornets to treacle; all but the
bluffer of the gang, the big, shaggy chap with the fire-red whiskers.
He indeed, out of envy, perhaps, of the newcomer, and thinking
such a "sweet and pleasant fellow," as he mockingly designated
him to the others, could hardly have the spirit of a gamecock, must
needs bestir himself in trying to get up an ugly row with him. Billy
forbore with him, and reassured with him in a pleasant way—he is
something like myself, Lieutenant, to whom aught like a quarrel is
hateful—but nothing served. So, in the second dogwatch one day
the Red Whiskers, in presence of the others, under pretence of
showing Billy just whence a sirloin steak was cut—for the fellow
had once been a butcher—insultingly gave him a dig under the
ribs. Quick as lightning Billy let fly his arm. I dare say he never
meant to do quite as much as he did, but anyhow he gave the burly
fool a terrible drubbing. It took about half a minute, I should think.
And, Lord bless you, the lubber was astonished at the celerity. And
will you believe it, Lieutenant, the Red Whiskers now really loves
Billy—loves him, or is the biggest hypocrite that ever I heard of.
But they all love him. Some of 'em do his washing, darn old trowsers

for him; the carpenter is at odd times making a pretty little chest of drawers for him. Anybody will do anything for Billy Budd; and it's the happy family here. Now, Lieutenant, if that young fellow goes, I know how it will be aboard the *Rights*. Not again very soon shall I, coming up from dinner, lean over the capstan smoking a quiet pipe—no, not very soon again, I think. Ay, Lieutenant, you are going to take away the jewel of 'em; you are going to take away my peacemaker.' And with that the good soul had really some ado in checking a rising sob.

'Well,' said the Lieutenant, who had listened with amused interest to all this, and now waxing merry with his tipple, 'well, blessed are the peacemakers, especially the fighting peacemakers! And such are the seventy-four beauties, some of which you see poking their noses out of the port-holes of yonder warship lying-to for me,' pointing through the cabin windows at the *Indomitable*. 'But courage! don't look so downhearted, man. Why, I pledge you in advance the royal approbation. Rest assured that His Majesty will be delighted to know that in a time when his hard-tack is not sought for by sailors with such avidity as should be; a time also when some shipmasters privily resent the borrowing from them of a tar or two for the service; His Majesty, I say, will be delighted to learn that *one* shipmaster at least cheerfully surrenders to the King the flower of his flock, a sailor who with equal loyalty makes no dissent. But where's my Beauty? Ah,' looking through the cabin's open door, 'here he comes; and, by Jove! lugging along his chest—Apollo with his portmanteau! My man,' stepping out to him, 'you can't take that big box aboard a warship. The boxes there are mostly shot-boxes. Put your duds in a bag, lad. Boot and saddle for the cavalryman, bag and hammock for the man-of-war's man.'

The transfer from chest to bag was made. And, after seeing his man into the cutter, and then following him down, the Lieutenant pushed off from the *Rights-of-Man*. That was the merchant ship's name; though by her master and crew abbreviated in sailor fashion into the *Rights*. The hard-headed Dundee owner was a staunch admirer of Thomas Paine, whose book in rejoinder to Burke's arraignment of the French Revolution had then been published for some time, and had gone everywhere. In christening his vessel after the title of Paine's volume, the man of Dundee was something like his contemporary shipowner, Stephen Girard of

Philadelphia, whose sympathies alike with his native land and its liberal philosophies he evinced by naming his ships after Voltaire, Diderot, and so forth.

But now when the boat swept under the merchantman's stern, and officer and oarsmen were noting, some bitterly and others with a grin, the name emblazoned there; just then it was that the new recruit jumped up from the bow where the coxswain had directed him to sit, and, waving his hat to his silent shipmates sorrowfully looking over at him from the taffrail, bade the lads a genial good-bye. Then making a salutation as to the ship herself, 'And good-bye to you too, old *Rights-of-Man!*'

'Down, sir,' roared the Lieutenant, instantly assuming all the rigour of his rank, though with difficulty repressing a smile.

To be sure, Billy's action was a terrible breach of naval decorum. But in that decorum he had never been instructed; in consideration of which the Lieutenant would hardly have been so energetic in reproof but for the concluding farewell to the ship. This he rather took as meant to convey a covert sally on the new recruit's part, a sly slur at impressment in general, and that of himself in especial. And yet, more likely, if satire it was in effect, it was hardly so by intention, for Billy, though happily endowed with the gaiety of high health, youth, and a free heart, was yet by no means of a satirical turn. The will to it and the sinister dexterity were alike wanting. To deal in double meaning and insinuations of any sort was quite foreign to his nature.

As to his enforced enlistment, that he seemed to take pretty much as he was wont to take any vicissitudes of weather. Like the animals, though no philosopher he was, without knowing it, practically a fatalist. And, it may be, that he rather liked this adventurous turn in his affairs which promised an opening into novel scenes and martial excitements.

Aboard the *Indomitable* our merchant-sailor was forthwith rated as an able seaman, and assigned to the starboard watch of the foretop. He was soon at home in the service, not at all disliked for his unpretentious good looks, and a sort of genial happy-go-lucky air. No merrier man in his mess; in marked contrast to certain other individuals included like himself among the impressed portion of the ship's company; for these when not actively employed were sometimes, and more particularly in the last dog-watch when the drawing near of twilight induced revery, apt to fall into a saddish mood which in some partook of sullenness. But they were not so young as our foretopman, and no few of them must have known a hearth of some sort, others may have had wives and children left, too probably, in uncertain circumstances, and hardly any but must have acknowledged kith and kin; while for Billy, as will shortly be seen, his entire family was practically invested in himself.

II

THOUGH our new-made foretopman was well received in the top and on the gun-decks, hardly here was he that cynosure he had previously been among those minor ships' companies of the merchant marine, with which companies only had he hitherto consorted.

He was young; and despite his all but fully developed frame, in aspect looked even younger than he really was. This was owing to a lingering adolescent expression in the as yet smooth face, all but feminine in purity of natural complexion, but where, thanks to his sea-going, the lily was quite suppressed, and the rose had some ado visibly to flush through the tan.

To one essentially such a novice in the complexities of factitious life, the abrupt transition from his former and simpler sphere to the ampler and more knowing world of a great warship—this might well have abashed him had there been any conceit or vanity in his composition. Among her miscellaneous multitude, the *Indomitable* mustered several individuals who, however inferior in grade, were of no common natural stamp, sailors more signally susceptive of that air which continuous martial discipline and repeated presence in battle can in some degree impart even to the average man. As the *Handsome Sailor* Billy Budd's position aboard the seventy-four was something analogous to that of a rustic beauty transplanted from the provinces and brought into competition with the high-born dames of the court. But this change of circumstances he scarce noted. As little did he observe that something about him provoked an ambiguous smile in one or two harder faces among the blue-jackets. Nor less unaware was he of the peculiar favourable effect his person and demeanour had upon the more intelligent gentlemen of the quarter-deck. Nor could this well have been otherwise. Cast in a mould peculiar to the finest physical examples of those Englishmen in whom the Saxon strain would seem not at all to partake of any Norman or other admixture, he showed in face that humane look of reposeful good-nature which the Greek sculptor in some instances gave to his heroic strong man, Hercules. But this again was subtly modified by another and pervasive quality. The ear, small and shapely, the arch of the foot, the curve in mouth and nostril, even the indurated hand dyed to the orange-tawny of the toucan's bill, a hand telling of the halyards and tar-buckets; but, above all, something in the mobile expression, and every chance attitude and movement, something suggestive of a mother eminently favoured by Love and the Graces; all this strangely indicated a lineage in direct contradiction to his lot. The mysteriousness here, became less mysterious through a matter of fact elicited when Billy at the capstan was being formally mustered into the service. Asked by the officer, a small, brisk little gentleman as it chanced, among other questions, his place of birth, he replied, 'Please, sir, I don't know.'

'Don't know where you were born? Who was your father?'

'God knows, sir.'

Struck by the straightforward simplicity of these replies, the officer next asked, 'Do you know anything about your beginning?'

'No, sir. But I have heard that I was found in a pretty silk-lined basket hanging one morning from the knocker of a good man's door in Bristol.'

'*Found*, say you? Well,' throwing back his head, and looking up and down the new recruit—'well, it turns out to have been a pretty good find. Hope they'll find some more like you, my man; the fleet sadly needs them.'

Yes, Billy Budd was a foundling, a presumable by-blow, and, evidently, no ignoble one. Noble descent was as evident in him as in a blood horse.

For the rest, with little or no sharpness of faculty or any trace of the wisdom of the serpent, nor yet quite a dove, he possessed a certain degree of intelligence along with the unconventional rectitude of a sound human creature—one to whom not yet has been proffered the questionable apple of knowledge. He was illiterate; he could not read, but he could sing, and like the illiterate nightingale was sometimes the composer of his own song.

Of self-consciousness he seemed to have little or none, or about as much as we may reasonably impute to a dog of St. Bernard's breed.

Habitually being with the elements and knowing little more of the land than as a beach, or, rather, that portion of the terraqueous globe providentially set apart for dance-houses, doxies and tapsters, in short, what sailors call a 'fiddlers' green,' his simple nature remained unsophisticated by those moral obliquities which are not in every case incomparable with that manufacturable thing known as respectability. But are sailor frequenters of fiddlers' greens without vices? No; but less often than with landsmen do their vices, so-called, partake of crookedness of heart, seeming less to proceed from viciousness than exuberance of vitality after long restraint, frank manifestations in accordance with natural law. By his original constitution, aided by the co-operating influences of his lot, Billy in many respects was little more than a sort of upright barbarian, much such perhaps as Adam presumably might have been ere the urbane Serpent wriggled himself into his company.

And here be it submitted that, apparently going to corroborate the doctrine of man's fall (a doctrine now popularly ignored), it is observable that where certain virtues pristine and unadulterate peculiarly characterise anybody in the external uniform of civilisation, they will upon scrutiny seem not to be derived from custom or convention but rather to be out of keeping with these, as if indeed exceptionally transmitted from a period prior to Cain's city and citified man. The character marked by such qualities has to an unvitiated taste an untampered-with flavour like that of berries, while the man thoroughly civilised, even in a fair specimen of the breed, has to the same moral palate a questionable smack as of a compounded wine. To any stray inheritor of these primitive qualities found, like Caspar Hauser, wandering dazed in any Christian capital of our time, the poet's famous invocation, near two thousand years ago, of the good rustic out of his latitude in the Rome of the Caesars, still appropriately holds:

> Faithful in word and thought,
> What hast Thee, Fabian, to the city brought.

Though our Handsome Sailor had as much of masculine beauty as one can expect anywhere to see; nevertheless, like the beautiful woman in one of Hawthorne's minor tales, there was just one thing amiss in him. No visible blemish, indeed, as with the lady; no, but an occasional liability to a vocal defect. Though in the hour of elemental uproar or peril, he was everything that a sailor should be, yet under sudden provocation of strong heart-feeling his voice, otherwise singularly musical, as if expressive of the harmony within, was apt to develop an organic hesitancy,—in fact, more or less of a stutter or even worse. In this particular Billy was a striking instance that the arch-interpreter, the envious marplot of Eden still has more or less to do with every human consignment to this planet of earth. In every case, one way or another, he is sure to slip in his little card, as much as to remind us—I too have a hand here.

The avowal of such an imperfection in the Handsome Sailor should be evidence not alone that he is not presented as a conventional hero, but also that the story in which he is the main figure is no romance.

III

AT the time of Billy Budd's arbitrary enlistment into the *Indomitable* that ship was on her way to join the Mediterranean fleet. No long time elapsed before the junction was effected. As one of that fleet the seventy-four participated in its movements, though at times on account of her superior sailing qualities, in the absence of frigates, dispatched on separate duty as a scout, and at times on less temporary service. But with all this the story has little concernment, restricted as it is to the inner life of one particular ship and the career of an individual sailor.

It was the summer of 1797. In the April of that year had occurred the commotion at Spithead, followed in May by a second and yet more serious outbreak in the fleet at the Nore. The latter is known, and without exaggeration in the epithet, as the Great Mutiny. It was indeed a demonstration more menacing to England than the contemporary manifestos and conquering and proselytising armies of the French Directory.

To the Empire, the Nore Mutiny was what a strike in the fire-brigade would be to London threatened by general arson. In a crisis when the Kingdom might well have anticipated the famous signal that some years later published along the naval line of battle what it was that upon occasion England expected of Englishmen; *that* was the time when at the mast-heads of the three-deckers and seventy-fours moored in her own roadstead—a fleet, the right arm of a Power then all but the sole free conservative one of the Old World, the blue-jackets, to be numbered by thousands, ran up with hurrahs the British colours with the union and cross wiped out; by that cancellation transmuting the flag of founded law and freedom defined, into the enemy's red meteor of unbridled and unbounded revolt. Reasonable discontent growing out of practical grievances in the fleet had been ignited into irrational combustion as by live cinders blown across the Channel from France in flames.

The event converted into irony for a time those spirited strains of Dibdin—as a song-writer no mean auxiliary to the English Government—at this European conjuncture, strains celebrating, among other things, the patriotic devotion of the British tar—

> And as for my life, 'tis the King's!

Such an episode in the Island's grand naval story her naval historians naturally abridge; one of them (G. P. R. James) candidly acknowledging that fain would he pass it over did not 'impartiality forbid fastidiousness.' And yet his mention is less a narration than a reference, having to do hardly at all with details. Nor are these readily to be found in the libraries. Like some other events in every age befalling states everywhere, including America, the Great Mutiny was of such character that national pride along with views of policy would fain shade it off into the historical background. Such events cannot be ignored, but there is a considerate way of historically treating them. If a well-constituted individual refrains from blazoning aught amiss or calamitous in his family, a nation in the like circumstance may without reproach be equally discreet.

Though after parleyings between Government and the ring-leaders, and concessions by the former as to some glaring abuses, the first uprising—that at Spithead—with difficulty was put down, or matters for a time pacified; yet at the Nore the unforeseen renewal of insurrection on a yet larger scale, and emphasised in the conferences that ensued by demands deemed by the authorities not only inadmissible but aggressively insolent, indicated, if the red flag did not sufficiently do so, what was the spirit animating the men. Final suppression, however, there was; but only made possible perhaps by the unswerving loyalty of the marine corps, and a voluntary resumption of loyalty among influential sections of the crews. To some extent the Nore Mutiny may be regarded as analogous to the distempering irruption of contagious fever in a frame constitutionally sound, and which anon throws it off.

At all events, among these thousands of mutineers were some of the tars who not so very long afterwards—whether wholly prompted thereto by patriotism, or pugnacious instinct, or by both—helped to win a coronet for Nelson at the Nile, and the naval crown of crowns for him at Trafalgar. To the mutineers those battles, and especially Trafalgar, were a plenary absolution, and a grand one; for that which goes to make up scenic naval display is heroic magnificence in arms. Those battles, especially Trafalgar, stand unmatched in human annals.

IV

Concerning 'The greatest sailor since the world began.'—

Tennyson.

IN this matter of writing, resolve as one may to keep to the main road, some by-paths have an enticement not readily to be withstood. Beckoned by the genius of Nelson I am going to err into such a by-path. If the reader will keep me company I shall be glad. At the least we can promise ourselves that pleasure which is wickedly said to be in sinning, for a literary sin the divergence will be.

Very likely it is no new remark that the inventions of our time have at last brought about a change in sea warfare in degree corresponding to the revolution in all warfare effected by the original introduction from China into Europe of gunpowder. The first European firearm, a clumsy contrivance, was, as is well known, scouted by no few of the knights as a base implement, good enough peradventure for weavers too craven to stand up crossing steel with steel in frank fight. But as ashore knightly valour, though shorn of its blazonry, did not cease with the knights, neither on the seas, though nowadays in encounters there a certain kind of displayed gallantry be fallen out of date as hardly applicable under changed circumstances, did the nobler qualities of such naval magnates as Don John of Austria, Doria, Van Tromp, Jean Bart, the long line of British admirals and the American Decaturs of 1812 become obsolete with their wooden walls.

Nevertheless, to anybody who can hold the Present at its worth without being inappreciative of the Past, it may be forgiven, if to such a one the solitary old hulk at Portsmouth, Nelson's *Victory*, seems to float there, not alone as the decaying monument of a fame incorruptible, but also as a poetic reproach, softened by its picturesqueness, to the *Monitors* and yet mightier hulls of the European ironclads. And this not altogether because such craft are unsightly, unavoidably lacking the symmetry and grand lines of the old battle-ships, but equally for other reasons.

There are some, perhaps, who while not altogether inaccessible to that poetic reproach just alluded to, may yet on behalf of the new order be disposed to parry it; and this to the extent of iconoclasm, if need be. For example, prompted by the sight of the star inserted in the *Victory's* deck designating the spot where the Great Sailor fell, these martial utilitarians may suggest considerations implying that Nelson's ornate publication of his person in battle was not only unnecessary, but not military, nay, savoured of foolhardiness and vanity. They may add, too, that at Trafalgar it was in effect nothing less than a challenge to death; and death came; and that but for his bravado the victorious admiral might possibly have survived the battle, and so, instead of having his sagacious dying injunctions overruled by his immediate successor in command, he himself when the contest was decided might have brought his shattered fleet to anchor, a proceeding which might have averted the deplorable loss of life by shipwreck in the elemental tempest that followed the martial one.

Well, should we set aside the more than disputable point whether for various reasons it was possible to anchor the fleet, then plausibly enough the Bethamites of war may urge the above.

But he *might have been* is but boggy ground to build on. And certainly in foresight as to the larger issue of an encounter, and anxious preparations for it—buoying the deadly way and mapping it out, as at Copenhagen—few commanders have been so painstakingly circumspect as this reckless declarer of his person in fight.

Personal prudence, even when dictated by quite other than

selfish considerations, is surely no special virtue in a military man; while an excessive love of glory, exercising to the uttermost the honest heart-felt sense of duty, is the first. If the name *Wellington* is not so much of a trumpet to the blood as the simpler name *Nelson*, the reason for this may perhaps be inferred from the above. Alfred in his funeral ode on the victor of Waterloo ventures not to call him the greatest soldier of all time, though in the same ode he invokes Nelson as 'the greatest sailor since the world began.'

At Trafalgar Nelson on the brink of opening the fight sat down and wrote his last brief will and testament. If under the presentiment of the most magnificent of all victories, to be crowned by his own glorious death, a sort of priestly motive led him to dress his person in the jewelled vouchers of his own shining deeds; if thus to have adorned himself for the altar and the sacrifice were indeed vainglory, then affectation and fustian is each truly heroic line in the great epics and dramas, since in such lines the poet but embodies in verse those exaltations of sentiment that a nature like Nelson, the opportunity being given, vitalises into acts.

V

THE outbreak at the Nore was put down. But not every grievance was redressed. If the contractors, for example, were no longer permitted to ply some practices peculiar to their tribe everywhere, such as providing shoddy cloth, rations not sound, or false in the measure; not the less impressment, for one thing, went on. By custom sanctioned for centuries, and judicially maintained by a Lord Chancellor as late as Mansfield, that mode of manning the fleet, a mode now fallen into a sort of abeyance but never formally renounced, it was not practicable to give up in those years. Its abrogation would have crippled the indispensable fleet, one wholly under canvas, no steam-power, its innumerable sails and thousands of cannon, everything in short, worked by muscle alone; a fleet the more insatiate in demand for men, because then multiplying its ships of all grades against contingencies present and to come of the convulsed Continent.

Discontent foreran the Two Mutinies, and more or less it lurkingly survived them. Hence it was not unreasonable to apprehend some return of trouble sporadic or general. One instance of such apprehensions: In the same year with this story, Nelson, then Vice-Admiral Sir Horatio, being with the fleet off the Spanish coast, was directed by the admiral in command to shift his pennant from the *Captain* to the *Theseus*; and for this reason: that the latter ship having newly arrived in the station from home where it had taken part in the Great Mutiny, danger was apprehended from the temper of the men; and it was thought that an officer like Nelson was the one, not indeed to terrorise the crew into base subjection, but to win them by force of his mere presence back to an allegiance, if not as enthusiastic as his own, yet as true. So it was, that for a time on more than one quarter-deck anxiety did exist. At sea precautionary vigilance was strained against relapse. At short notice an engagement might come on. When it did, the lieutenants assigned to batteries felt it incumbent on them in some instances to stand with drawn swords behind the men working the guns.

But on board the seventy-four in which Billy now swung his hammock very little in the manner of the men and nothing obvious in the demeanour of the officers would have suggested to an ordinary observer that the Great Mutiny was a recent event. In their general bearing and conduct the commissioned officers of a warship naturally take their tone from the commander, that is if he have that ascendency of character that ought to be his.

Captain the Honourable Edward Fairfax Vere, to give his full title, was a bachelor of forty or thereabouts, a sailor of distinction, even in a time prolific of renowned seamen. Though allied to the higher nobility, his advancement had not been altogether owing to influences connected with that circumstance. He had seen much service, been in various engagements, always acquitting himself as an officer mindful of the welfare of his men, but never tolerating an infraction of discipline; thoroughly versed in the science of his profession, and intrepid to the verge of temerity, though never injudiciously so. For his gallantry in the West Indian waters as flag-lieutenant under Rodney in that admiral's crowning victory over De Grasse, he was made a post-captain.

Ashore in the garb of a civilian, scarce anyone would have taken him for a sailor, more especially that he never garnished unprofessional talk with nautical terms, and grave in his bearing, evinced little appreciation of mere humour. It was not out of keeping with these traits that on a passage when nothing demanded his paramount action, he was the most undemonstrative of men. Any landsman observing this gentleman, not conspicuous by his stature and wearing no pronounced insignia, emerging from his retreat to the open deck, and noting the silent deference of the officers retiring to leeward, might have taken him for the King's guest, a civilian aboard the King's ship, some highly honourable discreet envoy on his way to an important post. But, in fact, this unobtrusiveness of demeanour may have proceeded from a certain unaffected modesty of manhood sometimes accompanying a resolute nature, a modesty evinced at all times not calling for pronounced action, and which shown in any rank of life suggests a virtue aristocratic in kind.

As with some others engaged in various departments of the world's more heroic activities, Captain Vere, though practical enough upon occasion, would at times betray a certain dreaminess of mood. Standing alone on the weather-side of the greater deck, one hand holding by the rigging, he would absently gaze off at the black sea. At the presentation to him then of some minor matter interrupting the current of his thoughts, he would show more or less irascibility; but instantly he would control it.

In the Navy he was popularly known by the appellation— Starry Vere. How such a designation happened to fall upon one who, whatever his sturdy qualities, was without any brilliant ones, was in this wise: a favourite kinsman, Lord Denton, a free-handed fellow, had been the first to meet and congratulate him upon his return to England from the West Indian cruise; and but the day previous turning over a copy of Andrew Marvell's poems had lighted, not for the first time however, upon the lines entitled 'Appelton House,' the name of one of the seats of their common ancestor, a hero in the German wars of the seventeenth century, in which poem occur the lines,

> This 'tis to have been from the first
> In a domestic heaven nursed,
> Under the discipline severe
> Of Fairfax and the starry Vere.

And so, upon embracing his cousin fresh from Rodney's victory, wherein he had played so gallant a part, brimming over with just family pride in the sailor of their house, he exuberantly exclaimed, 'Give ye joy, Ed; give ye joy, my starry Vere!' This got currency, and the novel prefix serving in familiar parlance readily to distinguish the *Indomitable's* captain from another Vere, his senior, a distant relative, and officer of like rank in the Navy, it remained permanently attached to the surname.

VI

IN view of the part that the commander of the *Indomitable* plays in scenes shortly to follow, it may be well to fill out that sketch of him outlined in the previous chapter. Aside from his qualities as a sea-officer Captain Vere was an exceptional character. Unlike no few of England's renowned sailors, long and arduous service with signal devotion to it, had not resulted in absorbing and *salting* the entire man. He had a marked leaning toward everything intellectual. He loved books, never going to sea without a newly replenished library, compact but of the best. The isolated leisure, in some cases so wearisome, falling at intervals to commanders even during a war-cruise, never was tedious to Captain Vere. With nothing of that literary taste which less heeds the thing conveyed than the vehicle, his bias was toward those books to which every serious mind of superior order occupying any active post of authority in the world, naturally inclines; books treating of actual men and events, no matter of what era—history, biography, and unconventional writers who, free from cant and convention, like Montaigne, honestly, and in the spirit of common sense, philosophise upon realities.

In this love of reading he found confirmation of his own more reserved thoughts—confirmation which he had vainly sought in social converse, so that as touching most fundamental topics, there had got to be established in him some positive convictions which he felt would abide in him essentially unmodified so long as his intelligent part remained unimpaired. In view of the humbled period in which his lot was cast, this was well for him. His settled convictions were as a dyke against those invading waters of novel opinion, social, political, and otherwise, which carried away as in a torrent no few minds in those days, minds by nature not inferior to his own. While other members of that aristocracy to which by birth he belonged were incensed at the innovators mainly because their theories were inimical to the privileged classes, Captain Vere disinterestedly opposed them, not alone because they seemed to him incapable of embodiment in lasting institutions, but at war with the world and the peace of mankind.

With minds less stored than his and less earnest, some officers of his rank, with whom at times he would necessarily consort, found him lacking in the companionable quality, a dry and bookish gentleman as they deemed. Upon any chance withdrawal from their company one would be apt to say to another something like this! 'Vere is a noble fellow, "Starry Vere." 'Spite the Gazettes Sir Horatio is at bottom scarce a better seaman or fighter. But between you and me now, don't you think there is a queer streak of the pedantic running through him? Yes, like the King's yarn in a coil of navy-rope.'

Some apparent ground there was for this sort of confidential criticism, since not only did the captain's discourse never fall into the jocosely familiar, but in illustrating any point touching the stirring personages and events of the time, he would cite some historical character or incident of antiquity with the same easy air that he would cite from the moderns. He seemed unmindful of the circumstance that to his bluff company such allusions, however pertinent they might really be, were altogether alien to men whose reading was mainly confined to the journals. But considerateness in such matters is not easy in natures constituted like Captain Vere's. Their honesty prescribes to them directness, sometimes far-reaching like that of a migratory fowl that in its flight never heeds when it crosses a frontier.

VII

THE lieutenants and other commissioned gentlemen forming Captain Vere's staff it is not necessary here to particularise, nor needs it to make mention of any of the warrant-officers. But among the petty officers was one who, having much to do with the story, may as well be forthwith introduced. This portrait I essay, but shall never hit it.

This was John Claggart, the master-at-arms. But that sea-title may to landsmen seem somewhat equivocal. Originally, doubtless, that petty officer's function was the instruction of the men in the use of arms, sword, or cutlass. But very long ago, owing to the advance in gunnery making hand-to-hand encounters less frequent, and giving to nitre and sulphur the pre-eminence over steel, that function ceased; the master-at-arms of a great warship becoming a sort of chief of police charged among other matters with the duty of preserving order on the populous lower gun-decks.

Claggart was a man of about five-and-thirty, somewhat spare and tall, yet of no ill figure upon the whole. His hand was too small and shapely to have been accustomed to hard toil. The face was a notable one; the features all except the chin, cleanly cut as those on a Greek medallion; yet the chin, beardless as Tecumseh's, had something of the strange protuberant heaviness in its make that recalled the prints of the Rev. Dr. Titus Oates, the historical deponent with the clerical drawl in the time of Charles II, and the fraud of the alleged Popish Plot. It served Claggart in his office that his eye could cast a tutoring glance. His brow was of the sort phrenologically associated with more than average intellect; silken jet curls partly clustering over it, making a foil to the pallor below, a pallor tinged with a faint shade of amber akin to the hue of time-tinted marbles of old.

This complexion singularly contrasting with the red or deeply bronzed visages of the sailors, and in part the result of his official seclusion from the sunlight, though it was not exactly displeasing, nevertheless seemed to hint of something defective or abnormal in the constitution and blood. But his general aspect and manner were so suggestive of an education and career incongruous with his naval function, that when not actively engaged in it he looked like a man of high quality, social and moral, who for reasons of his own was keeping incognito. Nothing was known of his former life. It might be that he was an Englishman; and yet there lurked a bit of accent in his speech suggesting that possibly he was not such by birth, but through naturalisation in early childhood. Among certain grizzled sea-gossips of the gun-decks and forecastle went a rumour perdue that the master-at-arms was a chevalier who had volunteered into the King's Navy by way of compounding for some mysterious swindle whereof he had been arraigned at the King's Bench. The fact that nobody could substantiate this report was, of course, nothing against its secret currency. Such a rumour once started on the gun-decks in reference to almost anyone below the rank of a commissioned officer would, during the period assigned to this narrative, have seemed not altogether wanting in credibility to the tarry old wiseacres of a man-of-war crew. And indeed a man of Claggart's accomplishments, without prior nautical experience entering the Navy at mature life, as he did, and necessarily allotted at the start to the lowest grade in it; a man, too, who never made allusion to his previous life ashore; these were circumstances which in the dearth of exact knowledge as to his true antecedents opened to the invidious a vague field for unfavourable surmise.

But the sailors' dog-watch gossip concerning him derived a vague plausibility from the fact that now for some period the British Navy could so little afford to be squeamish in the matter of keeping up the muster-rolls, that not only were press-gangs notoriously abroad both afloat and ashore, but there was little or no secret about another matter, namely, that the London police were at liberty to capture any able-bodied suspect, and any questionable fellow at large, and summarily ship him to the dock-yard or fleet. Furthermore, even among voluntary enlistments, there were instances where the motive thereto partook neither of patriotic impulse nor yet of a random desire to experience a bit of sea-life and martial adventure. Insolvent debtors of minor grade, together with the promiscuous lame ducks of morality, found in the Navy a convenient and secure refuge. Secure, because once enlisted aboard a King's ship, they were as much in sanctuary as the transgressor of the Middle Ages harbouring himself under the shadow of the altar. Such sanctioned irregularities, which for obvious reasons the Government would hardly think to parade at the time, and which consequently, and as affecting the least influential class of mankind, have all but dropped into oblivion, lends colour to something for the truth whereof I do not vouch, and hence have some scruple in stating; something I remember having seen in print, though the book I cannot recall; but the same thing was personally communicated to me now more than forty years ago by an old pensioner in a cocked hat, with whom I had a most interesting talk on the terrace at Greenwich, a Baltimore negro, a Trafalgar man. It was to this effect: In the case of a warship short of hands, whose speedy sailing was imperative, the deficient quota, in lack of any other way of making it good, would be eked out by drafts called direct from the jails. For reasons previously suggested it would not perhaps be easy at the present day directly to prove or disprove the allegation. But allowed as a verity, how significant would it be of England's straits at the time, confronted by these wars which like a flight of harpies rose shrieking from the din and dust of the fallen Bastille. That era appears measurably clear to us who look back at it, and but read of it. But to the grandfathers of us graybeards, the more thoughtful of them the genius of it presented an aspect like that of Camoëns' 'Spirit of the Cape,' an eclipsing menace mysterious and prodigious. Not America was exempt from apprehension. At the height of Napoleon's unexampled conquests, there were Americans who had fought at Bunker Hill who looked forward to the possibility that the Atlantic might prove no barrier against the ultimate schemes of this portentous upstart from the revolutionary chaos, who seemed in act of fulfilling judgment prefigured in the Apocalypse.

But the less credence was to be given to the gun-deck talk touching Claggart, seeing that no man holding his office in a man-of-war can ever hope to be popular with the crew. Besides, in derogatory comments upon one against whom they have a grudge, or for any reason or no reason mislike, sailors are much like landsmen, they are apt to exaggerate or romance it.

About as much was really known to the *Indomitable's* tars of the master-at-arms' career before entering the service as an astronomer knows about a comet's travels prior to its first observable appearance in the sky. The verdict of the sea-quidnuncs has been cited only by way of showing what sort of moral impression the man made upon rude uncultivated natures, whose conceptions of human wickedness were necessarily of the narrowest, limited to ideas of vulgar rascality—a thief among the swinging hammocks during a night-watch, or the man-brokers and land-sharks of the seaports.

It was no gossip, however, but fact, that though, as before hinted, Claggart upon his entrance into the navy was, as a novice, assigned to the least honourable section of a man-of-war's crew, embracing the drudges, he did not long remain there.

The superior capacity he immediately evinced, his constitutional sobriety, ingratiating deference to superiors, together with a peculiar ferreting genius manifested on a singular occasion, all this capped by a certain austere patriotism, abruptly advanced him to the position of master-at-arms.

Of this maritime chief of police the ship's corporals, so called, were the immediate subordinates, and compliant ones; and this, as is to be noted in some business departments ashore, almost to a degree inconsistent with entire moral volition. His place put various converging wires of underground influence under the chief's control, capable when astutely worked through his understrappers of operating to the mysterious discomfort, if nothing worse, of any of the sea-commonalty.

VIII

LIFE in the foretop well agreed with Billy Budd. There, when not actually engaged on the yards yet higher aloft, the topmen, who as such, had been picked out for youth and activity, constituted an aerial club, lounging at ease against the smaller stun'-sails rolled up into cushions, spinning yarns like the lazy gods, and frequently amused with what was going on in the busy world of the decks below. No wonder then that a young fellow of Billy's disposition was well content in such society. Giving no cause of offence to anybody, he was always alert at a call. So in the merchant service it had been with him. But now such punctiliousness in duty was shown that his top-mates would sometimes good-naturedly laugh at him for it. This heightened alacrity had its cause, namely: the impression made upon him by the first formal gangway-punishment he had ever witnessed, which befell the day following his impressment. It has been incurred by a little fellow, young, a novice, an after-guardsman absent from his assigned post when the ship was being put about, a dereliction resulting in a rather serious hitch to that manoeuvre, one demanding instantaneous promptitude in letting go and making fast. When Billy saw the culprit's naked back under the scourge gridironed with red welts, and worse; when he marked the dire expression in the liberated man's face, as with his woollen shirt flung over him by the executioner he rushed forward from the spot to bury himself in the crowd, Billy was horrified. He resolved that never through remissness would he make himself liable to such a visitation, or do or omit aught that might merit even verbal reproof. What then was his surprise and concern when ultimately he found himself getting into petty trouble occasionally about such matters as the stowage of his bag, or something amiss in his hammock, matters under the police oversight of the ship's corporals of the lower decks, and which brought down on him a vague threat from one of them.

So heedful in all things as he was, how could this be? He could not understand it, and it more than vexed him. When he spoke to his young topmates about it, they were either lightly incredulous, or found something comical in his unconcealed anxiety. 'Is it your bag, Billy?' said one; 'well, sew yourself up in it, Billy boy, and then you'll be sure to know if anybody meddles with it.'

Now there was a veteran aboard who, because his years began to disqualify him for more active work, had been recently assigned duty as mainmast-man in his watch, looking to the gear belayed at the rail round about that great spar near the deck. At off-times the foretopman had picked up some acquaintance with him, and now in his trouble it occurred to him that he might be the sort of person to go to for wise counsel. He was an old Dansker long anglicised in the service, of few words, many wrinkles and some honourable scars. His wizened face, time-tinted and weather-stormed to the complexion of an antique parchment, was here and there peppered blue by the chance explosion of a gun-cartridge in action. He was an *Agamemnon* man; some two years prior to the time of this story having served under Nelson when but Sir Horatio, in that ship immortal in naval memory, and which, dismantled and in parts broken up to her bare ribs, is seen a grand skeleton in Haydon's etching. As one of a boarding-party from the *Agamemnon* he had received a cut slantwise along one temple and cheek, leaving a long pale scar like a streak of dawn's light falling athwart the dark visage. It was on account of that scar and the affair in which it was known that he had received it, as well as from his blue-peppered complexion, that the Dansker went among the *Indomitable's* crew by the name of 'Board-her-in-the-smoke.'

Now the first time that his small weasel eyes happened to light on Billy Budd, a certain grim internal merriment set all his ancient wrinkles into antic play. Was it that his eccentric unsentimental old sapience, primitive in its kind, saw, or thought it saw, something which in contrast with the warship's environment looked oddly incongruous in the Handsome Sailor? But after slyly studying him at intervals, the old Merlin's equivocal merriment was modified by now. For now when the twain would meet, it would start in his face a quizzing sort of look, but it would be but momentary and sometimes replaced by an expression of speculative query as to what might eventually befall a nature like that, dropped into a world not without some man-traps and against whose subtleties simple courage lacking experience and address and without any touch of defensive ugliness, is of little avail; and where such innocence as man is capable of does yet in a moral emergency not always sharpen the faculties or enlighten the will.

However it was, the Dansker in his ascetic way rather took to Billy. Nor was this only because of a certain philosophic interest in such a character. There was another cause. While the old man's eccentricities, sometimes bordering on the ursine, repelled the juniors, Billy, undeterred thereby, would make advances, never passing the old *Agamemnon* man without a salutation marked by that respect which is seldom lost on the aged, however crabbed at times, or whatever their station in life. There was a vein of dry humour, or what not, in the mastman; and whether in freak of patriarchal irony touching Billy's youth and athletic frame, or for some other and more recondite reason, from the first in addressing him he always substituted Baby for Billy. The Dansker, in fact, being the originator of the name by which the foretopman eventually became known aboard ship.

Well then, in his mysterious little difficulty going in quest of the wrinkled one, Billy found him off duty in a dog-watch ruminating by himself, seated on a shot-box of the upper gun-deck, now and then surveying with a somewhat cynical regard certain of the more swaggering promenaders there. Billy recounted his trouble, again wondering how it all happened. The salt seer attentively listened, accompanying the foretopman's recitals with queer twitchings of his wrinkles and problematical little sparkles of his small ferret eyes. Making an end of his story, the foretopman asked, 'And now, Dansker, do tell me what you think of it.' The old man, shoving up the front of his tarpaulin and deliberately rubbing the long slant scar at the point where it entered the thin hair, laconically said, 'Baby Budd, *Jemmy Legs*' (meaning the master-at-arms) 'is down on you.'

'*Jemmy Legs!*' ejaculated Billy, his welkin eyes expanding; 'what for? Why, he calls me *the sweet and pleasant young fellow*, they tell me.'

'Does he so?' grinned the grizzled one; then said, 'Ay, Baby lad, a sweet voice has *Jemmy Legs*.'

'No, not always. But to me he has. I seldom pass him but there comes a pleasant word.'

'And that's because he's down upon you, Baby Budd.'

Such reiteration, along with the manner of it, incomprehensible to a novice, disturbed Billy almost as much as the mystery for which he had sought explanation. Something less unpleasingly oracular he tried to extract; but the old sea-Chiron, thinking perhaps that for the nonce he had sufficiently instructed his young Achilles, pursed his lips, gathered all his wrinkles together, and would commit himself to nothing further.

Years, and these experiences which befall certain shrewder men subordinated life-long to the will of superiors, all this had developed in the Dansker the pithy guarded cynicism that was his leading characteristic.

IX

THE next day an incident served to confirm Billy Budd in his incredulity as to the Dansker's strange summing-up of the case submitted.

The ship at noon going large before the wind was rolling on her course, and he, below at dinner and engaged in some sportful talk with the members of his mess, chanced in a sudden lurch to spill the entire contents of his soup-pan upon the new-scrubbed deck. Claggart, the master-at-arms, official ratan in hand, happened to be passing along the battery in a bay of which the mess was lodged, and the greasy liquid streamed just across his path. Stepping over it, he was proceeding on his way without comment, since the matter was nothing to take notice of under the circumstances, when he happened to observe who it was that had done the spilling. His countenance changed. Pausing, he was about to ejaculate something hasty at the sailor, but checked himself, and pointing down to the streaming soup, playfully tapped him from behind with his ratan, saying, in a low musical voice, peculiar to him at times, 'Handsomely done, my lad! And handsome is as handsome did it, too!' and with that passed on. Not noted by Billy as not coming within his view was the involuntary smile, or rather grimace, that accompanied Claggart's equivocal words. Aridly it drew down the thin corners of his shapely mouth. But everybody taking his remark as meant for humorous, and at which therefore as coming from a superior they were bound to laugh, 'with counterfeited glee,' acted accordingly; and Billy, tickled, it may be, by the allusion to his being the Handsome Sailor, merrily joined in; then addressing his messmates exclaimed, 'There, now, who says that Jemmy Legs is down on me!'

'And who said he was, Beauty?' demanded one Donald with some surprise. Whereat the foretopman looked a little foolish, recalling that it was only one person, Board-her-in-the-smoke, who has suggested what to him was the smoky idea that this pleasant master-at-arms was in any peculiar way hostile to him. Meantime that functionary resuming his path must have momentarily worn some expression less guarded than that of the bitter smile and, usurping the face from the heart, some distorting expression perhaps, for a drummer-boy heedlessly frolicking along from the opposite direction, and chancing to come into light collision with his person, was strangely disconcerted by his aspect. Nor was the impression lessened when the official, impulsively giving him a sharp cut with the ratan, vehemently exclaimed, 'Look where you go!'

X

WHAT was the matter with the master-at-arms? And be the matter what it might, how could it have direct relation to Billy Budd, with whom prior to the affair of the spilled soup he had never come into any special contact, official or otherwise? What indeed could the trouble have to do with one so little inclined to give offence as the merchant ship's *peacemaker*, even him who in Claggart's own phrase was 'the sweet and pleasant young fellow'? Yes, why should *Jemmy Legs*, to borrow the Dansker's expression, be *down* on the Handsome Sailor?

But, at heart and not for nothing, as the late chance encounter may indicate to the discerning, down on him, secretly down on him, he assuredly was.

Now to invent something touching the more private career of Claggart, something involving Billy Budd, of which something the latter should be wholly ignorant, some romantic incident implying that Claggart's knowledge of the young blue-jacket began at some period anterior to catching sight of him on board the seventy-four—all this, not so difficult to do, might avail in a way more or less interesting to account for whatever enigma may appear to lurk in the case. But, in fact, there was nothing of the sort. And yet the cause, necessarily to be assumed as the sole one assignable, is in its very realism as much charged with that prime element of Radcliffian romance, *the mysterious*, as any that the ingenuity of the author of the *Mysteries of Udolpho* could devise. For what can more partake of the mysterious than an antipathy spontaneous and profound such as is evoked in certain exceptional mortals by the mere aspect of some other mortal, however harmless he may be?—if not called forth by that very harmlessness itself.

Now there can exist no irritating juxtaposition of dissimilar personalities comparable to that which is possible aboard a great warship fully manned and at sea. There, every day, among all ranks, almost every man comes into more or less of contact with almost every other man. Wholly there to avoid even the sight of an aggravating object one must needs give it Jonah's toss, or jump overboard himself. Imagine how all this might eventually operate on some peculiar human creature the direct reverse of a saint?

But for the adequate comprehending of Claggart by a normal nature these hints are insufficient. To pass from a normal nature to him one must cross 'the deadly space between,' and this is best done by indirection.

Long ago an honest scholar, my senior, said to me in reference to one who like himself is now no more, a man so unimpeachably respectable that against him nothing was ever openly said, though among the few something was whispered, 'Yes, X—— is a nut not to be cracked by the tap of a lady's fan. You are aware that I am the adherent of no organised religion, much less of any philosophy built into a system. Well, for all that, I think that to try and get into X——, enter his labyrinth, and get out again, without a clue derived from some source other than what is known as *knowledge of the world*, that were hardly possible, at least for me.'

'Why,' said I, 'X——, however singular a study to some, is yet human, and knowledge of the world assuredly implies the knowledge of human nature, and in most of its varieties.'

'Yes, but a superficial knowledge of it, serving ordinary purposes. But for anything deeper, I am not certain whether to know the world and to know human nature be not two distinct branches of knowledge, which while they may coexist in the same heart, yet either may exist with little or nothing of the other. Nay, in a average man of the world, his constant rubbing with it blunts that fine spiritual insight indispensable to the understanding of the essential in certain exceptional characters, whether evil ones or good. In a matter of some importance I have seen a girl wind an old lawyer about her little finger. Nor was it the dotage of senile love. Nothing of the sort. But he knew law better than he knew the girl's heart. Coke and Blackstone hardly shed so much light into obscure spiritual places as the Hebrew prophets. And who were they? Mostly recluses.'

At the time my inexperience was such that I did not quite see the drift of all this. It may be that I see it now. And, indeed, if that lexicon which is based on Holy Writ were any longer popular, one might with less difficulty define and denominate certain phenomenal men. As it is, one must turn to some authority not liable to the charge of being tinctured with the Biblical element.

In a list of definitions included in the authentic translation of Plato, a list attributed to him, occurs this: 'Natural Depravity: a depravity according to nature.' A definition which though savouring of Calvinism, by no means involves Calvin's dogma as to total mankind. Evidently its intent makes it applicable but to individuals. Not many are the examples of this depravity which the gallows and jail supply. At any rate, for notable instances,—since these have no vulgar alloy of the brute in them, but invariably are dominated by intellectuality,—one must go elsewhere. Civilisation, especially if of the austerer sort, is auspicious to it. It folds itself in the mantle of respectability. It has its certain negative virtues serving as silent auxiliaries. It is not going too far to say that it is without vices or small sins. There is phenomenal pride in it that excludes them from anything—never mercenary or avaricious. In short, the depravity here meant partakes nothing of the sordid or sensual. It is is serious, but free from acerbity. Though no flatterer of mankind, it never speaks ill of it.

But the thing which in eminent instances signalises so exceptional a nature is this: though the man's even temper and discreet bearing would seem to intimate a mind peculiarly subject to the law of reason, not the less in his soul's recesses he would seem to riot in complete exemption from that law, having apparently little to do with reason further than to employ it as an ambidexter implement for effecting the irrational. That is to say: toward the accomplishment of an aim which in wantonness of malignity would seem to partake of the insane, he will direct a cool judgment sagacious and sound.

These men are true madmen, and of the most dangerous sort, for their lunacy is not continuous, but occasional; evoked by some special object; it is secretive and self-contained, so that when most active it is to the average mind not distinguished from sanity, and for the reason above suggested that whatever its aim may be, and the aim is never disclosed, the method and the outward proceeding is always perfectly rational.

Now something such was Claggart, in whom was the mania of an evil nature, not engendered by vicious training or corrupting books or licentious living, but born with him and innate, in short, 'a depravity according to nature.'

Can it be this phenomenon, disowned or not acknowledged, that in some criminal cases puzzles the courts? For this cause have our juries at times not only to endure the prolonged contentions of lawyers with their fees, but also the yet more perplexing strife of the medical experts with theirs? But why leave it to them? Why not subpoena as well the clerical proficients? Their vocation bringing them into peculiar contact with so many human beings, and sometimes in their least guarded hour, in interviews very much more confidential that those of physician and patient; this would seem to qualify them to know something about those intricacies involved in the question of moral responsibility; whether in a given case, say the crime proceeded from mania in the brain or rabies of the heart. As to any differences among themselves these clerical proficients might develop on the stand, these could hardly be greater than the direct contradictions exchanged between the remunerated medical experts.

Dark sayings are these, some will say. But why? It is because they somewhat savour of Holy Writ in its phrase 'mysteries of iniquity.'

The point of the story turning on the hidden nature of the master-at-arms has necessitated this chapter. With an added hint or two in connection with the accident of the mess, the resumed narrative must be left to vindicate as it may its own credibility.

XI

Pale ire, envy and despair.

THAT Claggart's figure was not amiss, and his face, save the chin, well moulded, has already been said. Of these favourable points he seemed not insensible, for he was not only neat but careful in his dress. But the form of Billy Budd was heroic; and if his face was without the intellectual look of the pallid Claggart's, not the less was it lit, like his, from within, though from a different source. The bonfire in his heart made luminous the rose-tan in his cheek.

In view of the marked contrast between the persons of the twain, it is more than probable that when the master-at-arms in the scene last given applied to the sailor the proverb '*Handsome is as handsome does,*' he there let escape an ironic inkling, not caught by the young sailors who heard it, as to what it was that had first moved him against Billy, namely, his significant personal beauty.

Now envy and antipathy, passions irreconcilable in reason, nevertheless in fact may spring conjoined like Chang and Eng in one birth. Is envy then such a monster? Well, though many an arraigned mortal has in hopes of mitigated penalty pleaded guilty to horrible actions, did ever anybody seriously confess to envy? Something there is in it universally felt to be more shameful than even felonious crime. And not only does everybody disown it, but the better sort are inclined to incredulity when it is in earnest imputed to an intelligent man. But since its lodgment is in the heart, not the brain, no degree of intellect supplies a guarantee against it. But Claggart's was no vulgar form of the passion. Nor, as directed toward Billy Budd, did it partake of that streak of apprehensive jealousy that marred Saul's visage perturbedly brooding on the comely young David. Claggart's envy struck deeper. If askance he eyed the good looks, cheery health, and frank enjoyment of young life in Billy Budd, it was because these happened to go along with a nature that, as Claggart magnetically felt, had in its simplicity never willed malice, or experienced the reactionary bite of that serpent. To him, the spirit lodged within Billy and looking out from his welkin eyes as from windows, that ineffability which made the dimple in his dyed cheek, suppled his joints, and danced in his yellow curls, made him pre-eminently the Handsome Sailor. One person excepted, the master-at-arms was perhaps the only man in the ship intellectually capable of adequately appreciating the moral phenomenon presented in Billy Budd, and the insight but intensified his passion, which assuming various secret forms within him, at times assumed that of cynic disdain—disdain of innocence. To be nothing more than innocent! Yet in an aesthetic way he saw the charm of it, the courageous free-and-easy temper of it, and fain would have shared it, but he despaired of it.

With no power to annul the elemental evil in himself, though he could hide it readily enough; apprehending the good, but powerless to be it; what recourse is left to a nature like Claggart's, surcharged with energy as such natures almost invariably are, but to recoil upon itself, and, like the scorpion for which the Creator alone is responsible, act out to the end its allotted part.

Passion, and passion in its profoundest, is not a thing demanding a palatial stage whereon to play its part. Down among the groundlings, among the beggars and rakers of the garbage, profound passion is enacted. And the circumstances that provoke it, however trivial or mean, are no measure of its power. In the present instance the stage is a scrubbed gun-deck, and one of the external provocations a man-of-war's man's spilled soup.

Now when the master-at-arms noticed whence came that greasy fluid streaming before his feet, he must have taken it—to some extent wilfully perhaps—not for the mere accident it assuredly was, but for the sly escape of a spontaneous feeling on Billy's part more or less answering to the antipathy on his own. In effect a foolish demonstration he must have thought, and very harmless, like the futile kick of a heifer, which yet were the heifer a shod stallion, would not be so harmless. Even so was it that into the gall of envy Claggart infused the vitriol of his contempt. But the incident confirmed to him certain tell-tale reports purveyed to his ear by *Squeak*, one of his more cunning corporals, a grizzled little man, so nicknamed by the sailors on account of his squeaky voice and sharp visage ferreting about the dark corners of the lower decks after interlopers, satirically suggesting to them the idea of a rat in a cellar.

Now his chief's employing him as an implicit tool in laying little traps for the worriment of the foretopman—for it was from the master-at-arms that the petty persecutions heretofore adverted to had proceeded—the corporal, having naturally enough concluded that his master could have no love for the sailor, made it his business, faithful understrapper that he was, to ferment the ill blood by perverting to his chief certain innocent frolics of the good-natured foretopman, besides inventing for his mouth sundry contumelious epithets he claimed to have overheard him let fall. The master-at-arms never suspected the veracity of these reports, more especially as to the epithets, for he well knew how secretly unpopular may become a master-at-arms—at least, a master-at-arms in those days, zealous in his function—and how the blue-jackets shoot at him in private their raillery and wit; the nickname by which he goes among them (*Jemmy Legs*) implying under the form of merriment their cherished disrespect and dislike.

In view of the greediness of hate for provocation, it hardly needed a purveyor to feed Claggart's passion. An uncommon prudence is habitual with the subtler depravity, for it has everything to hide. And in case of any merely suspected injury, its secretiveness voluntarily cuts it off from enlightenment or disillusion; and not unreluctantly, action is taken upon surmise as upon certainty. And the retaliation is apt to be in monstrous disproportion to the supposed offence; for when in anybody was revenge in its exactions aught else but an inordinate usurer. But how with Claggart's conscience? For though consciences are unlike as foreheads, every intelligence, not excluding the Scriptural devils who 'believe and tremble,' has one. But Claggart's conscience being but the lawyer to his will, made ogres of trifles, probably arguing that the motive imputed to Billy in spilling the soup just when he did, together with the epithets alleged, these, if nothing more, made a strong case against him; nay, justified animosity into a sort of retributive righteousness. The Pharisee is the Guy Fawkes prowling in the hid chambers underlying some natures like Claggart's. And they can really form no conception of an unreciprocated malice. Probably, the master-at-arms' clandestine persecution of Billy was started to try the temper of the man; but it had not developed any quality in him that enmity could make official use of, or ever pervert into even plausible self-justification; so that the occurrence at the mess, petty if it were, was a welcome one to that peculiar conscience assigned to be the private mentor of Claggart; and for the rest, not improbably, it put him upon new experiments.

XII

NOT many days after the last incident narrated, something befell Billy Budd that more gravelled him than aught that had previously occurred.

It was a warm night for the latitude; and the foretopman, whose watch at the time was properly below, was dozing on the uppermost deck whither he had ascended from his hot hammock—one of hundreds suspended so closely wedged together over a lower gun-deck that there was little or no swing to them. He lay as in the shadow of a hillside stretched under the lee of the *booms*, a piled ridge of spare spars, and among which the ship's largest boat, the launch, was stowed. Alongside of three other slumberers from below, he lay near one end of the booms which approached from the foremast; his station aloft on duty as a foretopman being just over the deck station of the forecastleman, entitling him according to usage to make himself more or less at home in that neighbour-hood.

Presently he was stirred into semi-consciousness by somebody, who must have previously sounded the sleep of the others, touching his shoulder, and then, as the foretopman raised his head, breathing into his ear in a quick whisper, 'Slip into the lee fore-chains, Billy; there is something in the wind. Don't speak. Quick. I will meet you there'; and disappeared.

Now Billy, like sundry other essentially good-natured ones, had some of the weaknesses inseparable from essential good-nature; and among these was a reluctance, almost an incapacity, of plumply saying *no* to an abrupt proposition not obviously absurd on the face of it, nor obviously unfriendly, nor iniquitous. And being of warm blood had not the phlegm to negate any proposition by unresponsive inaction. Like his sense of fear, his apprehension as to aught outside of the honest and natural was seldom very quick. Besides, upon the present occasion, the drouse from his sleep still hung upon him.

However it was, he mechanically rose, and sleepily wonder-ing what could be *in the wind*, betook himself to the designated place, a narrow platform, one of six, outside of the high bulwarks, and screened by the great dead-eyes and multiple columned lanyards of the shrouds and back-stays; and, in a great warship of that time, of dimensions commensurate to the ample hull's magnitude; a tarry balcony, in short, overhanging the sea, and so secluded that one mariner of the *Indomitable*, a nonconformist old tar of a serious turn, made it even in daytime his private oratory.

In this retired nook the stranger soon joined Billy Budd. There was no moon as yet; a haze obscured the starlight. He could not distinctly see the stranger's face. Yet from something in the outline and carriage, Billy took him to be, and correctly, one of the afterguard.

'Hist, Billy!' said the man, in the same quick, cautionary whisper as before; 'you were impressed, weren't you? Well, so was I'; and he paused, as to mark the effect. But Billy, not knowing exactly what to make of this, said nothing. Then the other: 'We are not the only impressed ones, Billy. There's a gang of us. Couldn't you—help—at a pinch?'

'What do you mean?' demanded Billy, here shaking off his drouse.

'Hist, hist!' the hurried whisper now growing husky; 'see here,' and the man held up two small objects faintly twinkling in the night light; 'see, they are yours, Billy, if you'll only——'

But Billy broke in, and in his resentful eagerness to deliver himself, his vocal infirmity somewhat intruded. 'D-D-Damme, I don't know what you are d-driving at, or what you mean, but you had better g-g-go where you belong!' For the moment the fellow, as confounded, did not stir; and Billy, springing to his feet, said, 'If you d-don't start, I'll t-t-t-oss you back over the r-rail!' There was no mistaking this, and the mysterious emissary decamped, disappearing in the direction of the mainmast in the shadow of the booms.

'Hallo, what's the matter?' here came growling from a forecastleman awakened from his deck-doze by Billy's raised voice. And as the foretopman reappeared, and was recognised by him, 'Ah, *Beauty*, is it you? Well, something must have been the matter, for you st-st-stuttered.'

'Oh,' rejoined Billy, now mastering the impediment; 'I found an afterguardsman in our part of the ship here, and I bid him be off where he belongs.'

'And is that all you did about it, foretopman?' gruffly demanded another, an irascible old fellow of brick-coloured visage and hair, and who was known to his associate forecastlemen as *Red Pepper*.

'Such sneaks I should like to marry to the gunner's daughter!' by that expression meaning that he would like to subject them to disciplinary castigation over a gun.

However, Billy's rendering of the matter satisfactorily accounted to these inquirers for the brief commotion, since of all the sections of a ship's company the forecastlemen, veterans for the most part, and bigoted in their sea-prejudices, are the most jealous in resenting territorial encroachments, especially on the part of any of the afterguard, of whom they have but a sorry opinion, chiefly landsmen, never going aloft except to reef or furl the mainsail, and in no wise competent to handle a marling-spike or turn in a *dead-eye*, say.

XIII

THIS incident sorely puzzled Billy Budd. It was an entirely new experience; the first time in his life that he had ever been personally approached in underhand intriguing fashion. Prior to this encounter he had known nothing of the afterguardsman, the two men being stationed wide apart, one forward and aloft during his watch, the other on deck and aft.

What could it mean? And could they really be guineas, those two glittering objects the interloper had held up to his (Billy's) eyes? Where could the fellow get guineas? Why, even buttons, spare buttons, are not so plentiful at sea. The more he turned the matter over, the more he was nonplussed, and made uneasy and discomforted. In his disgustful recoil from an overture which though he but ill comprehended he instinctively knew must involve evil of some sort, Billy Budd was like a young horse fresh from the pasture suddenly inhaling a vile whiff from some chemical factory, and by repeated snortings tries to get it out of his nostrils and lungs. This frame of mind barred all desire of holding further parley with the fellow, even were it but for the purpose of gaining some enlightenment as to his design in approaching him. And yet he was not without natural curiosity to see how such a visitor in the dark would look in broad day.

He espied him the following afternoon in his first dog-watch below, one of the smokers on that forward part of the upper gun-deck allotted to the pipe. He recognised him by his general cut and build, more than by his round freckled face and glassy eyes of pale blue veiled with lashes all but white. And yet Billy was a bit uncertain whether indeed it were he—yonder chap about his own age, chatting and laughing in free-hearted way, leaning against a gun; a genial young fellow enough to look at, and something of a rattle-brain, to all appearance. Rather chubby, too, for a sailor, even an afterguardsman. In short, the last man in the world, one would think, to be overburthened with thoughts, especially those perilous thoughts that must needs belong to a conspirator in any serious project, or even to the underling of such a conspirator.

Although Billy was not aware of it, the fellow with a sidelong watchful glance had perceived Billy first, and then noting that Billy was looking at him, thereupon nodded a familiar sort of friendly recognition as to an old acquaintance, without interrupting the talk he was engaged in with the group of smokers. A day or two afterwards, chancing in the evening promenade on a gun-deck to pass Billy, he offered a flying word of good-fellowship, as it were, which by its unexpectedness, and equivocalness under the circumstances, so embarrassed Billy, that he knew not how to respond to it, and let it go unnoticed.

Billy was now left more at a loss than before. The ineffectual speculations into which he was led were so disturbingly alien to him, that he did his best to smother them. It never entered his mind that here was a matter which, from its extreme questionableness, it was his duty as a loyal blue-jacket to report in the proper quarter. And, probably, had such a step been suggested to him, he would have been deterred from taking it by the thought, one of novice-magnanimity, that it would savour over-much of the dirty work of a tell-tale. He kept the thing to himself. Yet upon one occasion he could not forbear a little disburthening himself to the old Dansker, tempted thereto perhaps by the influence of a balmy night when the ship lay becalmed; the twain, silent for the most part, sitting together on deck, their heads propped against the bulwarks. But it was only a partial and anonymous account that Billy gave, the unfounded scruples above referred to preventing full disclosure to anybody. Upon hearing Billy's version, the sage Dansker seemed to divine more than he was told; and after a little meditation, during which his wrinkles were pursed as into a point, quite effacing for the time that quizzing expression his face sometimes wore—'Didn't I say so, Baby Budd?'

'Say what?' demanded Billy.

'Why, *Jemmy Legs* is *down* on you.'

'And what,' rejoined Billy in amazement, 'has *Jemmy Legs* to do with that cracked afterguardsman?'

'Ho, it was an afterguardsman, then. A cat's-paw, a cat's-paw!' And with that exclamation, which, whether it had reference to a light puff of air just then coming over the calm sea, or subtler relation to the afterguardsman, there is no telling. The old Merlin gave a twisting wrench with his black teeth at his plug of tobacco, vouchsafing no reply to Billy's impetuous question. For it was his wont to relapse into grim silence when interrogated in sceptical sort as to any of his sententious oracles, not always very clear ones, rather partaking of that obscurity which invests most Delphic deliverances from any quarter.

XIV

LONG experience had very likely brought this old man to that bitter prudence which never interferes in aught, and never gives advice.

Yet, despite the Dansker's pithy insistence as to the master-at-arms being at the bottom of these strange experiences of Billy on board the *Indomitable*, the young sailor was ready to ascribe them to almost anybody but the man who, to use Billy's own expression, 'always had a pleasant word for him.' This is to be wondered at. Yet not so much to be wondered at. In certain matters some sailors even in mature life remain unsophisticated enough. But a young seafarer of the disposition of our athletic foretopman, is much of a child-man. And yet a child's utter innocence is but its blank ignorance, and the innocence more or less wanes as intelligence waxes. But in Billy Budd intelligence, such as it was, had advanced, while yet his simple-mindedness remained for the most part unaffected. Experience is a teacher indeed; yet did Billy's years make his experience small. Besides, he had none of that intuitive knowledge of the bad which in natures not good or incompletely so, foreruns experience, and therefore may pertain, as in some instances it too clearly does pertain, even to youth.

And what could Billy know of man except of man as a mere sailor? And the old-fashioned sailor, the veritable man-before-the-mast, the sailor from boyhood up, he, though indeed of the same species as a landsman, is in some respects singularly distinct from him. The sailor is frankness, the landsman is finesse. Life is not a game with the sailor, demanding the long head; no intricate game of chess where few moves are made in straightforwardness, but ends are attained by indirection; an oblique, tedious, barren game, hardly worth that poor candle burnt out in playing it.

Yes, as a class, sailors are in character a juvenile race. Even their deviations are marked by juvenility. And this more especially holding true with the sailors of Billy's time. Then, too, certain things which apply to all sailors do more pointedly operate here and there upon the junior one. Every sailor, too, is accustomed to obey orders without debating them; his life afloat is externally ruled for him; he is not brought into that promiscuous commerce with mankind where unobstructed free agency on equal terms—equal superficially, at least— soon teaches one that unless upon occasion he exercises a distrust keen in proportion to the fairness of the appearance, some foul turn may be served him. A ruled, undemonstrative distrustfulness is so habitual, not with business-men so much, as with men who know their kind in less shallow relations than business, namely certain men of the world, that they come at last to employ it all but unconsciously; and some of them would very likely feel real surprise at being charged with it as one of their general characteristics.

XV

BUT after the little matter at the mess Billy Budd no more found himself in strange trouble at times about his hammock or his clothes-bag, or what not. While, as to that smile that occasionally sunned him, and the pleasant passing word, these were if not more frequent, yet if anything more pronounced than before.

But for all that, there were certain other demonstrations now. When Claggart's unobserved glance happened to light on belted Billy rolling along the upper gun-deck in the leisure of the second dog-watch, exchanging passing broadsides of fun with other young promenaders in the crowd, that glance would follow the cheerful sea-Hyperion with a settled meditative and melancholy expression, his eyes strangely suffused with incipient feverish tears. Then would Claggart look like the man of sorrows. Yes, and sometimes the melancholy expression would have in it a touch of soft yearning, as if Claggart could even have loved Billy but for fate and ban. But this was an evanescence, and quickly repented of, as it were, by an immitigable look, pinching and shrivelling the visage into the momentary semblance of a wrinkled walnut. But sometimes catching sight in advance of the foretopman coming in his direction, he would, upon their nearing, step aside a little to let him pass, dwelling upon Billy for the moment with the glittering dental satire of a guise. But upon any abrupt unforeseen encounter a red light would flash forth from his eye, like a spark from an anvil in a dusk smithy. That quick fierce light was a strange one, darted from orbs which in repose were of a colour nearest approaching a deeper violet, the softest of shades.

Though some of these caprices of the pit could not but be observed by their object, yet were they beyond the construing of such a nature. And the thews of Billy were hardly comparable with that sort of sensitive spiritual organisation which in some cases instinctively conveys to ignorant innocence an admonition of the proximity of the malign. He thought the master-at-arms acted in a manner rather queer at times. That was all. But the occasional frank air and pleasant word went for what they purported to be, the young sailor never having heard as yet of the 'too fair-spoken man.'

Had the foretopman been conscious of having done or said anything to provoke the ill-will of the official, it would have been different with him, and his sight might have been pursed if not sharpened.

So was it with him in yet another matter. Two minor officers, the armourer and captain of the hold, with whom he had never exchanged a word, his position on the ship not bringing him into contact with them; these men now for the first time began to cast upon Billy, when they chanced to encounter him, that peculiar glance which evidences that the man from whom it comes has been some way tampered with, and to the prejudice of him upon whom the glance lights. Never did it occur to Billy as a thing to be noted, or a thing suspicious, though he well knew the fact, that the armourer and captain of the hold, with the ship's yeoman, apothecary, and others of that grade, were by naval usage, messmates of the master-at-arms, men with ears convenient to his confidential tongue.

Our Handsome Sailor's manly forwardness upon occasion, and irresistible good-nature, indicating no mental superiority tending to excite an invidious feeling, bred general popularity, and this good-will on the part of most of his shipmates made him the less to concern himself about such mute aspects toward him as those whereto allusion has just been made.

As to the afterguardsman, though Billy for reasons already given necessarily saw little of him, yet when the two did happen to meet, invariably came the fellow's off-hand cheerful recognition, sometimes accompanied by a passing pleasant word or two. Whatever that equivocal young person's original design may really have been, or the design of which he might have been the deputy, certain it was from his manner upon these occasions, that he had wholly dropped it.

It was as if his precocity of crookedness (and every vulgar villain is precocious) had for once deceived him, and the man he had sought to entrap as a simpleton had, through his very simplicity, baffled him.

But shrewd ones may opine that it was hardly possible for Billy to refrain from going up to the afterguardsman and bluntly demanding to know his purpose in the initial interview, so abruptly closed in the fore-chains. Shrewd ones may also think it but natural in Billy to set about sounding some of the other impressed men of the ship in order to discover what basis, if any, there was for the emissary's obscure suggestions as to plotting disaffection aboard. Yes, the shrewd may so think. But something more, or rather, something else than mere shrewdness is perhaps needful for the due understanding of such a character as Billy Budd's.

As to Claggart, the monomania in the man—if that indeed it were—as involuntarily disclosed by starts in the manifestations detailed, yet in general covered over by his self-contained and rational demeanour; this, like a subterranean fire, was eating its way deeper and deeper in him. Something decisive must come of it.

XVI

AFTER the mysterious interview in the fore-chains, the one so abruptly ended there by Billy, nothing especially germane to the story occurred until the events now about to be narrated.

Elsewhere it has been said that owing to the lack of frigates (of course better sailers than line-of-battle ships) in the English squadron up the Straits at that period, the *Indomitable* seventy-four was occasionally employed not only as an available substitute for a scout, but at times on detached service of more important kind. This was not alone because of her sailing qualities, not common in a ship of her rate, but quite as much probably, that the character of her commander, it was thought, specially adapted him for any duty where under unforeseen difficulties a prompt initiative might have to be taken in some matter demanding knowledge and ability in addition to those qualities employed in good seamanship. It was on an expedition of the latter sort, a somewhat distant one, and when the *Indomitable* was almost at her furthest remove from the fleet, that in the latter part of an afternoon-watch she unexpectedly came in sight of a ship of the enemy. It proved to be a frigate. The latter, perceiving through the glass that the weight of men and metal would be heavily against her, invoking her light heels, crowded sail to get away. After a chase urged almost against hope, and lasting until about the middle of the first dog-watch, she signally succeeded in effecting her escape.

Not long after the pursuit had been given up, and ere the excitement incident thereto had altogether waned away, the master-at-arms, ascending from his cavernous sphere, made his appearance cap in hand by the main-mast, respectfully waiting the notice of Captain Vere, then solitary walking the weather-side of the quarter-deck, doubtless somewhat chafed at the failure of the pursuit. The spot where Claggart stood was the place allotted to men of lesser grades seeking some more particular interview either with the officer of the deck or the captain himself. But from the latter it was not often that a sailor or petty officer of those days would seek a hearing; only some exceptional cause would, according to established custom, have warranted that.

Presently, just as the commander, absorbed in his reflections, was on the point of turning aft in his promenade, he became sensible of Claggart's presence, and saw the doffed cap held in deferential expectancy. Here be it said that Captain Vere's personal knowledge of this petty officer had only begun at the time of the ship's last sailing from home, Claggart then for the first, in transfer from a ship detained for repairs, supplying on board the *Indomitable* the place of a previous master-at-arms disabled and ashore.

No sooner did the commander observe who it was that now so deferentially stood awaiting his notice, than a peculiar expression came over his face. It was not unlike that which uncontrollably will flit across the countenance of one at unawares encountering a person who though known to him indeed has hardly been long enough known for thorough knowledge, but something in whose aspect nevertheless now for the first provokes a vaguely repellent distaste. But coming to a stand, and resuming much of his wonted official manner, save that a sort of impatience lurked in the intonation of the opening word, he said, 'Well, what is it, master-at-arms?'

With the air of a subordinate grieved at the necessity of being a messenger of ill-tidings, and while conscientiously determined to be frank, yet equally resolved upon shunning overstatement, Claggart at this invitation, or rather summons to disburthen, spoke up. What he said, conveyed in the language of no uneducated man, was to the effect following, if not altogether in these words, namely: That during the chase and preparations for the possible encounter he had seen enough to convince him that at least one sailor aboard was a dangerous character in a ship mustering some who not only had taken a guilty part in the late serious trouble, but others also who, like the man in question, had entered His Majesty's service under another form than enlistment.

At this point Captain Vere with some impatience interrupted him:

'Be direct, man; say impressed men.'

Claggart made a gesture of subservience and proceeded. Quite lately he (Claggart) had begun to suspect that some sort of movement prompted by the sailor in question was covertly going on, but he had not thought himself warranted in reporting the suspicion so long as it remained indistinct. But from what he had that afternoon observed in the man referred to, the suspicion of something clandestine going on had advanced to a point less removed from certainty. He deeply felt, he added, the serious responsibility assumed in making a report involving such possible consequences to the individual mainly concerned, besides tending to augment those natural anxieties which every naval commander must feel in view of extraordinary outbreaks so recent as those which, he sorrowfully said it, it needed not to name.

Now at the first broaching of the matter Captain Vere, taken by surprise, could not wholly dissemble his disquietude, but as Claggart went on, the former's aspect changed into restiveness under something in the testifier's manner in giving his testimony. However, he refrained from interrupting him. And Claggart, continuing, concluded with this:

'God forbid, your honour, that the *Indomitable's* should be the experience of the——'

'Never mind that!' here peremptorily broke in the superior, his face altering with anger instantly, divining the ship that the other was about to name, one in which the Nore Mutiny had assumed a singularly tragical character that for a time jeopardised the life of its commander. Under the circumstances he was indignant at the purposed allusion. When the commissioned officers themselves were on all occasions very heedful how they referred to the recent event, for a petty officer unnecessarily to allude to it in the presence of his captain, this struck him as a most immodest presumption. Besides, to his quick sense of self-respect, it even looked under the circumstances something like an attempt to alarm him. Nor at that was he without some surprise that one who so far as he had hitherto come under his notice had shown considerable tact in his function, should in this particular evince such lack of it.

But these thoughts and kindred dubious ones flitting across his mind were suddenly replaced by an intuitional surmise, which though as yet obscure in form, served practically to affect his reception of the ill tidings. Certain it is, that long versed in everything pertaining to the complicated gun-deck life, which like every other form of life has its secret mines and dubious side, the side popularly disclaimed, Captain Vere did not permit himself to be unduly disturbed by the general tenor of his subordinate's report. Furthermore, if in view of recent events prompt action should be taken at the first palpable sign of recurring insubordination, for all that, not judicious would it be, he thought, to keep the idea of lingering disaffection alive by undue forwardness in crediting an informer, even if his own subordinate, and charged among other honours with police surveillance of the crew. This feeling would not perhaps have so prevailed with him were it not that upon a prior occasion the patriotic zeal officially evinced by Claggart had somewhat irritated him as appearing rather supersensitive and strained. Furthermore, something even in the official's self-possessed and somewhat ostentatious manner in making his specifications strangely reminded him of a bandsman, a perjured witness in a capital case before a court-martial ashore of which when a lieutenant he, Captain Vere, had been a member.

Now the peremptory check given to Claggart in the matter of the arrested allusion was quickly followed up by this: 'You say that there is at least one dangerous man aboard. Name him.'

'William Budd, a foretopman, your honour.'

'William Budd!' repeated Captain Vere with unfeigned astonishment; 'and mean you the man that Lieutenant Ratcliffe took from the merchantman not very long ago—the young fellow who seems to be so popular with the men—Billy, the Handsome Sailor, as they call him?'

'The same, your honour; but for all his youth and good looks, a deep one. Not for nothing does he insinuate himself into the good-will of his shipmates, since at the least they will at a pinch say a good word for him at all hazards. Did Lieutenant Ratcliffe happen to tell your honour of that adroit fling of Budd's jumping up in the cutter's bow under the merchantman's stern when he was being taken off? That sort of good-humoured air even masks that at heart he resents his impressment. You have but noted his fair cheek. A man-trap may be under his ruddy-tipped daisies.'

Now the *Handsome Sailor* as a signal figure among the crew had naturally enough attracted the captain's attention from the first. Though in general not very demonstrative to his officers, he had congratulated Lieutenant Ratcliffe upon his good fortune in lighting on such a fine specimen of the *genus homo*, who in the nude might have passed for a statue of young Adam before the Fall.

As to Billy's adieu to the ship *Rights-of-Man*, which the boarding lieutenant, in a deferential way, had indeed reported to him, Captain Vere, more as a good story than aught else (having mistakenly understood it as a satiric sally), had but thought so much the better of the impressed man for it; as a military sailor, admiring the spirit that could take an arbitrary enlistment so merrily and sensibly. The foretopman's conduct, too, so far as it had fallen under the captain's notice, had confirmed the first happy augury, while the new recruit's qualities as a *sailor-man* seemed to be such that he had thought of recommending him to the executive officer for promotion to a place that would more frequently bring him under his own observation, namely, the captaincy of the mizen-top, replacing there in the starboard-watch a man not so young whom partly for that reason he deemed less fitted for the post. Be it parenthesised here that since the mizen-topmen have not to handle such breadths of heavy canvas as the lower sails on the mainmast and foremast, a young man if of the right stuff not only seems best adapted to duty there, but, in fact, is generally selected for the captaincy of that top, and the company under him are light hands, and often but striplings. In sum, Captain Vere had from the beginning deemed Billy Budd to be what in the naval parlance of the time was called a '*King's bargain*,' that is to say, for His Britannic Majesty's Navy a capital investment at small outlay or none at all.

After a brief pause, during which the reminiscences above mentioned passed vividly through his mind, he weighed the import of Claggart's last suggestion conveyed in the phrase 'a man-trap under his ruddy-tipped daisies,' and the more he weighed it the less reliance he felt in the informer's good faith. Suddenly he turned upon him: 'Do you come to me, master-at-arms, with so foggy a tale? As to Budd, cite me an act or spoken word of his confirmatory of what you in general charge against him. Stay,' drawing nearer to him, 'heed what you speak. Just now and in a case like this, there is a yard-arm-end for the false witness.'

'Ah, your honour!' sighed Claggart, mildly shaking his shapely head as in sad deprecation of such unmerited severity of tone. Then bridling—erecting himself as in virtuous self-assertion, he circumstantially alleged certain words and acts which collectively, if credited, led to presumptions mortally inculpating Budd, and for some of these averments, he added, substantiating proof was not far.

With gray eyes impatient and distrustful, essaying to fathom to the bottom Claggart's calm violet ones, Captain Vere again heard him out; then for the moment stood ruminating. The mood he evinced, Claggart—himself for the time liberated from the other's scrutiny—steadily regarded with a look difficult to render—a look curious of the operation of his tactics, a look such as might have been that of the spokesman of the envious children of Jacob deceptively imposing upon the troubled patriarch the blood-dyed coat of young Joseph.

Though something exceptional in the moral quality of Captain Vere made him, in earnest encounter with a fellow-man, a veritable touchstone of that man's essential nature, yet now as to Claggart and what was really going on in him, his feeling partook less of intuitional conviction than of strong suspicion clogged by strange dubieties. The perplexity he evinced proceeded less from aught touching the man informed against—as Claggart doubtless opined—than from considerations how best to act in regard to the informer. At first, indeed, he was naturally for summoning that substantiation of his allegations which Claggart said was at hand. But such a proceeding would result in the matter at once getting abroad, which in the present stage of it, he thought, might undesirably affect the ship's company. If Claggart was a false witness—that closed the affair. And therefore, before trying the accusation, he would first practically test the accuser; and he thought this could be done in a quiet undemonstrative way.

The measure he determined upon involved a shifting of the scene, a transfer to a place less exposed to observation than the broad quarter-deck. For although the few gun-room officers there at the time had, in due observance of naval etiquette, withdrawn to leeward the moment Captain Vere had begun his promenade on the deck's weather-side; and though during the colloquy with Claggart they of course ventured not to diminish the distance; and though throughout the interview Captain Vere's voice was far from high, and Claggart's silvery and low; and the wind in the cordage and the wash of the sea helped the more to put them beyond earshot; nevertheless, the interview's continuance already had attracted observation from some topmen aloft, and other sailors in the waist or farther forward.

Having determined upon his measures, Captain Vere forthwith took action. Abruptly turning to Claggart he asked, 'Master-at-arms, is it now Budd's watch aloft?'

'No, your honour.'

Whereupon, 'Mr. Wilkes,' summoning the nearest midshipman, 'tell Albert to come to me.' Albert was the captain's hammock-boy, a sort of sea-valet, in whose discretion and fidelity his master had much confidence. The lad appeared. 'You know Budd, the foretopman?'

'I do, sir.'

'Go find him. It is his watch off. Manage to tell him out of ear-shot that he is wanted aft. Contrive it that he speaks to nobody. Keep him in talk yourself. And not till you get well aft here, not till then, let him know that the place where he is wanted is my cabin. You understand? Go. Master-at-arms, show yourself on the decks below, and when you think it time for Albert to be coming with his man, stand by quietly to follow the sailor in.'

XVII

NOW when the foretopman found himself closeted, as it were, in the cabin with the captain and Claggart, he was surprised enough. But it was a surprise unaccompanied by apprehension or distrust. To an immature nature, essentially honest and humane, forewarning intimations of subtler danger from one's kind came tardily, if at all. The only thing that took shape in the young sailor's mind was this: 'Yes, the captain, I have always thought, looks kindly upon me. Wonder if he's going to make me his coxswain. I should like that. And maybe now he is going to ask the master-at-arms about me.'

'Shut the door there, sentry,' said the commander. 'Stand without and let nobody come in. Now, master-at-arms, tell this man to his face what you told of him to me'; and stood prepared to scrutinise the mutually confronting visages.

With the measured step and calm collected air of an asylum physician approaching in the public hall some patient beginning to show indications of a coming paroxysm, Claggart deliberately advanced within short range of Billy, and mesmerically looking him in the eye, briefly recapitulated the accusation.

Not at first did Billy take it in. When he did the rose-tan of his cheek looked struck as by white leprosy. He stood like one impaled and gagged. Meanwhile the accuser's eyes, removing not as yet from the blue, dilated ones, underwent a phenomenal change, their wonted rich violet colour blurring into a muddy purple. Those lights of human intelligence losing human expression, gelidly protruding like the alien eyes of certain uncatalogued creatures of the deep.

The first mesmeric glance was one of surprised fascination; the last was as the hungry lurch of the torpedo-fish.

'Speak, man!' said Captain Vere to the transfixed one; struck by his aspect even more than by Claggart's. 'Speak! defend yourself.' Which appeal caused but a strange, dumb gesturing and gurgling in Billy; amazement at such an accusation so suddenly sprung on inexperienced nonage; this, and it may be horror at the accuser, serving to bring out his lurking defect, and in this instance for the time intensifying it into a convulsed tongue-tie; while the intent head and entire form, straining forward in an agony of ineffectual eagerness to obey the injunction to speak and defend himself, gave an expression to the face like that of a condemned vestal priestess in the moment of being buried alive, and in the first struggle against suffocation.

Though at the time Captain Vere was quite ignorant of Billy's liability to vocal impediment, he now immediately divined it, since vividly Billy's aspect recalled to him that of a bright young schoolmate of his whom he had seen struck by much the same startling impotence in the act of eagerly rising in the class to be foremost in response to a testing question put to it by the master. Going close up to the young sailor, and laying a soothing hand on his shoulder, he said, 'There is no hurry, my boy. Take your time, take your time.' Contrary to the effect intended, these words, so fatherly in tone, doubtless touching Billy's heart to the quick, prompted yet more violent efforts at utterance—efforts soon ending for the time in confirming the paralysis, and bringing to the face an expression which was as a crucifixion to behold. The next instant, quick as the flame from a discharged cannon at night, his right arm shot out, and Claggart dropped to the deck. Whether intentionally, or but owing to the young athlete's superior height, the blow had taken effect full upon the forehead, so shapely and intellectual-looking a feature in the master-at-arms; so that the body fell over lengthwise, like a heavy plank tilted from erectness. A gasp or two, and he lay motionless.

'Fated boy,' breathed Captain Vere, in tone so low as to be almost a whisper, 'what have you done! But here, help me.'

The twain raised the felled one from the loins up into a sitting position. The spare form flexibly acquiesced, but inertly. It was like handling a dead snake. They lowered it back. Regaining erectness, Captain Vere with one hand covering his face stood to all appearance as impassive as the object at his feet. Was he absorbed in taking in all the bearings of the event, and what was best not only now at once to be done, but also in the sequel? Slowly he uncovered his face; and the effect was as if the moon emerging from eclipse should reappear with quite another aspect than that which had gone into hiding. The father in him, manifested towards Billy thus far in the scene, was replaced by the military disciplinarian. In his official tone he bade the foretopman retire to a state-room aft (pointing it out), and there remain till thence summoned. This order Billy in silence mechanically obeyed. Then going to the cabin door where it opened on the quarter-deck, Captain Vere said to the sentry without, 'Tell somebody to send Albert here.' When the lad appeared his master so contrived it that he should not catch sight of the prone one. 'Albert,' he said to him, 'tell the surgeon I wish to see him. You need not come back till called.'

When the surgeon entered—a self-poised character of that grave sense and experience that hardly anything could take him aback—Captain Vere advanced to meet him, thus unconsciously interrupting his view of Claggart, and interrupting the other's wonted ceremonious salutation said, 'Nay tell me how it is with yonder man,' directing his attention to the prostrate one.

The surgeon looked, and for all his self-command, somewhat started at the abrupt revelation. On Claggart's always pallid complexion thick black blood was now oozing from mouth and ear. To the gazer's professional eyes it was unmistakably no living man that he saw.

'Is it so, then?' said Captain Vere, intently watching him. 'I thought it. But verify it.' Whereupon the customary tests confirmed the surgeon's first glance, who now looking up in unfeigned concern, cast a look of intense inquisitiveness upon his superior. But Captain Vere, with one hand to his brow, was standing motionless. Suddenly, catching the surgeon's arm convulsively, he exclaimed, pointing down to the body, 'It is the divine judgment of Ananias! Look!'

Disturbed by the excited manner he had never before observed in the *Indomitable*'s captain, and as yet wholly ignorant of the affair, the prudent surgeon nevertheless held his peace, only again looking an earnest interrogation as to what it was that had resulted in such a tragedy.

But Captain Vere was now again motionless, standing absorbed in thought. But again starting, he vehemently exclaimed, 'Struck dead by an angel of God. Yet the angel must hang!'

At these interjections, incoherences to the listener as yet unapprised of the antecedent events, the surgeon was profoundly discomforted. But now, as recollecting himself, Captain Vere in less harsh tone briefly related the circumstances leading up to the event.

'But come; we must dispatch,' he added; 'help me to remove him (meaning the body) to yonder compartment'—designating one opposite where the foretopman remained immured. Anew disturbed by a request that as implying a desire for secrecy seemed unaccountably strange to him, there was nothing for the subordinate to do but comply.

'Go now,' said Captain Vere, with something of his wonted manner, 'go now. I shall presently call a drum-head court. Tell the lieutenants what has happened, and tell Mr. Morton'— meaning the captain of marines. 'And charge them to keep the matter to themselves.'

Full of disquietude and misgivings, the surgeon left the cabin. Was Captain Vere suddenly affected in his mind, or was it but a transient excitement brought about by so strange and extraordinary a happening? As to the drum-head court, it struck the surgeon as impolitic, if nothing more. The thing to do, he thought, was to place Billy Budd in confinement, and in a way dictated by usage, and postpone further action in so extraordinary a case to such time as they should again join the squadron, and then transfer it to the admiral. He recalled the unwonted agitation of Captain Vere and his excited exclamations, so at variance with his normal manner. Was he unhinged? But assuming that he was, it were not so susceptible of proof. What then could he do? No more trying situation is conceivable than that of an officer subordinated under a captain whom he suspects to be, not mad indeed, but yet not quite unaffected in his intellect. To argue his order to him would be insolence. To resist him would be mutiny. In obedience to Captain Vere he communicated to the lieutenants and captain of marines what had happened, saying nothing as to the captain's state. They stared at him in surprise and concern.

Like him, they seemed to think that such a matter should be reported to the admiral.

Who in the rainbow can draw the line where the violet tint ends and the orange tint begins? Distinctly we see the difference of the colour, but where exactly does the first one visibly enter into the other? So with sanity and insanity. In pronounced cases there is no question about them. But in some cases, in various degrees supposedly less pronounced, to draw the line of demarcation few will undertake, though for a fee some professional experts will. There is nothing nameable but that some men will undertake to do for pay. In other words, there are instances where it is next to impossible to determine whether a man is sane or beginning to be otherwise.

Whether Captain Vere, as the surgeon professionally surmised, was really the sudden victim of any degree of aberration, one must determine for himself by such light as this narrative may afford.

XVIII

THE unhappy event which has been narrated could not have happened at a worse juncture. For it was close on the heel of the suppressed insurrections, an after-time very critical to naval authority, demanding from every English sea-commander two qualities not readily interfusable—prudence and rigour. Moreover, there was something crucial in the case.

In the jugglery of circumstances preceding and attending the event on board the *Indomitable*, and in the light of that martial code whereby it was formally to be judged, innocence and guilt, personified in Claggart and Budd, in effect changed places.

In the legal view, the apparent victim of the tragedy was he who had sought to victimise a man blameless; and the indisputable deed of the latter, navally regarded, constituted the most heinous of military crimes. Yet more. The essential right and wrong involved in the matter, the clearer that might be, so much the worse for the responsibility of a loyal sea-commander, inasmuch as he was authorised to determine the matter on that primitive legal basis.

Small wonder then that the *Indomitable's* captain, though in general a man of rigid decision, felt that circumspectness not less than promptitude was necessary. Until he could decide upon his course, and in each detail, and not only so, but until the concluding measure was upon the point of being enacted, he deemed it advisable, in view of all the circumstances, to guard as much as possible against publicity. Here he may or may not have erred. Certain it is, however, that subsequently in the confidential talk of more than one or two gun-rooms and cabins he was not a little criticised by some officers, a fact imputed by his friends, and vehemently by his cousin Jack Denton, to professional jealously of Starry Vere. Some imaginative ground for invidious comment there was. The maintenance of secrecy in the matter, the confining all knowledge of it for a time to the place where the homicide occurred—the quarter-deck cabin; in these particulars lurked some resemblance to the policy adopted in those tragedies of the palace which have occurred more than once in the capital founded by Peter the Barbarian, great chiefly by his crimes.

The case was such that fain would the *Indomitable's* captain have deferred taking any action whatever respecting it further than to keep the foretopman a close prisoner till the ship rejoined the squadron, and then submitting the matter to the judgment of his admiral.

But a true military officer is in one particular like a true monk. Not with more of self-abnegation will the latter keep his vows of monastic obedience than the former his vows of allegiance to martial duty.

Feeling that unless quick action was taken on it, the deed of the foretopman, as soon as it should be known on the gun-decks, would tend to awaken any slumbering embers of the Nore among the crew, a sense of the urgency of the case overruled in Captain Vere every other consideration. But though a conscientious disciplinarian he was no lover of authority for mere authority's sake. Very far was he from embracing opportunities for monopolising to himself the perils of moral responsibility, none at least that could properly be referred to an official superior, or shared with him by his official equals, or even subordinates. So thinking, he was glad it would not be at variance with usage to turn the matter over to a summary court of his own officers, reserving to himself, as the one on whom the ultimate accountability would rest, the right of maintaining a supervision of it, or formally or informally interposing at need. Accordingly a drum-head court was summarily convened, he electing the individuals composing it—the first lieutenant, the captain of marines, and the sailing-master.

In associating an officer of marines with the sea-lieutenant in a case having to do with a sailor, the commander perhaps deviated from general custom. He was prompted thereto by the circumstance that he took that soldier to be a judicious person, thoughtful and not altogether incapable of grappling with a difficult case unprecedented in his prior experience. Yet even as to him he was not without some latent misgiving, for withal he was an extremely good-natured man, an enjoyer of his dinner, a sound sleeper, and inclined to obesity. The sort of man who, though he would always maintain his manhood in battle, might not prove altogether reliable in a moral dilemma involving aught of the tragic. As to the first lieutenant and the sailing-master, Captain Vere could not but be aware that though honest natures, of approved gallantry upon occasion, their intelligence was mostly confined to the matter of active seamanship, and the fighting demands of their profession. The court was held in the same cabin where the unfortunate affair had taken place. This cabin, the commander's, embraced the entire area under the poop-deck. Aft, and on either side, was a small state-room—the one room temporarily a jail, and the other a dead-house—and a yet smaller compartment leaving a space between, expanding forward into a goodly oblong of length coinciding with the ship's beam. A skylight of moderate dimensions was overhead, and at each end of the oblong space were two sashed port-hole windows easily convertible back into embrasures for short carronades.

All being quickly in readiness, Billy Budd was arraigned, Captain Vere necessarily appearing as the sole witness in the case, and as such temporarily sinking his rank, though singularly maintaining it in a matter apparently trivial, namely, that he testified from the ship's weatherside, with that object having caused the court to sit on the lee-side. Concisely he narrated all that had led up to the catastrophe, omitting nothing in Claggart's accusation, and deposing as to the manner in which the prisoner had received it. At this testimony the three officers glanced with no little surprise at Billy Budd, the last man they would have suspected, either of mutinous design alleged by Claggart, or of the undeniable deed he himself had done. The first lieutenant taking judicial primary, and turning toward the prisoner, said,

'Captain Vere has spoken. Is it or is it not as Captain Vere says?'
In response came syllables not so much impeded in the utterance
as might have been anticipated. They were these:

'Captain Vere tells the truth. It is just as Captain Vere says, but
it is not as the master-at-arms said. I have eaten the King's bread,
and I am true to the King.'

'I believe you, my man,' said the witness, his voice indicating a
suppressed emotion not otherwise betrayed.

'God will bless you for that, your honour!' not without stammering, said Billy, and all but broke down. But immediately was
recalled to self-control by another question, to which with the same
emotional difficulty of utterance he said, 'No, there was no malice
between us. I never bore malice against the master-at-arms. I am
sorry that he is dead. I did not mean to kill him. Could I have used
my tongue I would not have struck him. But he foully lied to my face,
and in the presence of my captain, and I had to say something, and
I could only say it with a blow. God help me!'

In the impulsive above-board manner of the frank one the court
saw confirmed all that was implied in words that just previously
had perplexed them coming as they did from the testifier to the
tragedy, and promptly following Billy's impassioned disclaimer
of mutinous intent—Captain Vere's words, 'I believe you, my
man.'

Next, it was asked of him whether he knew of or suspected
aught savouring of incipient trouble (meaning mutiny, though
the explicit term was avoided) going on in any section of the ship's
company.

The reply lingered. This was naturally imputed by the court to
the same vocal embarrassment which had retarded or obstructed
previous answers. But in main it was otherwise here; the question
immediately recalling to Billy's mind the interview with the afterguardsman in the fore-chains. But an innate repugnance to playing
a part at all approaching that of an informer against one's own
shipmates—the same erring sense of uninstructed honour which
had stood in the way of his reporting the matter at the time, though
as a loyal man-of-war's man it was incumbent on him, and failure
so to do it charged against him and proven, would have subjected
him to the heaviest of penalties. This, with the blind feeling now his,
that nothing really was being hatched, prevailed with him. When
the answer came it was a negative.

'One question more,' said the officer of marines now first speaking, and with a troubled earnestnesss. 'You tell us that what the master-at-arms said against you was a lie. Now why should he have so lied, so maliciously lied, since you declare there was no malice between you?'

At that question, unintentionally touching on a spiritual sphere, wholly obscure to Billy's thoughts, he was nonplussed, evincing a confusion indeed that some observers, such as can be imagined, would have construed into involuntary evidence of hidden guilt. Nevertheless he strove some way to answer, but all at once relinquished the vain endeavour, at the same time turning an appealing glance towards Captain Vere, as deeming him his best helper and friend. Captain Vere, who had been seated for a time, rose to his feet, addressing the interrogator. 'The question you put to him comes naturally enough. But how can he rightly answer it, or anybody else? unless indeed it be he who lies within there,' designating the compartment where lay the corpse. 'But the prone one there will not rise to our summons. In effect though, as it seems to me, the point you make is hardly material. Quite aside from any conceivable motive actuating the master-at-arms, and irrespective of the provocation of the blow, a martial court must needs in the present case confine its attention to the blow's consequence, which consequence is to be deemed not otherwise than as the striker's deed!'

This utterance, the full significance of which it was not at all likely that Billy took in, nevertheless caused him to turn a wistful, interrogative look toward the speaker, a look in its dumb expressiveness not unlike that which a dog of generous breed might turn upon his master, seeking in his face some elucidation of a previous gesture ambiguous to the canine intelligence. Nor was the same utterance without marked effect upon the three officers, more especially the soldier. Couched in it seemed to them a meaning unanticipated, involving a prejudgment on the speaker's part. It served to augment a mental disturbance previously evident enough.

The soldier once more spoke, in a tone of suggestive dubiety addressing at once his associates and Captain Vere: 'Nobody is present—none of the ship's company, I mean, who might shed lateral light, if any is to be had, upon what remains mysterious in this matter.'

'That is thoughtfully put,' said Captain Vere; 'I see your drift. Ay, there is a mystery; but to use a Scriptural phrase, it is "a mystery of iniquity," a matter for psychological theologians to discuss. But what has a military court to do with it? Not to add that for us, any possible investigation of it is cut off by the lasting tongue-tie of—him—in yonder,' again designating the mortuary state-room. 'The prisoner's deed. With that alone we have to do.'

To this, and particularly the closing reiteration, the marine soldier, knowing not how aptly to reply, sadly abstained from saying aught. The first lieutenant, who at the outset had not unnaturally assumed primacy in the court, now over-rulingly instructed by a glance from Captain Vere, a glance more effective than words, resumed that primacy. Turning to the prisoner: 'Budd,' he said, and scarce in equable tones, 'Budd, if you have aught further to say for yourself, say it now.'

Upon this the young sailor turned another quick glance toward Captain Vere; then, as taking a hint from that aspect, a hint confirming his own instinct that silence was now best, replied to the lieutenant, 'I have said all, sir.'

The marine—the same who had been the sentinel without the cabin-door at the time that the foretopman, followed by the master-at-arms, entered it—he, standing by the sailor throughout their judicial proceedings, was now directed to take him back to the after-compartment originally assigned to the prisoner and his custodian. As the twain disappeared from view, the three officers, as partially liberated from some inward constraint associated with Billy's mere presence, simultaneously stirred in their seats. They exchanged looks of troubled indecision, yet feeling that decide they must and without long delay, for Captain Vere was for the time sitting unconsciously with his back toward them, apparently in one of his absent fits, gazing out from a sashed port-hole to windward upon the monotonous blank of the twilight sea. But the court's silence continuing, broken only at moments by brief consultations in low, earnest tones, this seemed to assure him and encourage him. Turning, he to and fro paced the cabin athwart; in the returning ascent to windward, climbing the slant deck in the ship's lee roll; without knowing it symbolising thus in his action a mind resolute to surmount difficulties even if against primitive instincts strong as the wind and the sea. Presently he came to a stand before the three. After scanning their faces he stood less as mustering his thoughts for expression, than as one only deliberating how best to put them to well-meaning men not intellectually mature, men with whom it was necessary to demonstrate certain principles that were axioms to himself. Similar impatience as to talking is perhaps one reason that deters some minds from addressing any popular assemblies; under which head is to be classed most legislatures in a democracy.

When speak he did, something both in the substance of what he said and his manner of saying it, showed the influence of unshared studies modifying and tempering the practical training of an active career. This, along with his phraseology now and then, was suggestive of the grounds whereon rested that imputation of a certain pedantry socially alleged against him by certain naval men of wholly practical cast, captains who nevertheless would frankly concede that His Majesty's Navy mustered no more efficient officers of their grade than *Starry Vere*.

What he said was to this effect: 'Hitherto I have been but the witness, little more; and I should hardly think now to take another tone, that of your coadjutor, for the time, did I not perceive in you—at the crisis too—a troubled hesitancy, proceeding, I doubt not, from the clashing of military duty with moral scruple—scruple vitalised by compassion. For the compassion, how can I otherwise but share it. But, mindful of paramount obligation, I strive against scruples that may tend to enervate decision. Not, gentlemen, that I hide from myself that the case is an exceptional one. Speculatively regarded, it well might be referred to a jury of casuists. But for us here, acting not as casuists or moralists, it is a case practical and under martial law practically to be dealt with.

'But your scruples! Do they move as in a dusk? Challenge them. Make them advance and declare themselves. Come now: do they impart something like this: If, mindless of palliating circumstances, we are bound to regard the death of the master-at-arms as the prisoner's deed, then does that deed constitute a capital crime whereof the penalty is a mortal one. But in natural justice is nothing but the prisoner's overt act to be considered? Now can we adjudge to summary and shameful death a fellow-creature innocent before God, and whom we feel to be so?—Does that state it aright? You sign sad assent. Well, I too feel that, the full force of that. It is Nature. But do these buttons that we wear attest that our allegiance is to Nature? No, to the King. Though the ocean, which is inviolate Nature primeval, though this be the element where we move and have our being as sailors, yet as the King's officers lies our duty in a sphere correspondingly natural? So little is that true, that in receiving our commissions we in the most important regards ceased to be natural free agents. When war is declared, are we the commissioned fighters previously consulted? We fight at command. If our judgments approve the war, that is but coincidence. So in other particulars. So now, would it be so much we ourselves that would condemn as it would be martial law operating through us? For that law and the rigour of it, we are not responsible. Our vowed responsibility is in this: That however pitilessly that law may operate, we nevertheless adhere to it and administer it.

'But the exceptional in the matter moves the heart within you. Even so, too, is mine moved. But let not warm hearts betray heads that should be cool. Ashore in a criminal case will an upright judge allow himself off the bench to be waylaid by some tender kinswoman of the accused seeking to touch him with her tearful plea? Well, the heart here is as that piteous woman. The heart is the feminine in man, and hard though it be, she must here be ruled out.'

He paused, earnestly studying them for a moment; then resumed.

'But something in your aspect seems to urge that it is not solely that heart that moves in you, but also the conscience, the private conscience. But tell me whether or not, occupying the position we do, private conscience should not yield to that imperial one formulated in the code under which alone we officially proceed?'

Here the three men moved in their seats, less convinced than agitated by the course of an argument troubling but the more the spontaneous conflict within. Perceiving which, the speaker paused for a moment; then abruptly changing his tone, went on.

'To steady us a bit, let us recur to the facts. In wartime at sea a man-of-war's man strikes his superior in grade, and the blow kills. Apart from its effect, the blow itself is, according to the Articles of War, a capital crime. Furthermore——'

'Ay, sir,' emotionally broke in the officer of marines, 'in one sense it was. But surely Budd purposed neither mutiny nor homicide.'

'Surely not, my good man. And before a court less arbitrary and more merciful than a martial one that plea would largely extenuate. At the Last Assizes it shall acquit. But how here? We proceed under the law of the Mutiny Act. In feature no child can resemble his father more than that Act resembles in spirit the thing from which it derives—War. In His Majesty's service—in this ship indeed—there are Englishmen forced to fight for the King against their will. Against their conscience, for aught we know. Though as their fellow-creatures some of us may appreciate their position, yet as Navy officers, what reck we of it? Still less recks the enemy. Our impressed men he would fain cut down in the same swath with our volunteers. As regards the enemy's naval conscripts, some of whom may even share our own abhorrence of the regicidal French Directory, it is the same on our side. War looks but to the frontage, the appearance. And the Mutiny Act, War's child, takes after the father. Budd's intent or non-intent is nothing to the purpose.

'But while, put to it by those anxieties in you which I cannot but respect, I only repeat myself—while thus strangely we prolong proceedings that should be summary, the enemy may be sighted and an engagement result. We must do; and one of two things must we do—condemn or let go.'

'Can we not convict and yet mitigate the penalty?' asked the junior lieutenant, here speaking, and falteringly, for the first.

'Lieutenant, were that clearly lawful for us under the circumstances, consider the consequences of such clemency. The people' (meaning the ship's company) 'have native sense; most of them are familiar with our naval usage and tradition; and how would they take it? Even could you explain to them—which our official position forbids—they, long moulded by arbitrary discipline, have not that kind of intelligence responsiveness that might qualify them to comprehend and discriminate. No, to the people the foretopman's deed, however it be worded in the announcement, will be plain homicide committed in a flagrant act of mutiny. What penalty for that should follow, they know. But it does not follow. *Why?* they will ruminate. You know what sailors are. Will they not revert to the recent outbreak at the Nore? Ay, they know the well-founded alarm—the panic it struck throughout England. Your clement sentence they would account pusillanimous. They would think that we flinch, that we are afraid of them—afraid of practising a lawful rigour singularly demanded at this juncture lest it should provoke new troubles. What shame to us such a conjecture on their part, and how deadly to discipline. You see then whither, prompted by duty and the law, I steadfastly drive. But I beseech you my friends, do not take me amiss. I feel as you do for this unfortunate boy. But did he know our hearts, I take him to be of that generous nature that he would feel even for us on whom in this military necessity so heavy a compulsion is laid.'

With that, crossing the deck, he resumed his place by the sashed port-hole, tacitly leaving the three to come to a decision. On the cabin's opposite side the troubled court sat silent. Loyal lieges, plain and practical, though at bottom they dissented from some points Captain Vere had put to them, they were without the faculty, hardly had the inclination to gainsay one whom they felt to be an earnest man, one, too, not less their superior in mind than in naval rank. But it is not improbable that even such of his words as were not without influence over them, came home to them less than his closing appeal to their instinct as sea-officers. He forecasted the practical consequences to discipline (considering the unconfirmed tone of the fleet at the time), if violent killing at sea by a man-of-war's man of a superior in grade were allowed to pass for aught else than a capital crime, and one demanding prompt infliction of the penalty.

Not unlikely they were brought to something more or less akin to that harassed frame of mind which in the year 1842 actuated the commander of the U.S. brig-of-war *Somers* to resolve, under the so-called Articles of War, Articles modelled upon the English Mutiny Act, to resolve upon the execution at sea of a midshipman and two petty officers as mutineers designing the seizure of the brig. Which resolution was carried out though in a time of peace and within not many days' sail of home. An act vindicated by a naval court of inquiry subsequently convened ashore. History, and here cited without comment. True, the circumstances on board the *Somers* were different from those on board the *Indomitable*. But the urgency felt, very well warranted or otherwise, was much the same.

Says a writer whom few know, 'Forty years after a battle it is easy for a non-combatant to reason about how it ought to have been fought. It is another thing personally and under fire to direct the fighting while involved in the obscuring smoke of it. Much so with respect to other emergencies involving considerations both practical and moral, and when it is imperative promptly to act. The greater the fog the more it imperils the steamer, and speed is put on though at the hazard of running somebody down. Little ween the snug card-players in the cabin of the responsibilities of the sleepless man on the bridge.'

In brief, Billy Budd was formally convicted and sentenced to be hung at the yard-arm in the early morning-watch, it being now night. Otherwise, as is customary in such cases, the sentence would forthwith have been carried out. In war-time on the field or in the fleet, a mortal punishment decreed by a drum-head court—on the field sometimes decreed by but a nod from the general—follows without delay on the heel of conviction without appeal.

XIX

IT was Captain Vere himself who of his own motion communicated the finding of the court to the prisoner; for that purpose going to the compartment where he was in custody, and bidding the marine there to withdraw for the time.

Beyond the communication of the sentence what took place at this interview was never known. But, in view of the character of the twain briefly closeted in that state-room, each radically sharing in the rarer qualities of one nature—so rare, indeed, as to be all but incredible to average minds, however much cultivated—some conjectures may be ventured.

It would have been in consonance with the spirit of Captain Vere should he on this occasion have concealed nothing from the condemned one; should he indeed have frankly disclosed to him the part he himself had played in bringing about the decision, at the same time revealing his actuating motives. On Billy's side it is not improbable that such a confession would have been received in much the same spirit that prompted it. Not without a sort of joy indeed he might have appreciated the brave opinion of him implied in his captain making such a confidant of him. Nor as to the sentence itself could he have been insensible that it was imparted to him as to one not afraid to die. Even more may have been. Captain Vere in the end may have developed the passion sometimes latent under an exterior stoical or indifferent. He was old enough to have been Billy's father. The austere devotee of military duty, letting himself melt back into what remains primeval in our formalised humanity, may in the end have caught Billy to his heart, even as Abraham may have caught young Isaac on the brink of resolutely offering him up in obedience to the exacting behest. But there is no telling the sacrament—seldom if in any case revealed to the gadding world wherever under circumstances at all akin to those here attempted to be set forth—two of great Nature's nobler order embrace. There is privacy at the time, inviolable to the survivor, and holy oblivion, the sequel to each diviner magnanimity, providentially covers all at last.

The first to encounter Captain Vere in the act of leaving the compartment was the senior lieutenant. The face he beheld, for the moment one expressive of the agony of the strong, was to that officer, though a man of fifty, a startling revelation. That the condemned one suffered less than he who mainly had effected the condemnation, was apparently indicated by the former's exclamation in the scene soon perforce to be touched upon.

Of a series of incidents within a brief term rapidly following each other, the adequate narration may take up a term less brief, especially if explanation or comment here and there seem requisite to the better understanding of such incidents. Between the entrance into the cabin of him who never left it alive, and him who when he did leave it left it as one condemned to die; between this and the closeted interview just given, less than an hour and a half had elapsed. It was an interval long enough, however, to awaken speculations among no few of the ship's company as to what it was that could be detaining in the cabin the master-at-arms and the sailor, for it was rumoured that both of them had been seen to enter it, and neither of them had been seen to emerge. This rumour had got abroad upon the gun-decks and in the tops; the people of a great warship being in one respect like villagers, taking microscopic note of every untoward movement or non-movement going on. When therefore in weather not at all tempestuous all hands were called in the second dog-watch, a summons under such circumstances not usual in those hours, the crew were not wholly unprepared for some announcement extraordinary, one having connection, too, with the continued absence of the two men from their wonted haunts.

There was a moderate sea at the time; and the moon newly risen, and near to being at its full, silvered the white spar-deck wherever not blotted by the clear-cut shadows horizontally thrown of fixtures and moving men. On either side the quarter-deck the marine guard under arms was drawn up; and Captain

Vere, standing in his place surrounded by all the ward-room officers, addressed his men. In so doing his manner showed neither more nor less than that properly pertaining to his supreme position aboard his own ship. In clear terms and concise he told them what had taken place in the cabin; that the master-at-arms was dead; that he who had killed him had been already tried by a summary court and condemned to death; and that the execution would take place in the early morning watch. The word *mutiny* was not named in what he said. He refrained, too, from making the occasion an opportunity for any preachment as to the maintenance of discipline, thinking, perhaps, that under existing circumstances in the Navy the consequence of violating discipline should be made to speak for itself.

Their captain's announcement was listened to by the throng of standing sailors in a dumbness like that of a seated congregation of believers in Hell listening to their clergyman's announcement of his Calvinistic text.

At the close, however, a confused murmur went up. It began to wax all but instantly, then at a sign, was pierced and suppressed by shrill whistles of the boatswain and his mates piping, 'Down one watch.'

To be prepared for burial Claggart's body was delivered to certain petty officers of his mess. And here, not to clog the sequel with lateral matters, it may be added that at a suitable hour, the master-at-arms was committed to the sea with every funeral honour properly belonging to his naval grade.

In this proceeding, as in every public one growing out of the tragedy, strict adherence to usage was observed. Nor in any point could it have been at all deviated from, either with respect to Claggart or Billy Budd, without begetting undesirable speculations in the ship's company, sailors, and more particularly man-of-war's men, being of all men the greatest sticklers for usage.

For similar cause all communication between Captain Vere and the condemned one ended with the closeted interview already given, the latter being now surrendered to the ordinary routine preliminary to the end. This transfer under guard from the captain's quarters was effected without unusual precautions—at least no visible ones.

If possible, not to let the men so much as surmise that their

officers anticipate aught amiss from them, is the tacit rule in a
military ship. And the more that some sort of trouble should really
be apprehended, the more do the officers keep that apprehension
to themselves; though not the less unostentatious vigilance may be
augmented.

   In the present instance the sentry placed over the prisoner had
strict orders to let no one have communication with him but the
chaplain. And certain unobtrusive measures were taken absolutely
to ensure this point.

XX

IN a seventy-four of the old order the deck known as the upper
gun-deck was the one covered over by the spar-deck, which last,
though not without its armament, was for the most part exposed
to the weather. In general it was at all hours free from hammocks;
those of the crew swinging on the lower gun-deck and berth-deck,
the latter being not only a dormitory but also the place for the
stowing of the sailors' bags, and on both sides lined with the large
chests or movable pantries of the many messes of the men.

   On the starboard side of the *Indomitable's* upper gun-deck,
behold Billy Budd under sentry lying prone in irons in one of
the bays formed by the regular spacing of the guns comprising
the batteries on either side. All these pieces were of the heavier
calibre of that period. Mounted on lumbering wooden carriages,
they were hampered with cumbersome harness of breeching and
strong side-tackles for running them out. Guns and carriages,
together with the long rammers and shorter lintstocks lodged in
loops overhead—all these, as customary, were painted black; and
the heavy hempen breechings tarred to the same tint, wore the like
livery of the undertaker. In contrast with the funereal tone of these
surroundings the prone sailor's exterior apparel, white *jumper* and
white duck trowsers, each more or less soiled, dimly glimmered
in the obscure light of the bay like a patch of discoloured snow
in early April lingering at some upland cave's black mouth. In
effect he is already in his shroud or the garments that shall serve
him in lieu of one. Over him, but scarce illuminating him, two
battle-lanterns swing from two massive beams of the deck above.
Fed with the oil supplied by the war-contractors (whose gains,

honest or otherwise, are in every land an anticipated portion of the harvest of death) with flickering splashes of dirty yellow light they pollute the pale moonshine all but ineffectually struggling in obstructed flecks through the open ports from which the tompioned cannon protrude. Other lanterns at intervals serve but to bring out somewhat the obscurer bays which, like small confessionals or side-chapels in a cathedral, branch from the long, dim-vistaed, broad aisle, between the two batteries of that covered tier.

Such was the deck where now lay the Handsome Sailor. Through the rose-tan of his complexion, no pallor could have shown. It would have taken days of sequestration from the winds and the sun to have brought about the effacement of that. But the skeleton in the cheek-bone at the point of its angle was just beginning delicately to be defined under the warm-tinted skin. In fervid hearts self-contained some brief experiences devour our human tissue as secret fire in a ship's hold consumes cotton in the bale.

But now, lying between the two guns, as nipped in the vice of fate, Billy's agony, mainly proceeding from a generous young heart's virgin experience of the diabolical incarnate and effective in some men—the tension of that agony was over now. It survived not the something healing in the closeted interview with Captain Vere. Without movement he lay as in a trance, that adolescent expression, previously noted as his, taking on something akin to the look of a slumbering child in the cradle when the warm hearth-glow of the still chamber of night plays on the dimples that at whiles mysteriously form in the cheek, silently coming and going there. For now and then in the gyved one's trance, a serene happy light born of some wandering reminiscence or dream would diffuse itself over his face, and then wane away only anew to return.

The chaplain coming to see him and finding him thus, and perceiving no sign that he was conscious of his presence, attentively regarded him for a space, then slipping aside, withdrew for the time, peradventure feeling that even he, the minister of Christ, though receiving his stipend from wars, had no consolation to proffer which could result in a peace transcending that which he beheld. But in the small hours he came again. And the prisoner, now awake to his surroundings, noticed his approach, and civilly, all but cheerfully, welcomed him. But it was to little purpose that in the interview following the good man sought to bring Billy Budd to some Godly understanding that he must die, and at dawn. True, Billy himself freely referred to his death as a thing close at hand; but it was something in the way that children will refer to death in general, who yet among their other sports will play a funeral with hearse and mourners. Not that like children Billy was incapable of conceiving what death really is. No, but he was wholly without irrational fear of it, a fear more prevalent in highly civilised communities than those so-called barbarous ones which in all respects stand nearer to unadulterate Nature. And, as elsewhere said, a barbarian Billy radically was; quite as much so (for all the costume) as his countrymen the British captives, living trophies made to march in the Roman triumph of Germanicus. Quite as much so as those later barbarians, young men probably, and picked specimens among the earlier British converts to Christianity, at least nominally such, and taken to Rome (as to-day converts from lesser isles of the sea may be taken to London), of whom the Pope of that time, admiring the strangeness of their personal beauty, so unlike the Italian stamp, their clear, ruddy complexions and curled flaxen locks, exclaimed, 'Angles' (meaning *English*, the modern derivative), 'Angles do you call them? And is it because they look so like Angels?' Had it been later in time one would think that the Pope had in mind Fra Angelico's seraphs, some of whom, plucking apples in gardens of Hesperides, have the faint rosebud complexion of the more beautiful English girls.

XXI

IF in vain the good chaplain sought to impress the young barbarian with ideas of death akin to those conveyed in the skull, dial, and cross-bones on old tombstones; equally futile to all appearance were his efforts to bring home to him the thought of salvation and a Saviour. Billy listened, but less out of awe or reverence, perhaps, than from a certain natural politeness; doubtless at bottom regarding all that in much the same way that most mariners of his class take any discourse, abstract or out of the common tone of the workaday world. And this sailor way of taking clerical discourse is not wholly unlike the way in which the pioneer of Christianity, full of transcendent miracles, was received long ago on tropic isles by any superior *savage* so called—a Tahitian, say, of Captain Cook's time or shortly after that time. Out of natural courtesy he received but did not appreciate. It was like a gift placed in the palm of an outstretched hand upon which the fingers do not close.

But the *Indomitable's* chaplain was a discreet man possessing the good sense of a good heart. So he insisted not on his vocation here. At the instance of Captain Vere, a lieutenant had apprised him of pretty much everything as to Billy; and since he felt that innocence was even a better thing than religion wherewith to go to judgment, he reluctantly withdrew; but in his emotion not without first performing an act strange enough in an Englishman, and under the circumstances yet more so in any regular priest. Stooping over, he kissed on the fair cheek his fellow-man, a felon in martial law, one who, though in the confines of death, he felt he could never convert to a dogma; nor for all that did he fear for his future.

Marvel not that having been made acquainted with the young sailor's essential innocence, the worthy man lifted not a finger to avert the doom of such a martyr to martial discipline. So to do would not only have been as idle as invoking the desert, but would also have been an audacious transgression of the bounds of his function, one as exactly prescribed to him by military law as that of the boatswain or any other naval officer. Bluntly put, a chaplain is the minister of the Prince of Peace serving in the host of the God of War—Mars. As such, he is as incongruous as a musket would be on the altar at Christmas. Why, then, is he there? Because he indirectly subserves the purpose attested by the cannon; because, too, he lends the sanction of the religion of the meek to that which practically is the abrogation of everything but force.

THE night so luminous on the spar-deck (otherwise on the cavernous ones below—levels so like the tiered galleries in a coal-mine) passed away. Like the prophet in the chariot disappearing in heaven and dropping his mantle to Elisha, the withdrawing night transferred its pale robe to the peeping day. A meek, shy light appeared in the east, where stretched a diaphanous fleece of white furrowed vapour. That light slowly waxed. Suddenly *one bells* was struck aft, responded to by one louder metallic stroke from forward. It was four o'clock in the morning. Instantly the silver whistles were heard summoning all hands to witness punishment. Up through the great hatchway, rimmed with racks of heavy shot, the watch-below came pouring, overspreading with the watch already on deck the space between the mainmast and foremast, including that occupied by the capacious launch and the black booms tiered on either side of it, boat and booms making a summit of observation for the powder-boys and younger tars. A different group comprising one watch of topmen leaned over the side of the rail of that sea-balcony, no small one in a seventy-four, looking down on the crowd below. Man or boy, none spake but in whispers, and few spake at all. Captain Vere—as before, the central figure among the assembled commissioned officers—stood nigh the break of the poop-deck, facing forward. Just below him on the quarter-deck the marines in full equipment were drawn up much as at the scene of the promulgated sentence.

At sea in the old time, the execution by halter of a military sailor was generally from the fore-yard. In the present instance, for special reasons, the main-yard was assigned. Under an arm of that yard the prisoner was presently brought up, the chaplain attending him. It was noted at the time, and remarked upon afterwards, that in this final scene the good man evinced little or nothing of the perfunctory. Brief speech indeed he had with the condemned one, but the genuine Gospel was less on his tongue than in his aspect and manner toward him. The final preparations personal to the latter being speedily brought to an end by two boatswain's-mates, the consummation impended. Billy stood facing aft. At the penultimate moment, his words, his only ones, words wholly unobstructed in the utterance, were these—'God bless Captain Vere!' Syllables so unanticipated coming from one with the ignominious hemp about his neck—a conventional felon's benediction directed aft toward the quarters of honour; syllables, too, delivered in the clear melody of a singing-bird on the point of launching from the twig, had a phenomenal effect, not unenhanced by the rare personal beauty of the young sailor, spiritualised now through late experiences so poignantly profound.

Without volition, as it were, as if indeed the ship's populace were the vehicles of some vocal current-electric, with one voice, from alow and aloft, came a resonant echo—'God bless Captain Vere!' And yet at that instant Billy alone must have been in their hearts, even as he was in their eyes.

At the pronounced words and the spontaneous echo that voluminously rebounded them, Captain Vere, either through stoic self-control or a sort of momentary paralysis induced by emotional shock, stood erectly rigid as a musket in the ship-armourer's rack.

The hull, deliberately recovering from the periodic roll to leeward, was just regaining an even keel, when the last signal, the preconcerted dumb one, was given. At the same moment it chanced that the vapoury fleece hanging low in the east, was shot through with a soft glory as of the fleece of the Lamb of God seen in mystical vision, and simultaneously therewith, watched by the wedged mass of upturned faces, Billy ascended; and ascending, took the full rose of the dawn.

In the pinioned figure, arrived at the yard-end, to the wonder of all, no motion was apparent save that created by the slow roll of the hull, in moderate weather so majestic in a great ship heavy-cannoned.

A DIGRESSION

When some days afterwards in reference to the singularity just mentioned, the purser, a rather ruddy, rotund person, more accurate as an accountant than profound as a philosopher, said at mess to the surgeon, 'What testimony to the force lodged in will-power,' the latter, spare and tall, one in whom a discreet causticity went along with a manner less genial than polite, replied, 'Your pardon, Mr. Purser. In a hanging scientifically conducted—and under special orders I myself directed how Budd's was to be effected—any movement following the completed suspension and

originating in the body suspended, such movement indicates
mechanical spasm in the muscular system. Hence the absence
of that is no more attributable to will-power, as you call it, than
to horse-power—begging your pardon.'

'But this muscular spasm you speak of, is not that in a degree
more or less invariable in these cases?'

'Assuredly so, Mr. Purser.'

'How then, my good sir, do you account for its absence in this
instance?'

'Mr. Purser, it is clear that your sense of singularity in this
matter equals not mine. You account for it by what you call will-
power, a term not yet included in the lexicon of science. For me
I do not with my present knowledge pretend to account for it
at all. Even should one assume the hypothesis that at the first
touch of the halyards the action of Budd's heart, intensified by
extraordinary emotion at its climax, abruptly stopped—much like
a watch when in carelessly winding it up you strain at the finish,
thus snapping the chain—even under that hypothesis how account
for the phenomenon that followed?'

'You admit, then, that the absence of spasmodic movement was
phenomenal?'

'It was phenomenal, Mr. Purser, in the sense that it was an
appearance, the cause of which is not immediately to be assigned.'

'But tell me, my dear sir,' pertinaciously continued the other,
'was the man's death effected by the halter, or was it a species of
euthanasia?'

'*Euthanasia*, Mr. Purser, is something like your will-power; I
doubt its authenticity as a scientific term—begging your pardon
again. It is at once imaginative and metaphysical—in short,
Greek. But,' abruptly changing his tone, 'there is a case in the sick-
bay that I do not care to leave to my assistants. Beg your pardon,
but excuse me.' And rising from the mess he formally withdrew.

XXIII

THE silence at the moment of execution, and for a moment or
two continuing thereafter, but emphasised by the regular wash
of the sea against the hull, or the flutter of a sail caused by the
helmsman's eyes being tempted astray, this emphasised silence

was gradually disturbed by a sound not easily to be verbally rendered. Whoever has heard the freshet-wave of a torrent suddenly swelled by pouring showers in tropical mountains, showers not shared by the plain; whoever has heard the first muffled murmur of its sloping advance through precipitous woods, may form some conception of the sound now heard. The seeming remoteness of its source was because of its murmurous indistinctness, since it came from close by, even from the men massed on the ship's open deck. Being inarticulate, it was dubious in significance further than it seemed to indicate some capricious revulsion of thought or feeling such as mobs ashore are liable to, in the present instance possibly implying a sullen revocation on the men's part of their involuntary echoing of Billy's benediction. But ere the murmur had time to wax into clamour it was met by a strategic command, the more telling that it came with abrupt unexpectedness.

'Pipe down the starboard watch, boatswain, and see that they go.'

Shrill as the shriek of the sea-hawk the whistles of the boatswain and his mates pierced that ominous low sound, dissipating it; and yielding to the mechanism of discipline the throng was thinned by one half. For the remainder, most of them were set to temporary employments connected with trimming the yards and so forth, business readily to be found upon occasion by any officer-of-the-deck.

Now each proceeding that follows a mortal sentence pronounced at sea by a drum-head court is characterised by promptitude not perceptibly merging into hurry, though bordering that. The hammock, the one which had been Billy's bed when alive, having already been ballasted with shot, and otherwise prepared to serve for his canvas coffin, the last office of the sea-undertakers, the sail-maker's mates, was now speedily completed. When everything was in readiness a second call for all hands, made necessary by the strategic movement before mentioned, was sounded, and now to witness burial.

The details of this closing formality it needs not to give. But when the tilted plank let slide its freight into the sea, a second strange human murmur was heard, blended now with another inarticulate sound proceeding from a certain larger sea-fowl, who, their attention having been attracted by the peculiar commotion in the water resulting from the heavy sloped dive of the shotted hammock into the sea, flew screaming to the spot. So near the hull did they come, that the stridor or bony creak of their gaunt double-jointed pinions was audible. As the ship under light airs passed on, leaving the burial spot astern, they still kept circling it low down with the moving shadow of their outstretched wings and the croaked requiem of their cries.

Upon sailors as superstitious as those of the age preceding ours, man-of-war's men, too, who had just beheld the prodigy of repose in the form suspended in air and now foundering in the deeps; to such mariners the action of the sea-fowl, though dictated by mere animal greed for prey, was big with no prosaic significance. An uncertain movement began among them, in which some encroachment was made. It was tolerated but for a moment. For suddenly the drum beat to quarters, which familiar sound happening at least twice every day, had upon the present occasion a signal peremptoriness in it. True martial discipline long continued superinduces in average man a sort of impulse of docility whose operation at the official tone of command much resembles in its promptitude the effect of an instinct.

The drum-beat dissolved the multitude, distributing most of them along the batteries of the two covered gun-decks. There, as wont, the gun crews stood by their respective cannon erect and silent. In due course the first officer, sword under arm and standing in his place on the quarter-deck, formally received the successive reports of the sworded lieutenants commanding the sections of batteries below; the last of which reports being made, the summed report he delivered with the customary salute to the commander. All this occupied time, which in the present case was the object of beating to quarters at an hour prior to the customary one. That such variance from usage was authorised by an officer like Captain Vere, a martinet as some deemed him, was evidence of the necessity for unusual action implied in what he deemed to be temporarily the mood of his men. 'With mankind,' he would say, 'forms, measured forms, are everything; and that is the import couched in the story of Orpheus with his lyre spell-binding the wild denizens of the woods.' And this he once applied to the disruption of forms going on across the Channel and the consequences thereof.

At this unwonted muster at quarters all proceeded as at the

regular hour. The band on the quarter-deck played a sacred air. After which the chaplain went through the customary morning service. That done, the drum beat the retreat, and toned by music and religious rites subserving the discipline and purpose of war, the men in their wonted orderly manner dispersed to the places allotted them when not at the guns.

And now it was full day. The fleece of low-hanging vapour had vanished, licked up by the sun that late had so glorified it. And the circumambient air in the clearness of its serenity was like smooth white marble in the polished block not yet removed from the marble-dealer's yard.

XXIV

THE symmetry of form attainable in pure fiction cannot so readily be achieved in a narration essentially having less to do with fable than with fact. Truth uncompromisingly told will always have its ragged edges; hence the conclusion of such a narration is apt to be less finished than an architectural finial.

How it fared with the Handsome Sailor during the year of the Great Mutiny has been faithfully given. But though properly the story ends with his life, something in way of sequel will not be amiss. Three brief chapters will suffice.

In the general re-christening under the Directory of the craft originally forming the navy of the French Monarchy, the *St. Louis* line-of-battle ship was named the *Athéiste*. Such a name, like some other substituted ones in the Revolutionary fleet, while proclaiming the infidel audacity of the ruling power, was yet, though not so intended to be, the aptest name, if one consider it, ever given to a warship; far more so indeed than the *Devastation*, the *Erebus* (the Hell), and similar names bestowed upon fighting-ships.

On the return passage to the English fleet from the detached cruise during which occurred the events already recorded, the *Indomitable* fell in with the *Athéiste*. An engagement ensued, during which Captain Vere, in the act of putting his ship alongside the enemy with a view of throwing his boarders across the bulwarks, was hit by a musket-ball from a port-hole of the enemy's main cabin. More than disabled, he dropped to the deck and was carried below to the same cock-pit where some of his men already lay. The senior lieutenant took command. Under him the enemy was finally captured, and though much crippled, was by rare good fortune successfully taken into Gibraltar, an English port not very distant from the scene of the fight. There Captain Vere with the rest of the wounded was put ashore. He lingered for some days, but the end came. Unhappily he was cut off too early for the Nile and Trafalgar. The spirit that 'spite its philosophic austerity may yet have indulged in the most secret of all passions, ambition, never attained to the fulness of fame.

Not long before death, while lying under the influence of that magical drug which, soothing the physical frame, mysteriously operates on the subtler element in man, he was heard to murmur words inexplicable to his attendant—'Billy Budd, Billy Budd.' That these were not the accents of remorse, would seem clear from what the attendant said to the *Indomitable's* senior officer of marines, who, as the most reluctant to condemn of the members of the drum-head court, too well knew, though here he kept the knowledge to himself, who Billy Budd was.

XXV

SOME few weeks after the execution, among other matters under the head of *News from the Mediterranean*, there appeared in a naval chronicle of the time, an authorised weekly publication, an account of the affair. It was doubtless for the most part written in good faith, though the medium, partly rumour, through which the facts must have reached the writer, served to deflect, and in part falsify them. Because it appeared in a publication now long ago superannuated and forgotten, and is all that hitherto has stood on human record to attest what manner of men respectively were John Claggart and Billy Budd, it is here reproduced.

On the tenth of the last month a deplorable occurrence took place on board H.M.S. *Indomitable*. John Claggart, the ship's master-at-arms, discovering that some sort of plot was incipient among an inferior section of the ship's company, and that the ringleader was one William Budd, he, Claggart, in the act of arraigning the man before the Captain was vindictively stabbed to the heart by the suddenly drawn sheath-knife of Budd.

The deed and the implement employed sufficiently suggest that though mustered into the service under an English name the assassin was no

Englishman, but one of those aliens adopting an English cognomen whom the present extraordinary necessities of the Service have caused to be admitted into it in considerable numbers.

The enormity of the crime and the extreme depravity of the criminal, appear the greater in view of the character of the victim, a middle-aged man, respectable and discreet, belonging to that minor official grade, the petty officers, upon whom, as none know better than the commissioned gentlemen, the efficiency of His Majesty's Navy so largely depends. His function was a responsible one; at once onerous and thankless, and his fidelity in it the greater because of his strong patriotic impulse. In this instance, as in so many other instances in these days, the character of the unfortunate man signally refutes, if refutation were needed, that peevish saying attributed to Dr. Johnson, that patriotism is the last refuge of a scoundrel.

The criminal paid the penalty of his crime. The promptitude of the punishment has proved salutary. Nothing amiss is now apprehended aboard H.M.S. *Indomitable*.

XXVI

EVERYTHING is for a season remarkable in navies. Any tangible object associated with some striking incident of the service, is converted into a monument. The spar from which the foretopman was suspended, was for some few years kept trace of by the blue-jackets. Then knowledge followed it from ship to dockyard and again from dockyard to ship, still pursuing it even when at last reduced to a mere dockyard boom. To them a chip of it was as a piece of the Cross. Ignorant though they were of the real facts of the happening, and not thinking but that the penalty was unavoidably inflicted from the naval point of view, for all that they instinctively felt that Billy was a sort of man as incapable of mutiny as of wilful murder. They recalled the fresh young image of the Handsome Sailor, that face never deformed by a sneer or subtler vile freak of the heart within! This impression of him was doubtless deepened by the fact that he was gone, and in a measure mysteriously gone. On the gun-decks of the *Indomitable* the general estimate of his nature and its unconscious simplicity eventually found rude utterance from another foretopman, one of his own watch, gifted as some sailors are, with an artless poetic temperament. The tarry hands made some lines, which, after circulating among the shipboard crew for a while, finally got rudely printed at Portsmouth as a ballad. The title given to it was the sailor's.

BILLY IN THE DARBIES

Good of the Chaplain to enter Lone Bay
And down on his marrow-bones here and pray
For the likes just o' me, Billy Budd.—But look:
Through the port comes the moon-shine astray!
It tips the guard's cutlass and silvers this nook;
But 'twill die in the dawning of Billy's last day,
A jewel-block they'll make of me to-morrow,
Pendant pearl from the yard-arm-end
Like the ear-drop I gave to Bristol-Molly—
Oh, 'tis me, not the sentence, they'll suspend.
Ay, ay, all is up; and I must up too
Early in the morning, aloft from alow.
On an empty stomach, now, never it would do.
They'll give me a nibble—bit o' biscuit ere I go.
Sure, a messmate will reach me the last parting cup;
But turning heads away from the hoist and the belay,
Heaven knows who will have the running of me up!
No pipe to those halyards—But aren't it all sham?
A blur's in my eyes; it is dreaming that I am.
A hatchet to my panzer? all adrift to go?
The drum roll to grog, and Billy never know?
But Donald he has promised to stand by the plank;
So I'll shake a friendly hand ere I sink.
But—no! It is dead then I'll be, come to think.
I remember Taff the Welshman when he sank.
And his cheek it was like the budding pink.
But me, they'll lash me in hammock, drop me deep
Fathoms down, fathoms down, how I'll dream fast asleep.
I feel it stealing now. Sentry, are you there?
Just ease these darbies at the wrist,
And roll me over fair.
I am sleepy and the oozy weeds about me twist.

END OF BOOK,
April 19, 1891.

Stephen Crane

THE RED BADGE OF COURAGE
An Episode of the American Civil War

1895

STEPHEN CRANE (1871–1900) spent most of his brief life struggling with adversity of one kind and another, but as a native of the settled, eastern region of the United States, one thing that never fell to his lot during his formative years was to hear a shot fired in anger. This celebrated writer about war had never been near any actual fighting (apart, as he said, from the football pitch) when he sat down to write *The Red Badge of Courage,* for which he absorbed much of the psychological insight from Tolstoy's *War and Peace* and from a book called *Battles and Leaders of the Civil War.* He had already brought out at his own expense, with borrowed money, *Maggie: A Girl of the Streets*—too sombre to find readers or purchasers to any useful extent until after the success of *The Red Badge of Courage* in 1895. The prestige brought to Crane by this masterpiece was sufficient to ensure the publication of a torrent of work in verse and prose; haunted by the approach of death from tuberculosis, he wrote book after book, as well as working as a war correspondent for the *Herald* and the *Tribune* (separate papers in those days). Before the outbreak of the Spanish–American War in 1898, there was an unofficial ('filibustering') military expedition there in 1896, and Crane was sent to cover this, but the ship was wrecked and it took him two days to be rescued, an experience he used in his story 'The Open Boat', described in its subtitle as 'A Tale Intended to be After the Fact' (1898).

Crane died in Germany, where he had gone in search of a cure. It is pleasant for English readers to know that he twice elected to spend periods in England, though sad to reflect that the second and longer of them, in 1899, resulted from the fact that in New York his personal character had become the target of ill-natured and slanderous gossip.

I

THE cold passed reluctantly from the earth, and the retiring fogs revealed an army stretched out on the hills, resting. As the landscape changed from brown to green, the army awakened, and began to tremble with eagerness at the noise of rumours. It cast its eyes upon the roads, which were growing from long troughs of liquid mud to proper thoroughfares. A river, amber-tinted in the shadow of its banks, purled at the army's feet; and at night, when the stream had become of a sorrowful blackness, one could see across it the red, eyelike gleam of hostile camp-fires set in the low brows of distant hills.

Once a certain tall soldier developed virtues and went resolutely to wash a shirt. He came flying back from a brook waving his garment bannerlike. He was swelled with a tale he had heard from a reliable friend, who had heard it from a truthful cavalryman, who had heard it from his trustworthy brother, one of the orderlies at division headquarters. He adopted the important air of a herald in red and gold.

'We're goin' t' move t'-morrah—sure,' he said pompously to a group in the company street.

'We're goin' 'way up the river, cut across, an' come around in behint 'em.'

To his attentive audience he drew a loud and elaborate plan of a very brilliant campaign. When he had finished, the blue-clothed men scattered into small arguing groups between the rows of squat brown huts. A negro teamster who had been dancing upon a cracker box with the hilarious encouragement of two score soldiers was deserted. He sat mournfully down. Smoke drifted lazily from a multitude of quaint chimneys.

'It's a lie! that's all it is—a thunderin' lie!' said another private loudly. His smooth face was flushed, and his hands were thrust sulkily into his trousers' pockets. He took the matter as an affront to him. 'I don't believe the derned old army's ever going to move. We're set. I've got ready to move eight times in the last two weeks, and we ain't moved yet.'

The tall soldier felt called upon to defend the truth of a rumour he himself had introduced. He and the loud one came near to fighting over it.

A corporal began to swear before the assemblage. He had just put a costly board floor in his house, he said. During the early spring he had refrained from adding extensively to the comfort of his environment because he had felt that the army might start on the march at any moment. Of late, however, he had been impressed that they were in a sort of eternal camp.

Many of the men engaged in a spirited debate. One outlined in a peculiarly lucid manner all the plans of the commanding general. He was opposed by men who advocated that there were other plans of campaign. They clamoured at each other, numbers making futile bids for the popular attention. Meanwhile, the soldier who had fetched the rumour bustled about with much importance. He was continually assailed by questions.

'What's up, Jim?'

'Th' army's goin' t' move.'

'Ah, what yeh talkin' about? How yeh know it is?'

'Well, yeh kin b'lieve me er not, jest as yeh like. I don't care a hang.'

There was much food for thought in the manner in which he replied. He came near to convincing them by disdaining to produce proofs. They grew much excited over it.

There was a youthful private who listened with eager ears to the words of the tall soldier and to the varied comments of his comrades. After receiving a fill of discussions concerning marches and attacks, he went to his hut and crawled through an intricate hole that served it as a door. He wished to be alone with some new thoughts that had lately come to him.

He lay down on a wide bunk that stretched across the end of the room. In the other end cracker boxes were made to serve as furniture. They were grouped about the fireplace. A picture from an illustrated weekly was upon the log walls, and three rifles were paralleled on pegs. Equipments hung on handy projections, and some tin dishes lay upon a small pile of firewood. A folded tent was serving as a roof. The sunlight, without, beating upon it, made it glow a light yellow shade. A small window shot an oblique square of whiter light upon the cluttered floor. The smoke from the fire at times neglected the clay chimney and wreathed into the room, and this flimsy chimney of clay and sticks made endless threats to set ablaze the whole establishment.

The youth was in a little trance of astonishment. So they were at last going to fight. On the morrow, perhaps, there would be a battle, and he would be in it. For a time he was obliged to labour to make himself believe. He could not accept with assurance an omen that he was about to mingle in one of those great affairs of the earth.

He had, of course, dreamed of battles all his life—of vague and bloody conflicts that had thrilled him with their sweep and fire. In visions he had seen himself in many struggles. He had imagined peoples secure in the shadow of his eagle-eyed prowess. But awake he had regarded battles as crimson blotches on the pages of the past. He had put them as things of the bygone with his thought-images of heavy crowns and high castles. There was a portion of the world's history which he had regarded as the time of wars, but it, he thought, had been long gone over the horizon and had disappeared for ever.

From his home his youthful eyes had looked upon the war in his own country with distrust. It must be some sort of a play affair. He had long despaired of witnessing a Greeklike struggle. Such would be no more, he had said. Men were better, or more timid. Secular and religious education had effaced the throat-grappling instinct, or else firm finance held in check the passions.

He had burned several times to enlist. Tales of great movements shook the land. They might not be distinctly Homeric, but there seemed to be much glory in them. He had read of marches, sieges, conflicts, and he had longed to see it all. His busy mind had drawn for him large pictures extravagant in colour, lurid with breathless deeds.

But his mother had discouraged him. She had affected to look with some contempt upon the quality of his war ardour and patriotism. She could calmly seat herself and with no apparent difficulty give him many hundreds of reasons why he was of vastly more importance on the farm than on the field of battle. She had had certain ways of expression that told him that her statements on the subject came from a deep conviction. Moreover, on her side, was his belief that her ethical motive in the argument was impregnable.

At last, however, he had made firm rebellion against this yellow light thrown upon the colour of his ambitions. The newspapers, the gossip of the village, his own picturings, had aroused him to an uncheckable degree. They were in truth fighting finely down there. Almost every day the newspapers printed accounts of a decisive victory.

One night, as he lay in bed, the winds had carried to him the clangouring of the church bell as some enthusiast jerked the rope frantically to tell the twisted news of a great battle. This voice of the people rejoicing in the night had made him shiver in a prolonged ecstasy of excitement. Later, he had gone down to his mother's room and had spoken thus: 'Ma, I'm going to enlist.'

'Henry, don't you be a fool,' his mother had replied. She had then covered her face with the quilt. There was an end to the matter for that night.

Nevertheless, the next morning he had gone to a town that was near his mother's farm and had enlisted in a company that was forming there. When he had returned home his mother was milking the brindle cow. Four others stood waiting. 'Ma, I've enlisted,' he had said to her diffidently. There was a short silence. 'The Lord's will be done, Henry.' she had finally replied, and had then continued to milk the brindle cow.

When he had stood in the doorway with his soldier's clothes on his back, and with the light of excitement and expectancy in his eyes almost defeating the glow of regret for the home bonds, he had seen two tears leaving their trails on his mother's scarred cheeks.

Still, she had disappointed him by saying nothing whatever about returning with his shield or on it. He had privately primed himself for a beautiful scene. He had prepared certain sentences which he thought could be used with touching effect. But her words destroyed his plans. She had doggedly peeled potatoes and addressed him as follows: 'You watch out, Henry, an' take good care of yerself in this here fighting business—you watch out, an' take good care of yerself. Don't go a-thinkin' you can lick the hull rebel army at the start, because yeh can't. Yer jest one little feller amongst a hull lot of others, and yeh've got to keep quiet an' do what they tell yeh. I know how you are, Henry.

'I've knet yeh eight pair of socks, Henry, and I've put in all yer best shirts, because I want my boy to be jest as warm and comf'able as anybody in the army. Whenever they get holes in 'em, I want yeh to send 'em rightaway back to me, so's I kin dern 'em.

'An' allus be careful an' choose yer comp'ny. There's lots of bad men in the army, Henry. The army makes 'em wild, and they like nothing better than the job of leading off a young feller like you, as ain't never been away from home much and has allus had a mother, an' a-learning 'em to drink and swear. Keep clear of them folks, Henry. I don't want yeh to ever do anything, Henry, that yeh would be 'shamed to let me know about. Jest think as if I was a-watchin' yeh. If yeh keep that in yer mind allus, I guess yeh'll come out about right.

'Yeh must allus remember yer father, too, child, an' remember he never drunk a drop of licker in his life, and seldom swore a cross oath.

'I don't know what else to tell yeh, Henry, excepting that yeh must never do no shirking, child, on my account. If so be a time comes when yeh have to be kilt or do a mean thing, why, Henry, don't think of anything 'cept what's right, because there's many a woman has to bear up 'ginst sech things these times, and the Lord'll take keer of us all. Don't fergit about the socks and the shirts, child; and I've put a cup of blackberry jam with yer bundle, because I knew yeh like it above all things. Good-bye, Henry. Watch out, and be a good boy.'

He had, of course, been impatient under the ordeal of this speech. It had not been quite what he expected, and he had borne it with an air of irritation. He departed feeling vague relief.

Still, when he had looked back from the gate, he had seen his mother kneeling among the potato parings. Her brown face, upraised, was stained with tears, and her spare form was quivering. He bowed his head and went on, feeling suddenly ashamed of his purposes.

From his home he had gone to the seminary to bid adieu to many schoolmates. They had thronged about him with wonder and admiration. He had felt the gulf now between them and had swelled with calm pride. He and some of his fellows who had donned blue were quite overwhelmed with privileges for all of one afternoon, and it had been a very delicious thing. They had strutted.

A certain light-haired girl had made vivacious fun at his martial spirit, but there was another and darker girl whom he had gazed at steadfastly, and he thought she grew demure and sad at sight of his blue and brass. As he had walked down the path between the rows of oaks, he had turned his head and detected her at a window watching his departure. As he perceived her, she had immediately begun to stare up through the high tree branches at the sky. He had seen a good deal of flurry and haste in her movement as she changed her attitude. He often thought of it.

On the way to Washington his spirit had soared. The regiment was fed and caressed at station after station until the youth had believed that he must be a hero. There was a lavish expenditure of bread and cold meats, coffee, and pickles and cheese. As he basked in the smiles of the girls and was patted and complimented by the old men, he had felt growing within him the strength to do mighty deeds of arms.

After complicated journeyings with many pauses, there had come months of monotonous life in a camp. He had had the belief that real war was a series of death struggles with small time in between for sleep and meals; but since his regiment had come to the field the army had done little but sit still and try to keep warm.

He was brought then gradually back to his old ideas. Greeklike struggles would be no more. Men were better, or more timid. Secular and religious education had effaced the throat-grappling instinct, or else firm finance held in check the passions.

He had grown to regard himself merely as a part of a vast blue demonstration. His province was to look out, as far as he could, for his personal comfort. For recreation he could twiddle his thumbs and speculate on the thoughts which must agitate the minds of the generals. Also, he was drilled and drilled and reviewed, and drilled and drilled and reviewed.

The only foes he had seen were some pickets along the river bank. They were a sun-tanned, philosophical lot, who sometimes shot reflectively at the blue pickets. When reproached for this afterward, they usually expressed sorrow, and swore by their gods that the guns had exploded without their permission. The youth, on guard duty one night, conversed across the stream with one of them. He was a slightly ragged man, who spat skilfully between his shoes and possessed a great fund of bland and infantile assurance. The youth liked him personally.

'Yank,' the other had informed him, 'yer a right dum good feller.' This sentiment, floating to him upon the still air, had made him temporarily regret war.

Various veterans had told him tales. Some talked of grey, bewhiskered hordes who were advancing with relentless curses and chewing tobacco with unspeakable valour; tremendous bodies of fierce soldiery who were sweeping along like the

Huns. Others spoke of tattered and eternally hungry men who fired despondent powders. 'They'll charge through hell's fire an' brimstone t' git a holt on a haversack, an' sech stomachs ain't a-lastin' long,' he was told. From the stories, the youth imagined the red, live bones sticking out through slits in the faded uniforms.

Still, he could not put a whole faith in veterans' tales, for recruits were their prey. They talked much of smoke, fire, and blood, but he could not tell how much might be lies. They persistently yelled 'Fresh fish!' at him, and were in no wise to be trusted.

However, he perceived now that it did not greatly matter what kind of soldiers he was going to fight, so long as they fought, which fact no one disputed. There was a more serious problem. He lay in his bunk pondering upon it. He tried to mathematically prove to himself that he would not run from a battle.

Previously he had never felt obliged to wrestle too seriously with this question. In his life he had taken certain things for granted, never challenging his belief in ultimate success, and bothering little about means and roads. But here he was confronted with a thing of moment. It had suddenly appeared to him that perhaps in a battle he might run. He was forced to admit that as far as war was concerned he knew nothing of himself.

A sufficient time before he would have allowed the problem to kick its heels at the outer portals of his mind, but now he felt compelled to give serious attention to it.

A little panic-fear grew in his mind. As his imagination went forward to a fight, he saw hideous possibilities. He contemplated the lurking menaces of the future, and failed in an effort to see himself standing stoutly in the midst of them. He recalled his visions of broken-bladed glory, but in the shadow of the impending tumult he suspected them to be impossible pictures.

He sprang from the bunk and began to pace nervously to and fro. 'Good Lord, what's th' matter with me?' he said aloud.

He felt that in this crisis his laws of life were useless. Whatever he had learned of himself was here of no avail. He was an unknown quantity. He saw that he would again be obliged to experiment as he had in early youth. He must accumulate information of himself, and meanwhile he resolved to remain close upon his guard lest those qualities of which he knew nothing should everlastingly disgrace him. 'Good Lord!' he repeated in dismay.

After a time the tall soldier slid dexterously through the hole.

The loud private followed. They were wrangling.

'That's all right,' said the tall soldier as he entered. He waved his hand expressively. 'You can believe me or not, jest as you like. All you got to do is to sit down and wait as quiet as you can. Then pretty soon you'll find out I was right.'

His comrade grunted stubbornly. For a moment he seemed to be searching for a formidable reply. Finally he said: 'Well, you don't know everything in the world, do you?'

'Didn't say I knew everything in the world,' retorted the other sharply. He began to stow various articles snugly into his knapsack.

The youth, pausing in his nervous walk, looked down at the busy figure. 'Going to be a battle, sure, is there, Jim?' he asked.

'Of course there is,' replied the tall soldier. 'Of course there is. You jest wait 'til tomorrow, and you'll see one of the biggest battles ever was. You jest wait.'

'Thunder!' said the youth.

'Oh, you'll see fighting this time, my boy, what'll be regular out-and-out fighting,' added the tall soldier, with the air of a man who is about to exhibit a battle for the benefit of his friends.

'Huh!' said the loud one from a corner.

'Well,' remarked the youth, 'like as not this story'll turn out jest like them others did.'

'Not much it won't,' replied the tall soldier, exasperated. 'Not much it won't. Didn't the cavalry all start this morning?' He glared about him. No one denied his statement. 'The cavalry started this morning,' he continued. 'They say there ain't hardly any cavalry left in camp. They're going to Richmond, or some place, while we fight all the Johnnies. It's some dodge like that. The regiment's got orders, too. A feller what seen 'em go to headquarters told me a little while ago. And they're raising blazes all over camp—anybody can see that.'

'Shucks!' said the loud one.

The youth remained silent for a time. At last he spoke to the tall soldier. 'Jim!'

'What?'

'How do you think the reg'ment 'll do?'

'Oh, they'll fight all right, I guess, after they once get into it,' said the other with cold judgement. He made a fine use of the third person. 'There's been heaps of fun poked at 'em because they're new, of course, and all that; but they'll fight all right, I guess.'

'Think any of the boys 'll run?' persisted the youth.

'Oh, there may be a few of 'em run, but there's them kind in every regiment, 'specially when they first goes under fire,' said the other in a tolerant way. 'Of course it might happen that the hull kit-and-boodle might start and run, if some big fighting came first-off, and then again they might stay and fight like fun. But you can't bet on nothing. Of course they ain't never been under fire yet, and it ain't likely they'll lick the hull rebel army all-to-oncet the first time; but I think they'll fight better than some, if worse that others. That's the way I figger. They call the reg'ment "Fresh fish" and everything; but the boys come of good stock, and most of 'em 'll fight like sin after they oncet git shootin',' he added, with a mighty emphasis on the last four words.

'Oh, you think you know—' began the loud soldier with scorn.

The other turned savagely upon him. They had a rapid altercation, in which they fastened upon each other various strange epithets.

The youth at last interrupted them. 'Did you ever think you might run yourself, Jim?' he asked. On concluding the sentence he laughed as if he had meant to aim a joke. The loud soldier also giggled.

The tall private waved his hand. 'Well,' said he profoundly, 'I've thought it might get too hot for Jim Conklin in some of them scrimmages, and if a whole lot of boys started and run, why, I s'pose I'd start and run. And if I once started to run, I'd run like the devil, and no mistake. But if everybody was a-standing and a-fighting, why, I'd stand and fight. Be jiminey, I would. I'll bet on it.'

'Huh!' said the loud one.

The youth of this tale felt gratitude for these words of his comrade. He had feared that all of the untried men possessed a great and correct confidence. He now was in a measure reassured.

II

THE next morning the youth discovered that his tall comrade had been the fast-flying messenger of a mistake. There was much scoffing at the latter by those who had yesterday been firm adherents of his views, and there was even a little sneering by men who had never believed the rumour. The tall one fought with a man from Chatfield Corners and beat him severely.

The youth felt, however, that his problem was in no wise lifted from him. There was, on the contrary, an irritating prolongation. The tale had created in him a great concern for himself. Now, with the newborn question in his mind, he was compelled to sink back into his old place as part of a blue demonstration.

For days he made ceaseless calculations, but they were all wondrously unsatisfactory. He found that he could establish nothing. He finally concluded that the only way to prove himself was to go into the blaze, and then figuratively to watch his legs to discover their merits and faults. He reluctantly admitted that he could not sit still and with a mental slate and pencil derive an answer. To gain it, he must have blaze, blood, and danger, even as a chemist requires this, that, and the other. So he fretted for an opportunity.

Meanwhile he continually tried to measure himself by his comrades. The tall soldier, for one, gave him some assurance. This man's serene unconcern dealt him a measure of confidence, for he had known him since childhood, and from his intimate knowledge he did not see how he could be capable of anything that was beyond him, the youth. Still, he thought that his comrade might be mistaken about himself. Or, on the other hand, he might be a man heretofore doomed to peace and obscurity, but, in reality, made to shine in war.

The youth would have liked to have discovered another who suspected himself. A sympathetic comparison of mental notes would have been a joy to him.

He occasionally tried to fathom a comrade with seductive sentences. He looked about to find men in the proper mood. All attempts failed to bring forth any statement which looked in any way like a confession to those doubts which he privately acknowledged in himself. He was afraid to make an open declaration of his concern, because he dreaded to place some unscrupulous confidant upon the high plane of the unconfessed from which elevation he could be derided.

In regard to his companions his mind wavered between two opinions, according to his mood. Sometimes he inclined to believing them all heroes. In fact, he usually admitted in secret the superior development of the higher qualities in others. He could conceive of men going very insignificantly about the world bearing a load of courage unseen, and, although he had known many of his comrades through boyhood, he began to fear that his judgement of them had been blind. Then, in other moments, he flouted these theories, and assured himself that his fellows were all privately wondering and quaking.

His emotions made him feel strange in the presence of men who talked excitedly of a prospective battle as of a drama they were about to witness, with nothing but eagerness and curiosity apparent in their faces. It was often that he suspected them to be liars.

He did not pass such thoughts without severe condemnation of himself. He dinned reproaches at times. He was convicted by himself of many shameful crimes against the gods of traditions.

In his great anxiety his heart was continually clamouring at what he considered the intolerable slowness of the generals. They seemed content to perch tranquilly on the river bank, and leave him bowed down by the weight of a great problem. He wanted it settled forthwith. He could not long bear such a load, he said. Sometimes his anger at the commanders reached an acute stage, and he grumbled about the camp like a veteran.

One morning, however, he found himself in the ranks of his prepared regiment. The men were whispering speculations and recounting the old rumours. In the gloom before the break of the day their uniforms glowed a deep purple hue. From across the river the red eyes were still peering. In the eastern sky there was a yellow patch like a rug laid for the feet of the coming sun; and against it, black and patternlike, loomed the gigantic figure of the colonel on a gigantic horse.

From off in the darkness came the trampling of feet. The youth could occasionally see dark shadows that moved like monsters. The regiment stood at rest for what seemed a long time. The youth grew impatient. It was unendurable the way these affairs were managed. He wondered how long they were to be kept waiting.

As he looked all about him and pondered upon the mystic gloom, he began to believe that at any moment the ominous distance might be aflare, and the rolling crashes of an engagement come to his ears. Staring once at the red eyes across the river, he conceived them to be growing larger, as the orbs of a row of dragons advancing. He turned toward the colonel and saw him lift his gigantic arm and calmly stroke his moustache.

At last he heard from along the road at the foot of the hill the clatter of a horse's galloping hoofs. It must be the coming of orders. He bent forward, scarce breathing. The exciting clickety-click, as it grew louder and louder, seemed to be beating upon his soul. Presently a horseman with jangling equipment drew rein before the colonel of the regiment. The two held a short, sharp-worded conversation. The men in the foremost ranks craned their necks.

As the horseman wheeled his animal and galloped away he turned to shout over his shoulder, 'Don't forget that box of cigars!' The colonel mumbled in reply. The youth wondered what a box of cigars had to do with war.

A moment later the regiment went swinging off into the darkness. It was now like one of those moving monsters wending with many feet. The air was heavy, and cold with dew. A mass of wet grass, marched upon, rustled like silk.

There was an occasional flash and glimmer of steel from the backs of all these huge crawling reptiles. From the road came creakings and grumblings as some surly guns were dragged away.

The men stumbled along still muttering speculations. There was a subdued debate. Once a man fell down, and as he reached for his rifle a comrade, unseeing, trod upon his hand. He of the injured fingers swore bitterly and aloud. A low, tittering laugh went among his fellows.

Presently they passed into a roadway and marched forward with easy strides. A dark regiment moved before them, and from behind also came the tinkle of equipments on the bodies of marching men.

The rushing yellow of the developing day went on behind their backs. When the sunrays at last struck full and mellowingly upon the earth, the youth saw that the landscape was streaked with two long, thin, black columns which disappeared on the brow of a hill in front and rearward vanished in a wood. They were like two serpents crawling from the cavern of the night.

The river was not in view. The tall soldier burst into praises of what he thought to be his powers of perception.

Some of the tall one's companions cried with emphasis that they, too, had evolved the same thing, and they congratulated themselves upon it. But there were others who said that the tall one's plan was not the true one at all. They persisted with other theories. There was a vigorous discussion.

The youth took no part in them. As he walked along in careless line he was engaged with his own eternal debate. He could not hinder himself from dwelling upon it. He was despondent and sullen, and threw shifting glances about him. He looked ahead, often expecting to hear from the advance the rattle of firing.

But the long serpents crawled slowly from hill to hill without bluster of smoke. A dun-coloured cloud of dust floated away to the right. The sky overhead was of a fairy blue.

The youth studied the faces of his companions, ever on the watch to detect kindred emotions. He suffered disappointment. Some ardour of the air which was causing the veteran commands to move with glee—almost with song—had infected the new regiment. The men began to speak of victory as of a thing they knew. Also, the tall soldier received his vindication. They were certainly going to come around in behind the enemy. They expressed commiseration for that part of the army which had been left upon the river bank, felicitating themselves upon being a part of a blasting host.

The youth, considering himself as separated from the others, was saddened by the blithe and merry speeches that went from rank to rank. The company wags all made their best endeavours. The regiment tramped to the tune of laughter.

The blatant soldier often convulsed whole files by his biting sarcasms aimed at the tall one.

And it was not long before all the men seemed to forget their mission. Whole brigades grinned in unison, and regiments laughed.

A rather fat soldier attempted to pilfer a horse from a dooryard. He planned to load his knapsack upon it. He was escaping with his prize when a young girl rushed from the house and grabbed the animal's mane. There followed a wrangle. The young girl, with pink cheeks and shining eyes, stood like a dauntless statue.

The observant regiment, standing at rest in the roadway, whooped at once, and entered whole-souled upon the side of the maiden. The men became so engrossed in this affair that they entirely ceased to remember their own large war. They jeered the piratical private, and called attention to various defects in his personal appearance; and they were wildly enthusiastic in support of the young girl.

To her, from some distance, came bold advice. 'Hit him with a stick.'

There were crows and catcalls showered upon him when he retreated without the horse. The regiment rejoiced at his downfall. Loud and vociferous congratulations were showered upon the maiden, who stood panting and regarding the troops with defiance.

At nightfall the column broke into regimental pieces, and the fragments went into the fields to camp. Tents sprang up like strange plants. Camp fires, like red, peculiar blossoms, dotted the night.

The youth kept from intercourse with his companions as much as circumstances would allow him. In the evening he wandered a few paces into the gloom. From this little distance the many fires, with the black forms of men passing to and fro before the crimson rays, made weird and satanic effects.

He lay down in the grass. The blades pressed tenderly against his cheek. The moon had been lighted and was hung in a treetop. The liquid stillness of the night enveloping him made him feel vast pity for himself. There was a caress in the soft winds; and the whole mood of the darkness, he thought, was one of sympathy for himself in his distress.

He wished, without reserve, that he was at home again making the endless rounds from the house to the barn, from the barn to the fields, from the fields to the barn, from the barn to the house. He remembered he had often cursed the brindle cow and her mates, and had sometimes flung milking stools. But, from his present point of view, there was a halo of happiness about each of their heads, and he would have sacrificed all the brass buttons on the continent to have been enabled to return to them. He told himself that he was not formed for a soldier. And he mused seriously upon the radical differences between himself and those men who were dodging implike around the fires.

As he mused thus he heard the rustle of grass, and, upon turning his head, discovered the loud soldier. He called out, 'Oh, Wilson!'

The latter approached and looked down. 'Why, hello, Henry; is it you? What you doing here?'

'Oh, thinking,' said the youth.

The other sat down and carefully lighted his pipe. 'You're getting blue, my boy. You're looking thundering peeked. What the dickens is wrong with you?'

'Oh, nothing,' said the youth.

The loud soldier launched then into the subject of the anticipated fight. 'Oh, we've got 'em now!' As he spoke his boyish face was wreathed in a gleeful smile, and his voice had an exultant ring. 'We've got 'em now. At last, by the eternal thunders, we'll lick 'em good!'

'If the truth was known,' he added, more soberly, '*they've* licked *us* about every clip up to now; but this time—this time—we'll lick 'em good!'

'I thought you was objecting to this march a little while ago,' said the youth coldly.

'Oh, it wasn't that,' explained the other. 'I don't mind marching, if there's going to be fighting at the end of it. What I hate is this getting moved here and moved there, with no good coming of it, as far as I can see, excepting sore feet and damned short rations.'

'Well, Jim Conklin says we'll get a plenty of fighting this time.'

'He's right for once, I guess, though I can't see how it come. This time we're in for a big battle, an we've got the best end of it, certain sure. Gee rod! how we will thump 'em!'

He arose and began to pace to and fro excitedly. The thrill of his enthusiasm made him walk with an elastic step. He was sprightly, vigorous, fiery in his belief in success. He looked into the future with clear, proud eye, and he swore with the air of an old soldier.

The youth watched him for a moment in silence. When he finally spoke his voice was as bitter as dregs. 'Oh, you're going to do great things, I s'pose!'

The loud soldier blew a thoughtful cloud of smoke from his pipe. 'Oh, I don't know,' he remarked with dignity; 'I don't know. I s'pose I'll do as well as the rest. I'm going to try like thunder.' He evidently complimented himself upon the modesty of this statement.

'How do you know you won't run when the time comes?' asked the youth.

'Run?' said the loud one; 'run?—of course not!' He laughed.

'Well,' continued the youth, 'lots of good-a-'nough men have thought they was going to do great things before the fight, but when the time come they skedaddled.'

'Oh, that's all true, I s'pose,' replied the other; 'but I'm not going to skedaddle. The man that bets on my running will lose his money, that's all.' He nodded confidently.

'Oh, shucks!' said the youth. 'You ain't the bravest man in the world, are you?'

'No, I ain't,' exclaimed the loud soldier indignantly; 'and I didn't say I was the bravest man in the world, neither. I said I was going to do my share of fighting—that's what I said. And I am, too. Who are you, anyhow? You talk as if you thought you was Napoleon Bonaparte.' He glared at the youth for a moment, and then strode away.

The youth called in a savage voice after his comrade: 'Well, you needn't git mad about it!' But the other continued on his way and made no reply.

He felt alone in space when his injured comrade had disappeared. His failure to discover any mite of resemblance in their view points made him more miserable than before. No one seemed to be wrestling with such a terrific personal problem. He was a mental outcast.

He went slowly to his tent and stretched himself on a blanket by the side of the snoring tall soldier. In the darkness he saw visions of a thousand-tongued fear that would babble at his back and cause him to flee, while others were going coolly about their country's business. He admitted that he would not be able to cope with this monster. He felt that every nerve in his body would be an ear to hear the voices, while other men would remain stolid and deaf.

And as he sweated with the pain of these thoughts, he could hear low, serene sentences. 'I'll bid five.' 'Make it six.' 'Seven.' 'Seven goes.'

He stared at the red, shivering reflection of a fire on the white wall of his tent until, exhausted and ill from the monotony of his suffering, he fell asleep.

III

WHEN another night came the columns, changed to purple streaks, filed across two pontoon bridges. A glaring fire wine-tinted the waters of the river. Its rays, shining upon the moving masses of troops, brought forth here and there sudden gleams of silver or gold. Upon the other shore a dark and mysterious range of hills was curved against the sky. The insect voices of the night sang solemnly.

After this crossing the youth assured himself that at any moment they might be suddenly and fearfully assaulted from the caves of the lowering woods. He kept his eyes watchfully upon the darkness.

But his regiment went unmolested to a camping place, and its soldiers slept the brave sleep of wearied men. In the morning they were routed out with early energy, and hustled along a narrow road that led deep into the forest.

It was during this rapid march that the regiment lost many of the marks of a new command.

The men had begun to count the miles upon their fingers, and they grew tired. 'Sore feet an' damned short rations, that's all,' said the loud soldier. There was perspiration and grumblings. After a time they began to shed their knapsacks. Some tossed them unconcernedly down; others hid them carefully, asserting their plans to return for them at some convenient time. Men extricated themselves from thick shirts. Presently few carried anything but their necessary clothing, blankets, haversacks, canteens, and arms and ammunition. There was sudden change from the ponderous infantry of theory to the light and speedy infantry of practice. The regiment, relieved of a burden, received a new impetus. But there was much loss of valuable knapsacks, and, on the whole, very good shirts.

But the regiment was not yet veteranlike in appearance. Veteran regiments in the army were likely to be very small aggregations of men. Once, when the command had first come to the field, some perambulating veterans, noting the length of their column, had accosted them thus: 'Hey, fellers, what brigade is that?' And when the men had replied that they formed a regiment and not a brigade, the older soldiers had laughed, and said, 'O Gawd!'

Also, there was too great a similarity in the hats. The hats of a regiment should properly represent the history of headgear for a period of years. And, moreover, there were no letters of faded gold speaking from the colours. They were new and beautiful, and the colour bearer habitually oiled the pole.

Presently the army again sat down to think. The odour of the peaceful pines was in the men's nostrils. The sound of monotonous axe blows rang through the forest, and the insects, nodding upon their perches, crooned like old women. The youth returned to his theory of a blue demonstration.

One grey dawn, however, he was kicked in the leg by the tall soldier, and then, before he was entirely awake, he found himself running down a wood road in the midst of men who were panting from the first effects of speed. His canteen banged rhythmically upon his thigh, and his haversack bobbed softly. His musket bounced a trifle from his shoulder at each stride and made his cap feel uncertain upon his head.

He could hear the men whisper jerky sentences: 'Say— what's all this—about?' 'What th' thunder—we—skeddadlin' this way fer?' 'Billie—keep off m' feet. Yeh run—like a cow.' And the loud soldier's shrill voice could be heard: 'What th' devil they in sich a hurry for?'

The youth thought the damp fog of early morning moved from the rush of a great body of troops. From the distance came a sudden spatter of firing.

He was bewildered. As he ran with his comrades he strenuously tried to think, but all he knew was that if he fell down those coming behind would tread upon him. All his faculties seemed to be needed to guide him over and past obstructions. He felt carried along by a mob.

The sun spread disclosing rays, and, one by one, regiments burst into view like armed men just born of the earth. The youth perceived that the time had come. He was about to be measured. For a moment he felt in the face of his great trial like a babe, and the flesh over his heart seemed very thin. He seized time to look about him calculatingly.

But he instantly saw that it would be impossible for him to escape from the regiment. It inclosed him. And there were iron laws of tradition and law on four sides. He was in a moving box.

As he perceived this fact it occurred to him that he had never wished to come to the war. He had not enlisted of his free will. He had been dragged by the merciless government. And now they were taking him out to be slaughtered.

The regiment slid down a bank and wallowed across a little stream. The mournful current moved slowly on, and from the water, shaded black, some white bubble eyes looked at the men.

As they climbed the hill on the farther side artillery began to boom. Here the youth forgot many things as he felt a sudden impulse of curiosity. He scrambled up the bank with a speed that could not be exceeded by a bloodthirsty man.

He expected a battle scene.

There were some little fields girted and squeezed by a forest. Spread over the grass and in among the tree trunks, he could see knots and waving lines of skirmishers who were running hither and thither and firing at the landscape. A dark battle line lay upon a sunstruck clearing that gleamed orange colour. A flag fluttered.

Other regiments floundered up the bank. The brigade was formed in line of battle, and after a pause started slowly through the woods in the rear of the receding skirmishers, who were continually melting into the scene to appear again farther on. They were always busy as bees, deeply absorbed in their little combats.

The youth tried to observe everything. He did not use care to avoid trees and branches, and his forgotten feet were constantly knocking against stones or getting entangled in briers. He was aware that these battalions with their commotions were woven red and startling into the gentle fabric of softened greens and browns. It looked to be a wrong place for a battle field.

The skirmishers in advance fascinated him. Their shots into thickets and at distant and prominent trees spoke to him of tragedies—hidden, mysterious, solemn.

Once the line encountered the body of a dead soldier. He lay upon his back staring at the sky. He was dressed in an awkward suit of yellowish brown. The youth could see that the soles of his shoes had been worn to the thinness of writing paper, and from a great rent in one the dead foot projected piteously. And it was as if fate had betrayed the soldier. In death it exposed to his enemies that poverty which in life he had perhaps concealed from his friends.

The ranks opened covertly to avoid the corpse. The invulnerable dead man forced a way for himself. The youth looked keenly at the ashen face. The wind raised the tawny beard. It moved as if a hand were stroking it. He vaguely desired to walk around and around the body and stare; the impulse of the living to try to read in dead eyes the answer to the Question.

During the march the ardour which the youth had acquired when out of view of the field rapidly faded to nothing. His curiosity was quite easily satisfied. If an intense scene had caught him with its wild swing as he came to the top of the bank, he might have gone roaring on. This advance upon Nature was too calm. He had opportunity to reflect. He had time in which to wonder about himself and to attempt to probe his sensations.

Absurd ideas took hold upon him. He thought that he did not relish the landscape. It threatened him. A coldness swept over his back, and it is true that his trousers felt to him that they were no fit for his legs at all.

A house standing placidly in distant fields had to him an ominous look. The shadows of the woods were formidable. He was certain that in this vista there lurked fierce-eyed hosts. The swift thought came to him that the generals did not know what they were about. It was all a trap. Suddenly those close forests would bristle with rifle barrels. Ironlike brigades would appear in the rear. They were all going to be sacrificed. The generals were stupids. The enemy would presently swallow the whole command. He glared about him, expecting to see the stealthy approach of his death.

He thought that he must break from the ranks and harangue his comrades. They must not all be killed like pigs; and he was sure it would come to pass unless they were informed of these dangers. The generals were idiots to send them marching into a regular pen. There was but one pair of eyes in the corps. He would step forth and make a speech. Shrill and passionate words came to his lips.

The line, broken into moving fragments by the ground, went calmly on through fields and woods. The youth looked at the men nearest him, and saw, for the most part, expressions of deep interest, as if they were investigating something that had fascinated them. One or two stepped with overvaliant airs as if they were already plunged into war. Others walked as upon thin ice. The greater part of the untested men appeared quiet and absorbed. They were going to look at war, the red animal—war, the blood-swollen god. And they were deeply engrossed in this march.

As he looked the youth gripped his outcry at his throat. He saw that even if the men were tottering with fear they would laugh at his warning. They would jeer him, and, if practicable, pelt him with missiles. Admitting that he might be wrong, a frenzied declamation of the kind would turn him into a worm.

He assumed, then, the demeanour of one who knows that he is doomed alone to unwritten responsibilities. He lagged, with tragic glances at the sky.

He was surprised presently by the young lieutenant of his company, who began heartily to beat him with a sword, calling out in a loud and insolent voice: 'Come, young man, get up into ranks there. No skulking 'll do here.' He mended his pace with suitable haste. And he hated the lieutenant, who had no appreciation of fine minds. He was a mere brute.

After a time the brigade was halted in the cathedral light of a forest. The busy skirmishers were still popping. Through the aisles of the wood could be seen the floating smoke from their rifles. Sometimes it went up in little balls, white and compact.

During this halt many men in the regiment began erecting tiny hills in front of them. They used stones, sticks, earth and anything they thought might turn a bullet. Some built comparatively large ones, while others seemed content with little ones.

This procedure caused a discussion among the men. Some wished to fight like duellists, believing it to be correct to stand erect and be, from their feet to their foreheads, a mark. They said they scorned the devices of the cautious. But the others scoffed in reply, and pointed to the veterans on the flanks who were digging at the ground like terriers. In a short time there was quite a barricade along the regimental fronts. Directly, however, they were ordered to withdraw from that place.

This astounded the youth. He forgot his stewing over the advance movement. 'Well, then, what did they march us out here for?' he demanded of the tall soldier. The latter with calm faith began a heavy explanation, although he had been compelled to leave a little protection of stones and dirt to which he had devoted much care and skill.

When the regiment was aligned in another position each man's regard for his safety caused another line of small entrenchments. They ate their noon meal behind a third one. They were moved from this one also. They were marched from place to place with apparent aimlessness.

The youth had been taught that a man became another thing in a battle. He saw his salvation in such a change. Hence this waiting was an ordeal to him. He was in a fever of impatience. He considered that there was denoted a lack of purpose on the part of the generals. He began to complain to the tall soldier. 'I can't stand this much longer,' he cried. 'I don't see what good it does to make us wear out our legs for nothin'.' He wished to return to camp, knowing that this affair was a blue demonstration; or else to go into a battle and discover that he had been a fool in his doubts, and was, in truth, a man of traditional courage. The strain of present circumstances he felt to be intolerable.

The philosophical tall soldier measured a sandwich of cracker and pork and swallowed it in a nonchalant manner.

'Oh, I suppose we must go reconnoitring around the country jest to keep 'em from getting too close, or to develop 'em, or something.'

'Huh!' said the loud soldier.

'Well,' cried the youth, still fidgeting, 'I'd rather do anything 'most than go tramping 'round the country all day doing no good to nobody and jest tiring ourselves out.'

'So would I,' said the loud soldier. 'It ain't right. I tell you if anybody with any sense was a-runnin' this army it—'

'Oh, shut up!' roared the tall private. 'You little fool. You little damn' cuss. You ain't had that there coat and them pants on for six months, and yet you talk as if—'

'Well, I wanta do some fighting anyway,' interrupted the other. 'I didn't come here to walk. I could 'ave walked to home—'round and 'round the barn, if I jest wanted to walk.'

The tall one, red-faced, swallowed another sandwich as if taking poison in despair.

But gradually, as he chewed, his face became again quiet and contented. He could not rage in fierce argument in the presence of such sandwiches. During his meals he always wore an air of blissful contemplation of the food he had swallowed. His spirit seemed then to be communing with the viands.

He accepted new environment and circumstance with great coolness, eating from his haversack at every opportunity. On the march he went along with the stride of a hunter, objecting to neither gait nor distance. And he had not raised his voice when he had been ordered away from three little protective piles of earth and stone, each of which had been an engineering feat worthy of being made sacred to the name of his grandmother.

In the afternoon the regiment went out over the same ground it had taken in the morning. The landscape then ceased to threaten the youth. He had been close to it and become familiar with it.

When, however, they began to pass into a new region, his fears of stupidity and incompetence reassailed him, but this time he doggedly let them babble. He was occupied with his problem, and in his desperation he concluded that the stupidity did not greatly matter.

Once he thought he had concluded that it would be better to get killed directly and end his troubles. Regarding death thus out of the corner of his eye, he conceived it to be nothing but rest, and he was filled with a momentary astonishment that he should have made an extraordinary commotion over the mere matter of getting killed. He would die; he would go to some place where he would be understood. It was useless to expect appreciation of his profound and fine senses from such men as the lieutenant. He must look to the grave for comprehension.

The skirmish-fire increased to a long clattering sound. With it was mingled far-away cheering. A battery spoke.

Directly the youth would see the skirmishers running. They were pursued by the sound of musketry fire. After a time the hot, dangerous flashes of the rifles were visible. Smoke clouds went slowly and insolently across the fields like observant phantoms. The din became crescendo, like the roar of an oncoming train.

A brigade ahead of them and on the right went into action with a rending roar. It was as if it had exploded. And thereafter it lay stretched in the distance behind a long grey wall, that one was obliged to look twice at to make sure that it was smoke.

The youth, forgetting his neat plan of getting killed, gazed spellbound. His eyes grew wide and busy with the action of the scene. His mouth was a little ways open.

Of a sudden he felt a heavy and sad hand laid upon his shoulder. Awakening from his trance of observation he turned and beheld the loud soldier.

'It's my first and last battle, old boy,' said the latter, with intense gloom. He was quite pale and his girlish lip was trembling.

'Eh?' murmured the youth in great astonishment.

'It's my first and last battle, old boy,' continued the loud soldier. 'Something tells me—'

'What?'

'I'm a gone coon this first time and—and I w-want you to take these here things—to—my—folks.' He ended in a quavering sob of pity for himself. He handed the youth a little packet done up in a yellow envelope.

'Why, what the devil—' began the youth again.

But the other gave him a glance as from the depths of a tomb, and raised his limp hand in a prophetic manner and turned away.

IV

THE brigade was halted in the fringe of a grove. The men crouched among the trees and pointed their restless guns out at the fields. They tried to look beyond the smoke.

Out of this haze they could see running men. Some shouted information and gestured as they hurried.

The men of the new regiment watched and listened eagerly, while their tongues ran on in gossip of the battle. They mouthed rumours that had flown like birds out of the unknown.

'They say Perry has been driven in with big loss.'

'Yes, Carrott went t' th' hospital. He said he was sick. That smart lieutenant is commanding "G" Company. Th' boys say they won't be under Carrott no more if they all have t' desert. They allus knew he was a—'

'Hannises' batt'ry is took.'

'It ain't either. I saw Hannises' batt'ry off on th' left not more 'n fifteen minutes ago.'

'Well—'

'Th' general, he ses he is goin' t' take th' hull cammand of th' 304th when we go inteh action, an' then he ses we'll do sech fightin' as never another one reg'ment done.'

'They say we're catchin' it over on th' left. They say th' enemy driv' our line inteh a devil of a swamp an' took Hannises' batt'ry.'

'No sech thing. Hannises' batt'ry was 'long here 'bout a minute ago.'

'That young Hasbrouck, he makes a good off'cer. He ain't afraid 'a nothin'.'

'I met one of th' 148th Maine boys an' he ses his brigade fit th' hull rebel army fer four hours over on th' turnpike road an' killed about five thousand of 'em. He ses one more sech fight as that an' th' war'll be over.'

'Bill wasn't scared either. No, sir! It wasn't that. Bill ain't a-gittin' scared easy. He was jest mad, that's what he was. When that feller trod on his hand, he up an' sed that he was willin' t' give his hand t' his country, but he be umbed if he was goin' t' have every dumb bushwacker in th' kentry walkin' 'round on it. So he went t' th' hospital disregardless of th' fight. Three fingers was crunched. Th' dern doctor wanted t' amputate 'm, an' Bill, he raised a heluva row, I hear. He's a funny feller.'

The din in front swelled to a tremendous chorus. The youth and his fellows were frozen to silence. They could see a flag that tossed in the smoke angrily. Near it were the blurred and agitated forms of troops. There came a turbulent stream of men across the fields. A battery changing position at a frantic gallop scattered the stragglers right and left.

A shell screaming like a storm banshee went over the huddled heads of the reserves. It landed in the grove, and exploding redly flung the brown earth. There was a little shower of pine needles.

Bullets began to whistle among the branches and nip at the trees. Twigs and leaves came sailing down. It was as if a thousand axes, wee and invisible, were being wielded. Many of the men were constantly dodging and ducking their heads.

The lieutenant of the youth's company was shot in the hand. He began to swear so wondrously that a nervous laugh went along the regimental line. The officer's profanity sounded conventional. It relieved the tightened senses of the new men. It was as if he had hit his fingers with a tack hammer at home.

He held the wounded member carefully away from his side so that the blood would not drip upon his trousers.

The captain of the company, tucking his sword under his arm, produced a handkerchief and began to bind with it the lieutenant's wound. And they disputed as to how the binding should be done.

The battle flag in the distance jerked about madly. It seemed to be struggling to free itself from an agony. The billowing smoke was filled with horizontal flashes.

Men running swiftly emerged from it. They grew in numbers until it was seen that the whole command was fleeing. The flag suddenly sank down as if dying. Its motion as it fell was a gesture of despair.

Wild yells came from behind the walls of smoke. A sketch in grey and red dissolved into a moblike body of men who galloped like wild horses.

The veteran regiments on the right and left of the 304th immediately began to jeer. With the passionate song of the bullets and the banshee shrieks of shells were mingled loud catcalls and bits of facetious advice concerning places of safety.

But the new regiment was breathless with horror. 'Gawd! Saunders's got crushed!' whispered the man at the youth's elbow. They shrank back and crouched as if compelled to await a flood.

The youth shot a swift glance along the blue ranks of the regiment. The profiles were motionless, carven; and afterward he remembered that the colour sergeant was standing with his legs apart, as if he expected to be pushed to the ground.

The following throng went whirling around the flank. Here and there were officers carried along on the stream like exasperated chips. They were striking about them with their swords and with their left fists, punching every head they could reach. They cursed like highwaymen.

A mounted officer displayed the furious anger of a spoiled child. He raged with his head, his arms, and his legs.

Another, the commander of the brigade, was galloping about bawling. His hat was gone and his clothes were awry. He resembled a man who has come from bed to go to a fire. The hoofs of his horse often threatened the heads of the running men, but they scampered with singular fortune. In this rush they were apparently all deaf and blind. They heeded not the largest and longest of the oaths that were thrown at them from all directions.

Frequently over this tumult could be heard the grim jokes of the critical veterans; but the retreating men apparently were not even conscious of the presence of an audience.

The battle reflection that shone for an instant in the faces on the mad current made the youth feel that forceful hands from heaven would not have been able to have held him in place if he could have got intelligent control of his legs.

There was an appalling imprint upon these faces. The struggle in the smoke had pictured an exaggeration of itself on the bleached cheeks and in the eyes wild with one desire.

The sight of this stampede exerted a floodlike force that seemed able to drag sticks and stones and men from the ground. They of the reserves had to hold on. They grew pale and firm, and red and quaking.

The youth achieved one little thought in the midst of this chaos. The composite monster which had caused the other troops to flee had not then appeared. He resolved to get a view of it, and then, he thought he might very likely run better than the best of them.

V

THERE were moments of waiting. The youth thought of the village street at home before the arrival of the circus parade on a day in the spring. He remembered how he had stood, a small, thrillful boy, prepared to follow the dingy lady upon the white horse, or the band in its faded chariot. He saw the yellow road, the lines of expectant people, and the sober houses. He particularly remembered an old fellow who used to sit upon a cracker box in front of the store and feign to despise such exhibitions. A thousand details of colour and form surged in his mind. The old fellow upon the cracker box appeared in middle prominence.

Someone cried, 'Here they come!'

There was rustling and muttering among the men. They displayed a feverish desire to have every possible cartridge ready to their hands. The boxes were pulled around into various positions, and adjusted with great care. It was as if seven hundred new bonnets were being tried on.

The tall soldier, having prepared his rifle, produced a red handkerchief of some kind. He was engaged in knitting it about his throat with exquisite attention to its position, when the cry was repeated up and down the line in a muffled roar of sound.

'Here they come! Here they come!' Gun locks clicked.

Across the smoke-infested fields came a brown swarm of running men who were giving shrill yells. They came on, stooping and swinging their rifles at all angles. A flag, tilted forward, sped near the front.

As he caught sight of them the youth was momentarily startled by a thought that perhaps his gun was not loaded. He stood trying to rally his faltering intellect so that he might recollect the moment when he had loaded, but he could not.

A hatless general pulled his dripping horse to a stand near the colonel of the 304th. He shook his fist in the other's face. 'You've got to hold 'em back!' he shouted, savagely; 'you've got to hold 'em back!'

In his agitation the colonel began to stammer. 'A-all r-right, General, all right, by Gawd! We-we'll do our—we-we'll d-d-do—do our best, General.' The general made a passionate gesture and galloped away. The colonel, perchance to relieve his feelings, began to scold like a wet parrot. The youth, turning swiftly to make sure that the rear was unmolested, saw the commander regarding his men in a highly resentful manner, as if he regretted above everything his association with them.

The man at the youth's elbow was mumbling, as if to himself: 'Oh, we're in for it now! oh, we're in for it now!'

The captain of the company had been pacing excitedly to and fro in the rear. He coaxed in schoolmistress fashion as to a congregation of boys with primers. His talk was an endless repetition. 'Reserve your fire, boys—don't shoot till I tell you— save your fire—wait till they get close up—don't be damned fools—'

Perspiration streamed down the youth's face, which was soiled like that of a weeping urchin. He frequently, with a nervous movement, wiped his eyes with his coat sleeve. His mouth was still a little ways open.

He got the one glance at the foe-swarming field in front of him, and instantly ceased to debate the question of his piece being loaded. Before he was ready to begin—before he had announced to himself that he was about to fight—he threw the obedient, well-balanced rifle into position and fired a first wild shot. Directly he was working at his weapon like an automatic affair.

He suddenly lost concern for himself, and forgot to look at a menacing fate. He became not a man but a member. He felt that something of which he was a part—a regiment, an army, a cause, or a country—was in a crisis. He was welded into a common personality which was dominated by a single desire. For some moments he could not flee no more than a little finger can commit a revolution from a hand.

If he had thought the regiment was about to be annihilated perhaps he could have amputated himself from it. But its noise gave him assurance. The regiment was like a firework that, once ignited, proceeds superior to circumstances until its blazing vitality fades. It wheezed and banged with a mighty power. He pictured the ground before it as strewn with the discomfited.

There was a consciousness always of the presence of his comrades about him. He felt the subtle battle brotherhood more potent even than the cause for which they were fighting.

It was a mysterious fraternity born of the smoke and danger of death.

He was at a task. He was like a carpenter who has made many boxes, making still another box, only there was furious haste in his movements. He, in his thought, was careering off in other places, even as the carpenter who as he works whistles and thinks of his friend or his enemy, his home or a saloon. And these jolted dreams were never perfect to him afterward, but remained a mass of blurred shapes.

Presently he began to feel the effects of the war atmosphere—a blistering sweat, a sensation that his eyeballs were about to crack like hot stones. A burning roar filled his ears.

Following this came a red rage. He developed the acute exasperation of a pestered animal, a well-meaning cow worried by dogs. He had a mad feeling against his rifle, which could only be used against one life at a time. He wished to rush forward and strangle with his fingers. He craved a power that would enable him to make a world-sweeping gesture and brush all back. His impotency appeared to him, and made his rage into that of a driven beast.

Buried in the smoke of many rifles his anger was directed not so much against men whom he knew were rushing toward him as against the swirling battle phantoms which were choking him, stuffing their smoke robes down his parched throat. He fought frantically for respite for his senses, for air, as a babe being smothered attacks the deadly blankets.

There was a blare of heated rage mingled with a certain expression on intentness on all faces. Many of the men were making low-toned noises with their mouths, and these subdued cheers, snarls, imprecations, prayers, made a wild, barbaric song that went as an undercurrent of sound, strange and chant-like with the resounding chords of the war march. The man at the youth's elbow was babbling. In it there was something soft and tender like the monologue of a babe. The tall soldier was swearing in a loud voice. From his lips came a black procession of curious oaths. Of a sudden another broke out in a querulous way like a man who has mislaid his hat. 'Well, why don't they support us? Why don't they send supports? Do they think—'

The youth in his battle sleep heard this as one who dozes hears.

There was a singular absence of heroic poses. The men bending and surging in their haste and rage were in every impossible attitude. The steel ramrods clanked and clanged with incessant din as the men pounded them furiously into the hot rifle barrels. The flaps of the cartridge boxes were all unfastened, and bobbed idiotically with each movement. The rifles, once loaded, were jerked to the shoulder and fired without apparent aim into the smoke or at one of the blurred and shifting forms which upon the field before the regiment had been growing larger and larger like puppets under a magician's hand.

The officers, at their intervals, rearward, neglected to stand in picturesque attitudes. They were bobbing to and fro roaring directions and encouragements. The dimensions of their howls were extraordinary. They expended their lungs with prodigal wills. And often they nearly stood upon their heads in their anxiety to observe the enemy on the other side of the tumbling smoke.

The lieutenant of the youth's company had encountered a soldier who had fled screaming at the first volley of his comrades. Behind the lines these two were acting a little isolated scene. The man was blubbering and staring with sheeplike eyes at the lieutenant, who had seized him by the collar and was pommelling him. He drove him back into the ranks with many blows. The soldier went mechanically, dully, with his animal-like eyes upon the officer. Perhaps there was to him a divinity expressed in the voice of the other—stern, hard, with no reflection of fear in it. He tried to reload his gun, but his shaking hands prevented. The lieutenant was obliged to assist him.

The men dropped here and there like bundles. The captain of the youth's company had been killed in an early part of the action. His body lay stretched out in the position of a tired man resting, but upon his face there was an astonished and sorrowful look, as if he thought some friend had done him an ill turn. The babbling man was grazed by a shot that made the blood stream widely down his face. He clapped both hands to his head. 'Oh!' he said, and ran. Another grunted suddenly as if he had been struck by a club in the stomach. He sat down and gazed ruefully. In his eyes there was mute, indefinite reproach. Farther up the line a man standing behind a tree, had had his knee joint splintered by a ball. Immediately he had dropped his rifle and gripped the tree with both arms. And there he remained, clinging desperately and crying for assistance that he might withdraw his hold upon the tree.

At last an exultant yell went along the quivering line. The firing dwindled from an uproar to a last vindictive popping. As the smoke slowly eddied away, the youth saw that the charge had been repulsed. The enemy were scattered into reluctant groups. He saw a man climb to the top of the fence, straddle the rail, and fire a parting shot. The waves had receded, leaving bits of dark *débris* upon the ground.

Some in the regiment began to whoop frenziedly. Many were silent. Apparently they were trying to contemplate themselves.

After the fever had left his veins, the youth thought that at last he was going to suffocate. He became aware of the foul atmosphere in which he had been struggling. He was grimy and dripping like a labourer in a foundry. He grasped his canteen and took a long swallow of the warmed water.

A sentence with variations went up and down the line. 'Well, we've helt 'em back. We've helt 'em back; derned if we haven't.' The men said it blissfully, leering at each other with dirty smiles.

The youth turned to look behind him and off to the right and off to the left. He experienced the joy of a man who at last finds leisure in which to look about him.

Under foot there were a few ghastly forms motionless. They lay twisted in fantastic contortions. Arms were bent and heads were turned in incredible ways. It seemed that the dead men must have fallen from some great height to get into such positions. They looked to be dumped out upon the ground from the sky.

From a position in the rear of the grove a battery was throwing shells over it. The flash of the guns startled the youth at first. He thought they were aimed directly at him. Through the trees he watched the black figures of the gunners as they worked swiftly and intently. Their labour seemed a complicated thing. He wondered how they could remember its formula in the midst of confusion.

The guns squatted in a row like savage chiefs. They argued with abrupt violence. It was a grim pow-wow. Their busy servants ran hither and thither.

A small procession of wounded men were going drearily toward the rear. It was a flow of blood from the torn body of the brigade.

To the right and to the left were the dark lines of other troops. Far in front he thought he could see lighter masses protruding in points from the forest. They were suggestive of unnumbered thousands.

Once he saw a tiny battery go dashing along the line of the horizon. The tiny riders were beating the tiny horses.

From a sloping hill came the sound of cheerings and clashes. Smoke welled slowly through the leaves.

Batteries were speaking with thunderous oratorical effort. Here and there were flags, the red in the stripes dominating. They splashed bits of warm colour upon the dark lines of troops.

The youth felt the old thrill at the sight of the emblem. They were like beautiful birds strangely undaunted in a storm.

As he listened to the din from the hillside, to a deep pulsating thunder that came from afar to the left, and to the lesser clamours which came from many directions, it occurred to him that they were fighting, too, over there, and over there, and over there. Heretofore he had supposed that all the battle was directly under his nose.

As he gazed around him the youth felt a flash of astonishment at the blue, pure sky and the sun-gleamings on the trees and fields. It was surprising that Nature had gone tranquilly on with her golden process in the midst of so much devilment.

VI

THE youth awakened slowly. He came gradually back to a position from which he could regard himself. For moments he had been scrutinizing his person in a dazed way as if he had never before seen himself. Then he picked up his cap from the ground. He wriggled in his jacket to make a more comfortable fit, and kneeling relaced his shoe. He thoughtfully mopped his reeking features.

So it was all over at last! The supreme trial had been passed. The red, formidable difficulties of war had been vanquished.

He went into an ecstasy of self-satisfaction. He had the most delightful sensations of his life. Standing as if apart from himself, he viewed that last scene. He perceived that the man who had fought thus was magnificent.

He felt that he was a fine fellow. He saw himself even with those ideals which he had considered as far beyond him. He smiled in deep gratification.

Upon his fellows he beamed tenderness and good will. 'Gee! ain't it hot, hey?' he said affably to a man who was polishing his streaming face with his coat sleeves.

'You bet!' said the other, grinning sociably. 'I never seen sech dumb hotness.' He sprawled out luxuriously on the ground. 'Gee, yes! An' I hope we don't have no more fightin' till a week from Monday.'

There were some handshakings and deep speeches with men whose features were familiar, but with whom the youth now felt the bonds of tied hearts. He helped a cursing comrade to bind up a wound of the shin.

But, of a sudden, cries of amazement broke out along the ranks of the new regiment. 'Here they come ag'in! Here they come ag'in!' The man who had sprawled upon the ground started up and said, 'Gosh!'

The youth turned quick eyes upon the field. He discerned forms begin to swell in masses out of a distant wood. He again saw the tilted flag speeding forward.

The shells, which had ceased to trouble the regiment for a time, came swirling again, and exploded in the grass or among the leaves of the trees. They looked to be strange war flowers bursting into fierce bloom.

The men groaned. The lustre faded from their eyes. Their smudged countenances now expressed a profound dejection. They moved their stiffened bodies slowly, and watched in sullen mood the frantic approach of the enemy. The slaves toiling in the temple of this god began to feel rebellion at his harsh tasks.

They fretted and complained each to each. 'Oh, say, this is too much of a good thing! Why can't somebody send us supports?'

'We ain't never goin' to stand this second banging. I didn't come here to fight the hull damn' rebel army.'

There was one who raised a doleful cry. 'I wish Bill Smithers had trod on my hand, insteader me treddin' on his'n.' The sore joints of the regiment creaked as it painfully floundered into position to repulse.

The youth stared. Surely, he thought, this impossible thing was not about to happen. He waited as if he expected the enemy to suddenly stop, apologize, and retire bowing. It was all a mistake.

But the firing began somewhere on the regimental line and ripped along in both directions. The level sheets of flame developed great clouds of smoke that tumbled and tossed in the mild wind near the ground for a moment, and then rolled through the ranks as through a gate. The clouds were tinged an earthlike yellow in the sun-rays and in the shadow were a sorry blue. The flag was sometimes eaten and lost in this mass of vapour, but more often it projected, sun-touched, resplendent.

Into the youth's eyes there came a look that one can see in the orbs of a jaded horse. His neck was quivering with nervous weakness and the muscles of his arms felt numb and bloodless. His hands, too, seemed large and awkward as if he was wearing invisible mittens. And there was a great uncertainty about his knee joints.

The words that comrades had uttered previous to the firing began to recur to him. 'Oh, say, this is too much of a good thing! What do they take us for—why don't they send supports? I didn't come here to fight the hull damned rebel army.'

He began to exaggerate the endurance, the skill, and the valour of those who were coming. Himself reeling from exhaustion, he was astonished beyond measure at such persistency. They must be machines of steel. It was very gloomy struggling against such affairs, wound up perhaps to fight until sundown.

He slowly lifted his rifle and catching a glimpse of the thick-spread field he blazed at a cantering cluster. He stopped then and began to peer as best he could through the smoke. He caught changing views of the ground covered with men who were all running like pursued imps, and yelling.

To the youth it was an onslaught of redoubtable dragons. He became like the man who lost his legs at the approach of the red and green monster. He waited in a sort of a horrified, listening attitude. He seemed to shut his eyes and wait to be gobbled.

A man near him who up to this time had been working feverishly at his rifle suddenly stopped and ran with howls. A lad whose face had borne an expression of exalted courage, the majesty of he who dares give his life, was, at an instant, smitten abject. He blanched like one who has come to the edge of a cliff at midnight and is suddenly made aware. There was a revelation.

He, too, threw down his gun and fled. There was no shame in his face. He ran like a rabbit.

Others began to scamper away through the smoke. The youth turned his head, shaken from his trance by this movement as if the regiment was leaving him behind. He saw the few fleeting forms.

He yelled then with fright and swung about. For a moment, in the great clamour, he was like a proverbial chicken. He lost the direction of safety. Destruction threatened him from all points.

Directly he began to speed toward the rear in great leaps. His rifle and cap were gone. His unbuttoned coat bulged in the wind. The flap of his cartridge box bobbed wildly, and his canteen, by its slender cord, swung out behind. On his face was all the horror of those things which he imagined.

The lieutenant sprang forward bawling. The youth saw his features wrathfully red, and saw him make a dab with his sword. His one thought of the incident was that the lieutenant was a peculiar creature to feel interested in such matters upon this occasion.

He ran like a blind man. Two or three times he fell down. Once he knocked his shoulder so heavily against a tree that he went headlong.

Since he had turned his back upon the fight his fears had been wondrously magnified. Death about to thrust him between the shoulder blades was far more dreadful than death about to smite him between the eyes. When he thought of it later, he conceived the impression that it is better to view the appalling than to be merely within hearing. The noises of the battle were like stones; he believed himself liable to be crushed.

As he ran on he mingled with others. He dimly saw men on his right and on his left, and he heard footsteps behind him. He thought that all the regiment was fleeing, pursued by these ominous crashes.

In his flight the sound of these following footsteps gave him his one meagre relief. He felt vaguely that death must make a first choice of the men who were nearest; the initial morsels for the dragons would be then those who were following him. So he displayed the zeal of an insane sprinter in his purpose to keep them in the rear. There was a race.

As he, leading, went across a little field, he found himself in a region of shells. They hurtled over his head with long wild screams. As he listened he imagined them to have rows of cruel teeth that grinned at him. Once one lit before him and the vivid lightning of the explosion effectually barred the way in his chosen direction. He grovelled on the ground and then springing up went careering off through some bushes.

He experienced a thrill of amazement when he came within view of a battery in action. The men there seemed to be in conventional moods, altogether unaware of the impending annihilation. The battery was disputing with a distant antagonist and the gunners were wrapped in admiration of their shooting. They were continually bending in coaxing postures over the guns. They seemed to be patting them on the back and encouraging them with words. The guns, stolid and undaunted, spoke with dogged valour.

The precise gunners were coolly enthusiastic. They lifted their eyes every chance to the smoke-wreathed hillock from whence the hostile battery addressed them. The youth pitied them as he ran. Methodical idiots! Machinelike fools! The refined joy of planting shells in the midst of the other battery's formation would appear a little thing when the infantry came swooping out of the woods.

The face of a youthful rider, who was jerking his frantic horse with an abandon of temper he might display in a placid barnyard, was impressed deeply upon his mind. He knew that he looked upon a man who would presently be dead.

Too, he felt a pity for the guns, standing, six good comrades, in a bold row.

He saw a brigade going to the relief of its pestered fellows. He scrambled upon a wee hill and watched it sweeping finely, keeping formation in difficult places. The blue of the line was crusted with steel colour, and the brilliant flags projected. Officers were shouting.

This sight also filled him with wonder. The brigade was hurrying briskly to be gulped into the infernal mouths of the war god. What manner of men were they, anyhow? Ah, it was some wondrous breed! Or else they didn't comprehend—the fools.

A furious order caused commotion in the artillery. An officer on a bounding horse made maniacal motions with his arms. The teams went swinging up from the rear, the guns were whirled about, and the battery scampered away. The cannon with their noses poked slantingly at the ground grunted and grumbled like stout men, brave but with objections to hurry.

The youth went on, moderating his pace since he had left the place of noises.

Later he came upon a general of division seated upon a horse that pricked its ears in an interested way at the battle. There was a great gleaming of yellow and patent leather about the saddle and bridle. The quiet man astride looked mouse-coloured upon such a splendid charger.

A jingling staff was galloping hither and thither. Sometimes the general was surrounded by horsemen and at other times he was quite alone. He looked to be much harassed. He had the appearance of a business man whose market is swinging up and down.

The youth went slinking around this spot. He went as near as he dared trying to overhear words. Perhaps the general, unable to comprehend chaos, might call upon him for information. And he could tell him. He knew all concerning it. Of a surety the force was in a fix, and any fool could see that if they did not retreat while they had opportunity—why—

He felt that he would like to thrash the general, or at least approach and tell him in plain words exactly what he thought him to be. It was criminal to stay calmly in one spot and make no effort to stay destruction. He loitered in a fever of eagerness for the division commander to apply to him.

As he warily moved about, he heard the general call out irritably: 'Tompkins, go over an' see Taylor, an' tell him not t' be in such an all-fired hurry; tell him t' halt his brigade in th' edge of th' woods; tell him t' detach a reg'ment—say I think th' centre 'll break if we don't help it out some; tell him t' hurry up.'

A slim youth on a fine chestnut horse caught these swift words from the mouth of his superior. He made his horse bound into a gallop almost from a walk in his haste to go upon his mission. There was a cloud of dust.

A moment later the youth saw the general bounce excitedly in his saddle.

'Yes, by heavens, they have!' The officer leaned forward. His face was aflame with excitement. 'Yes, by heavens, they've held 'im! They've held 'im!'

He began to blithely roar at his staff: 'We'll wallop 'im now. We'll wallop 'im now. We've got 'em sure.' He turned suddenly upon an aide: 'Here—you—Jones—quick—ride after Tompkins—see Taylor —tell him t' go in—everlastingly—like blazes—anything.'

As another officer sped his horse after the first messenger, the general beamed upon the earth like a sun. In his eyes was a desire to chant a paean. He kept repeating, 'They've held 'em, by heavens!'

His excitement made his horse plunge, and he merrily kicked and swore at it. He held a little carnival of joy on horseback.

VII

THE youth cringed as if discovered in a crime. By heavens, they had won after all! The imbecile line had remained and become victors. He could hear cheering.

He lifted himself upon his toes and looked in the direction of the fight. A yellow fog lay wallowing on the treetops. From beneath it came the clatter of musketry. Hoarse cries told of an advance.

He turned away amazed and angry. He felt that he had been wronged.

He had fled, he told himself, because annihilation approached. He had done a good part in saving himself, who was a little piece of the army. He had considered the time, he said, to be one in which it was the duty of every little piece to rescue itself if possible. Later the officers could fit the little pieces together again, and make a battle front. If none of the little pieces were wise enough to save themselves from the flurry of death at such a time, why, then, where would be the army? It was all plain that he had proceeded according to very correct and commendable rules. His actions had been sagacious things. They had been full of strategy. They were the work of a master's legs.

Thoughts of his comrades came to him. The brittle blue line had withstood the blows and won. He grew bitter over it. It seemed that the blind ignorance and stupidity of those little pieces had betrayed him. He had been overturned and crushed by their lack of sense in holding the position, when intelligent deliberation would have convinced them that it was impossible.

He, the enlightened man who looks afar in the dark, had fled because of his superior perceptions and knowledge. He felt a great anger against his comrades. He knew it could be proved that they had been fools.

He wondered what they would remark when later he appeared in camp. His mind heard howls of derision. Their destiny would not enable them to understand his sharper point of view.

He began to pity himself acutely. He was ill used. He was trodden beneath the feet of an iron injustice. He had proceeded with wisdom and from the most righteous motives under heaven's blue only to be frustrated by hateful circumstances.

A dull, animal-like rebellion against his fellows, war in the abstract, and fate grew within him. He shambled along with bowed head, his brain in a tumult of agony and despair. When he looked loweringly up, quivering at each sound, his eyes had the expression of those of a criminal who thinks his guilt and his punishment great, and knows that he can find no words.

He went from the fields into a thick wood, as if resolved to bury himself. He wished to get out of hearing of the crackling shots which were to him like voices.

The ground was cluttered with vines and bushes, and the trees grew close and spread out like bouquets. He was obliged to force his way with much noise. The creepers, catching against his legs, cried out harshly as their sprays were torn from the barks of trees. The swishing saplings tried to make known his presence to the world. He could not conciliate the forest. As he made his way, it was always calling out protestations. When he separated embraces of trees and vines the disturbed foliages waved their arms and turned their face leaves toward him. He dreaded lest these noisy motions and cries should bring men to look at him. So he went far, seeking dark and intricate places.

After a time the sound of musketry grew faint and the cannon boomed in the distance. The sun, suddenly apparent, blazed among the trees. The insects were making rhythmical noises. They seemed to be grinding their teeth in unison. A woodpecker stuck his impudent head around the side of a tree. A bird flew on light-hearted wing.

Off was the rumble of death. It seemed now that Nature had no ears.

This landscape gave him assurance. A fair field holding life.

It was the religion of peace. It would die if its timid eyes were compelled to see blood. He conceived Nature to be a woman with a deep aversion to tragedy.

He threw a pine cone at a jovial squirrel, and he ran with chattering fear. High in a treetop he stopped, and, poking his head cautiously from behind a branch, looked down with an air of trepidation.

The youth felt triumphant at this exhibition. There was the law, he said. Nature had given him a sign. The squirrel, immediately upon recognizing danger, had taken to his legs without ado. He did not stand stolidly baring his furry belly to the missile, and die with an upward glance at the sympathetic heavens. On the contrary, he had fled as fast as his legs could carry him; and he was but an ordinary squirrel, too—doubtless no philosopher of his race. The youth wended, feeling that Nature was of his mind. She re-enforced his argument with proofs that lived where the sun shone.

Once he found himself almost into a swamp. He was obliged to walk upon bog tufts and watch his feet to keep from the oily mire. Pausing at one time to look about him he saw, out at some black water, a small animal pounce in and emerge directly with a gleaming fish.

The youth went again into the deep thickets. The brushed branches made a noise that drowned the sounds of cannon. He walked on, going from obscurity into promises of a greater obscurity.

At length he reached a place where the high, arching boughs made a chapel. He softly pushed the green doors aside and entered. Pine needles were a gentle brown carpet. There was a religious half light.

Near the threshold he stopped, horror-stricken at the sight of a thing.

He was being looked at by a dead man who was seated with his back against a columnlike tree. The corpse was dressed in a uniform that once had been blue, but was now faded to a melancholy shade of green. The eyes, staring at the youth, had changed to the dull hue to be seen on the side of a dead fish. The mouth was open. Its red had changed to an appalling yellow. Over the grey skin of the face ran little ants. One was trundling some sort of a bundle along the upper lip.

The youth gave a shriek as he confronted the thing. He was for moments turned to stone before it. He remained staring into the liquid-looking eyes. The dead man and the living man exchanged a long look. Then the youth cautiously put one hand behind him and brought it against a tree. Leaning upon this he retreated, step by step, with his face still toward the thing. He feared that if he turned his back the body might spring up and stealthily pursue him.

The branches, pushing against him, threatened to throw him over upon it. His unguided feet, too, caught aggravatingly in brambles; and with it all he received a subtle suggestion to touch the corpse. As he thought of his hand upon it he shuddered profoundly.

At last he burst the bonds which had fastened him to the spot and fled, unheeding the underbrush. He was pursued by a sight of the black ants swarming greedily upon the grey face and venturing horribly near to the eyes.

After a time he paused, and, breathless and panting, listened. He imagined some strange voice would come from the dead throat and squawk after him in horrible menaces.

The trees about the portals of the chapel moved soughingly in a soft wind. A sad silence was upon the little guarding edifice.

VIII

THE trees began softly to sing a hymn of twilight. The sun sank until slanted bronze rays struck the forest. There was a lull in the noises of insects as if they had bowed their beaks and were making a devotional pause. There was silence save for the chanted chorus of the trees.

Then, upon this stillness, there suddenly broke a tremendous clangour of sounds. A crimson roar came from the distance.

The youth stopped. He was transfixed by this terrific medley of all noises. It was as if worlds were being rended. There was the ripping sound of musketry and the breaking crash of the artillery.

His mind flew in all directions. He conceived the two armies to be at each other panther fashion. He listened for a time. Then he began to run in the direction of the battle. He saw that it was an ironical thing for him to be running thus toward that which he had been at such pains to avoid. But he said, in substance, to himself that if the earth and the moon were about to clash, many persons would doubtless plan to get upon the roofs to witness the collision.

As he ran, he became aware that the forest had stopped its music, as if at last becoming capable of hearing the foreign sounds. The trees hushed and stood motionless. Everything seemed to be listening to the crackle and clatter and ear-shaking thunder. The chorus pealed over the still earth.

It suddenly occurred to the youth that the fight in which he had been was, after all, but perfunctory popping. In the hearing of this present din he was doubtful if he had seen real battle scenes. This uproar explained a celestial battle; it was tumbling hordes a-struggle in the air.

Reflecting, he saw a sort of humour in the point of view of himself and his fellows during the late encounter. They had taken themselves and the enemy very seriously and had imagined that they were deciding the war. Individuals must have supposed that they were cutting the letters of their names deep into everlasting tablets of brass, or enshrining their reputations for ever in the hearts of their countrymen, while, as to fact, the affair would appear in printed reports under a meek and immaterial title. But he saw that it was good, else, he said, in battle every one would surely run save forlorn hopes and their ilk.

He went rapidly on. He wished to come to the edge of the forest that he might peer out.

As he hastened, there passed through his mind pictures of stupendous conflicts. His accumulated thought upon such subjects was used to form scenes. The noise was as the voice of an eloquent being, describing.

Sometimes the brambles formed chains and tried to hold him back. Trees, confronting him, stretched out their arms and forbade him to pass. After its previous hostility this new resistance of the forest filled him with a fine bitterness. It seemed that Nature could not be quite ready to kill him.

But he obstinately took roundabout ways, and presently he was where he could see long grey walls of vapour where lay battle lines. The voices of cannon shook him. The musketry sounded in long irregular surges that played havoc with his ears. He stood regardant for a moment. His eyes had an awe-struck expression. He gawked in the direction of the fight.

Presently he proceeded again on his forward way. The battle was like the grinding of an immense and terrible machine to him. Its complexities and powers, its grim processes, fascinated him. He must go close and see it produce corpses.

He came to a fence and clambered over it. On the far side, the ground was littered with clothes and guns. A newspaper, folded up, lay in the dirt. A dead soldier was stretched with his face hidden in his arm. Farther off there was a group of four or five corpses keeping mournful company. A hot sun had blazed upon the spot.

In this place the youth felt that he was an invader. This forgotten part of the battle ground was owned by the dead men, and he hurried, in the vague apprehension that one of the swollen forms would rise and tell him to begone.

He came finally to a road from which he could see in the distance dark and agitated bodies of troops, smoke-fringed. In the lane was a bloodstained crowd streaming to the rear. The wounded men were cursing, groaning, and wailing. In the air, always, was a mighty swell of sound that it seemed could sway the earth. With the courageous words of the artillery and the spiteful sentences of the musketry mingled red cheers. And from this region of noises came the steady current of the maimed.

One of the wounded men had a shoeful of blood. He hopped like a schoolboy in a game. He was laughing hysterically.

One was swearing that he had been shot in the arm through the commanding general's mismanagement of the army. One was marching with an air imitative of some sublime drum major. Upon his features was an unholy mixture of merriment and agony. As he marched he sang a bit of doggerel in a high and quavering voice:

> Sing a song'a vic'try,
>   A pocketful'a bullets,
> Five an' twenty dead men
>   Baked in a—pie.

Parts of the procession limped and staggered to this tune.

Another had the grey seal of death already upon his face. His lips were curled in hard lines and his teeth were clinched. His hands were bloody from where he had pressed them upon his wound. He seemed to be awaiting the moment when he should pitch headlong. He stalked like the spectre of a soldier, his eyes burning with the power of a stare into the unknown.

There were some who proceeded sullenly, full of anger at their wounds, and ready to turn upon anything as an obscure cause.

An officer was carried along by two privates. He was peevish. 'Don't joggle so, Johnson, yeh fool,' he cried. 'Think m' leg is made of iron? If yeh can't carry me decent, put me down an' let someone else do it.'

He bellowed at the tottering crowd who blocked the quick march of his bearers. 'Say, make way there, can't yeh? Make way, dickens take it all.'

They sulkily parted and went to the roadsides. As he was carried past they made pert remarks to him. When he raged in reply and threatened them, they told him to be damned.

The shoulder of one of the tramping bearers knocked heavily against the spectral soldier who was staring into the unknown.

The youth joined this crowd and marched along with it. The torn bodies expressed the awful machinery in which the men had been entangled.

Orderlies and couriers occasionally broke through the throng in the roadway, scattering wounded men right and left, galloping on, followed by howls. The melancholy march was continually disturbed by the messengers, and sometimes by bustling batteries that came swinging and thumping down upon them, the officers shouting orders to clear the way.

There was a tattered man, fouled with dust, blood and powder stain from hair to shoes, who trudged quietly at the youth's side. He was listening with eagerness and much humility to the lurid descriptions of a bearded sergeant. His lean features wore an expression of awe and admiration. He was like a listener in a country store to wondrous tales told among the sugar barrels. He eyed the story-teller with unspeakable wonder. His mouth was agape in yokel fashion.

The sergeant, taking note of this, gave pause to his elaborate history while he administered a sardonic comment. 'Be keerful, honey, you'll be a-ketchin' flies,' he said.

The tattered man shrank back abashed.

After a time he began to sidle near to the youth, and in a different way try to make him a friend. His voice was gentle as a girl's voice and his eyes were pleading. The youth saw with surprise that the soldier had two wounds, one in the head, bound with a blood-soaked rag, and the other in the arm, making that member dangle like a broken bough.

After they had walked together for some time the tattered man mustered sufficient courage to speak. 'Was pretty good fight, wa'n't it?' he timidly said. The youth, deep in thought, glanced up at the bloody and grim figure with its lamb-like eyes. 'What?'

'Was pretty good fight, wa'n't it?'

'Yes,' said the youth shortly. He quickened his pace.

But the other hobbled industriously after him. There was an air of apology in his manner, but he evidently thought that he needed only to talk for a time, and the youth would perceive that he was a good fellow.

'Was pretty good fight, wa'n't it?' he began in a small voice, and then he achieved the fortitude to continue. 'Dern me if I ever see fellers fight so. Lawd, how they did fight! I knowed th' boys 'd like when they onct got square at it. Th' boys ain't had no fair chanct up t' now, but this time they showed what they was. I knowed it 'd turn out this way. Yeh can't lick them boys. No, sir! They're fighters, they be.'

He breathed a deep breath of humble admiration. He had looked at the youth for encouragement several times. He received none, but gradually he seemed to get absorbed in his subject.

'I was talkin' 'cross pickets with a boy from Georgie, oncet, an' that boy, he ses, "Your fellers 'll all run like hell when they oncet hearn a gun," he ses. "Mebbe they will," I ses, "but I don't b'lieve none of it." I ses; "an' b'jiminey," I ses back t' 'um, "mebbe your fellers 'll all run like hell when they oncet hearn a gun," I ses. He larfed. Well, they didn't run t'-day, did they, hey? No, sir! They fit, an' fit, an' fit.'

His homely face was suffused with a light of love for the army which was to him all things beautiful and powerful.

After a time he turned to the youth. 'Where yeh hit, ol' boy?' he asked in a brotherly tone.

The youth felt instant panic at this question, although at first its full import was not borne in upon him.

'What?' he asked.

'Where yeh hit?' repeated the tattered man.

'Why,' began the youth, 'I—I—that is—why—I—'

He turned away suddenly and slid through the crowd. His brow was heavily flushed, and his fingers were picking nervously at one of his buttons. He bent his head and fastened his eyes studiously upon the button as if it were a little problem.

The tattered man looked after him in astonishment.

IX

THE youth fell back in the procession until the tattered soldier was not in sight. Then he started to walk on with the others.

But he was amid wounds. The mob of men was bleeding. Because of the tattered soldier's question he now felt that his shame could be viewed. He was continually casting sidelong glances to see if the men were contemplating the letters of guilt he felt burned into his brow.

At times he regarded the wounded soldiers in an envious way. He conceived persons with torn bodies to be peculiarly happy. He wished that he, too, had a wound, a red badge of courage.

The spectral soldier was at his side like a stalking reproach. The man's eyes were still fixed in a stare into the unknown. His grey, appalling face had attracted attention in the crowd, and men, slowing to his dreary pace, were walking with him. They were discussing his plight, questioning him and giving him advice. In a dogged way he repelled them, signing to them to go on and leave him alone. The shadows of his face were deepening and his tight lips seemed holding in check the moan of great despair. There could be seen a certain stiffness in the movements of his body, as if he were taking infinite care not to arouse the passion of his wounds. As he went on, he seemed always looking for a place, like one who goes to choose a grave.

Something in the gesture of the man as he waved the bloody and pitying soldiers away made the youth start as if bitten. He yelled in horror. Tottering forward he laid a quivering hand upon the man's arm. As the latter slowly turned his wax-like features toward him, the youth screamed:

'Gawd! Jim Conklin!'

The tall soldier made a little commonplace smile. 'Hello, Henry,' he said.

The youth swayed on his legs and glared strangely. He stuttered and stammered. 'Oh, Jim—oh, Jim—oh, Jim—'

The tall soldier held out his gory hand. There was a curious red and black combination of new blood and old blood upon it. 'Where yeh been, Henry?' he asked. He continued in a monotonous voice,

'I thought mebbe yeh got keeled over. There's been thunder t' pay t'-day. I was worryin' about it a good deal.'

The youth still lamented. 'Oh, Jim—oh, Jim—oh, Jim—'

'Yeh know,' said the tall soldier, 'I was out there.' He made a careful gesture. 'An', Lord, what a circus! An', b'jiminey, I got shot—I got shot. Yes, b'jiminey, I got shot.' He reiterated this fact in a bewildered way, as if he did not know how it came about.

The youth put forth anxious arms to assist him, but the tall soldier went firmly on as if propelled. Since the youth's arrival as a guardian for his friend, the other wounded men had ceased to display much interest. They occupied themselves again in dragging their own tragedies toward the rear.

Suddenly, as the two friends marched on, the tall soldier seemed to be overcome by a terror. His face turned to a semblance of grey paste. He clutched the youth's arm and looked all about him, as if dreading to be overheard. Then he began to speak in a shaking whisper:

'I tell yeh what I'm 'fraid of, Henry—I'll tell yeh what I'm 'fraid of. I'm 'fraid I'll fall down—an' then yeh know—them damned artillery wagons—they like as not 'll run over me. That's what I'm 'fraid of—'

The youth cried out to him hysterically: 'I'll take care of yeh, Jim! I'll take care of yeh! I swear t' Gawd I will!'

'Sure—will yeh, Henry?' the tall soldier beseeched.

'Yes—yes—I tell yeh—I'll take care of yeh, Jim!' protested the youth. He could not speak accurately because of the gulpings in his throat.

But the tall soldier continued to beg in a lowly way. He now hung babelike to the youth's arm. His eyes rolled in the wildness of his terror. 'I was allus a good friend t' yeh, wa'n't I, Henry? I've allus been a pretty good feller, ain't I? An' it ain't much t' ask, is it? Jest t' pull me along outer th' road? I'd do it fer you, wouldn't I, Henry?'

He paused in piteous anxiety to await his friend's reply.

The youth had reached an anguish where the sobs scorched him. He strove to express his loyalty, but he could only make fantastic gestures.

However, the tall soldier seemed suddenly to forget all those fears. He became again the grim, stalking spectre of a soldier. He went stonily forward. The youth wished his friend to lean upon him, but the other always shook his head and strangely protested. 'No—no—no—leave me be—leave me be—'

His look was fixed again upon the unknown. He moved with mysterious purpose, and all of the youth's offers he brushed aside. 'No—no—leave me be—leave me be—'

The youth had to follow.

Presently the latter heard a voice talking softly near his shoulders. Turning he saw that it belonged to the tattered soldier. 'Ye'd better take 'im outa th' road, pardner. There's a batt'ry comin' helitywhoop down th' road an' he'll git runned over. He's a goner anyhow in about five minutes—yeh kin see that. Ye'd better take 'im outa th' road. Where th' blazes does he git his stren'th from?'

'Lord knows!' cried the youth. He was shaking his hands helplessly.

He ran forward presently and grasped the tall soldier by the arm. 'Jim! Jim!' he coaxed, 'come with me.'

The tall soldier weakly tried to wrench himself free. 'Huh,' he said vacantly. He stared at the youth for a moment. At last he spoke as if dimly comprehending. 'Oh! Inteh th' fields? Oh!'

He started blindly through the grass.

The youth turned once to look at the lashing riders and jouncing guns of the battery. He was startled from this view by a shrill outcry from the tattered man.

'Gawd! He's runnin'!'

Turning his head swiftly, the youth saw his friend running in a staggering and stumbling way toward a little clump of bushes. His heart seemed to wrench itself almost free from his body at this sight. He made a noise of pain. He and the tattered man began a pursuit. There was a singular race.

When he overtook the tall soldier he began to plead with all the words he could find. 'Jim—Jim—what are you doing—what makes you do this way—you'll hurt yourself.'

The same purpose was in the tall soldier's face. He protested in a dulled way, keeping his eyes fastened on the mystic place of his intentions. 'No—no—don't tech me—leave me be—leave me be—'

The youth, aghast and filled with wonder at the tall soldier, began quaveringly to question him. 'Where yeh goin', Jim? What you thinking about? Where you going? Tell me, won't you, Jim?'

The tall soldier faced about as upon relentless pursuers. In his eyes there was a great appeal. 'Leave me be, can't yeh? Leave me be fer a minnit.'

The youth recoiled. 'Why, Jim,' he said, in a dazed way, 'what's the matter with you?'

The tall soldier turned and, lurching dangerously, went on. The youth and the tattered soldier followed, sneaking as if whipped, feeling unable to face the stricken man if he should again confront them. They began to have thoughts of a solemn ceremony. There was something ritelike in these movements of the doomed soldier. And there was a resemblance in him to a devotee of a mad religion, blood-sucking, muscle-wrenching, bone-crushing. They were awed and afraid. They hung back lest he have at command a dreadful weapon.

At last, they saw him stop and stand motionless. Hastening up, they perceived that his face wore an expression telling that he had at last found the place for which he had struggled. His spare figure was erect; his bloody hands were quietly at his side. He was waiting with patience for something that he had come to meet. He was at the rendezvous. They paused and stood, expectant.

There was a silence.

Finally, the chest of the doomed soldier began to heave with a strained motion. It increased in violence until it was as if an animal was within and was kicking and tumbling furiously to be free.

This spectacle of gradual strangulation made the youth writhe, and once as his friend rolled his eyes, he saw something in them that made him sink wailing to the ground. He raised his voice in a last supreme call.

'Jim—Jim—Jim—'

The tall soldier opened his lips and spoke. He made a gesture. 'Leave me be—don't tech me—leave me be—'

There was another silence while he waited.

Suddenly, his form stiffened and straightened. Then it was shaken by a prolonged ague. He stared into space. To the two watchers there was a curious and profound dignity in the firm lines of his awful face.

He was invaded by a creeping strangeness that slowly enveloped him. For a moment the tremor of his legs caused him to dance a sort of hideous hornpipe. His arms beat wildly about his head in expression of implike enthusiasm.

His tall figure stretched itself to its full height. There was a slight rending sound. Then it began to swing forward, slow and straight, in the manner of a falling tree. A swift muscular contortion made the left shoulder strike the ground first.

The body seemed to bounce a little way from the earth. 'God!' said the tattered soldier.

The youth had watched, spellbound, this ceremony at the place of meeting. His face had been twisted into an expression of every agony he had imagined for his friend.

He now sprang to his feet and, going closer, gazed upon the pastelike face. The mouth was opened and the teeth showed in a laugh.

As the flap of the blue jacket fell away from the body, he could see that the side looked as if it had been chewed by wolves.

The youth turned, with sudden, livid rage, toward the battlefield. He shook his fist. He seemed about to deliver a philippic.

'Hell—'

The red sun was pasted in the sky like a wafer.

X

THE tattered man stood musing.

'Well, he was reg'lar jim-dandy fer nerve, wa'n't he,' said he finally in a little awestruck voice. 'A reg'lar jim-dandy.' He thoughtfully poked one of the docile hands with his foot. 'I wonner where he got 'is stren'th from? I never seen a man do like that before. It was a funny thing. Well, he was a reg'lar jim-dandy.'

The youth desired to screech out his grief. He was stabbed, but his tongue lay dead in the tomb of his mouth. He threw himself again upon the ground and began to brood.

The tattered man stood musing.

'Look-a-here, pardner,' he said, after a time. He regarded the corpse as he spoke. 'He's up an' gone, ain't 'e, an' we might as well begin t' look out fer ol' number one. This here thing is all over. He's up an' gone, ain't 'e? An' he's all right here. Nobody won't bother 'im. An' I must say I ain't enjoying any great health m'self these days.'

The youth, awakened by the tattered soldier's tone, looked

quickly up. He saw that he was swinging uncertainly on his legs and that his face had turned to a shade of blue.

'Good Lord!' he cried, 'you ain't goin' t'—not you, too.'

The tattered man waved his hand. 'Nary die,' he said. 'All I want is some pea soup an' a good bed. Some pea soup,' he repeated dreamfully.

The youth arose from the ground. 'I wonder where he came from. I left him over there.' He pointed. 'And now I find 'im here. And he was coming from over there, too.' He indicated a new direction. They both turned toward the body as if to ask of it a question.

'Well,' at length spoke the tattered man, 'there ain't no use in our stayin' here an' tryin' t' ask him anything.'

The youth nodded an assent wearily. They both turned to gaze for a moment at the corpse.

The youth murmured something.

'Well, he was a jim-dandy, wa'n't 'e?' said the tattered man as if in response.

They turned their backs upon it and started away. For a time they stole softly, treading with their toes. It remained laughing there in the grass.

'I'm commencin' t' feel pretty bad,' said the tattered man, suddenly breaking one of his little silences. 'I'm commencin' t' feel pretty damn' bad.'

The youth groaned. 'Oh Lord!' He wondered if he was to be the tortured witness of another grim encounter.

But his companion waved his hand reassuringly. 'Oh, I'm not goin' t' die yit! There's too much dependin' on me fer me t' die yit. No, sir! Nary die! I *can't!* Ye'd oughta see th' swad a' chil'ren I've got, an' all like that.'

The youth glancing at his companion could see by the shadow of a smile that he was making some kind of fun.

As they plodded on the tattered soldier continued to talk. 'Besides, if I died, I wouldn't die th' way that feller did. That was th' funniest thing. I'd jest flop down, I would. I never seen a feller die th' way that feller did.

'Yeh know Tom Jamison, he lives next door t' me up home. He's a nice feller, he is, an' we was allus good friends. Smart, too. Smart as a steel trap. Well, when we was a-fightin' this afternoon, all-of-a-sudden he begin t' rip up an' cuss an' beller at me. "Yer shot, yeh blamed infernal!"—he swear horrible—he ses t' me. I put up m' hand t' m' head an' when I looked at m' fingers, I seen, sure 'nough, I was shot. I give a holler an' begin t' run, but b'fore I could git away another one hit me in th' arm an' whirl' me clean 'round. I got skeared when they was all a-shootin' b'hind me an' I run t' beat all, but I cotch it pretty bad. I've an idee I'd a' been fightin' yit, if t'wasn't fer Tom Jamison.'

Then he made a calm announcement: 'There's two of 'em—little ones—but they're beginnin' t' have fun with me now. I don't b'lieve I kin walk much furder.'

They went slowly on in silence. 'Yeh look pretty peeked yerself,' said the tattered man at last. 'I bet yeh 've got a worser one than yeh think. Ye'd better take keer of yer hurt. It don't do t' let sech things go. It might be inside mostly, an' them plays thunder. Where is it located?' But he continued his harangue without waiting for a reply. 'I see' a feller git hit plum in th' head when my reg'ment was a-standin' at ease onct. An' everybody yelled out to 'im: Hurt, John? Are yeh hurt much? "No," ses he. He looked kinder surprised, an' he went on tellin' 'em how he felt. He sed he didn't feel nothin'. But, by dad, th' first thing that feller knowed he was dead. Yes, he was dead—stone dead. So, yeh wanta watch out. Yeh might have some queer kind 'a hurt yerself. Yeh can't never tell. Where is your'n located?'

The youth had been wriggling since the introduction of this topic. He now gave a cry of exasperation and made a furious motion with his hand. 'Oh, don't bother me!' he said. He was enraged against the tattered man, and could have strangled him. His companions seemed ever to play intolerable parts. They were ever upraising the ghost of shame on the stick of their curiosity. He turned toward the tattered man as one at bay. 'Now, don't bother me,' he repeated with desperate menace.

'Well, Lord knows I don't wanta bother anybody,' said the other. There was a little accent of despair in his voice as he replied, 'Lord knows I've got a 'nough m' own t' tend to.'

The youth, who had been holding a bitter debate with himself and casting glances of hatred and contempt at the tattered man, here spoke in a hard voice. 'Good-bye,' he said.

The tattered man looked at him in gaping amazement. 'Why— why, pardner, where yeh goin'?' he asked unsteadily. The youth looking at him, could see that he, too, like that other one, was beginning to act dumb and animal-like. His thoughts seemed to be floundering about in his head. 'Now—now—look—a—here, you Tom Jamison—now—I won't have this—this here won't do. Where—where yeh goin'?'

The youth pointed vaguely. 'Over there,' he replied.

'Well, now look—a—here—now,' said the tattered man, rambling on in idiot fashion. His head was hanging forward and his words were slurred. 'This thing won't do, now, Tom Jamison. It won't do. I know yeh, yeh pig-headed devil. Yeh wanta go trompin' off with a bad hurt. It ain't right—now—Tom Jamison—it ain't. Yeh wanta leave me take keer of yeh, Tom Jamison. It ain't—right—it ain't—fer yeh t' go—trompin' off—with a bad hurt—it ain't—ain't—ain't right—it ain't.'

In reply the youth climbed a fence and started away. He could hear the tattered man bleating plaintively.

Once he faced about angrily. 'What?'

'Look—a—here, now, Tom Jamison—now—it ain't—'

The youth went on. Turning at a distance he saw the tattered man wandering about helplessly in the field.

He now thought that he wished he was dead. He believed that he envied those men whose bodies lay strewn over the grass of the fields and on the fallen leaves of the forest.

The simple questions of the tattered man had been knife thrusts to him. They asserted a society that probes pitilessly at secrets until all is apparent. His late companion's chance persistency made him feel that he could not keep his crime concealed in his bosom. It was sure to be brought plain by one of those arrows which cloud the air and are constantly pricking, discovering, proclaiming those things which are willed to be for ever hidden. He admitted that he could not defend himself against this agency. It was not within the power of vigilance.

XI

HE became aware that the furnace roar of the battle was growing louder. Great brown clouds had floated to the still heights of air before him. The noise, too, was approaching. The woods filtered men and the fields became dotted.

As he rounded a hillock, he perceived that the roadway was now a crying mass of wagons, teams, and men. From the heaving tangle issued exhortations, commands, imprecations. Fear was sweeping it all along. The cracking whips bit and horses plunged and tugged. The white-topped wagons strained and stumbled in their exertions like fat sheep.

The youth felt comforted in a measure by this sight. They were all retreating. Perhaps, then, he was not so bad after all. He seated himself and watched the terror-stricken wagons. They fled like soft, ungainly animals. All the roarers and lashers served to help him to magnify the dangers and horrors of the engagement that he might try to prove to himself that the thing with which men could charge him was in truth a symmetrical act. There was an amount of pleasure to him in watching the wild march of this vindication.

Presently the calm head of a forward-going column of infantry appeared in the road. It came swiftly on. Avoiding the obstructions gave it the sinuous movement of a serpent. The men at the head butted mules with their musket stocks. They prodded teamsters indifferent to all howls. The men forced their way through parts of the dense mass by strength. The blunt head of the column pushed. The raving teamsters swore many strange oaths.

The commands to make way had the ring of a great importance in them. The men were going froward to the heart of the din. They were to confront the eager rush of the enemy. They felt the pride of their onward movement when the remainder of the army seemed trying to dribble down this road. They tumbled teams about with a fine feeling that it was no matter so long as their column got to the front in time. This importance made their faces grave and stern. And the backs of the officers were very rigid.

As the youth looked at them the black weight of his woe returned to him. He felt that he was regarding a procession of chosen beings. The separation was as great to him as if they had marched with weapons of flame and banners of sunlight. He could never be like them. He could have wept in his longings.

He searched about in his mind for an adequate malediction for the indefinite cause, the thing upon which men turn the words of final blame. It—whatever it was—was responsible for him, he said. There lay the fault.

The haste of the column to reach the battle seemed to the forlorn young man to be something much finer than stout fighting. Heroes, he thought, could find excuses in that long seething lane. They could retire with perfect self-respect and make excuses to the stars.

He wondered what those men had eaten that they could be in such haste to force their way to grim chances of death. As he watched his envy grew until he thought that he wished to change lives with one of them. He would have liked to have used a tremendous force, he said, throwing off himself and become a better. Swift pictures of himself, apart, yet in himself, came to him—a blue desperate figure leading lurid charges with one knee forward and a broken blade high—a blue, determined figure standing before a crimson and steel assault, getting calmly killed on a high place before the eyes of all. He thought of the magnificent pathos of his dead body.

These thoughts uplifted him. He felt the quiver of war desire. In his ears, he heard the ring of victory. He knew the frenzy of a rapid successful charge. The music of the trampling feet, the sharp voices, the clanking arms of the column near him made him soar on the red wings of war. For a few moments he was sublime.

He thought that he was about to start for the front. Indeed, he saw a picture of himself, dust-stained, haggard, panting, flying to the front at the proper moment to seize and throttle the dark, leering witch of calamity.

Then the difficulties of the thing began to drag at him. He hesitated, balancing awkwardly on one foot.

He had no rifle; he could not fight with his hands, said he resentfully to his plan. Well, rifles could be had for the picking. They were extraordinarily profuse.

Also, he continued, it would be a miracle if he found his regiment. Well, he could fight with any regiment.

He started forward slowly. He stepped as if he expected to tread upon some explosive thing. Doubts and he were struggling.

He would truly be a worm if any of his comrades should see him returning thus, the marks of his flight upon him. There was a reply that the intent fighters did not care for what happened rearward saving that no hostile bayonets appeared there. In the battle-blur his face would in a way be hidden, like the face of a cowled man.

But then he said that his tireless fate would bring forth, when the strife lulled for a moment, a man to ask of him an explanation. In imagination he felt the scrutiny of his companions as he painfully laboured through some lies.

Eventually, his courage expended itself upon these objections. The debates drained him of his fire.

He was not cast down by this defeat of his plan, for, upon studying the affair carefully, he could not but admit that the objections were very formidable.

Furthermore, various ailments had begun to cry out. In their presence he could not persist in flying high with the wings of war; they rendered it almost impossible for him to see himself in a heroic light. He tumbled headlong.

He discovered that he had a scorching thirst. His face was so dry and grimy that he thought he could feel his skin crackle. Each bone of his body had an ache in it, and seemingly threatened to break with each movement. His feet were like two sores. Also, his body was calling for food. It was more powerful than a direct hunger. There was a dull, weightlike feeling in his stomach, and, when he tried to walk, his head swayed and he tottered. He could not see with distinctness. Small patches of green mist floated before his vision.

While he had been tossed by many emotions, he had not been aware of ailments. Now they beset him and made clamour. As he was at last compelled to pay attention to them, his capacity for self-hate was multiplied. In despair, he declared that he was not like those others. He now conceded it to be impossible that he should ever become a hero. He was a craven loon. Those pictures of glory were piteous things. He groaned from his heart and went staggering off.

A certain mothlike quality within him kept him in the vicinity of the battle. He had a great desire to see, and to get news. He wished to know who was winning.

He told himself that, despite his unprecedented suffering, he had never lost his greed for a victory, yet, he said, in a half-apologetic manner to his conscience, he could not but know that a defeat for the army this time might mean many favourable things for him. The blows of the enemy would splinter regiments into fragments. Thus, many men of courage, he considered, would be obliged to desert the colours and scurry like chickens. He would appear as one of them. They would be sullen brothers in distress, and he could then easily believe he had not run any farther or faster than they. And if he himself could believe in his virtuous perfection, he conceived that there would be small trouble in convincing all others.

He said, as if in excuse for this hope, that previously the army had encountered great defeats and in a few months had shaken off all blood and tradition of them, emerging as bright and valiant as a new one; thrusting out of sight the memory of disaster, and appearing with the valour and confidence of unconquered legions. The shrilling voices of the people at home would pipe dismally for a time, but various generals were usually compelled to listen to these ditties. He of course felt no compunctions for proposing a general as a sacrifice. He could not tell who the chosen for the barbs might be, so he could centre no direct sympathy upon him. The people were afar and he did not conceive public opinion to be accurate at long range. It was quite probable they would hit the wrong man who, after he had recovered from his amazement would perhaps spend the rest of his days in writing replies to the songs of his alleged failure. It would be very unfortunate, no doubt, but in this case a general was of no consequence to the youth.

In a defeat there would be a roundabout vindication of himself. He thought it would prove, in a manner, that he had fled early because of his superior powers of perception. A serious prophet upon predicting a flood should be the first man to climb a tree. This would demonstrate that he was indeed a seer.

A moral vindication was regarded by the youth as a very important thing. Without salve, he could not, he thought, wear the sore badge of his dishonour through life. With his heart continually assuring him that he was despicable, he could not exist without making it, through his actions, apparent to all men.

If the army had gone gloriously on he would be lost. If the din meant that now his army's flags were tilted forward he was a condemned wretch. He would be compelled to doom himself to isolation. If the men were advancing, their indifferent feet were trampling upon his chances for a successful life.

As these thoughts went rapidly through his mind, he turned upon them and tried to thrust them away. He denounced himself as a villain. He said that he was the most unutterably selfish man in existence. His mind pictured the soldiers who would place their defiant bodies before the spear of the yelling battle fiend, and as he saw their dripping corpses on an imagined field, he said that he was their murderer.

Again he thought that he wished he was dead. He believed that he envied a corpse. Thinking of the slain, he achieved a great contempt for some of them, as if they were guilty for thus becoming lifeless. They might have been killed by lucky chances, he said, before they had had opportunities to flee or before they had been really tested.

Yet they would receive laurels from tradition. He cried out bitterly that their crowns were stolen and their robes of glorious memories were shams. However, he still said that it was a great pity he was not as they.

A defeat of the army had suggested itself to him as a means of escape from the consequences of his fall. He considered, now, however, that it was useless to think of such a possibility. His education had been that success for that mighty blue machine was certain; that it would make victories as a contrivance turns out buttons. He presently discarded all his speculations in the other direction. He returned to the creed of soldiers.

When he perceived again that it was not possible for the army to be defeated, he tried to bethink him of a fine tale which he could take back to his regiment, and with it turn the expected shafts of derision.

But, as he mortally feared these shafts, it became impossible for him to invent a tale he felt he could trust. He experimented with many schemes, but threw them aside one by one as flimsy. He was quick to see vulnerable places in them all.

Furthermore, he was much afraid that some arrow of scorn might lay him mentally low before he could raise his protecting tale.

He imagined the whole regiment saying: 'Where's Henry Fleming? He run, didn't 'e? Oh, my!' He recalled various persons who would be quite sure to leave him no peace about it. They would doubtless question him with sneers, and laugh at his stammering hesitation. In the next engagement they would try to keep watch of him to discover when he would run.

Wherever he went in camp, he would encounter insolent and lingeringly cruel stares. As he imagined himself passing near a crowd of comrades, he could hear someone say, 'There he goes!'

Then, as if the heads were moved by one muscle, all the faces turned toward him with wide, derisive grins. He seemed to hear someone make a humorous remark in a low tone. At it the others all crowed and cackled. He was a slang phrase.

XII

THE column that had butted stoutly at the obstacles in the roadway was barely out of the youth's sight before he saw dark waves of men come sweeping out of the woods and down through the fields. He knew at once that the steel fibres had been washed from their hearts. They were bursting from their coats and their equipments as from entanglements. They charged down upon him like terrified buffaloes.

Behind them blue smoke curled and clouded above the treetops, and through the thickets he could sometimes see a distant pink glare. The voices of the cannon were clamouring in interminable chorus.

The youth was horror-stricken. He stared in agony and amazement. He forgot that he was engaged in combating the universe. He threw aside his mental pamphlets on the philosophy of the retreated and rules for the guidance of the damned.

The fight was lost. The dragons were coming with invincible strides. The army, helpless in the matted thickets and blinded by the overhanging night, was going to be swallowed. War, the red animal, war, the blood-swollen god, would have bloated fill.

Within him something bade to cry out. He had the impulse to make a rallying speech, to sing a battle hymn, but he could only get his tongue to call into the air: 'Why—why—What— what's th' matter?'

Soon he was in the midst of them. They were leaping and scampering all about him. Their blanched faces shone in the dusk. They seemed, for the most part, to be very burly men. The youth turned from one to another of them as they galloped along. His incoherent questions were lost. They were heedless of his appeals. They did not seem to see him.

They sometimes grabbled insanely. One huge man was asking of the sky: 'Say, where de plank road? Where de plank road!' It was as if he had lost a child. He wept in his pain and dismay.

Presently, men were running hither and thither in all ways. The artillery booming, forward, rearward, and on the flanks made jumble of ideas of direction. Landmarks had vanished into the gathered gloom. The youth began to imagine that he had got into the centre of the tremendous quarrel, and he could perceive no way out of it. From the mouths of the fleeing men came a thousand wild questions, but no one made answers.

The youth, after rushing about and throwing interrogations at the heedless bands of retreating infantry, finally clutched a man by the arm. They swung around face to face.

'Why—why—' stammered the youth struggling with his balking tongue.

The man screamed: 'Let go me! Let go me!' His face was livid and his eyes were rolling uncontrolled. He was heaving and panting. He still grasped his rifle, perhaps having forgotten to release his hold upon it. He tugged frantically, and the youth being compelled to lean forward was dragged several paces.

'Let go me! Let go me!'

'Why—why—' stuttered the youth.

'Well, then!' bawled the man in lurid rage. He adroitly and fiercely swung his rifle. It crushed upon the youth's head. The man ran on.

The youth's fingers had turned to paste upon the other's arm. The energy was smitten from his muscles. He saw the flaming wings of lightning flash before his vision. There was a deafening rumble of thunder within his head.

Suddenly his legs seemed to die. He sank writhing to the ground. He tried to arise. In his efforts against the numbing pain he was like a man wrestling with a creature of the air.

There was a sinister struggle.

Sometimes he would achieve a position half erect, battle with the air for a moment, and then fall again, grabbing at the grass. His face was of a clammy pallor. Deep groans were wrenched from him.

At last, with a twisting movement, he got upon his hands and knees, and from thence, like a babe trying to walk, to his feet. Pressing his hands to his temples he went lurching over the grass.

He fought an intense battle with his body. His dulled senses wished him to swoon and he opposed them stubbornly, his mind portraying unknown dangers and mutilations if he should fall upon the field. He went tall soldier fashion. He imagined secluded spots where he could fall and be unmolested. To search for one he strove against the tide of his pain.

Once he put his hand to the top of his head and timidly touched the wound. The scratching pain of the contact made him draw a long breath through his clinched teeth. His fingers were dabbled with blood. He regarded them with a fixed stare.

Around him he could hear the grumble of jolted cannon as the scurrying horses were lashed toward the front. Once, a young officer on a besplashed charger nearly ran him down. He turned and watched the mass of guns, men, and horses sweeping in a wide curve toward a gap in a fence. The officer was making excited motions with a gauntleted hand. The guns followed the teams with an air of unwillingness, of being dragged by the heels.

Some officers of the scattered infantry were cursing and railing like fishwives. Their scolding voices could be heard above the din. Into the unspeakable jumble in the roadway rode a squadron of cavalry. The faded yellow of their facings shone bravely. There was a mighty altercation.

The artillery were assembling as if for a conference.

The blue haze of evening was upon the field. The lines of forest were long purple shadows. One cloud lay along the western sky partly smothering the red.

As the youth left the scene behind him, he heard the guns suddenly roar out. He imagined them shaking in black rage. They belched and howled like brass devils guarding a gate. The soft air was filled with the tremendous remonstrance. With it came the shattering peal of opposing infantry. Turning to look behind him, he could see sheets of orange light illumine the shadowy distance. There were subtle and sudden lightnings in the far air. At times he thought he could see heaving masses of men.

He hurried on in the dusk. The day had faded until he could barely distinguish a place for his feet. The purple darkness was filled with men who lectured and jabbered. Sometimes he could see them gesticulating against the blue and sombre sky. There seemed to be a great ruck of men and munitions spread about in the forest and in the fields.

The little narrow roadway now lay lifeless. There were overturned wagons like sun-dried boulders. The bed of the former torrent was choked with the bodies of horses and splintered parts of war machines.

It had come to pass that his wound pained him but little. He was afraid to move rapidly, however, for a dread of disturbing it. He held his head very still and took many precautions against stumbling. He was filled with anxiety, and his face was pinched and drawn in anticipation of the pain of any sudden mistake of his feet in the gloom.

His thoughts, as he walked, fixed intently upon his hurt. There was a cool, liquid feeling about it and he imagined blood moving slowly down under his hair. His head seemed swollen to a size that made him think his neck to be inadequate.

The new silence of his wound made much worriment. The little blistering voices of pain that had called out from the scalp were, he thought, definite in their expression of danger. By them he believed that he could measure his plight. But when they remained ominously silent he became frightened and imagined terrible fingers that clutched into his brain.

Amid it he began to reflect upon various incidents and conditions of the past. He bethought him of certain meals his mother had cooked at home, in which those dishes of which he was particularly fond had occupied prominent positions. He saw the spread table. The pine walls of the kitchen were glowing in the warm light from the stove. Too, he remembered how he and his companions used to go from the schoolhouse to the bank of a shaded pool. He saw his clothes in disorderly array upon the grass of the bank. He felt the swash of the fragant water upon his body. The leaves of the overhanging maple rustled with melody in the wii d of youthful summer.

He was overcome presently by a dragging weariness. His head hung forward and his shoulders were stooped as if he were bearing a great bundle. His feet shuffled along the ground.

He held continuous arguments as to whether he should lie down and sleep at some near spot, or force himself on until he reached a certain haven. He often tried to dismiss the question, but his body persisted in rebellion and his senses nagged at him like pampered babies.

At last he heard a cheery voice near his shoulder: 'Yeh seem t' be in a pretty bad way, boy?'

The youth did not look up, but he assented with thick tongue. 'Uh!'

The owner of the cheery voice took him firmly by the arm. 'Well,' he said, with a round laugh, 'I'm goin' your way. Th' hull gang is goin' your way. An' I guess I kin give yeh a lift.' They began to walk like a drunken man and his friend.

As they went along, the man questioned the youth and assisted him with the replies like one manipulating the mind of a child. Sometimes he interjected anecdotes. 'What reg'ment do yeh b'long teh? Eh? What's that? Th' 304th N' York? Why, what corps is that in? Oh, it is? Why, I thought they wasn't engaged t'-day—they're 'way over in th' centre. Oh, they was, eh? Well, pretty nearly everybody got their share a' fightin' t'-day. By dad, I give myself up fer dead any number 'a times. There was shootin' here an' shootin' there, an' hollerin' here an' hollerin' there, in th' damn' darkness, until I couldn't tell t' save m' soul which side I was on. Sometimes I thought I was sure 'nough from Ohier, an' other times I could a' swore I was from th' bitter end of Florida. It was th' most mixed up dern thing I ever see. An' these here hull woods is a reg'lar mess. It'll be a miracle if we find our reg'ment t'-night. Pretty soon, though, we'll meet a-plenty of guards an' provost guards, an' one thing an' another. Ho! there they go with an off'cer, I guess. Look at his hand a draggin'. He's got all th' war he wants, I bet. He won't be talkin' so big about his reputation an' all when they go t' sawin' off his leg. Poor feller! My brother's got whiskers jest like that. How did yeh git 'way over here, anyhow? Your reg'ment is a long way from here, ain't it? Well, I guess we can find it. Yeh know there was a boy killed in my comp'ny t'-day that I thought th' world an' all of. Jack was a nice feller. By ginger, it hurt like thunder t' see ol' Jack jest git knocked flat. We was a-standin' purty peaceable fer a spell, 'though there was men runnin' ev'ry way all 'round us, an' while we was a-standin' like that, 'long come a big fat feller. He began t' peck at Jack's elbow, an' he ses: "Say, where's th' road t' th' river?" An' Jack, he never paid no attention, an' th' feller kept on a-peckin' at his elbow an' sayin': "Say, where's th' road t' th' river?" Jack was a-lookin' ahead all th' time tryin' t' see th' Johnnies comin' through th' woods, an' he never paid no attention, t' this big fat feller fer a long time, but at last he turned 'round an' he ses: "Ah, go t' hell an' find th' road t' th' river!" An' jest then a shot slapped him bang on th' side th' head. He was a sergeant, too. Them was his last words. Thunder, I wish we was sure 'a findin' our reg'ments t'-night. It's goin' t' be long huntin'. But I guess we kin do it.'

In the search that followed, the man of the cheery voice seemed to the youth to possess a wand of a magic kind. He threaded the mazes of the tangled forest with a strange fortune. In encounter with guards and patrols he displayed the keenness of a detective and the valour of a gamin. Obstacles fell before him and became of assistance. The youth, with his chin still on his breast, stood woodenly by while his companion beat ways and means out of sullen things.

The forest seemed a vast hive of men buzzing about in frantic circles, but the cheery man conducted the youth without mistakes, until at last he began to chuckle with glee and self-satisfaction. 'Ah, there yeh are! See that fire?'

The youth nodded stupidly.

'Well, there's where you reg'ment is. An' now, good-bye, ol' boy, good luck t' yeh.'

A warm and strong hand clasped the youth's languid fingers for an instant, and then he heard a cheerful and audacious whistling as the man strode away. As he who had so befriended him was thus passing out of his life, it suddenly occurred to the youth that he had not once seen his face.

XIII

THE youth went slowly toward the fire indicated by his departed friend. As he reeled, he bethought him of the welcome his comrades would give him. He had a conviction that he would soon feel in his sore heart the barbed missiles of ridicule. He had no strength to invent a tale; he would be a soft target.

He made vague plans to go off into the deeper darkness and hide, but they were all destroyed by the voices of exhaustion and pain from his body. His ailments, clamouring, forced him to seek the place of food and rest, at whatever cost.

He swung unsteadily toward the fire. He could see the forms of men throwing black shadows in the red light, and as he went nearer it became known to him in some way that the ground was strewn with sleeping men.

Of a sudden he confronted a black and monstrous figure. A rifle barrel caught some glinting beams. 'Halt! halt!' He was dismayed for a moment, but he presently thought that he recognized the nervous voice. As he stood tottering before the rifle barrel, he called out: 'Why, hello, Wilson, you—you here?'

The rifle was lowered to a position of caution and the loud soldier came slowly forward. He peered into the youth's face. 'That you, Henry?'

'Yes it's—it's me.'

'Well, well, ol' boy,' said the other, 'by ginger, I'm glad t'see yeh! I give yeh up fer a goner. I thought yeh was dead sure enough.' There was husky emotion in his voice.

The youth found that now he could barely stand upon his feet. There was a sudden sinking of his forces. He thought he must hasten to produce his tale to protect him from the missiles already at the lips of his redoubtable comrades. So, staggering before the loud soldier, he began: 'Yes, yes, I've—I've had an awful time. I've been all over. Way over on th' right. Ter'ble fightin' over there. I had an awful time. I got separated from th' reg'ment. Over on th' right. I got shot. In th' head. I never see sech fightin'. Awful time. I don't see how I could a' got separated from th' reg'ment. I got shot, too.'

His friend had stepped forward quickly. 'What? Got shot? Why didn't yeh say so first? Poor ol' boy, we must—hol' on a minnit; what am I doin'. I'll call Simpson.'

Another figure at that moment loomed in the gloom. They could see that it was the corporal. 'Who yeh talkin' to, Wilson?' he demanded. His voice was anger-toned. 'Who yeh talkin' to? Yeh th' derndest sentinel—why—hello, Henry, you here? Why, I thought you was dead four hours ago! Great Jerusalem, they keep turnin' up every ten minutes or so! We thought we'd lost forty-two men by straight count, but if they keep on a-comin' this way, we'll git th' comp'ny all back by mornin' yit. Where was yeh?'

'Over on th' right. I got separated'—began the youth with considerable glibness.

But his friend had interrupted hastily. 'Yes, an' he got shot in th' head an' he's in a fix, an' we must see t' him right away.' He rested his rifle in the hollow of his left arm and his right around the youth's shoulder.

'Gee, it must hurt like thunder!' he said.

The youth leaned heavily upon his friend. 'Yes, it hurts— hurts a good deal,' he replied. There was a faltering in his voice.

'Oh,' said the corporal. He linked his arm in the youth's and drew him forward. 'Come on, Henry, I'll take keer 'a yeh.'

As they went on together the loud private called out after them: 'Put 'im t' sleep in my blanket, Simpson. An'—hol' on a minnit—here's my canteen. It's full 'a coffee. Look at his head by th' fire an' see how it looks. Maybe it's a pretty bad un. When I git relieved in a couple 'a minnits, I'll be over an' see t' him.'

The youth's senses were so deadened that his friend's voice sounded from afar and he could scarcely feel the pressure of the corporal's arm. He submitted passively to the latter's directing strength. His head was in the old manner hanging forward upon his breast. His knees wobbled.

The corporal led him into the glare of the fire. 'Now, Henry,' he said, 'let's have look at yer ol' head.'

The youth sat down obediently and the corporal, laying aside his rifle, began to fumble in the bushy hair of his comrade. He was obliged to turn the other's head so that the full flush of the fire light would beam upon it. He puckered his mouth with a critical air. He drew back his lips and whistled through his teeth when his fingers came in contact with the splashed blood and the rare wound.

'Ah, here we are!' he said. He awkwardly made further investigations. 'Jest as I thought,' he added, presently. 'Yeh've been grazed by a ball. It's raised a queer lump jest as if some feller had lammed yeh on th' head with a club. It stopped a-bleeding' long time ago. Th' most about it is that in th' morning' yeh'll feel that a number ten hat wouldn't fit yeh. An' your head 'll be all het up an' feel as dry as burnt pork. An' yeh may git a lot 'a other sicknesses, too, by mornin'. Yeh can't never tell. Still, I don't much think so. It's jest a damn' good belt on th' head, an' nothin' more. Now, you jest sit here an' don't move, while I go rout out th' relief. Then I'll send Wilson t' take keer 'a yeh.'

The corporal went away. The youth remained on the ground like a parcel. He stared with a vacant look into the fire.

After a time he aroused, for some part, and the things about him began to take form. He saw that the ground in the deep shadows was cluttered with men, sprawling in every conceivable posture. Glancing narrowly into the more distant darkness, he caught occasional glimpses of visages that loomed pallid and ghostly, lit with a phosphorescent glow. These faces expressed in their lines the deep stupor of the tired soldiers. They made them appear like men drunk with wine. This bit of forest might have appeared to an ethereal wanderer as a scene of the result of some frightful debauch.

On the other side of the fire the youth observed an officer asleep, seated bolt upright, with his back against a tree. There was something perilous in his position. Badgered by dreams, perhaps, he swayed with little bounces and starts, like an old, toddy-stricken grandfather in a chimney corner. Dust and stains were upon his face. His lower jaw hung down as if lacking strength to assume its normal position. He was the picture of an exhausted soldier after a feast of war.

He had evidently gone to sleep with his sword in his arms. These two had slumbered in an embrace, but the weapon had been allowed in time to fall unheeded to the ground. The brass-mounted hilt lay in contact with some parts of the fire.

Within the gleam of rose and orange light from the burning sticks were other soldiers, snoring and heaving, or lying death-like in slumber. A few pairs of legs were stuck forth, rigid and straight. The shoes displayed the mud or dust of marches and bits of rounded trousers, protruding from the blankets, showed rents and tears from hurried pitchings through the dense brambles.

The fire crackled musically. From it swelled light smoke. Overhead the foliage moved softly. The leaves, with their faces turned toward the blaze, were coloured shifting hues of silver, often edged with red. Far off to the right, through a window in the forest, could be seen a handful of stars lying, like glittering pebbles, on the black level of the night.

Occasionally, in this low-arched hall, a soldier would arouse and turn his body to a new position, the experience of his sleep having taught him of uneven and objectionable places upon the ground under him. Or, perhaps, he would lift himself to a sitting posture, blink at the fire for an unintelligent moment, throw a swift glance at his prostrate companion, and then cuddle down again with a grunt of sleepy content.

The youth sat in a forlorn heap until his friend, the loud young soldier, came, swinging two canteens by their light strings. 'Well, now, Henry, ol' boy,' said the latter, 'we'll have yeh fixed up in jest about a minnit.'

He had the bustling ways of an amateur nurse. He fussed around the fire and stirred the sticks to brilliant exertions. He made his patient drink largely from the canteen that contained the coffee. It was to the youth a delicious draught. He tilted his head afar back and held the canteen long to his lips. The cool mixture went caressingly down his blistered throat. Having finished, he sighed with comfortable delight.

The loud young soldier watched his comrade with an air of satisfaction. He later produced an extensive handkerchief from his pocket. He folded it into a manner of bandage and soused water from the other canteen upon the middle of it. This crude arrangement he bound over the youth's head, tying the ends in a queer knot at the back of the neck.

'There,' he said, moving off and surveying his deed, 'yeh look like th' devil, but I bet yeh feel better.'

The youth contemplated his friend with grateful eyes. Upon his aching and swelling head the cold cloth was like a tender woman's hand.

'Yeh don't holler ner say nothin',' remarked his friend approvingly. 'I know I'm a blacksmith at takin' keer 'a sick folks, an' yeh never squeaked. Yer a good un, Henry. Most 'a men would a' been in th' hospital long ago. A shot in th' head ain't foolin' business.'

The youth made no reply, but began to fumble with the buttons of his jacket.

'Well, come, now,' continued his friend, 'come on. I must put yeh t' bed an' see that yeh git a good night's rest.'

The other got carefully erect, and the loud young soldier led him among the sleeping forms lying in groups and rows. Presently he stooped and picked up his blankets. He spread the rubber one upon the ground and placed the woollen one about the youth's shoulders.

'There now,' he said, 'lie down an' git some sleep.'

The youth, with his manner of doglike obedience, got carefully down like a crone stooping. He stretched out with a murmer of relief and comfort. The ground felt like the softest couch.

But of a sudden he ejaculated: 'Hol' on a minnit! Where you goin' t' sleep?'

His friend waved his hand impatiently. 'Right down there by yeh.'

'Well, but hol' on a minnit,' continued the youth. 'What yeh goin' t' sleep in? I've got your—'

The loud young soldier snarled: 'Shet up an' go on t' sleep. Don't be makin' a damn' fool 'a yerself,' he said severely.

After the reproof the youth said no more. An exquisite drowsiness had spread through him. The warm comfort of the blanket enveloped him and made a gentle languor. His head fell forward on his crooked arm and his weighted lids went slowly down over his eyes. Hearing a splatter of musketry from the distance, he wondered indifferently if those men sometimes slept. He gave a long sigh, snuggled down into his blanket, and in a moment was like his comrades.

XIV

WHEN the youth awoke it seemed to him that he had been asleep for a thousand years, and he felt sure that he opened his eyes upon an unexpected world. Grey mists were slowly shifting before the first efforts of the sun-rays. An impending splendour could be seen in the eastern sky. An icy dew had chilled his face, and immediately upon arousing he curled farther down into his blankets. He stared for a while at the leaves overhead, moving in a heraldic wind of the day.

The distance was splintering and blaring with the noise of fighting. There was in the sound an expression of a deadly persistency, as if it had not begun and was not to cease.

About him were the rows and groups of men that he had dimly seen the previous night. They were getting a last draught of sleep before the awakening. The gaunt, careworn features and dusty figures were made plain by this quaint light at the dawning, but it dressed the skin of the men in corpselike hues and made the tangled limbs appear pulseless and dead. The youth started up with a little cry when his eyes first swept over this motionless mass of men, thick-spread upon the ground, pallid, and in strange postures. His disordered mind interpreted the hall of the forest as a charnel place. He believed for an instant that he was in the house of the dead, and he did not dare to move lest these corpses start up, squalling and squawking. In a second, however, he achieved his proper mind. He swore a complicated oath at himself. He saw that this sombre picture was not a fact of the present, but a mere prophecy.

He heard then the noise of a fire crackling briskly in the cold air, and, turning his head, he saw his friend pottering busily about a small blaze. A few other figures moved in the fog, and he heard the hard cracking of axe blows.

Suddenly there was a hollow rumble of drums. A distant bugle sang faintly. Similar sounds, varying in strength, came from near and far over the forest. The bugles called to each other like brazen gamecocks. The near thunder of the regimental drums rolled.

The body of men in the woods rustled. There was a general uplifting of heads. A murmuring of voices broke upon the air. In it there was much bass of grumbling oaths. Strange gods were addressed in condemnation of the early hours necessary to correct war. An officer's peremptory tenor rang out and quickened the stiffened movement of the men. The tangled limbs unravelled. The corpse-hued faces were hidden behind fists that twisted slowly in the eye sockets.

The youth sat up and gave vent to an enormous yawn. 'Thunder!' he remarked petulantly. He rubbed his eyes, and then putting up his hand felt carefully of the bandage over his wound. His friend, perceiving him to be awake, came from the fire. 'Well, Henry, ol' man, how do yeh fell this mornin'?' he demanded.

The youth yawned again. Then he puckered his mouth to a little pucker. His head, in truth, felt precisely like a melon, and there was an unpleasant sensation at his stomach.

'Oh, Lord, I feel pretty bad,' he said.

'Thunder!' exclaimed the other. 'I hoped ye'd feel all right this mornin'. Let's see th' bandage—I guess it's slipped.' He began to tinker at the wound in rather a clumsy way until the youth exploded.

'Gosh-dern it!' he said in sharp irritation; 'you're the hangdest man I ever saw! You wear muffs on your hands. Why in good thunderation can't you be more easy? I'd rather you'd stand off an' throw guns at it. Now, go slow, an' don't act as if you was nailing down carpet.'

He glared with insolent command at his friend, but the latter answered soothingly. 'Well, well, come now, an' git some grub,' he said. 'Then, maybe, yeh'll feel better.'

At the fireside the loud young soldier watched over his comrade's wants with tenderness and care. He was very busy marshalling the little black vagabonds of tin cups and pouring into them the streaming, iron-coloured mixture from a small and sooty tin pail. He had some fresh meat, which he roasted hurriedly upon a stick. He sat down then and contemplated the youth's appetite with glee.

The youth took note of a remarkable change in his comrade since those days of camp life upon the river bank. He seemed no more to be continually regarding the proportions of his personal prowess. He was not furious at small words that pricked his conceits. He was no more a loud young soldier. There was about him now a fine reliance. He showed a quiet belief in his purposes and his abilities. And this inward confidence evidently enabled him to be indifferent to little words of other men aimed at him.

The youth reflected. He had been used to regarding his comrade as a blatant child with an audacity grown from his inexperience, thoughtless, headstrong, jealous, and filled with a tinsel courage. A swaggering babe accustomed to strut in his own dooryard. The youth wondered where had been born these new eyes; when his comrade had made the great discovery that there were many men who would refuse to be subjected by him. Apparently, the other had now climbed a peak of wisdom from which he could perceive himself as a very wee thing. And the youth saw that ever after it would be easier to live in his friend's neighbourhood.

His comrade balanced his ebony coffee-cup on his knee. 'Well, Henry,' he said, 'what d'yeh think th' chances are? D'yeh think we'll wallop 'em?'

The youth considered for a moment. 'Day-b'fore-yestirday,' he finally replied, with boldness, 'you would a' bet you'd lick the hull kit-an'-boodle all by yourself.'

His friend looked a trifle amazed. 'Would I?' he asked. He pondered. 'Well, perhaps I would,' he decided at last. He stared humbly at the fire.

The youth was quite disconcerted at this surprising reception of his remarks. 'Oh, no, you wouldn't either,' he said, hastily trying to retrace.

But the other made a deprecating gesture. 'Oh, yeh needn't mind, Henry,' he said. 'I believe I was a pretty big fool in those days.' He spoke as after a lapse of years.

There was a little pause.

'All th' officers say we've got th' rebs in a pretty tight box,' said the friend, clearing his throat in a commonplace way. 'They all seem t' think we've got 'em jest where we want 'em.'

'I don't know about that,' the youth replied. 'What I seen over on th' right makes me think it was th' other way about. From where I was, it looked as if we was gettin' a good poundin' yestirday.'

'D'yeh think so?' inquired the friend. 'I thought we handled 'em pretty rough yestirday.'

'Not a bit,' said the youth. 'Why, lord, man, you didn't see nothing of the fight. Why!' Then a sudden thought came to him. 'Oh! Jim Conklin's dead.'

His friend started. 'What? Is he? Jim Conklin?'

The youth spoke slowly. 'Yes. He's dead. Shot in th' side.'

'Yeh don't say so. Jim Conklin . . . poor cuss!'

All about them were other small fires surrounded by men with their little black utensils. From one of these near came sudden sharp voices in a row. It appeared that two light-footed soldiers had been teasing a huge, bearded man, causing him to spill coffee upon his blue knees. The man had gone into a rage and had sworn comprehensively. Stung by his language, his tormentors had immediately bristled at him with a great show of resenting unjust oaths. Possibly there was going to be a fight.

The friend arose and went over to them, making pacific motions with his arms. 'Oh, here, now, boys, what's th' use?' he said. 'We'll be at th' rebs in less'n an hour. What's th' good fightin' 'mong ourselves?'

One of the light-footed soldiers turned upon him red-faced and violent. 'Yeh needn't come around here with yer preachin'. I s'pose yeh don't approve 'a fightin' since Charley Morgan licked yeh; but I don't see what business this here is 'a yours or anybody else.'

'Well, it ain't,' said the friend mildly. 'Still I hate t' see—'

That was a tangled argument.

'Well, he—,' said the two, indicating their opponent with accusative forefingers.

The huge soldier was quite purple with rage. He pointed at the two soldiers with his great hand, extended clawlike. 'Well, they—'

But during this argumentative time the desire to deal blows seemed to pass, although they said much to each other. Finally the friend returned to his old seat. In a short while the three antagonists could be seen together in an amiable bunch.

'Jimmie Rogers ses I'll have t' fight him after th' battle t'-day,' announced the friend as he again seated himself. 'He ses he don't allow no interferin' in his business. I hate t' see th' boys fightin' 'mong themselves.'

The youth laughed. 'Yer changed a good bit. Yeh ain't at all like yeh was. I remember when you an' that Irish feller—' He stopped and laughed again.

'No, I didn't use t' be that way,' said his friend thoughtfully. 'That's true 'nough.'

'Well, I didn't mean—' began the youth.

The friend made another deprecatory gesture. 'Oh, yeh needn't mind, Henry.'

There was another little pause.

'Th' reg'ment lost over half th' men yestirday,' remarked the friend eventually. 'I thought 'a course they was all dead, but, laws, they kep' a-comin' back last night until it seems, after all, we didn't lose but a few. They'd been scattered all over, wanderin' around in th' woods, fightin' with other reg'ments, an' everything. Jest like you done.'

'So?' said the youth.

XV

THE regiment was standing at order arms at the side of a lane, waiting for the command to march, when suddenly the youth remembered the little packet enwrapped in a faded yellow envelope which the loud young soldier with lugubrious words had entrusted to him. It made him start. He uttered an exclamation and turned toward his comrade.

'Wilson!'

'What?'

His friend, at his side in the ranks, was thoughtfully staring down the road. From some cause his expression was at that moment very meek. The youth, regarding him with sidelong glances, felt impelled to change his purpose. 'Oh, nothing,' he said.

His friend turned his head in some surprise. 'Why, what was yeh goin' t' say?'

'Oh, nothing,' repeated the youth.

He resolved not to deal the little blow. It was sufficient that the fact made him glad. It was not necessary to knock his friend on the head with the misguided packet.

He had been possessed of much fear of his friend, for he saw how easily questionings could make holes in his feelings. Lately, he had assured himself that the altered comrade would not tantalize him with a persistent curiosity, but he felt certain that during the first period of leisure his friend would ask him to relate his adventures of the previous day.

He now rejoiced in the possession of a small weapon with which he could prostrate his comrade at the first signs of a cross-examination. He was master. It would now be he who could laugh and shoot the shafts of derision.

The friend had, in a weak hour, spoken with sobs of his own death. He had delivered a melancholy oration previous to his funeral, and had doubtless in the packet of letters, presented various keepsakes to relatives. But he had not died, and thus he had delivered himself into the hands of the youth.

The latter felt immensely superior to his friend, but he inclined to condescension. He adopted toward him an air of patronizing good humour.

His self-pride was now entirely restored. In the shade of its flourishing growth he stood with braced and self-confident legs, and since nothing could now be discovered he did not shrink from an encounter with the eyes of judges, and allowed no thoughts of his own to keep him from an attitude of manfulness. He had performed his mistakes in the dark, so he was still a man.

Indeed, when he remembered his fortunes of yesterday, and looked at them from a distance he began to see something fine there. He had licence to be pompous and veteranlike.

His panting agonies of the past he put out of his sight.

In the present, he declared to himself that it was only the doomed and the damned who roared with sincerity at circumstance. Few but they ever did it. A man with a full stomach and the respect of his fellows had no business to scold about anything he might think to be wrong in the ways of the universe, or even with the ways of society. Let the unfortunates rail; the others may play marbles.

He did not give a great deal of thought to these battles that lay directly before him. It was not essential that he should plan his ways in regard to them. He had been taught that many obligations of a life were easily avoided. The lessons of yesterday had been that retribution was a laggard and blind. With these facts before him he did not deem it necessary that he should become feverish over the possibilities of the ensuing twenty-four hours. He could leave much to chance. Besides, a faith in himself had secretly blossomed. There was a little flower of confidence growing within him. He was now a man of experience. He had been out among the dragons, he said, and he assured himself that they were not so hideous as he had imagined them. Also, they were inaccurate; they did not sting with precision. A stout heart often defied, and defying, escaped.

And, furthermore, how could they kill him who was the chosen of gods and doomed to greatness?

He remembered how some of the men had run from the battle. As he recalled their terror-struck faces he felt a scorn for them. They had surely been more fleet and more wild than was absolutely necessary. They were weak mortals. As for himself, he had fled with discretion and dignity.

He was aroused from this reverie by his friend, who, having hitched about nervously and blinked at the trees for a time, suddenly coughed in an introductory way, and spoke.

'Fleming!'

'What?'

The friend put his hand up to his mouth and coughed again. He fidgeted in his jacket.

'Well,' he gulped, at last, 'I guess yeh might as well give me back them letters.' Dark, prickling blood had flushed into his cheeks and brow.

'All right, Wilson,' said the youth. He loosened two buttons of his coat, thrust in his hand, and brought forth the packet. As he extended it to his friend the latter's face was turned from him.

He had been slow in the act of producing the packet because during it he had been trying to invent a remarkable comment upon the affair. He could conjure nothing of sufficient point. He was compelled to allow his friend to escape unmolested with his packet. And for this he took unto himself considerable credit. It was a generous thing.

His friend at his side seemed suffering great shame. As he contemplated him, the youth felt his heart grow more strong and stout. He had never been compelled to blush in such manner for his acts; he was an individual of extraordinary virtues.

He reflected, with condescending pity: 'Too bad! Too bad! The poor devil, it makes him feel tough!'

After this incident, and as he reviewed the battle pictures he had seen, he felt quite competent to return home and make the hearts of the people glow with stories of war. He could see himself in a room of warm tints telling tales to listeners. He could exhibit laurels. They were insignificant; still, in a district where laurels were infrequent, they might shine.

He saw his gaping audience picturing him as the central figure in blazing scenes. And he imagined the consternation and the ejaculations of his mother and the young lady at the seminary as they drank his recitals. Their vague feminine formula for beloved ones doing brave deeds on the field of battle without risk of life would be destroyed.

XVI

A SPUTTERING of musketry was always to be heard. Later, the cannon had entered the dispute. In the fog-filled air their voices made a thudding sound. The reverberations were continued. This part of the world led a strange, battleful existence.

The youth's regiment was marched to relieve a command that had lain long in some damp trenches. The men took positions behind a curving line of rifle pits that had been turned up, like a large furrow, along the line of woods. Before them was a level stretch, peopled with short, deformed stumps. From the woods beyond came the dull popping of the skirmishers and pickets, firing in the fog. From the right came the noise of a terrific fracas.

The men cuddled behind the small embankment and sat in easy attitudes awaiting their turn. Many had their backs to the firing. The youth's friend lay down, buried his face in his arms, and almost instantly, it seemed, he was in a deep sleep.

The youth leaned his breast against the brown dirt and peered over at the woods and up and down the line. Curtains of trees interfered with his ways of vision. He could see the low line of trenches but for a short distance. A few idle flags were perched on the dirt hills. Behind them were rows of dark bodies with a few heads sticking curiously over the top.

Always the noise of skirmishers came from the woods on the front and left, and the din on the right had grown to frightful proportions. The guns were roaring without an instant's pause for breath. It seemed that the cannon had come from all parts and were engaged in a stupendous wrangle. It became impossible to make a sentence heard.

The youth wished to launch a joke—a quotation from newspapers. He desired to say, 'All quiet on the Rappahannock,' but the guns refused to permit even a comment upon their uproar. He never successfully concluded the sentence. But at last the guns stopped, and among the men in the rifle pits rumours again flew, like birds, but they were now for the most part black creatures who flapped their wings drearily near to the ground and refused to rise on any wings of hope. The men's faces grew doleful from the interpreting of omens. Tales of hesitation and uncertainty on the part of those high in place and responsibility came to their ears. Stories of disaster were borne into their minds with many proofs. This din of musketry on the right, growing like a released genie of sound, expressed and emphasized the army's plight.

The men were disheartened and began to mutter. They made gestures expressive of the sentence: 'Ah, what more can we do?' And it could always be seen that they were bewildered by the alleged news and could not fully comprehend a defeat.

Before the grey mists had been totally obliterated by the sun-rays, the regiment was marching in a spread column that was retiring carefully through the woods. The disordered, hurrying lines of the enemy could sometimes be seen down through the groves and little fields. They were yelling, shrill and exultant.

At this sight the youth forgot many personal matters and became greatly enraged. He exploded in loud sentences. 'B'jiminey, we're generaled by a lot 'a lunkheads.'

'More than one feller has said that t'-day,' observed a man.

His friend, recently aroused, was still very drowsy. He looked behind him until his mind took in the meaning of the movement. Then he sighed. 'Oh, well, I s'pose we got licked,' he remarked sadly.

The youth had a thought that it would not be handsome for him to freely condemn other men. He made an attempt to restrain himself, but the words upon his tongue were too bitter. He presently began a long and intricate denunciation of the commander of the forces.

'Mebbe, it wa'n't all his fault—not all together. He did th' best he knowed. It's our luck t' git licked often,' said his friend in a weary tone. He was trudging along with stooped shoulders and shifting eyes like a man who has been caned and kicked.

'Well, don't we fight like the devil? Don't we do all that men can?' demanded the youth loudly.

He was secretly dumbfounded at this sentiment when it came from his lips. For a moment his face lost its valour and he looked guiltily about him. But no one questioned his right to deal in such words, and presently he recovered his air of courage. He went on to repeat a statement he had heard going from group to group at the camp that morning. 'The brigadier said he never saw a new reg'ment fight the way we fought yestirday, didn't he? And we didn't do better than many another reg'ment, did we? Well, then, you can't say it's th' army's fault, can you?'

In his reply, the friend's voice was stern. "A course not,' he said. 'No man dare say we don't fight like th' devil. No man will ever dare say it. Th' boys fight like hell-roosters. But still—still, we don't have no luck.'

'Well, then, if we fight like the devil an' don't ever whip, it must be the general's fault,' said the youth grandly and decisively. 'And I don't see any sense in fighting and fighting and fighting, yet always losing through some derned old lunk-head of a general.'

A sarcastic man who was tramping at the youth's side, then spoke lazily. 'Mebbe yeh think yeh fit th' hull battle yestirday, Fleming,' he remarked.

The speech pierced the youth. Inwardly he was reduced to an abject pulp by these chance words. His legs quaked privately. He cast a frightened glance at the sarcastic man.

'Why, no,' he hastened to say in a conciliating voice. 'I don't think I fought the whole battle yesterday.'

But the other seemed innocent of any deeper meaning. Apparently, he had no information. It was merely his habit. 'Oh!' he replied in the same tone of calm derision.

The youth, nevertheless, felt a threat. His mind shrank from going near to the danger, and thereafter he was silent. The significance of the sarcastic man's words took from him all loud moods that would make him appear prominent. He became suddenly a modest person.

There was low-toned talk among the troops. The officers were impatient and snappy, their countenances clouded with the tales of misfortune. The troops, sifting through the forest, were sullen. In the youth's company once a man's laugh rang out. A dozen soldiers turned their faces quickly toward him and frowned with vague displeasure.

The noise of firing dogged their footsteps. Sometimes, it seemed to be driven a little way, but it always returned again with increased insolence. The men muttered and cursed, throwing black looks in its direction.

In a clear space the troops were at last halted. Regiments and brigades, broken and detached through their encounters with thickets, grew together again and lines were faced toward the pursuing bark of the enemy's infantry.

This noise, following like the yellings of eager, metallic hounds, increased to a loud and joyous burst, and then, as the sun went serenely up the sky, throwing illuminating rays into the gloomy thickets, it broke forth into prolonged pealings. The woods began to crackle as if afire.

'Whoop-a-dadee,' said a man, 'here we are! Everybody fightin'. Blood an' destruction.'

'I was willin' t' bet they'd attack as soon as th' sun got fairly up,' savagely asserted the lieutenant who commanded the youth's company. He jerked without mercy at his little moustache. He strode to and fro with dark dignity in the rear of his men, who were lying down behind whatever protection they had collected.

A battery had trundled into position in the rear and was thoughtfully shelling the distance. The regiment, unmolested as yet, awaited the moment when the grey shadows of the woods before them should be slashed by the lines of flame. There was much growling and swearing.

'Good Gawd,' the youth grumbled, 'we're always being chased around like rats! It makes me sick. Nobody seems to know where we go or why we go. We just get fired around from pillar to post and get licked here and get licked there, and nobody knows what it's done for. It makes a man feel like a damn' kitten in a bag. Now, I'd like to know what the eternal thunders we was marched into these woods for anyhow, unless it was to give the rebs a regular pot shot at us. We came in here and got our legs all tangled up in these cussed briers, and then we begin to fight and the rebs had an easy time of it. Don't tell me it's just luck! I know better. It's this derned old—'

The friend seemed jaded, but he interrupted his comrade with a voice of calm confidence. 'It'll turn out all right in th' end,' he said.

'Oh, the devil it will! You always talk like a dog-hanged parson. Don't tell me! I know—'

At this time there was an interposition by the savage-minded lieutenant, who was obliged to vent some of his inward dissatisfaction upon his men. 'You boys shut right up! There no need 'a your wastin' your breath in long-winded arguments about this an' that an' th' other. You've been jawin' like a lot 'a old hens. All you've got t' do is to fight, an' you'll get plenty 'a that t' do in about ten minutes. Less talkin' an' more fightin' is what's best for you boys. I never saw sech gabbling jackasses.'

He paused, ready to pounce upon any man who might have the temerity to reply. No words being said, he resumed his dignified pacing.

'There's too much chin music an' too little fightin' in this war, anyhow,' he said to them, turning his head for a final remark.

The day had grown more white, until the sun shed his full radiance upon the thronged forest. A sort of a gust of battle came sweeping toward that part of the line where lay the youth's regiment. The front shifted a trifle to meet it squarely. There was a wait. In this part of the field there passed slowly the intense moments that precede the tempest.

A single rifle flashed in a thicket before the regiment. In an instant it was joined by many others. There was a mighty song of clashes and crashes that went sweeping through the woods. The guns in the rear, aroused and enraged by shells that had been thrown burrlike at them, suddenly involved themselves in a hideous altercation with another band of guns. The battle roar settled to a rolling thunder, which was a single, long explosion.

In the regiment there was a peculiar kind of hesitation denoted in the attitudes of the men. They were worn, exhausted, having slept but little and laboured much. They rolled their eyes toward the advancing battle as they stood awaiting the shock. Some shrank and flinched. They stood as men tied to stakes.

XVII

THIS advance of the enemy had seemed to the youth like a ruthless hunting. He began to fume with rage and exasperation. He beat his foot upon the ground, and scowled with hate at the swirling smoke that was approaching like a phantom flood. There was a maddening quality in this seeming resolution of the foe to give him no rest, to give him no time to sit down and think. Yesterday he had fought and had fled rapidly. There had been many adventures. For today he felt that he had earned opportunities for contemplative repose. He could have enjoyed portraying to uninitiated listeners various scenes at which he had been a witness or ably discussing the processes of war with other proved men. Too it was important that he should have time for physical recuperation. He was sore and stiff from his experiences. He had received his fill of all exertions, and he wished to rest.

But those other men seemed never to grow weary; they were fighting with their old speed. He had a wild hate for the relentless foe. Yesterday, when he had imagined the universe to be against him, he had hated it, little gods and big gods; today he hated the army of the foe with the same great hatred. He was not going to be badgered of his life, like a kitten chased by boys, he said. It was not well to drive men into final corners; at those moments they could all develop teeth and claws.

He leaned and spoke into his friend's ear. He menaced the woods with a gesture. 'If they keep on chasing us, by Gawd, they'd better watch out. Can't stand *too* much.'

The friend twisted his head and made a calm reply. 'If they keep on a-chasin' us they'll drive us all inteh th' river.'

The youth cried out savagely at this statement. He crouched behind a little tree, with his eyes burning hatefully and his teeth set in a curlike snarl. The awkward bandage was still about his head, and upon it, over his wound, there was a spot of dry blood. His hair was wondrously tousled, and some straggling, moving locks hung over the cloth of the bandage down toward his forehead. His jacket and shirt were open at the throat, and exposed his young bronzed neck. There could be seen spasmodic gulpings at his throat.

His fingers twined nervously about his rifle. He wished that it was an engine of annihilating power. He felt that he and his companions were being taunted and derided from sincere convictions that they were poor and puny. His knowledge of his inability to take vengeance for it made his rage into a dark and stormy spectre, that possessed him and made him dream of abominable cruelties. The tormentors were flies sucking insolently at his blood, and he thought that he would have given his life for a revenge of seeing their faces in pitiful plights.

The winds of battle had swept all about the regiment, until the one rifle, instantly followed by others, flashed in its front. A moment later the regiment roared forth its sudden and valiant retort. A dense wall of smoke settled slowly down. It was furiously slit and slashed by the knifelike fire from the rifles.

To the youth the fighters resembled animals tossed for a death struggle into a dark pit. There was a sensation that he and his fellows, at bay, were pushing back, always pushing fierce onslaughts of creatures who were slippery. Their beams of crimson seemed to get no purchase upon the bodies of their foes; the latter seemed to evade them with ease, and come through, between, around, and about with unopposed skill.

When, in a dream, it occurred to the youth that his rifle was an impotent stick, he lost sense of everything but his hate, his desire to smash into pulp the glittering smile of victory which he could feel upon the faces of his enemies.

The blue smoke-swallowed line curled and writhed like a snake stepped upon. It swung its ends to and fro in an agony of fear and rage.

The youth was not conscious that he was erect upon his feet. He did not know the direction of the ground. Indeed, once he even lost the habit of balance and fell heavily. He was up again immediately. One thought went through the chaos of his brain at the time. He wondered if he had fallen because he had been shot. But the suspicion flew away at once. He did not think more of it.

He had taken up a first position behind the little tree, with a direct determination to hold it against the world. He had not deemed it possible that his army could that day succeed, and from this he felt the ability to fight harder. But the throng had surged in all ways, until he lost directions and locations, save that he knew where lay the enemy.

The flames bit him, and the hot smoke broiled his skin. His rifle barrel grew so hot that ordinarily he could not have borne it upon his palms; but he kept on stuffing cartridges into it, and pounding them with his clanking, bending ramrod. If he aimed at some changing form through the smoke, he pulled his trigger with a fierce grunt, as if he were dealing a blow of the fist with all his strength.

When the enemy seemed falling back before him and his fellows, he went instantly forward, like a dog who, seeing his foes lagging, turns and insists upon being pursued. And when he was compelled to retire again, he did it slowly, sullenly, taking steps of wrathful despair.

Once he, in his intent hate, was almost alone, and was firing, when all those near him had ceased. He was so engrossed in his occupation that he was not aware of a lull.

He was recalled by a hoarse laugh and a sentence that came to his ears in a voice of contempt and amazement. 'Yeh infernal fool, don't yeh know enough t' quit when there ain't anything t' shoot at? Good Gawd!'

He turned then, and, pausing with his rifle thrown half into position, looked at the blue line of his comrades. During this moment of leisure they seemed all to be engaged in staring with astonishment at him. They had become spectators. Turning to the front again he saw, under the lifted smoke, a deserted ground.

He looked bewildered for a moment. Then there appeared upon the glazed vacancy of his eyes a diamond point of intelligence. 'Oh,' he said, comprehending.

He returned to his comrades and threw himself upon the ground. He sprawled like a man who had been thrashed. His flesh seemed strangely on fire, and the sounds of the battle continued in his ears. He groped blindly for his canteen.

The lieutenant was crowing. He seemed drunk with fighting. He called out to the youth: 'By heavens, if I had ten thousand wild cats like you I could tear th' stomach outa this war in less'n a week!' He puffed out his chest with large dignity as he said it.

Some of the men muttered and looked at the youth in awestruck ways. It was plain that as he had gone on loading and firing and cursing without the proper intermission, they had found time to regard him. And they now looked upon him as a war devil.

The friend came staggering to him. There was some fright and dismay in his voice. 'Are yeh all right, Fleming? Do yeh feel all right? There ain't nothin' th' matter with yeh, Henry, is there?'

'No,' said the youth with difficulty. His throat seemed full of knobs and burrs.

These incidents made the youth ponder. It was revealed to him that he had been a barbarian, a beast. He had fought like a pagan who defends his religion. Regarding it, he saw that it was fine, wild, and, in some ways, easy. He had been a tremendous figure, no doubt. By this struggle he had overcome obstacles which he had admitted to be mountains. They had fallen like paper peaks, and he was now what he called a hero. And he had not been aware of the process. He had slept and, awakening, found himself a knight.

He lay and basked in the occasional stares of his comrades. Their faces were varied in degrees of blackness from the burned powder. Some were utterly smudged. They were reeking with perspiration, and their breaths came hard and wheezing. And from these soiled expanses they peered at him.

'Hot work! Hot work!' cried the lieutenant deliriously. He walked up and down, restless and eager. Sometimes his voice could be heard in a wild, incomprehensible laugh.

When he had a particularly profound thought upon the science of war he always unconsciously addressed himself to the youth.

There was some grim rejoicing by the men. 'By thunder, I bet this army'll never see another new reg'ment like us!'

'You bet!'

> *'A dog, a woman, an' a walnut tree,*
> *Th' more yeh beat 'em, th' better they be!*

That's like us.'

'Lost a piler men, they did. If an ol' woman swep' up th' woods she'd git a dustpanful.'

'Yes, an' if she'll come around ag'in in 'bout an hour she'll git a pile more.'

The forest still bore its burden of clamour. From off under the trees came the rolling clatter of the musketry. Each distant thicket seemed a strange porcupine with quills of flame. A cloud of dark smoke, as from smouldering ruins, went up toward the sun now bright and gay in the blue, enamelled sky.

XVIII

THE ragged line had respite for some minutes, but during its pause the struggle in the forest became magnified until the trees seemed to quiver from the firing and the ground to shake from the rushing of the men. The voices of the cannon were mingled in a long and interminable row. It seemed difficult to live in such an atmosphere. The chests of the men strained for a bit of freshness, and their throats craved water.

There was one shot through the body, who raised a cry of bitter lamentation when came this lull. Perhaps he had been calling out during the fighting also, but at that time no one had heard him. But now the men turned at the woeful complaints of him upon the ground.

'Who is it? Who is it?'

'It's Jimmie Rogers. Jimmie Rogers.'

When their eyes first encountered him there was a sudden halt, as if they feared to go near. He was thrashing about in the grass, twisting his shuddering body into many strange postures. He was screaming loudly. This instant's hesitation seemed to fill him with a tremendous, fantastic contempt, and he damned them in shrieked sentences.

The youth's friend had a geographical illusion concerning a stream, and he obtained permission to go for some water. Immediately canteens were showered upon him. 'Fill mine, will yeh?' 'Bring me some, too.' 'And me, too.' He departed, ladened. The youth went with his friend, feeling a desire to throw his heated body on to the stream and, soaking there, drink quarts.

They made a hurried search for the supposed stream, but did not find it. 'No water here,' said the youth. They turned without delay and began to retrace their steps.

From their position as they again faced toward the place of the fighting, they could of course comprehend a greater amount of the battle than when their visions had been blurred by the hurling smoke of the line. They could see dark stretches winding along the land, and on one cleared space there was a row of guns making grey clouds, which were filled with large flashes of orange-coloured flame. Over some foliage they could see the roof of a house. One window, glowing a deep murder red, shone squarely through the leaves. From the edifice a tall leaning tower of smoke went far into the sky.

Looking over their own troops, they saw mixed masses slowly getting into regular form. The sunlight made twinkling points of the bright steel. To the rear there was a glimpse of a distant roadway as it curved over a slope. It was crowded with retreating infantry. From all the interwoven forest arose the smoke and bluster of the battle. The air was always occupied by a blaring.

Near where they stood shells were flip-flapping and hooting. Occasional bullets buzzed in the air and spanged into tree trunks. Wounded men and other stragglers were slinking through the woods.

Looking down an aisle of the grove, the youth and his companion saw a jangling general and his staff almost ride upon a wounded man, who was crawling on his hands and knees. The general reined strongly at his charger's opened and foamy mouth and guided it with dexterous horsemanship past the man. The latter scrambled in wild and torturing haste. His strength evidently failed him as he reached a place of safety. One of his arms suddenly weakened, and he fell, sliding over upon his back. He lay stretched out, breathing gently.

A moment later the small, creaking cavalcade was directly in front of the two soldiers. Another officer, riding with the skilful abandon of a cowboy, galloped his horse to a position directly before the general. The two unnoticed foot soldiers made a little show of going on, but they lingered near in the desire to overhear the conversation. Perhaps, they thought, some great inner historical things would be said.

The general, whom the boys knew as the commander of their division, looked at the other officer and spoke coolly, as if he were criticizing his clothes. 'Th' enemy's formin' over there for another charge,' he said. 'It'll be directed against Whiterside, an' I fear they'll break through there unless we work like thunder t' stop them.'

The other swore at his restive horse, and then cleared his throat. He made a gesture toward his cap. 'It'll be hell t' pay stoppin' them,' he said shortly.

'I presume so,' remarked the general. Then he began to talk rapidly and in a lower tone. He frequently illustrated his words with a pointing finger. The two infantrymen could hear nothing until finally he asked: 'What troops can you spare?'

The officer who rode like a cowboy reflected for an instant. 'Well,' he said, 'I had to order in th' 12th to help th' 76th, an' I haven't really got any. But there's th' 304th. They fight like a lot 'a mule drivers. I can spare them best of any.'

The youth and his friend exchanged glances of astonishment.

The general spoke sharply. 'Get 'em ready, then. I'll watch developments from here, an' send you word when t' start them. It'll happen in five minutes.'

As the other officer tossed his fingers toward his cap and wheeling his horse, started away, the general called out to him in a sober voice: 'I don't believe many of your mule drivers will get back.'

The other shouted something in reply. He smiled.

With scared faces, the youth and his companion hurried back to the line.

These happenings had occupied an incredibly short time, yet the youth felt that in them he had been made aged. New eyes were given to him. And the most startling thing was to learn suddenly that he was very insignificant. The officer spoke of the regiment as if he referred to a broom. Some part of the woods needed sweeping, perhaps, and he merely indicated a broom in a tone properly indifferent to its fate. It was war, no doubt, but it appeared strange.

As the two boys approached the line, the lieutenant perceived them and swelled with wrath. 'Fleming—Wilson—how long does it take yeh to git water, anyhow—where yeh been to?'

But his oration ceased as he saw their eyes, which were large with great tales. 'We're goin' t' charge—we're goin' t' charge!' cried the youth's friend, hastening with his news.

'Charge?' said the lieutenant. 'Charge? Well, b' Gawd! Now; this is real fightin'.' Over his soiled countenance there went a boastful smile. 'Charge? Well, b' Gawd!'

A little group of soldiers surrounded the two youths. 'Are we, sure 'nough? Well, I'll be derned! Charge? What fer? What at? Wilson, you're lyin'.'

'I hope to die,' said the youth, pitching his tones to the key of angry remonstrance. 'Sure as shooting, I tell you.'

And his friend spoke in re-enforcement. 'Not by a blame sight, he ain't lyin'. We heard 'em talkin'.'

They caught sight of two mounted figures a short distance from them. One was the colonel of the regiment and the other was the officer who had received orders from the commander of the division. They were gesticulating at each other. The soldier, pointing at them, interpreted the scene.

One man had a final objection: 'How could yeh hear 'em talkin'?' But the men, for a large part, nodded, admitting that previously the two friends had spoken truth.

They settled back into reposeful attitudes with airs of having accepted the matter. And they mused upon it, with a hundred varieties of expression. It was an engrossing thing to think about. Many tightened their belts carefully and hitched at their trousers.

A moment later the officers began to bustle among the men, pushing them into a more compact mass and into a better alignment. They chased those that straggled and fumed at a few men who seemed to show by their attitudes that they had decided to remain at that spot. They were like critical shepherds struggling with sheep.

Presently, the regiment seemed to draw itself up and heave a deep breath. None of the men's faces were mirrors of large thoughts. The soldiers were bended and stooped like sprinters before a signal. Many pairs of glinting eyes peered from the grimy faces toward the curtains of the deeper woods. They seemed to be engaged in deep calculations of time and distance.

They were surrounded by the noises of the monstrous altercation between the two armies. The world was fully interested in other matters. Apparently, the regiment had its small affair to itself.

The youth, turning, shot a quick, inquiring glance at his friend. The latter returned to him the same manner of look. They were the only ones who possessed an inner knowledge. 'Mule drivers—hell t' pay—don't believe many will get back.' It was an ironical secret. Still, they saw no hesitation in each other's faces, and they nodded a mute and unprotesting assent when a shaggy man near them said in a meek voice: 'We'll git swallowed.'

XIX

THE youth stared at the land in front of him. Its foliages now seemed to veil powers and horrors. He was aware of the machinery of orders that started the charge, although from the corners of his eyes he saw an officer, who looked like a boy a-horseback, come galloping, waving his hat. Suddenly he felt a straining and heaving among the men. The line fell slowly forward like a toppling wall, and, with a convulsive gasp that was intended for a cheer, the regiment began its journey. The youth was pushed and jostled for a moment before he understood the movement at all, but directly he lunged ahead and began to run.

He fixed his eye upon a distant and prominent clump of trees where he had concluded the enemy were to be met, and he ran toward it as toward a goal. He had believed throughout that it was a mere question of getting over an unpleasant matter as quickly as possible, and he ran desperately, as if pursued for a murder. His face was drawn hard and tight with the stress of his endeavour. His eyes were fixed in a lurid glare. And with his soiled and disordered dress, his red and inflamed features surmounted by the dingy rag with its spot of blood, his wildly swinging rifle and banging accoutrements, he looked to be an insane soldier.

As the regiment swung from its position out into a cleared space the woods and thickets before it awakened. Yellow flames leaped toward it from many directions. The forest made a tremendous objection.

The line lurched straight for a moment. Then the right wing sprung forward; it in turn was surpassed by the left. Afterward the centre careered to the front until the regiment was a wedge-shaped mass, but an instant later the opposition of the bushes, trees, and uneven places on the ground split the command and scattered it into detached clusters.

The youth, light-footed, was unconsciously in advance. His eyes still kept note of the clump of trees. From all places near it the clannish yell of the enemy could be heard. The little flames of rifles leaped from it. The song of the bullets was in the air and shells snarled among the tree-tops. One tumbled directly into the middle of a hurrying group and exploded in crimson fury. There was an instant's spectacle of a man, almost over it, throwing up his hands to shield his eyes.

Other men, punched by bullets, fell in grotesque agonies. The regiment left a coherent trail of bodies.

They had passed into a clearer atmosphere. There was an effect like a revelation in the new appearance of the landscape. Some men working madly at a battery were plain to them, and the opposing infantry's lines were defined by the grey walls and fringes of smoke.

It seemed to the youth that he saw everything. Each blade of the green grass was bold and clear. He thought that he was aware of every change in the thin, transparent vapour that floated idly in sheets. The brown or grey trunks of the trees showed each roughness of their surfaces. And the men of the regiment, with their starting eyes and sweating faces, running madly, or falling, as if thrown headlong, to queer, heaped-up corpses—all were comprehended. His mind took a mechanical but firm impression, so that afterward everything was pictured and explained to him, save why he himself was there.

But there was a frenzy made from this furious rush. The men, pitching forward insanely, had burst into cheerings, moblike and barbaric, but tuned in strange keys that can arouse the dullard and the stoic. It made a mad enthusiasm that, it seemed, would be incapable of checking itself before granite and brass. There was the delirium that encounters despair and death, and is heedless and blind to the odds. It is a temporary but sublime absence of selfishness. And because it was of this order was the reason, perhaps, why the youth wondered, afterward, what reasons he could have had for being there.

Presently the straining pace ate up the energies of the men. As if by agreement, the leaders began to slacken their speed. The volleys directed against them had had a seeming windlike effect. The regiment snorted and blew. Among some stolid trees it began to falter and hesitate. The men, staring intently, began to wait for some of the distant walls of smoke to move and disclose to them the scene. Since much of their strength and their breath had vanished, they returned to caution. They were become men again.

The youth had a vague belief that he had run miles, and he thought, in a way, that he was now in some new and unknown land.

The moment the regiment ceased its advance the protesting splutter of musketry became a steadied roar. Long and accurate fringes of smoke spread out. From the top of a small hill came level belchings of yellow flame that caused an inhuman whistling in the air.

The men, halted, had opportunity to see some of their comrades dropping with moans and shrieks. A few lay under foot, still or wailing. And now for an instant the men stood, their rifles slack in their hands, and watched the regiment dwindle. They appeared dazed and stupid. This spectacle seemed to paralyse them, overcome them with a fatal fascination. They stared woodenly at the sights, and, lowering their eyes, looked from face to face. It was a strange pause, and a strange silence.

Then, above the sounds of the outside commotion, arose the roar of the lieutenant. He strode suddenly forth, his infantile features black with rage.

'Come on yeh fools!' he bellowed. 'Come on! Yeh can't stay here. Yeh must come on.' He said more, but much of it could not be understood.

He started rapidly forward, with his head turned toward the men. 'Come on,' he was shouting. The men stared with blank and yokel-like eyes at him. He was obliged to halt and retrace his steps. He stood then with his back to the enemy and delivered gigantic curses into the faces of the men. His body vibrated from the weight and force of his imprecations. And he could string oaths with the facility of a maiden who strings beads.

The friend of the youth aroused. Lurching suddenly forward and dropping to his knees, he fired an angry shot at the persistent woods. This action awakened the men. They huddled no more like sheep. They seemed suddenly to bethink them of their weapons, and at once commenced firing. Belaboured by their officers, they began to move forward. The regiment, involved like a cart involved in mud and muddle, started unevenly with many jolts and jerks. The men stopped now every few paces to fire and load, and in this manner moved slowly on from trees to trees.

The flaming opposition in their front grew with their advance until it seemed that all forward ways were barred by the thin leaping tongues, and off to the right an ominous demonstration could sometimes be dimly discerned. The smoke lately generated was in confusing clouds that made it difficult for the regiment to proceed with intelligence. As he passed through each curling mass the youth wondered what would confront him on the farther side.

The command went painfully forward until an open space interposed between them and the lurid lines. Here, crouching and cowering behind some trees, the men clung with desperation, as if threatened by a wave. They looked wild-eyed, and as if amazed at this furious disturbance they had stirred. In the storm there was an ironical expression of their importance. The faces of the men, too, showed a lack of a certain feeling of responsibility for being there. It was as if they had been driven. It was the dominant animal failing to remember in the supreme moments the forceful causes of various superficial qualities. The whole affair seemed incomprehensible to many of them.

As they halted thus the lieutenant again began to bellow profanely. Regardless of the vindictive threats of the bullets, he went about coaxing, berating, and bedamning. His lips, that were habitually in a soft and childlike curve, were now writhed into unholy contortions. He swore by all possible deities.

Once he grabbed the youth by the arm. 'Come on, yeh lunkhead!' he roared. 'Come on! We'll all git killed if we stay here. We've on'y got t' go across that lot. An' then'—the remainder of his idea disappeared in a blue haze of curses.

The youth stretched forth his arm. 'Cross there?' His mouth was puckered in doubt and awe.

'Certainly. Jest 'cross th' lot! We can't stay here,' screamed the lieutenant. He poked his face close to the youth and waved his bandaged hand. 'Come on!' Presently he grappled with him as if for a wrestling bout. It was as if he planned to drag the youth by the ear on to the assault.

The private felt a sudden unspeakable indignation against his officer. He wrenched fiercely and shook him off.

'Come on yerself, then,' he yelled. There was a bitter challenge in his voice.

They galloped together down the regimental front. The friend scrambled after them. In front of the colours the three men began to bawl: 'Come on! come on!' They danced and gyrated like tortured savages.

The flag, obedient to these appeals, bended its glittering form and swept toward them. The men wavered in indecision for a moment, and then with a long, wailful cry the dilapidated regiment surged forward and began its new journey.

Over the field went the scurrying mass. It was a handful of men splattered into the faces of the enemy. Toward it instantly sprang the yellow tongues. A vast quantity of blue smoke hung before them. A mighty banging made ears valueless.

The youth ran like a madman to reach the woods before a bullet could discover him. He ducked his head low, like a football player. In his haste his eyes almost closed, and the scene was a wild blur. Pulsating saliva stood at the corners of his mouth.

Within him, as he hurled himself forward, was born a love, a despairing fondness for this flag which was near him. It was a creation of beauty and invulnerability. It was a goddess, radiant, that bended its form with an imperious gesture to him. It was a woman, red and white, hating and loving, that called him with the voice of his hopes. Because no harm could come to it he endowed it with power. He kept near, as if it could be a saver of lives, and an imploring cry went from his mind.

In the mad scramble he was aware that the colour sergeant flinched suddenly, as if struck by a bludgeon. He faltered, and then became motionless, save for his quivering knees.

He made a spring and a clutch at the pole. At the same instant his friend grabbed it from the other side. They jerked at it, stout and furious, but the colour sergeant was dead, and the corpse would not relinquish its trust. For a moment there was a grim encounter. The dead man, swinging with bended back, seemed to be obstinately tugging, in ludicrous and awful ways, for the possession of the flag.

It was past in an instant of time. They wrenched the flag furiously from the dead man, and, as they turned again, the corpse swayed forward with bowed head. One arm swung high, and the curved hand fell with heavy protest on the friend's unheeding shoulder.

XX

WHEN the two youths turned with the flag they saw that much of the regiment had crumbled away, and the dejected remnant was coming back. The men, having hurled themselves in projectile fashion, had presently expended their forces. They slowly retreated, with their faces still toward the spluttering woods, and their hot rifles still replying to the din. Several officers were giving orders, their voices keyed to screams.

'Where in hell yeh goin'?' the lieutenant was asking in a sarcastic howl. And a red-bearded officer, whose voice of triple brass could plainly be heard, was commanding: 'Shoot into 'em! Shoot into 'em, Gawd damn their souls!' There was a *mêlée* of screeches, in which the men were ordered to do conflicting and impossible things.

The youth and his friend had a small scuffle over the flag. 'Give it t' me!' 'No, let me keep it!' Each felt satisfied with the other's possession of it, but each felt bound to declare, by an offer to carry the emblem, his willingness to further risk himself. The youth roughly pushed his friend away.

The regiment fell back to the stolid trees. There it halted for a moment to blaze at some dark forms that had begun to steal upon its track. Presently it resumed its march again, curving among the tree trunks. By the time the depleted regiment had again reached the first open space they were receiving a fast and merciless fire. There seemed to be mobs all about them.

The greater part of the men, discouraged, their spirits worn by the turmoil, acted as if stunned. They accepted the pelting of the bullets with bowed and weary heads. It was of no purpose to strive against walls. It was of no use to batter themselves against granite. And from this consciousness that they had attempted to conquer an unconquerable thing there seemed to arise a feeling that they had been betrayed. They glowered with bent brows, but dangerously, upon some of the officers, more particularly upon the red-bearded one with the voice of triple brass.

However, the rear of the regiment was fringed with men, who continued to shoot irritably at the advancing foes. They seemed resolved to make every trouble. The youthful lieutenant was perhaps the last man in the disordered mass. His forgotten back was toward the enemy. He had been shot in the arm. It hung straight and rigid. Occasionally he would cease to remember it, and be about to emphasize an oath with a sweeping gesture. The multiplied pain caused him to swear with incredible power.

The youth went along with slipping, uncertain feet. He kept watchful eyes rearward. A scowl of mortification and rage was upon his face. He had thought of a fine revenge upon the officer who had referred to him and his fellow as mule drivers. But he saw that it could not come to pass. His dreams had collapsed when the mule drivers, dwindling rapidly, had wavered and h sitated on the little clearing, and then had recoiled. And now the retreat of the mule drivers was a march of shame to him.

A dagger-pointed gaze from without his blackened face was held toward the enemy, but his greater hatred was riveted upon the man, who, not knowing him, had called him a mule driver.

When he knew that he and his comrades had failed to do anything in successful ways that might bring the little pangs of a kind of remorse upon the officer, the youth allowed the rage of the baffled to possess him. This cold officer upon a monument, who dropped epithets unconcernedly down, would be finer as a dead man, he thought. So grievous did he think it that he could never possess the secret right to taunt truly in answer.

He had pictured red letters of curious revenge. 'We *are* mule drivers, are we?' And now he was compelled to throw them away.

He presently wrapped his heart in the cloak of his pride and kept the flag erect. He harangued his fellows, pushing against their chests with his free hand. To those he knew well he made frantic appeals, beseeching them by name. Between him and the lieutenant, scolding and near to losing his mind with rage, there was felt a subtle fellowship and equality. They supported each other in all manner of hoarse, howling protests.

But the regiment was a machine run down. The two men babbled at a forceless thing. The soldiers who had heart to go slowly were continually shaken in their resolves by a knowledge that comrades were slipping with speed back to the lines. It was difficult to think of reputation when others were thinking of skins. Wounded men were left crying on this black journey.

The smoke fringes and flames blustered always. The youth, peering once through a sudden rift in a cloud, saw a brown mass of troops, interwoven and magnified until they appeared to be thousands. A fierce-hued flag flashed before his vision.

Immediately, as if the uplifting of the smoke had been pre-arranged, the discovered troops burst into a rasping yell, and a hundred flames jetted toward the retreating band. A rolling grey cloud again interposed as the regiment doggedly replied. The youth had to depend again upon his misused ears, which were trembling and buzzing from the *mêlée* of musketry and yells.

The way seemed eternal. In the clouded haze men became panic-stricken with the thought that the regiment had lost its path, and was proceeding in a perilous direction. Once the men who headed the wild procession turned and came pushing back against their comrades, screaming that they were being fired upon from points which they had considered to be toward their own lines. At this cry a hysterical fear and dismay beset the troops. A soldier, who heretofore had been ambitious to make the regiment into a wise little band that would proceed calmly amid the huge-appearing difficulties, suddenly sank down and buried his face in his arms with an air of bowing to a doom. From another a shrill lamentation rang out filled with profane allusions to a general. Men ran hither and thither, seeking with their eyes roads of escape. With serene regularity, as if controlled by a schedule, bullets buffed into men.

The youth walked stolidly into the midst of the mob, and with his flag in his hands took a stand as if he expected an attempt to push him to the ground. He unconsciously assumed the attitude of the colour bearer in the fight of the preceding day. He passed over his brow a hand that trembled. His breath did not come freely. He was choking during this small wait for the crisis.

His friend came to him. 'Well, Henry, I guess this is good-bye—John.'

'Oh, shut up, you damned fool!' replied the youth, and he would not look at the other.

The officers laboured like politicians to beat the mass into a proper circle to face the menaces. The ground was uneven and torn. The men curled into depressions and fitted themselves snugly behind whatever would frustrate a bullet.

The youth noted with vague surprise that the lieutenant was standing mutely with his legs far apart and his sword held in the manner of a cane. The youth wondered what had happened to his vocal organs that he no more cursed.

There was something curious in this little intent pause of the lieutenant. He was like a babe which, having wept its fill, raises its eyes and fixes upon a distant toy. He was engrossed in this contemplation, and the soft under lip quivered from self-whispered words.

Some lazy and ignorant smoke curled slowly. The men, hiding from the bullets, waited anxiously for it to lift and disclose the plight of the regiment.

The silent ranks were suddenly thrilled by the eager voice of the youthful lieutenant bawling out: 'Here they come! Right on to us, b' Gawd!' His further words were lost in a roar of wicked thunder from the men's rifles.

The youth's eyes had instantly turned in the direction indicated by the awakened and agitated lieutenant, and he had seen the haze of treachery disclosing a body of soldiers of the enemy. They were so near that he could see their features. There was a recognition as he looked at the types of faces. Also he perceived with dim amazement that their uniforms were rather gay in effect, being light grey, accented with a brilliant-hued facing. Too, the clothes seemed new.

These troops had apparently been going forward with caution, their rifles held in readiness, when the youthful lieutenant had discovered them and their movement had been interrupted by the volley from the blue regiment. From the moment's glimpse, it was derived that they had been unaware of the proximity of their dark-suited foes or had mistaken the direction. Almost instantly they were shut utterly from the youth's sight by the smoke from the energetic rifles of his companions. He strained his vision to learn the accomplishment of the volley, but the smoke hung before him.

The two bodies of troops exchanged blows in the manner of a pair of boxers. The fast angry firings went back and forth. The men in blue were intent with the despair of their circumstances and they seized upon the revenge to be had at close range. Their thunder swelled loud and valiant. Their curving front bristled with flashes and the place resounded with the clangour of their ramrods. The youth ducked and dodged for a time and achieved a few unsatisfactory views of the enemy. There appeared to be many of them and they were replying swiftly. They seemed moving toward the blue regiment, step by step. He seated himself gloomily on the ground with his flag between his knees.

As he noted the vicious, wolflike temper of his comrades he had a sweet thought that if the enemy was about to swallow the regimental broom as a large prisoner, it could at least have the consolation of going down with bristles forward.

But the blows of the antagonist began to grow more weak. Fewer bullets ripped the air, and finally, when the men slackened to learn of the fight, they could see only dark, floating smoke. The regiment lay still and gazed. Presently some chance whim came to the pestering blur, and it began to coil heavily away. The men saw a ground vacant of fighters. It would have been an empty stage if it were not for a few corpses that lay thrown and twisted into fantastic shapes upon the sward.

At sight of this tableau, many of the men in blue sprang from behind their covers and made an ungainly dance of joy. Their eyes burned and a hoarse cheer of elation broke from their dry lips.

It had begun to seem to them that events were trying to prove that they were impotent. These little battles had evidently endeavoured to demonstrate that the men could not fight well. When on the verge of submission to these opinions, the small duel had showed them that the proportions were not impossible, and by it they had revenged themselves upon their misgivings and upon the foe.

The impetus of enthusiasm was theirs again. They gazed about them with looks of uplifted pride, feeling new trust in the grim, always confident weapons in their hands. And they were men.

XXI

PRESENTLY they knew that no fighting threatened them. All ways seemed once more opened to them. The dusty blue lines of their friends were disclosed a short distance away. In the distance there were many colossal noises, but in all this part of the field there was a sudden stillness.

They perceived that they were free. The depleted band drew a long breath of relief and gathered itself into a bunch to complete its trip.

In this last length of journey the men began to show strange emotions. They hurried with nervous fear. Some who had been dark and unfaltering in the grimmest moments now could not conceal an anxiety that made them frantic. It was perhaps that they dreaded to be killed in insignificant ways after the times for proper military deaths had passed. Or, perhaps, they thought it would be too ironical to get killed at the portals of safety. With backward looks of perturbation, they hastened.

As they approached their own lines there was some sarcasm exhibited on the part of a gaunt and bronzed regiment that lay resting in the shade of trees. Questions were wafted to them.

'Where th' hell yeh been?'

'What yeh comin' back fer?'

'Why didn't yeh stay there?'

'Was it warm out there, sonny?'

'Goin' home now, boys?'

One shouted in taunting mimicry: 'Oh, mother, come quick an' look at th' sojers!'

There was no reply from the bruised and battered regiment, save that one man made broadcast challenges to fist fights and the red-bearded officer walked rather near and glared in great swashbuckler style at a tall captain in the other regiment. But the lieutenant suppressed the man who wished to fist fight, and the tall captain, flushing at the little fanfare of the red-bearded one, was obliged to look intently at some trees.

The youth's tender flesh was deeply stung by these remarks. From under his creased brows he glowered with hate at the mockers. He meditated upon a few revenges. Still, many in the regiment hung their heads in criminal fashion, so that it came to pass that the men trudged with sudden heaviness, as if they bore upon their bended shoulders the coffin of their honour. And the youthful lieutenant, recollecting himself, began to mutter softly in black curses.

They turned when they arrived at their old position to regard the ground over which they had charged.

The youth in this contemplation was smitten with a large astonishment. He discovered that the distances, as compared with the brilliant measurings of his mind, were trivial and ridiculous. The stolid trees, where much had taken place, seemed incredibly near. The time, too, now that he reflected, he saw to have been short. He wondered at the number of emotions and events that had been crowded into such little spaces. Elfin thoughts must have exaggerated and enlarged everything, he said.

It seemed, then, that there was bitter justice in the speeches of the gaunt and bronzed veterans. He veiled a glance of disdain at his fellows who strewed the ground, choking with dust, red from perspiration, misty-eyed, dishevelled.

They were gulping at their canteens, fierce to wring every mite of water from them, and they polished at their swollen and watery features with coat sleeves and bunches of grass.

However, to the youth there was a considerable joy in musing upon his performances during the charge. He had had very little time previously in which to appreciate himself, so that there was now much satisfaction in quietly thinking of his actions. He recalled bits of colour that in the flurry had stamped themselves unawares upon his engaged senses.

As the regiment lay heaving from its hot exertions the officer who had named them as mule drivers came galloping along the line. He had lost his cap. His tousled hair streamed wildly, and his face was dark with vexation and wrath. His temper was displayed with more clearness by the way in which he managed his horse. He jerked and wrenched savagely at his bridle, stopping the hard-breathing animal with a furious pull near the colonel of the regiment. He immediately exploded in reproaches which came unbidden to the ears of the men. They were suddenly alert, being always curious about black words between officers.

'Oh, thunder, MacChesnay, what an awful bull you made of this thing!' began the officer. He attempted low tones, but his indignation caused certain of the men to learn the sense of his words. 'What an awful mess you made! Good Lord, man, you stopped about a hundred feet this side of a very pretty success! If your men had gone a hundred feet farther you would have made a great charge, but as it is—what a lot of mud diggers you've got anyway!'

The men, listening with bated breath, now turned their curious eyes upon the colonel. They had a ragamuffin interest in this affair.

The colonel was seen to straighten his form and put one hand forth in oratorical fashion. He wore an injured air; it was as if a deacon had been accused of stealing. The men were wiggling in an ecstasy of excitement.

But of a sudden the colonel's manner changed from that of a deacon to that of a Frenchman. He shrugged his shoulders. 'Oh, well, general, we went as far as we could,' he said calmly.

'As far as you could? Did you, b' Gawd?' snorted the other. 'Well, that wasn't very far, was it? he added, with a glance of cold contempt into the other's eyes. 'Not very far, I think. You were intended to make a diversion in favour of Whiterside. How well you succeeded your own ears can now tell you.' He wheeled his horse and rode stiffly away.

The colonel, bidden to hear the jarring noises of an engagement in the woods to the left, broke out in vague damnations.

The lieutenant, who had listened with an air of impotent rage to the interview, spoke suddenly in firm and undaunted tones. 'I don't care what a man is—whether he is a general or what—if he says th' boys didn't put up a good fight out there he's a damned fool.'

'Lieutenant,' began the colonel, severely, 'this is my own affair, and I'll trouble you—'

The lieutenant made an obedient gesture. 'All right, colonel, all right,' he said. He sat down with an air of being content with himself.

The news that the regiment had been reproached went along the line. For a time the men were bewildered by it. 'Good thunder!' they ejaculated, staring at the vanishing form of the general. They conceived it to be a huge mistake.

Presently, however, they began to believe that in truth their efforts had been called light. The youth could see this conviction weigh upon the entire regiment until the men were like cuffed and cursed animals, but withal rebellious.

The friend, with a grievance in his eye, went to the youth. 'I wonder what he does want,' he said. 'He must think we went out there an' played marbles! I never see sech a man!'

The youth developed a tranquil philosophy for these moments of irritation. 'Oh, well,' he rejoined, 'he probably didn't see nothing of it at all and got mad as blazes, and concluded we were a lot of sheep, just because we didn't do what he wanted done. It's a pity old Grandpa Henderson got killed yestirday—he'd have known that we did our best and fought good. It's just our awful luck, that's what.'

'I should say so,' replied the friend. He seemed to be deeply wounded at an injustice. 'I should say we did have awful luck! There's no fun in fightin' fer people when everything yeh do—no matter what—ain't done right. I have a notion t' stay behind next time an' let 'em take their ol' charge an' go t' th' devil with it.'

The youth spoke soothingly to his comrade. 'Well, we both did good. I'd like to see the fool what'd say we both didn't do as good as we could!'

'Of course we did,' declared the friend stoutly. 'An' I'd break th' feller's neck if he was as big as a church. But we're all right, anyhow, for I heard one feller say that we two fit th' best in th' reg'ment, an' they had a great argument 'bout it. Another feller, 'a course, he had t' up an' say it was a lie—he seen all what was goin' on an' say never seen us from th' beginnin' t' th' end. An' a lot more struck in an' ses it wasn't a lie—we did fight like thunder, an' they give us quite a send-off. But this is what I can't stand—these everlastin' ol' soldiers, titterin' an' laughin', an' then that general, he's crazy.'

The youth exclaimed with sudden exasperation: 'He's a lunkhead! He makes me mad. I wish he'd come along next time. We'd show 'im what—'

He ceased because several men had come hurrying up. Their faces expressed a bringing of great news.

'O Flem, yeh jest oughta heard!' cried one, eagerly.

'Heard what?' said the youth.

'Yeh jest oughta heard!' repeated the other, and he arranged himself to tell his tidings. The others made an excited circle. 'Well, sir, th' colonel met your lieutenant right by us—it was damnedest thing I ever heard—an' he ses: "Ahem! ahem!" he ses. "Mr. Hasbrouck!" he ses, "by th' way, who was that lad what carried th' flag?" he ses. There, Flemin', what d' yeh think 'a that? "Who was th' lad what carried th' flag?" he ses, an' th' lieutenant, he speaks up right away: "That's Flemin', an' he's a jimhickey," he ses, right away. What? I say he did. "A jimhickey," he ses—those 'r his words. He did, too. I say he did. If you kin tell this story better than I kin, go ahead an' tell it. Well, then, keep yer mouth shet. Th' lieutenant, he ses: "He's a jimhickey," an' th' colonel, he ses: "Ahem! ahem! he is, indeed, a very good man t' have, ahem! He kep' th' flag

'way t' th' front. I saw 'im. He's a good un," ses th' colonel.
"You bet," ses th' lieutenant, "he an' a feller named Wilson
was at th' head 'a th' charge, an' howlin' like Indians all th'
time," he ses. "Head 'a th' charge all th' time," he ses. "A
feller named Wilson," he ses. There, Wilson, m'boy, put that
in a letter an' send it hum t' yer mother, hay? "A feller named
Wilson," he ses. An' th' colonel, he ses: "Were they, indeed?
Ahem! ahem! My sakes!" he ses. "At th' head 'a th' reg'ment?"
he ses. "They were," ses th' lieutenant. "My sakes!" ses th'
colonel. He ses: "Well, well, well," he ses, "those two babies?"
"They were," ses th' lieutenant. "Well, well," ses th' colonel,
"they deserve t' be major-generals," he ses. "They deserve t' be
major-generals."'

The youth and his friend had said: 'Huh!' 'Yer lyin', Thomp-
son.' 'Oh, go t' blazes!' 'He never sed it.' 'Oh, what a lie!' 'Huh!'
But despite these youthful scoffings and embarrassments, they
knew that their faces were deeply flushing from thrills of pleasure.
They exchanged a secret glance of joy and congratulation.

They speedily forgot many things. The past held no pictures
of error and disappointment. They were very happy, and their
hearts swelled with grateful affection for the colonel and the
youthful lieutenant.

XXII

WHEN the woods again began to pour forth the dark-hued
masses of the enemy the youth felt serene self-confidence. He
smiled briefly when he saw men dodge and duck at the long
screechings of shells that were thrown in giant handfuls over
them. He stood, erect and tranquil, watching the attack begin
against a part of the line that made a blue curve along the
side of an adjacent hill. His vision being unmolested by smoke
from the rifles of his companions, he had opportunities to see
parts of the hard fight. It was a relief to perceive at last from
whence came some of these noises which had been roared into
his ears.

Off a short way he saw two regiments fighting a little separate
battle with two other regiments. It was in a cleared space, wearing
a set-apart look. They were blazing as if upon a wager, giving and

taking tremendous blows. The firings were incredibly fierce and rapid. These intent regiments apparently were oblivious of all larger purposes of war, and were slugging each other as if at a matched game.

In another direction he saw a magnificent brigade going with the evident intention of driving the enemy from a wood. They passed in out of sight and presently there was a most awe-inspiring racket in the wood. The noise was unspeakable. Having stirred this prodigious uproar, and, apparently, finding it too prodigious, the brigade, after a little time, came marching airily out again with its fine formation in nowise disturbed. There were no traces of speed in its movements. The brigade was jaunty and seemed to point a proud thumb at the yelling wood.

On a slope to the left there was a long row of guns, gruff and maddened, denouncing the enemy, who, down through the woods, were forming for another attack in the pitiless monotony of conflicts. The round red discharges from the guns made a crimson flare and a high, thick smoke. Occasional glimpses could be caught of groups of the toiling artillerymen. In the rear of this row of guns stood a house, calm and white, amid bursting shells. A congregation of horses, tied to a long railing, were tugging frenziedly at their bridles. Men were running hither and thither.

The detached battle between the four regiments lasted for some time. There chanced to be no interference, and they settled their dispute by themselves. They struck savagely and powerfully at each other for a period of minutes, and then the lighter-hued regiments faltered and drew back, leaving the dark-blue lines shouting. The youth could see the two flags shaking with laughter amid the smoke remnants.

Presently there was a stillness, pregnant with meaning. The blue lines shifted and changed a trifle and stared expectantly at the silent woods and fields before them. The hush was solemn and churchlike, save for a distant battery that, evidently unable to remain quiet, sent a faint rolling thunder over the ground. It irritated, like the noises of unimpressed boys. The men imagined that it would prevent their perched ears from hearing the first words of the new battle.

Of a sudden the guns on the slope roared out a message of warning. A spluttering sound had begun in the woods. It swelled with amazing speed to a profound clamour that involved the earth in noises. The splitting crashes swept along the lines until an interminable roar was developed. To those in the midst of it it became a din fitted to the universe. It was the whirring and thumping of gigantic machinery, complications among the smaller stars. The youth's ears were filled up. They were incapable of hearing more.

On an incline over which a road wound he saw wild and desperate rushes of men perpetually backward and forward in riotous surges. These parts of the opposing armies were two long waves that pitched upon each other madly at dictated points. To and fro they swelled. Sometimes, one side by its yells and cheers would proclaim decisive blows, but a moment later the other side would be all yells and cheers. Once the youth saw a spray of light forms go in houndlike leaps toward the waving blue lines. There was much howling, and presently it went away with a vast mouthful of prisoners. Again, he saw a blue wave dash with such thunderous force against a grey obstruction that it semed to clear the earth of it and leave nothing but trampled sod. And always in their swift and deadly rushes to and fro the men screamed and yelled like maniacs.

Particular pieces of fence or secure positions behind collections of trees were wrangled over, as gold thrones or pearl bedsteads. There were desperate lunges at these chosen spots seemingly every instant, and most of them were bandied like light toys between the contending forces. The youth could not tell from the battle flags flying like crimson foam in many directions which colour of cloth was winning.

His emaciated regiment bustled forth with undiminished fierceness when its time came. When assaulted again by bullets, the men burst out in a barbaric cry of rage and pain. They bent their heads in aims of intent hatred behind the projected hammers of their guns. Their ramrods clanged loud with fury as their eager arms pounded the cartridges into the rifle barrels. The front of the regiment was a smoke-wall penetrated by the flashing points of yellow and red.

Wallowing in the fight, they were in an astonishingly short time besmudged. They surpassed in stain and dirt all their previous appearances. Moving to and fro with strained exertion, jabbering the while, they were, with their swaying bodies, black faces, and glowing eyes, like strange and ugly fiends jigging heavily in the smoke.

The lieutenant, returning from a tour after a bandage, produced from a hidden receptacle of his mind new and portentous oaths suited to the emergency. Strings of expletives he swung lash-like over the backs of his men, and it was evident that his previous efforts had in nowise impaired his resources.

The youth, still the bearer of the colours, did not feel his idleness. He was deeply absorbed as a spectator. The crash and swing of the great drama made him lean forward, intent-eyed, his face working in small contortions. Sometimes he prattled, words coming unconsciously from him in grotesque exclamations. He did not know that he breathed; that the flag hung silently over him, so absorbed was he.

A formidable line of the enemy came within dangerous range. They could be seen plainly—tall, gaunt men with excited faces running with long strides toward a wandering fence.

At sight of this danger the men suddenly ceased their cursing monotone. There was an instant of strained silence before they threw up their rifles and fired a plumping volley at the foes. There had been no order given; the men, upon recognizing the menace, had immediately let drive their flock of bullets without waiting for word of command.

But the enemy were quick to gain the protection of the wandering line of fence. They slid down behind it with remarkable celerity, and from this position they began briskly to slice up the blue men.

These latter braced their energies for a great struggle. Often, white clinched teeth shone from the dusky faces. Many heads surged to and fro, floating upon a pale sea of smoke. Those behind the fence frequently shouted and yelped in taunts and gibelike cries, but the regiment maintained a stressed silence. Perhaps, at this new assault the men recalled the fact that they had been named mud diggers, and it made their situation thrice bitter. They were breathlessly intent upon keeping the ground and thrusting away the rejoicing body of the enemy. They fought swiftly and with a despairing savageness denoted in their expressions.

The youth had resolved not to budge whatever should happen. Some arrows of scorn that had buried themselves in his heart had generated strange and unspeakable hatred. It was clear to him that his final and absolute revenge was to be achieved by his dead body lying, torn and gluttering, upon the field. This was to be a poignant retaliation upon the officer who had said 'mule drivers', and later 'mud diggers', for in all the wild graspings of his mind for a unit responsible for his sufferings and commotions he always seized upon the man who had dubbed him wrongly. And it was his idea, vaguely formulated, that his corpse would be for those eyes a great and salt reproach.

The regiment bled extravagantly. Grunting bundles of blue began to drop. The orderly sergeant of the youth's company was shot through the cheeks. Its supports being injured, his jaw hung afar down, disclosing in the wide cavern of his mouth a pulsing mass of blood and teeth. And with all he made attempts to cry out. In his endeavour there was a dreadful earnestness, as if he conceived that one great shriek would make him well.

The youth saw him presently go rearward. His strength seemed in nowise impaired. He ran swiftly, casting wild glances for succour.

Others fell down about the feet of their companions. Some of the wounded crawled out and away, but many lay still, their bodies twisted into impossible shapes.

The youth looked once for his friend. He saw a vehement young man, powder-smeared and frowzled, whom he knew to be him. The lieutenant, also, was unscathed in his position at the rear. He had continued to curse, but it was now with the air of a man who was using his last box of oaths.

For the fire of the regiment had begun to wane and drip. The robust voice, that had come strangely from the thin ranks, was growing rapidly weak.

XXIII

THE COLONEL came running along back of the line. There were other officers following him. 'We must charge'm!' they shouted. 'We must charge'm!' they cried with resentful voices, as if anticipating a rebellion against this plan by the men.

The youth, upon hearing the shouts, began to study the distance between him and the enemy. He made vague calculations. He saw that to be firm soldiers they must go forward. It would be death to stay in the present place, and with all the circumstances to go backward would exalt too many others. Their hope was to push the galling foes away from the fence.

He expected that his companions, weary and stiffened, would have to be driven to this assault, but as he turned toward them he perceived with a certain surprise that they were giving quick and unqualified expressions of assent. There was an ominous, clanging overture to the charge when the shafts of the bayonets rattled upon the rifle barrels. At the yelled words of command the soldiers sprang forward in eager leaps. There was new and unexpected force in the movement of the regiment. A knowledge of its faded and jaded condition made the charge appear like a paroxysm, a display of the strength that comes before a final feebleness. The men scampered in insane fever of haste, racing as if to achieve a sudden success before an exhilarating fluid should leave them. It was a blind and despairing rush by the collection of men in dusty and tattered blue, over a green sward and under a sapphire sky, toward a fence, dimly outlined in smoke, from behind which spluttered the fierce rifles of enemies.

The youth kept the bright colours to the front. He was waving his free arm in furious circles, the while shrieking mad calls and appeals, urging on those that did not need to be urged, for it seemed that the mob of blue men hurling themselves on the dangerous group of rifles were again grown suddenly wild with an enthusiasm of unselfishness. From the many firings starting toward them, it looked as if they would merely succeed in making a great sprinkling of corpses on the grass between their former position and the fence. But they were in a state of frenzy, perhaps because of forgotten vanities, and it made an exhibition of sublime recklessness. There was no obvious questioning, nor figurings, nor diagrams. There was, apparently, no considered loopholes. It appeared that the swift wings of their desires would have shattered against the iron gates of the impossible.

He himself felt the daring spirit of a savage religion mad. He was capable of profound sacrifices, a tremendous death. He had no time for dissections, but he knew that he thought of the bullets only as things that could prevent him from reaching the place of his endeavour. There were subtle flashings of joy within him that thus should be his mind.

He strained all his strength. His eyesight was shaken and dazzled by the tension of thought and muscle. He did not see anything excepting the mist of smoke gashed by the little knives of fire, but he knew that in it lay the aged fence of a vanished farmer protecting the snuggled bodies of the grey men.

As he ran a thought of the shock of contact gleamed in his mind. He expected a great concussion when the two bodies of troops crashed together. This became a part of his wild battle madness. He could feel the onward swing of the regiment about him and he conceived of a thunderous, crushing blow that would prostrate the resistance and spread consternation and amazement for miles. The flying regiment was going to have a catapultian effect. This dream made him run faster among his comrades, who were giving vent to hoarse and frantic cheers.

But presently he could see that many of the men in grey did not intend to abide the blow. The smoke, rolling, disclosed men who ran, their faces still turned. These grew to a crowd, who retired stubbornly. Individuals wheeled frequently to send a bullet at the blue wave.

But at one part of the line there was a grim and obdurate group that made no movement. They were settled firmly down behind posts and rails. A flag, ruffled and fierce, waved over them and their rifles dinned fiercely.

The blue whirl of men got very near, until it seemed that in truth there would be a close and frightful scuffle. There was an expressed disdain in the opposition of the little group, that changed the meaning of the cheers of the men in blue. They became yells of wrath, directed, personal. The cries of the two parties were now in sound an interchange of scathing insults.

They in blue showed their teeth; their eyes shone all white. They launched themselves as at the throats of those who stood resisting. The space between dwindled to an insignificant distance.

The youth had centred the gaze of his soul upon that other flag. Its possession would be high pride. It would express bloody minglings, near blows. He had a gigantic hatred for those who made great difficulties and complications. They caused it to be as a craved treasure of mythology, hung amid tasks and contrivances of danger.

He plunged like a mad horse at it. He was resolved it should not escape if wild blows and darings of blows could seize it. His own emblem, quivering and aflare, was winging toward the other. It seemed there would shortly be an encounter of strange beaks and claws, as of eagles.

The swirling body of blue men came to a sudden halt at close and disastrous range and roared a swift volley. The group in grey was split and broken by this fire, but its riddled body still fought. The men in blue yelled again and rushed in upon it.

The youth, in his leapings, saw, as through a mist, a picture of four or five men stretched upon the ground or writhing upon their knees with bowed heads as if they had been stricken by bolts from the sky. Tottering among them was the rival colour bearer, whom the youth saw had been bitten vitally by the bullets of the last formidable volley. He perceived this man fighting a last struggle, the struggle of one whose legs are grasped by demons. It was a ghastly battle. Over his face was the bleach of death, but set upon it was the dark and hard lines of desperate purpose. With this terrible grin of resolution he hugged his precious flag to him and was stumbling and staggering in his design to go the way that led to safety for it.

But his wounds always made it seem that his feet were retarded, held, and he fought a grim fight, as with invisible ghouls fastened greedily upon his limbs. Those in advance of the scampering blue men, howling cheers, leaped at the fence. The despair of the lost was in his eyes as he glanced back at them.

The youth's friend went over the obstruction in a tumbling heap and sprang at the flag as a panther at prey. He pulled at it and, wrenching it free, swung up its red brilliancy with a mad cry of exultation even as the colour bearer, gasping, lurched over in a final throe and, stiffening convulsively, turned his dead face to the ground. There was much blood upon the grass blades.

At the place of success there began more wild clamourings of cheers. The men gesticulated and bellowed in an ecstasy. When they spoke it was as if they considered their listener to be a mile away. What hats and caps were left to them they often slung high in the air.

At one part of the line four men had been swooped upon, and they now sat as prisoners. Some blue men were about them in an eager and curious circle. The soldiers had trapped strange birds, and there was an examination. A flurry of fast questions was in the air.

One of the prisoners was nursing a superficial wound in the foot. He cuddled it, baby-wise, but he looked up from it often to curse with an astonishing utter abandon straight at the noses of his captors. He consigned them to red regions; he called upon the pestilential wrath of strange gods. And with it all he was singularly free from recognition of the finer points of the conduct of prisoners of war. It was as if a clumsy clod had trod upon his toe and he conceived it to be his privilege, his duty, to use deep, resentful oaths.

Another, who was a boy in years, took his plight with great calmness and apparent good nature. He conversed with the men in blue, studying their faces with his bright and keen eyes. They spoke of battle and conditions. There was an acute interest in all their faces during this exchange of view points. It seemed a great satisfaction to hear voices from where all had been darkness and speculation.

The third captive sat with a morose countenance. He preserved a stoical and cold attitude. To all advances he made one reply without variation, 'Ah, go t' hell!'

The last of the four was always silent, and, for the most part, kept his face turned in unmolested directions. From the views the youth received he seemed to be in a state of absolute dejection. Shame was upon him, and with it profound regret that he was, perhaps, no more to be counted in the ranks of his fellows. The youth could detect no expression that would allow him to believe that the other was giving a thought to his narrowed future, the pictured dungeons, perhaps, and starvations and brutalities, liable to the imagination. All to be seen was shame for captivity and regret for the right to antagonize.

After the men had celebrated sufficiently they settled down behind the old rail fence, on the opposite side to the one from which their foes had been driven. A few shot perfunctorily at distant marks.

There was some long grass. The youth nestled in it and rested, making a convenient rail support the flag. His friend, jubilant and glorified, holding his treasure with vanity, came to him there. They sat side by side and congratulated each other.

XXIV

THE roarings that had stretched in a long line of sound across the face of the forest began to grow intermittent and weaker. The stentorian speeches of the artillery continued in some distant encounter, but the crashes of the musketry had almost ceased. The youth and his friend of a sudden looked up, feeling a deadened form of distress at the waning of these noises, which had become a part of life. They could see changes going on among the troops. There were marchings this way and that way. A battery wheeled leisurely. On the crest of a small hill was the thick gleam of many departing muskets.

The youth arose. 'Well, what now, I wonder?' he said. By his tone he seemed to be preparing to resent some new monstrosity in the way of dins and smashes. He shaded his eyes with his grimy hand and gazed over the field.

His friend also arose and stared. 'I bet we're goin' t' git along out of this an' back over th' river,' said he.

'Well, I swan!' said the youth.

They waited, watching. Within a little while the regiment received orders to retrace its way. The men got up grunting from the grass, regretting the soft repose. They jerked their stiffened legs, and stretched their arms over their heads. One man swore as he rubbed his eyes. They all groaned 'O Lord!' They had as many objections to this change as they would have had to a proposal for a new battle.

They trampled slowly back over the field across which they had run in a mad scamper.

The regiment marched until it had joined its fellows. The reformed brigade, in column, aimed through a wood at the road. Directly they were in a mass of dust-covered troops, and were trudging along in a way parallel to the enemy's lines as these had been defined by the previous turmoil.

They passed within view of a stolid white house, and saw in front of it groups of their comrades lying in wait behind a neat breastwork. A row of guns were booming at a distant enemy. Shells thrown in reply were raising clouds of dust and splinters. Horsemen dashed along the line of entrenchments.

At this point of its march the division curved away from the

field and went winding off in the direction of the river. When
the significance of this movement had impressed itself upon the
youth he turned his head and looked over his shoulder toward the
trampled and *débris*-strewed ground. He breathed a breath of new
satisfaction. He finally nudged his friend. 'Well, it's all over,' he
said to him.

His friend gazed backward. 'B'Gawd, it is,' he assented. They
mused.

For a time the youth was obliged to reflect in a puzzled and
uncertain way. His mind was undergoing a subtle change. It
took moments for it to cast off its battleful ways and resume
its accustomed course of thought. Gradually his brain emerged
from the clogged clouds, and at last was enabled to more closely
comprehend himself and circumstance.

He understood then that the existence of shot and countershot
was in the past. He had dwelt in a land of strange, squalling
upheavals and had come forth. He had been where there was
red of blood and black of passion, and he was escaped. His first
thoughts were given to rejoicings at this fact.

Later he began to study his deeds, his failures, and his
achievements. Thus, fresh from scenes where many of his usual
machines of reflection had been idle, from where he had proceeded
sheeplike, he struggled to marshal all his acts.

At last they marched before him clearly. From this present view
point he was enabled to look at them in spectator fashion and to
criticize them with some correctness, for his new condition had
already defeated certain sympathies.

Regarding his procession of memory, he felt gleeful and
unregretting, for in it his public deeds were paraded in great
and shining prominence. Those performances which had been
witnessed by his fellows marched now in wide purple and gold,
having various deflections. They went gaily with music. It was
pleasure to watch these things. He spent delightful minutes
viewing the gilded images of memory.

He saw that he was good. He recalled with a thrill of joy the
respectful comments of his fellows upon his conduct.

Nevertheless, the ghost of his flight from the first engagement
appeared to him and danced. There were small shoutings in his
brain about these matters. For a moment he blushed, and the light
of his soul flickered with shame.

A spectre of reproach came to him. There loomed the dogging memory of the tattered soldier—he who, gored by bullets and faint for blood, had fretted concerning an imagined wound in another; he who had loaned his last of strength and intellect for the tall soldier; he who, blind with weariness and pain, had been deserted in the field.

For an instant a wretched chill of sweat was upon him at the thought that he might be detected in the thing. As he stood persistently before his vision, he gave vent to a cry of sharp irritation and agony.

His friend turned. 'What's the matter, Henry?' he demanded. The youth's reply was an outburst of crimson oaths.

As he marched along the little branch-hung roadway among his prattling companions this vision of cruelty brooded over him. It clung near him always and darkened his view of these deeds in purple and gold. Whichever way his thoughts turned they were followed by the sombre phantom of the desertion in the fields. He looked stealthily at his companions, feeling sure that they must discern in his face evidences of this pursuit. But they were plodding in ragged array, discussing with quick tongues the accomplishments of the late battle.

'Oh, if a man should come up an' ask me, I'd say we got a dum good lickin'.'

'Lickin'—in yer eye! We ain't licked, sonny. We're going down here aways, swing aroun', an' come in behint 'em.'

'Oh, hush, with your comin' in behint 'em. I've seen all 'a that I wanta. Don't tell me about comin' in behint—'

'Bill Smithers, he ses he'd rather been in ten hundred battles than been in that heluva hospital. He ses they got shootin' in th' night-time, an' shells dropped plum among 'em in th' hospital. He ses sech hollerin' he never see.'

'Hasbrouck? He's th' best off'cer in this here reg'ment. He's a whale.'

'Didn't I tell yeh we'd come aroun' in behint 'em? Didn't I tell yeh so? We—'

'Oh, shet yer mouth!'

For a time this pursuing recollection of the tattered man took all elation from the youth's veins. He saw his vivid error, and he was afraid that it would stand before him all his life. He took no share in the chatter of his comrades, nor did he look at them or know them, save when he felt sudden suspicion that they were seeing his thoughts and scrutinizing each detail of the scene with the tattered soldier.

Yet gradually he mustered force to put the sin at a distance. And at last his eyes seemed to open to some new ways. He found that he could look back upon the brass and bombast of his earlier gospels and see them truly. He was gleeful when he discovered that he now despised them.

With this conviction came a store of assurance. He felt a quiet manhood, non-assertive but of sturdy and strong blood. He knew that he would no more quail before his guides wherever they should point. He had been to touch the great death, and found that, after all, it was but the great death. He was a man.

So it came to pass that as he trudged from the place of blood and wrath his soul changed. He came from hot ploughshares to prospects of clover tranquilly, and it was as if hot ploughshares were not. Scars faded as flowers.

It rained. The procession of weary soldiers became a bedraggled train, despondent and muttering, marching with churning effort in a trough of liquid brown mud under a low, wretched sky. Yet the youth smiled, for he saw that the world was a world for him, though many discovered it to be made of oaths and walking sticks. He had rid himself of the red sickness of battle. The sultry nightmare was in the past. He had been an animal blistered and sweating in the heat and pain of war. He turned now with a lover's thirst to images of tranquil skies, fresh meadows, cool brooks—an existence of soft and eternal peace.

Over the river a golden ray of sun came through the hosts of leaden rain clouds.

Anton Pavlovich Chekhov
MY LIFE
A Provincial's Story

1897

ANTON CHEKHOV (1860–1904), unlike the other great Russian genius represented in these pages, came from a background of penury, the grandson of a serf and the son of an unsuccessful tradesman. As a medical student in Moscow, he paid some of his expenses by writing short humorous sketches in the newspapers of the day, and generally lived a struggling existence; he remarked once, in later life, that the security and comfort that the property-owning classes take for granted the poor achieve, if they achieve them at all, 'at the cost of their youth'. Chekhov qualified as a doctor in 1884, the same year, ironically, in which he began to exhibit the symptoms of tuberculosis.

By that time his work as a writer was becoming recognized and he had broadened its scope far beyond the comic, though humour always retained its place in his work and the rich, haunting, complex, indefinable manner one thinks of as 'Chekhovian' contains a note of laughter as well as the notes of profound melancholy, irony, resignation, and sudden white-hot anger. *My Life*, his longest story, shows his characteristic blend of all these elements.

Chekhov crammed his short life with experience. In 1890 he undertook an arduous voyage to Sakhalin Island, a penal settlement on the Pacific coast, and wrote a report on the conditions there. Two years later he bought a farm at Malikhovo, south of Moscow, and involved himself in country life, taking a special interest in educational and charitable work. His connection with the theatre belongs to his last ten years; *The Seagull* (1896), *Uncle Vanya* (1897), and in 1904 *The Three Sisters* and *The Cherry Orchard*, were star offerings of the Moscow Arts Theatre, one of whose actresses, Olga Knipper, became his wife in 1901.

Chekhov's plays, ceaselessly performed in the theatres of the world, are probably even more famous than his stories; but the stories have the wider range. They stretch all the way from the harsh, bleak realism of his studies of poverty in 'Peasants' and 'In the Ravine' and the unflinching portrayal of suffering in 'Ward No. 6' (a story that helped to shape the mind of Lenin) to 'The Lady with the Dog', a tender and lyrical story that takes us, socially, closer to the world of the plays.

I

'I ONLY keep you here out of respect for your esteemed father,' the director told me. 'Otherwise you'd have been sent flying long ago.'

'Sir,' I replied, 'you flatter me unduly if you think I can defy the laws of gravity.' Then I heard him say, 'Take this character away, he gets on my nerves.'

I was dismissed two days later, and that made nine jobs I had had since reaching man's estate, to the great grief of my father, the city architect.

I had worked in various government offices, but all nine jobs had been exactly alike and involved sitting down, copying, listening to stupid, insensitive remarks and waiting to be sacked.

Father was sitting back in his armchair with his eyes closed when I went to see him. His gaunt, emaciated face, with a bluish-grey shadow where he shaved, was the picture of meekness and resignation and he looked like an elderly Catholic organist. He did not answer my greeting or open his eyes.

'If my dear wife, your mother, were still alive,' he said, 'your way of life would be a constant thorn in her flesh. I see the workings of Providence in her premature death. Tell me, wretched youth,' he went on, opening his eyes, 'what, pray, am I to do with you?'

When I was younger my friends and relations had known what to do with me, some advising me to volunteer for the army, while others wanted me to work in a chemist's shop or a telegraph office. But now I was turned twenty-five and even a bit grey at the temples, now I had actually been a volunteer, a chemist's assistant and a telegraph operator, I had used up my chances in life, it seemed, so they stopped advising me and just sighed or shook their heads.

'Who do you think you are?' Father went on. 'By your age most young men have a position in life, but look at you, you penniless lout, living on your father.'

He made his usual speech about young men nowadays being doomed—doomed by atheism, materialism and inordinate conceit— and about how amateur theatricals should be banned for distracting them from religion and duty.

'You'll come with me tomorrow, you'll tell the director you're sorry and you'll promise to work properly,' he ended. 'You must regularize your position in society before another day has passed.'

'Do you mind if I say something?' I asked sullenly, expecting nothing good from this conversation. 'What does your "position in society" come to? Simply the privileges conferred by capital and education. Poor, uneducated people earn their living by manual labour. Why should I be different? That's what I don't see.'

'When you talk about manual labour you sound stupid and vulgar,' said Father irritably. 'Look here, you nit-wit, can't you get it into your thick skull that there's more to it than brute strength? You also have the divine spirit within you—the sacred flame that sets you quite apart from an ass or a reptile and gives you an affinity with the sublime. And what produced this flame? Thousands of years' effort by the best of mankind. Your great-grandfather, General Poloznev, fought at Borodino. Your great-uncle was a poet, public speaker and marshal of the nobility, your uncle's a teacher, and lastly I, your father, am an architect. Don't tell me we Poloznevs have all handed on this sacred flame just for you to put it out!'

'Be fair,' I said. 'Millions of people do work with their hands.'

'Let them! That's all they're fit for! Anyone—a complete idiot or criminal even—can work with his hands. Such work is the hallmark of slaves and barbarians, while the sacred flame is granted only to the few.'

There was no point in going on. Father worshipped himself and no words could sway him unless they came out of his own mouth. Besides, I was pretty sure that these high-handed references to manual labour were prompted less by any notion about sacred flames than by a secret dread that I might become a labourer and set the whole town talking about me. But the main thing was that other men of my age had all graduated long ago and were doing well—the son of the manager of the State Bank was an established civil servant already—while I, my father's only son, was a nobody.

There was no point in going on with this unpleasant conversation, but I sat there feebly protesting and hoping to make my point in the end. The problem was simple and straightforward enough, goodness knows—how was I to earn my living? That's all. But this simplicity went unnoticed as the mellifluous sentences rolled on, all about Borodino, sacred flames and my father's uncle, a forgotten poet whose verse had been wretched, bogus stuff. And rude remarks about nit-wits and their thick skulls were made at my expense.

But I did so much want to be understood. In spite of everything I loved my father and sister. I had been asking them for advice ever since I was a child and by now the habit was so ingrained that it was with me for life. Right or wrong, I was always afraid of annoying them—and afraid because Father was now so upset that his stringy neck had turned red and he might have a stroke.

'Sitting in a stuffy room, copying and competing with a typewriter,' I pronounced. 'What a disgrace and humiliation for a man of my age! There's no sacred flame about that.'

'It is brain work all the same,' Father said. 'But enough! This conversation must cease. In any case I warn you that if you won't go back to the office and if you follow your own contemptible inclinations, my daughter and I will banish you from our hearts. I'll cut you out of my will too, and by God I mean it!'

'Your will doesn't matter to me,' I said in all sincerity, to show the absolute purity of the motives which I wished to rule my life. 'I renounce my inheritance in advance.'

Somehow, to my astonishment, these words hurt Father terribly. He turned crimson.

'How dare you talk to me like that, you idiot!' he shouted in a thin, shrill voice. 'You good-for-nothing!' And with a practised hand, quickly and deftly, he slapped my face twice. 'You forget yourself!'

When Father beat me as a child I was made to stand to attention and look him in the face. And I was so flabbergasted when he struck me nowadays that I always drew myself up and tried to look him in the eye as if I were still in the nursery. My father was old and very thin, but those slender muscles must have been tough as whip-cord because the blows really hurt.

I reeled back into the hall and he snatched up his umbrella and struck me several blows on the head and shoulders. Then my sister opened the drawing-room door to see what the noise was about, but turned away at once with a look of pity and terror, not saying a word in my defence.

I did not intend to go back to the office and I did mean to start a new life as a worker. And nothing was going to stop me. I only had to choose a job, and that did not seem so very difficult, for I felt I had plenty of strength and stamina to tackle the toughest work. I was going to live as a worker with all the monotony, hunger and smells. I should have to rough it. I should always be worried about earning enough to make ends meet, and coming home from work along Great Dvoryansky Street I might well find myself envying Dolzhikov the engineer, who worked with his brain. Who could tell? At the moment I enjoyed thinking about these future tribulations.

At one time intellectual activity had fired my imagination and I had seen myself as a teacher, doctor or writer, but those dreams had never come true. I was passionately addicted to such intellectual pleasures as reading and the theatre. But could I do brain work? I don't know. At school I had an absolute aversion to Greek and had to be taken away in the fourth form. For a long time I had private tutors trying to get me into the fifth form. Then I worked in various offices, doing absolutely nothing most of the day, and was told that was brain work.

Nothing I did as pupil or clerk needed any mental effort, talent, special ability or creative drive. It was all mechanical. I regard that kind of brain work as lower than manual labour, I despise it and do not think it can justify an idle, carefree life for one moment, being simply a sham—another form of idleness in fact. Very likely I just don't know what real brain work is.

Evening came on. We lived in Great Dvoryansky Street, the city's main thoroughfare, where the local smart set paraded in the evening for want of a decent municipal park. And a splendid street it was, almost as good as a park. On both sides grew poplars, especially sweet-scented after rain. Acacias, lilac bushes, wild cherries and apple-trees hung out over fences and railings. Twilight in May, the young, green leaves and the shadows, the scent of lilac, the humming of insects, the stillness and the warmth—spring comes round every year, it's true, but it seems so fresh and wonderful each time. I stood at the garden gate watching people stroll by. I had grown up with most of them and we had played together as children. But they might be a bit put off by me now in my cheap, unfashionable clothes with narrow trousers tucked into large, clumsy boots—people called me 'drain-pipes'. Besides, I had a bad name in town because I lacked social standing and was always playing billiards in low dives. Having twice been hauled off to the local police station probably didn't help much either, though I had done absolutely nothing to deserve it.

Someone was playing the piano in Mr. Dolzhikov's flat in the large house opposite. It was growing dark and stars twinkled in the sky. I saw Father walk slowly past with my sister on his arm, returning the bows of passers-by. He wore an old top-hat with a broad upturned brim.

'Just look,' he said to my sister, pointing at the sky with the umbrella that he had been hitting me with. 'Look at the sky. Even the tiniest star is a world of its own. Man is indeed insignificant compared with the universe.'

He sounded as if he enjoyed being insignificant and found it most flattering. What a mediocrity! He was the only architect we had, I am sorry to say, and not one decent house had been built in our town in the fifteen or twenty years I could remember.

When he was asked to plan a house, he usually drew the ballroom and drawing-room first. In the old days boarding-school girls couldn't dance at all unless they started at the stove, and in the same way his creative thinking could not develop unless he started with ballroom and drawing-room. He would tack on dining-room, nursery and study, all linked by doors which inevitably turned them into corridors, each room with two, even three, doors too many. His imagination must have been muddled, chaotic and stunted. He always seemed to feel that something was missing and resorted to various kinds of annexes which he planted on top of each other. I can still see those narrow entrance halls, poky little passages and crooked little staircases leading to mezzanines where you could not stand upright, with three huge steps instead of a floor—like the shelves in a Russian bath-house. The kitchens must always be in the basement with vaulted ceilings and brick floors, the façades had a stubborn, crusty expression, their lines stiff and timid, and the roofs were low and squashed, while the plump, hefty-looking chimneys were incomplete without wire caps and squeaky black cowls.

Somehow all these houses built by Father, each so like the next, vaguely evoked his top-hat and the austere, stiff lines of the back of his neck. The town became accustomed to Father's incompetence in time. It took root and became the local style.

Father also brought this style into my sister's life. To start with he gave her the name Cleopatra, just as he had named me Misail.

When she was a child he would scare her with talk about the stars, the wise men of old and our ancestors, and would explain at some length the nature of life and duty. Now that she was twenty-six he was still at it. No one might take her arm except himself, and he somehow imagined that an eligible young man must come along sooner or later to seek her hand out of respect for his moral calibre. She adored Father, feared him, and thought him highly intelligent.

It grew quite dark and the street gradually emptied. The music stopped in the house opposite us and the gates were flung wide open. A troika bowled off down our street with a dashing air, its bells softly jingling. The engineer and his daughter had gone for a spin. Time for bed.

I had my own room in our house, but lived in a shed tacked onto a brick outbuilding. Very likely it had been put up as a harness room originally, for there were huge pegs driven into the walls, but it was no longer needed as such. For thirty years Father had been stacking newspapers there. He had them bound, heaven knows why, in half-yearly batches and let no one touch them. Living there, I ran into Father and his guests less often. I felt that not having a proper room and not going into the house for dinner every day took some of the sting out of Father's talk about my being a burden to him.

My sister was waiting for me. Without telling Father, she had brought me some supper, a small piece of cold veal and a slice of bread. They were always on about 'counting your copecks' in our house—'taking care of your roubles' and that sort of stuff. These clichés rather got my sister down and she thought only of economizing, so we ate badly. She put the plate on the table, sat on my bed and burst into tears.

'Oh Misail,' she said, 'what are you doing to us?'

She did not cover her face. The tears fell onto her breast and hands and she looked miserable. She threw herself down on the pillow and let the tears come, shaking all over and sobbing.

'That's another job you've walked out of . . .' she said. 'Oh, how dreadful.'

'But my dear sister, you must see . . .' I said. Her tears filled me with despair.

Then of course my lamp had to run out of paraffin. It had started smoking, and was about to go out. The old pegs on the walls looked grim and their shadows flickered.

'Don't be too hard on us,' said my sister, getting up. 'Father's terribly upset and I'm ill, nearly out of my mind. What will become of you?' she asked, sobbing and holding out her hands. 'Please, I beg you for our dear mother's sake, go back to the office.'

'I can't, Cleopatra,' I said, on the verge of giving in. 'I can't.'

'Why not?' my sister went on. 'Why not? Look, if you didn't get on with your boss, find another job. For instance, why not go and work on the railway? I've just been talking to Anyuta Blagovo and she says they're sure to take you on there. She's even promised to put in a word for you. For God's sake, Misail, do think about it. Give it some thought, please.'

After a little more talk I gave in. I said I had never thought of a job on the new railway and didn't mind having a go.

She smiled happily through her tears and pressed my hand, and then went on crying, unable to stop. I fetched some paraffin from the kitchen.

II

NO one in town was more addicted to amateur theatricals, concerts and *tableaux vivants* for charity than the Azhogins, who owned a house in Great Dvoryansky Street. They provided the premises, did the organizing, and bore the expense. The family was rich and owned land, having about eight thousand acres in the district with a magnificent manor-house and garden, but they disliked the country and lived in town all year round.

There was the mother—a tall, lean, genteel woman with short hair, short blouse and narrow skirt in the English fashion—and three daughters who were called not by name, but simply by 'Eldest', 'Middle' and 'Youngest'. Short-sighted and round-shouldered, they all had hideous sharp chins and dressed like their mother. They lisped unattractively. But despite all this they needs must be in every show and were always doing something for charity—acting, reciting, singing. They were very earnest, never smiled, and even acted in musical comedies without a spark of life, looking as businesslike as if they were auditing accounts.

I liked our theatricals, especially the numerous rehearsals— somewhat chaotic, but great fun and always followed by supper. I had no hand in choosing plays or casting, for my job was off stage, painting scenery, copying parts, prompting and doing the make-up. I was also put in charge of sound effects—thunder, nightingale song and all that. Having neither social standing nor respectable clothes, I always kept to myself at rehearsals, lurking in the wings, too shy to speak.

I painted scenery in the Azhogins' shed or yard, helped by a house-painter or, as he called himself, 'decorating contractor', one Andrew Ivanov. He was about fifty, tall, very thin and pale, with a sunken chest, sunken temples and dark blue rings under his eyes. He looked slightly frightening. He suffered from some wasting disease and every autumn and spring people said he was fading away, but he would have a spell in bed and then get up again.

'Still alive, you see,' he would say with an air of surprise.

In town he was called Radish, which was said to be his real surname. He was as fond of the theatre as I was, and would drop everything when he heard that a show was in the air, and go to the Azhogins' to paint scenery.

The day after my talk with my sister I worked all day at the Azhogins'. The rehearsal was to start at 7 p.m. All the company met in the ballroom an hour before that, and three sisters—Eldest, Middle and Youngest—were walking up and down the stage reading from notebooks. Radish, in a long reddish-brown overcoat with a scarf round his neck, stood leaning his head against a wall, reverently watching the stage. Mrs. Azhogin went up to each guest in turn and made polite remarks. She had a trick of staring you in the face and speaking quietly as though revealing a secret.

'It must be hard work painting scenery,' she said quietly, coming up to me. 'I was just talking to Mrs. Mufke about superstitions when you came in. God knows, my whole life has been one long fight against superstition. Just to show the servants how silly such fears are, I always light three candles in my room and begin any important venture on the thirteenth of the month.'

Mr. Dolzhikov's daughter came in—a beautiful, buxom, fair-haired girl, 'dressed Paris fashion', as people put it locally. She did not act, but they put a chair on the stage for her at rehearsals, and performances never started till she appeared in the front row, dazzling and breath-taking in her fine clothes. Coming from the metropolis, she was allowed to pass remarks at rehearsal and did so with a smile of charming condescension, obviously thinking our shows a sort of child's game. She had studied singing at the

St. Petersburg Conservatoire, it was said, and had even sung for a whole winter in a private opera house. I found her very attractive and could hardly take my eyes off her at rehearsals and performances.

I had already picked up a notebook to prompt from when my sister suddenly appeared. She came up without taking off her hat and coat and asked if I would please go with her.

I went. Anyuta Blagovo stood in the doorway back-stage. She also had her hat on, and wore a dark veil. She was the daughter of a Deputy Judge who had served in our town for some time, pretty well since the local court was first set up. Tall and well-built, Anyuta was thought essential for *tableaux vivants* and when she represented a fairy or 'Glory' her face burnt with shame. But she took no part in theatricals. She did sometimes drop in at rehearsals for a moment on some errand, but never came into the hall and it was obvious now that she had looked in only for a moment.

'My father's been talking about you,' she said dryly, blushing and not looking at me. 'Dolzhikov says he'll give you a job on the railway. Will you see him tomorrow? He'll be at home.'

I bowed and thanked her for her trouble.

'You can leave that,' she said, pointing to my notebook.

Anyuta and my sister went up to Mrs. Azhogin and they all whispered for a minute or two with an occasional glance at me. This was some sort of consultation.

'Yes indeed,' said Mrs. Azhogin quietly, coming up to me and staring me in the face. 'Yes indeed, if this is keeping you from serious work,'—she took the notebook from my hands—'you can hand over to someone else. It's all right, my dear man. Be off, and good luck to you.'

I said goodbye and went out feeling awkward. On my way downstairs I saw Anyuta Blagovo and my sister leaving in a hurry and talking excitedly—no doubt about my railway job. My sister had never been at a rehearsal before and very likely felt guilty, scared of Father finding out that she had been at the Azhogins' without his permission.

About half-past twelve next day I went to see Dolzhikov. A man-servant showed me into a very fine room which served the engineer as both drawing-room and office. It was all so soft, elegant and—to someone as unused to it as I was—even a bit strange. There were expensive carpets, huge armchairs, bronzes, pictures, gilt and plush frames. The walls were covered with photographs of very beautiful women and people with fine, intelligent faces in relaxed poses. A door from the drawing-room led straight to a balcony facing the garden. There were lilac-bushes, a table laid for lunch, lots of bottles and a bunch of roses. It smelt of spring and expensive cigars—the very smell of happiness. 'Here's a man who really has lived,' everything seemed to say. 'He has worked hard and earned such happiness as this world can offer.'

The engineer's daughter was sitting at the desk reading a newspaper.

'You want Father?' she asked. 'He's having a shower, but he'll be here in a minute. Won't you sit down?'

I did.

'I believe you live opposite?' she said after a short pause.

'Yes.'

'I watch you every day from the window for som·thing to do. I hope you don't mind,' she went on, looking at her paper. 'I often see you and your sister. She looks so kind and seems to be so intent on what she's doing.'

Dolzhikov came in, rubbing his neck with a towel.

'It's Mr. Poloznev, Daddy,' his daughter said.

'Yes, yes, Blagovo told me.' He turned to me briskly, but did not offer to shake hands. 'Now look here, what do you want out of me? What are these "jobs" I keep hearing about? You're a funny lot,' he went on in a loud voice as if telling me off. 'A score of you come here every day. Think I'm running an office? I'm running a railway, my dear sirs. It's a tough job of work and I need mechanics, fitters, navvies, carpenters, tunnellers. All you people can do is sit on your backsides and write! Oh, you're all great writers!'

He had an air of well-being like his carpets and armchairs. Plump, healthy, rosy-cheeked, broad-chested, well-scrubbed, he looked like a china figure of a coachman in his cotton print shirt and wide trousers tucked inside his boots. He had not a grey hair on his head. He had a full, curly beard, a hooked nose and dark, clear, innocent eyes.

'What good are you?' he went on. 'You're no damn good at all. Oh yes, I'm an engineer. I've made my way in life. But before I ran the railway I sweated my guts out for years. I've been an engine-driver and I worked two years in Belgium as a common greaser. Judge for yourself, man—what work can I give you?'

'You're right of course . . .' I muttered, greatly put out. Those clear, innocent eyes were too much for me.

'Can you at least work a telegraph?' he asked after a moment's thought.

'Yes, I've been a telegraph clerk.'

'Well, we'll see. You'd better go to Dubechnya for the moment. I have someone there, but he's no damn good.'

'What will my duties be?' I asked.

'We'll see. You run along there for the moment and I'll fix things up. But I won't have you going on the booze, mind. And don't come bothering me or I'll boot you out.'

He moved off without even a nod. I bowed to him and his daughter, who was reading the paper, and went out. I was so fed up that when my sister asked how I had got on with Dolzhikov I just could not speak.

I rose at sunrise to walk to Dubechnya. There was no one in our street—everyone was still in bed—and my footsteps sounded lonely and hollow. The dew-drenched poplars filled the air with soft fragrance. I was sad and did not feel like leaving town. I loved my native town—it was a place of warmth and beauty to me. I loved the green leaves, the quiet sunny mornings, the bells ringing. But the people bored me. I lived with them, but we had nothing in common and at times they made me feel sick. I disliked them, couldn't make them out at all.

What kept these sixty-five thousand people going? That's what I couldn't see. Kimry got its living by boots, I knew. Tula made samovars and guns, Odessa was a port. But what our town was and what it did, I had no idea. Great Dvoryansky Street and a couple of the smarter streets were kept going on capital and civil servants' salaries paid by the government. But what of the other eight streets that ran parallel for a couple of miles and vanished behind the hill? What did they live on? That's what baffled me.

The way these people lived was shameful beyond words. There was no park, no theatre, no decent orchestra. No one went inside the town library or club reading-room except for a few Jewish youths, so magazines and new books lay around uncut for months. Well-off professional people slept in cramped, stuffy bedrooms on wooden, bug-infested beds. They kept their children in revoltingly dirty rooms called nurseries, and servants, even old and respected ones, slept on the kitchen floor under rags. On fast days their houses smelled of sturgeon fried in sunflower oil and on other days of *bortsch*. Their food tasted awful and their drinking-water was unwholesome. At the town hall, governor's office, bishop's palace and all over town they had been going on for years about how we had no good, cheap water and must borrow two hundred thousand roubles from the government to lay on a proper supply. Very rich people—our town had about three dozen, who were known to gamble away whole estates at cards—also drank tainted water and talked excitedly about this loan, in fact they never stopped. It made no sense to me. I should have thought they would have found it easier to go ahead and put up the two hundred thousand out of their own pockets.

I did not know one honest man in the whole town.

My father took bribes, thinking they were offered out of respect for his moral calibre. And if boys wanted to be moved into a higher form at school they boarded out with their teachers and paid through the nose. At recruiting time the military commander's wife took bribes from the young men. She was not above accepting a few drinks either, and was once too drunk to get off her knees in church. The doctors also took bribes at call-up time. The town medical officer and the vet levied a regular tax on butchers' shops and restaurants, and there was a brisk trade in exemption certificates at the local college. The higher clergy took bribes from the lower and from churchwardens. If you applied to the municipal offices, the citizens' bureau, the health centre or any other institution, they would shout after you, 'Remember to say thank you', and you would go back and hand over thirty or forty copecks.

Those who took no bribes—high officials of the law-courts, say—were arrogant and held out two fingers instead of shaking hands. They were callous and narrow-minded, played cards, drank a lot and married rich girls. And they had an evil, corrupting influence on their surroundings, there was no doubt about that.

Only the young women had an air of integrity, being mostly honourable, decent, high-minded girls. But they knew nothing of life and thought bribes were offered out of respect for people's moral calibre. After marriage they let themselves go and aged quickly, hopelessly swamped in the morass of this vulgar, commonplace existence.

III

THEY were building a railway in our district and on Saturday nights hordes of riff-raff loafed about the town. People called them navvies and were afraid of them.

I have often seen one of these toughs hauled off to the police station with no cap on and blood all over his face, while the *corpus delicti*—a samovar or wet underwear fresh from the washing-line—was carried behind. The navvies usually swarmed round the taverns and markets. They ate, drank and swore, and when a woman of easy virtue went past they pursued her with piercing whistles.

Our shop-assistants tried to amuse this starving rabble by giving dogs and cats vodka or tying an empty paraffin can to a dog's tail and whistling, whereupon the dog bolted down the street as if it had a fiend from hell at its heels. Squealing with terror with the can clattering after it, it would run far out into the country till it dropped. There were some dogs in our town that shook all the time and kept their tails between their legs. These, it was said, hadn't quite seen the joke. They had gone mad.

They were building the station about three miles from town. The engineers had wanted a fifty thousand rouble bribe, it was said, to bring the line right up to town, but the town council would not go above forty and they had fallen out over the odd ten thousand roubles. Now the townsfolk were sorry, as they had to build a road to the station and the estimate for that came to a lot more.

Sleepers and rails had been laid along the whole line and service trains ran, carrying building material and workers. Now they were just waiting for the bridges which Dolzhikov was building and one or two uncompleted stations.

Dubechnya, as our first station was called, was a dozen miles from town. I walked there. Caught by the morning sun, the cornfields shone bright green. It was cheerful, flat country, with the station, hillocks and far-away farms clearly outlined in the distance.

It was so pleasant to be out in the country. I longed for this feeling of freedom to soak into me, if only for one morning, to save me from thinking about events in town, or about how hard life was and how hungry I felt. I have never known anything so frustrating as those moments of acute hunger, when thoughts of higher things become strangely mixed with thoughts of porridge, rissoles and fried fish. And here was I standing alone in the fields, looking up at a lark which floated motionless in the air trilling away as if it had hysterics, while I thought, 'I wouldn't mind a bit of bread and butter'. Or I would sit by the wayside and close my eyes so that I could rest and listen to the magical sounds of May, and would suddenly remember the smell of hot potatoes. I did not usually have enough to eat for someone as tall and hefty as I was, so my main feeling during the day was hunger. Perhaps that is why I understood so well how many people work only to get their daily bread and can talk of nothing but food.

At Dubechnya they were plastering the inside of the station and putting a wooden upper storey on the pumping shed. It was hot and smelt of quicklime. Workmen were loafing about among piles of shavings and rubble, and a signalman was asleep near his little hut with the sun beating down on his face. There were no trees. A faint hum came from the telegraph wires on which a few hawks were perched here and there. Not knowing what to do, I strolled among the piles of rubble like everyone else. I remembered asking the engineer about my duties and being told, 'We'll see'. But how could you 'see' about anything in this dump? The plasterers spoke of a foreman and one Fedot Vasilyev, but that meant nothing to me and I became more and more fed up—physically depressed, as when you are conscious of your arms, legs and great hulking body, but do not know what to do with them or where to put them.

I walked about for two hours at least and then noticed a row of telegraph poles leading off to the right from the station and ending by a white stone wall a mile or so away. That was the office, some of the men told me, and, as I finally worked out, it was where I should be heading.

It was an old estate long abandoned. The wall was of spongy white stone, thoroughly weathered and broken in places. There was a lodge with a blank wall facing outwards and a rusty roof with shiny tin patches dotted about on it. The gates opened onto a wide yard—a mass of weeds—and onto an old manor-house with sunblinds in the windows and a high roof red with rust. Twin lodges stood one on each side of the house. One was boarded up, but the windows of the other one were open, washing hung on the line and calves were wandering about. The last telegraph pole stood in the yard, and a wire led to the window of the lodge with the blank wall facing outwards. The door was open and I went in.

There was some character sitting at a table by a telegraph apparatus. He had dark, curly hair and wore a canvas jacket. He gave me a sullen scowl, but immediately smiled.

'Hallo, Better-than-nothing,' he said.

This was Ivan Cheprakov, an old school friend of mine who had been expelled for smoking when he was in the second form. We used to catch goldfinches, greenfinches and linnets together in autumn and sell them in the market in the early morning while our parents were still in bed. We ambushed flocks of migrating starlings, firing small shot at them and picking up the wounded, some of which died in dreadful agony—I still remember them squeaking in the cage at night. When any recovered we put them up for sale and swore blind that they were males. At market once I had only one starling left which I kept trying to sell and eventually let go for a copeck. 'Better than nothing, anyway,' I said to console myself, putting the copeck in my pocket. It was then that urchins and schoolchildren nicknamed me Better-than-nothing. Urchins and shopkeepers still used the name to jeer at me, though no one except me remembered where it came from.

Cheprakov was not very strongly built. He was narrow-chested, round-shouldered, long-legged. His tie looked like a piece of string, he wore no waistcoat and his boots were in poorer shape and more down-at-heel than my own. He had an unblinking stare and always looked ready to pounce. He was always fussing.

'Hold on a moment,' he would say in his fidgety way. 'Now just you listen to me. Er, what was it I was saying just now?'

We had a talk and I learnt that not long ago the Cheprakovs had owned the estate on which I now was. It was only in the previous autumn that Mr. Dolzhikov had got hold of it. He thought it better to put money into land than to keep it in cash and had already bought three sizeable mortgaged estates in our district. When she sold the place, Cheprakov's mother had reserved the right to live in one of the lodges for two years and had secured a job in the office for her son.

'Buying this place was nothing.' Cheprakov was referring to the engineer. 'If you knew how much money he makes out of the contractors alone! Nobody's safe.'

Then he took me to dinner, having decided after a lot of fuss that I should share the lodge with him and board with his mother.

'She's a bit stingy,' he said. 'But she won't charge you much.'

His mother's quarters were very cramped and tiny. The whole place, hall and entrance-lobby included, was cluttered up with furniture brought from the big house after the sale, all old-fashioned mahogany stuff. Mrs. Cheprakov, a very stout middle-aged woman with slanting Chinese eyes, sat in a large armchair by the window, knitting a stocking. She greeted me ceremoniously.

Cheprakov introduced me. 'This is Mr. Poloznev, Mother. He's going to work here.'

'Are you a gentleman?' she asked in a strange, disagreeable voice. It sounded as if there was fat gurgling in her throat.

'Yes.'

'Then please sit down.'

It was a poor sort of dinner—only sour curd pie and milk soup. Our hostess kept winking in a curious way, first one eye, then the other. She spoke and ate, but she was somehow dead all over and even seemed to smell like a corpse. There was only a faint flicker of life, a dim feeling that she was the lady of the manor, had owned serfs and been a general's wife—'my lady' to the servants. When these pitiful embers flared up for a second she would say to her son, 'Now Ivan, that's no way to hold your knife'.

Or she took a deep breath and addressed me in the affected style of a society hostess trying to amuse a guest.

'We sold the estate, you know. A pity of course, we're so fond of it, but Dolzhikov has promised to make Ivan stationmaster at Dubechnya, so we shan't be leaving. We shall live at the station, which is as good as living on our estate. The engineer's so kind. He's very good-looking too, don't you think?'

Not long ago the Cheprakovs had lived in style, but all that changed when the general died. Mrs. Cheprakov quarrelled with the neighbours, became involved in lawsuits, stopped paying her managers and work-people, and was terrified of being robbed. In ten years or so Dubechnya had changed out of all recognition.

Behind the big house was an old garden, gone to seed and choked with weeds and bushes. I strolled along the terrace, which was still firm and beautiful, and saw through a french window a room with a parquet floor, probably the drawing-room. There was an old-fashioned upright piano and there were engravings in broad mahogany frames—that was all. Nothing was left of the old flower-beds except peonies and poppies that raised their white and crimson heads above the grass. Young maples and elms, nibbled by cows, grew over the paths, reaching out and crowding each other. The garden was densely overgrown and seemed impenetrable, but this was only near the house, where poplars and pines still stood with old lime-trees all of an age, sole relics of former avenues. Farther out the garden was cleared for mowing and was less dank, one's eyes and mouth were not assailed by cobwebs, and now and then a breeze stirred. The farther you went, the more it opened up. Here cherries and plums grew wild. There were spreading apple-trees disfigured by props and canker, and pear-trees too spindly, it seemed, to be pear-trees at all. This part of the garden was let to women who sold fruit in town and was guarded from thieves and starlings by a sort of village idiot who lived there in a shack.

The garden opened up into a real meadow sloping down to a river overgrown with green reeds and willow. There was a milldam with a deep millpond full of fish. An angry roar came from the small thatched mill and there was a furious croaking of frogs. An occasional ripple ruffled water smooth as glass, and water-lilies quivered, stirred by playful fish. Beyond the stream was the small village of Dubechnya. The still, blue millpond was inviting with its cool, quiet promise.

And now all this—millpond, mill, delightful riverside—belonged to the engineer.

So I started my new job. I received and forwarded telegrams, filled in returns and made fair copies of indents, complaints and statements sent to the office by foremen and workmen who could hardly write their own names. Most of the time I did nothing but walk up and down waiting for telegrams or got a boy to sit in the lodge and strolled in the garden till he ran to tell me that the machine was clicking. I ate at Mrs. Cheprakov's. Meat was seldom served, we had nothing but milk dishes, and Wednesdays and Fridays were fast days when special pink 'lenten' plates were used. Mrs. Cheprakov had this trick of always winking and I felt uneasy in her presence.

There was little enough work in the lodge for one, so Cheprakov just dozed or went duck-shooting by the millpond. He got drunk every evening in the village or at the station and before going to bed stared in the mirror and shouted, 'Hallo, Ivan Cheprakov'.

When drunk he turned very pale and kept rubbing his hands and giving a neighing laugh. He used to strip and run round the fields naked for a lark. He ate flies and said that they had quite a nice tang to them.

IV

ONE day after dinner he dashed breathlessly into the lodge.

'You'd better run along,' he said. 'Your sister's here.'

I went out. And there by the porch of the big house was a hired cab from town. My sister had arrived with Anyuta Blagovo and a man in a military tunic, whom I recognized when I came nearer as Anyuta's brother, an army doctor.

'We've come out for a picnic,' he said. 'Hope you don't mind.'

Anyuta and my sister wanted to ask how I was getting on, but neither spoke. They just looked at me and I said nothing too. They saw that I disliked the place and tears came into my sister's eyes. Anyuta Blagovo blushed. We went into the garden with the doctor leading the way.

'What air!' he said ecstatically. 'Goodness me, what air!'

He still looked like a student. He walked and talked like a student and his grey eyes—like the best type of student's—had a lively, frank, open look. Beside his tall, good-looking sister he seemed frail and thin. His beard was thin, as was his voice—a thin, but quite pleasant tenor. He had been with his regiment, but was home on leave now and said he was going to St. Petersburg in the autumn to take a higher degree. He was a family man with a wife and three children, having married young, as a second-year student. It was said in town that his family life was unhappy and that he was separated from his wife.

'What's the time?' My sister was worried. 'We'd better go back early. Daddy said I could come to see my brother on condition that I was back by six.'

'Oh, confound Daddy!' sighed the doctor.

I put on the samovar and we sat and had tea on a rug in front of the terrace of the big house. The doctor knelt down and drank out of his saucer and said he called this sheer bliss. Then Cheprakov fetched a key and opened the french windows and we all went inside. The house was gloomy and mysterious and smelt of fungus. Our footsteps sounded hollow, as if there was a cellar beneath the floor. The doctor stood by the piano and touched the keys, which gave back a faint, quavering chord, a bit fuzzy, but melodious. He tried his voice and sang a song, frowning and tapping his foot impatiently whenever he hit a dead key. My sister forgot about going home and walked up and down excitedly.

'Oh, I'm so happy,' she said. 'So very, very happy.'

She sounded surprised, not believing, it seemed, that she could be gay like other people. I had never seen her so happy in all my life. She even looked prettier. She was not much to look at in profile because her nose and mouth seemed to jut out, and she always looked as if she was blowing. But she had lovely dark eyes, a pale, very delicate complexion and a kind, sad look that was most appealing. When she spoke she seemed attractive, even beautiful. We both took after our mother, being broad-shouldered, strong and tough. But her pallor came from ill health. She was always coughing and I sometimes caught in her eyes the look of a person who is seriously ill, but for some reason doesn't want you to know it.

There was something childlike and naïve in her gaiety now, as if childhood's joys, suppressed and stifled by our strict upbringing, had suddenly awoken inside her and found an outlet.

When evening came on and the horses were brought round, my sister grew quiet and seemed to shrivel up. She got into the carriage and sat down looking like a prisoner in the dock.

When they had all gone and the place was quiet, it struck me that Anyuta Blagovo had not said a word to me all day.

'A wonderful girl,' I thought. 'Wonderful!'

St. Peter's Fast began and we ate only lenten food. My idleness and the uncertainty of my position had brought on a physical depression. Dissatisfied with myself, listless and hungry, I drifted round the estate. I was only waiting till I was in the right mood to leave.

Late one afternoon when Radish was with us in the lodge, Dolzhikov unexpectedly came in, very sunburnt and covered with grey dust. Having spent three days on his section of the line, he had just come to Dubechnya by rail and walked over from the station to see us. A cab was coming from town to fetch him, and while waiting for it he went round the grounds with his manager, giving orders in a loud voice. Then he sat in our lodge for a whole hour writing letters. While he was there some telegrams came for him and he tapped out the answers himself. We three stood to attention and said nothing.

'What a mess!' he said with a scornful glance at the records. 'I'm moving the office to the station in a fortnight, but what to do with you lot I really don't know.'

'I do try, sir,' said Cheprakov.

'So I've noticed.'

The engineer looked at me.

'All you're good for,' he went on, 'is drawing your salary. You think because you have friends in the right places you can hope for a quick shove up the ladder. Well, no one gets a leg up from me. No one ever put himself out on my account. Before I ran the railway I was an engine-driver and I worked in Belgium as a common greaser. Hey, you there, what are you doing here?' he asked, turning to Radish. 'Boozing with this lot, I suppose.'

For some reason he called all working men 'You there'. As for me and Cheprakov, he despised our sort and called us a lot of drunken swine behind our backs. He was harsh with all his low-grade clerks, fining them and coolly giving them notice without saying why.

In the end his carriage arrived. As he left he said that he was going to sack the lot of us in a fortnight and called his manager an oaf, then sprawled back in his carriage and bowled off to town.

'Look here, Andrew, why don't you give me a job?' I asked Radish.

'All right.'

So we set off for town together. When we had left the station and manor-house some way behind, I asked why he had just been to Dubechnya.

'Firstly, some of my lads are working on the railway, and secondly, I went to pay the general's widow her interest. I borrowed fifty roubles off her last year and now I pay her a rouble a month.' ·

The painter stopped and seized me by a button.

'The way I look at it is this, mate,' he went on. 'Anyone, worker or gent, who lends money at interest, is a bad man and the truth is not in him.'

Gaunt, pale, terrifying, Radish closed his eyes and shook his head.

'Grass doth wither,' he proclaimed with a sagacious air, 'iron doth rust and lies do rot the soul. Lord, save us sinners.'

V

RADISH was an impractical man. He hadn't much sense. He took on more jobs than he could handle, then lost his head when it came to settling up and so was almost always out of pocket. He did painting, glazing, wall-papering and even took on roof work, and I remember him running round for three days looking for roofers—all for the sake of some twopenny-halfpenny job. He was a first-class workman and had been known to earn as much as ten roubles a day. He might have been pretty well off but for this urge to be a boss at all costs and call himself a contractor.

He was paid by the job, but he paid me and the other men daily—between seventy copecks and one rouble. In hot, dry weather we did outside jobs, mainly roof-painting. I was new to this and my feet burnt as if I was walking on hot bricks, but if I put on felt boots they got even hotter. That was only at the start. Later on I became used to it and it all went like a dream. I was living among people who had to work. They could not avoid it. They slaved away like cart-horses, often without seeing the moral purpose of work and never once bringing the word 'work' into their conversation. Among them I felt a bit of a cart-horse myself. What I was doing had to be done, I felt, and there was no getting out of it. This feeling obsessed me more and more, making life easier and removing all my doubts.

At the start everything was fresh and absorbing, as if I had been reborn. I could sleep on the ground or go barefoot, a most pleasant sensation. I could stand in an ordinary crown without anyone minding, and when a cab horse fell down in the street I ran and helped to pull it up without caring if my clothes got dirty. Above all, I was earning my own living and was not a burden to anyone else.

Painting roofs, especially with our own materials, was thought a very rewarding job, so even skilled men like Radish did not turn up their noses at this rough, boring work. Walking on a roof in shorts, he looked like a stork with his scraggy purple legs. I often heard him heave a sigh as he plied the brush and said, 'Woe, woe unto us sinners!'

He was as much at home on a roof as on the ground, being wonderfully nimble, though ill and white as a corpse. He painted the dome and cupolas of a church just like a young man, using no scaffolding—only ladders and rope. It was rather frightening to see him standing up there so far from the ground, stretching himself to his full height and declaring for the benefit of some person unknown, 'Grass doth wither, iron doth rust and lies do rot the soul.'

Sometimes he ruminated and answered his thoughts aloud. 'Anything's possible. Yes, anything's possible.'

When I went home from work, everyone sitting about on benches near gateways—shop assistants, errand-boys and their masters—pursued me with jeers and abuse. This upset me at first and seemed quite monstrous.

'Better-than-nothing!' I heard on all sides. 'Where's yer paint-brush, mister?'

No one treated me more unkindly than those who not so long ago had themselves been working men, earning their living by unskilled labour. Among the shops I might have water thrown over me accidentally on purpose when I went past the ironmonger's, and someone once actually hurled a stick at me. One time a white-haired old fish merchant barred my way.

'I don't care about you, you idiot,' he said with a dirty look. 'It's your father I'm sorry for.'

For some reason my friends were embarrassed to meet me. Some thought me a freak or clown. Others felt sorry for me. Others again did not know how to treat me, and it was hard to make them out.

One afternoon I ran across Anyuta Blagovo in a side road near Great Dvoryansky Street. I was on my way to work, carrying two long brushes and a bucket of paint. Anyuta flared up when she saw me.

'Pray don't bow to me in the street . . .' she said in an edgy, severe, quavering voice without offering to shake hands, her eyes suddenly bright with tears. 'If you must go in for this sort of thing, you must . . . I don't care. But kindly keep out of my way.'

I had left great Dvoryansky Street now and was boarding in the suburb of Makarikha with my old nanny Karpovna, a kind-hearted but lugubrious old woman who always thought that something awful was going to happen, feared all dreams without exception, and even saw bad omens in the bees and wasps that flew into her room. The fact that I had become a worker boded no good, or so she thought.

'You're finished,' she used to say, shaking her head sadly. 'Done for.'

She shared her cottage with her adopted son, the butcher Prokofy, a hulking, clumsy fellow of about thirty with red hair and a bristly moustache. If we met in the hall he never spoke, but moved aside respectfully, and when he was drunk he gave me a military salute. When he had supper in the evening I could hear him grunting and sighing through the board partition as he downed glass after glass of vodka.

'Ma,' he would call in a low voice.

'Well?' Karpovna would answer. Her love for her adopted son knew no bounds. 'What is it, sonny?'

'I'll do the decent thing by you, Ma. All this earthly life I'll keep you in your old age in this vale of tears and when you die I'll pay for your funeral, honest I will.'

I was up before dawn each day and went to bed early. We decorators ate heartily and slept soundly. But for some reason my heart used to beat loudly at night. I did not quarrel with my mates. Swear words, fouls oaths and things like 'damn your eyes!' or 'rot your guts!' were all in the day's work. Still, we got on well together. The lads thought I was some sort of religious crank and pulled my leg good-humouredly. They declared that even my own father had disowned me, and then told me that they rarely put their nose inside a church and that many of them had not been to confession in ten years. They tried to justify such slackness by saying that painters were the black sheep of the human flock.

The men thought highly of me and respected me. What they obviously liked was that I neither smoked nor drank, and led a quiet, orderly life, but they were a little shocked when I would not steal linseed oil with them or join them in wheedling tips from the people that we worked for. Stealing employers' oil and paint was common practice among house-painters—to them it was not really stealing at all. Funnily enough, even someone as upright as Radish always took some whiting and oil when he finished work, and even respectable old men, with houses of their own in Makarikha, thought nothing of asking for a tip. It was a sorry, shameful business when the boys were starting or finishing a job and all rushed off to crawl to some little worm and thank him humbly for the ten copecks that he handed them.

They behaved like sly courtiers with the people whose houses they painted and almost every day I was reminded of Shakespeare's Polonius.

'Looks like rain,' a client would say with a glance at the sky.

'Oh yes sir, definitely,' the painters would agree.

'I don't know though, those aren't rain clouds. Perhaps it won't rain after all.'

'Oh no sir. Definitely not.'

Behind their clients' backs the attitude was usually ironical. For instance, if they saw a gentleman sitting on his balcony with a newspaper, they would say, 'Sits reading the paper, but I bet he's got nothing to eat.'

I never visited my family. When I returned from work I often found short, anxious notes from my sister about Father. One day he had been unusually thoughtful at dinner and had eaten nothing. Or he had fallen over. Or had locked himself in his room and not come out for a long time. This sort of news disturbed me and stopped me sleeping. Sometimes I even walked past our house in Great Dvoryansky Street at night, peering into the dark windows and trying to make out whether all was well at home. My sister came to see me on Sundays, but furtively, pretending to be visiting Nanny instead of me. If she came into my room she was always very pale, with tear-stained eyes, and began crying at once.

'Father will never get over it,' she said. 'If, God forbid, anything happens to him, you'll have it on your conscience all your life. It's terrible, Misail. For our mother's sake, mend your ways, I beg you.'

'My dear good sister,' I said. 'How can I mend my ways when I know I'm obeying my conscience? Try and understand.'

'I know you're obeying your conscience. But couldn't you do it a bit differently so as not to annoy people?'

'Oh dearie me!' the old woman would sigh in the other room. 'You're done for. Bad times are coming, my dears, bad times indeed.'

VI

ONE Sunday Dr. Blagovo suddenly visited me. He was wearing a
military tunic over a silk shirt, and patent leather top-boots.

'I've come to see you,' he began, pumping my hand like a student.
'I hear of you every day and I've kept meaning to come over for a
"heart to heart". This town is no end of a bore. They're all half
dead and there's no one to talk to. My God, isn't it hot!' he went
on, taking off his tunic and standing there in his silk shirt. 'Let's
have a talk about things, old man.'

I felt bored myself. For a long while I had wanted to pass the
time of day with someone other than a house-painter and I was
really glad to see him.

'To start with, I'm completely on your side,' he said, sitting on
my bed. 'I thoroughly respect your way of life. No one appreciates
you in this town. But what else can you expect? As you know
yourself, they're a prize collection of gargoyles here, with very few
exceptions. But I saw what you were like at once, at that picnic.
You're a thoroughly honest, decent, high-minded person.

'I respect you,' he went on ecstatically, 'and I'm greatly
honoured to shake your hand. No one makes a sharp break like
you without first going through a complex emotional experience.
If you are to carry on as you do, trying to live up to your beliefs
all the time, you have to put your heart and soul into the thing
day after day. Now tell me this for a start. If you devoted all
this will-power, effort and potential to something else—turning
yourself into a great scholar or artist, for instance—don't you
think that would give your life greater depths and scope and make
it more productive in every way?'

We talked, and when the subject of manual work cropped up
I expressed myself as follows. 'The strong must not enslave the
weak and the minority must not be parasites on the majority or
vampires forever sucking their blood. In fact everyone without
exception—strong and weak, rich and poor—should do his bit
equally in the struggle for existence.' This brought me to the point
that manual work is the greatest leveller of all if everyone is made
to do his bit.

'So your idea is that every single person should do manual work?'
asked the doctor.

'Yes.'

'Well, let's suppose all of us, including the élite—the thinkers and great scholars—play our part in the struggle for existence and spend our time breaking stones or painting roofs. Don't you think that might be a serious threat to progress?'

'Where's the threat?' I asked. 'Surely progress consists in good works and obeying the moral law. If you don't enslave anyone, if you aren't a burden to anyone, what more progress do you need?'

'But look here!' Blagovo exploded, jumping to his feet. 'Just look here! If a snail in its shell spends its time trying to lead a better life, fiddling around with moral laws—is that what you call progress?'

'Why "fiddling around"?' I was offended. 'If you stop making your neighbour feed you, clothe you, carry you about and defend you from your enemies, surely that *is* progress in the context of a life built entirely on slavery. I think that's real progress, perhaps the only kind man can have or needs.'

'Mankind has infinite scope for progress in this world. To talk about the sort of progress which we "can have"—progress limited by our needs or by short-term theories—well, that's odd to say the least.'

'If, as you make out, the bounds of progress are infinite, its aims must be vague,' I said. 'Fancy living without knowing definitely what you're living for!'

'Have it your own way. But my ignorance is less of a bore than your knowledge. I'm climbing a ladder called progress, civilization, culture. I'm going higher and higher and I don't know exactly where I'm heading, but really, this wonderful ladder alone makes life worth living. Now you know what you're living for. You want one lot of people to stop enslaving another, you want the artist and the man who mixes his colours to eat the same food. But that side of life's so dim, grey and commonplace, can't you see? Can't you see it's disgusting to live for that alone? If one lot of insects enslaves another, to hell with them! They can eat each other alive for all I care. We shouldn't be thinking about them at all—they'll all die and rot, won't they, however hard you try to save them from slavery? We should be thinking about the great Unknown that awaits man in the distant future.'

Blagovo argued hotly, but had something quite different on his mind, I could see that.

'Your sister can't be coming,' he said, with a look at his watch. 'She was at our place yesterday and said she was coming out here. You keep on and on about slavery,' he continued. 'But that's a special problem and mankind always solves such problems gradually, in due course.'

So we got on to the gradual approach. I said that every man decided for himself whether to do good or evil without waiting for mankind to evolve a solution gradually.

'What's more,' I said, 'your gradual approach cuts both ways. The gradual evolution of humane ideas has gone hand in hand with the gradual growth of other ideas of quite a different kind. Serfdom has gone, but capitalism is spreading. Ideas of freedom are enjoying a great vogue, but now, as in the days of the Mongols, the majority still feeds, clothes and protects the minority, while remaining hungry, unclothed and unprotected itself.

'The system fits in beautifully with any trend or current you like, because the art of enslavement is being gradually perfected as well. True, we don't flog our servants in the stables any more, but we do evolve new refinements of slavery—or at least we're pretty good at finding justifications for it in individual instances. Ideas are all very well, but if now, at the end of the nineteenth century, it should become possible to foist our more unpleasant bodily functions onto the workers as well, then foist away we would. After which of course we should defend ourselves by saying that if "the élite of thinkers and great scholars" were to waste their precious time on these functions, progress might be seriously threatened.'

At this point my sister arrived. She seemed agitated and alarmed at seeing the doctor and said at once that she must go home to Father.

'Look here, Cleopatra,' urged Blagovo, pressing both hands to his heart, 'your dear Daddy won't burst if you spend half an hour or so with me and your brother.'

He was completely natural with us and his high spirits were infectious. After a moment's thought my sister laughed and suddenly cheered up as on the day of the picnic. We went into the fields and lay down on the grass to go on with our talk, looking at the town, where all the west-facing windows seemed bright gold because the sun was setting.

After this Blagovo always appeared when my sister came to see me and they greeted each other as if they had met in my room by accident. While I argued with the doctor, my sister listened with a happy, enthralled, interested look and seemed greatly affected. I felt that a new world was gradually opening up before her, a world that she had never even dreamt of and was now trying to fathom. When the doctor was not there she was always quiet and sad, and when she sat and cried on my bed these days she never told me why.

In August Radish told us to prepare to leave for the railway line. A couple of days before we received our 'marching orders', Father came to see me. He sat down, without looking at me, and slowly wiped his red face. Then he took a copy of the local *Herald* out of his pocket. Slowly, emphasizing each word, he read out an item about the son of the manager of the State Bank who was the same age as me and had been made a head of department in the treasury office.

'And look at you,' he said, folding the newspaper. 'Pauper! Tramp! Scoundrel! Even working men and farm labourers get an education so they can make their way in life. And you, a Poloznev, despite your distinguished, illustrious ancestors, are heading for the rubbish dump. But I didn't come here to talk to you, I've washed my hands of you,' he went on in a strangled voice, standing up. 'I've come to ask where your sister is, you scoundrel. She went out after dinner, but it's nearly eight and she still isn't back. She goes out quite often now without a word to me. She's less respectful than she was, and I put that down to your vicious, evil influence. Where is she?'

He was carrying the umbrella that I knew so well. I was at my wits' end and jumped to attention, feeling like a schoolboy and expecting Father to hit me, but he saw me looking at the umbrella and that probably stopped him.

'Live as you please,' he said. 'I shall not give you my blessing.'

'Oh dearie dearie me,' my old nanny muttered behind the door. 'You poor unhappy boy! No good will come of this, I feel it in my bones.'

I worked on the railway line. It rained non-stop all through August and it was damp and cold. They could not get the crops in, and on the large farms which used reaping machines the wheat was not in stooks, but just lay about in heaps. I remember those miserable heaps growing darker and darker every day and the grain sprouting in them. It was hard work. The torrential rain ruined everything that we managed to do. They would not let us eat or sleep in the station buildings, so we sheltered in filthy, damp dugouts, where the navvies had lived earlier in the summer. At night I could not sleep for the cold and the woodlice crawling over my face and arms. When we worked near the bridges a whole gang of navvies would visit us in the evenings, just to beat up the painters, which was their idea of fun. They beat us up and stole our brushes. They tried to provoke us to fight by ruining our work, for instance by daubing the signal-boxes with green paint.

To make matters worse, Radish took to paying us very irregularly. All the painting work on this sector had been put in the hands of a contractor. That contractor sub-contracted to someone else, who subcontracted further to Radish for a consideration of about twenty per cent. The work paid badly anyway, quite apart from the rain. Time was wasted and we could not get on with the job, but Radish had undertaken to pay the men daily. The hungry painters nearly beat him up. They called him a bloodsucking swindler, a regular Judas, while he, poor fellow, just sighed, lifted up his hands in despair and kept going to Mrs. Cheprakov for more money.

VII

AUTUMN came—dark, wet and muddy. Work was hard to come by and I sometimes sat at home doing nothing for three days on end, or took on odd jobs outside the decorating line like shifting earth for ballast at twenty copecks a day. Dr. Blagovo had gone off to St. Petersburg and my sister had stopped coming to see me. Radish was at home, ill in bed and thinking that every day would be his last.

The general mood was autumnal too. As a worker I saw only the seamy side of town life, and perhaps that is why I could not help making discoveries nearly every day that drove me quite frantic. It turned out that fellow citizens of mine who had never impressed me one way or the other before, or who had seemed quite decent folk, were mean and cruel and up to all kinds of dirty tricks. We working men were duped, swindled, made to wait for hours in cold vestibules or kitchens, insulted and treated with the utmost rudeness.

That autumn I papered the reading-room and two other rooms at the club. I was paid seven copecks a piece, but was told to sign for twelve and refused.

'No more of your lip, you blackguard, or I'll bash your dirty face in,' said a distinguished-looking gentleman with gold-rimmed spectacles, who must have been on the committee.

A servant whispered that I was the son of Poloznev the architect and he looked ashamed of himself and blushed, but regained his composure at once.

'Oh, to hell with him!' he said.

The shops palmed off their rotten meat on us workers—and their stale flour and used tea-leaves. We were shoved around by the police in church. In hospital the nurses and junior medical staff sponged on us, and if we could not afford to bribe them they got their own back by dishing up our food on filthy plates. Feeling entitled to treat us like dirt, the most junior post-office clerk shouted roughly and rudely at us. ('You! Just you wait! Where do you think you're going?') Even the yard-dogs were hostile and rushed at us with extra viciousness. But what really shocked me in my new situation was the blatant unfairness of everything—what the common people mean when they say that someone is 'lost to shame'. Few days passed without some piece of sharp practice. The tradesmen who sold us linseed-oil, our bosses, the other workmen and even our clients—all were on the fiddle. We had no rights—there was no question of that, needless to say—and always had to ask for our wages like beggars, standing cap in hand at the back door.

One evening I was papering a room next to the reading-room in the club and was about to knock off when Mr. Dolzhikov's daughter came in carrying a bundle of books.

I bowed.

'Oh, good evening,' she said, recognizing me at once and holding out her hand. 'How nice to see you.'

She smiled and stared, fascinated and puzzled, at my smock, paste-bucket, and wallpaper spread on the floor. I was a little taken aback and she was rather ill at ease too.

'Excuse me staring like this,' she said. 'I've heard so much about you, especially from Dr. Blagovo—he's quite crazy about you. I've met your sister too—such a dear, sweet girl, but I just couldn't make her see that there's nothing dreadful about you leading the simple life. Far from it, you've become the most interesting man in town.'

She took another look at the paste-bucket and wallpaper and went on.

'I asked Dr. Blagovo to put me in touch with you, but he must have forgotten or been too busy. Anyway, we have met before. Why not look me up some time? I'd be most obliged if you would, I'd so much like to talk to you. I'm not hard to get on with,' she said, holding out her hand, 'and I hope you'll feel at home with me. Father's away in St. Petersburg.'

She went into the reading-room, her dress rustling. I went home and could not sleep for a long time.

That cheerless autumn some good soul, obviously wanting to help me out a bit, sent me tea, lemons, cakes and roast grouse from time to time. Karpovna said that these things were always brought by a soldier, but who sent them she didn't know. The soldier would ask if I was well. Did I have a proper meal every day? Had I warm clothing? Then again, when the frosts came the soldier brought a soft knitted scarf while I was out. The scarf had a faint, delicate scent and I guessed who my good fairy was. It was lily-of-the-valley, Anyuta Blagovo's favourite scent.

As winter approached there was more work to be had and things were looking up. Radish revived and we did a job together in the cemetery chapel, preparing the icon-stand for gilding. It was a clean, quiet job—'a piece of cake,' the men called it. You could get through plenty of work in a day and time sped past unnoticed. There was no swearing, laughter or loud talk. The place itself made us want to be quiet and well-behaved, and inspired calm, serious thoughts. We stood or sat, absorbed in our work, still as statues. There was a deathly hush, as befits a cemetery, and a dropped tool or sputtering icon-lamp gave out a harsh, hollow sound that made us look round. After a long silence there might be a sound like buzzing bees—the slow, soft chanting of the requiem for a dead baby at the back of the church. The artist—he was painting a dove with stars round it on a cupola—would start whistling softly and then suddenly stop, remembering where he was. 'Anything's possible, anything at all,' Radish would sigh in answer to his thoughts. Or bells tolled slowly and lugubriously above our heads and the painters said that it must be for a rich man's funeral.

I spent my days in this stillness in the twilight of the church, and during the long evenings I played billiards or went to the theatre and sat in the gallery, wearing the new woollen suit that

I had bought with my earnings. Concerts and performances had already begun at the Azhogins', and now Radish painted scenery on his own. He told me all about the plays and *tableaux vivants* that he saw there and I listened enviously. I longed to attend rehearsals, but could not bring myself to go to the Azhogins'.

A week before Christmas Dr. Blagovo came round. Again we argued and spent the evenings playing billiards. He took his coat off to play, unbuttoning his shirt at the front and somehow generally trying to look like a thoroughgoing rake. He did not drink much, but made a great to-do about it, contriving to spend twenty roubles an evening in a cheap dive like the 'Volga'.

My sister took to visiting me again. She and the doctor both seemed surprised to run across each other, but her happy, apologetic air showed that these meetings were no accident.

'Look here, why do you never go and see Masha Dolzhikov?' the doctor asked me as we were playing billiards one evening. 'You've no idea what a clever girl she is—so charming, natural, kind-hearted.'

I described the reception that I had had from her father in the spring.

'Don't be silly,' the doctor laughed. 'She's quite unlike her father, you know. Really, old boy, you mustn't hurt her feelings. Do call on her some time. How about us going along together tomorrow evening? What do you say?'

I let him talk me into it. Next evening I put on my new suit and set off with some trepidation to see Miss Dolzhikov. The footman no longer struck me as quite so high and mighty, nor did the furniture look so splendid as on the morning when I had come asking for a job. Miss Dolzhikov was expecting me and greeted me like an old friend with a firm, friendly handclasp. She was wearing a grey woollen dress with full sleeves. Her hair—we called the style 'dog's ears' when it came into vogue in our town a year later—was combed back from the temples onto her ears. It made her face seem broader, and this time I thought that she looked very much like her father, who had a broad, ruddy face and an expression rather like a coachman's. She looked beautiful and elegant, but not particularly young—she seemed about thirty, though in fact she was no more than twenty-five.

'How nice of the doctor, I am grateful to him,' she said as she asked me to sit down. 'You wouldn't have come but for him. I'm bored to death. Father's gone away and left me on my own and I don't know what to do with myself in this town.'

Then she asked where I was working, how much I earned and where I lived.

'You manage on your wages then?' she asked.

'Yes.'

'Lucky man,' she sighed. 'I think all the evil in this world comes from idleness, boredom and having nothing to fill your mind. What else can you expect if you're used to sponging on other people? Don't think I'm just saying this for effect. Being rich is a dull, disagreeable business, I really mean it. "Make to yourselves friends of the mammon of unrighteousness,"—they say that because there's no such thing as righteous wealth and never can be.'

She gave the furniture a cold, solemn look, as if wanting to count it, and went on.

'Comfort and luxury can cast a magic spell. They gradually drag you down, even if you're strong-willed. Father and I once led ordinary, humble lives, but look at us now! Isn't it fantastic!' She shrugged her shoulders. 'We run through twenty thousand a year. In the provinces!'

'One's forced to look on comfort and luxury as the privilege of capital and education,' I said. 'Now I think that decent amenities could go with any kind of work, even the hardest and dirtiest. Your father's rich, but as he says himself, he had to put in time as an engine-driver and a common greaser.'

She smiled and shook her head doubtfully.

'Father sometimes eats bread dipped in kvass,' she said. 'It's a fad of his.'

The door-bell rang and she stood up.

'Rich and educated people should work like everyone else,' she went on. 'And any comforts should be shared out equally. We should do away with privilege. Oh well, that's quite enough clever talk. Tell me something amusing. Tell me about your decorators. What are they like? Funny?'

The doctor came in and I started telling them about the decorators, but lack of practice cramped my style and I spoke earnestly and lifelessly, like an ethnographer. The doctor also told a few funny stories of his own about working-class life—staggering, weeping, kneeling and even lying on the floor to imitate a drunk. It was as good as a play. Masha watched him and laughed till she cried. Then he played the piano and sang in his pleasant, light tenor while Masha stood by and chose the songs, putting him right when he made a mistake.

'You sing too, I hear,' I said to her.

'"Sing too"!' the doctor was horrified. 'She's a wonderful singer—a real artist—and you talk about her "singing too". Dear me, we *have* put our foot in it!'

'I did study seriously once,' she answered me. 'But I've given it up now.'

Sitting on a low stool, she spoke of her life in St. Petersburg and impersonated some well-known singers, mimicking their voices and styles. She did a sketch of the doctor in her album and then one of me. She drew rather badly, but both came out good likenesses. She laughed, joked and grimaced charmingly. This suited her better than talking about the mammon of unrighteousness and I felt that there had been something second-hand and not quite sincere in her recent remarks about riches and comfort. She was a superb comic actress. I found myself comparing her with our local young women. Even Anyuta Blagovo, though beautiful and stately, was not in the same class. There was a big gap between them—one might have been a fine garden rose and the other a wild briar.

The three of us had supper together. Masha and the doctor drank red wine and champagne, then went on to coffee and brandy. They clinked glasses and drank to friendship, intelligence, progress and freedom, without getting drunk. They only became red in the face and kept laughing over nothing till the tears ran down their cheeks. Not wanting to seem a killjoy, I had some wine too.

'Really brilliant, gifted people know how to live,' said Masha. 'They go their own way. But average people—people like me— don't know anything and can't do anything on their own. All they can do is spot some significant social movement and float with the stream.'

'Don't tell me you can spot something non-existent,' said the doctor.

'Non-existent? When we're just too blind to see!'

'You think so, do you? Trends are an invention of modern literature. We haven't any.'

They began arguing.

'We haven't any significant social trends and never have had,' shouted the doctor. 'There's no end to the things modern literature has invented. It's even dreamt up certain mysterious intellectuals who toil away in our countryside, though you can search our villages high and low without finding more than the occasional clodhopper in a jacket or black frock-coat who can't write a three-letter word without making four spelling mistakes. Cultural life in Russia hasn't even begun. Things are no better than they were five hundred years ago, for we're still savages and louts, all of us—nonentities! Trends and movements there may be, but what tenth-rate, dismal stuff—all tied up with some dirty little racket! Don't tell me you take that sort of thing seriously! If you feel you've spotted a significant trend and mean to follow it by devoting your life to the latest crazes, such as freeing insects from slavery or abstaining from beef rissoles, then I can only congratulate you, madam. What we need is study, study and yet more study. And significant social trends can wait a bit. We're not really up to that sort of thing yet and quite honestly we're out of our depth with it.'

'You may be, but I'm not,' said Masha. 'God, you are a bore this evening!'

'Our job is to study, I tell you. We must try to amass as much knowledge as we can because important social trends and knowledge go together. And man's future happiness can come only from knowledge. Here's to learning!'

'One thing's quite clear—we must somehow change our lives,' said Masha after a moment's thought. 'Life hasn't been worth living so far. Let's not talk about it.'

The cathedral clock struck two as we left.

'Do you like her?' asked the doctor. 'She's splendid, isn't she?'

On Christmas Day, we had dinner with Masha and then went to see her almost every day during the holidays. We were her only visitors—she was right when she said that the doctor and I were the only people she knew in town. We talked most of the time. Sometimes the doctor brought a book or magazine and read to us. Actually he was the first educated man I had ever met. How well informed he was I cannot judge, but he was always bringing out things he knew, wanting others to share them. On medical subjects he was quite different from any of the local doctors. It was his freshness and originality that struck one somehow and I felt he had it in him to become a real scholar if he wanted. He was probably the only person with any real influence on me at that time. Meeting him and reading the books that he lent me, I felt more and more the need for knowledge to inspire my cheerless labours. I found it odd that I had once not known, say, that the world was made up of sixty elements, or what oil and paint consisted of—odd too that I had somehow managed without this knowledge. The doctor's friendship was good for my character as well. We were always arguing. I usually stuck to my guns, but thanks to him I came to see that I didn't know everything, and tried to work out principles of the utmost strictness so that the voice of my conscience should be clear and save me from woolly-mindedness.

The doctor may have been the best and most cultivated man in town, but he was far from perfect all the same. There was something a little crude and brash about his manners, his argumentativeness, his bland tenor voice and even his general friendliness. When he took off his coat and went about in his silk shirt or threw the waiter a tip in a restaurant, it always struck me that there was something pretty barbarous about him, culture or no culture.

Early in the new year, he left one morning to go back to St. Petersburg. After dinner my sister called on me. She did not take off her fur coat and cap, and just sat there not saying anything, very pale, staring fixedly before her. She was feeling the cold and was clearly overwrought.

'You must have caught a chill,' I said.

Her eyes filled with tears and she stood up and went to see Karpovna without a word to me, as if I had offended her. A little later I heard her voice raised in bitter complaint.

'What have I lived for all this time, Nanny? What's the point? I've wasted my youth, haven't I? I've spent my best years keeping accounts, pouring tea, counting pennies and entertaining visitors. And I thought these were the most important things in life. Do understand, Nanny. I have needs like any other person, I want a bit of real life—and they've made me into a sort of housekeeper. Can't you see how awful it is!'

She hurled the keys into my room and they fell jingling to the floor. They were the keys of the sideboard, the kitchen cupboard, the cellar and the tea-caddy—keys my mother used to carry.

'Oh goodness gracious me!' The old woman was horrified. 'Holy saints above!'

On her way out my sister came into my room to pick up the keys.

'I'm sorry,' she said. 'I don't know what's come over me lately.'

VIII

LATE one evening I came home from Masha's to find a young police inspector in my room. He wore a new uniform and was sitting at my table looking through a book.

'Ah, at last! he said, standing up and stretching. 'This makes the third time I've been here. The Governor orders you to report to him tomorrow at 9 a.m. precisely. Without fail.'

He made me sign an undertaking to obey the Governor's order and left.

The inspector's late visit and this unexpected summons to the Governor thoroughly depressed me. Since early childhood I have been terrified of policemen, officers of the law and court officials, and I was as worried now as if I had really done something wrong. And I just could not sleep. Nanny and Prokofy could not sleep either—they were too upset. Nanny had earache too. She kept groaning and several times started to cry with pain. Hearing that I was awake, Prokofy came cautiously into my room with a lamp and sat down by the table.

'You need a spot of pepper vodka,' he said after a moment's thought. 'A drink never comes amiss in this vale of tears. A drop of that vodka in her ear would do Ma a power of good too.'

At about half-past two he got ready to fetch meat from the slaughter-house. I knew I should have no sleep before daybreak now, and joined him so as to kill time till nine o'clock. We walked with a lantern. His assistant Nikolka—a lad of thirteen with blue blotches on his face from frostbite, a fearful young tough from the look of him—drove after us in the sledge, urging on the horse in a husky voice.

'You'll be punished at the Governor's, bound to be,' Prokofy told me on the way. 'Governors, bishops, officers, doctors—they all have their own rules. To every trade its own tricks. But you don't toe your line at all and you won't get away with that.'

The slaughter-house was beyond the cemetery and so far I had seen it only from a distance. There were three gloomy sheds with a grey fence round them and when the wind came from that quarter on a hot summer day the stench was enough to choke you. We went into the yard, but it was too dark to see the sheds. I kept meeting horses and sledges, some empty, some loaded with meat. Men walked about with lanterns, swearing like troopers. Oaths no less foul came from Prokofy and Nikolka and the air rang with continuous swearing, coughing and the neighing of horses.

There was a smell of dung and carcasses. It was thawing and the snow was mixed up with mud and in the dark I felt I was walking in pools of blood.

We piled our sledge full of meat and made for the butcher's stall in the market. Dawn was breaking. Cooks with baskets and elderly women in cloaks passed by one after the other. Cleaver in hand, wearing a bloodstained white apron, Prokofy swore fearful oaths, crossed himself in the direction of the church, and bellowed for the whole market to hear that he was letting his meat go at cost price, or even at a loss. He gave short weight and short change, as the cooks could well see, but, deafened by his yells, they raised no objection beyond calling him a shark. He assumed picturesque poses, brandishing his terrible cleaver and giving a ferocious yell each time he crashed it down. I was afraid that he might really chop off someone's head or hand.

I spent the morning at the butcher's. When at last I went to the Governor's, my fur coat smelt of meat and blood and I felt as if someone had given me a spear and told me to go and kill a bear. I remember a tall staircase with a striped carpet and a young official in a tail-coat with shiny buttons silently motioning me towards a door with both hands and running to announce me. I went into a large reception-room. It was luxuriously appointed, but cold and tasteless. The bright yellow window-curtains and tall, narrow mirrors on the walls were particular eyesores. Governors might come and governors might go, but the furnishings clearly went on for ever.

The young official again motioned me to a door with both hands and I made my way towards a large green table. Behind it stood a general with the Order of St. Vladimir at his throat.

'I've asked you to come here, Mr. Poloznev . . .' he began, holding a letter and opening his mouth wide like the letter O. 'I've asked you to come here to give you the following information. Your worthy father has made written and oral application to the provincial marshal of nobility, asking him to send for you and point out the discrepancy between your behaviour and the rank of gentleman which you are privileged to hold. His Excellency

Alexander Pavlovich rightly supposed that your behaviour might be a bad example. He was also aware that mere exhortation on his part might be inadequate and that serious official action was called for. He has therefore put before me his views about you in this letter. Those views I share.'

He said all this quietly and deferentially, holding himself erect as if I was his superior officer and looking at me with no trace of severity. His face was flabby, worn and wrinkled, there were bags under his eyes and his hair was dyed. From the look of him he might have been any age from forty to sixty.

'I trust,' he went on, 'that you will appreciate the tact of our worthy Alexander Pavlovich in consulting me privately and unofficially. I have also invited you here unofficially and am speaking to you not as Governor, but as one who sincerely respects your father. So pray change your way of life and return to the duties proper to your rank. Or else keep out of mischief by moving to some part of the country where you're unknown and can do what you like. Otherwise I shall have to take extreme measures.'

He stood there for half a minute in silence, looking at me open-mouthed.

'Are you a vegetarian?' he asked.

'No sir, I eat meat.'

He sat down and drew a document towards him. I bowed and left.

There was no point in going to work before dinner, so I went home to bed, but was unable to sleep because of a disagreeable, painful feeling brought on by the slaughter-house and my talk with the Governor. I waited till evening and went, gloomy and distraught, to see Masha. I told her about my visit to the Governor. She looked as if she could not believe her ears and suddenly gave a loud, happy, ringing laugh as only good-natured people can—people who see the funny side of things.

'What a story!' she said, laughing so much that she could hardly stand up and leaning over her table. 'If one could only tell it in St. Petersburg!'

WE often met these days—twice daily. She came to the cemetery almost every afternoon and read the inscriptions on crosses and tombs while she waited for me. Sometimes she came inside the church and stood by me watching me work. The silence, the painters' and gilders' simple craft, Radish's grave disquisitions and the fact that I looked just like the other men, worked like them in waistcoat and worn shoes, and was treated as one of them—she found all this new and appealing. Once when she was there the artist, up aloft painting a dove, shouted, 'Misail, let's have some of the white.'

I took him some white paint and as I climbed back down the rickety scaffolding she looked at me, smiling and moved to tears.

'What a sweet person you are,' she said.

I have a childhood memory of a green parrot belonging to a rich man who lived in our town, a beautiful bird that escaped from its cage and was about the town for a whole month, flying lazily from garden to garden, lonely and homeless. Masha reminded me of that bird.

'I've nowhere to go these days except the cemetery,' she told me with a laugh. 'I'm sick to death of this town. There's all that reciting, singing and childish prattle at the Azhogins'—I can't stand that stuff these days. Your sister keeps herself to herself, Miss Blagovo dislikes me for some reason and I don't like the theatre. So where else can I go?'

I visited her with my hands black, and smelling of paint and turpentine. That she liked. She also wanted me to wear my ordinary working kit whenever I went to see her. But those clothes cramped my drawing-room style and I felt as awkward as if I was in uniform, so I always put on my new suit when I was going to see her. That she disliked.

'You must admit you're not quite happy in your new role,' she said to me once. 'You feel awkward and ill at ease in workman's clothes. Tell me, isn't that because you're not sure of yourself—not satisfied? And the kind of work you've picked on, this painting bug you've got, does that really satisfy you either? I know paint makes things look nicer and last longer,' she laughed. 'But these things do belong to our local plutocrats, don't they? And they are luxuries, let's face it. Besides, you've often said yourself that everyone should earn his bread with his own hands. But you don't earn bread. You earn money. Why don't you stick to the literal meaning of what you say? Bread is what you should be earning—in fact you should be ploughing, sowing, reaping, threshing or doing something directly connected with farm work like looking after cows, digging or building log huts. . . .'

She opened a pretty little cupboard which stood near her desk.

'I want to tell you my secret,' she said. 'That's what all this has been leading up to. Look—here's my agricultural library, all about field-work, vegetable plots, orchards, cattle-yards and bee-keeping. I find it terribly interesting and I know the whole theory of it already. It's my dearest wish, my great dream, to go over to Dubechnya at the beginning of March. It's marvellous there! Fabulous! Don't you think so? The first year I'll just have a look round and get the feel of things, but the year after that I'm going to do a job of work myself—going to "put my back into it". Father's promised to give me Dubechnya and I shall do just what I like there.'

Blushing, laughing and nearly crying with excitement, she mused aloud about her future life in Dubechnya and how interesting it would be. I envied her. March was near, the days were drawing out, and melting snow dripped from the roofs in the bright noon sun. There was a smell of spring and I longed to be in the country myself.

When she told me that she was moving to Dubechnya I saw myself being left alone in town and felt jealous of her book-cupboard and farming. I knew nothing about farming and I disliked it. I nearly told her that tilling the soil was a form of slavery, but I remembered that Father often said something of the sort and held my peace.

Lent began. Victor Dolzhikov the engineer, whose existence I had almost forgotten, turned up unexpectedly from St. Petersburg without so much as a warning telegram. When I arrived as usual that evening, he was walking up and down the drawing-room telling some story. With his well-scrubbed look and his hair cut short, he seemed ten years younger. Kneeling down, his daughter was taking boxes, scent-bottles and books out of suitcases and handling them to Paul, the man-servant. When I saw the engineer I couldn't help taking a step backward, but he held out both hands.

'Well, well, well! Look who's here!' he said, baring his firm, white, coachman's teeth in a smile. 'Glad to see you, Mr. Painter. Masha's told me all about it—she certainly has been singing your praises.'

He took my arm. 'I see your point and I'm all for it,' he went on. 'It's a sight more sensible and honest to be a decent workman than to churn out red tape by the yard and wear a ribbon in your hat. I worked in Belgium myself with these two hands and then spent two years as an engine-driver. . . .'

He wore a short jacket and had slippers on and walked about, rubbing his hands, with a slight roll as if he had gout. He hummed and purred to himself, and kept hugging himself with pleasure at being back home at last and having had a shower-bath, a thing he much enjoyed.

'Oh, I don't deny it,' he said to me at supper. 'You're all charming, delightful people, I don't deny it at all. But why is it, my dear sirs, that the moment you take up manual work or peasant welfare, somehow all it really boils down to is being some sort of religious crank? Don't tell me you don't belong to some such movement. You don't drink vodka for instance. That can only mean one thing—you're a nonconformist.'

I had a vodka to please him, and some wine too. We sampled cheeses, salami, pâté, pickles and sundry delicatessen brought by the engineer, and the wines that had arrived from abroad in his absence. The wine was excellent. The engineer managed to get his wine and cigars from abroad duty free and someone sent him caviare and dried sturgeon for nothing. His flat was rent free because the owner supplied paraffin to the railway. From their general air, he and his daughter had all the best things in life for the asking—free, gratis and for nothing.

I still went to see them, though I was less keen on going now. The engineer put me off—I never felt at ease with him. Those clear, innocent eyes were altogether too much and his tiresome remarks sickened me. And I was depressed to think that this well-fed, ruddy-cheeked person had been my boss not so long ago and had been outrageously rude to me. True, he now put his arm round me, slapped me heartily on the shoulder, and was in favour of my way of life, but I felt that he still thought me a worm and only put up with me to please his daughter. Since I could not laugh or say what I liked, I more or less kept my mouth shut, expecting him to call me 'You there' any moment, as he did his servant Paul.

My petty provincial pride was hurt. I, a proletarian, a house-painter, now visited the rich every day, though we had nothing in common and the whole town looked on them as foreigners. I drank expensive wine there and ate outlandish food. All this was more than my conscience could stomach. On my way there I pulled a long face and avoided people in the street, scowling at them as though I really was some sort of religious crank. When I went home from the engineer's I used to feel ashamed of having done myself so well.

But I chiefly feared falling in love. Walking down the street, working or talking to my mates, I could only think of going to see Masha that evening. I thought of her voice, her laughter, her way of walking. Before visiting her I always spent a long time tying my tie in front of Nanny's crooked looking-glass and thinking how repulsive my new suit was. I really suffered, despising myself at the same time for worrying about such trifles. When she shouted from another room that she wasn't dressed and asked me to wait, I could hear her putting on her clothes and felt panicky, as if the ground was giving way beneath me. When I saw a woman in the street, even far away, I could not help comparing, and I found all our girls and women vulgar, absurdly dressed and lacking in poise. These comparisons made me feel proud, for Masha was the pick of the bunch! At night I dreamt of the two of us.

One evening at supper we polished off a whole lobster with the engineer's help. On my way home afterwards I remembered the engineer twice calling me 'my dear fellow' over supper. They were kind to me there, but they would have been just as kind, I decided, to some miserable big dog that had lost its master. They found me amusing, but the moment they tired of me they would kick me out like a stray dog. I was ashamed and felt so hurt that I was ready to cry. I felt insulted. Looking up at the sky, I swore to end all this.

I did not go to Dolzhikov's next day. Late in the evening—it was raining and already quite dark—I took a walk along Great Dvoryansky Street and looked at the windows. At the Azhogins' everyone seemed to have gone to bed, though a light shone in a window at the end. That would be old Mrs. Azhogin embroidering by the light of three candles and thinking that she was carrying on the fight against superstition. Our house was in darkness, but at the Dolzhikovs' opposite us the windows were bright, though nothing could be seen inside for flowers and curtains.

I went on patrolling the street, drenched by the cold March rain, and heard Father come home from his club. He knocked on the gate. A minute later a light showed in a window and I saw my sister hurry along with a lamp, patting her thick hair with one hand as she went. Then Father stalked up and down the drawing-room, talking and rubbing his hands, while my sister sat quite still in an armchair thinking and not listening.

Then they went away. The lights went out.

I looked round at the engineer's house. That too was dark now. In the rain and darkness I felt utterly lonely and abandoned to the whim of fate. All I had ever done or desired, all I had ever thought and said—how trivial it seemed compared with this loneliness, compared with my sufferings now and those which lay ahead. Alas, the deeds and thoughts of living creatures are of far less consequence than their miseries.

Without being quite clear what I was doing, I gave a frantic tug at the bell on Dolzhikov's gate. It broke and I dashed down the street like a naughty boy, terrified. I was sure that they would come straight out to see who it was, but when I paused for breath at the end of the street I heard only the rain and a watchman banging his sheet of iron somewhere far away.

For a whole week I stayed away from the Dolzhikovs. I sold my new suit. There was no painting work to be had and I was living from hand to mouth again, earning ten or twenty copecks a day doing odd jobs—heavy, irksome work. Floundering knee deep in cold mud, straining every muscle, I tried to stifle my memories, as if in revenge for all the cheeses and tinned delicacies that they had regaled me with at the engineer's. But as soon as I was in bed, hungry and wet, my sinful imagination would begin to conjure up marvellous, seductive scenes. I would realize to my astonishment that I was in love—passionately—and fall into a sound, healthy sleep, feeling that all this penal servitude only made my body younger and stronger.

One evening there was an unseasonable fall of snow and the north wind blew as if winter was about to return. Coming back from work, I found Masha sitting in my room in her fur coat, with both hands in her muff.

'Why have you stopped coming?' she asked, raising her clear, intelligent eyes. A thrill of joy went through me and I stood stiffly to attention, as when Father was about to hit me. She looked into my face and her eyes showed that she understood why I was so moved.

'Why have you stopped coming?' she said again. 'Since you won't come to me I've come to you.'

She stood up and came close to me.

'Don't desert me,' she said, and her eyes filled with tears. 'I'm lonely, so utterly lonely.'

She burst into tears and hid her face in her muff.

'I'm so lonely!' she said. 'Things have got me down, they really have. I've no one except you. Don't desert me.'

She looked for a handkerchief to wipe her eyes and smiled. For a time we said nothing. Then I put my arms round her and kissed her, scratching my cheek on her hat-pin.

We started talking as if we had been close friends for a long, long time.

X

A FEW days later, to my utter delight, she sent me to Dubechnya. Walking to the station, and later in the train, I kept laughing for no reason and people stared at me as if I was drunk. It was snowing and there were morning frosts, but the roads were no longer white and rooks hovered overhead, cawing.

My first idea was to fix up quarters for Masha and myself in one of the lodges at the side of the house, the one opposite Mrs. Cheprakov's, but it turned out that pigeons and ducks had moved in some time ago and it would have meant destroying a lot of nests to clean the place out. Like it or not, we had to move into the cheerless rooms of the large house with their venetian blinds. The villagers called it 'the big house'. It had over twenty rooms, but no furniture except an upright piano and a child's armchair in the attic. Even if Masha brought all her furniture from town we should never get rid of the grim, empty, cold feeling.

I chose three small rooms with windows facing the garden and worked from early morning to night, clearing them out, putting in new glass, papering the walls and filling in cracks and holes in the floors. It was pleasant, easy work. Now and then I would run down to the river to see if the ice was shifting and I kept fancying that the starlings had arrived. At night I thought about Masha and listened, enraptured and enthralled, to the rats scurrying and the wind soughing and banging above the ceiling. It sounded as if there was an old ghost coughing in the attic.

The snow was deep. A lot more fell at the end of March, but swiftly melted as if by magic. The spring floods swirled past and by the beginning of April starlings were chattering and yellow butterflies flew about the garden. The weather was wonderful. Every afternoon I went to meet Masha in town. And how I enjoyed treading barefoot on the road, which was drying out and still soft. When I was half way there I used to sit down and look at the town, not venturing nearer, for the sight of it upset me. I kept wondering what my friends would think when they heard of my love. What would Father say? What troubled me most was the thought of life having grown so complex that I had lost control over it. It was like a balloon sweeping me off God knows where. I no longer thought about how to earn my keep and how to live. I thought about—well I honestly can't remember what.

When Masha's carriage arrived, I got in with her and we drove off to Dubechnya, happy and carefree. Or I waited for the sun to set and went home, fed up, bored, wondering why she hadn't come. Then unexpectedly, at the gate or in the garden, a charming apparition would greet me—Masha, who, it turned out, had come by rail after all and walked from the station. That was always a great occasion. She wore a simple woollen dress and a scarf round her head, and carried an ordinary umbrella, but she was laced in and slender, and wore expensive foreign boots. She was a clever actress playing the part of a provincial housewife.

We would inspect our establishment and try to allot the rooms and plan the paths, vegetable plot and beehives. We already had our hens, ducks and geese which we loved because they were ours. Everything was ready for sowing—oats, clover, timothy grass, buckwheat and vegetables. We always spent a long time inspecting all this and discussing the harvest prospects. Masha's every word seemed extremely clever and delightful.

These were the happiest days of my life.

A few weeks after Easter we were married in our parish church at Kurilovka, the village about two miles from Dubechnya. Masha wanted a quiet wedding. At her wish the ushers were village lads, the parish clerk managed the singing, and she drove us back from the church in a jolting trap.

We only had one guest from town, my sister Cleopatra—Masha had sent her a note two or three days before the wedding. My sister wore a white dress and gloves. During the ceremony she was greatly moved and quietly wept tears of joy. Her expression was motherly and infinitely kind. Our happiness excited her and she smiled as if she was inhaling sweet, intoxicating fumes. Looking at her during the ceremony, I realized that to her love, yes love, was the most important thing in the world. It was what she always secretly longed for—timidly, but with all her heart. She put her arms round Masha and kissed her. Not knowing how to express her emotions, she said I was 'good, so very good.'

She changed into her ordinary clothes before leaving and took me into the garden to talk to me alone.

'Father's hurt because you didn't write,' she said. 'You should have asked for his blessing. But he's really very pleased—says this marriage will raise your standing in society and Masha's influence will make you take things more seriously. We talk only of you in the evenings these days and last night he even called you "our Misail". It gave me so much pleasure. He seems to have some plan in mind. I think he wants to set an example of generosity by being the first to propose a reconciliation. He'll be out to see you in a day or two, very likely.'

She quickly made the sign of the cross over me several times.

'Well, God be with you,' she said. 'Be happy. Anyuta Blagovo's a very clever girl and she says this marriage of yours is another ordeal sent by God. Well, so it may be. Family life can't all be happiness. There's bound to be suffering as well, you can't help that.'

Masha and I saw her off and walked a couple of miles with her. Then we turned back, walking slowly and saying nothing, as if we were resting. Masha held my arm. We felt relaxed and didn't want to talk about love any more. After the wedding we had become closer and dearer to each other than ever and we felt as if nothing could separate us.

'Your sister's very nice,' said Masha. 'But she looks as if her life has been one long agony. Your father must be an awful man.'

I started telling her how my sister and I had been brought up and how our childhood really had been meaningless and painful. When she heard about Father hitting me not so long ago she shuddered and pressed closer to me.

'Don't tell me any more,' she said. 'It's too horrible.'

We were inseparable now. We lived in the three rooms of the big house and bolted the door to the empty rooms in the evenings, as if they housed a stranger whom we feared. I rose at crack of dawn each day and got down to a job at once—mending carts, making garden paths, digging flower-beds or painting the roof of the house. When the time came to sow oats I tried my hand at double-ploughing, harrowing and sowing. I made a good job of it and kept up with our labourer. I used to get so tired. The biting cold wind and rain made my face and feet burn for hours and I dreamt of ploughland at nights. But working in the fields was not my idea of fun. I knew nothing about farming. I disliked it, perhaps because townsmen's blood flows in my veins and my ancestors have never tilled the soil.

Nature—fields, meadows, vegetable-plots—I loved dearly. But the peasant, turning the sod with his plough and urging on his miserable horse—the ragged, damp peasant, craning his neck—that was my idea of brute strength at its crudest and most barbarous. Watching his clumsy movements, I found myself thinking of that legendary life long ago before man knew the use of fire. The grim bull, moving among the peasants' cows, horses careering through the village with thundering hooves—they scared me stiff. Everything at all large, strong and angry—a horned ram, a gander or a watch-dog—seemed a symbol of this same barbarous, brute force. This prejudice affected me most in bad weather when heavy clouds lowered over the black ploughland. Above all, when I was ploughing or sowing and two or three people stood watching me work, I could not feel that what I was doing really mattered all that much. I felt that I was just amusing myself. I preferred jobs round the yard and liked painting the roof most.

I used to walk through the garden and meadow to our mill. It was rented to Stephen, a dark, handsome, sturdy-looking peasant from Kurilovka with a thick black beard. He disliked running a mill—said it bored him and there was no money in it. He only lived there so that he need not live at home. He was a saddler and carried a pleasant smell of tar and leather round with him. He was no great talker, but a listless sluggish person, always sitting on the river bank or in his doorway and humming to himself. His wife and mother-in-law—pale, droopy, meek creatures—sometimes came over from Kurilovka to see him. They made him low bows and addressed him with great respect. In reply he neither moved nor spoke, but sat to one side on the bank, quietly humming. An hour or two would pass without a word spoken, then mother-in-law and wife would whisper together, stand up and look at him for some time, expecting him to turn round. They would bow low and say 'goodbye, Stephen' in honeyed, sing-song tones.

Then they would go. Stephen used to make off with the bundle of rolls or shirt that they had brought him, sighing.

'Women!' he would remark with a wink in their direction.

The mill had two sets of mill-stones and worked all day and night. I used to help Stephen. I liked the work and was glad to take over when he was away.

XI

A WET spell followed the warm, fine weather and May was rainy and cold. The noise of the mill-wheels and rain made one lazy and sleepy. The vibrating floor and the smell of flour made for drowsiness too. My wife came over twice a day, wearing a short fur-lined jacket and a pair of wellington boots, and always said the same thing.

'Call this summer! It's worse than October.'

We drank tea or made some porridge or sat for hours without speaking, waiting for the rain to stop. Once when Stephen was away at a fair, Masha spent the night at the mill. We had no idea what time it was when we got up because the whole sky was shrouded in rain-clouds, but sleepy cocks were crowing in Dubechnya and corncrakes were calling in the meadow. It was very early indeed.

I went down to the mill-pond with my wife and pulled out the fish-trap that we had seen Stephen throw in the night before. A large perch was floundering in it and a crayfish writhed about, clawing upwards with its pincers.

'Let them go,' said Masha. 'Let them be happy too.'

The day seemed very long because we had got up so early and then done nothing—it seemed the longest day of my life. Late in the afternoon Stephen came back and I went home to the manor-house.

'Your father was here today,' Masha told me.

'Then where is he now?'

'Gone. I wouldn't see him.'

I stood there without speaking. She saw that I was sorry for Father.

'One must be consistent,' she said. 'I wouldn't see him and sent him a message not to bother coming again.'

A moment later I was through the gate and on my way to town to straighten things out with Father. It was muddy, slippery, cold. Suddenly, for the first time since the wedding, I felt sad, and the thought that perhaps something was wrong with my life flashed through my brain, which was exhausted by this long, grey day. I was worn out and gradually gave way to indolence and faint-heartedness till I did not want to move or think. After walking a bit farther, I decided not to bother and turned back.

The engineer was standing in the middle of the yard in a leather coat with a hood.

'Where's the furniture?' he shouted. 'There was some splendid Empire stuff here. There were pictures, vases. But the place has been picked clean. I bought the estate with the furniture, damn her!'

Mrs. Cheprakov's odd-job-man Moses, a young fellow of about twenty-five, thin, with a pock-marked face and insolent little eyes, stood near him crumpling his cap. One of his cheeks was bigger that the other as though he had been lying on it too long.

'I'm afraid, sir, you did purchase it without the furniture, sir,' he said feebly. 'I happen to remember.'

'Shut up, you!' shouted the engineer, turning crimson and shaking with anger. The echo of his shout reverberated from the garden.

XII

WHEN I did a job in the garden or yard, Moses always stood near by, his hands behind his back, watching me with a lazy, insolent look in his little eyes. It annoyed me so much I used to stop work and go away.

This Moses was Mrs. Cheprakov's lover according to Stephen. I had noticed that anyone who came to borrow money always applied to him first. I once saw some fellow, black all over—he must have been a coal-heaver—prostrate himself in front of Moses. After some whispering he would sometimes hand over money on his own initiative, without telling his mistress, which made me think he must do occasional business on the side.

He went shooting in our garden under our very windows, helped himself to stuff from our larder and took our horses without so much as by your leave. We were furious and felt that we couldn't call the place our own. Masha would go white.

'Don't tell me we have to put up with these swine for another eighteen months,' she would say.

Mrs. Cheprakov's son Ivan was a guard on our railway. He had grown very thin and weak that winter. One drink was enough to make him tipsy these days and he felt the cold when out of the sun. He was ashamed of his guard's uniform and loathed wearing it, but thought his job worth while as he could steal candles and sell them. He viewed my new status with mixed feelings—wonder, envy and a vague hope that something of the sort might come his way. He pursued Masha with admiring glances and asked what I had for dinner these days. A sad, sickly look showed on his ugly, emaciated face and he moved his fingers as though he was testing the feel of my luck.

'Tell you what, Better-than-nothing,' he said in his fidgety way, forever relighting his cigarette—there was always a mess where he stood because it took him dozens of matches to light up once. 'I'm in a pretty poor way these days, you know. Worst of all, any jumped-up little second lieutenant can shout, "Hey, you! Guard! You there!" I've heard a thing or two in trains, old boy, I can tell you! I know one thing, though—life's a rotten business. Mother's been the ruin of me. A doctor in the train once told me immoral parents always have drunken or criminal children. And that's about the size of it.'

Once he staggered into our yard, breathing heavily, with a blank look, his eyes rolling. He laughed and cried and raved as if delirious. All I could make of this rigmarole was, 'My mother! Where's my mother?' which he brought out tearfully—like a child that has lost his mother in a crowd. I brought him into our garden and laid him under a tree, and Masha and I took turns to sit with him all day and night. He was in a bad way and the sight of his pale, damp face made Masha feel sick.

'Have we really got these swine round the place for another eighteen months?' she asked. 'Oh, how ghastly! Ghastly!'

What a trial the peasants were! And how badly they let us down at the very start, in those spring months when we so longed to be happy! My wife was building them a school, so I sketched out the plan of a school for sixty boys. The council passed it, but advised us to build at Kurilovka, the large village only two miles away. It so happened that the Kurilovka school—attended by children from four villages of which Dubechnya was one—was old and overcrowded and the floor was so rotten that you had to watch your step.

At the end of March, Masha was made trustee of the Kurilovka school at her own wish and in early April we held three meetings to persuade the peasants that their school was old and overcrowded and a new one should be put up. A local councillor and an inspector of state schools came along and put the same point. After each meeting the peasants crowded round us and asked us to stand them a keg of vodka. We felt hot in the crowd. Soon we grew tired and went home, annoyed and somewhat embarrassed.

In the end the peasants did set aside land for the school and undertook to cart all building material from town with their own horses. On the first Sunday after the spring sowing, carts left Kurilovka and Dubechnya to fetch bricks for the foundations. The men left at crack of dawn and came back late at night, drunk and talking about what an awful time they had had.

Needless to say the rain and cold went on all through May with the roads a shocking mess and mud everywhere. The carts usually turned into our yard when they came back from town, and quite an ordeal that was! A pot-bellied nag would appear in the gateway, splaying its front legs. Before coming into the yard it seemed to bow, after which a wet, slimy-looking thirty-foot beam would slither in on a long, low trailer. A peasant, muffled up against the rain, with his coat-tails tucked inside his belt, would walk alongside, not looking where he was going and stepping in all the puddles. A second cart would appear, carrying planks, then a third one with a beam and a fourth.

Bit by bit the space in front of the house became jammed with horses, beams and planks. Peasants and their women, heads muffled, skirts tucked up, stared balefully at our windows, making a great hullabaloo and demanding to see the missus.

Their language was atrocious. Moses stood by, looking as if our discomfiture was all great fun.

'No more carting for us!' yelled the men. 'We're dead beat! She can get the stuff herself!'

Pale-faced and terrified, Masha thought that they were going to break into the house. She would send them the money for half a keg of vodka, whereupon the noise always died down and one after another the long beams crawled back out of the yard again.

My wife always worried when I left for the site.

'The men are in an ugly mood,' she would say. 'They might do you an injury. Wait a moment, I'm coming with you.'

We would drive off to Kurilovka together and the carpenters would ask us for a tip. The framework was ready and it was time the foundations were laid, but the bricklayers had not come and the carpenters grumbled at the delay. When at last bricklayers did appear, it turned out that there was no sand—we had somehow forgotten it would be needed. The peasants made the most of our predicament, demanding thirty copecks a load, though it was only a few hundred yards from the site to the river where they fetched the stuff. And we needed over five hundred loads.

There was no end to the muddling, swearing and cadging, and my wife was furious. The foreman-bricklayer, an old fellow of seventy called Titus Petrov, took her by the arm.

'Now look'ee here, I tell you!' said he. 'Just you get me that sand and I'll have a dozen of the lads here in a jiffy and the job'll be done in a couple of days. Look'ee here, I say!'

Well, they did bring the sand. And a couple of days did pass. Then four days, then a week. But there was still a yawning hole in place of those promised foundations.

'This is driving me crazy!' said my wife in great distress. 'What frightful, frightful people!'

In the middle of this chaos Victor Dolzhikov came to see us, bringing hampers of wine and *delicatessen*. He ate a leisurely meal and took a nap on the terrace. The workmen shook their heads at his snores and said, 'How do you like that!'

Masha was never pleased to see him. She distrusted him, yet took his advice. He would get up from his after-dinner nap in a bad mood and make nasty remarks about our way of running things or say how sorry he was to have bought Dubechnya and lost so much money on it. At such times poor Masha looked agonized. While she complained, he yawned and said the peasants needed a good thrashing.

He called our married life a farce—a piece of childish self-indulgence.

'She's done this sort of thing before,' he told me. 'She once saw herself as an opera singer and ran away from home. I was two months hunting for her. Spent a thousand roubles on telegrams alone, my dear man.'

He no longer called me a nonconformist or 'Mr. Painter'. And he no longer approved of my living as a workman.

'You're a funny chap,' he said. 'There's something wrong with you. I don't venture to prophesy, but you'll come to a bad end.'

At night Masha slept badly and was always sitting brooding by our bedroom window. There was no more laughter at supper, no more charming grimaces. I was miserable. When it rained, every drop seemed to go right through me and I felt like falling on my knees and apologizing to Masha for the weather. I felt equally guilty when the peasants kicked up a row in the yard.

For hours on end I sat in one place, thinking what a marvellous, splendid woman Masha was. I loved her passionately. Everything she did or said fascinated me. She was given to quiet, studious pursuits and liked reading or studying for hours on end. Though she knew farming only from books, her knowledge amazed us all. The advice that she gave was always to the point and helped to improve our methods. And with all this went such a generous nature, such good taste and good humour—the kind of good humour only found in well-educated people.

To a woman like Masha with her sound, practical brain, the chaos of our lives and all these petty cares and squabbles were sheer agony. I saw this and I could not sleep at night either. My mind was active, a lump came into my throat, and I would toss about, not knowing what to do.

Sometimes I galloped off to town and brought Masha books, newspapers, chocolates or flowers. Or I went fishing with Stephen and spent hours in the rain, wading neck-deep in cold water after some special sort of fish to vary our diet. I sank to pleading with the peasants not to make a noise, plied them with vodka, bribed them, made them all sorts of promises. And did a host of other silly things.

In the end the rain stopped and the ground dried out. Sometimes I rose at about four in the morning and went into the garden where the flowers sparkled with dew. Birds sang, insects hummed, and there was not a cloud in the sky. The garden, meadows and river were lovely, but I could not get the peasants and the carts and the engineer out of my mind. Masha and I sometimes drove off to the fields in a racing trap to look at the oats, she at the reins and I sitting behind. She held her shoulders rather high and the wind played with her hair.

'Keep to the right!' she shouted to anyone coming the other way.'

'You're a real driver,' I told her once.

'Very likely. After all, my grandfather—the engineer's father—was one. Didn't you know?' she asked, turning to me and starting to mimic the way coachmen shout and sing.

'Splendid!' I thought as I listened to her. 'Absolutely splendid!' Then I remembered the peasants and their carts and the engineer. . . .

XIII

DR. BLAGOVO arrived on his bicycle and my sister took to coming out. There was more talk about manual labour, progress and the mysterious Unknown awaiting mankind in the distant future.

The doctor did not like us farming because it left less time for arguing, and said that ploughing, mowing and grazing calves were no work for a free man. In due course, he said, mankind would assign these cruder aspects of the life-struggle to animals and machines and would spend all its time on scientific research. My sister kept asking us to let her go home early and when she stayed late or spent the night there was no end of a fuss.

'Heavens, what a child you are,' Masha reproached her. 'This is really too silly.'

'I know,' my sister agreed. 'I can see how silly it is, but what if I just can't help myself? I feel I'm doing wrong.'

Haymaking made my whole body ache because the work was new to me. Sitting and talking on the terrace with the others in the evening, I was always falling asleep. They would roar with laughter, wake me up and sit me down at the supper table, but drowsiness still came over me. I felt like one in a trance—seeing lights, faces, plates and hearing voices that made no sense. I rose early in the mornings and picked up my scythe at once or went over to the building site and worked there all day.

When I stayed at home on Sundays or other holidays, I noticed that my wife and sister were hiding something from me and actually seemed to be avoiding me. Masha was as loving as ever, but she had something on her mind that she kept from me. The peasants were getting more and more on her nerves, there was no doubt about that, and she was finding the life more depressing, but she had stopped complaining to me. She would rather talk to the doctor than me these days—why, I had no idea.

At haymaking and harvesting-time it was the custom in our province for farm-workers to go to the big house in the evenings for a round of vodka—even the young girls had a glass. We did not keep up this practice, so mowers and peasant women hung about our yard till late at night waiting for their vodka and then went off swearing. Meanwhile Masha, frowning grimly, kept quiet or muttered irritably to the doctor, 'Savages! Brutes!'

Newcomers to the country always meet a cool, almost hostile reception, like new boys at school, and this is what happened to us. At first we were taken for stupid, silly people who had only bought an estate because we did not know what to do with our money.

We were a laughing-stock. The peasants grazed their cattle in our woods and even in our garden. They drove our cows and horses off to the village, then came and demanded money for the damage that they had done. The inhabitants of an entire village would come into the yard and make a row about our trespassing on 'old Bull Neck Meadow' or some such place when we cut hay. Not knowing the exact boundaries of our own property yet, we took their word for it and paid for the damage. Then it would turn out that we had been mowing our own land after all. They stripped the bark from the lime-trees in our wood. One Dubechnya man, a thoroughpaced shark who sold vodka without a licence, bribed our labourers to help him work all sorts of dirty swindles on us by changing the new wheels on our carts for old, running off with our ploughing harness, then selling it back to us, and so on.

But the incidents at the Kurilovka building site upset us most, with women stealing planks, bricks, tiles and iron at night. The village elder would take witnesses and search their huts and they would be fined two roubles apiece at a village meeting. Then the money would be spent on drinks all round for the village.

Masha was furious when she heard. 'What swine!' she used to say to the doctor or my sister. 'It's awful! Ghastly!'

I often heard her saying how sorry she was that she ever started building that school.

'Do get one thing straight, Masha,' the doctor would urge. 'If you build that school and go round doing good, it's not the peasants you do it for. You do it for civilization, for the future. And the worse those peasants are, the more reason there is for building them a school, don't you see?'

But he didn't sound at all sure of himself and I felt that he hated the peasants as much as Masha did.

Masha often went to the mill and took my sister with her, both of them laughing and saying that they went to look at Stephen because he was so handsome. It was only in masculine company that he was so taciturn and slow off the mark, as it turned out, for with women he was very free and easy and rattled away like anything.

One day I went to the river to bathe and chanced to overhear them. Masha and Cleopatra, both in white, were sitting on the bank in the broad shade of a willow, while Stephen stood near by talking, with his hands behind his back.

'Call them peasants human?' he said. 'They ain't, begging your pardon. Brutes and cheats, that's what they are. What kind of life does the peasant live? Eating and drinking is all he thinks of—cheap grub and a chance to shout his silly head off at the tavern. He ain't go no conversation, no manners, no dignity. A clodhopper, that's what he is! He lives in filth, his wife lives in filth and his children live in filth. Goes to bed with his clothes on, he does, fishes the spuds out of the stew with his fingers and drinks kvass with beetles in it—can't even bother to blow them away!'

'But he's so poor, you see,' my sister put in.

'What's that got to do with it? True, he's hard up, but there's different ways of being hard up, miss. If someone's in prison, say, or blind or crippled—well, that's something you wouldn't wish on anyone. But if he's free and has his head screwed on, if he has eyes in his head and his two hands and his strength and his God—then what else does he need?

'It's not poverty, miss, it's all self-indulgence and ignorance. If decent, educated folk like you take pity on him and decide to help him out, the low creature will only spend your money on drink. Worse still, he'll open a dram-shop of his own and use your money to rob his mates. You talk about poverty. But what about your rich peasant? Does he live any better? He's just as big a swine, begging your pardon, the brawling, bawling, bullying lout, broader than he's long, him and his fat, red snout! I'd like to take a swing at the blackguard and knock his teeth out, that I would. Take Larion from Dubechnya. He's well off, but I bet he strips your trees along with the poorest of them. He's a foul-mouthed fellow, his children are the same, and when he's drunk he falls flat on his face in a puddle and sleeps it off.

'They're worthless, miss, the whole lot of them, it's sheer hell living in a village with them. I'm sick and tired of that village. I've food to eat and clothes on my back, thanks be to God above. I've served my time in the dragoons, done a three years' stint as village elder and now I'm free as a bird. I live where I like. I won't live in the village and no one can make me. People go on about my wife. They say I ought to live in a hut with my wife. Why should I? I ain't her hired man.'

'Tell us, Stephen, did you marry for love?' asked Masha.

'Love! What—in a village?' Stephen answered with a laugh. 'If you really want to know, miss, this is my second marriage. I don't come from Kurilovka. I'm from Zalegoshch, but I became a Kurilovka man when I got married. The thing was, my father wouldn't divide up his land and there were five of us brothers. So I said goodbye and made myself scarce. Went to another village to live with my wife's family. My first wife died young.'

'How was that?'

'Sheer stupidity. Kept crying, she did, crying all the time for no reason at all. And took ill, always drinking herbal stuff to make herself pretty. Must have harmed her innards. And my second wife, the one at Kurilovka—why, there's nothing to her. She's just a peasant woman from the village—that's all. I thought she was all right when we were courting. She's young, I thought, and clean-looking, and they live decently. Her mother seemed to belong to some funny religious sect and drank coffee, but the main thing was, you see, they did live decently. So I got married. Next day we're sitting down to dinner and I ask my mother-in-law for a spoon. She hands me one and I see her wipe it with her finger. So much for you, I think. And so much for my "living decently"! I stayed on there for a year and then left.

'Perhaps I should have married a town girl,' he went on after a bit. 'They say a wife should help her husband. But what do I need with help? I help myself. I want someone to talk to. And I don't mean just a lot of blah, blah, blah, either. I mean something with a bit of sense and feeling to it. What's the use of living if you can't have a good talk?'

Stephen suddenly stopped and started his weary, monotonous humming. This meant that he had spotted me.

Masha often went to the mill and obviously enjoyed talking to Stephen. What she liked about him was that when he cursed those peasants he meant every word he said. Whenever she came back from the mill the village idiot who guarded our orchard shouted, 'Ah, there goes our lass. Hullo there, wench!' And he barked at her like a dog.

She used to stop and look at him carefully as if she found an answer to her thoughts in this idiot barking. Very likely it had the same appeal for her as Stephen's curses. There was always news for her at home—the village geese had trampled on the cabbage in our kitchen-garden, say, or Larion had stolen the reins. She would shrug her shoulders.

'What do you expect from these people?' she asked sardonically.

She was furious and things were really beginning to get her down, but I was growing used to the peasants and found myself more and more drawn to them. They were mainly highly strung, irritable people who had had a raw deal and whose imaginations had been crushed. Ignorant men with limited, dull horizons, they all had the same obsession with grey earth, grey days, black bread. They tried to cheat, but showed as much sense over it as an ostrich sticking its head in the sand and thinking that it can't be seen. They couldn't even count. They wouldn't take twenty roubles to help with our haymaking, but would do it for half a keg of vodka, when for twenty roubles they could buy four whole kegs.

Oh yes, there was dirt, drunkenness, stupidity and cheating, but all the same you felt that by and large the peasant's life had a firm, healthy base. He might look like some great lumbering beast as he followed his wooden plough. He might dull his wits with vodka. Still, when you looked closer, you saw something vital

and significant there which was lacking in Masha and the doctor
for instance. I mean his belief that what really matters on this earth
is truth, and that truth and nothing but the truth can save him and
our whole people. This is why he loves justice more than anything
in the world. I used to tell my wife that she could not see the glass
for the dirty marks on the pane. She either gave no answer or just
hummed like Stephen.

Pale with indignation, this clever, good-natured girl would
talk to the doctor in quavering tones about drunkenness and
dishonesty. She had such a short memory, that's what I found
so staggering. How could she forget that her father the engineer
also drank—heavily too—or that Dubechnya had been bought on
the proceeds of a whole chain of monstrous, barefaced swindles?
How could she?

XIV

MY sister too lived a life of her own which she carefully hid from
me. She and Masha often whispered to each other. When I went
near her she seemed to cringe, and a pleading, guilty look came
into her eyes. Obviously she had something on her mind to make
her afraid or ashamed. By sticking close to Masha she managed
to avoid meeting me in the garden and being left alone with me.
I hardly had a chance to talk to her except at dinner.

One evening I was coming quietly through the garden on my
way back from the building site in the dusk. My sister was walking
near a spreading old apple-tree, making no sound—she might
have been a ghost. Nor did she notice me or hear my steps. She
wore black and was walking up and down quickly, in a straight
line, looking at the ground. An apple fell from a tree. The sound
made her jump and she paused, holding her hands to her temples.
It was then that I went up to her.

Tears came to my eyes and somehow my thoughts turned to our
mother and our childhood. A feeling of great tenderness suddenly
swept over me and I put my arm round her shoulders and kissed
her.

'What's the matter?' I asked. 'You're unhappy, I've seen that
for some time. Tell me, what's wrong.'

'I'm frightened . . .' she said, shuddering.

'But what's the matter?' I insisted. 'For God's sake come out with it.'

'All right, I'll tell you, I'll tell you all about it. I can't bear keeping things from you, it distresses me. Misail, I'm in love . . .' she went on in a whisper. 'I love him, I love him. . . . I'm happy, but why am I so scared?'

Steps were heard and Dr. Blagovo appeared between the trees in a silk shirt and top-boots—they had clearly arranged to meet here by the apple-tree. Seeing him, she rushed towards him impulsively with an agonized cry as if someone was trying to take him from her.

'Vladimir! Vladimir!'

She clung to him and gazed hungrily into his eyes, and only then did I notice how pale and thin she had grown of late. What really brought it home to me was the lace collar that I remembered from some time back—it hung more loosely than ever round her long, thin neck. The doctor was embarrassed, but recovered at once and stroked her hair.

'There, there . . .' he said. 'Why so upset? I'm here now, you see.'

We did not speak, but just looked at each other in some embarrassment. Then we all three walked off together.

'Civilized life hasn't even started in Russia,' the doctor was telling me. 'Old people try to console themselves—if there's nothing doing now, they say, something was at least going on in the forties and sixties. That's all very well for the old, but you and I are young and we aren't yet in our second childhood, so we can't comfort ourselves with such illusions. Russia began in 862 A.D. but *civilized* Russia still hasn't got off the mark at all, as I see it.'

I did not follow his arguments. It was all a bit odd somehow. I did not want to believe that my sister was in love and that here she was walking along, holding a stranger's arm and gazing fondly at him. My sister, that highly strung, terrified, downtrodden, enslaved creature, loved a married man with children. I felt vaguely sorry—what about, I don't quite know. I felt a distaste for the doctor's company somehow and could not see what future this love might have.

XV

MASHA and I drove over to Kurilovka for the dedication of the school.

'Autumn, autumn, autumn . . .' said Masha quietly, looking round her. 'Summer's over. The birds have gone and only the willows are green.'

Summer was indeed over. The days were fine and warm, but there was a nip in the morning air, shepherds wore their sheepskin coats and dew lay all day long on the asters in our garden. There were plaintive sounds all the time, but whether they were from shutters grumbling on their rusty hinges or cranes flying past, you could not tell. It was a wonderful sensation, it made you feel so full of life.

'Summer's over . . .' said Masha. 'Now you and I can see where we stand. We've done a lot of work, a lot of thinking. We're better for it—all credit to us—and we've managed to lead better lives. But has our progress had any noticeable effect on life around us? Has it done anyone else any good? No. Ignorance, physical uncleanliness, drunkenness, the appallingly high infant mortality-rate—none of that's changed. You've ploughed and sowed, while I've spent money and read books, but what good has that been to anyone? All our work, all our fine ideas have clearly been only for ourselves.'

This kind of argument disturbed me and I did not know what to think.

'We've been sincere from start to finish,' I said. 'You can't go wrong if you're sincere.'

'No one's denying that. We had the right ideas, but were wrong in the way we applied them. The main thing is, we've gone about things in the wrong way, haven't we? You want to help people, but by buying an estate you lose all chance of helping them from the outset. Then if you work, dress and eat like a peasant, you somehow lend your support to those heavy, clumsy clothes, ghastly huts and stupid beards.

'On the other hand, suppose you work for a long time, give your life to it and achieve some practical results in the end. What do those results mean? What *can* they mean in the face of such elemental forces as wholesale ignorance, famine, cold and degeneracy? They're a drop in the ocean! What's needed here is quite a different line of attack, something powerful, bold, swift. If you really want to be some use, leave your usual narrow daily round and try to influence the masses directly. What's really needed is noisy, vigorous propaganda. Why is art—music for instance—so alive? Why is it so popular and genuinely powerful? Because your musician or singer makes his impact on thousands at a time.

'Wonderful, wonderful art!' she went on, looking thoughtfully at the sky. 'Art gives you wings—sweeps you off far, far away. If you're sick and tired of filth and petty, niggling concerns—if you're baffled, aggrieved, indignant—you can only find peace and satisfaction in beauty.'

The weather was bright and cheerful as we reached Kurilovka. They were threshing in some of the farm-yards and there was a smell of rye straw. There was a bright red mountain-ash beyond some wattle fences and wherever you looked the trees were gold and red. The church bells were ringing and icons were being carried in procession to the school. You could hear them singing, 'Holy Mother, Intercessor.' The air was clear and the pigeons flew high.

The service was held in a classroom. Then the Kurilovka peasants brought Masha an icon, and those of Dubechnya gave her a large loaf of bread and a gilt salt-cellar. Masha burst into tears.

'If we've said anything we shouldn't or been any trouble, pray forgive us,' said one old man, bowing to her and me.

As we drove home Masha kept looking back at the school. The green roof, painted by me, remained in sight for a long time, glittering in the sunlight. Glancing at it now, Masha was saying goodbye, I felt.

XVI

SHE packed and went to town that evening.

She had taken to going to town often lately and spending the night there. I could not work while she was away, my arms felt limp and weak, our huge yard seemed like some dismal, disgusting waste plot and the garden was full of angry noises. The house, the trees, the horses—none of these were 'ours' to me while she was away.

I did not leave the house, but just sat at her table near the cupboard with her books on farming—old favourites no longer needed, they seemed to look at me with such embarrassment. For hours on end, while it struck seven, eight, nine, and the pitch-black autumn night darkened the windows, I looked at her old glove or the pen that she had always used, or her little scissors. I did nothing and saw quite clearly that anything I'd done before—ploughing, mowing or felling—had only been done because she wanted it. If she had sent me to clean out a deep well, standing waist-deep in water, I would have plunged straight in without bothering whether the job needed doing or not. Now that she was no longer near me, Dubechnya seemed sheer chaos, with its ruins, untidiness, banging shutters and round-the-clock pilfering. Why work in a place like that? Why should I? Why bother my head about the future when I felt the ground slipping from under my feet, felt that my role in Dubechnya was played out—felt in fact that I was heading for the same fate as those books on farming. And what agony the lonely night hours were! I listened and worried, expecting any moment to hear a voice shouting that it was time I left. Dubechnya was no loss, but I mourned my lost love, for the autumn of our love had clearly come. What happiness to love and be loved! And how dreadful to feel yourself falling off that lofty pinnacle.

Masha came back from town next afternoon. Annoyed about something, but trying to hide it, she only asked why all the double window-frames had been put in for winter—said it was enough to choke anyone. So I took two frames out. Though not hungry, we sat down to supper.

'Go and wash your hands. You smell of putty,' my wife said.

She had brought some new illustrated magazines from town and we looked at them together after supper. There were supplements with fashion-plates and patterns which Masha glanced through and put on one side to look at properly later. But one dress with a wide, smooth, bell-shaped skirt and full sleeves caught her fancy and she gazed at it for a minute with grave attention.

'That's not bad,' she said.

'Yes, it would really suit you,' I said. 'It really would.'

I looked fondly at the dress, admiring this grey blob just because she liked it.

'It's a wonderful, splendid dress!' I went on fondly. 'Lovely, marvellous Masha! Darling Masha!

My tears splashed on the picture.

'My splendid Masha . . .' I muttered. 'My lovely, darling Masha. . . .'

She went to bed and I sat up for an hour looking at the illustrations.

'You shouldn't have taken those frames out,' she said from the bedroom. 'It might be cold. There, just feel that draught!'

I read something from the 'miscellaneous' column—a recipe for cheap ink and something about the largest diamond in the world. My eye was caught once more by the picture of the dress that she had liked and I imagined her at a ball with a fan, music, painting and literature. How small and brief my own role seemed!

Our meeting and married life had only been one episode, and there would be plenty more of them in the life of this vigorous, gifted woman. As I have said already, all the best things in life were at her service, hers for the asking. Even ideas and intellectual fashions only served her as a source of pleasure, lending variety to her life, while I was just the cab-driver who had conveyed her from one amusement to another. Now I was no longer needed and she would sail away, leaving me high and dry.

As if in answer to my thoughts a frantic yell came from outside.

'He-e-elp!'

It was a shrill voice, like a woman's. As if mimicking it, the wind, moaning in the chimney, gave out the same shrill note. Half a minute passed and through the howling wind I heard the cry again.

'He-e-elp!'

This time it seemed to come from the far end of the yard.

'Do you hear that, Misail?' my wife asked quietly. 'Do you hear?'

She came out of the bedroom in her nightdress with her hair down and listened, looking at the dark window.

'Someone's being murdered,' she said. 'This really is the last straw.'

I took my gun and went out. It was very dark outside and the wind was so strong that I could hardly stand. I went over to the gate and listened. The trees roared, the wind whistled, and a low, lazy howl came from the garden—the village idiot's dog, no doubt. Outside the gate it was pitch dark with not one light on the railway-line. From near the lodge where the railway office had been last year suddenly came a strangled cry.

'He-e-elp!'

'Who's there?' I shouted.

Two men were struggling. One was shoving, the other resisting and both were breathing hard.

'Let go!' said one of them and I recognized Ivan Cheprakov. It was he who had been shouting in that shrill voice like a woman's. 'Let go, blast you, or I'll bite your hands!'

I recognized the other one as Moses. Separating them, I could not resist hitting him twice in the face and he fell down. Then he stood up and I hit him again.

'Gentleman was trying to kill me,' he muttered. 'Trying to get into his Mum's chest of drawers, he was. . . . I'm aiming to lock him up in the lodge, sir, to be on the safe side, like.'

Cheprakov was drunk and did not recognize me. He drew deep breaths, as if filling his lungs to shout 'help' again.

I left them and went back to the house where my wife was lying on the bed, now fully dressed. I told her what had happened outside, not even hiding the fact that I had hit Moses.

'It's so frightening living in the country,' she said. 'What a confoundedly long night this is.'

A little later we heard the cry again.

'He-e-elp!'

'I'll go and separate them,' I said.

'No, they can tear each other's throats out for all I care,' she said with a look of disdain.

She gazed at the ceiling, listening, and I sat near her, not daring to open my mouth, feeling that this cry for help outside and the long night were all my fault.

We said nothing and I waited impatiently for a glimmer of dawn in the windows. Meanwhile Masha looked as if she had just come out of a trance and was wondering how a clever, well-educated, decent person like her ever became involved with a set of contemptible mediocrities in this miserable provincial dump. How could she sink to letting one of these people attract her and be his wife for more than six months? Myself, Moses, Cheprakov—we were all the same to her, I felt. That drunken, savage cry for help summed it all up—me, our marriage, our farming and the filthy autumn weather. When she sighed or moved into a more comfortable position I read in her face, 'Oh, hurry up, morning!'

In the morning she left.

I stayed on at Dubechnya for another three days waiting for her. Then I piled all our things in one room, locked it, and walked to town. When I rang the engineer's bell it was already evening and on Great Dvoryansky Street the lamps were lit. There was no one in, Paul told me. Mr. Dolzhikov had gone to St. Petersburg and Miss Masha must be at rehearsal at the Azhogins'.

I remember how nervous I was as I went on to the Azhogins'. I remember my heart throbbing and fluttering as I mounted the stairs and stood for a while on the top landing, not venturing inside that temple of the muses. In the ballroom—on a small table, on the grand piano and on stage—candles were burning, everywhere in threes. The first performance was billed for the thirteenth and this first rehearsal was on Monday, an unlucky day. All part of the struggle against superstition.

The drama-fanciers were there already. The eldest, middle and youngest sisters were walking about the stage and reading out their parts from notebooks. Radish stood a little apart, quite still, with the side of his head against a wall, reverently watching the stage as he waited for them to start rehearsing. Nothing had changed.

I set off to pay my respects to the lady of the house, but everyone suddenly began hushing and gesticulating to me to step quietly. There was silence. The piano lid was put up and a lady sat down, screwing up her short-sighted eyes at the music. Then my dear Masha went up to the piano. She was superbly dressed and looked beautiful, but in some new and special way, for she was nothing like the Masha who had come out to see me at the mill that spring. She began singing, 'O radiant night, why do I love thee?'

This was the very first time since we had met that I had heard her sing. She had a fine, mellow, strong voice and as she sang I felt as if I was eating a sweet, ripe, fragrant melon. When she finished, everyone clapped and she smiled delightedly, fluttering her eyes, turning the pages of the music and smoothing her dress. She was like a bird that has broken out of its cage at last and preens its wings in freedom. Her hair was combed back behind her ears and she had a truculent, challenging look, as if she wanted to defy us all or shout at us as she shouted at her horses, 'Come on, my beauties!'

At that moment she must have looked just like her grandfather the coachman.

'You here too?' she said, offering her hand. 'Did you hear me sing? Well, what do you think? It's a good thing you're here,' she went on without waiting for an answer. 'I'm leaving tonight for St. Petersburg. I shan't be away long—you don't mind my going, do you?'

At midnight I took her to the station. She embraced me affectionately—to thank me for not asking unnecessary questions, most likely—and promised to write. I held her hands for a while and kissed them, hardly able to keep back my tears and not saying a word.

When she had gone I stood watching the lights disappear and caressed her in my imagination.

'Darling Masha,' I said in a low voice. 'Wonderful Masha. . . .'

I spent the night at Karpovna's house in Makarikha. Next morning Radish and I upholstered some furniture for a rich businessman who was marrying his daughter to a doctor.

XVII

MY sister came to tea on Sunday afternoon.

'I read a lot these days,' she said, showing me some books that she had borrowed from the public library on the way. 'I'm so grateful to your wife and Vladimir for making me aware of myself. They've been my salvation, made me feel like a real person at last. There was a time when I lay awake at nights worrying. "Oh dear", I'd think, "we've used too much sugar this week. Oh, what if I put too much salt on the cucumbers?" Now I can't sleep either, but I've other things on my mind. It's agony to think that half my life has gone by in this stupid, feeble way. I despise my past life. I'm ashamed of it, and I think of Father as an enemy these days. Oh, I'm so grateful to your wife. And what about Vladimir? He's such a wonderful man. They've opened my eyes.'

'It's bad that you can't sleep at night,' I said.

'You mean I'm ill? Not at all. Vladimir listened to my chest and gave me a clean bill of health, but health isn't what counts, it isn't all that important. . . . Am I doing the right thing? That's what I want to know.'

She needed moral support, that was clear enough. With Masha gone and Dr. Blagovo in St. Petersburg there was no one left in town except me to tell her that she was on the right track. She would stare into my eyes and try to read my secret thoughts. And if I was pensive in her presence or said nothing she always thought that it was her fault and felt depressed. I always had to be on my guard and when she asked me if she was doing right, I hastened to assure her that she was and that I greatly respected her.

'Do you know, they've given me a part at the Azhogins'?' she went on. 'I want to act. I want to live—in fact I want to experience everything. I'm no good at all and my part's only ten lines, but still this is a far, far better and nobler thing than pouring out tea five times a day and seeing if the cook's been eating too much. Above all, Father must be shown that I'm capable of protest.'

After tea she lay down on my bed for some time with her eyes shut, very pale.

'How weak of me,' she said, getting up. 'Vladimir says all the women and girls in this town are anaemic from sheer idleness. Isn't Vladimir clever? He's right, he's so so right. We must work!'

Two days later she turned up for rehearsal at the Azhogins' with a notebook, wearing a black dress, a coral necklace and a brooch that looked like a piece of puff-pastry from a distance. She had large earrings, each with a jewel shining in it. It embarrassed me to look at her and what struck me was the lack of taste. I was not the only one to notice those unfortunate earrings and jewels and her strange get-up, for I saw smiles and heard someone laugh and say, 'Cleopatra of Egypt'.

She was trying to be urbane, nonchalant, at ease, but that only made her look grotesque and affected. Her natural and becoming air had deserted her.

'I just told Father I was going to rehearsal,' she began, coming up to me. 'He shouted at me—said he wouldn't give me his blessing and actually came near to striking me. Just fancy, I don't know my part,' she said, looking at the notebook. 'I'm bound to make a mess of it. And so I've burnt my boats,' she went on, much agitated. 'I've burnt my boats. . . .'

She thought that everyone was looking at her, staggered by the momentous step she had taken and expecting something extraordinary from her. No one ever does notice people as drab and trivial as she and I, but you could never get her to see that.

She was not on until the third act and her part—that of a guest, a provincial busybody—just involved standing by a door for a short time, as if eavesdropping, and then making a short speech. For at least an hour and a half before she was due on—while people came and went on the stage, recited, drank tea and argued—she did not leave my side, constantly mumbling her part and nervously crumpling the notebook.

Thinking that everyone was watching her and waiting for her to go on, she patted her hair with shaking hand.

'I'm sure to make a mess of it . . . .' she told me. 'I feel awful, you've no idea. I'm so terrified, it's as if I was going to be led out to execution.'

Her cue came at last.

'Cleopatra Poloznev! You're on,' said the stage-manager.

She walked into the centre of the stage looking horrorstruck, ugly and clumsy, and stood for half a minute as if paralysed, not moving at all except for the large ear-rings swinging from her ears.

'You may use your notebook as it's the first time,' someone said.

Seeing that she was shaking too much to speak or open her notebook and was not concerned with her part at all, I was about to go and have a word with her when suddenly she fell on her knees in the middle of the stage and burst out sobbing.

All was agitation and uproar. Only I stood there leaning against the scenery at one side, overwhelmed by these proceedings. I hadn't the faintest idea what to do. I saw them pick her up and take her off. I saw Anyuta Blagovo come up to me—I had not noticed her in the hall before and she seemed to have sprung from nowhere. She wore her hat and veil and had her usual look of having just dropped in for a moment.

'I told her not to take a part,' she said angrily, jerking out each word abruptly and blushing. 'It's sheer lunacy! Why didn't you stop her?'

Mrs. Azhogin rushed up, looking thin and flat-chested in a short blouse with short sleeves and tobacco ash down the front.

'My dear, this is too ghastly,' she said, wringing her hands and staring into my face as usual. 'Ghastly! Your sister's in a certain condition . . . she's, er, pregnant! Please take her away, do you mind . . . ?'

She was actually panting with emotion. Her three daughters, just as thin and flat-chested as their mother, stood near by, huddled timidly together. They were paralysed with fright. You might have thought an escaped convict had been caught in their house. ('Oh, what a disgrace!' 'Oh, what a dreadful business!') Yet this worthy family had spent its life fighting superstition. Three candles, the number thirteen and unlucky Monday—these in their view clearly exhausted the catalogue of human superstition and error.

'Please . . . do you mind . . . ?' said Mrs. Azhogin, pursing her lips as she said 'do you'. 'Do you mind taking her home?'

XVIII

SOON after that my sister and I went downstairs. I tried to shield her with my coat and we hurried along, choosing side streets where there were no lamps and avoiding passers-by. We might have been running away. She had stopped crying and looked at me dry-eyed. It was only about twenty minutes' walk to Makarikha where I was taking her and, curiously enough, we managed to call to mind our entire lives in that short time. We went into everything, considered where we stood and made plans. . . .

We decided that we could not go on living in this town and would move somewhere else as soon as I had some money. People had already gone to bed in some houses, and in others they were playing cards. We hated and feared those houses. We spoke of the fanaticism, hard hearts and worthlessness of these respectable families, these lovers of dramatic art whom we had so alarmed.

'Are these stupid, cruel, lazy, dishonest people any better than the drunken, superstitious Kurilovka peasants?' I asked. 'Are they any better than animals, which also panic when some accident disturbs their monotonous lives bounded by instincts?'

What would have become of my sister now if she had gone on living at home? Talking to Father and meeting people she knew every day—what torments she would have endured! I could just picture it. Then I remembered people, all of whom I knew, whose lives had been made more and more of a misery by their nearest and dearest. I remembered the tortured dogs going mad, the live sparrows thrown into water after street urchins had plucked out all their feathers. I remembered the long, long procession of obscure, slow agonies that I had observed continuously in this town ever since I was a boy.

I just could not see what kept these sixty thousand citizens going. Why did they read the Gospels? Why did they say their prayers? Or read books and magazines? Not one word of what has been said and written since the beginning of time can have done them any good if we still find the same darkness of the soul and hatred of freedom as a hundred or three hundred years ago. A master carpenter spends his whole life building houses in the town, but he will go on mispronouncing the terms of his trade till his dying day. Likewise these sixty thousand townspeople have been reading and hearing about truth, mercy and freedom for generations, yet their entire progress from cradle to grave is one long lie. And they torment each other, fearing and hating freedom as if it was their worst enemy.

'Well, my fate is decided,' my sister said when we reached home. 'I can't go back *there* after what's happened. God, isn't that marvellous! I feel so much easier in my mind.'

She went straight to bed. Tears shone on her eyelashes, but she looked happy. She slept sweetly and soundly and obviously really was relaxed and easier in her mind. It was a long, long time since she had slept like that.

Thus began our life together. She was always singing and saying how well she felt. We borrowed books from the library, but I took them back unread because she could not read these days. She only felt like dreaming and talking of the future. She darned my underwear of helped Karpovna at the stove. She was always humming or talking about her Vladimir—how clever, well mannered and kind he was, and how amazingly learned. I would agree, though I no longer liked her doctor. She wanted to do a job and earn her own living. She said that she was going to be a schoolmistress or nurse as soon as she was well enough, and she meant to scrub floors and do the washing. She was quite devoted to her baby. He wasn't even born yet, but she already knew what his eyes and hands were like and how he laughed. She liked talking about education. As Vladimir was the best man in the world, everything she said about education boiled down to making her boy as fascinating as his father. We had no end of discussions and whatever she said was exciting and exhilarating to her. I sometimes cheered up too without knowing why.

I suppose her dreaminess infected me. I did not read anything either, but just mooned about. Tired as I was, I used to walk up and down the room in the evenings with my hands in my pockets, talking about Masha.

'When do you think she'll be back?' I would ask my sister. 'I think she'll be here by Christmas at the latest. What is there for her to do there?'

'She must be coming very soon, or else she'd write.'

'Very true,' I always agreed, knowing full well that there was nothing to bring Masha back to our town.

I missed her dreadfully. Unable to deceive myself any longer, I tried to get other people to deceive me. My sister waited for her doctor and I waited for Masha, and we both talked and laughed all the time without noticing that we were keeping Karpovna awake. She lay on her stove.

'The samovar was humming this morning, oh dearie me it was,' she kept muttering. 'That means bad luck, my dears. Bad luck, that means.'

No one came near us except the postman who brought my sister letters from the doctor, and Prokofy who sometimes looked in during the evening, stared at my sister without speaking, then went off.

'Every class should stick to its own rules,' he would say from his kitchen. 'And them as is too proud to understand that will find this life a vale of tears.'

He loved this phrase, 'Vale of tears'. I was going through the market one day—Christmas week had arrived—when he called me over to his butcher's stall. Without offering to shake hands, he announced that he had something important to discuss. Vodka and frost had made his face red, and by him at the counter stood Nikolka—he of the villainous face—holding a bloody knife.

'I want a word or two with you,' Prokofy began. 'This business can't go on because you can see for yourself that this here vale of tears is going to get you and us a bad name. Ma's too sorry for you of course to say anything unpleasant about your sister moving to other quarters on account of her being in the family way. But I don't want her around any more because her behaviour is something what I can't approve of.'

I took the point and left his stall. That day my sister and I moved to Radish's place. We could not afford a cab, so we walked and I carried our stuff in a bundle on my back. My sister did not carry anything, but kept panting and coughing and asking if we would get there soon.

XIX

A LETTER did arrive from Masha in the end.

My dear, kind M. (she wrote), my good, gentle 'angel of mercy', as the old painter calls you, goodbye. Father and I are going to America for the Exhibition. In a few days I shall see the ocean—it's dreadful to think how far from Dubechnya. It's distant and unfathomable like the sky and I so long to go there, to be free. I feel on top of the world, I'm crazy—you can see for yourself what a muddle this letter is.

My dear, please give me my freedom. Please hurry up and break the thread that still binds us together. Meeting you and knowing you was like a ray of sunshine that lit up my existence. But becoming your wife was a mistake, as you see yourself. The thought of my mistake depresses me. I beg you on my knees, my generous darling, please, please send a wire quickly before I sail over the ocean. Say you agree to put right our common mistake and remove this one stone which weighs down my wings. My father will make the arrangements and he promises not to bother you too much with formalities. So may I be free to do as I like? Do say yes.

Be happy and God bless you. Forgive me my sins.

I'm alive and well. I spend money like water and do lots of silly things. I thank God every minute of the day that a bad woman like me has no children. I'm still singing and doing rather well at it, but my singing isn't just a hobby. No, it's my haven, my cell where I retreat to find peace. King David had a ring with the inscription, 'All things pass'. When I'm sad those words cheer me up, and when I'm cheerful they make me sad. I've got myself a ring like that with Hebrew letters on it, a talisman to prevent me being carried away too much. Things pass. Life too will pass, so one doesn't need anything. Perhaps one needs nothing but a sense of freedom, because when someone's free he needs nothing, nothing at all. So do break the thread. My best love to you and your sister. Forgive and forget

your M.

My sister lay in one room and Radish, who had been ill again and was getting better, lay in another. Just as I received this letter my sister went quietly into the painter's room, sat down beside him and started reading aloud. She read him Ostrovsky or Gogol every day, and he solemnly listened, gazing into space, not laughing.

'All things are possible, indeed they are,' he muttered from time to time with a shake of his head.

When a play portrayed something base or ugly, he jabbed his finger at the book. 'That's lies for you,' he would gloat. 'That's what lying does for you.'

He liked plays for their plot, their moral and their complex artistic structure, and was full of admiration for the authors, whom he never named, always referring to them as 'he'. ('How neatly he tied all that up.')

This time my sister only read one page quietly and could not go on because her voice gave out. Radish took her arm and moved his parched lips.

'The soul of the righteous man is white and smooth as chalk,' he said in hoarse, barely audible tones. 'But the soul of the sinful man is like unto pumice-stone. The soul of the righteous man is like clear oil, but the soul of the sinful man is like tar. We must labour, we must mourn, we must fall sick,' he went on.

'He who labours not and mourns not, shall not inherit the Kingdom of Heaven. Woe, woe unto them that are well fed, woe unto the mighty, woe unto the rich, woe unto the money-lenders, for the Kingdom of Heaven is not theirs. Grass doth wither, iron doth rust. . . .'

'And lies do rot the soul,' my sister went on with a laugh.

I read the letter again. Then the soldier came into the kitchen—the one who twice a week brought us tea, French bread and grouse, all smelling of scent, from an unknown source. I was out of work and had to stay at home for days on end, and whoever sent us those rolls must have known that we were hard up.

I heard my sister talking to the soldier and laughing happily. Then she ate a roll, lying down.

'Anyuta Blagovo and I,' said she, 'knew from the start that you were right to turn down your job and become a painter. But we feared to say so out loud. Tell me, what is it that stops people saying what they think—what is this strange compulsion? Take Anyuta Blagovo. She loves you, adores you and knows that you're absolutely right. She loves me like a sister and knows I'm doing the right thing too—and envies me, I dare say, in her heart of hearts. But something stops her visiting us. She shuns us and she's scared.'

My sister folded her arms on her breast.

'If you only knew how she loves you!' she said excitedly. 'I'm the only person she's told about her love—and then secretly, in the dark. She used to take me to a dark avenue in the garden and whisper how precious you are to her. She'll never marry because she loves you, you'll see. Aren't you sorry for her?'

'Yes.'

'It's she who sent the bread. She really is a funny girl. Why make such a secret of it? I was funny and silly myself once, but now I've left that place and I'm afraid of no one. I think and say what I like and I'm happy. Living at home I had no idea what happiness was, but now I wouldn't change places with a queen.'

Blagovo arrived. He had obtained his higher medical degree and was now staying with his father in our town. He was on holiday and said he was soon going to St. Petersburg, as he wanted to work on inoculation for typhus—and cholera too, I think. He meant to finish his training abroad and then become a professor. He had left the army and wore generously cut cheviot jackets, very wide trousers and superb ties. My sister was crazy about his pins and studs and the red silk handkerchief that he kept in his top jacket pocket—as a jaunty touch, presumably. Having nothing else to do one day, we tried to remember how many suits he had, and decided that it was at least ten.

He obviously still loved my sister, but never, even in jest, suggested taking her to St. Petersburg or abroad. I could not see what was going to happen to her if she survived—or to her child. But she was forever mooning about and gave the future no serious thought. She said that he should go where he liked. So long as he was happy he might even desert her. What had already happened was enough for her.

When he came to see us, he usually listened most carefully to her chest and saw that she drank milk with drops in it. He did the same this time, listening to her chest and making her drink her glass of milk with something in it that made our rooms smell of creosote afterwards.

'There's a good girl,' he said, taking the glass from her. 'You shouldn't talk too much. You've been chattering away like nobody's business lately. Try not to talk, will you?'

She laughed. Then he came into Radish's room where I was sitting and gave me a friendly pat on the shoulder.

He bent over the sick man. 'Well, how are things, old fellow?'

'Well, sir . . .' said Radish, moving his lips slowly. 'Permit me to report, sir. . . . We none of us live for ever, it's all God's will. . . . Permit me to tell you the truth . . . you won't go to heaven, sir.'

'Never mind,' joked the doctor. 'Someone has to go to hell.'

Suddenly a strange feeling came over me and I seemed to be dreaming. It was a winter night and I was in the slaughter-house yard, standing by Prokofy. He smelt of pepper vodka. I tried to pull myself together and rubbed my eyes, whereupon I saw myself going for my interview with the Governor. Nothing of this sort has ever happened to me before or since and I can only put down these strange, dreamlike memories to nervous exhaustion. I lived through the scene at the slaughter-house and my interview with the Governor, dimly conscious all the time that none of it was real.

When I came to, I found myself outside, standing by a street-lamp with the doctor.

'Oh, what a miserable business,' he was saying, with tears streaming down his cheeks. 'She's so cheerful, always laughing, full of hope. But her condition's hopeless, old boy. Your friend Radish hates me, thinks I've treated her badly and is always trying to bring it home to me. He's right in his way, but I have my own point of view too and don't regret the past a bit. One must love—we should all love, shouldn't we? There'd be no life without love, and anyone who fears love and runs away from it, well, he's not free.'

He gradually turned to other topics, talking about science and his thesis, which had gone down well in St. Petersburg. He was quite carried away as he talked, forgetting my sister, his own troubles and me. Life fascinated him.

'Masha has America and her ring with the inscription on it,' I thought, 'and he has his higher degree and academic career. Only my sister and I are stuck in the old rut.'

I said goodbye to him and went up to a street-lamp to read the letter again. And I remembered her so vividly coming to see me at the mill one spring morning and lying down with her fur jacket over her, wanting to look like a simple peasant woman. Then there had been another morning when we were pulling a fish-trap out of the water and huge raindrops fell on us from the riverside willows and made us laugh. . . .

The lights were out in our house in Great Dvoryansky Street. I climbed the fence and went through the back door into the kitchen, as in the old days, to fetch a lantern. There was no one in the kitchen. By the stove the samovar was hissing in readiness for Father. 'Who pours out Father's tea these days?' I wondered. I took the lantern, went out to the shack, made up a bed from old newspapers and lay down. The pegs on the walls looked as stern as ever and their shadows flickered. It was cold. I felt as if my sister was just about to come in with my supper, but then I suddenly remembered that she was ill in bed in Radish's house, and it seemed strange that I should have climbed the fence and be lying in this unheated shed. My head was swimming and grotesque visions passed before my eyes.

The bell rang. I remembered how it sounded from child-hood—first the wire rustling on the wall, then the short, plaintive note in the kitchen. Father must have come back from his club. I got up and went into the kitchen. When Aksinya the cook saw me she threw up her arms and burst out crying for some reason.

'My boy!' she said softly. 'My dear! Oh goodness me!'

In her agitation she started crumpling her apron. There were gallon jars of berries in vodka standing in the window. I poured out a cupful and gulped it down, for I badly needed a drink.

Aksinya had just scrubbed the table and benches, and the kitchen smelt like any other bright, cosy kitchen where the cook keeps things spick and span. This smell and the chirp of crickets always attracted us children to the kitchen and put us in the mood for fairy-tales and card games. . . .

'But where's Cleopatra?' asked Aksinya softly, flustered and holding her breath. 'And where's your cap, my dear? I hear your wife's gone off to St. Petersburg.'

She had worked for us in Mother's time and used to bath Cleopatra and me. She still thought of us as children who had to be told what to do. In about a quarter of an hour she had put to me all the arguments which, wise old servant that she was, she had been piling up in the quiet of the kitchen since our last meeting. She said that the doctor could be made to marry Cleopatra—he only needed to be given a bit of a fright. And then, if the application was drawn up properly, the bishop would dissolve his first marriage. She said that I should sell Dubechnya without telling my wife and put the money into a bank account of my own, and that Father might forgive my sister and me if we threw ourselves at his feet and asked him properly. She said that we should offer a special service to Our Lady. . . .

'Now go and talk to him, dear,' she said, hearing Father cough. 'Go and talk to him—bow down before him. Your head won't fall off.'

I went. Father was sitting at a table sketching out the plan of a villa with Gothic windows and a fat turret like the watch-tower of a fire-station, something thoroughly stick-in-the-mud and second-rate. I went into his study and stood where I could see this sketch. Why I had called on Father I did not know, but when I saw his lean face, red neck and shadow on the wall, I remember, I wanted to throw my arms round his neck and prostrate myself before him as Aksinya had instructed me. But the sight of that villa with its Gothic windows and fat turret held me back.

'Good evening,' I said.

He looked at me and immediately looked down at his sketch.

'What do you want?' he asked after a while.

'I've come to say that my sister's very ill. She can't live long,' I added in a hollow voice.

'What do you expect?' sighed Father, taking off his spectacles and putting them on the table. 'You reap what you have sown.'

'What you have sown,' he repeated, getting up from the table, 'you reap. Remember coming to see me two years ago? In this very room I asked you, implored you to leave the path of error. I reminded you of duty, honour, and what you owe to those ancestors whose traditions we should hold sacred. And did you listen to me? You scorned my advice, stubbornly clinging to your false ideas. Furthermore, you also led your sister into your own evil ways and made her lose her virtue and all sense of shame. Now you're both in trouble. Well, what do you expect? What you have sown you reap!'

He walked up and down the study as he spoke, probably thinking that I had come to apologize—perhaps beg for my sister and myself. Cold and shivering feverishly, I could hardly find my voice.

'I must ask you to remember something too,' I said hoarsely. 'On this very spot I implored you to try and see my point of view and help me decide how to live and what to live for. You replied by bringing in our ancestors and my great-uncle the poet. Now I tell you your only daughter's dying, you're off about ancestors and traditions again. . . . How can you be so frivolous in your old age when you haven't all that long to live—some five or ten years perhaps?'

'What have you come for?' asked my father sternly, obviously offended at being called frivolous.

'I don't know. I love you and I'm sorry we're so far apart, more sorry than I can say—so I came. I still love you, but my sister's finished with you. She can't forgive you and she never will. Your very name fills her with disgust for the past and for life itself.'

'Well, whose fault is that?' Father shouted. 'It's all your doing, you scoundrel.'

'All right,' I said, 'we'll call it my fault. I admit I'm very much to blame. But why is your way of life—which you think binding on us too—so dismal and mediocre? You've been building houses for thirty years now, but why do none of them contain people who could tell me how to live decently? There isn't an honest man in the whole town! Those houses of yours are sinks of iniquity where mothers and daughters have their lives made a misery and children are tortured.

'My poor mother!' I went on frantically. 'My poor sister! A man must dull his wits with vodka, cards and tittle-tattle, must be a vile hypocrite, must have spent dozens of years drawing up plan after plan, not to notice the horrors lurking inside these houses. Our town's been here for hundreds of years and all that time it hasn't given the country one useful citizen! Not one! Anything the least bit bright and lively has pretty short shrift from you! This is a town of shopkeepers, publicans, office-clerks and hypocrites. It's no use to anyone. If the earth suddenly swallowed it up, no one would care.'

'I won't listen to you, you scoundrel!' said Father, taking a ruler from the table. 'You're drunk! How dare you come and see your father in this condition! I tell you for the last time—and you can pass it on to your depraved sister—you'll get nothing out of me. I've hardened my heart to my disobedient children and if they suffer for their disobedience and obstinacy, they'll have no sympathy from me. You can go back where you came from! You were sent to punish me—such was God's will—but I suffer this affliction humbly. Like Job, I take comfort in my sufferings and in unceasing labour. Mend your ways or never darken my doors again. I'm a fair-minded man and I tell you all this for your own good. And if you want it to do you any good, just you remember these words—and what I said before—for as long as you live.'

I gave up and left. What happened that night or the next day I do not remember.

I am told that I wandered the streets bareheaded, staggering and singing noisily, with crowds of boys running after me and shouting, 'Better-than-nothing! Better-than-nothing!'

XX

IF I wanted to have a ring I should choose the inscription, 'Nothing passes away'. In my view nothing does pass away entirely and the smallest step we take influences our present and future.

My experiences have not been in vain. The townspeople have been touched by my great misfortunes and the way I have put up with them. No one calls me 'Better-than-nothing' any more and they do not laugh at me or throw water at me when I go past the shops. They are used to my being a worker and no longer find it funny if a gentleman carries paint-buckets and puts in windows. Far from it—they like giving me jobs and I rate as a first-class workman these days and the best contractor after Radish. His health is better and he still paints belfry domes without scaffolding, but cannot manage his men any more. I run round town looking for jobs instead of him these days. I hire men and fire them and borrow money at high interest. Now that I am a contractor myself, I see how a man can run round town for three days chasing up roofers for the sake of some twopenny-halfpenny job. People are civil to me and speak to me politely. When I work on a house I am given tea and they send to ask if I want a meal. Children and girls often come and give me sad, quizzical looks.

One day I was working in the Governor's garden, painting a summer-house to look like marble. The Governor was taking a stroll and came into the summer-house. Having nothing better to do, he started talking to me and I reminded him how he had once summoned me for interview. He stared at my face for a moment, then opened his mouth like the letter O and shrugged his shoulders.

'I don't remember,' he said.

I look older now. I do not talk much, I am austere and stern, and I rarely laugh. They say that I have begun to look like Radish and, like him, bore my mates with my futile exhortations.

Masha Dolzhikov, my ex-wife, now lives abroad and her father the engineer is building a line somewhere in eastern Russia and buying estates there. Dr. Blagovo is abroad too. Dubechnya has reverted to Mrs. Cheprakov, who bought it back after getting the engineer to knock twenty per cent off the price. Moses wears a bowler hat these days. He often comes to town on business in a racing trap and stops by the bank. He is said to have bought up a mortgaged estate and is always enquiring about Dubechnya at the bank because he means to buy that as well.

The wretched Ivan Cheprakov drifted about town for some time doing nothing, always on the booze. I did try to fix him up with us and he joined us for a time painting roofs and putting in windows. He rather took to it actually and stole his linseed-oil, asked for his tips and drank his dram like any other self-respecting decorator. But he soon grew thoroughly fed up with the work and went back to Dubechnya. Later on some of the lads told me that he had been trying to get them to help him kill Moses one night and rob Mrs. Cheprakov.

Father has aged a great deal. He is very bent and goes for walks near his house in the evenings. I never visit him.

During the cholera epidemic Prokofy dosed shopkeepers with pepper vodka and tar and charged them for it. I read in our newspaper that he had been flogged for making nasty remarks about doctors while sitting in his meat stall. His shop-boy Nikolka died of cholera. Karpovna is still alive, and she still loves and fears her Prokofy. When she sees me she shakes her head sadly. 'You'll come to a bad end!' she sighs.

Every working day I am at it from morning to night. On holidays, in fine weather, I pick up my little niece—my sister expected a boy, but had a girl—and walk slowly to the cemetery. There I stand or sit, gazing for a while at the grave so dear to me and tell the little girl that her mother lies there.

I sometimes find Anyuta Blagovo at the graveside. We greet each other and stand in silence or talk about Cleopatra and her little girl and how sad life is. Then we leave the cemetery and walk along in silence and she walks more slowly so as to be with me as long as possible. The little girl, gay and happy, screwing up her eyes in the bright sunlight and laughing, holds out her hands to Anyuta. We stop and both fondle the dear child.

As we enter the town Anyuta Blagovo, flushed and agitated, says goodbye to me. Then she goes her way alone—dignified and prim. No one in the street would think to look at her that she had just been walking at my side and had even fondled the little girl.

Joseph Conrad

HEART OF DARKNESS

1902

TEODOR JOSEF KONRAD KORZENIOWSKI (1857–1924), who adopted the name 'Joseph Conrad' after settling in England, was born of Polish peasant parents living in the Ukraine. His father's political views caused friction with the Russian government, who effectively ruled the Ukraine, and the family suffered a period of exile in Arctic Russia, where Conrad's mother died when he was seven. He and his father returned to Poland, but shortly afterwards his father also died, and Conrad was brought up by an uncle. Always fascinated by tales of a seafaring life, at the age of sixteen Conrad found his way to Marseilles, joined the crew of a French ship, and began a twenty-year career at sea in the course of which he became a British subject (1886) and a master mariner. In 1894 he settled in England and began his work as an author, at first against a background of slow recognition and financial worry. His work was soon noticed by good judges, including many eminent men of letters, but it was nearly another twenty years before the public began to buy his books in sufficient quantities to give him a secure living. In 1913 his novel *Chance* had a success in New York, later repeated in London, and the book-buying public took him up as a result; it is a love story, unusually for Conrad, as well as a tale of adventure at sea.

The hesitation of the English-speaking public before the work of Conrad is to some extent understandable. English was his third language, so that his handling of it, though perfectly correct, was always slightly inflexible. He always claimed that English was an impossible language to learn because the words were loaded with so much suggestion, familiar only to native and lifelong speakers; his favourite example was 'oaken'—the equivalent word in any other language would simply mean 'made of oak' but in English it shimmered with indefinable overtones. (At least, it did then. Does it still do so now?) Not only that, Conrad's whole approach to the novel is un-English; perhaps it is not surprising that his first success was in America. English novelists, like English people, feel more at home with characters real or imagined when they can set them firmly in their social class, and it is a rare English novel that does not convey very clearly, from the beginning, what class the various characters belong to and how it influences them and their behaviour. Conrad never seems to consider such matters; many of his stories are set on shipboard, where the hierarchy of ship's discipline overrides all other considerations, or in the remote and lawless places of the earth, where the human being, bereft of any guidance from habit and tradition, faced often with extreme situations, must draw on the resources of his own nature with no help from any surrounding structure.

The result was a kind of novel rather rare in the nineteenth century but more common in the twentieth, partly owing to the influence of Conrad himself: the story of violence and adventure which does not stay within the neatly ruled lines of the slam-bang action story but, working with the same kind of plot, fills in the emotional and moral dimensions very much as a play like *Hamlet* fills in those dimensions in the crude framework of the Elizabethan revenge play. The novels of Hemingway, Graham Greene, or Georges Simenon would probably not have been quite as they are if Conrad had not existed.

Heart of Darkness is one of his most universally admired works.

I

THE *Nellie*, a cruising yawl, swung to her anchor without a flutter of the sails, and was at rest. The flood had made, the wind was nearly calm, and being bound down the river, the only thing for it was to come to and wait for the turn of the tide.

The sea-reach of the Thames stretched before us like the beginning of an interminable waterway. In the offing the sea and the sky were welded together without a joint, and in the luminous space the tanned sails of the barges drifting up with the tide seemed to stand still in red clusters of canvas sharply peaked, with gleams of varnished spirits. A haze rested on the low shores that ran out to sea in vanishing flatness. The air was dark above Gravesend, and farther back still seemed condensed into a mournful gloom, brooding motionless over the biggest, and the greatest, town on earth.

The Director of Companies was our captain and our host. We four affectionately watched his back as he stood in the bows looking to seaward. On the whole river there was nothing that looked half so nautical. He resembled a pilot, which to a seaman is trustworthiness personified. It was difficult to realize his work was not out there in the luminous estuary, but behind him, within the brooding gloom.

Between us there was, as I have already said somewhere, the bond of the sea. Besides holding our hearts together through long periods of separation, it had the effect of making us tolerant of each other's yarns—and even convictions. The Lawyer—the best of old fellows—had, because of his many years and many virtues, the only cushion on deck, and was lying on the only rug. The Accountant had brought out already a box of dominoes, and was toying architecturally with the bones. Marlow sat cross-legged right aft, leaning against the mizzen-mast. He had sunken cheeks, a yellow complexion, a straight back, an ascetic aspect, and, with his arms dropped, the palms of hands outwards, resembled an idol. The director, satisfied the anchor had good hold, made his way aft and sat down amongst us. We exchanged a few words lazily. Afterwards there was silence on board the yacht. For some reason or other we did not begin that game of dominoes. We felt meditative, and fit for nothing but placid staring. The day was ending in a serenity of still and exquisite brilliance. The water shone pacifically; the sky, without a speck, was a benign immensity of unstained light; the very mist on the Essex marshes was like a gauzy and radiant fabric, hung from the wooded rises inland, and draping the low shores in diaphanous folds. Only the gloom to the west, brooding over the upper reaches, became more sombre every minute, as if angered by the approach of the sun.

And at last, in its curved and imperceptible fall, the sun sank low, and from glowing white changed to a dull red without rays and without heat, as if about to go out suddenly, stricken to death by the touch of that gloom brooding over a crowd of men.

Forthwith a change came over the waters, and the serenity became less brilliant but more profound. The old river in its broad reach rested unruffled at the decline of day, after ages of good service done to the race that peopled its banks, spread out in the tranquil dignity of a waterway leading to the uttermost ends of the earth. We looked at the venerable stream not in the vivid flush of a short day that comes and departs for ever, but in the august light of abiding memories. And indeed nothing is easier for a man who has, as the phrase goes, 'followed the sea' with reverence and affection, than to evoke the great spirit of the past upon the lower reaches of the Thames. The tidal current runs to and fro in its unceasing service, crowded with memories of men and ships it had borne to the rest of home or to the battles of the sea. It had known and served all the men of whom the nation is proud, from Sir Francis Drake to Sir John Franklin, knights all, titled and untitled—the great knights-errant of the sea. It had borne all the ships whose names are like jewels flashing in the night of time, from the *Golden Hind* returning with her round flanks full of treasure, to be visited by the Queen's Highness and thus pass out of the gigantic tale, to the *Erebus* and *Terror*, bound on other conquests—and that never returned. It had known the ships and the men. They had sailed from Deptford, from Greenwich, from Erith—the adventurers and the settlers; kings' ships and the ships of men on 'Change; captains, admirals, the dark 'interlopers' of the Eastern trade, and the commissioned 'generals' of East India fleets. Hunters for gold or pursuers of fame, they all had gone out on that stream, bearing the sword, and often the torch, messengers of the might within the land, bearers of a spark from the sacred fire. What greatness had not floated on the ebb of that river into the mystery of an unknown earth! . . . The dreams of men, the seed of commonwealths, the germs of empires.

The sun set; the dusk fell on the stream, and lights began to appear along the shore. The Chapman lighthouse, a three-legged thing erect on a mud-flat, shone strongly. Lights of ships moved in the fairway—a great stir of lights going up and going down. And farther west on the upper reaches the place of the monstrous town was still marked ominously on the sky, a brooding gloom in sunshine, a lurid glare under the stars.

'And this also,' said Marlow suddenly, 'has been one of the dark places of the earth.'

He was the only man of us who still 'followed the sea.' The worst that could be said of him was that he did not represent his class. He was a seaman, but he was a wanderer, too, while most seamen lead, if one may so express it, a sedentary life. Their minds are of the stay-at-home order, and their home is always with them—the ship; and so is their country—the sea. One ship is very much like another, and the sea is always the same. In the immutability of their surroundings the foreign shores, the foreign faces, the changing immensity of life, glide past, veiled not by a sense of mystery but by a slightly disdainful ignorance; for there is nothing mysterious to a seaman unless it be the sea itself, which is the mistress of his existence and as inscrutable as Destiny. For the rest, after his hours of work, a casual stroll or a casual spree on shore suffices to unfold for him the secret of a whole continent, and generally he finds the secret not worth knowing. The yarns of seamen have a direct simplicity, the whole meaning of which lies within the shell of a cracked nut. But Marlow was not typical (if his propensity to spin yarns be excepted), and to him the meaning of an episode was not inside like a kernel but outside, enveloping the tale which brought it out only as a glow brings out a haze, in the likeness of one of these misty haloes that sometimes are made visible by the spectral illumination of moonshine.

His remark did not seem at all surprising. It was just like Marlow. It was accepted in silence. No one took the trouble to grunt even; and presently he said, very slow—

'I was thinking of very old times, when the Romans first came here, nineteen hundred years ago—the other day. . . . Light came out of this river since—you say Knights? Yes; but it is like a running blaze on a plain, like a flash of lightning in the clouds. We live in the flicker—may it last as long as the old earth keeps rolling! But darkness was here yesterday. Imagine the feelings of a commander of a fine—what d'ye call 'em?—trireme in the Mediterranean, ordered suddenly to the north; run overland across the Gauls in a hurry; put in charge of one of these craft the legionaries—a wonderful lot of handy men they must have been, too—used to build, apparently by the hundred, in a month or two, if we may believe what we read. Imagine him here—the very end of the world, a sea the colour of lead, a sky the colour of smoke, a kind of ship about as rigid as a concertina—and going up this river with stores, or orders, or what you like. Sand-banks, marshes, forests, savages,—precious little to eat fit for a civilized man, nothing but Thames water to drink. No Falernian wine here, no going ashore. Here and there a military camp lost in a wilderness, like a needle in a bundle of hay—cold, fog, tempests, disease, exile, and death,—death skulking in the air, in the water, in the bush. They must have been dying like flies here. Oh, yes—he did it. Did it very well, too, no doubt, and without thinking much about it either, except afterwards to brag of what he had gone through in his time, perhaps. They were men enough to face the darkness. And perhaps he was cheered by keeping his eye on a chance of promotion to the fleet at Ravenna by-and-by, if he had good friends in Rome and survived the awful climate. Or think of a decent young citizen in a toga—perhaps too much dice, you know—coming out here in the train of some prefect, or tax-gatherer, or trader even, to mend his fortunes. Land in a swamp, march through the woods, and in some inland post feel the savagery, the utter savagery, had closed round him,—all that mysterious life of the wilderness that stirs in the forest, in the jungles, in the hearts of wild men. There's no initiation either into such mysteries. He has to live in the midst of the incomprehensible, which is also detestable. And it has a fascination, too, that goes to work upon him. The fascination of the abomination—you know, imagine the growing regrets, the longing to escape, the powerless disgust, the surrender, the hate.'

He paused.

'Mind,' he began again, lifting one arm from the elbow, the palm of the hand outwards, so that, with his legs folded before him, he had the pose of a Buddha preaching in European clothes and without a lotus-flower—'Mind, none of us would feel exactly like this. What saves us is efficiency—the devotion to efficiency. But these chaps were not much account, really. They were no colonists; their administration was merely a squeeze, and nothing more, I suspect. They were conquerors, and for that you want only brute force—nothing to boast of, when you have it, since your strength is just an accident arising from the weakness of others. They grabbed what they could get for the sake of what was to be got. It was just robbery with violence, aggravated murder on a great scale, and men going at it blind—as is very proper for those who tackle a darkness. The conquest of the earth, which mostly means the taking it away from those who have a different complexion or slightly flatter noses than ourselves, is not a pretty thing when you look into it too much. What redeems it is the idea only. An idea at the back of it; not a sentimental pretence but an idea; and an unselfish belief in the idea—something you can set up, and bow down before, and offer a sacrifice to. . . .'

He broke off. Flames glided in the river, small green flames, red flames, white flames, pursuing, overtaking, joining, crossing each other—then separating slowly or hastily. The traffic of the great city went on in the deepening night upon the sleepless river. We looked on, waiting patiently—there was nothing else to do till the end of the flood; but it was only after a long silence, when he said, in a hesitating voice, 'I suppose you fellows remember I did once turn fresh-water sailor for a bit,' that we knew we were fated, before the ebb began to run, to hear about one of Marlow's inconclusive experiences.

'I don't want to bother you much with what happened to me personally,' he began, showing in this remark the weakness of many tellers of tales who seem so often unaware of what their audience would best like to hear; 'yet to understand the effect of it on me you ought to know how I got out there, what I saw, how I went up that river to the place where I first met the poor chap. It was the farthest point of navigation and the culminating point of my experience. It seemed somehow to throw a kind of light on everything about me—and into my thoughts. It was sombre enough, too—and pitiful—not extraordinary in any way—not very clear either. No, not very clear. And yet it seemed to throw a kind of light.

'I had then, as you remember, just returned to London after a lot of Indian Ocean, Pacific, China Seas—a regular dose of the

East—six years or so, and I was loafing about, hindering you fellows in your work and invading your homes, just as though I had got a heavenly mission to civilize you. It was very fine for a time, but after a bit I did get tired of resting. Then I began to look for a ship—I should think the hardest work on earth. But the ships wouldn't even look at me. And I got tired of that game, too.

'Now when I was a little chap I had a passion for maps. I would look for hours at South America, or Africa, or Australia, and lose myself in all the glories of exploration. At that time there were many blank spaces on the earth, and when I saw one that looked particularly inviting on a map (but they all look that) I would put my finger on it and say, When I grow up I will go there. The North Pole was one of these places, I remember. Well, I haven't been there yet, and shall not try now. The glamour's off. Other places were scattered about the Equator, and in every sort of latitude all over the two hemispheres. I have been in some of them, and . . . well, we won't talk about that. But there was one yet—the biggest, the most blank, so to speak—that I had a hankering after.

'True, by this time it was not a blank space any more. It had got filled since my boyhood with rivers and lakes and names. It had ceased to be a blank space of delightful mystery—a white patch for a boy to dream gloriously over. It had become a place of darkness. But there was in it one river especially, a mighty big river, that you could see on the map, resembling an immense snake uncoiled, with its head in the sea, its body at rest curving afar over a vast country, and its tail lost in the depths of the land. And as I looked at the map of it in a shop-window, it fascinated me as a snake would a bird—a silly little bird. Then I remembered there was a big concern, a Company for trade on that river. Dash it all! I thought to myself, they can't trade without using some kind of craft on that lot of fresh water—steamboats! Why shouldn't I try to get charge of one? I went on along Fleet Street, but could not shake off the idea. The snake had charmed me.

'You understand it was a Continental concern, that Trading society; but I have a lot of relations living on the Continent, because it's cheap and not so nasty as it looks, they say.

'I am sorry to own I began to worry them. This was already a fresh departure for me. I was not used to get things that way, you know. I always went my own road and on my own legs where I had a mind to go. I wouldn't have believed it of myself; but, then—you see—I felt somehow I must get there by hook or by crook. So I worried them. The men said "My dear fellow," and did nothing. Then—would you believe it?—I tried the women. I, Charlie Marlow, set the women to work—to get a job. Heavens! Well, you see, the notion drove me. I had an aunt, a dear enthusiastic soul. She wrote: "It will be delightful. I am ready to do anything, anything for you. It is a glorious idea. I know the wife of a very high personage in the Administration, and also a man who had lots of influence with," etc., etc. She was determined to make no end of fuss to get me appointed skipper of a river steamboat, if such was my fancy.

'I got my appointment—of course; and I got it very quick. It appears the Company had received news that one of their captains had been killed in a scuffle with the natives. This was my chance, and it made me the more anxious to go. It was only months and months afterwards, when I made the attempt to recover what was left of the body, that I heard the original quarrel arose from a misunderstanding about some hens. Yes, two black hens. Fresleven—that was the fellow's name, a Dane—thought himself wronged somehow in the bargain, so he went ashore and started to hammer the chief of the village with a stick. Oh, it didn't surprise me in the least to hear this, and at the same time to be told that Fresleven was the gentlest, quietest creature that ever walked on two legs. No doubt he was; but he had been a couple of years already out there engaged in the noble cause, you know, and he probably felt the need at last of asserting his self-respect in some way. Therefore he whacked the old nigger mercilessly, while a big crowd of his people watched him, thunderstruck, till some man—I was told the chief's son—in desperation at hearing the old chap yell, made a tentative jab with a spear at the white man—and of course it went quite easy between the shoulder-blades. Then the whole population cleared into the forest, expecting all kinds of calamities to happen, while, on the other hand, the steamer Fresleven commanded left also in a bad panic, in charge of the engineer, I believe. Afterwards nobody seemed to trouble much about Fresleven's remains, till I got out and stepped into his shoes. I couldn't let it rest, though; but when an opportunity offered at last to meet my predecessor, the grass growing through his ribs was tall enough to hide his bones. They were all there. The supernatural being had not been touched after he fell. And the village was deserted, the huts gaped black, rotting, all askew within the fallen enclosures. A calamity had come to it, sure enough. The people had vanished. Mad terror had scattered them, men, women, and children, through the bush, and they had never returned. What became of the hens I don't know either. I should think the cause of progress got them, anyhow. However, through this glorious affair I got my appointment, before I had fairly begun to hope for it.

'I flew around like mad to get ready, and before forty-eight hours I was crossing the Channel to show myself to my employers, and sign the contract. In a very few hours I arrived in a city that always makes me think of a whited sepulchre. Prejudice no doubt. I had no difficulty in finding the Company's offices. It was the biggest thing in the town, and everybody I met was full of it. They were going to run an over-sea empire, and make no end of coin by trade.

'A narrow and deserted street in deep shadow, high houses, innumerable windows with venetian blinds, a dead silence, grass sprouting between the stones, imposing carriage archways right and left, immense double doors standing ponderously ajar. I slipped through one of these cracks, went up a swept and ungarnished staircase, as arid as a desert, and opened the first door I came to. Two women, one fat and the other slim, sat on straw-bottomed chairs, knitting black wool. The slim one got up and walked straight at me—still knitting with down-cast eyes—and only just as I began to think of getting out of her way, as you would for a somnambulist, stood still, and looked up. Her dress was as plain as an umbrella-cover, and she turned around without a word and preceded me into a waiting-room. I gave my name, and looked about. Deal table in the middle, plain chairs all round the walls, on one end a large shining map, marked with all the colours of a rainbow. There was a vast amount of red—good to see at any time, because one knows that some real work is done in there, a deuce of a lot of blue, a little green, smears of orange, and, on the East Coast, a purple patch, to show where the jolly pioneers of progress drink the jolly lager-beer. However, I wasn't going into any of these. I was going into the yellow. Dead in the centre. And the river was there—fascinating—deadly—like a snake. Ough! A door opened, a white-haired secretarial head, but wearing a compassionate expression, appeared, and a skinny forefinger beckoned me into the sanctuary. Its light was dim, and a heavy writing-desk squatted in the middle. From behind that structure came out an impression of pale plumpness in a frock-coat. The great man himself. He was five feet six, I should judge, and had his grip on the handle-end of ever so many millions. He shook hands, I fancy, murmured vaguely, was satisfied with my French. *Bon voyage.*

'In about forty-five seconds I found myself again in the waiting-room with the compassionate secretary, who, full of desolation and sympathy, made me sign some document. I believe I undertook amongst other things not to disclose any trade secrets. Well, I am not going to.

'I began to feel slightly uneasy. You know I am not used to such ceremonies, and there was something ominous in the atmosphere. It was just as though I had been let into some conspiracy—I don't know—something not quite right; and I was glad to get out. In the outer room the two women knitted black wool feverishly. People were arriving, and the younger one was walking back and forth introducing them. The old one sat on her chair. Her flat cloth slippers were propped up on a foot-warmer, and a cat reposed on her lap. She wore a starched white affair on her head, had a wart on one cheek, and silver-rimmed spectacles hung on the tip of her nose. She glanced at me above the glasses. The swift and indifferent placidity of that look troubled me. Two youths with foolish and cheery countenances were being piloted over, and she threw at them the same quick glance of unconcerned wisdom. She seemed to know all about them and about me, too. An eerie feeling came over me. She seemed uncanny and fateful. Often far away there I thought of these two, guarding the door of Darkness, knitting black wool as for a warm pall, one introducing, introducing continuously to the unknown, the other scrutinizing the cheery and foolish faces with unconcerned old eyes. *Ave!* Old knitter of black wool. *Morituri te salutant.* Not many of those she looked at ever saw her again—not half, by a long way.

'There was yet a visit to the doctor. "A simple formality," assured me the secretary, with an air of taking an immense part in all my sorrows. Accordingly a young chap wearing his hat over the left eyebrow, some clerk I suppose,—there must have been clerks in the business, though the house was as still as a house in a city of the dead—came from somewhere up-stairs, and led me forth. He was shabby and careless, with ink-stains on the sleeves of his jacket, and his cravat was large and billowy, under a chin shaped like the toe of an old boot. It was a little too early for the doctor, so I proposed a drink, and thereupon he developed a vein of joviality. As we sat over our vermouths he glorified the Company's business, and by-and-by I expressed casually my surprise at him not going out there. He became very cool and collected all at once. "I am not such a fool as I look, quoth Plato to his disciples," he said sententiously, emptied his glass with great resolution, and we rose.

'The old doctor felt my pulse, evidently thinking of something else the while. "Good, good for there," he mumbled, and then with a certain eagerness asked me whether I would let him measure my head. Rather surprised, I said Yes, when he produced a thing like calipers and got the dimensions back and front and every way, taking notes carefully. He was an unshaven little man in a threadbare coat like a gaberdine, with his feet in slippers, and I thought him a harmless fool. "I always ask leave, in the interests of science, to measure the crania of those going out there," he said. "And when they come back, too?" I asked. "Oh, I never see them," he remarked; "and, moreover, the changes take place inside, you know." He smiled, as if at some quiet joke. "So you are going out there. Famous. Interesting, too." He gave me a searching glance, and made another note. "Ever any madness in your family?" he asked, in a matter-of-fact tone. I felt very annoyed. "Is that question in the interests of science, too?" "It would be," he said, without taking notice of my irritation, "interesting for science to watch the mental changes of individuals, on the spot, but . . ." "Are you an alienist?" I interrupted. "Every doctor should be—a little," answered that original, imperturbably. "I have a little theory which you Messieurs who go out there must help me to prove. This is my share in the advantages my country shall reap from the possession of such a magnificent dependency. The mere wealth I leave to others. Pardon my questions, but you are the first Englishman coming under my observation . . ." I hastened to assure him I was not in the least typical. "If I were," said I, "I wouldn't be talking like this with you." "What you say is rather profound, and probably erroneous," he said, with a laugh. "Avoid irritation more than exposure to the sun. Adieu. How do you English say, eh? Good-bye. Ah! Good-bye. Adieu. In the tropics one must before everything keep calm." . . . He lifted a warning forefinger. . . . "*Du calme, du calme. Adieu.*"

'One thing more remained to do—say good-bye to my excellent

aunt. I found her triumphant. I had a cup of tea—the last decent cup of tea for many days—and in a room that most soothingly looked just as you would expect a lady's drawing-room to look, we had a long quiet chat by the fireside. In the course of these confidences it became quite plain to me I had been represented to the wife of the high dignitary, and goodness knows to how many more people besides, as an exceptional and gifted creature—a piece of good fortune for the Company—a man you don't get hold of every day. Good heavens! and I was going to take charge of a two-penny-half-penny river-steamboat with a penny whistle attached! It appeared, however, I was also one of the Workers, with a capital—you know. Something like an emissary of light, something like a lower sort of apostle. There had been a lot of such rot let loose in print and talk just about that time, and the excellent woman, living right in the rush of all that humbug, got carried off her feet. She talked about "weaning those ignorant millions from their horrid ways," till, upon my word, she made me quite uncomfortable. I ventured to hint that the Company was run for profit.

' "You forget, dear Charlie, that the labourer is worthy of his hire," she said, brightly. It's queer how out of touch with truth women are. They live in a world of their own, and there had never been anything like it, and never can be. It is too beautiful altogether, and if they were to set it up it would go to pieces before the first sunset. Some confounded fact we men have been living contentedly with ever since the day of creation would start up and knock the whole thing over.

'After this I got embraced, told to wear flannel, be sure to write often, and so on—and I left. In the street—I don't know why—a queer feeling came to me that I was an impostor. Odd thing that I, who used to clear out for any part of the world at twenty-four hours' notice, with less thought than most men give to the crossing of a street, had a moment—I won't say of hesitation, but of startled pause, before this commonplace affair. The best way I can explain it to you is by saying that, for a second or two, I felt as though, instead of going to the centre of a continent, I were about to set off for the centre of the earth.

'I left in a French steamer, and she called in every blamed port they have out there, for, as far as I could see, the sole purpose of landing soldiers and custom-house officers. I watched the coast.

Watching a coast as it slips by the ship is like thinking about an enigma. There it is before you—smiling, frowning, inviting, grand, mean, insipid, or savage, and always mute with an air of whispering. Come and find out. This one was almost featureless, as if still in the making, with an aspect of monotonous grimness. The edge of a colossal jungle, so dark-green as to be almost black, fringed with white surf, ran straight, like a ruled line, far, far away along a blue sea whose glitter was blurred by a creeping mist. The sun was fierce, the land seemed to glisten and drip with steam. Here and there greyish-whitish specks showed up clustered inside the white surf, with a flag flying above them perhaps. Settlements some centuries old, and still no bigger than pin-heads on the untouched expanse of their background. We pounded along, stopped, landed soldiers; went on, landed custom-house clerks to levy toll in what looked like a God-forsaken wilderness, with a tin shed and a flag-pole lost in it; landed more soldiers—to take care of the custom-house clerks, presumably. Some, I heard, got drowned in the surf; but whether they did or not, nobody seemed particularly to care. They were just flung out there, and on we went. Every day the coast looked the same, as though we had not moved; but we passed various places—trading places—with names like Gran' Bassam, Little Popo; names that seemed to belong to some sordid farce acted in front of a sinister back-cloth. The idleness of a passenger, my isolation amongst all these men with whom I had no point of contact, the oily and languid sea, the uniform sombreness of the coast, seemed to keep me away from the truth of things, within the toil of a mournful and senseless delusion. The voice of the surf heard now and then was a positive pleasure, like the speech of a brother. It was something natural, that had its reason, that had a meaning. Now and then a boat from the shore gave one a momentary contact with reality. It was paddled by black fellows. You could see from afar the white of their eyeballs glistening. They shouted, sang; their bodies streamed with perspiration; they had faces like grotesque masks—these chaps; but they had bone, muscle, a wild vitality, an intense energy of movement, that was as natural and true as the surf along their coast. They wanted no excuse for being there. They were a great comfort to look at. For a time I would feel I belonged still to a world of straightforward facts; but the feeling would not last long. Something would turn up to scare it away. Once, I remember, we came upon a man-of-war anchored off the coast. There wasn't even a shed there, and she was shelling the bush. It appears the French had one of their wars going on thereabouts. Her ensign drooped limp like a rag; the muzzles of the long six-inch guns stuck out all over the low hull; the greasy, slimy swell swung her up lazily and let her down, swaying her thin masts. In the empty immensity of earth, sky, and water, there she was, incomprehensible, firing into a continent. Pop, would go one of the six-inch guns; a small flame would dart and vanish, a little white smoke would disappear, a tiny projectile would give a feeble screech—and nothing happened. Nothing could happen. There was a touch of insanity in the proceeding, a sense of lugubrious drollery in the sight; and it was not dissipated by somebody on board assuring me earnestly there was a camp of natives—he called them enemies!—hidden out of sight somewhere.

'We gave her her letters (I heard the men in that lonely ship were dying of fever at the rate of three a-day) and went on. We called at some more places with farcical names, where the merry dance of death and trade goes on in a still and earthy atmosphere as of an overheated catacomb; all along the formless coast bordered by dangerous surf, as if Nature herself had tried to ward off intruders; in and out of rivers, streams of death in life, whose banks were rotting into mud, whose waters, thickened into slime, invaded the contorted mangroves, that seemed to writhe at us in the extremity of an impotent despair. Nowhere did we stop long enough to get a particularized impression, but the general sense of vague and oppressive wonder grew upon me. It was like a weary pilgrimage amongst hints for nightmares.

'It was upward of thirty days before I saw the mouth of the big river. We anchored off the seat of the government. But my work would not begin till some two hundred miles farther on. So as soon as I could I made a start for a place thirty miles higher up.

'I had my passage on a little sea-going steamer. Her captain was a Swede, and knowing me for a seaman, invited me on the bridge. He was a young man, lean, fair, and morose, with lanky hair and a shuffling gait. As we left the miserable little wharf, he tossed his head contemptuously at the shore. "Been living there?" he asked. I said, "Yes." "Fine lot these government chaps—are they not?" he went on, speaking English with great precision and considerable bitterness. "It is funny what some people will do for a few francs a month. I wonder what becomes of that kind when it goes up country?" I said to him I expected to see that soon. "So-o-o!" he exclaimed. He shuffled athwart, keeping one eye ahead vigilantly. "Don't be too sure," he continued. "The other day I took up a man who hanged himself on the road. He was a Swede, too." "Hanged himself! Why, in God's name?" I cried. He kept on looking out watchfully. "Who knows? The sun too much for him, or the country perhaps."

'At last we opened a reach. A rocky cliff appeared, mounds of turned-up earth by the shore, houses on a hill, others with iron roofs, amongst a waste of excavations, or hanging to the declivity. A continuous noise of the rapids above hovered over this scene of inhabited devastation. A lot of people, mostly black and naked, moved about like ants. A jetty projected into the river. A blinding sunlight drowned all this at times in a sudden recrudescence of glare. "There's your company's station," said the Swede, pointing to three wooden barrack-like structures on the rocky slope. "I will send your things up. Four boxes did you say? So. Farewell."

'I came upon a boiler wallowing in the grass, then found a path leading up the hill. It turned aside for the boulders, and also for an undersized railway-truck lying there on its back with its wheels in the air. One was off. The thing looked as dead as the carcass of some animal. I came upon more pieces of decaying machinery, a stack of rusty rails. To the left a clump of trees made a shady spot, where dark things seemed to stir feebly. I blinked, the path was steep. A horn tooted to the right, and I saw the black people run. A heavy and dull detonation shook the ground, a puff of smoke came out of the cliff, and that was all. No change appeared on the face of the rock. They were building a railway. The cliff was not in the way or anything; but this objectless blasting was all the work going on.

'A slight clinking behind me made me turn my head. Six black men advanced in a file, toiling up the path. They walked erect and slow, balancing small baskets full of earth on their heads, and the clink kept time with their footsteps. Black rags were wound round their loins, and the short ends behind waggled to and fro like tails. I could see every rib, the joints of their limbs were like knots in a rope; each had an iron collar on his neck, and all were connected together with a chain whose bights swung between them, rhythmically clinking. Another report from the cliff made me think suddenly of that ship of war I had seen firing into a continent. It was the same kind of ominous voice; but these men could by no stretch of imagination be called enemies. They were called criminals, and the outraged law, like the bursting shells, had come to them, an insoluble mystery from the sea. All their meagre breasts panted together, the violently dilated nostrils quivered, the eyes stared stonily up-hill. They passed me within six inches, without a glance, with that complete, deathlike indifference of unhappy savages. Behind this raw matter one of the reclaimed, the product of the new forces at work, strolled despondently, carrying a rifle by its middle. He had a uniform jacket with one button off, and seeing a white man on the path, hoisted his weapon to his shoulder with alacrity. This was simple prudence, white men being so much alike at a distance that he could not tell who I might be. He was speedily reassured, and with a large, white, rascally grin, and a glance at his charge, seemed to take me into partnership in his exalted trust. After all, I also was a part of the great cause of these high and just proceedings.

'Instead of going up, I turned and descended to the left. My idea was to let that chain-gang get out of sight before I climbed the hill. You know I am not particularly tender; I've had to strike and to fend off. I've had to resist and to attack sometimes—that's only one way of resisting—without counting the exact cost, according to the demands of such sort of life as I had blundered into. I've seen the devil of violence, and the devil of greed, and the devil of hot desire; but, by all the stars! these were strong, lusty, red-eyed devils, that swayed and drove men—men, I tell you. But as I stood on this hillside, I foresaw that in the blinding sunshine of that land I would become acquainted with a flabby, pretending, weak-eyed devil of a rapacious and pitiless folly. How insidious he could be, too, I was only to find out several months later and a thousand miles farther. For a moment I stood appalled, as though by a warning. Finally I descended the hill, obliquely, towards the trees I had seen.

'I avoided a vast artificial hole somebody had been digging on the slope, the purpose of which I found it impossible to divine. It wasn't a quarry or a sandpit, anyhow. It was just a hole. It might have been connected with the philanthropic desire of giving the criminals something to do. I don't know. Then I nearly fell into a very narrow ravine, almost no more than a scar in the hillside. I discovered that a lot of imported drainage-pipes for the settlement had been tumbled in there. There wasn't one that was not broken.

It was a wanton smash-up. At last I got under the trees. My purpose was to stroll into the shade for a moment; but no sooner within than it seemed to me I had stepped into the gloomy circle of some Inferno. The rapids were near, and an uninterrupted, uniform, headlong, rushing noise filled the mournful stillness of the grove, where not a breath stirred, not a leaf moved, without a mysterious sound—as though the tearing pace of the launched earth had suddenly become audible.

'Black shapes crouched, lay, sat between the trees leaning against the trunks, clinging to the earth, half coming out, half effaced within the dim light, in all the attitudes of pain, abandonment, and despair. Another mine on the cliff went off, followed by a slight shudder of the soil under my feet. The work was going on. The work! And this was the place where some of the helpers had withdrawn to die.

'They were dying slowly—it was very clear. They were not enemies, they were not criminals, they were nothing earthly now,—nothing but black shadows of disease and starvation, lying confusedly in the greenish gloom. Brought from all the recesses of the coast in all the legality of time contracts, lost in uncongenial surroundings, fed on unfamiliar food, they sickened, became inefficient, and were then allowed to crawl away and rest. These moribund shapes were free as air—and nearly as thin. I began to distinguish the gleam of the eyes under the trees. Then, glancing down, I saw a face near my hand. The black bones reclined at full length with one shoulder against the tree, and slowly the eyelids rose and the sunken eyes looked up at me, enormous and vacant, a kind of blind, white flicker in the depths of the orbs, which died out slowly. The man seemed young—almost a boy—but you know with them it's hard to tell. I found nothing else to do but to offer him one of my good Swede's ship's biscuits I had in my pocket. The fingers closed slowly on it and held—there was no other movement and no other glance. He had tied a bit of white worsted round his neck—why? Where did he get it? Was it a badge—an ornament—a charm—a propitiatory act? Was there any idea at all connected with it? It looked startling round his black neck, this bit of white thread from beyond the seas.

'Near the same tree two more bundles of acute angles sat with their legs drawn up. One, with his chin propped on his knees, stared at nothing, in an intolerable and appalling manner: his brother phantom rested its forehead, as if overcome with a great weariness; and all about others were scattered in every pose of contorted collapse, as in some picture of a massacre or a pestilence. While I stood horror-struck, one of these creatures rose to his hands and knees, and went off on all-fours towards the river to drink. He lapped out of his hand, then sat up in the sunlight, crossing his shins in front of him, and after a time let his woolly head fall on his breastbone.

'I didn't want any more loitering in the shade, and I made haste towards the station. When near the buildings I met a white man, in such an unexpected elegance of get-up that in the first moment I took him for a sort of vision. I saw a high starched collar, white cuffs, a light alpaca jacket, snowy trousers, a clean necktie, and varnished boots. No hat. Hair parted, brushed, oiled, under a green-lined parasol held in a big white hand. He was amazing, and had a penholder behind his ear.

'I shooks hands with this miracle, and I learned he was the Company's chief accountant, and that all the book-keeping was done at this station. He had come out for a moment, he said, "to get a breath of fresh air". The expression sounded wonderfully odd, with its suggestion of sedentary desk-life. I wouldn't have mentioned the fellow to you at all, only it was from his lips that I first heard the name of the man who is so indissolubly connected with the memories of that time. Moreover, I respected the fellow. Yes; I respected his collars, his vast cuffs, his brushed hair. His appearance was certainly that of a hairdresser's dummy; but in the great demoralization of the land he kept up his appearance. That's backbone. His starched collars and got-up shirt-fronts were achievements of character. He had been out nearly three years; and, later, I could not help asking him how he managed to sport such linen. He has just the faintest blush, and said modestly, "I've been teaching one of the native women about the station. It was difficult. She had a distaste for the work." Thus this man had verily accomplished something. And he was devoted to his books, which were in apple-pie order.

'Everything else in the station was in a muddle,—heads, things, buildings. Strings of dusty niggers with splay feet arrived and departed; a stream of manufactured goods, rubbishy cottons, beads, and brass-wire sent into the depths of darkness, and in return came a precious trickle of ivory.

'I had to wait in the station for ten days—an eternity. I lived in a hut in the yard, but to be out of the chaos I would sometimes get into the accountant's office. It was built of horizontal planks, and so badly put together that, as he bent over his high desk, he was barred from neck to heels with narrow strips of sunlight. There was no need to open the big shutter to see. It was hot there, too; big flies buzzed fiendishly, and did not sting, but stabbed. I sat generally on the floor, while, of faultless appearance (and even slightly scented), perching on a high stool, he wrote, he wrote. Sometimes he stood up for exercise. When a truckle-bed with a sick man (some invalid agent from up-country) was put in there, he exhibited a gentle annoyance. "The groans of this sick person," he said, "distract my attention. And without that it is extremely difficult to guard against clerical errors in this climate."

'One day he remarked, without lifting his head, "In the interior you will no doubt meet Mr. Kurtz." On my asking who Mr. Kurtz was, he said he was a first-class agent; and seeing my disappointment at this information, he added slowly, laying down his pen, "He is a very remarkable person." Further questions elicited from him that Mr. Kurtz was at present in charge of a trading post, a very important one, in the true ivory-country, at "the very bottom of there. Sends in as much ivory as all the others put together . . ." He began to write again. The sick man was too ill to groan. The flies buzzed in a great peace.

'Suddenly there was a growing murmur of voices and a great tramping of feet. A caravan had come in. A violent babble of uncouth sounds burst out on the other side of the planks. All the carriers were speaking together, and in the midst of the uproar the lamentable voice of the chief agent was heard "giving it up" tearfully for the twentieth time that day. . . . He rose slowly. "What a frightful row," he said. He crossed the room gently to look at the sick man, and returning, said to me, "He does not hear." "What! Dead?" I asked, startled. "No, not yet," he answered, with great composure. Then, alluding with a toss of the head to the tumult in the station-yard, "When one has got to make correct entries, one comes to hate those savages—hate them to the death." He remained thoughtful for a moment. "When you see Mr. Kurtz," he went on, "tell him from me that everything here"—he glanced at the desk—"is very satisfactory. I don't like to write to him—with those messengers of ours you never know who may get hold of your letter—at that Central Station." He stared at me for a moment with his mild, bulging eyes. "Oh, he will go far, very far," he began again. "He will be a somebody in the Administration before long. They, above—the Council in Europe, you know—mean him to be."

'He turned to his work. The noise outside had ceased, and presently in going out I stopped at the door. In the steady buzz of flies the homeward-bound agent was lying flushed and insensible; the other, bent over his books, was making correct entries of perfectly correct transactions; and fifty feet below the doorstep I could see the still tree-tops of the grove of death.

'Next day I left that station at last, with a caravan of sixty men, for a two-hundred-mile tramp.

'No use telling you much about that. Paths, paths, everywhere; a stamped-in network of paths spreading over the empty land, through long grass, through burnt grass, through thickets, down and up chilly ravines, up and down stony hills ablaze with heat; and a solitude, a solitude, nobody, not a hut. The population had cleared out a long time ago. Well, if a lot of mysterious niggers armed with all kinds of fearful weapons suddenly took to travelling on the road between Deal and Gravesend, catching the yokels right and left to carry heavy loads for them, I fancy every farm and cottage thereabouts would get empty very soon. Only here the dwellings were gone, too. Still I passed through several abandoned villages. There's something pathetically childish in the ruins of grass walls. Day after day, with the stamp and shuffle of sixty pair of bare feet behind me, each pair under a 60-lb. load. Camp, cook, sleep, strike camp, march. Now and then a carrier dead in harness, at rest in the long grass near the path, with an empty water-gourd and his long staff lying by his side. A great silence around and above. Perhaps on some quiet night the tremor of far-off drums, sinking, swelling, a tremor vast, faint; a sound weird, appealing, suggestive, and wild—and perhaps with as profound a meaning as the sound of bells in a Christian country. Once a white man in an unbuttoned uniform, camping on the path with an armed escort of lank Zanzibaris, very hospitable and festive—not to say drunk. Was looking after the upkeep of the road he declared. Can't say I saw any road or any upkeep, unless the body of a middle-aged negro, with a bullet-hole in the forehead, upon which I absolutely stumbled three miles farther on, may be considered as a permanent improvement. I had a white companion, too, not a bad chap, but rather too fleshy and with the exasperating habit of fainting on the hot hillsides, miles away from the least bit of shade and water. Annoying, you know, to hold your own coat like a parasol over a man's head while he is coming-to. I couldn't help asking him once what he meant by coming there at all. "To make money, of course. What do you think?" he said, scornfully. Then he got fever, and had to be carried in a hammock slung under a pole. As he weighed sixteen stone I had no end of rows with the carriers. They jibbed, ran away, sneaked off with their loads in the night—quite a mutiny. So, one evening, I made a speech in English with gestures, not one of which was lost to the sixty pairs of eyes before me, and the next morning I started the hammock off in front all right. An hour afterwards I came upon the whole concern wrecked in a bush—man, hammock, groans, blankets, horrors. The heavy pole had skinned his poor nose. He was very anxious for me to kill somebody, but there wasn't the shadow of a carrier near. I remember the old doctor,—"It would be interesting for science to watch the mental changes of individuals, on the spot." I felt I was becoming scientifically interesting. However, all that is to no purpose. On the fifteenth day I came in sight of the big river again, and hobbled into the Central Station. It was on a back water surrounded by scrub and forest, with a pretty border of smelly mud on one side, and on the three others enclosed by a crazy fence of rushes. A neglected gap was all the gate it had, and the first glance at the place was enough to let you see the flabby devil was running that show. White men with long staves in their hands appeared languidly from amongst the buildings, strolling up to take a look at me, and then retired out of sight somewhere. One of them, a stout, excitable chap with black moustaches, informed me with great volubility and many digressions, as soon as I told him who I was, that my steamer was at the bottom of the river. I was thunderstruck. What, how, why? Oh, it was "all right." The "manager himself" was there. All quite correct. "Everybody had behaved splendidly: splendidly!"—"you must," he said in agitation, "go and see the general manager at once. He is waiting!"

'I did not see the real significance of that wreck at once. I fancy I see it now but I am not sure—not at all. Certainly the affair was too stupid—when I think of it—to be altogether natural. Still. . . . But at the moment it presented itself simply as a confounded nuisance.

The steamer was sunk. They had started two days before in a sudden hurry up the river with the manager on board, in charge of some volunteer skipper, and before they had been out three hours they tore the bottom out of her on stones, and she sank near the south bank. I asked myself what I was to do there, now my boat was lost. As a matter of fact, I had plenty to do in fishing my command out of the river. I had to set about it the very next day. That, and the repairs when I brought the pieces to the station, took some months.

'My first interview with the manager was curious. He did not ask me to sit down after my twenty-mile walk that morning. He was commonplace in complexion, in feature, in manners, and in voice. He was of middle size and of ordinary build. His eyes, of the usual blue, were perhaps remarkably cold, and he certainly could make his glance fall on one as trenchant and heavy as an axe. But even at these times the rest of his person seemed to disclaim the intention. Otherwise there was only an indefinable, faint expression of his lips, something stealthy—a smile—not a smile—I remember it, but I can't explain. It was unconscious, this smile was, though just after he had said something it got intensified for an instant. It came at the end of his speeches like a seal applied on the words to make the meaning of the commonest phrase appear absolutely inscrutable. He was a common trader, from his youth up employed in these parts—nothing more. He was obeyed, yet he inspired neither love nor fear, nor even respect. He inspired uneasiness. That was it! Uneasiness. Not a definite mistrust—just uneasiness—nothing more. You have no idea how effective such a . . . a . . . faculty can be. He had no genius for organizing, for initiative, or for order even. That was evident in such things as the deplorable state of the station. He had no learning, and no intelligence. His position had come to him—why? Perhaps because he was never ill. . . . He had served three terms of three years out there. . . . Because triumphant health in the general rout of constitutions is a kind of power in itself. When he went home on leave he rioted on a large scale—pompously. Jack ashore—with a difference—in externals only. This one could gather from his casual talk. He originated nothing, he could keep the routine going—that's all. But he was great. He was great by this little thing that it was impossible to tell what could control such a man. He never gave that secret away. Perhaps there was nothing within him. Such a suspicion made one pause—for out there there were no external checks. Once when various tropical diseases had laid low almost every "agent" in the station, he was heard to say, "Men who come out here should have no entrails." He sealed the utterance with that smile of his, as though it had been a door opening into a darkness he had in his keeping. You fancied you had seen things—but the seal was on. When annoyed at meal-times by the constant quarrels of the white men about precedence, he ordered an immense round table to be made, for which a special house had to be built. This was the station's mess-room. Where he sat was the first place—the rest were nowhere. One felt this to be his unalterable conviction. He was neither civil nor uncivil. He was quiet. He allowed his "boy"—an overfed young negro from the coast—to treat the white men, under his very eyes, with provoking insolence.

'He began to speak as soon as he saw me. I had been very long on the road. He could not wait. Had to start without me. The up-river stations had to be relieved. There had been so many delays already that he did not know who was dead and who was alive, and how they got on—and so on, and so on. He paid no attention to my explanations, and, playing with a stick of sealing-wax, repeated several times that the situation was "very grave, very grave." There were rumours that a very important station was in jeopardy, and its chief, Mr. Kurtz, was ill. Hoped it was not true. Mr. Kurtz was. . . . I felt weary and irritable. Hang Kurtz, I thought. I interrupted him by saying I had heard of Mr. Kurtz on the coast. "Ah! So they talk of him down there," he murmured to himself. Then he began again, assuring me Mr. Kurtz was the best agent he had, an exceptional man, of the greatest importance to the Company; therefore I could understand his anxiety. He was, he said, "very, very uneasy." Certainly he fidgeted on his chair a good deal, exclaimed, "Ah, Mr. Kurtz!" broke the stick of sealing-wax and seemed dumbfounded by the accident. Next thing he wanted to know "how long it would take to" . . . I interrupted him again. Being hungry, you know, and kept on my feet, too, I was getting savage. "How could I tell?" I said. "I hadn't even seen the wreck yet—some months, no doubt." All this talk seemed to me so futile. "Some months," he said. "Well, let us say three months before we can make a start. Yes. That ought to do the affair." I flung out of his hut (he lived all alone in a clay hut with a sort of verandah) muttering to myself my opinion of him. He was a chattering idiot. Afterwards I took it back when it was borne in upon me startlingly with what extreme nicety he had estimated the time requisite for the "affair."

'I went to work the next day, turning, so to speak, my back on that station. In that way only it seemed to me I could keep my hold on the redeeming facts of life. Still, one must look about sometimes; and then I saw this station, these men strolling aimlessly about in the sunshine of the yard. I asked myself sometimes what it all meant. They wandered here and there with their absurd long staves in their hands, like a lot of faithless pilgrims bewitched inside a rotten fence. The word "ivory" rang in the air, was whispered, was sighed. You would think they were praying to it. A taint of imbecile rapacity blew through it all, like a whiff from some corpse. By Jove! I've never seen anything so unreal in my life. And outside, the silent wilderness surrounding this cleared speck on the earth struck me as something great and invincible, like evil or truth, waiting patiently for the passing away of this fantastic invasion.

'Oh, these months! Well, never mind. Various things happened. One evening a grass shed full of calico, cotton prints, beads, and I don't know what else, burst into a blaze so suddenly that you would have thought the earth had opened to let an avenging fire consume all that trash. I was smoking my pipe quietly by my dismantled steamer, and saw them all cutting capers in the light, with their arms lifted high, when the stout man with moustaches came tearing down to the river, a tin pail in his hand, assured me that everybody was "behaving splendidly, splendidly," dipped about a quart of water and tore back again. I noticed there was a hole in the bottom of his pail.

'I strolled up. There was no hurry. You see the thing had gone off like a box of matches. It had been hopeless from the very first. The flame had leaped high, driven everybody back, lighted up everything—and collapsed. The shed was already a heap of embers glowing fiercely. A nigger was being beaten near by. They said he had caused the fire in some way; be that as it may, he was screeching most horribly. I saw him, later, for several days, sitting in a bit of shade looking very sick and trying to recover himself: afterwards he arose and went out—and the wilderness without a sound took him into its bosom again. As I approached the glow from the dark I found myself at the back of two men, talking. I heard the name of Kurtz pronounced, then the words, "take advantage of this unfortunate accident." One of the men was the manager. I wished him a good evening. "Did you ever see anything like it—eh? it is incredible," he said, and walked off. The other man remained. He was a first-class agent, young, gentlemanly, a bit reserved, with a forked little beard and a hooked nose. He was stand-offish with the other agents, and they on their side said he was the manager's spy upon them. As to me, I had hardly ever spoken to him before. We got into talk, and by-and-by we strolled away from the hissing ruins. Then he asked me to his room, which was in the main building of the station. He struck a match, and I perceived that this young aristocrat had not only a silver-mounted dressing-case but also a whole candle all to himself. Just at the time the manager was the only man supposed to have any right to candles. Native mats covered the clay walls; a collection of spears, assegais, shields, knives was hung up in trophies. The business intrusted to this fellow was the making of bricks—so I had been informed; but there wasn't a fragment of a brick anywhere in the station, and he had been there more than a year—waiting. It seems he could not make bricks without something, I don't know what—straw maybe. Anyways, it could not be found there, and as it was not likely to be sent from Europe, it did not appear clear to me what he was waiting for. An act of special creation perhaps. However, they were all waiting—all the sixteen or twenty pilgrims of them—for something; and upon my word it did not seem an uncongenial occupation, from the way they took it, though the only thing that ever came to them was disease—as far as I could see. They beguiled the time by backbiting and intriguing against each other in a foolish kind of way. There was an air of plotting about that station, but nothing came of it, of course. It was as unreal as everything else—as the philanthropic pretence of the whole concern, as their talk, as their government, as their show of work. The only real feeling was a desire to get appointed to a trading-post where ivory was to be had, so that they could earn percentages. They intrigued and slandered and hated each other only on that account,—but as to effectually lifting a little finger—oh, no. By heavens! there is something after all in the world allowing one man to steal a horse while another must not look at a halter. Steal a horse straight out. Very well. He has done it. Perhaps he can ride. But there is a way of looking at a halter that would provoke the most charitable of saints into a kick.

'I had no idea why he wanted to be sociable, but as we chatted in there it suddenly occurred to me the fellow was trying to get at something—in fact, pumping me. He alluded constantly to Europe, to the people I was supposed to know there—putting leading questions as to my acquaintances in the sepulchral city, and so on. His little eyes glittered like mica discs—with curiosity—though he tried to keep up a bit of superciliousness. At first I was astonished, but very soon I became awfully curious to see what he would find out from me. I couldn't possibly imagine what I had in me to make it worth his while. It was very pretty to see how he baffled himself, for in truth my body was full only of chills, and my head had nothing in it but that wretched steamboat business. It was evident he took me for a perfectly shameless prevaricator. At last he got angry, and, to conceal a movement of furious annoyance, he yawned. I rose. Then I noticed a small sketch in oils, on a panel, representing a woman, draped and blindfolded, carrying a lighted torch. The background was sombre—almost black. The movement of the woman was stately, and the effect of the torch-light on the face was sinister.

'It arrested me, and he stood by civilly, holding an empty half-pint champagne bottle (medical comforts) with the candle stuck in it. To my question he said Mr. Kurtz had painted this—in this very station more than a year ago—while waiting for means to go to his trading-post. "Tell me, pray," said I, "who is this Mr. Kurtz?"

' "The chief of the Inner Station," he answered in a short tone, looking away. "Much obliged," I said, laughing. "And you are the brickmaker of the Central Station. Everyone knows that." He was silent for a while. "He is a prodigy," he said at last. "He is an emissary of pity, and science, and progress, and devil knows what else. We want," he began to declaim suddenly, "for the guidance of the cause intrusted to us by Europe, so to speak, higher intelligence, wide sympathies, a singleness of purpose." "Who says that?" I asked. "Lots of them," he replied. "Some even write that; and so *he* comes here, a special being, as you ought to know." "Why ought I to know?" I interrupted, really surprised. He paid no attention. "Yes. To-day he is chief of the best station, next year he will be assistant-manager, two years more and . . . but I daresay you know what he will be in two years' time. You are of the new gang—the gang of virtue. The same people who sent him specially also recommended you. Oh, don't say no. I've my own eyes to trust." Light dawned upon me. My dear aunt's influential acquaintances were producing an unexpected effect upon that young man. I nearly burst into a laugh. "Do you read the Company's confidential correspondence?" I asked. He hadn't a word to say. It was great fun. "When Mr. Kurtz," I continued, severely, "is General Manager, you won't have the opportunity."

'He blew the candle out suddenly, and we went outside. The moon had risen. Black figures strolled about listlessly, pouring water on the glow, whence proceeded a sound of hissing; steam ascended in the moonlight, the beaten nigger groaned somewhere. "What a row the brute makes!" said the indefatigable man with the moustaches, appearing near us. "Serve him right. Transgression—punishment —bang! Pitiless, pitiless. That's the only way. This will prevent all conflagrations for the future. I was just telling the manager. . . ." He noticed my companion, and became crestfallen all at once. "Not in bed yet," he said, with a kind of servile heartiness; "it's so natural. Ha! Danger—agitation." He vanished. I went on to the river-side, and the other followed me. I heard a scathing murmur at my ear. "Heap of muffs—go to." The pilgrims could be seen in knots gesticulating, discussing. Several had still their staves in their hands. I verily believed they took these sticks to bed with them. Beyond the fence the forest stood up spectrally in the moonlight, and through the dim stir, through the faint sounds of that lamentable courtyard, the silence of the land went home to one's very heart—its mystery, its greatness, the amazing reality of its concealed life. The hurt nigger moaned feebly somewhere near by, and then fetched a deep sigh that made me mend my pace away from there. I felt a hand introducing itself under my arm. "My dear sir," said the fellow, "I don't want to be misunderstood, and especially by you, who will see Mr. Kurtz long before I can have that pleasure. I wouldn't like him to get a false idea of my disposition. . . ."

'I let him run on, this papier-mâché Mephistopheles, and it seemed to me that if I tried I could poke my forefinger through him, and would find nothing inside but a little loose dirt, maybe. He, don't you see, had been planning to be assistant-manager by-and-by under the present man, and I could see that the coming of that Kurtz had upset them both not a little. He talked precipitately, and I did not try to stop him. I had my shoulders against the wreck of my steamer, hauled up on the slope like a carcass of some big river animal. The smell of mud, of primeval mud, by Jove! was in my nostrils, the high stillness of primeval forest was before my eyes; there were shiny patches on the black creek. The moon had spread over everything a thin layer of silver—over the rank grass, over the mud, upon the wall of matted vegetation standing higher than the wall of a temple, over the great river I could see through a sombre gap glittering, glittering, as it flowed broadly by without a murmur. All this was great, expectant, mute, while the man jabbered about himself. I wondered whether the stillness on the face of the immensity looking at us two were meant as an appeal or as a menace. What were we who had strayed in here? Could we handle that dumb thing, or would it handle us? I felt how big, how confoundedly big, was that thing that couldn't talk, and perhaps was deaf as well. What was in there? I could see a little ivory coming out from there, and I had heard Mr. Kurtz was in there. I had heard enough about it, too—God knows! Yet somehow it didn't bring any image with it—no more than if I had been told an angel or a fiend was in there. I believed it in the same way one of you might believe there are inhabitants in the planet Mars. I knew once a Scotch sailmaker who was certain, dead sure, there were people in Mars. If you asked him for some idea how they looked and behaved, he would get shy and mutter something about "walking on all-fours." If you as much as smiled, he would—though a man of sixty—offer to fight you. I would not have gone so far as to fight for Kurtz, but I went for him near enough to a lie. You know I hate, detest, and can't bear a lie, not because I am straighter than the rest of us, but simply because it appals me. There is a taint of death, a flavour of mortality in lies—which is exactly what I hate and detest in the world—what I want to forget. It makes me miserable and sick, like biting something rotten would do. Temperament, I suppose. Well, I went near enough to it by letting the young fool there believe anything he liked to imagine as to my influence in Europe. I became in an instant as much of a pretence as the rest of the bewitched pilgrims. This simply because I had a notion it somehow would be of help to that Kurtz whom at the time I did not see—you understand. He was just a word for me. I did not see the man in the name any more than you do. Do you see him? Do you see the story? Do you see anything? It seems to me I am trying to tell you a dream—making a vain attempt, because no relation of a dream can convey the dream-sensation, that commingling of absurdity, surprise, and bewilderment in a tremor of struggling revolt, that notion of being captured by the incredible which is of the very essence of dreams. . . .'

He was silent for a while.

'. . . No, it is impossible; it is impossible to convey the life-sensation of any given epoch of one's existence—that which makes its truth, its meaning—its subtle and penetrating essence. It is impossible. We live, as we dream—alone. . . .'

He paused again as if reflecting, then added—

'Of course in this you fellows see more than I could then. You see me, whom you know. . . .'

It had become so pitch dark that we listeners could hardly see one another. For a long time already he, sitting apart, had been no more to us than a voice. There was not a word from anybody. The others might have been asleep, but I was awake. I listened, I listened on the watch for the sentence, for the word, that would give me the clue to the faint uneasiness inspired by this narrative that seemed to shape itself without human lips in the heavy night-air of the river.

'. . . Yes—I let him run on,' Marlow began again, 'and think what he pleased about the powers that were behind me. I did! And there was nothing behind me! There was nothing but that wretched, old, mangled steamboat I was leaning against, while he talked fluently about "the necessity for every man to get on." "And when one comes out here, you conceive, it is not to gaze at the moon." Mr. Kurtz was a "universal genius," but even a genius would find it easier to work with "adequate tools—intelligent men." He did not make bricks—why, there was a physical impossibility in the way—as I was well aware; and if he did secretarial work for the manager, it was because "no sensible man rejects wantonly the confidence of his superiors." Did I see it? I saw it. What more did I want? What I really wanted was rivets, by heaven! Rivets. To get on with the work—to stop the hole. Rivets I wanted. There were cases of them down at the coast—cases—piled up—burst—split! You kicked a loose rivet at every second step in that station yard on the hillside. Rivets had rolled into the grove of death. You could fill your pockets with rivets for the trouble of stooping down—and there wasn't one rivet to be found where it was wanted. We had plates that would do, but nothing to fasten them with. And every week the messenger, a lone negro, letter-bag on shoulder and staff in hand, left our station for the coast. And several times a week a coast caravan came in with trade goods—ghastly glazed calico that made you shudder only to look at it, glass beads value about a penny a quart, confounded spotted cotton handkerchiefs. And no rivets. Three carriers could have brought all that was wanted to set that steamboat afloat.

'He was becoming confidential now, but I fancy my unresponsive attitude must have exasperated him at last, for he judged it necessary to inform me he feared neither God nor devil, let alone any mere man. I said I could see that very well, but what I wanted was a certain quantity of rivets—and rivets were what really Mr. Kurtz wanted, if he had only known it. Now letters went to the coast every week. . . . "My dear sir," he cried, "I write from dictation." I demanded rivets. There was a way—for an intelligent man. He changed his manner; became very cold, and suddenly began to talk about a hippopotamus; wondered whether sleeping on board the steamer (I stuck to my salvage night and day) I wasn't disturbed. There was an old hippo that had the bad habit of getting out on the bank and roaming at night over the station grounds. The pilgrims used to turn out in a body and empty every rifle they could lay hands on at him. Some even had sat up o' nights for him. All this energy was wasted, though. "That animal has a charmed life," he said; "but you can say this only of brutes in this country. No man—you apprehend me?—no man here bears a charmed life." He stood there for a moment in the moonlight with his delicate hooked nose set a little askew, and his mica eyes glittering without a wink, then, with a curt Goodnight, he strode off. I could see he was disturbed and considerably puzzled, which made me feel more hopeful than I had been for days. It was a great comfort to turn from that chap to my influential friend, the battered, twisted, ruined, tin-pot steamboat. I clambered on board. She rang under my feet like an empty Huntley & Palmer biscuit-tin kicked along a gutter; she was nothing so solid in make, and rather less pretty in shape, but I had expended enough hard work on her to make me love her. No influential friend would have served me better. She had given me a chance to come out a bit—to find out what I could do. No, I don't like work. I had rather laze about and think of all the fine things that can be done. I don't like work—no man does—but I like what is in the work,—the chance to find yourself. Your own reality—for yourself, not for others—what no other man can ever know. They can only see the mere show, and never can tell what it really means.

'I was not surprised to see somebody sitting aft, on the deck, with his legs dangling over the mud. You see I rather chummed with the few mechanics there were in that station, whom the other pilgrims naturally despised—on account of their imperfect manners, I suppose. This was the foreman—a boiler-maker by trade—a good worker. He was a lank, bony, yellow-faced man, with big intense eyes. His aspect was worried, and his head was as bald as the palm of my hand; but his hair in falling seemed to have stuck to his chin, and had prospered in the new locality, for his beard hung down to his waist. He was a widower with six young children (he had left them in charge of a sister of his to come out there), and the passion of his life was pigeon-flying. He was an enthusiast and a connoisseur. He would rave about pigeons. After work hours he used sometimes to come over from his hut for a talk about his children and his pigeons; at work, when he had to crawl in the mud under the bottom of the steamboat, he would tie up that beard of his in a kind of white serviette he brought for the purpose. It had loops to go over his ears. In the evening he could be seen squatted on the bank rinsing that wrapper in the creek with great care, then spreading it solemnly on a bush to dry.

'I slapped him on the back and shouted "We shall have rivets!" He scrambled to his feet exclaiming "No! Rivets!" as though he couldn't believe his ears. Then in a low voice, "You . . . eh?" I don't know why we behaved like lunatics. I put my finger to the side of my nose and nodded mysteriously. "Good for you!" he cried, snapped his fingers above his head, lifting one foot. I tried a jig. We capered on the iron deck. A frightful clatter came out of that hulk, and the virgin forest on the other bank of the creek sent it back in a thundering roll upon the sleeping station. It must have made some of the pilgrims sit up in their hovels. A dark figure obscured the lighted doorway of the manager's hut, vanished, then, a second or so after, the doorway itself vanished, too. We stopped, and the silence driven away by the stamping of our feet flowed back again from the recesses of the land. The great wall of vegetation, an exuberant and entangled mass of trunks, branches, leaves, boughs, festoons, motionless in the moonlight, was like a rioting invasion of soundless life, a rolling wave of plants, piled up, crested, ready to topple over the creek to sweep every little man of us out of his little existence. And it moved not. A deadened burst of mighty splashes and snorts reached us from afar, as though an ichthyosaurus had been taking a bath of glitter in the great river. "After all," said the boiler-maker in a reasonable tone, "why shouldn't we get the rivets?" Why not, indeed! I did not know of any reason why we shouldn't. "They'll come in three weeks," I said, confidently.

'But they didn't. Instead of rivets there came an invasion, an infliction, a visitation. It came in sections during the next three weeks, each section headed by a donkey carrying a white man in new clothes and tan shoes, bowing from that elevation right and left to the impressed pilgrims. A quarrelsome band of footsore sulky niggers trod on the heels of the donkey; a lot of tents, camp-stools, tin boxes, white cases, brown bales would be shot down in the courtyard, and the air of mystery would deepen a little over the muddle of the station. Five such instalments came, with their absurd air of disorderly flight with the loot of innumerable outfit shops and provision stores, that, one would think, they were lugging, after a raid, into the wilderness for equitable division. It was an inextricable mess of things decent in themselves but that human folly made look like spoils of thieving.

'This devoted band called itself the Eldorado Exploring Expedition, and I believe they were sworn to secrecy. Their talk, however, was the talk of sordid buccaneers: it was reckless without hardihood, greedy without audacity, and cruel without courage; there was not an atom of foresight or of serious intention in the whole batch of them, and they did not seem aware these things are wanted for the work of the world. To tear treasure out of the bowels of the land was their desire, with no more moral purpose at the back of it than there is in burglars breaking into a safe. Who paid the expenses of the noble enterprise I don't know; but the uncle of our manager was leader of that lot.

'In exterior he resembled a butcher in a poor neighbourhood, and his eyes had a look of sleepy cunning. He carried his fat paunch with ostentation on his short legs, and during the time his gang infested the station spoke to no one but his nephew. You could see these two roaming about all day long with their heads close together in an everlasting confab.

'I had given up worrying myself about the rivets. One's capacity for that kind of folly is more limited than you would suppose. I said

Hang!—and let things slide. I had plenty of time for meditation, and now and then I would give some thought to Kurtz. I wasn't very interested in him. No. Still, I was curious to see whether this man, who had come out equipped with moral ideas of some sort, would climb to the top after all and how he would set about his work when there.'

II

'ONE evening as I was lying flat on the deck of my steamboat, I heard voices approaching—and there were the nephew and the uncle strolling along the bank. I laid my head on my arm again, and had nearly lost myself in a doze, when somebody said in my ear, as it were: "I am as harmless as a little child, but I don't like to be dictated to. Am I the manager—or am I not? I was ordered to send him there. It's incredible." . . . I became aware that the two were standing on the shore alongside the forepart of the steamboat, just below my head. I did not move; it did not occur to me to move: I was sleepy. "It *is* unpleasant," grunted the uncle. "He has asked the Administration to be sent there," said the other, "with the idea of showing what he could do; and I was instructed accordingly. Look at the influence that man must have. Is it not frightful?" They both agreed it was frightful, then made several bizarre remarks: "Make rain and fine weather—one man—the Council—by the nose"—bits of absurd sentences that got the better of my drowsiness, so that I had pretty near the whole of my wits about me when the uncle said, "The climate may do away with this difficulty for you. Is he alone there?" "Yes," answered the manager; "he sent his assistant down the river with a note to me in these terms: 'Clear this poor devil out of the country, and don't bother sending more of that sort. I had rather be alone than have the kind of men you can dispose of with me.' It was more than a year ago. Can you imagine such impudence!" "Anything since then?" asked the other, hoarsely. "Ivory," jerked the nephew; "lots of it—prime sort—lots—most annoying, from him." "And with that?" questioned the heavy rumble. "Invoice," was the reply fired out, so to speak. Then silence. They had been talking about Kurtz.

'I was broad awake by this time, but, lying perfectly at ease, remained still, having no inducement to change my position.

"How did that ivory come all this way?" growled the elder man, who seemed very vexed. The other explained that it had come with a fleet of canoes in charge of an English half-caste clerk Kurtz had with him; that Kurtz had apparently intended to return himself, the station being by that time bare of goods and stores, but after coming three hundred miles, had suddenly decided to go back, which he started to do alone in a small dugout with four paddlers, leaving the half-caste to continue down the river with the ivory. The two fellows there seemed astounded at anybody attempting such a thing. They were at a loss for an adequate motive. As to me, I seemed to see Kurtz for the first time. It was a distinct glimpse: the dugout, four paddling savages, and the lone white man turning his back suddenly on the headquarters, on relief, on thoughts of home—perhaps; setting his face towards the depths of the wilderness, towards his empty and desolate station. I did not know the motive. Perhaps he was just simply a fine fellow who stuck to his work for its own sake. His name, you understand, had not been pronounced once. He was "that man." The half-caste, who, as far as I could see, had conducted a difficult trip with great prudence and pluck, was invariably alluded to as "that scoundrel." The "scoundrel" had reported that the "man" had been very ill—had recovered imperfectly. . . . The two below me moved away then a few paces, and strolled back and forth at some little distance. I heard: "Military post—doctor—two hundred miles—quite alone now—unavoidable delays—nine months—no news—strange rumours." They approached again, just as the manager was saying, "No one, as far as I know, unless a species of wandering trader—a pestilential fellow, snapping ivory from the natives." Who was it they were talking about now? I gathered in snatches that this was some man supposed to be in Kurtz's district, and of whom the manager did not approve. "We will not be free from unfair competition till one of these fellows is hanged for an example," he said. "Certainly," grunted the other; "get him hanged! Why not? Anything—anything can be done in this country. That's what I say; nobody here, you understand, *here*, can endanger your position. And why? You stand the climate—you outlast them all. The danger is in Europe; but there before I left I took care to——" They moved off and whispered, then their voices rose again. "The extraordinary series of delays is not my fault. I did my best." The fat man sighed. "Very sad." "And the pestiferous absurdity of his talk," continued the other; "he bothered me enough when he was here. 'Each station should be like a beacon on the road towards better things, a centre for trade of course, but also for humanizing, improving, instructing.' Conceive you—that ass! And he wants to be manager! No, it's——" Here he got choked by excessive indignation, and I lifted my head the least bit. I was surprised to see how near they were—right under me. I could have spat upon their hats. They were looking on the ground, absorbed in thought. The manager was switching his leg with a slender twig: his sagacious relative lifted his head. "You have been well since you came out this time?" he asked. The other gave a start. "Who? I? Oh! Like a charm—like a charm. But the rest—oh, my goodness! All sick. They die so quick, too, that I haven't the time to send them out of the country—it's incredible!" "H'm. Just so," grunted the uncle. "Ah! my boy, trust to this—I say, trust to this." I saw him extend his short flipper of an arm for a gesture that took in the forest, the creek, the mud, the river,—seemed to beckon with a dishonouring flourish before the sunlit face of the land a treacherous appeal to the lurking death, to the hidden evil, to the profound darkness of its heart. It was so startling that I leaped to my feet and looked back at the edge of the forest, as though I had expected an answer of some sort to that black display of confidence. You know the foolish notions that come to one sometimes. The high stillness confronted these two figures with its ominous patience, waiting for the passing away of a fantastic invasion.

'They swore aloud together—out of sheer fright, I believe—then pretending not to know anything of my existence, turned back to the station. The sun was low and leaning forward side by side, they seemed to be tugging painfully uphill their two ridiculous shadows of unequal length, that trailed behind them slowly over the tall grass without bending a single blade.

'In a few days the Eldorado Expedition went into the patient wilderness, that closed upon it as the sea closes over a diver. Long afterwards the news came that all the donkeys were dead. I know nothing as to the fate of the less valuable animals. They, no doubt, like the rest of us, found what they deserved. I did not inquire. I was then rather excited at the prospect of meeting Kurtz very soon. When I say very soon I mean it comparatively. It was just two months from the day we left the creek when we came to the bank below Kurtz's station.

'Going up that river was like travelling back to the earliest beginnings of the world, when vegetation rioted on the earth and the big trees were kings. An empty stream, a great silence, an impenetrable forest. The air was warm, thick, heavy, sluggish. There was no joy in the brilliance of sunshine. The long stretches of the waterway ran on, deserted, into the gloom of overshadowed distances. On silvery sandbanks hippos and alligators sunned themselves side by side. The broadening waters flowed through a mob of wooded islands; you lost your way on that river as you would in a desert, and butted all day long against shoals, trying to find the channel, till you thought yourself bewitched and cut off for ever from everything you had known once—somewhere—far away—in another existence perhaps. There were moments when one's past came back to one, as it will sometimes when you have not a moment to spare to yourself; but it came in the shape of an unrestful and noisy dream, remembered with wonder amongst the overwhelming realities of this strange world of plants, and water, and silence. And this stillness of life did not in the least resemble a peace. It was the stillness of an implacable force brooding over an inscrutable intention. It looked at you with a vengeful aspect. I got used to it afterwards; I did not see it any more; I had no time. I had to keep guessing at the channel; I had to discern, mostly by inspiration, the signs of hidden banks; I watched for sunken stones; I was learning to clap my teeth smartly before my heart flew out, when I shaved by a fluke some infernal sly old snag that would have ripped the life out of the tin-pot steamboat and drowned all the pilgrims; I had to keep a look-out for the signs of dead wood we could cut up in the night for next day's steaming. When you have to attend to things of that sort, to the mere incidents of the surface, the reality—the reality, I tell you—fades. The inner truth is hidden—luckily, luckily. But I felt it all the same; I felt often its mysterious stillness watching me at my monkey tricks, just as it watches you fellows performing on your respective tight-ropes for—what is it? half-a-crown a tumble——'

'Try to be civil, Marlow,' growled a voice, and I knew there was at least one listener awake besides myself.

'I beg your pardon. I forgot the heartache which makes up the rest of the price. And indeed what does the price matter, if the trick be well done? You do your tricks very well. And I didn't do badly either, since I managed not to sink that steamboat on my first trip. It's a wonder to me yet. Imagine a blindfolded man set to drive a van over a bad road. I sweated and shivered over that business considerably, I can tell you. After all, for a seaman, to scrape the bottom of the thing that's supposed to float all the time under his care is the unpardonable sin. No one may know of it, but you never forget the thump—eh? A blow on the very heart. You remember it, you dream of it, you wake up at night and think of it—years after—and go hot and cold all over. I don't pretend to say that steamboat floated all the time. More than once she had to wade for a bit, with twenty cannibals splashing around and pushing. We had enlisted some of these chaps on the way for a crew. Fine fellows—cannibals—in their place. They were men one could work with, and I am grateful to them. And, after all, they did not eat each other before my face: they had brought along a provision of hippo-meat which went rotten, and made the mystery of the wilderness stink in my nostrils. Phoo! I can sniff it now. I had the manager on board and three or four pilgrims with their staves—all complete. Sometimes we came upon a station close by the bank, clinging to the skirts of the unknown, and the white men rushing out of a tumbledown hovel, with great gestures of joy and surprise and welcome, seemed very strange—had the appearance of being held there captive by a spell. The word ivory would ring in the air for a while—and on we went again into the silence, along empty reaches, round the still bends, between the high walls of our winding way, reverberating in hollow claps the ponderous beat of the stern-wheel. Trees, trees, millions of trees, massive, immense, running up high; and at their foot, hugging the bank against the stream, crept the little begrimed steamboat, like a sluggish beetle crawling on the floor of a lofty portico. It made you feel very small, very lost, and yet it was not altogether depressing, that feeling. After all, if you were small, the grimy beetle crawled on—which was just what you wanted it to do. Where the pilgrims imagined it crawled to I don't know. To some place where they expected to get something, I bet! For me it crawled towards Kurtz—exclusively; but when the steam-pipes started leaking we crawled very slow. The reaches opened before us and closed behind, as if the forest had stepped leisurely across the water to bar the way for our return. We penetrated deeper and deeper into the heart of darkness. It was very quiet there. At night sometimes the roll of drums behind the curtain of trees would run up the river and remain sustained faintly, as if hovering in the air high over our heads, till the first break of day. Whether it meant war, peace, or prayer we could not tell. The dawns were heralded by the descent of a chill stillness; the wood-cutters slept, their fires burned low; the snapping of a twig would make you start. We were wanderers on prehistoric earth, on an earth that wore the aspect of an unknown planet. We could have fancied ourselves the first of men taking possession of an accursed inheritance, to be subdued at the cost of profound anguish and of excessive toil. But suddenly, as we struggled round a bend, there would be a glimpse of rush walls, of peaked grass-roofs, a burst of yells, a whirl of black limbs, a mass of hands clapping, of feet stamping, of bodies swaying, of eyes rolling, under the droop of heavy and motionless foliage. The steamer toiled along slowly on the edge of a black and incomprehensible frenzy. The prehistoric man was cursing us, praying to us, welcoming us—who could tell? We were cut off from the comprehension of our surroundings; we glided past like phantoms, wondering and secretly appalled, as sane men would be before an enthusiastic outbreak in a madhouse. We could not understand because we were too far and could not remember, because we were travelling in the night of first ages, of those ages that are gone, leaving hardly a sign—and no memories.

'The earth seemed unearthly. We are accustomed to look upon the shackled form of a conquered monster, but there—there you could look at a thing monstrous and free. It was unearthly, and the men were——No, they were not inhuman. Well, you know, that was the worst of it—this suspicion of their not being inhuman. It would come slowly to one. They howled and leaped, and spun, and made horrid faces; but what thrilled you was just the thought of their humanity—like yours—the thought of your remote kinship with this wild and passionate uproar. Ugly. Yes, it was ugly enough; but if you were man enough you would admit to yourself that there was in you just the faintest trace of a response to the terrible frankness of that noise, a dim suspicion of there being a meaning in it which you—you so remote from the night of first ages—could comprehend. And why not? The mind of man is capable of anything—because everything is in it, all the past as well as all the future. What was there after all? Joy, fear, sorrow, devotion, valour, rage—who can tell?—but truth—truth stripped of its cloak of time. Let the fool gape and shudder—the man knows and can look on without a wink. But he must at least be as much of a man as these on the shore. He must meet that truth with his own true stuff—with his own inborn strength. Principles won't do. Acquisitions, clothes, pretty rags—rags that would fly off at the first good shake. No; you want a deliberate belief. An appeal to me in this fiendish row—is there? Very well; I hear; I admit, but I have a voice, too, and for good or evil mine is the speech that cannot be silenced. Of course, a fool, what with sheer fright and fine sentiments, is always safe. Who's that grunting? You wonder I didn't go ashore for a howl and a dance? Well, no—I didn't. Fine sentiments, you say? Fine sentiments, be hanged! I had no time. I had to mess about with white-lead and strips of woollen blanket helping to put bandages on those leaky steampipes—I tell you. I had to watch the steering, and circumvent those snags, and get the tin-pot along by hook or by crook. There was surface-truth enough in these things to save a wiser man. And between whiles I had to look after the savage who was fireman. He was an improved specimen; he could fire up a vertical boiler. He was there below me, and, upon my word, to look at him was as edifying as seeing a dog in a parody of breeches and a feather hat, walking on his hind-legs. A few months of training had done for that really fine chap. He squinted at the steam-gauge and at the water-gauge with an evident effort of intrepidity—and he had filed teeth, too, the poor devil, and the wool of his pate shaved into queer patterns, and three ornamental scars on each of his cheeks. He ought to have been clapping his hands and stamping his feet on the bank, instead of which he was hard at work, a thrall to strange witchcraft, full of improving knowledge. He was useful because he had been instructed; and what he knew was this—that should the water in that transparent thing disappear, the evil spirit inside the boiler would get angry through the greatness of his thirst, and take a terrible vengeance. So he sweated and fired up and watched the glass fearfully (with an impromptu charm, made of rags, tied to his arm, and a piece of polished bone, as big as a watch, stuck flatways through his lower lip), while the wooded banks slipped past us slowly, the short noise was left behind, the interminable miles of silence—and we crept on, towards Kurtz. But the snags were thick, the water was treacherous and shallow, the boiler seemed indeed to have a sulky devil in it, and thus neither that fireman nor I had any time to peer into our creepy thoughts.

'Some fifty miles below the Inner Station we came upon a hut of reeds, an inclined and melancholy pole, with the unrecognizable tatters of what had been a flag of some sort flying from it, and a neatly stacked wood-pile. This was unexpected. We came to the bank, and on the stack of firewood found a flat piece of board with some faded pencil-writing on it. When deciphered it said: "Wood for you. Hurry up. Approach cautiously." There was a signature, but it was illegible—not Kurtz—a much longer word. Hurry up. Where? Up the river? "Approach cautiously." We had not done so. But the warning could not have been meant for the place where it could be only found after approach. Something was wrong above. But what—and how much? That was the question. We commented adversely upon the imbecility of that telegraphic style. The bush around said nothing, and would not let us look very far, either. A torn curtain of red twill hung in the doorway of the hut, and flapped sadly in our faces. The dwelling was dismantled; but we could see a white man had lived there not very long ago. There remained a rude table—a plank on two posts; a heap of rubbish reposed in a dark corner, and by the door I picked up a book. It had lost its covers, and the pages had been thumbed into a state of extremely dirty softness; but the back had been lovingly stitched afresh with white cotton thread, which looked clean yet. It was an extraordinary find. Its title was, *An Inquiry into some Points of Seamanship*, by a man Tower, Towson—some such name—Master in his Majesty's Navy. The matter looked dreary reading enough, with illustrative diagrams and repulsive tables of figures, and the copy was sixty years old. I handled this amazing antiquity with the greatest possible tenderness, lest it should dissolve in my hands. Within, Towson or Towser was inquiring earnestly into the breaking strain of ships' chains and tackle, and other such matters. Not a very enthralling book; but at the first glance you could see there a singleness of intention, an honest concern for the right way of going to work, which made these humble pages, thought out so many years ago, luminous with another than a professional light. The simple old sailor, with his talk of chains and purchases, made me forget the jungle and the pilgrims in a delicious sensation of having come upon something unmistakably real. Such a book being there was wonderful enough; but still more astounding were the notes pencilled in the margin, and plainly referring to the text. I couldn't believe my eyes! They were in cipher! Yes, it looked like cipher. Fancy a man lugging with him a book of that description into this nowhere and studying it—and making notes—in cipher at that! It was an extravagant mystery.

'I had been dimly aware for some time of a worrying noise, and when I lifted my eyes I saw the wood-pile was gone, and the manager, aided by all the pilgrims, was shouting at me from the river-side. I slipped the book into my pocket. I assure you to leave off reading was like tearing myself away from the shelter of an old and solid friendship.

'I started the lame engine ahead. "It must be this miserable trader—this intruder," exclaimed the manager, looking back malevolently at the place we had left. "He must be English," I said. "It will not save him from getting into trouble if he is not careful," muttered the manager darkly. I observed with assumed innocence that no man was safe from trouble in this world.

'The current was more rapid now, the steamer seemed at her last gasp, the stern-wheel flopped languidly, and I caught myself listening on tiptoe for the next beat of the float, for in sober truth I expected the wretched thing to give up every moment. It was like watching the last flickers of a life. But still we crawled. Sometimes I would pick out a tree a little way ahead to measure our progress towards Kurtz by, but I lost it invariably before we got abreast. To keep the eyes so long on one thing was too much for human patience. The manager displayed a beautiful resignation. I fretted and fumed and took to arguing with myself whether or no I would talk openly with Kurtz; but before I could come to any conclusion it occurred to me that my speech or my silence, indeed any action of mine, would be a mere futility. What did it matter what any one knew or ignored? What did it matter who was manager? One gets sometimes such a flash of insight. The essentials of this affair lay deep under the surface, beyond my reach, and beyond my power of meddling.

'Towards the evening of the second day we judged ourselves about eight miles from Kurtz's station. I wanted to push on; but the manager looked grave, and told me the navigation up there was so dangerous that it would be advisable, the sun being very low already, to wait where we were till next morning. Moreover, he pointed out that if the warning to approach cautiously were to be followed, we must approach in daylight—not at dusk, or in the dark. This was sensible enough. Eight miles meant nearly three hours' steaming for us, and I could also see suspicious ripples at the upper end of the reach. Nevertheless, I was annoyed beyond expression at the delay, and most unreasonably, too, since one night more could not matter much after so many months. As we had plenty of wood, and caution was the word, I brought up in the middle of the stream. The reach was narrow, straight, with high sides like a railway cutting. The dusk came gliding into it long before the sun had set. The current ran smooth and swift, but a dumb immobility sat on the banks. The living trees, lashed together by the creepers and every living bush of the undergrowth, might have been changed into stone, even to the slenderestt wig, to the lightest leaf. It was not sleep—it seemed unnatural, like a state of trance. Not the faintest sound of any kind could be heard. You looked on amazed, and began to suspect yourself of being deaf—then the night came suddenly, and struck you blind as well. About three in the morning some large fish leaped, and the loud splash made me jump as though a gun had been fired. When the sun rose there was a white fog, very warm and clammy, and more blinding than the night. It did not shift or drive; it was just there, standing all round you like something solid. At eight or nine, perhaps, it lifted as a shutter lifts. We had a glimpse of the towering multitude of trees, of the immense matted jungle, with the blazing little ball of the sun, hanging over it—all perfectly still—and then the white shutter came down again, smoothly, as if sliding in greased grooves. I ordered the chain, which we had begun to heave in, to be paid out again. Before it stopped running with a muffled rattle, a cry, a very loud cry, as of infinite desolation, soared slowly in the opaque air. It ceased. A complaining clamour, modulated in savage discords, filled our ears. The sheer unexpectedness of it made my hair stir under my cap. I don't know how it struck the others: to me it seemed as though the mist itself had screamed, so suddenly, and apparently from all sides at once, did this tumultuous and mournful uproar arise. It culminated in a hurried outbreak of almost intolerably excessive shrieking, which stopped short, leaving us stiffened in a variety of silly attitudes, and obstinately listening to the nearly as appalling and excessive silence. "Good God! What is the meaning——" stammered at my elbow one of the pilgrims,—a little fat man, with sandy hair and red whiskers, who wore side-spring boots, and pink pyjamas tucked into his socks. Two others remained open-mouthed a whole minute, then dashed into the little cabin, to rush out incontinently and stand darting scared glances, with Winchesters at "ready" in their hands. What we could see was just the steamer we were on, her outlines blurred as though she had been on the point of dissolving, and a misty strip of water, perhaps two feet broad, around her—and that was all. The rest of the world was nowhere, as far as our eyes and ears were concerned. Just nowhere. Gone, disappeared, swept off without leaving a whisper or a shadow behind.

'I went forward, and ordered the chain to be hauled in short, so as to be ready to trip the anchor and move the steamboat at once if necessary. "Will they attack?" whispered an awed voice. "We will be all butchered in this fog," murmured another. The faces twitched with the strain, the hands trembled slightly, the eyes forgot the wink. It was very curious to see the contrast of expressions of the white men and of the black fellows of our crew, who were as much strangers to that part of the river as we, though their homes were only eight hundred miles away. The whites, of course greatly discomposed, had besides a curious look of being painfully shocked by such an outrageous row. The others had an alert, naturally interested expression; but their faces were essentially quiet, even those of the one or two who grinned as they hauled at the chain. Several exchanged short, grunting phrases, which seemed to settle the matter to their satisfaction. Their headman, a young, broad-chested black, severely draped in dark-blue fringed cloths, with fierce nostrils and his hair all done up artfully in oily ringlets, stood near me. "Aha!" I said, just for good fellowship's sake. "Catch 'im," he snapped, with a bloodshot widening of his eyes and a flash of sharp teeth—"catch 'im. Give 'im to us." "To you, eh?" I asked; "what would you do with them?" "Eat 'im!" he said, curtly, and, leaning his elbow on the rail, looked out into the fog in a dignified and profoundly pensive attitude. I would no doubt have been properly horrified, had it not occurred to me that he and his chaps must be very hungry: that they must have been growing increasingly hungry for at least this month past. They had been engaged for six months (I don't think a single one of them had any clear idea of time, as we at the end of countless ages have. They still belonged to the beginnings of time—had no inherited experience to teach them as it were), and of course, as long as there was a piece of paper written over in accordance with some farcical law or other made down the river, it didn't enter anybody's head to trouble how they would live. Certainly they had brought with them some rotten hippo-meat, which couldn't have lasted very long, anyway, even if the pilgrims hadn't, in the midst of a shocking hullabaloo, thrown a considerable quantity of it overboard. It looked like a high-handed proceeding; but it was really a case of legitimate self-defence. You can't breathe dead hippo waking, sleeping, and eating, and at the same time keep your precarious grip on existence. Besides that, they had given them every week three pieces of brass wire, each about nine inches long; and the theory was they were to buy their provisions with that currency in river-side villages. You can see how *that* worked. There were either no villages, or the people were hostile, or the director, who like the rest of us fed out of tins, with an occasional old he-goat thrown in, didn't want to stop the steamer for some more or less recondite reason. So, unless they swallowed the wire itself, or made loops of it to snare the fishes with, I don't see what good their extravagant salary could be to them. I must say it was paid with a regularity worthy of a large and honourable trading company. For the rest, the only thing to eat—though it didn't look eatable in the least—I saw in their possession was a few lumps of some stuff like half-cooked dough, of a dirty lavender colour, they kept wrapped in leaves, and now and then swallowed a piece of, but so small that it seemed done more for the looks of the thing than for any serious purpose of sustenance. Why in the name of all the gnawing devils of hunger they didn't go for us—they were thirty to five—and have a good tuck in for once, amazes me now when I think of it. They were big powerful men, with not much capacity to weigh the consequences, with courage, with strength, even yet, though their skins were no longer glossy and their muscles no longer hard. And I saw that something restraining, one of those human secrets that baffle probability, had come into play there. I looked at them with a swift quickening of interest—not because it occurred to me I might be eaten by them before very long, though I own to you that just then I perceived—in a new light, as it were—how unwholesome the pilgrims looked, and I hoped, yes, I positively hoped, that my aspect was not so—what shall I say?—so—unappetizing: a touch of fantastic vanity which fitted well with the dream-sensation that pervaded all my days at that time. Perhaps I had a little fever, too. One can't live with one's finger everlastingly on one's pulse. I had often "a little fever," or a little touch of other things—the playful paw-strokes of the wilderness, the preliminary trifling before the more serious onslaught which came in due course. Yes; I looked at them as you would on any human being, with a curiosity of their impulses, motives, capacities, weaknesses, when brought to the test of an inexorable physical necessity. Restraint! What possible restraint? Was it superstition, disgust, patience, fear—or some kind of primitive honour? No fear can stand up to hunger, no patience can wear it out, disgust simply does not exist where hunger is; and as to superstition, beliefs, and what you may call principles, they are less than chaff in a breeze. Don't you know the devilry of lingering starvation, its exasperating torment, its black thoughts, its sombre and brooding ferocity? Well, I do. It takes a man all his inborn strength to fight hunger properly. It's really easier to face bereavement, dishonour, and the perdition of one's soul—than this kind of prolonged hunger. Sad, but true. And these chaps, too, had no earthly reason for any kind of scruple. Restraint! I would just as soon have expected restraint from a hyena prowling amongst the corpses of a battlefield. But there was the fact facing me—the fact dazzling, to be seen, like the foam on the depths of the sea, like a ripple on an unfathomable enigma, a mystery greater—when I thought of it—than the curious, inexplicable note of desperate grief in this savage clamour that had swept by us on the river-bank, behind the blind whiteness of the fog.

'Two pilgrims were quarrelling in hurried whispers as to which bank. "Left." "No, no; how can you? Right, right, of course." "It is very serious," said the manager's voice behind me; "I would be desolated if anything should happen to Mr. Kurtz before we came up." I looked at him, and had not the slightest doubt be was sincere. He was just the kind of man who would wish to preserve appearances. That was his restraint. But when he muttered something about going on at once, I did not even take the trouble to answer him. I knew, and he knew, that it was impossible. Were we to let go our hold of the bottom, we would be absolutely in the air—in space. We wouldn't be able to tell where we were going to—whether up or down stream, or across—till we fetched against one bank or the other,—and then we wouldn't know at first which it was. Of course I made no move. I had no mind for a smash-up. You couldn't imagine a more deadly place for a shipwreck. Whether drowned at once or not, we were sure to perish speedily in one way or another. "I authorize you to take all the risk," he said, after a short silence. "I refuse take to any," I said, shortly; which was just the answer he expected, though its tone might have surprised him. "Well, I must defer to your judgment. You are captain," he said, with marked civility. I turned my shoulder to him in sign of my appreciation, and looked into the fog. How long would it last? It was the most hopeless look-out. The approach to this Kurtz grubbing for ivory in the wretched bush was beset by as many dangers as though he had been an enchanted princess sleeping in a fabulous castle. "Will they attack, do you think?" asked the manager, in a confidential tone.

'I did not think they would attack, for several obvious reasons. The thick fog was one. If they left the bank in their canoes they would get lost in it, as we would be if we attempted to move. Still, I had also judged the jungle of both banks quite impenetrable—and yet eyes were in it, eyes that had seen us. The river-side bushes were certainly very thick; but the undergrowth behind was evidently penetrable. However, during the short lift I had seen no canoes anywhere in the reach—certainly not abreast of the steamer. But what made the idea of attack inconceivable to me was the nature of the noise—of the cries we had heard. They had not the fierce character boding of immediate hostile intention. Unexpected, wild, and violent as they had been, they had given me an irresistible impression of sorrow. The glimpse of the steamboat had for some reason filled those savages with unrestrained grief. The danger, if any, I expounded, was from our proximity to a great human passion let loose. Even extreme grief may ultimately vent itself in violence—but more generally takes the form of apathy. . . .

'You should have seen the pilgrims stare! They had no heart to grin, or even to revile me: but I believe they thought me gone mad—with fright, maybe. I delivered a regular lecture. My dear boys, it was no good bothering. Keep a look-out? Well, you may guess I watched the fog for the signs of lifting as a cat watches a mouse; but for anything else our eyes were of no more use to us than if we had been buried miles deep in a heap of cotton-wool. It felt like it, too—choking, warm, stifling. Besides, all I said, though it sounded extravagant, was absolutely true to fact. What we afterwards alluded to as an attack was really an attempt at repulse. The action was very far from being aggressive—it was not even defensive, in the usual sense: it was undertaken under the stress of desperation, and in its essence was purely protective.

'It developed itself, I should say, two hours after the fog lifted, and its commencement was at a spot, roughly speaking, about a mile and a half below Kurtz's station. We has just floundered and flopped round a bend, when I saw an islet, a mere grassy hummock of bright green, in the middle of the stream. It was the only thing of the kind; but as we opened the reach more, I perceived it was the head of a long sandbank, or rather of a chain of shallow patches stretching down the middle of the river. They were discoloured, just awash, and the whole lot was seen just under the water, exactly as a man's backbone is seen running down the middle of his back under the skin. Now, as far as I did see, I could go to the right or to the left of this. I didn't know either channel, of course. The banks looked pretty well alike, the depth appeared the same; but as I has been informed the station was on the west side, I naturally headed for the western passage.

'No sooner had we fairly entered it than I became aware it was much narrower than I had supposed. To the left of us there was the long uninterrupted shoal, and to the right a high, steep bank heavily overgrown with bushes. Above the bush the trees stood in serried ranks. The twigs overhung the current thickly, and from distance to distance a large limb of some tree projected rigidly over the stream. It was then well on in the afternoon, the face of the forest was gloomy, and a broad strip of shadow had already fallen on the water. In this shadow we steamed up—very slowly, as you may imagine. I sheered her well inshore—the water being deepest near the bank, as the sounding-pole informed me.

'One of my hungry and forbearing friends was sounding in the bows just below me. This steamboat was exactly like a decked scow. On the deck, there were two little teak-wood houses, with doors and windows. The boiler was in the fore-end, and the machinery right astern. Over the whole there was a light roof, supported on stanchions. The funnel projected through that roof, and in front of the funnel a small cabin built of light planks served for a pilot-house. It contained a couch, two camp-stools, a loaded Martini-Henry leaning in one corner, a tiny table, and the steering-wheel. It had a wide door in front and a broad shutter at each side. All these were always thrown open, of course. I spent my days perched up there on the extreme fore-end of that roof, before the door. At night I slept, or tried to, on the couch. An athletic black belonging to some coast tribe, and educated by my poor predecessor, was the helmsman. He sported a pair of brass earrings, wore a blue cloth wrapper from the waist to the ankles, and thought all the world of himself. He was the most unstable kind of fool I had ever seen. He steered with no end of a swagger while you were by; but if he lost sight of you, he became instantly the prey of an abject funk, and would let that cripple of a steamboat get the upper hand of him in a minute.

'I was looking down at the sounding-pole, and feeling much annoyed to see at each try a little more of it stick out of that river, when I saw my poleman give up the business suddenly, and stretch himself flat on the deck, without even taking the trouble to haul his pole in. He kept hold on it though, and it trailed in the water. At the same time the fireman, whom I could also see below me, sat down abruptly before his furnace and ducked his head. I was amazed. Then I had to look at the river mighty quick, because there was a snag in the fairway. Sticks, little sticks, were flying about—thick: they were whizzing before my nose, dropping below me, striking behind me against my pilot-house. All this time the river, the shore, the woods, were very quiet—perfectly quite. I could only hear the heavy splashing thump of the stern-wheel and the patter of these things. We cleared the snag clumsily. Arrows, by Jove! We were being shot at! I stepped in quickly to close the shutter on the land-side. That fool-helmsman, his hands on the spokes, was lifting his knees high, stamping his feet, champing his mouth, like a reined-in horse. Confound him! And we were staggering within ten feet of the bank. I had to lean right out to swing the heavy shutter, and I saw a face amongst the leaves on the level with my own, looking at me very fierce and steady; and then suddenly, as though a veil had been removed from my eyes, I made out, deep in the tangled gloom, naked breasts, arms, legs, glaring eyes,—the bush was swarming with human limbs in movement, glistening, of bronze colour. The twigs shook, swayed, and rustled, the arrows flew out of them, and then the shutter came to. "Steer her straight,"

I said to the helmsman. He held his head rigid, face forward; but his eyes rolled, he kept on, lifting and setting down his feet gently, his mouth foamed a little. "Keep quiet!" I said in a fury. I might just as well have ordered a tree not to sway in the wind. I darted out. Below me there was a great scuffle of feet on the iron deck; confused exclamations; a voice screamed, "Can you turn back?" I caught sight of a V-shaped ripple on the water ahead. What? Another snag! A fusillade burst out under my feet. The pilgrims had opened with their Winchesters, and were simply squirting lead into that bush. A deuce of a lot of smoke came up and drove slowly forward. I swore at it. Now I couldn't see the ripple or the snag either. I stood in the doorway, peering, and the arrows came in swarms. They might have been poisoned, but they looked as though they wouldn't kill a cat. The bush began to howl. Our wood-cutters raised a warlike whoop; the report of a rifle just at my back deafened me. I glanced over my shoulder, and the pilot-house was yet full of noise and smoke when I made a dash at the wheel. The fool-nigger had dropped everything, to throw the shutter open and let off that Martini-Henry. He stood before the wide opening, glaring, and I yelled at him to come back, while I straightened the sudden twist out of that steamboat. There was no room to turn even if I had wanted to, the snag was somewhere very near ahead in that confounded smoke, there was no time to lose, so I just crowded her into the bank—right into the bank, where I knew the water was deep.

'We tore slowly along the overhanging bushes in a whirl of broken twigs and flying leaves. The fusillade below stopped short, as I had foreseen it would when the squirts got empty. I threw my head back to a glinting whizz that traversed the pilot-house, in at one shutter-hole and out at the other. Looking past that mad helmsman, who was shaking the empty rifle and yelling at the shore, I saw vague forms of men running bent double, leaping, gliding, distinct, incomplete, evanescent. Something big appeared in the air before the shutter, the rifle went overboard, and the man stepped back swiftly, looked at me over his shoulder in an extraordinary, profound, familiar manner, and fell upon my feet. The side of his head hit the wheel twice, and the end of what appeared a long cane clattered round and knocked over a little camp-stool. It looked as though after wrenching that thing from somebody ashore he had lost his balance in the effort. The thin smoke had blown away, we were clear of the snag, and looking ahead I could see that in another hundred yards or so I would be free to sheer off, away from the bank; but my feet felt so very warm and wet that I had to look down. The man had rolled on his back and stared straight up at me; both his hands clutched that cane. It was the shaft of a spear that, either thrown or lunged through the opening, had caught him in the side just below the ribs; the blade had gone in out of sight, after making a frightful gash; my shoes were full; a pool of blood lay very still, gleaming dark-red under the wheel; his eyes shone with an amazing lustre. The fusillade burst out again. He looked at me anxiously, gripping the spear like something precious, with an air of being afraid I would try to take it away from him. I had to make an effort to free my eyes from his gaze and attend to the steering. With one hand I felt above my head for the line of the steam whistle, and jerked out screech after screech hurriedly. The tumult of angry and warlike yells was checked instantly, and then from the depths of the woods went out such a tremulous and prolonged wail of mournful fear and utter despair as may be imagined to follow the flight of the last hope from the earth. There was a great commotion in the bush; the shower of arrows stopped, a few dropping shots rang out sharply—then silence, in which the languid beat of the stern-wheel came plainly to my ears. I put the helm hard a-starboard at the moment when the pilgrim in pink pyjamas, very hot and agitated, appeared in the doorway. "The manager sends me——" he began in an official tone, and stopped short. "Good God!" he said, glaring at the wounded man.

'We two whites stood over him, and his lustrous and inquiring glance enveloped us both. I declare it looked as though he would presently put to us some question in an understandable language; but he died without uttering a sound, without moving a limb, without twitching a muscle. Only in the very last moment, as though in response to some sign we could not see, to some whisper we could not hear, he frowned heavily, and that frown gave to his black death-mask an inconceivably sombre, brooding, and menacing expression. The lustre of inquiring glance faded swiftly into vacant glassiness. "Can you steer?" I asked the agent eagerly. He looked very dubious; but I made a grab at his arm, and he understood at once I meant him to steer whether or no. To tell you the truth, I was morbidly anxious to change my shoes and socks.

"He is dead," murmured the fellow, immensely impressed. "No doubt about it," said I, tugging like mad at the shoe-laces. "And by the way, I suppose Mr. Kurtz is dead as well by this time."

'For the moment that was the dominant thought. There was a sense of extreme disappointment, as though I had found out I had been striving after something altogether without a substance. I couldn't have been more disgusted if I had travelled all this way for the sole purpose of talking with Mr. Kurtz. Talking with. . . . I flung one shoe overboard, and became aware that that was exactly what I had been looking forward to—a talk with Kurtz. I made the strange discovery that I had never imagined him as doing, you know, but as discoursing. I didn't say to myself, "Now I will never see him," or "Now I will never shake him by the hand," but, "now I will never hear him." The man presented himself as a voice. Not of course that I did not connect him with some sort of action. Hadn't I been told in all the tones of jealousy and admiration that he had collected, bartered, swindled, or stolen more ivory than all the other agents together? That was not the point. The point was in his being a gifted creature, and that of all his gifts the one that stood out pre-eminently, that carried with it a sense of real presence, was his ability to talk, his words—the gift of expression, the bewildering, the illuminating, the most exalted and the most contemptible, the pulsating stream of light, or the deceitful flow from the heart of an impenetrable darkness.

'The other shoe went flying unto the devil-god of that river. I thought, By Jove! it's all over. We are too late; he has vanished—the gift has vanished, by means of some spear, arrow, or club. I will never hear that chap speak after all,—and my sorrow had a startling extravagance of emotion, even such as I had noticed in the howling sorrow of these savages in the bush. I couldn't have felt more of lonely desolation somehow, had I been robbed of a belief or had missed my destiny in life. . . .Why do you sigh in this beastly way, somebody? Absurd? Well, absurd. Good Lord! mustn't a man ever——Here, give me some tobacco.' . . .

There was a pause of profound stillness, then a match flared, and Marlow's lean face appeared, worn, hollow, with downward folds and dropped eyelids, with an aspect of concentrated attention; and as he took vigorous draws at his pipe, it seemed to retreat and advance out of the night in the regular flicker of the tiny flame. The match went out.

'Absurd!' he cried. 'This is the worst of trying to tell. . . . Here you all are, each moored with two good addresses, like a hulk with two anchors, a butcher round one corner, a policeman round another, excellent appetites, and temperature normal—you hear—normal from year's end to year's end. And you say, Absurd! Absurd be—exploded! Absurd! My dear boys, what can you expect from a man who out of sheer nervousness had just flung overboard a pair of new shoes! Now I think of it, it is amazing I did not shed tears. I am, upon the whole, proud of my fortitude. I was cut to the quick at the idea of having lost the inestimable privilege of listening to the gifted Kurtz. Of course I was wrong. The privilege was waiting for me. Oh, yes, I heard more than enough. And I was right, too. A voice. He was very little more than a voice. And I heard—him—it—this voice—other voices—all of them were so little more than voices—and the memory of that time itself lingers around me, impalpable, like a dying vibration of one immense jabber, silly, atrocious, sordid, savage, or simply mean, without any kind of sense. Voices, voices—even the girl herself—now——'

He was silent for a long time.

'I laid the ghost of his gifts at last with a lie,' he began, suddenly. 'Girl! What? Did I mention a girl? Oh, she is out of it—completely. They—the women I mean—are out of it—should be out of it. We must help them to stay in that beautiful world of their own, lest ours gets worse. Oh, she had to be out of it. You should have heard the disinterred body of Mr. Kurtz saying, "My Intended." You would have perceived directly then how completely she was out of it. And the lofty frontal bone of Mr. Kurtz! They say the hair goes on growing sometimes, but this—ah—specimen, was impressively bald. The wilderness had patted him on the head, and, behold, it was like a ball—an ivory ball; it had caressed him, and—lo!—he had withered; it had taken him, loved him, embraced him, got into his veins, consumed his flesh, and sealed his soul to its own by the inconceivable ceremonies of some devilish initiation. He was its spoiled and pampered favourite. Ivory? I should think so. Heaps of it, stacks of it. The old mud shanty was bursting with it. You would think there was not a single tusk left either above or below the ground in the whole country. "Mostly fossil," the manager had remarked, disparagingly. It was no more fossil than I am; but they call it fossil when it is dug up. It appears these niggers do bury the tusks sometimes—but evidently they couldn't bury this parcel deep enough to save the gifted Mr. Kurtz from his fate. We filled the steamboat with it, and had to pile a lot on the deck. Thus he could see and enjoy as long as he could see, because the appreciation of this favour had remained with him to the last. You should have heard him say, "My ivory." Oh yes, I heard him. "My Intended, my ivory, my station, my river, my——" everything belonged to him. It made me hold my breath in expectation of hearing the wilderness burst into a prodigious peal of laughter that would shake the fixed stars in their places. Everything belonged to him—but that was a trifle. The thing was to know what he belonged to, how many powers of darkness claimed him for their own. That was the reflection that made you creepy all over. It was impossible—it was not good for one either—trying to imagine. He had taken a high seat amongst the devils of the land—I mean literally. You can't understand. How could you?—with solid pavement under your feet, surrounded by kind neighbours ready to cheer you or to fall on you, stepping delicately between the butcher and the policeman, in the holy terror of scandal and gallows and lunatic asylums—how can you imagine what particular region of the first ages a man's untrammelled feet may take him into by the way of solitude—utter solitude without a policeman—by the way of silence—utter silence, where no warning voice of a kind neighbour can be heard whispering of public opinion? These little things make all the great difference. When they are gone you must fall back upon your own innate strength, upon your own capacity for faithfulness. Of course you may be too much of a fool to go wrong—too dull even to know you are being assaulted by the powers of darkness. I take it, no fool ever made a bargain for his soul with the devil: the fool is too much of a fool, or the devil too much of a devil—I don't know which. Or you may be such a thunderingly exalted creature as to be altogether deaf and blind to anything but heavenly sights and sounds. Then the earth for you is only a standing place—and whether to be like this is your loss or your gain I won't pretend to say. But most of us are neither one nor the other. The earth for us is a place to live in, where we must put up with sights, with sounds, with smells, too, by Jove!—breathe dead hippo, so to speak, and not be contaminated. And there, don't you see? your strength comes in, the faith in your ability for the digging of unostentatious holes to bury the stuff in—your power of devotion, not to yourself, but to an obscure, back-breaking business. And that's difficult enough. Mind, I am not trying to excuse or even explain—I am trying to account to myself for—for—Mr. Kurtz—for the shade of Mr. Kurtz. This initiated wraith from the back of Nowhere honoured me with its amazing confidence before it vanished altogether. This was because it could speak English to me. The original Kurtz had been educated partly in England, and—as he was good enough to say himself—his sympathies were in the right place. His mother was half-English, his father was half-French. All Europe contributed to the making of Kurtz; and by-and-by I learned that, most appropriately, the International Society for the Suppression of Savage Customs had intrusted him with the making of a report, for its future guidance. And he had written it, too. I've seen it. I've read it. It was eloquent, vibrating with eloquence, but too high-strung, I think. Seventeen pages of close writing he had found time for! But this must have been before his—let us say—nerves, went wrong, and caused him to preside at certain midnight dances ending with unspeakable rites, which—as far as I reluctantly gathered from what I heard at various times—were offered up to him—do you understand?—to Mr. Kurtz himself. But it was a beautiful piece of writing. The opening paragraph, however, in the light of later information, strikes me now as ominous. He began with the argument that we whites, from the point of development we had arrived at, "must necessarily appear to them [savages] in the nature of supernatural beings—we approach them with the might as of a deity," and so on, and so on. "By the simple exercise of our will we can exert a power for good practically unbounded," etc. etc. From that point he soared and took me with him. The peroration was magnificent, though difficult to remember, you know. It gave me the notion of an exotic Immensity ruled by an august Benevolence. It made me tingle with enthusiasm. This was the unbounded power of eloquence—of words—of burning noble words. There were no practical hints to interrupt the magic current of phrases, unless a kind of note at the foot of the last page, scrawled evidently much later, in an unsteady hand, may be regarded as the exposition of a method. It was very simple, and at the end of that moving appeal to every altruistic sentiment it blazed at you, luminous and terrifying, like a flash of lightning in a serene sky: "Exterminate all the brutes!" The curious part was that he had apparently forgotten all about that valuable postscriptum, because, later on, when he in a sense came to himself, he repeatedly entreated me to take good care of "my pamphlet" (he called it), as it was sure to have in the future a good influence upon his career. I had full information about all these things, and, besides, as it turned out, I was to have the care of his memory. I've done enough for it to give me the indisputable right to lay it, if I choose, for an everlasting rest in the dust-bin of progress, amongst all the sweepings and, figuratively speaking, all the dead cats of civilization. But then you see, I can't choose. He won't be forgotten. Whatever he was, he was not common. He had the power to charm or frighten rudimentary souls into an aggravated witch-dance in his honour; he could also fill the small souls of the pilgrims with bitter misgivings: he had one devoted friend at least, and he had conquered one soul in the world that was neither rudimentary nor tainted with self-seeking. No; I can't forget him, though I am not prepared to affirm the fellow was exactly worth the life we lost in getting to him. I missed my late helmsman awfully,—I missed him even while his body was still lying in the pilot-house. Perhaps you will think it passing strange this regret for a savage who was no more account than a grain of sand in a black Sahara. Well, don't you see, he had done something, he had steered; for months I had him at my back—a help—an instrument. It was a kind of partnership. He steered for me—I had to look after him, I worried about his deficiencies, and thus a subtle bond had been created, of which I only became aware when it was suddenly broken. And the intimate profundity of that look he gave me when he received his hurt remains to this day in my memory—like a claim of distant kinship affirmed in a supreme moment.

'Poor fool! If he had only left that shutter alone. He had no restraint, no restraint—just like Kurtz—a tree swayed by the wind. As soon as I had put on a dry pair of slippers, I dragged him out, after first jerking the spear out of his side, which operation I confess I performed with my eyes shut tight. His heels leaped together over the little door-step; his shoulders were pressed to my breast; I hugged him from behind desperately. Oh! he was heavy, heavy; heavier than any man on earth, I should imagine. Then without more ado I tipped him overboard. The current snatched him as though he had been a wisp of grass, and I saw the body roll over twice before I lost sight of it for ever. All the pilgrims and the manager were then congregated on the awning-deck about the pilot-house, chattering at each other like a flock of excited magpies, and there was a scandalized murmur at my heartless promptitude. What they wanted to keep that body hanging about for I can't guess. Embalm it, maybe. But I had also heard another, and a very ominous, murmur on the deck below. My friends the wood-cutters were likewise scandalized, and with a better show of reason—though I admit that the reason itself was quite inadmissible. Oh, quite! I had made up my mind that if my late helmsman was to be eaten, the fishes alone should have him. He had been a very second-rate helmsman while alive, but now he was dead he might have become a first-class temptation, and possibly cause some startling trouble. Besides, I was anxious to take the wheel, the man in pink pyjamas showing himself a hopeless duffer at the business.

'This I did directly the simple funeral was over. We were going half-speed, keeping right in the middle of the stream, and I listened to the talk about me. They had given up Kurtz, they had given up the station; Kurtz was dead, and the station had been burnt—and so on—and so on. The red-haired pilgrim was beside himself with the thought that at least this poor Kurtz had been properly avenged. "Say! We must have made a glorious slaughter of them in the bush. Eh? What do you think? Say?" He positively danced, the bloodthirsty little gingery beggar. And he had nearly fainted when he saw the wounded man! I could not help saying, "You made a glorious lot of smoke, anyhow." I had seen, from the way the tops of the bushes rustled and flew, that almost all the shots had gone too high. You can't hit anything unless you take aim and fire from the shoulder; but these chaps fired from the hip with their eyes shut. The retreat, I maintained—and I was right—was caused by the screeching of the steam-whistle. Upon this they forgot Kurtz, and began to howl at me with indignant protests.

'The manager stood by the wheel murmuring confidentially about the necessity of getting well away down the river before dark at all events, when I saw in the distance a clearing on the river-side and the outlines of some sort of building. "What's this?" I asked. He clapped his hands in wonder. "The station!" he cried. I edged in at once, still going half-speed.

'Through my glasses I saw the slope of a hill interspersed with rare trees and perfectly free from undergrowth. A long decaying building on the summit was half buried in the high grass; the large holes in the peaked roof gaped black from afar; the jungle and the woods made a background. There was no enclosure or fence of any kind; but there had been one apparently, for near the house half-a-dozen slim posts remained in a row, roughly trimmed, and with their upper ends ornamented with round carved balls. The rails, or whatever there had been between, had disappeared. Of course the forest surrounded all that. The river-bank was clear, and on the water-side I saw a white man under a hat like a cart-wheel beckoning persistently with his whole arm. Examining the edge of the forest above and below, I was almost certain I could see movements—human forms gliding here and there. I steamed past prudently, then stopped the engines and let her drift down. The man on the shore began to shout, urging us to land. "We have been attacked," screamed the manager. "I know—I know. It's all right," yelled back the other, as cheerful as you please. "Come along. It's all right. I am glad."

'His aspect reminded me of something I had seen—something funny I had seen somewhere. As I manoeuvred to get alongside, I was asking myself, "What does this fellow look like?" Suddenly I got it. He looked like a harlequin. His clothes had been made of some stuff that was brown holland probably, but it was covered with patches all over, with bright patches, blue, red, and yellow,—patches on the back, patches on the front, patches on elbows, on knees; coloured binding around his jacket, scarlet edging at the bottom of his trousers; and the sunshine made him look extremely gay and wonderfully neat withal, because you could see how beautifully all this patching had been done. A beardless, boyish face, very fair, no features to speak of, nose peeling, little blue eyes, smiles and frowns chasing each other over that open countenance like sunshine and shadow on a wind-swept plain. "Look out, captain!" he cried; "there's a snag lodged in here last night." What! Another snag? I confess I swore shamefully. I had nearly holed my cripple, to finish off that charming trip. The harlequin on the bank turned his little pug-nose up to me. "You English?" he asked, all smiles. "Are you?" I shouted from the wheel. The smiles vanished, and he shook his head as if sorry for my disappointment. Then he brightened up. "Never mind!"

he cried, encouragingly. "Are we in time?" I asked. "He is up there," he replied, with a toss of the head up the hill, and becoming gloomy all of a sudden. His face was like the autumn sky, overcast one moment and bright the next.

'When the manager, escorted by the pilgrims, all of them armed to the teeth, had gone to the house this chap came on board. "I say, I don't like this. These natives are in the bush," I said. He assured me earnestly it was all right. "They are simple people," he added; "well, I am glad you came. It took me all my time to keep them off." "But you said it was all right," I cried. "Oh, they meant no harm," he said; and as I stared he corrected himself, "Not exactly." Then vivaciously, "My faith, your pilot-house wants a clean up!" In the next breath he advised me to keep enough steam on the boiler to blow the whistle in case of any trouble. "One good screech will do more for you than all your rifles. They are simple people," he repeated. He rattled away at such a rate he quite overwhelmed me. He seemed to be trying to make up for lots of silence, and actually hinted, laughing, that such was the case. "Don't you talk with Mr. Kurtz?" I said. "You don't talk with that man—you listen to him," he exclaimed with severe exaltation. "But now——" He waved his arm, and in the twinkling of an eye was in the uttermost depths of despondency. In a moment he came up again with a jump, possessed himself of both my hands, shook them continuously, while he gabbled: "Brother sailor . . . honour . . . pleasure . . . delight . . . introduce myself . . . Russian . . . son of an arch-priest . . . Government of Tambov . . . What? Tobacco! English tobacco; the excellent English Tobacco! Now, that's brotherly. Smoke? Where's a sailor that does not smoke?"

'The pipe soothed him, and gradually I made out he had run away from school, had gone to sea in a Russian ship; ran away again; served some time in English ships; was now reconciled with the arch-priest. He made a point of that. "But when one is young one must see things, gather experience, ideas; enlarge the mind." "Here!" I interrupted. "You can never tell! Here I met Mr. Kurtz," he said, youthfully solemn and reproachful. I held my tongue after that. It appears he had persuaded a Dutch trading-house on the coast to fit him out with stores and goods, and had started for the interior with a light heart, and no more idea of what would happen to him than a baby. He had been wandering about that river for nearly two years alone, cut off from everybody and everything. "I am not so young as I look. I am twenty-five," he said. "At first old Van Shuyten would tell me to go to the devil," he narrated with keen enjoyment; "but I stuck to him, and talked and talked, till at last he got afraid I would talk the hind-leg off his favourite dog, so he gave me some cheap things and a few guns, and told me he hoped he would never see my face again. Good old Dutchman, Van Shuyten. I've sent him one small lot of ivory a year ago, so that he can't call me a little thief when I get back. I hope he got it. And for the rest I don't care. I had some wood stacked for you. That was my old house. Did you see?"

'I gave him Towson's book. He made as though he would kiss me, but restrained himself. "The only book I had left, and I thought I had lost it," he said, looking at it ecstatically. "So many accidents happen to a man going about alone, you know. Canoes get upset sometimes—and sometimes you've got to clear out so quick when the people get angry." He thumbed the pages. "You made notes in Russian?" I asked. He nodded. "I thought they were written in cipher," I said. He laughed, then became serious. "I had lots of trouble to keep these people off," he said. "Did they want to kill you?" I asked. "Oh, no!" he cried, and checked himself. "Why did they attack us?" I pursued. He hesitated, then said shamefacedly, "They don't want him to go." "Don't they?" I said, curiously. He nodded a nod full of mystery and wisdom. "I tell you," he cried, "this man has enlarged my mind." He opened his arms wide, staring at me with his little blue eyes that were perfectly round.'

III

'I LOOKED at him, lost in astonishment. There he was before me, in motley, as though he had absconded from a troupe of mimes, enthusiastic, fabulous. His very existence was improbable, inexplicable, and altogether bewildering. He was an insoluble problem. It was inconceivable how he had existed, how he had succeeded in getting so far, how he had managed to remain—why he did not instantly disappear. "I went a little farther," he said, "then still a little farther—till I had gone so far that I don't know how I'll ever get back. Never mind. Plenty time. I can manage. You take Kurtz away quick—quick—I tell you."

The glamour of youth enveloped his particoloured rags, his destitution, his loneliness, the essential desolation of his futile wanderings. For months—for years—his life hadn't been worth a day's purchase; and there he was gallantly, thoughtlessly alive, to all appearance indestructible solely by the virtue of his few years and of his unreflecting audacity. I was seduced into something like admiration—like envy. Glamour urged him on, glamour kept him unscathed. He surely wanted nothing from the wilderness but space to breathe in and to push on through. His need was to exist, and to move onwards at the greatest possible risk, and with a maximum of privation. If the absolutely pure, uncalculating, unpractical spirit of adventure had ever ruled a human being, it ruled this be-patched youth. I almost envied him the possession of this modest and clear flame. It seemed to have consumed all thought of self so completely, that even while he was talking to you, you forgot that it was he—the man before your eyes—who had gone through these things. I did not envy him his devotion to Kurtz, though. He had not meditated over it. It came to him, and he accepted it with a sort of eager fatalism. I must say that to me it appeared about the most dangerous thing in every way he had come upon so far.

'They had come together unavoidably, like two ships becalmed near each other, and lay rubbing sides at last. I suppose Kurtz wanted an audience, because on a certain occasion, when encamped in the forest, they had talked all night, or more probably Kurtz had talked. "We talked of everything," he said, quite transported at the recollection. "I forgot there was such a thing as sleep. The night did not seem to last an hour. Everything! Everything! . . . Of love, too." "Ah, he talked to you of love!" I said, much amused. "It isn't what you think," he cried, almost passionately. "It was in general. He made me see things—things."

'He threw his arms up. We were on deck at the time, and the headman of my wood-cutters, lounging near by, turned upon him his heavy and glittering eyes. I looked around, and I don't know why, but I assure you that never, never before, did this land, this river, this jungle, the very arch of this blazing sky, appear to me so hopeless and so dark, so impenetrable to human thought, so pitiless to human weakness. "And, ever since, you have been with him, of course?" I said.

'On the contrary. It appears their intercourse had been very much broken by various causes. He had, as he informed me proudly, managed to nurse Kurtz through two illnesses (he alluded to it as you would to some risky feat), but as a rule Kurtz wandered alone, far in the depths of the forest. "Very often coming to this station, I had to wait days and days before he would turn up," he said. "Ah, it was worth waiting for!—sometimes." "What was he doing? exploring or what?" I asked. "Oh, yes, of course;" he had discovered lots of villages, a lake, too—he did not know exactly in what direction; it was dangerous to inquire too much—but mostly his expeditions had been for ivory. "But he had no goods to trade with by that time," I objected. "There's a good lot of cartridges left even yet," he answered, looking away. "To speak plainly, he raided the country," I said. He nodded. "Not alone, surely!" He muttered something about the villages round that lake. "Kurtz got the tribe to follow him did he?" I suggested. He fidgeted a little. "They adored him," he said. The tone of these words was so extraordinary that I looked at him searchingly. It was curious to see his mingled eagerness and reluctance to speak of Kurtz. The man filled his life, occupied his thoughts, swayed his emotions. "What can you expect?" he burst out; "he came to them with thunder and lightning, you know—and they had never seen anything like it—and very terrible. He could be very terrible. You can't judge Mr. Kurtz as you would an ordinary man. No, no, no! Now—just to give you an idea—I don't mind telling you, he wanted to shoot me, too, one day—but I don't judge him." "Shoot you!" I cried. "What for?" "Well, I had a small lot of ivory the chief of that village near my house gave me. You see I used to shoot game for them. "Well, he wanted it, and wouldn't hear reason. He declared he would shoot me unless I gave him the ivory and then cleared out of the country, because he could do so, and had a fancy for it, and there was nothing on earth to prevent him killing whom he jolly well pleased. And it was true, too. I gave him the ivory. What did I care! But I didn't clear out. No, no. I couldn't leave him. I had to be careful, of course, till we got friendly again for a time. He had his second illness then. Afterwards I had to keep out of the way; but I didn't mind. He was living for the most part in those villages on the lake. When he came down to the river, sometimes he would take to me, and sometimes it was better for me to be careful. This man suffered too much. He hated all this, and somehow he couldn't get away. When I had a chance I begged him to try and leave while there was time; I offered to go back with him. And he would say yes, and then he would remain; go off on another ivory hunt; disappear for weeks; forget himself amongst these people—forget himself—you know." "Why! he's mad," I said. He protested indignantly. Mr. Kurtz couldn't be mad. If I had heard him talk, only two days ago, I wouldn't dare hint at such a thing. . . . I had taken up my binoculars while we talked, and was looking at the shore, sweeping the limit of the forest at each side and at the back of the house. The consciousness of there being people in that bush, so silent, so quiet—as silent and quiet as the ruined house on the hill—made me uneasy. There was no sign on the face of nature of this amazing tale that was not so much told as suggested to me in desolate exclamations, completed by shrugs, in interrupted phrases, in hints ending in deep sighs. The woods were unmoved, like a mask—heavy, like the closed door of a prison—they looked with their air of hidden knowledge, of patient expectation, of unapproachable silence. The Russian was explaining to me that it was only lately that Mr. Kurtz had come down to the river, bringing along with him all the fighting men of that lake tribe. He had been absent for several months—getting himself adored, I supposed—and had come down unexpectedly, with the intention to all appearance of making a raid either across the river or down stream. Evidently the appetite for more ivory had got the better of the—what shall I say?—less material aspirations. However he had got much worse suddenly. "I heard he was lying helpless, and so I came up—took my chance," said the Russian. "Oh, he is bad, very bad." I directed my glass to the house. There were no signs of life, but there was the ruined roof, the long mud wall peeping above the grass, with three little square window-holes, no two of the same size; all this brought within reach of my hand, as it were. And then I made a brusque movement, and one of the remaining posts of that vanished fence leaped up in the field of my glass. You remember I told you I had been struck at the distance by certain attempts at ornamentation, rather remarkable in the ruinous aspect of the place. Now I had suddenly a nearer view, and its first result was to make me throw my head back as if before a blow. Then I went carefully from post to post with my glass, and I saw my mistake. These round knobs were not ornamental but symbolic; they were expressive and puzzling, striking and disturbing—food for thought and also for the vultures if there had been any looking down from the sky; but at all events for such ants as were industrious enough to ascend the pole. They would have been even more impressive, those heads on the stakes, if their faces had not been turned to the house. Only one, the first I had made out, was facing my way. I was not so shocked as you may think. The start back I had given was really nothing but a movement of surprise. I had expected to see a knob of wood there, you know. I returned deliberately to the first I had seen—and there it was, black, dried, sunken, with closed eyelids,—a head that seemed to sleep at the top of that pole, and, with the shrunken dry lips showing a narrow white line of the teeth, was smiling, too, smiling continuously at some endless and jocose dream of that eternal slumber.

'I am not disclosing any trade secrets. In fact, the manager said afterwards that Mr. Kurtz's methods had ruined the district. I have no opinion on that point, but I want you clearly to understand that there was nothing exactly profitable in these heads being there. They only showed that Mr. Kurtz lacked restraint in the gratification of his various lusts, that there was something wanting in him—some small matter which, when the pressing need arose, could not be found under his magnificent eloquence. Whether he knew of this deficiency himself I can't say. I think the knowledge came to him at last—only at the very last. But the wilderness had found him out early, and had taken on him a terrible vengeance for the fantastic invasion. I think it had whispered to him things about himself which he did not know, things of which he had no conception till he took counsel with this great solitude—and the whisper had proved irresistibly fascinating. It echoed loudly within him because he was hollow at the core. . . . I put down the glass, and the head that had appeared near enough to be spoken to seemed at once to have leaped away from me into inaccessible distance.

'The admirer of Mr. Kurtz was a bit crestfallen. In a hurried, indistinct voice he began to assure me he had not dared to take these—say, symbols—down. He was not afraid of the natives; they would not stir till Mr. Kurtz gave the word. His ascendancy was extraordinary. The camps of these people surrounded the place, and the chiefs came every day to see him. They would crawl. . . .

"I don't want to know anything of the ceremonies used when approaching Mr. Kurtz," I shouted. Curious, this feeling that came over me that such details would be more intolerable than those heads drying on the stakes under Mr. Kurtz's windows. After all, that was only a savage sight, while I seemed at one bound to have been transported into some lightless region of subtle horrors, where pure, uncomplicated savagery was a positive relief, being something that had a right to exist—obviously—in the sunshine. The young man looked at me with surprise. I suppose it did not occur to him that Mr. Kurtz was no idol of mine. He forgot I hadn't heard any of these splendid monologues on, what was it? on love, justice, conduct of life—or what not. If it had come to crawling before Mr. Kurtz, he crawled as much as the veriest savage of them all. I had no idea of the conditions, he said: these heads were the heads of rebels. I shocked him excessively by laughing. Rebels! What would be the next definition I was to hear? There had been enemies, criminals, workers—and these were rebels. Those rebellious heads looked very subdued to me on their sticks. "You don't know how such a life tries a man like Kurtz," cried Kurtz's last disciple. "Well, and you?" I said. "I! I! I am a simple man. I have no great thoughts. I want nothing from anybody. How can you compare me to? . . ." His feelings were too much for speech, and suddenly he broke down. "I don't understand," he groaned. "I've been doing my best to keep him alive, and that's enough. I had no hand in all this. I have no abilities. There hasn't been a drop of medicine or a mouthful of invalid food for months here. He was shamefully abandoned. A man like this, with such ideas. Shamefully! Shamefully! I—I—haven't slept for the last ten nights. . . ."

'His voice lost itself in the calm of the evening. The long shadows of the forest had slipped down hill while we talked, had gone far beyond the ruined hovel, beyond the symbolic row of stakes. All this was in the gloom, while we down there were yet in the sunshine, and the stretch of the river abreast of the clearing glittered in a still and dazzling splendour, with a murky and overshadowed bend above and below. Not a living soul was seen on the shore. The bushes did not rustle.

'Suddenly round the corner of the house a group of men appeared, as though they had come up from the ground. They waded waist-deep in the grass, in a compact body, bearing an improvised stretcher in their midst. Instantly, in the emptiness of the landscape, a cry arose whose shrillness pierced the still air like a sharp arrow flying straight to the very heart of the land; and, as if by enchantment, streams of human beings—of naked human beings—with spears in their hands, with bows, with shields, with wild glances and savage movements, were poured into the clearing by the dark-faced and pensive forest. The bushes shook, the grass swayed for a time, and then everything stood still in attentive immobility.

' "Now, if he does not say the right thing to them we are all done for," said the Russian at my elbow. The knot of men with the stretcher had stopped, too, half-way to the steamer, as if petrified. I saw the man on the stretcher sit up, lank and with an uplifted arm, above the shoulders of the bearers. "Let us hope that the man who can talk so well of love in general will find some particular reason to spare us this time," I said. I resented bitterly the absurd danger of our situation, as if to be at the mercy of that atrocious phantom had been a dishonouring necessity. I could not hear a sound, but through my glasses I saw the thin arm extended commandingly, the lower jaw moving, the eyes of that apparition shining darkly far in its bony head that nodded with grotesque jerks. Kurtz—Kurtz—that means short in German—don't it? Well, the name was as true as everything else in his life—and death. He looked at least seven feet long. His covering had fallen off, and his body emerged from it pitiful and appalling as from a winding-sheet. I could see the cage of his ribs all astir, the bones of his arm waving. It was as though an animated image of death carved out of old ivory had been shaking its hand with menaces at a motionless crowd of men made of dark and glittering bronze. I saw him open his mouth wide—it gave him a weirdly voracious aspect, as though he had wanted to swallow all the air, all the earth, all the men before him. A deep voice reached me faintly. He must have been shouting. He fell back suddenly. The stretcher shook as the bearers staggered forward again, and almost at the same time I noticed that the crowd of savages was vanishing without any perceptible movement of retreat, as if the forest that had ejected these beings so suddenly had drawn them in again as the breath is drawn in a long aspiration.

'Some of the pilgrims behind the stretcher carried his arms—two shot-guns, a heavy rifle, and a light revolver-carbine—the thunderbolts of that pitiful Jupiter. The manager bent over him murmuring as he walked beside his head. They laid him down in one of the little cabins—just a room for a bedplace and a camp-stool or two, you know. We had brought his belated correspondence, and a lot of torn envelopes and open letters littered his bed. His hand roamed feebly amongst these papers. I was struck by the fire of his eyes and the composed languor of his expression. It was not so much the exhaustion of disease. He did not seem in pain. This shadow looked satiated and calm, as though for the moment it had had its fill of all the emotions.

'He rustled one of the letters, and looking straight in my face said, "I am glad." Somebody had been writing to him about me. These special recommendations were turning up again. The volume of tone he emitted without effort, almost without the trouble of moving his lips, amazed me. A voice! a voice! It was grave, profound, vibrating, while the man did not seem capable of a whisper. However, he had enough strength in him—factitious no doubt—to very nearly make an end of us, as you shall hear directly.

'The manager appeared silently in the doorway; I stepped out at once and he drew the curtain after me. The Russian, eyed curiously by the pilgrims, was staring at the shore. I followed the direction of his glance.

'Dark human shapes could be made out in the distance, flitting indistinctly against the gloomy border of the forest, and near the river two bronze figures, leaning on tall spears, stood in the sunlight under fantastic head-dresses of spotted skins, warlike and still in statuesque repose. And from right to left along the lighted shore moved a wild and gorgeous apparition of a woman.

'She walked with measured steps, draped in striped and fringed cloths, treading the earth proudly, with a slight jingle and flash of barbarous ornaments. She carried her head high; her hair was done in the shape of a helmet; she had brass leggings to the knee, brass wire gauntlets to the elbow, a crimson spot on her tawny cheek, innumerable necklaces of glass beads on her neck; bizarre things, charms, gifts of witch-men, that hung about her, glittered and trembled at every step. She must have had the value of several elephant tusks upon her. She was savage and superb, wild-eyed and magnificent; there was something ominous and stately in her deliberate progress. And in the hush that had fallen suddenly upon the whole sorrowful land, the immense wilderness, the colossal body of the fecund and mysterious life seemed to look at her, pensive, as though it had been looking at the image of its own tenebrous and passionate soul.

'She came abreast of the steamer, stood still, and faced us. Her long shadow fell to the water's edge. Her face had a tragic and fierce aspect of wild sorrow and of dumb pain mingled with the fear of some struggling, half-shaped resolve. She stood looking at us without a stir, and like the wilderness itself, with an air of brooding over an inscrutable purpose. A whole minute passed, and then she made a step forward. There was a low jingle, a glint of yellow metal, a sway of fringed draperies, and she stopped as if her heart had failed her. The young fellow by my side growled. The pilgrims murmured at my back. She looked at us all as if her life had depended upon the unswerving steadiness of her glance. Suddenly she opened her bared arms and threw them up rigid above her head, as though in an uncontrollable desire to touch the sky, and at the same time the swift shadows darted out on the earth, swept around on the river, gathering the steamer into a shadowy embrace. A formidable silence hung over the scene.

'She turned away slowly, walked on, following the bank, and passed into the bushes to the left. Once only her eyes gleamed back at us in the dusk of the thickets before she disappeared.

' "If she had offered to come aboard I really think I would have tried to shoot her," said the man of patches, nervously. "I had been risking my life every day for the last fortnight to keep her out of the house. She got in one day and kicked up a row about those miserable rags I picked up in the storeroom to mend my clothes with. I wasn't decent. At least it must have been that, for she talked like a fury to Kurtz for an hour, pointing at me now and then. I don't understand the dialect of this tribe. Luckily for me, I fancy Kurtz felt too ill that day to care, or there would have been mischief. I don't understand. . . . No—it's too much for me. Ah, well, it's all over now."

'At this moment I heard Kurtz's deep voice behind the curtain: "Save me!—save the ivory, you mean. Don't tell me. Save *me!* Why, I've had to save you. You are interrupting my plans now. Sick! Sick! Not so sick as you would like to believe. Never mind. I'll carry my ideas out yet—I will return. I'll show you what can be done. You with your little peddling notions—you are interfering with me. I will return. I. . . ."

'The manager came out. He did me the honour to take me under the arm and lead me aside. "He is very low, very low," he said. He considered it necessary to sigh, but neglected to be consistently sorrowful. "We have done all we could for him—haven't we? But there is no disguising the fact, Mr. Kurtz has done more harm than good to the Company. He did not see the time was not ripe for vigorous action. Cautiously, cautiously—that's my principle. We must be cautious yet. The district is closed to us for a time. Deplorable! Upon the whole, the trade will suffer. I don't deny there is a remarkable quantity of ivory—mostly fossil. We must save it, at all events—but look how precarious the position is—and why? Because the method is unsound." "Do you," said I, looking at the shore, "call it 'unsound method?' " "Without doubt," he exclaimed, hotly. "Don't you?" . . . "No method at all," I murmured after a while. "Exactly," he exulted. "I anticipated this. Shows a complete want of judgment. It is my duty to point it out in the proper quarter." "Oh," said I, "that fellow—what's his name?—the brickmaker, will made a readable report for you." He appeared confounded for a moment. It seemed to me I had never breathed an atmosphere so vile, and I turned mentally to Kurtz for relief—positively for relief. "Nevertheless I think Mr. Kurtz is a remarkable man," I said with emphasis. He started, dropped on me a cold heavy glance, said very quietly, "he *was*," and turned his back on me. My hour of favour was over; I found myself lumped along with Kurtz as a partisan of methods for which the time was not ripe: I was unsound! Ah! but it was something to have at least a choice of nightmares.

'I had turned to the wilderness really, not to Mr. Kurtz, who, I was ready to admit, was as good as buried. And for a moment it seemed to me as if I also were buried in a vast grave full of unspeakable secrets. I felt an intolerable weight oppressing my breast, the smell of the damp earth, the unseen presence of victorious corruption, the darkness of an impenetrable night. . . . The Russian tapped me on the shoulder. I heard him mumbling and stammering something about "brother seaman—couldn't conceal—knowledge of matters that would affect Mr. Kurtz's reputation." I waited. For him evidently Mr. Kurtz was not in his grave; I suspect that for him

Mr. Kurtz was one of the immortals. "Well!" said I at last, "speak out. As it happens, I am Mr. Kurtz's friend—in a way."

'He stated with a good deal of formality that had we not been "of the same profession," he would have kept the matter to himself without regard to consequences. "He suspected there was an active ill will towards him on the part of these white men that——" "You are right," I said, remembering a certain conversation I had overheard. "The manager thinks you ought to be hanged." He showed a concern at this intelligence which amused me at first. "I had better get out of the way quietly," he said, earnestly. "I can do no more for Kurtz now, and they would soon find some excuse. What's to stop them? There's a military post three hundred miles from here." "Well, upon my word," said I, "perhaps you had better go if you have any friends amongst the savages near by." "Plenty," he said. "They are simple people—and I want nothing, you know." He stood biting his lip, then: "I don't want any harm to happen to these whites here, but of course I was thinking of Mr. Kurtz's reputation—but you are a brother seaman and——" "All right," said I, after a time. "Mr. Kurtz's reputation is safe with me." I did not know how truly I spoke.

'He informed me, lowering his voice, that it was Kurtz who had ordered the attack to be made on the steamer. "He hated sometimes the idea of being taken away—and then again. . . . But I don't understand these matters. I am a simple man. He thought it would scare you away—that you would give it up, thinking him dead. I could not stop him. Oh, I had an awful time of it this last month." "Very well," I said. "He is all right now." "Ye-e-es," he muttered, not very convinced apparently. "Thanks," said I; "I shall keep my eyes open." "But quiet—eh?" he urged, anxiously. "It would be awful for his reputation if anybody here——" I promised a complete discretion with great gravity. "I have a canoe and three black fellows waiting not very far. I am off. Could you give me a few Martini-Henry cartridges?" I could, and did, with proper secrecy. He helped himself, with a wink at me, to a handful of my tobacco. "Between sailors—you know—good English tobacco." At the door of the pilot-house he turned round—"I say, haven't you a pair of shoes you could spare?" He raised one leg. "Look." The soles were tied with knotted strings sandal-wise under his bare feet. I rooted out an old pair, at which he looked with admiration before tucking it under his left arm. One of his pockets (bright red) was bulging with cartridges, from the other (dark blue) peeped "Towson's Inquiry," etc., etc. He seemed to think himself excellently well equipped for a renewed encounter with the wilderness. "Ah! I'll never, never meet such a man again. You ought to have heard him recite poetry—his own, too, it was, he told me. Poetry!" He rolled his eyes at the recollection of these delights. "Oh, he enlarged my mind!" "Goodbye," said I. He shook hands and vanished in the night. Sometimes I ask myself whether I had ever really seen him—whether it was possible to meet such a phenomenon! . . .

'When I woke up shortly after midnight his warning came to my mind with its hint of danger that seemed, in the starred darkness, real enough to make me get up for the purpose of having a look round. On the hill a big fire burned, illuminating fitfully a crooked corner of the station-house. One of the agents with a picket of a few of our blacks, armed for the purpose, was keeping guard over the ivory; but deep within the forest, red gleams that wavered, that seemed to sink and rise from the ground amongst confused columnar shapes of intense blackness, showed the exact position of the camp where Mr. Kurtz's adorers were keeping their uneasy vigil. The monotonous beating of a big drum filled the air with muffled shocks and a lingering vibration. A steady droning sound of many men chanting each to himself some weird incantation came out from the black, flat wall of the woods as the humming of bees comes out of a hive, and had a strange narcotic effect upon my half-awake senses. I believe I dozed off leaning over the rail, till an abrupt burst of yells, an overwhelming outbreak of a pent-up and mysterious frenzy, woke me up in a bewildered wonder. It was cut short all at once, and the low droning went on with an effect of audible and soothing silence. I glanced casually into the little cabin. A light was burning within, but Mr. Kurtz was not there.

'I think I would have raised an outcry if I had believed my eyes. But I didn't believe them at first—the thing seemed so impossible. The fact is I was completely unnerved by a sheer blank fright, pure abstract terror, unconnected with any distinct shape of physical danger. What made this emotion so overpowering was—how shall I define it?—the moral shock I received, as if something altogether monstrous, intolerable to thought and odious to the soul, had been thrust upon me unexpectedly. This lasted of course the merest fraction of a second, and then the usual sense of commonplace, deadly danger, the possibility of a sudden onslaught and massacre, or something of the kind, which I saw impending, was positively welcome and composing. It pacified me, in fact, so much, that I did not raise an alarm.

'There was an agent buttoned up inside an ulster and sleeping on a chair on deck within three feet of me. The yells had not awakened him; he snored very slightly; I left him to his slumbers and leaped ashore. I did not betray Mr. Kurtz—it was ordered I should never betray him—it was written I should be loyal to the nightmare of my choice. I was anxious to deal with this shadow by myself alone,—and to this day I don't know why I was so jealous of sharing with any one the peculiar blackness of that experience.

'As soon as I got on the bank I saw a trail—a broad trail through the grass. I remember the exultation with which I said to myself, "He can't walk—he is crawling on all-fours—I've got him." The grass was wet with dew. I strode rapidly with clenched fists. I fancy I had some vague notion of falling upon him and giving him a drubbing. I don't know. I had some imbecile thoughts. The knitting old woman with the cat obtruded herself upon my memory as a most improper person to be sitting at the other end of such an affair. I saw a row of pilgrims squirting lead in the air out of Winchesters held to the hip. I thought I would never get back to the steamer, and imagined myself living alone and unarmed in the woods to an advanced age. Such silly things—you know. And I remember I confounded the beat of the drum with the beating of my heart, and was pleased at its calm regularity.

'I kept to the track though—then stopped to listen. The night was very clear; a dark blue space, sparkling with dew and starlight, in which black things stood very still. I thought I could see a kind of motion ahead of me. I was strangely cocksure of everything that night. I actually left the track and ran in a wide semicircle (I verily believe chuckling to myself) so as to get in front of that stir, of that motion I had seen—if indeed I had seen anything. I was circumventing Kurtz as though it had been a boyish game.

'I came upon him, and, if he had not heard me coming, I would have fallen over him, too, but he got up in time. He rose, unsteady, long, pale, indistinct, like a vapour exhaled by the earth, and swayed slightly, misty and silent before me; while at my back the fires loomed between the trees, and the murmur of many voices issued from the forest. I had cut him off cleverly; but when actually confronting him I seemed to come to my senses, I saw the danger in its right proportion. It was by no means over yet. Suppose he began to shout? Though he could hardly stand, there was still plenty of vigour in his voice. "Go away—hide yourself," he said, in that profound tone. It was very awful. I glanced back. We were within thirty yards from the nearest fire. A black figure stood up, strode on long black legs, waving long black arms, across the glow. It had horns—antelope horns, I think—on its head. Some sorcerer, some witch-man, no doubt: it looked fiend-like enough. "Do you know what you are doing?" I whispered. "Perfectly," he answered, raising his voice for that single word: it sounded to me far off and yet loud, like a hail through a speaking-trumpet. If he makes a row we are lost, I thought to myself. This clearly was not a case for fisticuffs, even apart from the very natural aversion I had to beat that Shadow—this wandering and tormented thing. "You will be lost," I said—"utterly lost." One gets sometimes such a flash of inspiration, you know. I did say the right thing, though indeed he could not have been more irretrievably lost than he was at this very moment, when the foundations of our intimacy were being laid—to endure—to endure—even to the end—even beyond.

' "I had immense plans," he muttered irresolutely. "Yes," said I; "but if you try to shout I'll smash your head with——" There was not a stick or a stone near. "I will throttle you for good," I corrected myself. "I was on the threshold of great things," he pleaded, in a voice of longing, with a wistfulness of tone that made my blood run cold. "And now for this stupid scoundrel——" "Your success in Europe is assured in any case," I affirmed, steadily. I did not want to have the throttling of him, you understand—and indeed it would have been very little use for any practical purpose. I tried to break the spell—the heavy, mute spell of the wilderness—that seemed to draw him to its pitiless breast by the awakening of forgotten and brutal instincts, by the memory of gratified and monstrous passions. This alone, I was convinced, had driven him out to the edge of the forest, to the bush, towards the gleam of fires, the throb of drums, the drone of weird incantations; this alone had beguiled his unlawful soul beyond the bounds of permitted aspirations. And, don't you see, the terror of the position was not in being knocked on the head—though I had a very lively sense of that danger, too—but in this, that I had to deal with a being to whom I could not appeal in the name of anything high or low. I had, even like the niggers, to invoke him—himself—his own exalted and incredible degradation. There was nothing either above or below him, and I knew it. He had kicked himself loose of the earth. Confound the man! he had kicked the very earth to pieces. He was alone, and I before him did not know whether I stood on the ground or floated in the air. I've been telling you what we said—repeating the phrases we pronounced—but what's the good? They were common everyday words—the familiar, vague sounds exchanged on every waking day of life. But what of that? They had behind them, to my mind, the terrific suggestiveness of words heard in dreams, of phrases spoken in nightmares. Soul! If anybody had ever struggled with a soul, I am the man. And I wasn't arguing with a lunatic either. Believe me or not, his intelligence was perfectly clear—concentrated, it is true, upon himself with horrible intensity, yet clear; and therein was my only chance—barring, of course, the killing him there and then, which wasn't so good, on account of unavoidable noise. But his soul was mad. Being alone in the wilderness, it had looked within itself, and, by heavens! I tell you, it had gone mad. I had—for my sins, I suppose—to go through the ordeal of looking into it myself. No eloquence could have been so withering to one's belief in mankind as his final burst of sincerity. He struggled with himself, too. I saw it,—I heard it. I saw the inconceivable mystery of a soul that knew no restraint, no faith, and no fear, yet struggling blindly with itself. I kept my head pretty well; but when I had him at last stretched on the couch, I wiped my forehead, while my legs shook under me as though I had carried half a ton on my back down that hill. And yet I had only supported him, his bony arm clasped round my neck—and he was not much heavier than a child.

'When next day we left at noon, the crowd, of whose presence behind the curtain of trees I had been acutely conscious all the time, flowed out of the woods again, filled the clearing, covered the slope with a mass of naked, breathing, quivering, bronze bodies. I steamed up a bit, then swung downstream, and two thousand eyes followed the evolutions of the splashing, thumping, fierce river-demon beating the water with its terrible tail and breathing black smoke into the air. In front of the first rank, along the river, three men, plastered with bright red earth from head to foot, strutted to and fro restlessly. When we came abreast again, they faced the river, stamped their feet, nodded their horned heads, swayed their scarlet bodies; they shook towards the fierce river-demon a bunch of black feathers, a mangy skin with a pendent tail—something that looked like a dried gourd; they shouted periodically together strings of amazing words that resembled no sounds of human language; and the deep murmurs of the crowd, interrupted suddenly, were like the responses of some satanic litany.

'We had carried Kurtz into the pilot-house: there was more air there. Lying on the couch, he stared through the open shutter. There was an eddy in the mass of human bodies, and the woman with helmeted head and tawny cheeks rushed out to the very brink of the stream. She put out her hands, shouted something, and all that wild mob took up the shout in a roaring chorus of articulated, rapid, breathless utterance.

' "Do you understand this?" I asked.

'He kept on looking out past me with fiery, longing eyes, with a mingled expression of wistfulness and hate. He made no answer, but I saw a smile, a smile of indefinable meaning, appear on his colourless lips that a moment after twitched convulsively. "Do I not?" he said slowly, gasping, as if the words had been torn out of him by a supernatural power.

'I pulled the string of the whistle, and I did this because I saw the pilgrims on deck getting out their rifles with an air of anticipating a jolly lark. At the sudden screech there was a movement of abject terror through that wedged mass of bodies. "Don't! don't you frighten them away," cried someone on deck disconsolately. I pulled the string time after time. They broke and ran, they leaped, they crouched, they swerved, they dodged the flying terror of the sound. The three red chaps had fallen flat, face down on the shore, as though they had been shot dead. Only the barbarous and superb woman did not so much as flinch, and stretched tragically her bare arms after us over the sombre and glittering river.

'And then that imbecile crowd down on the deck started their little fun, and I could see nothing more for smoke.

'The brown current ran swiftly out of the heart of darkness, bearing us down towards the sea with twice the speed of our upward progress; and Kurtz's life was running swiftly, too, ebbing, ebbing out of his heart into the sea of inexorable time. The manager was very placid, he had no vital anxieties now, he took us both in with a comprehensive and satisfied glance: the "affair" had come off as well as could be wished. I saw the time approaching when I would be left alone of the party of "unsound method." The pilgrims looked upon me with disfavour. I was, so to speak, numbered with the dead. It is strange how I accepted this unforeseen partnership, this choice of nightmares forced upon me in the tenebrous land invaded by these mean and greedy phantoms.

'Kurtz discoursed. A voice! a voice! It rang deep to the very last. It survived his strength to hide in the magnificent folds of eloquence the barren darkness of his heart. Oh, he struggled! he struggled! The wastes of his weary brain were haunted by shadowy images now—images of wealth and fame revolving obsequiously round his unextinguishable gift of noble and lofty expression. My Intended, my station, my career, my ideas—these were the subjects for the occasional utterances of elevated sentiments. The shade of the original Kurtz frequented the beside of the hollow sham, whose fate it was to be buried presently in the mould of primeval earth. But both the diabolic love and the unearthly hate of the mysteries it had penetrated fought for the possession of that soul satiated with primitive emotions, avid of lying fame, of sham distinction, of all the appearances of success and power.

'Sometimes he was contemptibly childish. He desired to have kings meet him at railway-stations on his return from some ghastly Nowhere, where he intended to accomplish great things. "You show them you have in you something that is really profitable, and then there will be no limits to the recognition of your ability," he would say. "Of course you must take care of the motives—right motives—always." The long reaches that were like one and the same reach, monotonous bends that were exactly alike, slipped past the steamer with their multitude of secular trees looking patiently after this grimy fragment of another world, the forerunner of change, of conquest, of trade, of massacres, of blessings. I looked ahead—piloting. "Close the shutter," said Kurtz suddenly one day; "I can't bear to look at this." I did so. There was a silence. "Oh, but I will wring your heart yet!" he cried at the invisible wilderness.

'We broke down—as I had expected—and had to lie up for repairs at the head of an island. This delay was the first thing that shook Kurtz's confidence. One morning he gave me a packet of papers and a photograph—the lot tied together with a shoe-string. "Keep this for me," he said. "This noxious fool" (meaning the manager) "is capable of prying into my boxes when I am not looking." In the afternoon I saw him. He was lying on his back with closed eyes, and I withdrew quietly, but I heard him mutter, "Live rightly, die, die. . . ." I listened. There was nothing more. Was he rehearsing some speech in his sleep, or was it a fragment of a phrase from some newspaper article? He had been writing for the papers and meant to do so again, "for the furthering of my ideas. It's a duty."

'His was an impenetrable darkness. I looked at him as you peer down at a man who is lying at the bottom of a precipice where the sun never shines. But I had not much time to give him, because I was helping the engine-driver to take to pieces the leaky cylinders, to straighten a bent connecting-rod, and in other such matters. I lived in an infernal mess of rust, filings, nuts, bolts, spanners, hammers, ratchet-drills—things I abominate, because I don't get on with them. I tended the little forge we fortunately had aboard; I toiled wearily in a wretched scrap-heap—unless I had the shakes too bad to stand.

'One evening coming in with a candle I was startled to hear him say a little tremulously, "I am lying here in the dark waiting for death." The light was within a foot of his eyes. I forced myself to murmur, "Oh, nonsense!" and stood over him as if transfixed.

'Anything approaching the change that came over his features I have never seen before, and hope never to see again. Oh, I wasn't touched. I was fascinated. It was as though a veil had been rent. I saw on that ivory face the expression of sombre pride, of ruthless power, of craven terror—of an intense and hopeless despair. Did he live his life again in every detail of desire, temptation, and surrender during that supreme moment of complete knowledge? He cried in a whisper at some image, at some vision—he cried out twice, a cry that was no more than a breath—

'"The horror! The horror!"

'I blew the candle out and left the cabin. The pilgrims were dining in the mess-room, and I took my place opposite the manager, who lifted his eyes to give me a questioning glance, which

I successfully ignored. He leaned back, serene, with that peculiar smile of his sealing the unexpressed depths of his meanness. A continuous shower of small flies streamed upon the lamp, upon the cloth, upon our hands and faces. Suddenly the manager's boy put his insolent black head in the doorway, and said in a tone of scathing contempt—

'"Mistah Kurtz—he dead."

'All the pilgrims rushed out to see. I remained, and went on with my dinner. I believe I was considered brutally callous. However, I did not eat much. There was a lamp in there—light, don't you know—and outside it was so beastly, beastly dark. I went no more near the remarkable man who had pronounced a judgment upon the adventures of his soul on this earth. The voice was gone. What else had been there? But I am of course aware that next day the pilgrims buried something in a muddy hole.

'And then they very nearly buried me.

'However, as you see, I did not go to join Kurtz there and then. I did not. I remained to dream the nightmare out to the end, and to show my loyalty to Kurtz once more. Destiny. My destiny! Droll thing life is—that mysterious arrangement of merciless logic for a futile purpose. The most you can hope from it is some knowledge of yourself—that comes too late—a crop of unextinguishable regrets. I have wrestled with death. It is the most unexciting contest you can imagine. It takes place in an impalpable greyness, with nothing underfoot, with nothing around, without spectators, without clamour, without glory, without the great desire of victory, without the great fear of defeat, in a sickly atmosphere of tepid scepticism, without much belief in your own right, and still less in that of your adversary. If such is the form of ultimate wisdom, then life is a greater riddle than some of us think it to be. I was within a hair's-breadth of the last opportunity for pronouncement, and I found with humiliation that probably I would have nothing to say. This is the reason why I affirm that Kurtz was a remarkable man. He had something to say. He said it. Since I had peeped over the edge myself, I understand better the meaning of his stare, that could not see the flame of the candle, but was wide enough to embrace the whole universe, piercing enough to penetrate all the hearts that beat in the darkness. He had summed up—he had judged. "The horror!" He was a remarkable man. After all, this was the expression of some sort of belief; it had candour, it had conviction, it had a vibrating note of revolt in its whisper, it had the appalling face of a glimpsed truth—the strange commingling of desire and hate. And it is not my own extremity I remember best—a vision of greyness without form filled with physical pain, and a careless contempt for the evanescence of all things—even of this pain itself. No! It is his extremity that I seem to have lived through. True, he had made that last stride, he had stepped over the edge, while I had been permitted to draw back my hesitating foot. And perhaps in this is the whole difference; perhaps all the wisdom, and all truth, and all sincerity, are just compressed into that inappreciable moment of time in which we step over the threshold of the invisible. Perhaps! I like to think my summing-up would not have been a word of careless contempt. Better his cry—much better. It was an affirmation, a moral victory paid for by innumerable defeats, by abominable terrors, by abominable satisfactions. But it was a victory! That is why I have remained loyal to Kurtz to the last, and even beyond, when a long time after I heard once more, not his own voice, but the echo of his magnificent eloquence thrown to me from a soul as translucently pure as a cliff of crystal.

'No, they did not bury me, though there is a period of time which I remember mistily, with a shuddering wonder, like a passage through some inconceivable world that had no hope in it and no desire. I found myself back in the sepulchral city resenting the sight of people hurrying through the streets to filch a little money from each other, to devour their infamous cookery, to gulp their unwholesome beer, to dream their insignificant and silly dreams. They trespassed upon my thoughts. They were intruders whose knowledge of life was to me an irritating pretence, because I felt so sure they could not possibly know the things I knew. Their bearing, which was simply the bearing of commonplace individuals going about their business in the assurance of perfect safety, was offensive to me like the outrageous flauntings of folly in the face of a danger it is unable to comprehend. I had no particular desire to enlighten them, but I had some difficulty in restraining myself from laughing in their faces, so full of stupid importance. I daresay I was not very well at that time. I tottered about the streets—there were various affairs to settle—grinning bitterly at perfectly respectable persons. I admit my behaviour was inexcusable, but then my temperature was seldom normal in these days. My dear aunt's endeavours to "nurse up my strength" seemed altogether beside the mark. It was not my strength that wanted nursing, it was my imagination that wanted soothing. I kept the bundle of papers given me by Kurtz, not knowing exactly what to do with it. His mother had died lately, watched over, as I was told, by his Intended. A clean-shaved man, with an official manner and wearing gold-rimmed spectacles, called on me one day and made inquiries, at first circuitous, afterwards suavely pressing, about what he was pleased to denominate certain "documents." I was not surprised, because I had had two rows with the manager on the subject out there. I had refused to give up the smallest scrap out of that package, and I took the same attitude with the spectacled man. He became darkly menacing at last, and with much heat argued that the Company had the right to every bit of information about its "territories." And said he, "Mr. Kurtz's knowledge of unexplored regions must have been necessarily extensive and peculiar—owing to his great abilities and to the deplorable circumstances in which he had been placed: therefore——" I assured him Mr. Kurtz's knowledge, however extensive, did not bear upon the problems of commerce or administration. He invoked then the name of science. "It would be an incalculable loss if," etc., etc. I offered him the report on the "Suppression of Savage Customs," with the postscriptum torn off. He took it up eagerly, but ended by sniffing at it with an air of contempt. "This is not what we had a right to expect," he remarked. "Expect nothing else," I said. "There are only private letters." He withdrew upon some threat of legal proceedings, and I saw him no more; but another fellow, calling himself Kurtz's cousin, appeared two days later, and was anxious to hear all the details about his dear relative's last moments. Incidentally he gave me to understand that Kurtz had been essentially a great musician. "There was the making of an immense success," said the man, who was an organist, I believe, with lank grey hair flowing over a greasy coat-collar. I had no reason to doubt his statement; and to this day I am unable to say what was Kurtz's profession, whether he ever had any—which was the greatest of his talents. I had taken him for a painter who wrote for the papers, or else for a journalist who could paint—but even the cousin (who took snuff during the interview) could not tell me what he had been—exactly. He was a universal genius—on that point I agreed with the old chap, who thereupon blew his nose noisily into a large cotton handkerchief and withdrew in senile agitation, bearing off some family letters and memoranda without importance. Ultimately a journalist anxious to know something of the fate of his "dear colleague" turned up. This visitor informed me Kurtz's proper sphere ought to have been politics "on the popular side." He had furry straight eyebrows, bristly hair cropped short, an eye-glass on a broad ribbon, and, becoming expansive, confessed his opinion that Kurtz really couldn't write a bit—"but heavens! how that man could talk. He electrified large meetings. He had faith—don't you see?—he had the faith. He could get himself to believe anything—anything. He would have been a splendid leader of an extreme party." "What party?" I asked. "Any party," answered the other. "He was an—an—extremist." Did I not think so? I assented. Did I know, he asked, with a sudden flash of curiosity, "what it was that had induced him to go out there?" "Yes," said I, and forthwith handed him the famous Report for publication, if he thought fit. He glanced through it hurriedly, mumbling all the time, judged "it would do," and took himself off with this plunder.

'Thus I was left at last with a slim packet of letters and the girl's portrait. She struck me as beautiful—I mean she had a beautiful expression. I know that the sunlight can be made to lie, too, yet one felt that no manipulation of light and pose could have conveyed the delicate shade of truthfulness upon those features. She seemed ready to listen without mental reservation, without suspicion, without a thought for herself. I concluded I would go and give her back her portrait and those letters myself. Curiosity? Yes; and also some other feeling perhaps. All that had been Kurtz's had passed out of my hands: his soul, his body, his station, his plans, his ivory, his career. There remained only his memory and his Intended—and I wanted to give that up, too to the past, in a way—to surrender personally all that remained of him with me to that oblivion which is the last word of our common fate. I don't defend myself. I had no clear perception of what it was I really wanted. Perhaps it was an impulse of unconscious loyalty, or the fulfilment of one of these ironic necessities that lurk in the facts of human existence. I don't know. I can't tell. But I went.

'I thought his memory was like the other memories of the dead that accumulate in every man's life—a vague impress on the brain of shadows that had fallen on it in their swift and final passage; but before the high and ponderous door, between the tall houses of a street as still and decorous as a well-kept alley in a cemetery, I had a vision of him on the stretcher, opening his mouth voraciously, as if to devour all the earth with all its mankind. He lived then before me; he lived as much as he had ever lived—a shadow insatiable of splendid appearances, of frightful realities; a shadow darker that the shadow of the night, and draped nobly in the folds of a gorgeous eloquence. The vision seemed to enter the house with me—the stretcher, the phantom-bearers, the wild crowd of obedient worshippers, the gloom of the forests, the glitter of the reach between the murky bends, the beat of the drum, regular and muffled like the beating of a heart—the heart of a conquering darkness. It was a moment of triumph for the wilderness, an invading and vengeful rush which, it seemed to me, I would have to keep back alone for the salvation of another soul. And the memory of what I had heard him say afar there, with the horned shapes stirring at my back, in the glow of fires, within the patient woods, those broken phrases came back to me, were heard again in their ominous and terrifying simplicity. I remembered his abject pleading, his abject threats, the colossal scale of his vile desires, the meanness, the torment, the tempestuous anguish of his soul. And later on I seemed to see his collected languid manner, when he said one day, "This lot of ivory now is really mine. The Company did not pay for it. I collected it myself at a very great personal risk. I am afraid they will try to claim it as theirs though. H'm. It is a difficult case. What do you think I ought to do—resist? Eh? I want no more than justice." . . . He wanted no more than justice—no more than justice. I rang the bell before a mahogany door on the first floor, and while I waited he seemed to stare at me out of the glassy panel—stare with that wide and immense stare embracing, condemning, loathing all the universe. I seemed to hear the whispered cry, "The horror! The horror!"

'The dusk was falling. I had to wait in a lofty drawing-room with three long windows from floor to ceiling that were like three luminous and bedraped columns. The bent gilt legs and backs of the furniture shone in indistinct curves. The tall marble fireplace had a cold and monumental whiteness. A grand piano stood massively in a corner; with dark gleams on the flat surfaces like a sombre and polished sarcophagus. A high door opened—closed. I rose.

'She came forward, all in black, with a pale head, floating towards me in the dusk. She was in mourning. It was more than a year since his death, more than a year since the news came; she seemed as though she would remember and mourn for ever. She took both my hands in hers and murmured, "I had heard you were coming." I noticed she was not very young—I mean not girlish. She had a mature capacity for fidelity, for belief, for suffering. The room seemed to have grown darker, as if all the sad light of the cloudy evening had taken refuge on her forehead. This fair hair, this pale visage, this pure brow, seemed surrounded by an ashy halo from which the dark eyes looked out at me. Their glance was guileless, profound, confident, and trustful. She carried her sorrowful head as though she were proud of that sorrow, as though she would say, I—I alone know how to mourn for him as he deserves. But while we were still shaking hands, such a look of awful desolation came upon her face that I perceived she was one of those creatures that are not the playthings of Time. For her he had died only yesterday. And, by Jove! the impression was so powerful that for me, too, he seemed to have died only yesterday—nay, this very minute. I saw her and him in the same instant of time—his death and her sorrow—I saw her sorrow in the very moment of his death. Do you understand? I saw them together—I heard them together. She had said, with a deep catch of the breath, "I have survived" while my strained ears seemed to hear distinctly, mingled with her tone of despairing regret, the summing up whisper of his eternal condemnation. I asked myself what I was doing there, with a sensation of panic in my heart as though I had blundered into a place of cruel and absurd mysteries not fit for a human being to behold. She motioned me to a chair. We sat down. I laid the packet gently on the little table, and she put her hand over it. . . . "You knew him well," she murmured, after a moment of mourning silence.

' "Intimacy grows quickly out there," I said. "I knew him as well as it is possible for one man to know another."

' "And you admired him," she said. "It was impossible to know him and not to admire him. Was it?"

' "He was a remarkable man," I said, unsteadily. Then before the appealing fixity of her gaze, that seemed to watch for more words on my lips, I went on, "It was impossible not to——"

' "Love him," she finished eagerly, silencing me into an appalled dumbness. "How true! how true! But when you think that no one knew him so well as I! I had all his noble confidence. I knew him best."

' "You knew him best," I repeated. And perhaps she did. But with every word spoken the room was growing darker, and only her forehead, smooth and white, remained illumined by the unextinguishable light of belief and love.

' "You were his friend," she went on. "His friend," she repeated, a little louder. "You must have been, if he had given you this, and sent you to me. I feel I can speak to you—and oh! I must speak. I want you—you who have heard his last words—to know I have been worthy of him. . . . It is not pride. . . . Yes! I am proud to know I understood him better than any one on earth—he told me so himself. And since his mother died I have had no one—no one—to—to——"

'I listened. The darkness deepened. I was not even sure whether he had given me the right bundle. I rather suspect he wanted me to take care of another batch of his papers which, after his death, I saw the manager examining under the lamp. And the girl talked, easing her pain in the certitude of my sympathy; she talked as thirsty men drink. I had heard that her engagement with Kurtz had been disapproved by her people. He wasn't rich enough or something. And indeed I don't know whether he had not been a pauper all his life. He had given me some reason to infer that it was his impatience of comparative poverty that drove him out there.

' ". . . Who was not his friend who had heard him speak once?" she was saying. "He drew men towards him by what was best in them." She looked at me with intensity. "It is the gift of the great," she went on, and the sound of her low voice seemed to have the accompaniment of all the other sounds, full of mystery, desolation, and sorrow, I had ever heard—the ripple of the river, the soughing of the trees swayed by the wind, the murmurs of the crowds, the faint ring of incomprehensible words cried from afar, the whisper of a voice speaking from beyond the threshold of an eternal darkness. "But you have heard him! You know!" she cried.

' "Yes, I know," I said with something like despair in my heart, but bowing my head before the faith that was in her, before that great and saving illusion that shone with an unearthly glow in the darkness, in the triumphant darkness from which I could not have defended her—from which I could not even defend myself.

' "What a loss to me—to us!"—she corrected herself with beautiful generosity; then added in a murmur, "To the world." By the last gleams of twilight I could see the glitter of her eyes, full of tears—of tears that would not fall.

' "I have been very happy—very fortunate—very proud," she went on. "Too fortunate. Too happy for a little while. And now I am unhappy for—for life."

'She stood up; her fair hair seemed to catch all the remaining light in a glimmer of gold. I rose, too.

' "And of all this," she went on, mournfully, "of all his promise, and of all his greatness, of his generous mind, of his noble heart, nothing remains—nothing but a memory. You and I——"

' "We shall always remember him," I said, hastily.

' "No!" she cried. "It is impossible that all this should be lost—that such a life should be sacrificed to leave nothing—but sorrow. You know what vast plans he had. I knew of them, too—I could not perhaps understand—but others knew of them. Something must remain. His words, at least, have not died."

' "His words will remain," I said.

' "And his example," she whispered to herself. "Men looked up to him—his goodness shone in every act. His example——"

' "True," I said; "his example, too. Yes, his example. I forgot that."

' "But I do not. I cannot—I cannot believe—not yet. I cannot believe that I shall never see him again, that nobody will see him again, never, never, never."

'She put out her arms as if after a retreating figure, stretching them back and with clasped pale hands across the fading and narrow sheen of the window. Never see him! I saw him clearly enough then. I shall see this eloquent phantom as long as I live, and I shall see her, too, a tragic and familiar Shade, resembling in this gesture another one, tragic also, and bedecked with powerless charms, stretching bare brown arms over the glitter of the infernal stream, the stream of darkness. She said suddenly very low, "He died as he lived."

' "His end," said I, with dull anger stirring in me, "was in every way worthy of his life."

' "And I was not with him," she murmured. My anger subsided before a feeling of infinite pity.

' "Everything that could be done——" I mumbled.

' "Ah, but I believed in him more than any one on earth— more than his own mother, more than—himself. He needed me! Me! I would have treasured every sigh, every word, every sign, every glance."

'I felt like a chill grip on my chest. "Don't," I said, in a muffled voice.

' "Forgive me. I—I—have mourned so long in silence—in silence. . . . You were with him—to the last? I think of his loneliness. Nobody near to understand him as ¨ would have understood. Perhaps no one to hear. . . ."

' "To the very end," I said, shakily. "I heard his very last words. . . ." I stopped in a fright.

' "Repeat them," she murmured in a heart-broken tone. "I want—I want—something—something—to—to live with."

'I was on the point of crying at her, "Don't you hear them?" The dusk was repeating them in a persistent whisper all around us, in a whisper that seemed to swell menacingly like the first whisper of a rising wind. "The horror! the horror!"

' "His last word—to live with," she insisted. "Don't you under-stand I loved him—I loved him—I loved him!"

'I pulled myself together and spoke slowly.

' "The last word he pronounced was—your name."

'I heard a light sigh and then my heart stood still, stopped dead short by an exulting and terrible cry, by the cry of inconceivable triumph and of unspeakable pain. "I knew it—I was sure!" . . . She knew. She was sure. I heard her weeping; she had hidden her face in her hands. It seemed to me that the house would collapse before I could escape, that the heavens would fall upon my head. But nothing happened. The heavens do not fall for such a trifle. Would they have fallen, I wonder, if I had rendered Kurtz that justice which was his due? Hadn't he said he wanted only justice? But I couldn't. I could not tell her. It would have been too dark—too dark altogether. . . .'

Marlow ceased, and sat apart, indistinct and silent, in the pose of a meditating Buddha. Nobody moved for a time. 'We have lost the first of the ebb,' said the Director, suddenly. I raised my head. The offing was barred by a black bank of clouds, and the tranquil waterway leading to the uttermost ends of the earth flowed sombre under an overcast sky—seemed to lead into the heart of an immense darkness.